Silent Stranger

Silent Stranger

Silent Stranger
BY PEGGY DARTY

If the Prospect Pleases
BY SALLY LAITY

Hold on My Heart
BY JOANN A. GROTE

Meet Me with a Promise
BY JOANN A. GROTE

HeavenSent
FROM
Crossings

Silent Stranger
Copyright © 1998 by Barbour Publishing, Inc.

If the Prospect Pleases
Copyright © 1998 by Barbour Publishing, Inc.

Hold on My Heart
Copyright © 2002 by JoAnn A. Grote

Meet Me with a Promise
Copyright © 2002 by JoAnn A. Grote

This edition was especially created in 2005 for Crossings by arrangement with Barbour Publishing, Inc.

Published by Crossings Book Club, 501 Franklin Avenue, New York, New York 11530.

ISBN: 1-58288-168-5

Printed in the United States of America

Silent Stranger

Silent Stranger

BY PEGGY DARTY

$\mathcal{R}$ uth Wright stepped from the general store onto the narrow boardwalk of Dawson in the Northwest Territories. Dawson had sprung up at the junction of the Yukon and Klondike Rivers soon after gold was discovered on Bonanza Creek, and the word had spread like wildfire across Canada, Alaska, and the United States since July 1897. Over the last year, people had poured into the territory—Ruth and her father included—and now the settlement had become a rowdy little town. Today Dawson was buzzing with excitement over the weekly arrival of a boat from "outside," for with the boat came mail, food, mining supplies, and news from all over the world.

Tucking a strand of auburn hair under her bonnet, she drew herself up to her five feet, seven inches and turned her slender body toward the wharf for she, too, was interested in the boat's arrival.

"Good afternoon, Ruth." Mrs. Greenwood stopped her. She was short, heavyset in middle age, and rumored to be the town gossip. "Who's at the clinic today?"

"It's been a quiet day, Mrs. Greenwood. Just a few routine calls. No major ailments." She took a secret delight in suppressing information from Mrs. Greenwood.

"Well, you and the doc better get ready! With all the new folks arriving, there'll be brawls in the street tonight."

Ruth glanced at her. "Maybe not."

Despite Mrs. Greenwood's negative opinion about the passengers, she joined Ruth in walking toward the dock, where the *Bella* was nudging its way into the shoreline. People eagerly gathered up and down the shore watching.

"As usual, the men outnumber the women," Mrs. Greenwood said with a heavy sigh.

Ruth did not reply as she studied the strangers meandering tentatively down the gangplank. Watching, she tried to guess the professions of those arriving. It was easy to spot the miners—denim trousers, flannel shirts, felt hats. Then there were the men who had come to open shops; on their arms were women dressed in the fashion of the day.

"Hmmph," Mrs. Greenwood snorted. "They'll find out their city garb won't work here," she said as she and Ruth both stared at the fashionably high, stiff collars, narrow corseted waists, and wide bouffant skirts. "Look! Some of them are even wearing those disgraceful skirts!"

In cities, the fashion now was toward shorter skirts that showed the ankles.

"At least the knickers underneath will keep them warm," Ruth laughed, glad for her own. "Those were all the fad when I left Seattle."

"I call them bloomers," Mrs. Greenwood said under her breath. "I'm glad to see that not all of them are trying to be fashionmongers," she commented grudgingly. Mrs. Greenwood had gained ten pounds since Ruth had known her, and she couldn't help wonder if some of her criticism was due to her own dissatisfaction with herself.

"Reckon they'll be shedding those corsets soon enough," Mrs. Greenwood stated with pride. Automatically Ruth touched her waist, thinking how most of the women in Dawson had shed their corsets by mutual agreement, choosing comfort over fashion. It was difficult enough to keep the clothes clean and presentable, with having to deal with the mud of the streets and the occasional misfired stream of tobacco juice.

Ruth's eyes skimmed the crowd, recalling how she must have looked on the day she and her father arrived in June: She had worn her best silk dress with brush braid and interlined with buckram, which made the skirt swing wide when she walked.

An amused grin slipped over her full lips. She had worn the dress only once since her arrival nearly two months ago. At that time only those with money—like Ruth and her father, Dr. Wright, affectionately called Doc—could afford to arrive in Dawson City by boat. Many of the other inhabitants had come over the most difficult route, yet the cheapest. They had booked passage, one way or another, by steamer to Skagway, then struggled over the seven hundred miles to the Klondike by White Pass or Chilkoot Pass, each a challenge for human survival.

Somehow they had arrived, frostbitten, heavily bearded, and practically threadbare. They brought very little, having to shed their belongings piece by piece to lighten their load on the tortuous pass. When finally they stumbled in from the Klondike, thin as rails, many were in need of her father's medical attention. There was one other doctor in town, a fortyish widower by the name of Arthur Bradley, but Doc Wright's clinic was the busier one.

"Looks like the same kind of people," Mrs. Greenwood sighed.

As Ruth watched the boat's passengers disperse among the crowd, her eyes lingered on one young man in particular. He was tall with broad shoulders and long legs, and he wore the clothes of a laborer or a miner—denim trousers, red woolen shirt with long sleeves, and a black felt hat. She glimpsed thick, golden hair beneath the hat as he turned to speak with a huge, burly man beside him whose clothes were ragged and whose felt hat was smashed low on his forehead.

They had exited the gangplank and were now lost in the crowd.

"You heading home now?" Mrs. Greenwood asked as they turned back toward Front Street.

"Yes, actually I should have gone back sooner."

"And Mr. Greenwood will be wondering what's happened to me," she said, quickening her short steps. "I have to tell him about the boat."

Mrs. Greenwood was always on a mission for news. Her husband was one of the town assayers, and when Mrs. Greenwood ran low on conversation, he could pick up the slack. He knew the extent of everyone's wealth, particularly if their wealth came from gold dust or nuggets measured at his hands. He also knew which men were losing their shirts or had already busted and gone home. As it happened, the Greenwoods were Ruth's neighbors, which added to her discomfort. Her father merely seemed amused by the two.

As they parted company and Mrs. Greenwood turned down a side street to her husband's office, Ruth shifted the brown-papered bundle of supplies in her arms and hurried toward home. As she retraced her steps, she looked around her, wondering how the new arrivals aboard the *Bella* would regard Dawson. This was a town of white tents—most of them dirty by now—some hastily thrown up log dwellings, a few crude saloons, and a couple of hotels in various stages of development. Where there had once been a rough wilderness, the stampede for gold had brought thousands of people pouring into the territory. The screech of saws cutting across wood filled her ears as men worked day and night to construct dwellings. Every day brought a new adventure. It was the most exciting period of Ruth's twenty-one years.

Ruth had reached the end of the block and was now facing their two-story log house, the only two-story house in Dawson. The first floor of the house was used for the clinic; the upstairs provided two bedrooms, a living room-dining room combination, and a kitchen. Her father had spared no expense when he commissioned the hasty building of the house before their arrival. He had paid dearly for the indoor toilet and well-insulated plumbing, but Ruth was eternally grateful. She couldn't bear to think of traipsing to the outhouses she saw behind most buildings. Her father felt by combining office and home, the luxury was warranted.

She noted there were no horses at the hitching rail, which could or could not indicate patients within the clinic. She climbed the porch steps of the simple log house and caught her breath. It had been a long walk and she was tired. Pausing at the horsehair mat, she scraped the mud from her rubber boots and opened the door.

Crossing the hall, she peered into the large front room of the clinic. The clinic was basically an office and a waiting room. An overstuffed sofa and table were balanced by several straight-backed chairs. Her father got up from behind his cluttered desk at the opposite end of the room and came to meet her.

"Has Dr. Bradley stolen your patients?" She looked around, teasing her father. "You must have cut off the wrong toe and Mrs. Greenwood got wind of it!"

Her father laughed, enjoying his daughter's humor. "Dr. Bradley is

welcome to some of the load," he said, chuckling. "Here, let me help."
He scooped the packages from her arms.

"The *Bella* just arrived," she said, removing her cape and placing it
on the coat tree.

"I pray there was a generous amount of food for the merchants to
stock their shelves," Doc was saying.

Ruth nodded as she looked at the tall man before her. Kind hazel
eyes reflected the charm of his youth, but that youth had vanished
with the death of Mary Ruth Wright three years ago and with the
long work-filled days that had been so much a part of his life. Thick
brows and dark lashes matched the darkness of his hair, although
more gray than black now covered his head. His dark coat, superbly
tailored, no longer concealed the paunch at his waist, but Ruth's
smile merely widened. Her father enjoyed eating, and she loved
cooking.

"Seriously, did anyone come by?" she asked, glancing around the
clinic and noting that her father had already tidied things up. Her eyes
lifted to the wooden bookcase that held numerous medical books and
journals. One or two were askew, as though he had consulted them at
some point during the day.

"Ned Joiner from the blacksmith shop. He got careless with the
hammer and smashed his thumb. No permanent damage. All in all,
I'd say it's been a rather dull day."

"Then I'm glad. You work too hard."

He was staring at her thoughtfully now. "Ruth, I couldn't manage
without you. I hope you realize that."

"I do realize it. Besides, you don't take care of yourself very well.
You need me to boss you around," she teased.

He chuckled. "Then I'll allow you to do that. But first, I'll take this
package up to the kitchen for you."

"No, thank you." She wrestled the package from him. "You stretch
out in the chair and put your feet up."

Strangely, he obeyed, tilting his head curiously at her as he took
his seat.

"Why are you looking at me that way?" she asked frankly.

He smiled. "It's just that you remind me so much of your beautiful mother—the auburn hair, the heart-shaped face, the way you move and talk and think."

"Thank you," she replied, touched by the compliment. Her mother was the kindest person she had ever known and, like her father, Ruth had been devastated by her death.

"But I have your eyes," she reminded him, and they both laughed. "Well, I must start supper."

She climbed the steps to their apartment on the second floor. Entering the living room, her eyes moved over the simple wooden furniture they had purchased from local carpenters. It was a far cry from the fine pieces they had left behind, but in Dawson City, everyone had to start all over again.

She hurried to the kitchen, depositing her goods on the cabinet. The kitchen always gave her a sense of contentment, perhaps because in Seattle the kitchen had been the center of their family life. Her mother loved to cook and had dispensed with kitchen help, even though most families of their status hired cooks and maids. The only concession her mother made was hiring a cleaning lady for their large home. The kitchen belonged to Ruth and her mother. Unable to conceive another child after Ruth, her mother had tried to make up for their small family by constantly entertaining.

The sound of horse hooves outside brought her to the window. She parted the muslin curtain and peered down. Her eyes widened. To her surprise, the man she had spotted on the gangplank of the *Bella* was slowly getting down from a brown sorrel with a well-tended harness. Yes, it was him—and now she could see that he was even taller as her eyes scanned the long legs that stretched to brown cowhide boots. His red shirt strained against well-toned muscles as he hitched his horse at the log rail. Then suddenly his eyes moved upward to the window where she stood gawking.

Ruth stepped back, realizing she shouldn't be so judgmental of Mrs. Greenwood, for at the moment she was burning with curiosity. She heard his knock, and then her father's steps crossed the hall to the front door. She walked to the open door and stood listening.

"I'm Doc Wright." Her father's voice floated up to her.

"I'm Joe Spencer," he said, speaking slowly. "I hurt my back down at the dock just now. Thought I should get it checked."

"Then come in and let's have a look."

Ruth could hear them crossing the hall, and then the clinic door closed. She supposed if her father needed her, he would call for her. She stopped at the counter, picking up a narrow black satin ribbon. Suddenly conscious of the wispy strands of auburn hair dangling at her collar, she gripped the ribbon with her teeth and swept her hair back from her face, securing it at the nape of her neck with the ribbon.

Her curiosity about the man downstairs lingered as she rolled up the long sleeves of her blouse. He was a southerner; she could tell from his accent.

She rinsed her hands in the wash pan, wondering if he had seriously injured his back; from the way he moved, she would guess it was a strain. She dried her hands on a cup towel then turned to check the dough she had left rising near the stove. As she pressed her thumb into the fat dough and made a fingerprint, she reached for the rolling pin. Scrambled eggs with biscuits and a tin of molasses settled the question of supper. How could she manage an invitation to the stranger? Or was he married? Her heart sank. Probably.

The door opened again, and she heard her father speaking. "Just apply that liniment and don't lift anything heavy. If you want to stop in tomorrow, I'll have a larger bottle. Some of my medical supplies should have come in on the boat. Say, want to come up and have a cup of coffee?"

There was a moment's hesitation while she grabbed the teakettle.

"If it's no bother."

"No bother at all. We drink a lot of coffee here," he was saying as the men climbed the stairs.

Ruth had poured hot water from the teakettle into the tin coffeepot and now had it back on the stove. She was spooning coffee grounds into the pot as their footsteps entered the living room. "Have a seat," her father was saying. "You need to bend your knees and ease yourself slowly onto the sofa. Protect that back." Doc poked his head around the door. "Could we—"

"I'm making coffee," she said, smiling at him.

"Thank you." He grinned then turned back to the living room.

"How long have you been here, Doc?" The smooth voice of the stranger drifted to her.

"My daughter and I came up from Seattle in June. I'd spent my life there. After the Panic in '93, the country was in a depression. It seemed the Pacific Northwest was especially slow to recover. Many of my patients couldn't even pay their medical bills, but I wouldn't turn them away. They were people I'd known for years."

Listening from the kitchen, Ruth nodded, thinking about how tenderhearted her father had always been. She checked to be sure the water was boiling then grabbed tall mugs from the cupboard.

"When the *Portland* steamed into Seattle last year—July 17 it was—with news of the Klondike gold strike, Seattle went crazy. Salespeople bolted over the counters; firemen and policemen threw down their uniforms; even the mayor resigned. I heard that one preacher walked out on his congregation!"

Both men laughed at that, and from the kitchen Ruth listened, enjoying the sound of Joe Spencer's laughter. Everything about this stranger fascinated her.

"San Francisco was much the same way," Joe replied.

"I think everyone was hungry for change," Doc continued. "The idea of gold and adventure appealed to all of us. I heard the Yukon was desperate for doctors, so my daughter and I left as soon as we could have our place built. But then, after all I'd heard about the Klondike and its thriving towns, Ruth and I were pretty disappointed when we got here. From the boat this place just looked like one big swamp sprawled along a riverbank." He chuckled.

"I reckon the first settlers here had a real vision about what the town could become," Joe said. "It seems to be thriving now."

"Yes, it is," Doc agreed. "And you're right, Joe Ladue had a real vision when he put up a warehouse and a sawmill. He knew what he was doing, that's for sure. My biggest gripe with Dawson, I guess, is those who try to get rich on the settlers."

"Yes, sir. I'd heard men complain about how the merchants had tripled the prices on everything. When I went into the mercantile this afternoon, I almost dropped the sack of secondhand nails when the clerk priced them at eight dollars a pound."

"It's ridiculous," Doc replied, his voice filled with contempt.

"As a matter of fact, sir, you have the best price in town for services rendered."

"Thank you. That's a nice thing to say. I just came to help, that's all."

"The people here are fortunate you made that decision, Dr. Wright."

"Just call me Doc. Everyone does."

"Do you dabble in mining at all, Doc?"

Her father hesitated. As Ruth pulled the coffeepot from the burner, she wondered if her father would admit that he owned a claim. A half-starved miner had collapsed on their doorstep while waiting for the next boat out. In payment for services, he had given Doc the claim, which appeared useless and had nearly killed him.

"I don't have time to think about mining." Doc sidestepped the question. "I'm not inclined to hire someone to build a shaft down into the earth or wade through the frozen streams in winter. And I certainly don't want to do that."

"I feel sure you'll end up with more money in this profession," the stranger said.

Ruth stared at the thin curl of smoke drifting up from the spout of the coffeepot, suffusing her pale cheeks with color. *Keep talking*, she silently pleaded. She loved his accent.

Her father peered around the door, glancing at the coffeepot.

"It's ready," she said.

"Ruth, won't you come in and join us?" He walked over to get the tray from the cupboard.

Her eyes darted to him then back to the mugs. "All right."

Placing the mugs on a tray, along with spoons and sugar, she followed her father into the living room. The tray was a far cry from her mother's silver service she had used so many times; a silver service in Dawson City would be subject to theft, not to mention the fact that it would look oddly out of place.

Joe Spencer stood as she entered, almost startling her with his good manners. She placed the tray on the coffee table then straightened, dropping her hands to her sides.

"Mr. Spencer, this is my daughter, Ruth Wright."

"How do you do?" she said, smiling at him.

"Hello." He nodded politely. "Thank you for the coffee."

"We don't have cream," she said, glancing back at the tray.

"I drink it black. Since coming north, I've learned to be happy with the bare necessities. It suits me fine." He spoke with confidence as his eyes lingered on Ruth. She turned to the tray.

"And where is home for you?" Doc asked, leaning back on the sofa, studying him thoughtfully.

"Richmond, Virginia," he said. "Thank you." His eyes met Ruth's as she handed him a mug of coffee.

His eyes were a clear, bright blue. He had thick brown brows and darker brown lashes, a slim straight nose, full lips, and a square chin. He was unquestionably the most handsome man she had seen in a very long time. If ever. She turned and handed her father his coffee, then took her mug and sat in the nearest chair, studying Joe Spencer over her mug.

"How did you get all the way to Dawson from Richmond?" Doc asked curiously.

"I went to California five years ago at the invitation of my uncle, who was working on a ranch out from San Francisco. I enjoyed the life of a cowhand for a few years, but after my uncle died, I left the ranch and went into San Francisco looking for work. I heard about the Klondike strike and decided I wanted to give it a try. So I worked as a carpenter and saved every cent I made until I could board the ship."

"You were wise to choose the ship rather than trying to cross Chilkoot Pass on foot as so many are doing."

Joe Spencer shook his head. "I had already heard horror stories about that route. A fellow I worked with at the lumber yard joined some guys who were going up in '96. He almost died trying to get over the pass. He turned around and came home with tuberculosis and an amputated foot due to frostbite."

Doc nodded. "I fear we're in for a winter of such maladies." He paused, glancing over at Ruth. Then his eyes returned to Joe Spencer. "Did you come alone?" he asked.

Ruth glanced at her father, thinking he was almost as curious as she was about this stranger with the southern accent.

"I did, but I've made friends. In fact, one of my friends, Ivan Bertoff, will be going out to the mining district with me when I leave tomorrow." His eyes drifted slowly to Ruth. "How do you like living here, Miss Wright?" he asked.

Surprised by his question, she swallowed the hot coffee too quickly and almost choked. She kept her composure, however, as she licked her lips and looked at him. "I like it."

"It must seem quite a change from Seattle," he said as his eyes drifted over her face.

She reached up to push a lock of auburn hair back from her forehead. "It is, but I enjoy the satisfaction of helping others. My father is a wonderful doctor."

"I've already benefitted from his services." He finished his coffee and came slowly to his feet. "I've imposed for long enough. I must get busy gathering the supplies I'll need. What time would you like me to come in tomorrow?"

Doc shrugged. "We don't make appointments here. It's first come, first serve."

Joe laughed. "Then I'll see you in the morning." He turned to Ruth. "It was a pleasure meeting you."

Their eyes locked and Ruth felt something strange and different as she looked at Joe Spencer, something she had never felt before. "Thank you," she said.

He turned and nodded at Doc then headed for the door, hat in hand. Doc followed him back down the stairs as Ruth returned to the kitchen, trying to sort out her feelings. He had told them very little about himself. He hadn't mentioned a wife, but how could a man so handsome reach—at least thirty years of age she guessed—and remain single?

Joe Spencer tried to ignore the ache in his back as he weaved his way through the crowd. Glancing around, he recognized some of the boat passengers, but many of the men on the street were obviously miners. With tanned faces and thick beards, they wore tattered clothing and surveyed the newly arriving people through narrowed eyes.

He kept thinking of the Wrights and feeling a sense of regret that he wouldn't allow himself to get to know them better. But he had to be careful; already, he worried he had told them too much. Still, there was something about them that made him feel at home and comfortable; he longed to enjoy their hospitality, take advantage of their kindness. But he would be taking advantage and he knew that; he could stay nowhere for long. The secrets in his past dogged him like predators; memories howled like the wolves on a cold night, and he had spent many cold nights alone in the woods, listening to the wolves howl.

Joe located the Bank of British North America, which was actually a large tent with a board plank for a counter and an old trunk for a safe—both proof of how new Dawson City was. Joe's eyes widened. Around the trunk, Joe spotted several sacks of gold on the sawdust floor.

He reached deep into the pocket of his denim trousers and withdrew a deerskin bag of gold dust. He offered the bag to the assayer, wanting to convert some of his gold dust to cash for a deposit in the bank. For spending money, the common practice was to use gold dust. When an impressive sum had been opened in his account, he thanked the clerk and left.

Just down the street he spotted the Alaska Commercial Company and entered. The store was a large, square room filled with shoppers milling about the counter, which ran the length of one side. Although the days were still long and the air was crisp but not cold, the potbellied stove in the corner held a low fire. Two well-dressed men from the boat were conversing with three miners, each hungry for news the other had to offer. Joe turned toward the shelves, consulting the list he pulled from the pocket of his shirt, and began to stack up the items: sugar, flour, salt, canned milk, beans, tea. He added a hefty slab of bacon then paused, glancing toward another array of shelves. Consulting his list again, he walked over to select a pick, shovel, and a metal pan. What other tools did he need? He frowned, trying to concentrate despite the boisterous crowd.

Joe had been forced to leave his other supplies behind in Skagway, but he had brought what he needed most: the gold dust. He turned to the cashier and slowly withdrew another deerskin bag from the pocket of his denim trousers. He handed the bag to the clerk and waited; as he did, his eyes made a slow, careful sweep of the room. There were no familiar faces; Ivan still had not appeared.

The clerk weighed the gold dust on scales positioned on a thick, black velvet cloth. Joe wondered how much gold dust ended up on that cloth by the end of the day. He watched the scales tip and noted the look of surprise on the clerk's face. The man cast his eyes over the crowd and leaned toward Joe. "About ninety dollars," he whispered.

Joe nodded. "Will you total my supplies and see if this is enough?"

Joe knew it would be. If not, there was another pouch of gold dust, but he needed that to survive through the winter.

"Could you tell me where I could obtain some good dogs?" he asked the clerk while the man packaged up his supplies.

"Try Arvin Christensen. His place is on the south end of town, first road to the right. Has a white banner in his yard advertising his business."

"Thanks," Joe said. "And what about a place to stay?"

"Try Mattie's Roadhouse. It's the best we have to offer until the hotel is completed. She's down at the south end, too, but you better hurry. With the boat coming in, she may be filled up already."

"Thanks again," he said.

His good luck was still holding when he obtained the last cot in the boardinghouse. The log structure was actually four large rooms with as many cots as Mattie could cram into each room. For the ladies who had accompanied their men, another room awaited them. This room was strictly for males, and already six were sprawled on the cots, snoring loudly.

Joe pushed his supplies up under the cot and hesitated, wondering if it would be safe to leave them while he checked on the dogs.

The ache in his back had intensified after carrying the load, and he could no longer pass up the cot. The dogs could wait, he decided, as he removed his boots and stretched out on the cot.

When he closed his eyes, he saw Ruth Wright, and this surprised him. He had been impressed by her beauty—the fair skin that was enhanced even more by thick auburn hair and deep hazel eyes. And yet it was the depth he sensed in the woman that drew him even more. She had to be brave and adventurous—and unselfish—to accompany her father here to the frozen north. She obviously had no idea what was in store for her. No doubt, she would be on the first boat when spring breakup came and there was boat travel again.

It didn't matter, he told himself. He had a plan, and no woman would fit into his plan. Not ever again.

2

*R*uth and Doc shared their simple meal in relative silence in the glow of the lantern. Doc had been in the process of buttering a biscuit when suddenly he laid down his knife and looked across the small table. "I hope the winter here won't be too harsh for you. We haven't yet experienced the cold and—"

She put up her hand. "Father, I am no longer the forgetful young girl who dashes off without mittens or muff. I find Dawson exciting. And I'm very proud of what you're doing here. Like you, I'm far more interested in seeing a sick person restored to good health than sitting by a cozy fire in Seattle, pricking my thumb with a needle."

He sighed, leaning back in the wooden chair. "We're going to have some gruesome illnesses to treat. Frostbitten hands and feet, consumption, scurvy, perhaps even tuberculosis."

"Please." She pressed a hand to her stomach. "I'm trying to enjoy my meal."

"Sorry." He grinned, acknowledging her mock humor. "Do you think we have enough food to last the winter?" he asked suddenly.

"You are determined to be a worrywart, aren't you?" she gently scolded.

His brow was creased with concern as he glanced toward the wooden shelves behind the pantry curtain.

"We can't crowd one more item on those shelves, Father. I'd say we could live comfortably for two years!"

He sighed. "It's just that once the Yukon freezes over, which will be soon, there will be no more boats coming in. We'll be cut off from the outside world. There'll be no—"

"Father, I'm not worried," she said quickly, wanting to turn his thoughts in another direction. "If a stocked pantry had been of primary importance, I would have married William Manchester and grown fat and bored with him."

He did not laugh, as she had expected. He merely stared at her for a moment, as though trying to be certain she meant what she was saying.

She tilted her head and stared at him. "Why won't you believe that I really wanted to come here? That I didn't make the trip just for you?"

Slowly, a weary smile tilted his lips and some of the age in his face faded. "I want to believe that. But I keep thinking that you didn't want to hold me back; you knew I wouldn't leave you behind unmarried. And if you wouldn't marry William—"

"Father." She threw down her napkin as her temper began to flare. "William Manchester may have been considered attractive and well educated by a lot of Seattle women, but I did not love him. And I knew I never would. I want to feel what you and Mother felt for one another." She bit her lip, lost in thought.

Tears glistened in her father's hazel eyes before he quickly lowered his head. "I pray that you will have that someday," he said quietly. "To be truthful, I will never get over losing your mother. This adventure to the Klondike has been good for me, but I still long for Mary Ruth every day of my life."

She swallowed hard and her temper vanished as quickly as it had appeared. "I miss her, too, Father, but we have to go on. We're doing a good work here, a Christian service to these people, which must please Mother to no end. You know she is watching from heaven," she added softly, thinking she would read from her mother's Bible at bedtime.

"Yes," he said, unashamedly wiping the tears from his eyes. "And I'm glad you didn't marry William if you didn't love him."

"I didn't. He was aggressive, overpowering, and opinionated. I'll tell you something else, which I hope will end this discussion once and for all. I was certain that William would miss the benefits of his clubs and social events more than he would miss me; still, I decided to put him to the test. I told him if he really loved me, I'd like him to accompany us to the Klondike. I even promised to return with him in a year. He was quick to agree with me that this was not the life for him. So you see, if he had really loved me, he wouldn't have backed down so easily."

Doc nodded. "You're absolutely right." Something flashed in his eyes as he studied her face. "What did you think of Joe Spencer?"

She fought the color rising on her cheeks, telegraphing her feelings. "I don't know him, so how could I make a judgment?" She got up from the table, clearing away the dishes.

Her father stood, too, chuckling softly.

"Why are you laughing?" She whirled on him.

"I just had an amusing thought, that's all. I'm going downstairs to look through one of the new journals that came in by boat."

With that, he had disappeared, leaving her to her thoughts. She stared at the fluffy biscuits remaining in the pan and thought of Joe Spencer. What was he doing at this hour? Was he at the Bonanza Saloon like so many other men? Or was he already settled in someplace for the night?

After cleaning the kitchen, she picked up the mug that she had set apart from the others, the mug that Joe Spencer had held. Her slim fingers traced the round curve of the mug, relishing the thought that his lips had touched the enameled surface. Shaking herself back to reality, she quickly put the mug in the cabinet and went to her bedroom.

As she undressed and prepared for bed, she picked up her mother's Bible and turned the wick up on the lantern. She opened the Bible to Psalm 119, which had been one of her mother's favorites. Her eyes skimmed down the verses and lingered on those she had marked.

"Thy word have I hid in mine heart, that I might not sin against thee.

Blessed art thou, O Lord: teach me thy statutes.

With my lips have I declared all the judgments of thy mouth.

I have rejoiced in the way of thy testimonies, as much as in all riches.

I will meditate in thy precepts, and have respect unto thy ways.

I will delight myself in thy statutes: I will not forget thy word.

Deal bountifully with thy servant, that I may live, and keep thy word.

Open thou mine eyes, that I may behold wondrous things out of thy law."

Ruth paused, staring at the next verse, which seemed so appropriate for her.

"I am a stranger in the earth: hide not thy commandments from me."

She stopped reading and stared into space. She was a stranger to this country, to this way of life. There were times she felt frightened by that, although she would never admit as much to her father. But now this verse had given her comfort. She knew the word of God. She had grown up at her mother's knee, having the Bible read to her. It had always been a source of comfort to her, and just reading the verses from her mother's Bible tonight had given her such peace and joy.

She closed the Bible and smiled to herself, basking in the radiance of God's love.

Ruth returned the Bible to the nightstand and blew softly into the globe, extinguishing the flame. Snuggling deeper under the quilts, she closed her eyes and said her prayers. Her last thought before she drifted into sleep was that she was more grateful than ever that she had not married William Manchester.

❧

The next morning Ruth took extra care as she chose a favorite green dress of soft wool topped by the fashionably high, stiff collar. She even resorted to her corset today, for the special liniment her father had ordered had been delivered last night. When Joe Spencer came to their clinic, her father would check his back and apply the liniment again. And she wanted to look appealing. She had been grateful to learn that Joe had paid cash for her father's services. That was always a relief.

Her father was willing to take anything as payment from his patients, ranging from a sick dog to a lame mule. This held true regardless of how many times he had seen the patient or the extent of his care for that patient. The next needy miner who came to his door would more than likely be the recipient of the dog or mule. Failing all else, he even wrote No Charge on certain charts. He was a good Christian man, unable to turn a needy soul from their door.

The temperature had dropped below freezing in the night, and her fingers were stiff with cold as she fumbled for a ribbon. Tossing her auburn hair back from her face, she gathered it into one thick mass. She slipped the ribbon under her hair and pulled it tight, tying it into a bow at the nape of her neck.

Her father was an early riser, and he had left coffee for her on the stove. She had covered the leftover biscuits from last night, and now she plucked one from the pan, enjoying its fluffy taste. She poured herself a mug of coffee and sat down at the table, trying to organize her thoughts. It was not yet eight, and there were no patients downstairs, so she devoted her energy to preparing a stew that could simmer in the Dutch oven until lunch. Her potato stew was usually good, so she went to the cabinet, jammed with food, and retrieved some potatoes and located a paring knife. Humming to herself, she went to work.

❧

Joe Spencer had decided to wait another day before heading into the hills. He had slept comfortably on the cot and was pleased to learn that Mattie could be trusted. She had agreed to lock his supplies in her bedroom closet, freeing him up to do more shopping today and stop off at Doc Wright's clinic one last time.

His first mission was to check out the dogs. He didn't have to have a sled and dogs to carry supplies, but it would be good if he could find what he needed at the right price. He headed for the place he had been told about the day before. It was easy to follow the sound of dogs barking as he sloshed through the mud where the boardwalk ended, making his way to the log house where a white banner in the front yard advertised Malamutes For Sale.

A tall bearded man in denim trousers and a red flannel shirt stood in the front yard, surveying the sky.

"Hello," Joe called. "I wanted to see your dogs."

"How many?" the man asked, looking him over.

Joe hesitated, uncertain. "I don't know yet. Also, do you have a sled for sale?"

"Matter of fact, I do." The man motioned him around the side of the house to the backyard. Enclosed in a log fence were four brown and white malamutes, along with four other dogs of mixed breed. All appeared to be in good health.

"Man just sold me his sled and the eight dogs there. The dogs are well trained. They can pull a load for eight hours."

Joe frowned. "That's a long time."

"And a heavy load, too," the man said, ignoring the sympathy in Joe's voice.

Joe studied the dogs, pleased to see that their coats were lush, well tended, their eyes bright. He had always had a soft spot in his heart for dogs.

"How much for the sled and dogs?" He turned back to the man.

"Two thousand."

Joe stared at him. "That's ridiculous."

The man shrugged. "I'll get that much, perhaps more as winter sets in."

Joe sighed, tallying up his money. Even though he had a comfortable nest egg, he was not going to submit to such an exorbitant price. He cast another glance toward the dogs, regretting that he was unable to purchase them.

"How much does it take to feed those dogs?" he asked curiously.

"Man said he gave them lots of fish and maybe a thousand pounds of bacon over a year's time."

Joe whistled. "That's better than I'll be eating," he said wryly. "Can't afford them," he said and turned to leave. Then another thought occurred to him. "What about one dog? Do you have just one good malamute for sale?"

This took the man by surprise. "One dog can't pull much."

"No, but he could be a good companion."

"I've got a good male over here." He led Joe around to another enclosure where a brown and white malamute with soft brown eyes won

Joe's heart at first sight. Joe leaned down to rub the top of his brown head and study the white muzzle of fur around his eyes and mouth.

"He's twenty-six inches at the shoulders, weighs seventy-four pounds," Christensen announced.

Joe checked out the white underside of the dog's body and the sturdy white legs. He appeared to be a strong, healthy dog, and he was a friendly one, licking at Joe's hand. Joe's eyes skimmed over the brown back to the white tail curled over his back. He looked back at the almond-shaped eyes, filled with soul, and couldn't resist. "I'll take him," he said, without asking the price.

An hour later, with his new malamute leading the way, Joe gripped the leash and headed toward Doc's clinic.

～❧

Ruth listened to her father's lecture on vitamin C to Lucky Herndon, a local miner who was a frequent patient. The nickname Lucky had been a cruel joke on someone's part for the thin, bedraggled man seemed always in a streak of bad luck. Today he had come in complaining of aching muscles and showing bruises on his skin. Lucky was dressed as usual in patched denims, faded gray shirt, and dirt-encrusted boots. Doc had checked him over and assessed the bruises on his skin. Then he had looked in his mouth and shaken his head at Lucky's bleeding gums.

"You've got scurvy, Lucky," Doc said with a sigh.

"Scurvy?" Lucky croaked. Nervously, he removed his battered gray hat and raked through his thin hair that overlapped his collar. His long face seemed to lengthen as the jaw sagged. "That's bad news, ain't it?"

"Could be worse. How long you been without fruit?" Doc asked, closing his black bag.

Lucky shook his head. "I can't remember."

"Well, let me tell you something, Lucky. Don't even think about going back to that claim until you go to the store and get some decent food in your system. Ruth, do we have any oranges left?"

Ruth nodded and went upstairs to the pantry. Oranges were selling for one dollar each, and she doubted the poor man could afford them. There were half a dozen on their shelf, so she removed half of them and headed back downstairs. When she returned, her father was giving him a bottle of pills.

Just then the front door opened, and she turned to see Joe Spencer, who had just stepped into the hall. Her heart jumped at the sight of him, and she wondered what she was going to do about these crazy feelings she was experiencing each time she saw the man.

"Hello." He smiled at her.

"Hello." She smiled back.

"Want to see my new dog?" he asked her.

"Sure," she said then laughed.

It was a surprising question, but she followed him out to the front porch, where a handsome malamute sat, surveying the surroundings. She knelt, stroking his thick fur. "Hi there," she said then glanced up at Joe. "What's his name?"

"I'm going to call him Kenai," he answered.

She lifted a brow. "Kenai?"

He shrugged then propped a broad shoulder against the door jamb. "After a beautiful peninsula."

"That's a nice name," she said as she continued to stroke the dog's fur, yet her eyes had never left Joe's face.

Ruth held his gaze for a few more seconds. He was wearing fresh clothes—another pair of denim trousers, a brown wool shirt, and matching hat. He was clean-shaven, unlike so many she had seen.

The door behind him opened and the miner stumbled out, holding a sack.

"Now take your medicine and eat those oranges," Doc warned. "Come back and see me next week."

"Thanks, Doc." His faded blue eyes swept Doc then Ruth. "Thanks, ma'am."

"You're welcome." Ruth stood, brushing her hands.

"Nice dog," Doc said, glancing down. "How's your back, Spencer?"

"Better. A decent bed helped," Joe added as he and Ruth followed Doc back inside.

Ruth noticed as they entered the hall that the scent of the potato stew wafted pleasantly over the downstairs. She wanted to invite Joe to lunch, but she felt it was her father's place to do that.

"Father, I'm going to check on lunch. It will be ready soon," she added.

He nodded then looked at Joe. "Want to stay and join us? I'd like to hear more about San Francisco."

Joe glanced at Ruth as she lifted her skirts to climb the stairs. "Yes, sir, I'd be pleased to stay if it's not an imposition."

She glanced back over her shoulder. "No, it isn't."

❧

Later, as the three of them sat around the kitchen table, Ruth tried to conceal the joy she felt over having Joe with them. She could hardly keep her eyes from his handsome face, and he seemed to be looking her way a lot.

She lifted the platter of corn bread and offered him a slice.

"Thank you," he said. Again, his eyes lingered on her face for a fraction of a second.

"So," her father spoke up, "we were going to talk about San Francisco. I haven't been there in years. What's it like now?"

"The people are depressed over the money situation, the same way you mentioned folks are in Seattle. When news of the gold strike here reached the city, it caused a major upheaval. Everyone quit their jobs and tried to book passage on the first boat out."

He paused for a sip of coffee.

"I finally got passage on an old coal tanker and had the pleasure of breathing coal dust all the way to Skagway. Seemed like where there was space for one man, four were crammed in. In fact, there were about eight hundred people on that old clunker."

"And you got off in Skagway?"

"I did, along with a lot of other people waiting for another ship going farther north. If your clinic was located there, you would have been in business night and day," Joe added then searched his mind for another topic to quickly change the subject. "What do you treat most people for here, Dr. Wright?"

Doc dipped in his stew again. "Scurvy. I imagine it will soon be frostbite when the harsh winter sets in." He looked up at Joe. "If you don't have a hot water bottle, that would be a good investment. Mrs. Mulrooney sells them at her road-house on the edge of town. She was smart to think of bringing hot water bottles to sell." He winked at his daughter. "Ruth, why didn't you think of that?"

Ruth got up to refill the coffee cups. "You didn't give me a lot of time to think of hot water bottles," she replied lightly.

❧

Joe watched Ruth and her father, admiring the way they got along together. He had been without family for a very long time, and he found himself drawn to the doctor and his daughter—particularly the daughter—in a way that could prove dangerous for him. He concentrated on his food, trying to goad himself into leaving as soon as it would be polite to do so.

"Father, what's wrong?" Ruth had asked.

He looked up. Doc's face had turned gray, and for a moment, he said nothing.

"Do you have some food caught in your throat?" she asked, hurrying to his side.

Joe stood, staring down at the man, wondering what he could do. But then Doc shook his head and took a deep breath. "Just a slight case of indigestion, I think." He pushed his plate back and looked at his daughter. "You feed me too well."

Joe watched him carefully, noticing that the color had not returned to his face, although his smile and the pleasant hazel eyes seemed to convince his daughter. Narrowing his eyes, Joe studied him for another moment. He was a doctor; he, of all people, should know if something were wrong, and he claimed to have indigestion. Something nagged at Joe, however; something he could not pinpoint. Then he remembered. He had seen that gray color last year on the face of an older gentleman before he toppled onto the saloon table and died.

"I didn't prepare a dessert," she said, a note of apology in her voice.

Joe shook his head. "I don't care for sweets, but thank you. As a matter of fact, I really should get on with my errands, although I feel it's impolite to eat and leave."

"It's quite all right," she said. Then she turned to Joe and startled him senseless with her next statement. "We attend midweek prayer services tonight. Would you like to join us?"

Joe's mind raced. How could he pretend he was leaving town tonight when he had admitted a few minutes ago that he was departing at first light tomorrow? And at the moment, he couldn't even think of an excuse not to join them. He glanced quickly at her father. The man's color still was not good, and Joe found himself filled with concern for another individual for the first time in a year.

"We would like that," her father added seriously.

Joe touched the soft napkin to his lips, still searching his mind for an excuse and still finding none. "Where are the services held?" he asked.

"Up on the north end of town," Doc replied, "next to the tent that advertises blankets for sale. Services are held in one of the few clean white tents in Dawson. At the present, it's the only church we have, such as it is, but by next year there will be a building on that spot."

Joe nodded, feeling the pull of Ruth's eyes. He could see that she wanted him to join them, and for some reason he didn't understand, he decided to go.

"All right, thank you for inviting me." He hesitated then decided to be truthful. "I used to be a Christian—"

"Used to be?" Ruth tilted her head and gazed at him with questioning eyes.

He shifted uncomfortably. "Well, I still am. What I meant was, I was raised to attend church, but I haven't gone in . . . quite a while. If my mother were alive, she would be grateful to you for inviting me." His voice softened at the mention of his mother. Nothing in his life had been the same since she died.

He pushed back his chair. "I have some errands to run this afternoon. What time do services start?"

"We start early," Doc replied. "Six this evening. The preacher works days at the docks, so he's usually too tired to be long-winded."

Joe smiled, coming to his feet. He looked at Ruth again. "Thank you for a nice meal." He looked back at Doc, relieved to see that the color was returning to his face. He looked normal again. Maybe it was only indigestion, after all. "And thank you for treating my back. Oh," he reached into his pocket, "I forgot to pay you today."

Doc shook his head. "You paid yesterday. This was just a follow-up visit. And the pleasure of your company has been payment enough. See you tonight."

Joe hesitated. "Very well. Thanks for inviting me," he added, glancing at Ruth.

"By the way," Ruth said, going to the cabinet, "I have something for Kenai." She handed him a small bowl of leftovers. "You can keep the bowl," she added with a smile.

He stared into the oval face, mesmerized by the way her deep auburn hair made her skin look as soft as cream, and the eyes were a hazel color that was quite unusual. Joe wished he had the time to get to know her, to give over to the feelings that were nudging at his heart. But he didn't. He took the bowl from her and smiled. "Kenai will be grateful," he said.

They said their good-byes and Joe hurried down the stairs to the hall, bowl in hand. He thought about what nice people the Wrights were and how he wished he had met them a year ago. If he had, his life might have been drastically different. But he had not. And he had to live with the man he had become.

3

*R*uth and her father had chosen a seat on the middle bench, with her father seated next to the aisle. The crowd was sparse tonight, despite the arrival of the boat, which should have added to the small congregation. In contrast, the saloons were livelier than usual, having absorbed many of the boat's passengers.

Inside the tent that served as their church, the minister, Grant Sprayberry, stood at the front of the benches, Bible in hand, ready to conduct the service. He led the songs, as well. There were no musical instruments, so it was fortunate for everyone that he had a strong voice and an ear for music. Since there were no hymnals, he took requests for favorite hymns. First, he asked if anyone was in need of special prayer. Ruth vaguely heard the requests, lowered her head during prayer time, and tried to join in mentally.

Still, this was difficult, because Ruth was beginning to feel anxious. She and her father had waited outside the tent for Joe until time for the service, but he had not appeared. Doc had made an excuse for him, but Ruth was embarrassed and humiliated by his failure to show up. How could he eat their meal, accept their kindness, then be so rude? Was it possible that something had come up? She remembered his hesitation when she first invited him, and now she suspected that he had not wanted to come but was reluctant to refuse. So he had taken the easy way out.

"What's our song for tonight?" Pastor Sprayberry asked.

"How about 'Rock of Ages'?" someone in the rear of the church called out.

"'Rock of Ages' it is." Pastor Sprayberry smiled. He was a tall, middle-aged man with a wife and two daughters. When the pastor smiled, his entire face lit up, and he was smiling now.

Ruth tried to recall the verses to the hymn, since most hymns were sung by memory.

Rock of ages, cleft for me, Let me hide myself in thee . . .

"Excuse me."

She turned to see Joe Spencer standing in the aisle beside her father.

Doc nodded and Joe stepped in front of him, attempting to slip quietly past Ruth to fill the empty space on the other side of her.

"Sorry I'm late," he whispered.

She merely smiled and began to sing the hymn. All voices were lifted joyfully in praise, and while Joe did not open his mouth to sing, he seemed to be standing very still beside her.

After three verses of the hymn, the pastor opened his Bible and began to read from Psalms. He had chosen a favorite Psalm—the Twenty-third—and most people seemed to know it by heart, as they read along with him.

Ruth was holding her mother's Bible, and she shared the open page with Joe. He did not take a corner of the Bible; he merely followed the verses with his eyes. Then the pastor began to speak about the journey of life, emphasizing the importance of having the Lord as our shepherd, taking each verse and relating it to life's daily journey. When he had finished the simple, yet heartwarming message, he took requests for another hymn.

Doc Wright spoke up. "'Amazing Grace.'"

Ruth smiled sadly. It was her mother's favorite hymn, and she and her father had always liked it, as well.

Amazing grace! How sweet the sound, That saved a wretch like me . . .

She lifted her voice in song, feeling joy stir through her soul.

I once was lost, but now am found, Was blind, but now I see.

At the end of the first stanza, she glanced at Joe. Quickly, her eyes flew back to the front of the tent where Grant Sprayberry stood. She didn't want to make Joe self-conscious by having him know she had seen him in a vulnerable moment. But there was no mistaking it; he had tears in his eyes.

Joe swallowed hard, lowered his eyes, and hoped that Ruth had not seen the emotion that seemed to be flooding through him. What was wrong with him? First, the woman beside him had turned his head since he first met her. Being near her left him feeling as though he wanted to stand at her side for . . . well, for a long time. Now, he was reacting to the message, to the hymns, to the simple words the man had spoken. Well, he couldn't react, he couldn't feel anything. Not now; most of all, *not now*.

He concentrated on his hands, on the long fingers laced together before him. He thought of the mining claim, how rich he would be. He even forced himself to remember the cute little gal he had met in Skagway, although he couldn't even remember her name.

"We are so glad you could come." The soft voice beside him pulled his thoughts back to the moment. He turned and looked at her. She had tilted her head back to look at him, and her hazel eyes sparkled in a way that made his heart beat faster.

He cleared his throat, trying to summon back the manners his mother had taught him growing up. "Thank you for inviting me," he responded.

He looked over her head and saw that people were leaving now; it was his chance to get out, and he was eager to do that. He could feel her eyes lingering on his face for another few seconds, but he didn't look back at her. He pretended an interest in the people who had attended the service, but in truth, it didn't matter.

"Glad you could join us." Doc extended his hand for a shake.

"Thank you. I'm sorry I was late." He glanced quickly at Ruth then turned back to her father. "My partner wants to leave Dawson this evening, so I had to pack."

"When will you be returning?" Doc asked.

Joe shook his head. "I'm not sure."

Did her shoulders slump slightly at his reply, or had he imagined it?

"Go easy with your back," Doc said, stepping into the aisle.

To his relief, Joe saw that the pastor was engaged in conversation with an elderly woman at the front bench. He was terrified that they might drag him up and introduce him to the preacher, and then every-one might start asking about his salvation. He had been embarrassed like that once when he was seven, and he had never forgotten it.

They moved with the crowd, out of the tent, into the lingering daylight of an August day. He looked up at the sky as he placed his broad-brimmed hat back on his head. Only another hour, two if they were lucky, of daylight. He had to say goodbye and leave.

"Well, thanks again," he said to Ruth, trying to sound more formal with her.

"You're welcome. Take care," she said, extending her hand.

He was surprised by that gesture, surprised even more by the softness of her hand in his, and how much he liked the feel of her slim fingers. Then she had withdrawn her hand and was stepping back from him.

"Good-bye," he said, touching the brim of his hat as he looked from Ruth to Doc Wright. Then he turned and walked toward his horse. It was a sorrel, not particularly handsome, just serviceable, but with a good heart, like his dog Kenai, who waited for him at the boardinghouse.

"Good-bye," her voice called out, but he tried not to hear her.

And all the way back to the boardinghouse, he tried to shut out the murmurings of his conscience and the pain in his heart.

∽❧

Ruth and her father sat at the kitchen table having a bedtime snack. A patient had been waiting on their doorstep once they arrived back at the clinic. Tom Haroldson, a sixteen-year-old boy, had taken a fall and sprained his ankle while helping his father unload a wagon of sup-plies. Doc had bound the ankle carefully while Ruth handed him gauze, and now they had closed up the clinic and were free to relax.

"You're a good cook," her father said, taking one last bite of the huckleberry cobbler she had whipped up when they returned from church.

"Thanks."

Ruth had been filled with energy that she needed to vent, and after the clinic, the kitchen was the most appropriate spot to vent her energy, or frustration, whichever it happened to be. She was feeling a bit of both as she toyed with the dessert on her plate and thought about Joe Spencer. She gave up trying to finish the cobbler and laid her fork across the plate.

"Father," she looked up, "when you first met Mother, how did you feel about her?"

His eyes widened at her sudden question, but as usual he took their conversation in stride and always answered her patiently. She was grateful for that.

She watched him thoughtfully as he leaned back in the chair, and his hazel eyes drifted into space, seeing something that she could not. After a while, he spoke in a soft, gentle voice, one that held the tenderness of a deep love.

"I met her at the home of a friend in Seattle. You've heard the story. But how did I feel?" He heaved a deep sigh. "I thought she had the sweetest spirit of any woman I had ever encountered. I sensed this as we began to talk, and I knew I had never met anyone like her."

He closed his eyes for a moment. When he opened them again, he looked directly at Ruth. "She was pretty, of course, and she could have taken her pick of men." A slow, pleased smile crinkled his face. "Thank God, she chose me."

"I know why," Ruth said softly, placing her elbows on the table, lacing her fingers together to cup her chin. "I would have chosen you if I had been Mother."

Doc's smile widened even more, and for a moment, he said nothing; he merely stared at her. Then he glanced down at the cobbler and took another bite. "Does this question have anything to do with Joe Spencer?" He glanced back at her. "I saw the look in your eyes, Ruth; in fact, I've been watching you all evening."

She reached for her fork, dragging it over the brown crust of the cobbler. "He seems like a nice man, and there aren't many of those around," she said, trying to sound casual.

Doc nodded. "That's true. And he's a gentleman; I like that. But we know very little about him, even though he spent an hour here today, had lunch with us, and joined us at prayer meeting. Still . . ." His voice trailed and now he seemed to be avoiding her eyes.

Ruth didn't like the look of concern on his face or the guarded tone of his voice.

"We haven't had a chance to get to know him," she pointed out. "We've just met him."

"True," he said, lifting his eyes to her face again. "So you must give yourself time to get to know him before you let your heart sweep you away."

"*Fa-ther!*" She lifted an eyebrow and pretended to be dismayed by his words. "Surely you don't think I'm foolish enough to fall for a man I don't know!"

He studied her face for a moment, then the worried lines along his brow softened as the smile touched his face again. "Sorry. A father has to be protective," he said, winking at her.

"Even when his daughter is twenty-one years of age? Please give me credit for not having made a bad choice yet."

They laughed together; but even as she spoke the words, the anxious tone of her voice was apparent to her own ears. She supposed her father heard it as well.

❧

Joe surveyed the area that had been home to Ivan the previous winter. Situated on higher ground, the area was walled in by spruce and birch trees on three sides, with a view of the broad valley below. Salmonberry and huckleberry bushes grew in abundance on the ridges.

Glancing back to the creek below, his eyes moved over the scarred stumps of spruce trees, long since cut down for firewood. There, at the edge of the bank, a spruce stump had been axed clean and carved in the wood in jagged print was the name *Ivan Bertoff*. This marked his claim; and to Joe's utter surprise, nobody had bothered it. It was the habit of most claims to have a description attached to the name, but since Ivan could not write, he had done well to print his name, which was the extent of his education.

Leaning back, swatting at a pestering mosquito, Joe recalled how he had harbored doubts about the stake even being here when Ivan first told him about his claim. But Ivan had told him the truth about everything. He had even described the tiny log hut he had built as a home for the past winter; now Joe would help Ivan expand it into a decent cabin for the two of them.

Joe ran a hand across his forehead as a troublesome thought took root: How badly would he and Ivan get on one another's nerves during the long cold winter that stretched ahead?

With that question in mind, he turned and looked across at Ivan stretched out on the ground, taking a nap. Ivan was a large man, weighing at least two hundred fifty pounds, and he stood six feet, five or maybe six inches. At fifty years of age, only a fringe of black hair rimmed his large shiny head; however, the black hair grew in abundance on his handlebar mustache. He had shed his flannel shirt, and now the stained undershirt strained across his wide chest and protruding stomach above brown corduroy trousers that had seen better days. He snored loudly, oblivious to the occasional mosquito or gnat nipping at his face.

Joe sighed and sat down on a flat rock to assess his situation. He had met Ivan in a saloon in Skagway. Ivan was a loner, friendly to no one; but if not for Joe, he would have bled to death in an alley behind the Last Dollar Saloon. Joe had found him, face down, a deep cut in the center of his back, his pockets emptied. Ivan had come to Skagway for supplies to keep from paying the high prices in Dawson and had nearly paid for it with his life. With assistance, Joe had dragged him to his tent, summoned help, and eventually saved his life. He had hoped, by this act, to make restitution for the life he had taken in Skagway.

Joe swatted at a mosquito and turned his gaze back to the stake, which Ivan swore marked an abundance of gold. Ivan claimed to have found color in the streams, panned it, and followed its source to this property. As for the claim itself, they would build a shaft and work the claim together, splitting the profits. The small amount of money Ivan had after last winter was stolen from him that night in the alley. Joe had won his trust by saving his life, and in return, Ivan was willing to make him a partner in what he was certain was a real bonanza.

After Ivan had produced a tiny piece of gold tucked deep in his boot, Joe had studied it thoughtfully.

"Bite it," Ivan instructed. "Then you know."

Joe looked from Ivan back to the wrinkled piece of metal. He had heard that gold would bend between the teeth if it were real. Amused, he had washed the nugget, placed it between his teeth, and gently bitten down. The nugget bent.

Ivan laughed, pleased to have proven his word. Operating on instinct, Joe had agreed. After all, he needed to stay on the move; and despite his efforts at mining in Skagway, he had lost money. He believed Ivan, for Ivan had no reason to mention the claim if it were not true. He could simply have healed at Joe's tent then said good-bye. Instead, he had wanted to show his gratitude; furthermore, he had noticed that Joe had a little money.

"Ahh . . ." Ivan struggled to a sitting position and looked across at him.

"Have a good nap?" Joe asked with a grin.

Ivan gave a wag of his bald head and turned to stare at their efforts so far. Fortunately, there was still enough timber around for adding on to his cabin. They had spent hours chopping down the spruce trees and cutting the trees into logs for the ends and sides of the cabin. The hut Joe had spotted when they first arrived was developed into a liveable cabin.

"You sleep?" Ivan squinted at him as he lifted a hammy hand to swat at a mosquito.

Joe shook his head. "No, but I'm ready to work again."

Joe drove himself relentlessly and he knew it. The past few days had been even worse, for in the back of his mind, he kept seeing Ruth Wright's face, and he kept hearing the voice of the pastor at the prayer service.

Sighing, he came to his feet. He could work as hard as Ivan, who was as strong as a moose, and he would. The month of September had come, and the days were already beginning to grow shorter, colder.

In the days that followed, Joe and Ivan worked side by side, from early until late, until exhaustion finally forced them to relinquish the task. They proved to be quite compatible, for neither had much to say, and the comfortable silence that enveloped them eased the strain of working and living together twenty-four hours a day.

Their work was simple yet complex, since they worked with only two sharp axes and two saws. They had no nails or spikes with which to build the cabin. Therefore, they had to notch the logs. Diligently, they worked, flattening three-inch strips across the bottom and top of each spruce log to ensure the fit of the logs when stacked upon one another. They filled the cracks with a thick layer of moss with the hope of shutting out the black flies and mosquitoes that nagged them now and the icy winds and snows that would torment in winter.

When the cabin was finished, Joe suggested they improve upon Ivan's small plank table. They built another one then made long boxes for their sleeping rolls. When Joe finally crawled into the sleeping roll, his back ached almost unbearably, even though he had applied Doc's liniment. Still, he did not think of his back or of his work; instead, his thoughts turned toward Ruth Wright, and the pain seemed to ease as he closed his eyes and the vision of her lovely face filled his memory.

4

"uth, I wanted to ask you something." Mrs. Greenwood had caught up as Ruth and Doc were leaving the tent after the Sunday service.

Reminding herself that the sermon had been on loving one's neighbor, Ruth turned sweetly to face Mrs. Greenwood.

"Good morning, Mrs. Greenwood. And how are you today?" Ruth smiled at the plump woman whose black silk dress stretched tautly across the bodice, threatening to pop the buttons.

"I am well, thank you. I want to invite you and your father to join Mr. Greenwood and me for lunch. I'm inviting Dr. Bradley as well," she added, beaming with satisfaction. It amazed Ruth that Mrs. Greenwood seemed to think she was doing everyone a favor with her efforts at matchmaking.

Behind the smile, Ruth gritted her teeth. What was she going to do about Mrs. Greenwood's self-appointed mission to play cupid between Ruth and Dr. Bradley, their competition? Of course, he wasn't really competition, because it took both doctors to tend to the patients in and around Dawson City.

"I . . . think we'll be busy, won't we, Father?" She turned, looking for her father. To her disappointment, he was engaged in conversation with Arthur Bradley.

"I'll just ask," Mrs. Greenwood said. Whirling, she rushed upon the two men, surprising them with the invitation before either could provide an excuse.

Ruth was uncomfortable with the situation. Dr. Bradley had been attempting to court her for the past month, but she had managed to avoid him. He stood about five feet, ten inches, was slight of build, with a long face, thin brown hair, and pale green eyes. He was a pleasant Canadian from Victoria, who had lost his wife to typhoid fever soon after their arrival in Dawson City last July. He had been too grieved to notice anyone until recently, but now she felt his eyes upon her and she didn't know how to respond. She was certain she could never be romantically interested in him.

"We've been invited out for lunch, Ruth," her father called to her, unable to escape the Greenwoods.

"Did you decide not to rest?" Ruth asked, holding her smile in place. "When we left home, you said you needed to get back and lie down, that you're exhausted from the week."

Doc hesitated, obviously caught in the dilemma.

"Then you'll be glad to know the meal is already prepared and waiting on the stove," Mrs. Greenwood shot back at her then turned to Dr. Bradley. "We'll excuse you busy people soon after you eat," she said, fairly beaming at him.

Ruth's eyes lingered on Mrs. Greenwood's round face. Her protruding blue eyes were fixed on Dr. Bradley as though she considered him to be the catch of the century.

Dr. Bradley, obviously embarrassed, nodded and thanked her profusely for her luncheon invitation while casting a quick glance toward Ruth.

Ruth was thoroughly embarrassed by Mrs. Greenwood's obvious attempts to pair up Ruth and the most eligible bachelor in Dawson City. It took every ounce of willpower to hold her temper. She lived up to the reputation of a redhead having a temper, and she was engaged in a mental tug-of-war between minding the pastor's sermon or minding her own will. She could feel the blood rushing to her cheeks. It felt as though her smile had tightened to a grimace of pain. Saying nothing more, she merely looked at her father with an expression that spoke volumes.

"What else could I do?" he muttered under his breath as he tucked her hand in his arm and they made their way to the Greenwood home.

Mrs. Greenwood had seated Ruth opposite Dr. Bradley, with her father at her side, while the Greenwoods occupied opposite ends of the table. Ruth touched the lace tablecloth, appreciating the luxury here in Dawson City. Her eyes moved on to the huge serving platter where a moose roast was surrounded with carrots and potatoes. She was grateful that someone else was willing to go to the trouble of a nice meal for her, and she turned her eyes back to Mrs. Greenwood, determined to be a bit nicer.

"This is very kind of you, Mrs. Greenwood," she said, smiling at the plump woman whose round cheeks were reddened from the heat of the kitchen.

"My pleasure. Mr. Greenwood, will you say grace?"

Everyone bowed their head while thanks were offered for the meal. Then, upon conclusion of the prayer, Ruth unfolded her napkin and laid it across the lap of her gray taffeta dress.

"Dr. Bradley, we've hardly had a chance to talk," Doc said, opening the conversation.

"We stay much too busy, don't we? And I'd like everyone to call me Arthur," he said as his eyes slid to Ruth.

"Arthur," Mrs. Greenwood spoke up, "do you miss Victoria? I hear it's such a beautiful city with the lovely gardens and all."

Sadness gripped his features for a moment as he nodded. "Yes, I do. And I miss Katherine terribly."

"Arthur, may I tell you what helped me when I lost my wife?" Doc asked gently.

The man looked up, his expression bleak. "Please do."

"My pastor recommended that I read the epistles of Paul in the New Testament. Paul was a man who survived shipwrecks, beatings, imprisonment, and starvation. In fact, he suffered numerous adversities and yet he was able to maintain an inner peace throughout his tribulations. Knowing that a man had suffered through so much and kept his faith helped me to hang on to mine. By reading those epistles, I found a peace that I thought was impossible. There isn't a day that passes that I don't long for Mary Ruth, but I have been able to start over and I, too, have found peace."

Arthur stared at Doc for a moment then nodded. "I appreciate your telling me that. Perhaps I will make that effort, as well."

Silence fell, and for a moment even Mrs. Greenwood seemed at a loss for words.

"Which route did you travel getting here?" Doc asked, moving to another subject. "I'm always curious about the various routes people use because it's such a treacherous journey."

"Yes, it is," Arthur agreed. "We took a steamer from Victoria, and actually the trip was quite pleasant. When weather and sea permitted, we stood on deck admiring the scenery. Everything went extremely well until someone on the boat got sick, and then an epidemic of typhoid spread. Fortunately, there was another doctor traveling as far as Lake Bennet. We were able to save some, but we lost many others. We had only been here three days when Katherine came down with typhoid." He dropped his eyes to his lap. "I did not have the facilities or the proper medicine for her. I will regret this trip until my dying day."

Ruth stared at him, moved by his words. She was suddenly filled with compassion for him, and she made a silent vow to be nicer to him. He was not interested in courting her, she decided; he was merely lonely.

Ruth was thinking about what he had said as she looked at him. He seemed so frail for this kind of lifestyle, and she couldn't help wondering why he had wanted to come to this wild frontier. She did not ask him that; instead, she thought of Victoria and how she had always longed to visit the gardens there.

"Do you consider returning to Victoria?" she asked gently.

He nodded. "Yes, I do. I have decided to give myself another year here, and then if I still am not happy, I will return."

Mrs. Greenwood cleared her throat. "Then we must see that you are happy," she said with unnecessary emphasis as she glanced boldly at Ruth. "We need your services here. Dr. Wright can't possibly handle all the people if the exodus continues as they say it will."

"I agree we need his help," Doc said. "However, I think our exodus will soon shut down for the winter. Already the Yukon is starting to freeze over, and Chilkoot and White Pass will be too treacherous in the dead of winter."

"So many people are talking about the scarcity of food." Mr. Greenwood entered the conversation at last. "Nell, do we have enough?"

Everyone stopped chewing and looked at Mrs. Greenwood. "I believe so. What about you people?" She glanced from Doc and Ruth to Arthur.

"I'm afraid I haven't planned very well," Arthur admitted. "Nevertheless, if I continue to be paid in sacks of flour and sugar," a wry grin touched his mouth, "I should fare well."

Doc chuckled. "I imagine we'll soon prefer to be paid in food rather than money."

The rest of the meal passed pleasantly, and after Mrs. Greenwood's bread pudding, Ruth noticed her father had begun to yawn. Everyone had finished the meal and was getting up from the table. She began to help Mrs. Greenwood clear the dishes as the men wandered into the small living room.

"Mrs. Greenwood, exactly when did you come to Dawson?" she asked conversationally, regretting the anger she had felt toward her earlier.

Mrs. Greenwood tilted her head back thoughtfully. "We came in '97, got a head start on getting our cabin built here. Clarence had heard about the strike, of course, and being an assayer, he knew he had a good future here." Her plump face held a wide grin as she spoke.

Ruth nodded. "I'm sure he does." Ruth had heard, through her father, that Mr. Greenwood, as an assayer, was getting rich from collecting remnants of gold dust that gathered on his velvet cloth, not to mention the particles he swept up from the board floor.

"Dear, you must join our sewing circle," Mrs. Greenwood was saying as she scraped the leftover food into a large pail for their dogs.

Ruth had opened her mouth to offer a reply, but she never got the chance. The woman plunged into a discourse on one of the women who was a member of the circle, relating some outrageous gossip.

Ruth glanced toward the living area where the men were seated. She had a chance to look Arthur Bradley over more carefully, since he sat with his back to her. She had to admire the courage required of him to continue on here after losing his wife. He was in a noble profession, like her father, and she admired that, just as she admired the man. Maybe in time she could think of him in a more romantic way. It would certainly make sense for the two of them.

Mrs. Greenwood droned on as Ruth turned back to dry a dish. Suddenly, Ruth's thoughts moved in another direction, and she found herself recalling a handsome bronze face, piercing blue eyes, and golden hair. Joe Spencer. She sighed heavily. It was difficult to believe that she would chose a poor miner over a prosperous doctor whose background seemed more compatible with her own.

Thinking of Joe, she reminded herself that he might not be poor; or if he were low on funds now, he could strike a bonanza like a few men had already done in this area. But then, what did it matter? Money was not the measure of a man.

Her eyes drifted back to the men talking pleasantly in the living room. Even Arthur Bradley was laughing softly. She thought of Joe again, recalling the sheen of tears in his blue eyes. *What had made him sad?* she wondered. And when would she see him again?

She forced her thoughts back to Mrs. Greenwood's prattle, and as they finished in the kitchen, she was relieved to hear her father say he was overdue for his Sunday afternoon nap.

As they prepared to leave, Arthur approached her, looking unsure of himself. "I told your father I'd like to come for a visit sometime to see how his clinic is set up."

She nodded. "Feel free to do that." She realized this was the moment she should have invited him for a meal, but she chose not to do that. Before she could consider Arthur as a suitor, she had to get Joe Spencer out of her head.

❧

One day had begun to flow into another as Joe worked beside Ivan digging through the hard earth, hoping to hit a streak of gold. At night, they built a fire and kept it going. By morning, the fire had served to thaw the ground five to six inches deep so they could start to shovel their way down, making a shaft. They dug fervently until they reached frozen ground again. The following night they built another fire; the next day they dug.

It was a monotonous process of grueling work. Sometimes Joe's back ached so miserably he could hardly sleep. Still, he had spotted some flecks of gold in the black gravel, and now he was filled with hope. This fueled his determination to keep going until they were twenty feet down and four feet wide. This would be their shaft. At this point, they would no longer use a shovel but rather a windlass for getting the dirt out. They took turns in the shaft, shoveling out the rocks and frozen dirt that had melted from the fire. Ivan had made a pigtail hook on the end of the rope attached to the bucket that hauled up the dirt. One man loaded the bucket while the other operated the windlass at the top of the shaft, hauling the bucket to the surface.

Both Ivan and Joe kept their eyes strained for the sight of gold, so much so that they often dreamed about it at night; but through it all, he never stopped thinking of Ruth Wright.

～❦～

The first snow of the season had come, and Ruth stared out at the swirling snowflakes beyond her window, drawing her shawl tighter around her. She and her father were comfortable and warm in their house, and for that she was grateful. Looking out on the inhabitants of Dawson Creek, huddling into their coats and rushing toward their destination, she wondered just how low the temperature would drop. Already the men wore their fur caps, twill parkas, and heavy mackinaws. Most had shaved their beards. Miners had been warned that in winter their beards would freeze to their face.

The snow did not last, however, and to everyone's surprise the sun burst forth, thawing out the snow, making it possible for the boat that had been docked for a week to depart.

"Ruth," her father entered the room, "check our pantry again."

She turned and glanced at her father as he sank into the chair, looking weary although it was only ten in the morning. He had already seen three patients, however, and she wondered if he were hungry.

"Do you want an early lunch?" she asked.

He shook his head. "I'm not hungry. I'm just concerned about the food supply. Yesterday, I saw a notice on the board by the trading company that troubled me."

Ruth looked at him curiously. "What is it?"

"Today's boat will probably be the last one until spring. The notice warned those who did not have a supply of food to last the winter to leave Dawson." His hazel eyes were troubled as he looked across at Ruth. "There is a general fear of starvation, so we must be careful."

Ruth nodded then wondered why her father was so generous to his patients if he had concerns about their food. She had watched thin men and women haul tinned goods from their clinic by the armload. Still, she was not worried. She knew her father was doing the Christian thing by giving hungry people food.

She had examined their pantry just this morning as she was planning the day's meals. The shelves were still fully stocked, although there were some obvious spaces where tinned goods had once been, the results of her father's generosity. It didn't matter. She would be a smart cook, and her father had a promise from one of the merchants that there was a supply of food tucked in a back room for the doctors and merchants.

She smiled at him, aware that he needed her reassurance. "We will be fine, Father. There's plenty of food in our pantry, and I have learned how to economize."

He sighed with relief. "I'm glad to hear that." He ran a hand across his forehead. "Ruth, I think I'll lie down for a few minutes. Keep an eye on the clinic, please."

"Of course," she said. Her eyes followed him with concern. He seemed to be moving slowly today, and she knew he worried too much about her and about his patients.

After he had gone to his room, she went to the kitchen to stir the hash simmering in the iron skillet. She loved the smell of onions and potatoes that filled her kitchen. Since this was one of her father's favorite meals, perhaps it would boost his energy.

She went to the window and glanced out. There was no one approaching their door. Still, she should go downstairs and wait in the clinic while her father rested. They kept medicine in the supply cabinet and her father worried about theft.

Halfway down the stairs, she thought she heard her father call her name. She hesitated, her hand on the banister. Then she heard the unmistakable sound of a loud groan. Lifting her skirts, she flew back up the stairs.

"Father?" she called out as she entered the quiet living room. Hurrying on to his bedroom, her eyes flew to his bed and her breath caught. *"Father!"*

His legs were extended from the bed onto the floor, while his upper torso remained slumped against the bed. It looked as though he had made an attempt to get up then given up.

"Father? What is it?" She rushed to the bed.

When she looked into his face, fear slammed into her. His eyes were open, staring at the ceiling. For a split second she froze, unable to move. She had watched men die in her role as nurse, but she refused to believe what her knowledge suggested to her now. Seizing his limp hand, she began to rub it earnestly, calling his name all the while. He did not respond, did not move. And now his eyes were glazed. She put a hand to his neck, seeking the pulse point, finding none.

A cry escaped her as she flew into the living room, grabbing her cloak from its hook. Down the stairs and out the door she went, not bothering to lock the door, disobeying her father's cardinal rule. All she could think of was reaching Arthur Bradley's office two blocks down the street.

The people she passed along the way were a blur; someone called to her. She ran wildly, oblivious to the cold penetrating her dress and shawl, to the harsh wind biting her face. She was too numb with fear to feel anything other than the need to get help.

Her breath jerked in her throat, sending gasps of cold air down to pierce her lungs. She burst into the door marked Dr. Bradley and found him examining a patient. At her abrupt entrance, Arthur Bradley removed the stethoscope from the man's chest and stared at her.

"What is it?" he asked, taking in her windblown hair, her white face.

"Father!" Her voice was a whimper, but he understood and grabbed his coat.

"What about me, Doctor?" The patient called after him.

Ignoring him, Arthur grabbed his black bag and ran out the door with Ruth. She tried to explain what had happened as they ran the distance, but her voice was breaking in sobs.

"Don't try to talk," Arthur said as they raced along the boardwalks, attracting stares as they hurried up the hill to Ruth's house.

Her legs were weakening, more from her emotion than exhaustion. Arthur glanced at her. "Slow down. I'll get there as quickly as I can."

She lagged back, her chest aching from the hard run, her cheeks oddly cold. She pressed her fingers against her cheeks and felt the moisture. She blinked, aware for the first time that she was crying, and now the cold air struck her wet cheeks, chilling her more. In the distance, she could hear the boat's whistle, signaling its departure; and she recalled her father's last warning about this being the last day to leave town.

What's wrong with me? she thought wildly. *Why have I stopped thinking of Father's condition? Of Arthur racing on ahead? Why am I standing on the boardwalk staring back at the boat dock?*

Someone touched her arm. She whirled. It was Mrs. Greenwood. "Dear, is something wrong? You're obviously upset, and you're out without your coat."

Ruth swallowed, giving way to the sobs that wracked her body. "It's Father," she said. "I must get home."

Breaking free of Mrs. Greenwood, she took a breath and forced herself to hurry on. A second burst of energy propelled her, and she tried to think about what must be done. Her father had gone into a coma for some reason; that was it. Dr. Bradley—Arthur—would know what to do. He would give him some kind of medicine, an injection; he would do something to save the man who was the center of her world. And she would be eternally grateful to Arthur. She would accept his invitations, even try to return his interest if only he would save her father.

Those were the thoughts flying through her brain as she reached the house, climbed to the front porch on shaky knees, then stumbled through the front door.

The house was quiet, quieter than she had ever heard it. A different kind of quiet.

Then Arthur was coming down the stairs, his black bag in his hand. Her eyes dropped to the bag then returned to his face. She saw it then, the look of pity, of . . . sympathy.

"No," she said, sinking into the nearest chair. "He's going to be all right." Her words were muffled behind her palms as she cupped her face in her hands, giving way to sobs again. "It can't be," she cried. But she had known the truth before she left the house, and now Arthur confirmed her worst fears.

"I'm sorry." His voice sounded distant in her ringing ears. "It appears to have been a heart attack. He's . . . gone."

"Please, God . . . ," she pleaded, burying her face deeper in her hands, unwilling to accept it, unwilling to believe it. She had already given up her mother, wasn't that enough? Why her father? Why *now*? He was too young. "No," she said brokenly, shaking her head wildly. She felt an arm around her shoulder, and she heard his voice again.

"I'm so sorry."

The door was opening, and she could hear Mrs. Greenwood's voice, but she refused to look at her or to listen to Arthur.

"I'm going to give you an injection, Ruth." His voice was weaker now as another arm embraced her, a heavier arm. "You're going into shock." The words made no sense to her, just as nothing else did.

Her sleeve was being pushed up, and the woman beside her was speaking gently. Something pricked her arm, but she scarcely felt it. The woman continued to talk, and the man said something as well, but it didn't matter. Nothing mattered. She slumped against the arms that held her as her senses hurried toward the comforting darkness that enveloped her.

$$5$$

oe and Ivan were getting low on food and supplies, and both were in need of a new pair of rubber overshoes. Long since out of kerosene for their lantern, they had to dig by candlelight. Joe jumped at the excuse to go into Dawson, for it had been two months since he had been to town. Ivan, preferring solitude, was happy to leave this task to Joe.

Bundled into a heavy parka, Joe spent an extra minute petting Kenai, who seemed to be taking the cold well, and promised him a thick bone on his return.

Eight hours later, his felt hat lowered on his forehead to protect him against the wind and huddled into his parka, he rode into Dawson.

The little town of Dawson was a welcome sight to him after weeks out in the bush. He turned his horse in at the hitching rail before Miss Mattie's Roadhouse. As he swung down from the horse, a blast of wind whipped across his face, and he quickened his steps, hoping there was a spare cot.

To his good fortune, there was one cot left, and a pot of hot coffee waited on the stove for those coming in from the cold.

"Warm yourself," Miss Mattie said, motioning him onto a bench at the long wooden table.

She was a stout woman who usually dressed in her husband's trousers and flannel shirts and wore her hair slicked back in a bun. Her lack of femininity in appearance was compensated for in her tasty food and clean, comfortable home.

"Thank you," Joe said, easing down onto the bench and sipping at the coffee. "Mighty good," he said, giving her his best smile.

She hesitated for a moment, staring into his face. Then she

glanced back at the stove. "Got some dumplings on the stove if you're hungry."

Joe hesitated, not wanting to impose, and yet he hadn't eaten since last night. He recalled his meal of cold beans and hard tack and his stomach growled.

Miss Mattie, unaccustomed to being argued with, was already dipping out some dumplings in a small tin pan.

"Better stock up with groceries before you head back," she said, placing the pan down before him. "No more boats are coming in till spring, and the stores are already starting to ration food. It will get scarce. Did last winter."

He nodded; then as he tasted the dumplings, he realized that renting a cot did not cover good food as well. "Miss Mattie, I don't feel right eating your food unless you add a little more to my bill. Please do that."

Her gray eyes shot to him, then she shrugged. "All right. Another dollar will cover you. How long did you say you'll be staying here?"

Joe was enjoying the taste of the rich dumplings so much that it took a moment for him to swallow and reply. "Just long enough to pick up some supplies." Then his thoughts moved on to one of his reasons for returning to Dawson. Ruth Wright. "I may need to stop in at Doc Wright's clinic and get him to check my back again."

She whirled from the stove and looked at him with an expression of surprise. "Haven't you—no, you've been out in the bush," she said, answering her own question. "Guess you can't keep up with the town news. Doc Wright died almost two months ago. Heart attack."

Joe almost dropped his fork. He stared at Miss Mattie for a moment. "What about . . . what will happen to his clinic?"

Miss Mattie sighed and shrugged. "It's closed down. There's only one doctor left, Arthur Bradley, and he's still wet behind the ears. I shouldn't say that. Most folks think he's all right. He just suffers in comparison to Doc Wright." Her chest heaved beneath the flannel shirt. "It's a tragedy for Dawson City that we've lost Doc."

Joe stared into space, shaking his head. "He was a nice man. I liked him a lot." He cleared his throat. "What about his daughter? Is she still here?"

"The last boat had pulled out the day he died." She shook her head. "It's a shame she couldn't go back to Seattle. I heard she was all tore up about Doc's death." She was pouring flour into a large bowl. Then she added two handfuls of sugar. "She's a good nurse, though. I hear she wouldn't see anybody for a while, then Dr. Bradley persuaded her to go to work for him in his clinic. Nell Greenwood says they'll probably team up. Nell's the town crier, you know."

Joe arched an eyebrow. "No, I don't know her."

"Then you've missed being grilled about where you come from and what you're doing here."

"Is that right?" He made a mental note to avoid the woman at all costs.

"Yep. Nell keeps up with everybody's business."

"What do you mean about Miss Wright and Dr. Bradley teaming up?" Joe frowned, hoping this meant they would team up as the local nurse and doctor.

Miss Mattie turned back to the stove. "Dr. Bradley and Ruth Wright are sharing Thanksgiving dinner with the Greenwoods. Nell says there's a romance in the making. Dr. Bradley's a widower, you know?" she asked, glancing back over her shoulder.

Joe stared into his plate. "No, I don't know him." Nor did he want to know him if Ruth was interested in him. "Where does he come from?" he couldn't resist asking.

"Victoria. He's a nice man, little too nice for Dawson, if you ask me."

Joe nodded. He could see how Ruth would have a lot in common with someone like that, and if she worked in his clinic, perhaps it would help her to survive a long, cruel winter.

"Don't you like my dumplings?" Miss Mattie asked, thrusting her hands on her hips and staring at his half-filled plate.

"They're wonderful. I think my stomach just shrunk a bit since I've been doing my own cooking."

He picked up the fork and tried to resume his meal with enthusiasm, but he was merely going through the motions in order not to offend Miss Mattie. His thoughts were centered on Ruth, and he found himself filled with a mix of emotions. He had been unable to get her out of his mind since leaving Dawson City. In fact, his plan had been to clean up a bit then head right over to the clinic. Miss Mattie's bad news had changed everything.

He stared at the scarred plank boards of the eating table. Doc Wright had been a good, decent man. Joe was saddened by the news of his death. He was glad he had attended church with them, and yet he had sensed a cautiousness about the man where his daughter was concerned. Joe could certainly understand why. Doc had gone out of his way to be kind to him, and yet Joe had watched a wall of reserve going up when he caught Joe staring at Ruth.

Thinking back, he recalled that it had been Ruth who invited him to church, and she had smiled at him as though she liked him. Doc had noticed that, of course.

Joe sighed, pushing his plate aside. In comparison with this city-bred doctor, he had nothing to offer. No matter how much he wanted to see Ruth Wright, he must force himself to stay away from her now. She would be much better off with Bradley.

He came slowly to his feet, feeling tired to the bone. "You asked how long I'll be here. I'll only be staying the night. As soon as I round up what I need, I'll be riding out in the morning."

Miss Mattie nodded. "Then I'll have you some hot biscuits on the stove."

"Thanks," he said, trying to smile.

His heart was not in his smile nor his words. He felt a keen disappointment welling up inside. He should be accustomed to the feeling by now, but he was not. Particularly not where Ruth Wright was concerned. Being in her presence had awakened something deep in his soul. It was as though a candle had been lit in the darkness. He had been happy. But now the candle had been extinguished.

❧

Ruth stood in the Dawson City cemetery staring bleakly at her father's grave. A cold wind raced across the frozen Yukon and snatched at the hood of her black woolen cloak. The hood gave way and now her auburn hair was exposed to the elements, but she didn't care. Nor did she care that she had lost weight and looked as devastated as she felt.

As she stared at the mound of dirt that covered her father, thick tears streamed down her cold cheeks. Absently, she thrust her kid glove into the deep pocket of her skirt and withdrew the crumpled lace handkerchief he had given her, one of many Christmas gifts last year.

She touched the soft handkerchief to her eyes, then her nose, and sniffed hard.

"Good-bye for today, Father," she spoke softly. "I know you and Mother are together . . . safe and happy . . . together in heaven."

While that knowledge brought her comfort, at the same time she was filled with the deepest sense of loneliness and despair that she had ever known. She was completely alone here in this frozen country, cut off from the world until late next spring or whenever the weather warmed enough to thaw the Yukon River. Alone except for Arthur, who had been so very kind to her.

She took a deep quivering breath, refusing to allow pity or regret to get a foothold in her heart. She was glad she had come here with her father; she would feel worse if she had thwarted his last dream.

She pulled her hood over her head and turned from the grave. Squaring her shoulders, she drew her slender body erect, trying to call forth the strength she knew she would need to survive. As she walked back toward home, she paid little attention to the people hurrying in and out of shops or the occasional miner and his mule or his dogs. She thought of stopping in to see Arthur on this Sunday. It would be nice to visit on a day when the clinic was closed. But she wasn't even up to attending church services this morning, and now she didn't feel like a social call. All she wanted was to lock herself in her house, curl up in bed, and sleep. Arthur told her that wasn't healthy, that she must go on with her life. It was exactly what her father would say. In fact, her father had liked Arthur and would be pleased to know that he was calling on her.

She sighed. In time, God would restore her if she clung to His promises and kept reading her mother's Bible. It was all that gave her comfort and hope now. As she reached her house, she quickened her pace, climbing the steps and unlocking the door.

She was going to put the teakettle on and make a pot of tea. She was trying to drink more tea and less coffee, since coffee was being rationed at the mercantile. She still had a good supply in the pantry, but she knew she must be saving with it.

As always, the echo of her footsteps on the boards in the hall reminded her of how quiet the house was and how alone she felt. Arthur had offered to buy the house, but she didn't know where that would leave her, and she wasn't ready to think about a permanent relationship with him. Not yet. Perhaps in time.

∿

Joe strapped his newly purchased supplies onto the horse and glanced up at the sky. He had been pleased to see sunshine when he awoke and peered through the window by his cot. When he entered Miss Mattie's kitchen, she had informed him that it was going to be a pleasant day. Her hot coffee and thick biscuits had reinforced her prediction.

He placed his boot into the stirrup and pulled himself into the saddle. Turning the horse's head, he trotted through town, trying to forget that he must pass the clinic in the next block. Miss Mattie's words had stayed with him throughout the night. It should have been his best night's sleep in weeks, but he had slept fitfully. The room was warm, the cot was comfortable, and the men occupying other cots had not snored loudly enough to bother him. Ruth Wright bothered him. What would happen to her?

It was not his business, he told himself as he approached her frame house, yet he couldn't resist a quick glance in that direction. The house looked forlorn, with the curtains drawn and no one coming or going. His eyes strayed to the front door, and he thought about how welcome he had felt when he walked through that door and how good the Wrights had been to him. He continued to stare at the house, hoping that a curtain would part, that he would see her face framed in the window. Then he would feel he had an excuse to stop by and say hello. But the curtains remained closed and the door did not open.

He turned his eyes back to the road before him. Soon he would be out of Dawson City, heading back to the crude cabin he shared with Ivan for the winter. That knowledge brought a weight to his heart, and for a moment he could hardly resist the temptation to go back to the Wright house to speak with Ruth.

No, he had made himself a promise not to interfere in her life now. He drew a deep breath and forced his eyes toward the other travelers along the road. Occasionally, he met another miner coming or going, their faces haggard, their eyes weary.

The craze for gold—it gripped all of them and held them tight. It kept them digging into the frozen ground, hauling up bucket after bucket of dirt, searching, hoping, praying for the sight of gold flecks, nuggets, or yes—a vein of gold that would transport them from rags to riches.

Glancing at the last tent on the edge of town, his eyes froze. It was the tent that served as a church, the church he had attended with the Wrights. The tent was emptying of people, and he realized this was Sunday and the service had just concluded.

He pulled on the reins to halt his sorrel and sat back in the saddle, staring at the people coming out of the tent. Ruth was not among them. Had she stopped going to church? He frowned. That possibility troubled him; it would mean she was as distraught as Miss Mattie had indicated.

His eyes lifted to the snow-covered roof of the tent. Ruth and her father had brought him here, opened a door in his heart that he thought he had firmly closed. Still, that door they had opened was ajar, and he had been nagged by a longing to return to God. Once upon a time there had been peace in his life, peace when he had lived by God's rules. But for a long time he had lived by his own rules.

It took several seconds for him to realize that he and his horse had come to a dead halt in the center of the road, that he was simply staring at the strangers who must think his behavior odd.

He turned his eyes to the road ahead, but something more important lingered in his mind. Doc Wright and his daughter had brought something good back into his life, if only for a short while. He had found peace inside that tent during their little church service. He wasn't back on the spiritual path yet, but he felt the call, as surely as he felt the call to search for Klondike gold.

He shifted in his saddle and glanced back over his shoulder. The very least he could do was express his sympathy to her and his thanks for what she and her father had done for him. There was something wrong about riding into town and then leaving without at least paying his respects.

Gently, he turned the horse's head and trotted back toward Ruth Wright's house.

$\mathcal{R}$uth stood at the stove, stirring the stew. She had decided to make use of some remnants in the pantry, making an odd mix of what she could find. She cooked conservatively these days, but she had no appetite, and even if she did, she knew she had to be careful with her food supply.

She heard the whinny of a horse and removed her wooden spoon and laid it on the spoon rest. Wearily, she walked to the window to look down, wondering which patient had not heard about her father's death. She had turned so many away, although on three occasions she had been able to help. She had served as midwife for two babies and bandaged up one minor cut.

When her glance fell on Joe Spencer getting down from his horse, her breath caught. For a moment she stood mesmerized, watching him slowly loop the reins of his horse around the log hitching rail. Then suddenly she came alive. Her hands flew to her hair, patting it back into the chignon as she turned and hurried down the steps to the front door, just as he began to knock.

Of course she had thought of him many times the past weeks, wondered about him. Still, she had resigned herself to the fact that it would be a long time before she saw him again, if ever. Like so many others, she thought he might have given up and left Dawson.

Turning the key in the lock, she opened the door and looked into his serious blue eyes. For the first time in days, she felt a little smile creep over her mouth.

"Hello," she said as he removed his hat. "Come in."

He hesitated for a moment, scraping the soles of his boots on the mat. She found herself thinking of the many others who never bothered to do that.

She held the door back for him as he stepped inside the hall, and she stepped back from him then closed the door. The cold air whipped in with him, bringing a smell of spruce and horseflesh and a pleasant soap. He was wearing a heavy parka over jeans and chaps; his boots were clean.

He was staring at the closed door of the clinic. She wondered for a moment if he knew, but the sadness in his eyes told her that he did.

"Would you like a cup of tea?" she asked.

He looked back at her, his hat pressed against his chest. "Thank you. I'd like that very much."

She nodded. "Come on up."

He paused long enough to hook his hat and coat on the hall tree, then he followed her up the stairs.

Lifting her skirts to climb the stairs, she wondered fleetingly if this was proper, having Joe Spencer up to her kitchen when they were alone in the house. Proper no longer mattered in this situation. She was glad to see this man, and she wanted to know what he had been doing since she last saw him.

As they entered the living room, the warmth from the cook stove reached them. She glanced over her shoulder. "I don't heat the downstairs now."

He nodded. "Good idea. Miss Wright . . . ," he began then faltered.

She knew what he was trying to say and tried to smile. "I'm glad you stopped by," she answered, turning toward the kitchen. "Did you just arrive?"

His boots echoed over the wooden boards as he entered the kitchen. "No. I came last night. I needed supplies."

She was pouring tea into the cup, and now she glanced over the curl of steam as she handed the cup to him. "I see," she said, registering the fact that he hadn't rushed right over as she had dared to hope.

He cleared his throat as she poured herself a cup of tea and motioned him toward the kitchen table.

"Actually, I had planned to stop in when I arrived late yesterday," he was saying as he settled into a chair opposite her at the table. "Then I heard the bad news about your father . . ."

She dropped her eyes, staring into the dark tea.

"I wanted to come and tell you how sorry I am," he said in a gentle voice. "You must be completely grief stricken."

She nodded, averting her eyes. "I am." She swallowed hard. Surely there were no tears left, but she could feel her throat tighten in a threat. "I've had an awful time adjusting. In fact, for the first two weeks, I couldn't even leave the house. I just sat here and cried." She took a deep breath and then looked at him. "I've gone to work at Dr. Bradley's clinic and that seems to help. At least, it keeps my mind off my own situation."

"What are your plans?"

She sighed. "My plans? I'm afraid I don't have any plans." She lifted her eyes and looked around the kitchen. "I've sold most of the medical supplies to Dr. Bradley." She wondered why he suddenly dropped his eyes to the tea, not looking at her. "I've kept a few necessary items—gauze, first aid supplies, that sort of thing. Is there anything you might like to take back to camp?" she asked suddenly.

He looked up, appearing surprised by the question. "I . . . don't think so."

"How is your back?" she asked, sipping her tea for the first time.

He shrugged. "It still aches when I abuse it." He grinned. "But the liniment helped a lot."

"Good." Her eyes locked with his for a moment as silence fell. Then she remembered her stew. "I was about to have an early lunch. Could I offer you a bowl of stew?"

He hesitated, glanced at the stove, then shook his head. "I had breakfast at Miss Mattie's."

"Then my cooking can't compare to hers, I'm afraid."

"Sure it does," he answered quickly, too quickly, and they both smiled. "I just don't want to impose," he added softly, smiling at her.

She shook her head. "You aren't. To be honest, I get tired of eating alone."

"Oh." She saw the question in his eyes, but then he glanced toward the pot of stew. "In that case, I would be honored to join you." He placed his teacup on the table. "May I wash up?"

She indicated the pan of water on the basin. "Sure."

Ruth stood and began to assemble the bowls and spoons, feeling something awaken in her heart again. She had felt completely numb ever since she walked into the room and found her father on the bed, breathing his last breath. In fact, she had begun to wonder if her heart, like the frozen ground, would ever thaw again. Now, as she busily dipped the stew into bowls and heard his movements in the background, she felt the cold begin to break inside her. She felt a nudge of warmth, a ray of hope.

When they sat down at the table, she offered grace. Then, as she unfolded her napkin and glanced at him, she found herself recalling the prayer service, the look in his eyes when the service ended. She knew he had been touched, and now she felt as though she should return to that moment. Perhaps that was the reason God had placed him in her life.

"When are you leaving?" she asked, already hating the thought.

"Today," he responded, looking across at her. "I wish I could stay longer. In fact," he lowered his eyes to his spoon as he dipped into the stew, "if I had known about . . ." He looked up at her. "I would have come into Dawson for your father's funeral if I had known."

"Thank you," she said, touched by his kindness. "Pastor Sprayberry conducted a graveside service reading Father's favorite verses. After Mother's death, Father told me not to be sad for him when his time came. He thought the end of one's life should be a celebration—"

"A celebration?" Joe Spencer was obviously taken aback.

"Yes, he believed that we should be thankful for a person's life, then celebrate his passing to a better world."

He chewed for a moment, staring at her, obviously thinking about what she had said. "That makes a lot of sense. It's too bad more people don't have that kind of attitude."

She lifted a shoulder in a weak shrug. "Well, of course there's the grief in a loved one's passing . . . but I know he's with Mother." She looked at Joe and this time there was no stopping the tears that formed in her eyes. "They were so devoted to one another. They must be very happy to be reunited."

His eyes widened as he put down his soup spoon and tilted his head, studying her thoughtfully. "That must be very comforting to you."

"Yes, it's comforting," she agreed, "but it's a truth that I feel very deeply. I know they're together in heaven."

He dropped his eyes to his napkin, saying nothing in response.

She leaned forward in her chair, curious to know his thoughts. "How do you feel about those things? Or is that too personal?"

When he looked back at her, a gentle smile crossed his lips, lighting his blue eyes. "You've been very open with me. It would be selfish on my part not to share my thoughts with you."

She blinked, surprised by his statement. She was just beginning to realize what a tender, caring person he was. She was hungry to know more about him, to know everything.

"I don't usually talk about this," he said, "but somehow I feel comfortable talking with you. I've already told you my father died soon after he returned from war, that I was a baby."

"Yes, I've thought of what you said about reading his diary. I think that must have been so special."

He nodded. "It was. But then when my mother died . . ." He broke off, frowning.

She studied the way the skin between his brows puckered with the frown, and she saw the blue eyes dim with the memory. She could feel his sadness, as real as her own, and at that moment, she knew they shared a bond that was special.

"What happened when your mother died?" she prompted.

"I suppose each of us reacted differently. My older brothers seemed to go on with their lives, even though they missed her as I did. But somehow . . ." He shook his head. "I don't know, somehow my life just wasn't the same anymore. I grew restless, tired of Richmond. I wasn't willing to work as a clerk in a store as my brothers were doing. You see, we lost everything in the war. Our plantation was confiscated by the government, all our horses and cattle. Mother took in work as a seamstress soon after I was born. Her father supported us as best he could, but we struggled. Always. I wanted to make a different life for myself. I didn't want to struggle the way others did."

He drained his teacup and Ruth got up to refill it.

"Thank you." He smiled at her.

"I had an uncle who had gone out west right after the war," he continued. "Over the years, his letters fired my imagination. I left the South and I can't say that I've really missed it."

She nodded. "So how long did you work in California?"

He picked up the cup and sipped his tea. "I worked my way from Virginia to California," he answered with a smile. "That took a while. Then soon after I got to the ranch where my uncle worked, he died."

"Really?" She sighed. "Your life has been pretty difficult, hasn't it?"

He shrugged. "I don't mean to sound tragic. I never knew my uncle, really. What about you? Did you leave family in Seattle?"

She blinked, trying to follow the quick change of thoughts. "Just an uncle and aunt, and half a dozen cousins."

"Do you plan to return?" he asked, watching her closely.

She nodded. "Probably. I'm not certain I'll go back to Seattle, however." Like Joe, she wasn't ready to face the memories that would accompany her when she went to the large lonely house they had left behind. She had written to ask her uncle to look into selling it. She knew she was going to need the funds.

"I see," he said, pushing his bowl back.

She heard the note of reserve in his tone and wondered what had brought about his change of mood. The fact that she would probably return to the States?

"What are *your* plans?" she asked quickly.

He leaned back in the chair and looked at her, saying nothing for a moment. "My plans are to work my claim for as long as it takes. I believe the gold is there," he said. "And I'm determined not to stop digging until I find it."

His words saddened Ruth, for now she saw in his face the same kind of fierce emotion that seemed to drive so many people here in Dawson, even the merchants.

"Ah, you want to be rich like everyone else who has come here?" she asked.

His expression changed, and she sounded more harsh than she had intended. Still, she had spoken her thoughts honestly.

"Why else would anyone come here?" he asked, an edge to his tone.

She studied him for a moment, wondering if he thought that was the only reason she and her father had come. She was about to set him straight when he suddenly came to his feet.

"I appreciate your hospitality. The stew was delicious. And I enjoyed the company," he said. This time, however, his smile was more reserved.

"Thank you," she said, standing. "And thank you for stopping by."

Silence stretched between them, and for a moment, she thought he might say something. The moment passed, however, as he turned for the door. "Take care of yourself," he said, glancing back over his shoulder.

"You, too," she said, clasping her fingers before her as she followed him through the living room and down the front steps. She watched as he retrieved his coat and hat from the hall tree. "What kind of living conditions do you have at the mine site?" she asked curiously.

"A very small, rather crude cabin," he drawled, buttoning his coat. "I imagine it will shrink even more as the winter progresses. I share it with Ivan," he added, planting his hat firmly on his head and looking her over once more.

"Well . . ." She crossed her arms, wondering what was left to say. "Good luck."

"Thank you."

She watched his expression change once again. The reserve seemed to be slipping, and now his eyes held an emptiness as he glanced at her one last time.

"Good-bye," he finally said, his voice gentle and soft.

"Good-bye," she replied, staring after him as he turned and walked out the door.

For a long time, she stood in the door, oblivious to the cold, watching as he mounted the horse and rode off. Then something her father had said returned to haunt her. *We don't really know him, Ruth.*

She realized how true that was. Each time she felt as though she was on the brink of knowing him well, perhaps on a deeper level than most other people, something happened. She was unsure if she said something that stopped his flow of words, or if he had the ability to shut out painful memories, to stop himself just short of letting anyone see his soul.

When he was out of sight, she closed the door and locked it. Then she pressed her back to the door and stared into space. Her feelings for him were as strong as before, but this time she sensed something more: He was a very complicated man. There were layers to this man that would have to be uncovered before she could allow herself to really care for him.

Shivering, she headed back up the stairs thinking how uncomplicated Arthur Bradley was in comparison. While their conversations were never very exciting, and certainly she did not feel physically attracted to him as she did with Joe, there was something very comforting about being with Arthur. Was it because of his medical background? Was the comfort she found with him due to the familiarity of being in a clinic, hearing the talk she had heard all of her life? Or was it because she knew he cared for her, and she found security in knowing that?

She sighed as she reached the kitchen and stared at Joe's empty bowl and cup. He was, after all, just another money-hungry miner. He had no real mission in life, as she and her father had or even as Arthur had. While Arthur had never gotten around to reading the Bible, as her father had suggested, he was a good man.

She picked up Joe's dishes and took them to the basin, forcing herself to wash them quickly this time, rather than hold the cup as a silly souvenir like she had done before. Joe's visit had served to frustrate and confuse her in one way; in another way, the mystique surrounding him seemed to underscore the logic of returning Arthur's affections.

Joe rode back to camp, regretting his visit to Ruth. He was glad he'd had the good manners to pay his respects, but he should have left it at that. He should never have stayed for lunch and an hour of conversation. The lady at the boardinghouse had been right. She did have plans with Bradley; otherwise, why was she hedging about returning to Seattle? *Probably waiting on a marriage proposal*, he told himself bitterly.

He tried to tell himself other things as well: that she was merely pretending that she and her father hadn't been drawn here by the money they would make, that she had regarded him with a certain disdain when he was honest about his reason for being here. He bunched his shoulders together, tugged his hat lower on his forehead as a blast of cold wind hit him. While sitting in the cozy kitchen with her, a wonderful contentment had settled over him. He had felt a sense of home, of caring for someone again. Yes, for an hour, he had felt a frightening pull toward Ruth Wright. He had even been on the brink of telling her many things about himself. He was grateful he had come to his senses in the nick of time. Confiding in her would have been a mistake.

He was not interested in her, he told himself. She was less appealing since she had lost weight. Still, she rode with him, in his thoughts, in his memory; and she was to remain there until he saw her again.

❧

Ruth had accepted the Greenwoods' invitation to join them for Thanksgiving dinner, although the food was less abundant this time, and everyone knew why. The main topic of conversation in Dawson was the fear of running out of food before a boat could bring in more supplies in the spring. Nevertheless, the Greenwoods managed a nice meal, and she had been grateful. She had brought along a loaf of bread and a rice pudding, which Arthur complimented profusely.

"Didn't I see that blond stranger enter your house this week?" Mrs. Greenwood asked bluntly, startling all of them.

Ruth chewed her food, taking her time in replying. "Yes, he stopped in to pay his respects," she answered coolly.

"Well, it might pay to be leery of him," Mr. Greenwood spoke up. "There's something funny going on with that claim."

Ruth looked up quickly. "Why do you say that?"

"The claim belongs to someone else."

Ruth looked at him, wondering why he had spoken in a sinister tone, as though there was something suspicious about Joe. "He has a partner. I'm sure the claim is filed under that man's name," she said, sounding more defensive than she intended. She realized that all three were staring at her, and she guessed they wondered how she happened to know. "He mentioned having a partner to my father and me on the first day he came to the clinic," she added slowly, "with an injured back."

There, that should shut them up, she thought, glancing down the table to Mr. Greenwood who was as thin and gaunt as his wife was plump.

"Well, I just wondered," said Mr. Greenwood with a light shrug.

"Ruth," Arthur picked up the conversation tactfully, "we'll probably be seeing a number of patients tomorrow who have overindulged in Thanksgiving dinners."

She smiled at him, grateful for the kind way he seemed to understand when she needed a change of subject.

"What with the shortage of food, you may not have many patients," Mrs. Greenwood added, coming in from the kitchen with a platter of jam cake.

Ruth smiled then, for she had not had jam cake since she left Seattle, and she was grateful for the Greenwoods' kindness. The least she could do was overlook their tendency to mind other people's business. They were probably unaware of how prevalent their habit was. The day passed pleasantly then, and Arthur even offered to accompany her to the cemetery, where she paid her respects to her father and tried not to cry over the Thanksgivings past. When he walked her home, he seemed to sense her need to be alone then, and he did not linger for an invitation to come inside.

"I'll see you tomorrow," he said at the door.

She nodded. "Arthur, thank you for being so kind."

He smiled at her with tenderness filling his green eyes. "It's easy to be kind to you, Ruth. I long to help you in any way I can."

"I know that," she answered quickly. "Thank you."

After she had gone inside and locked the door, she felt a lingering worry over what to do about Arthur. She could see that he was growing very fond of her, and she wasn't sure how she felt about him. As she had said, she was grateful for his kindness, and she appreciated all he was doing for her. Unfortunately, she could not dredge up any romantic notions toward him. Nor did she imagine that she ever would. Still, she had to be realistic, she told herself, lifting her skirts to climb the stairs. Eager to get her corset off, for she was unaccustomed to wearing one these days, she told herself that her father would be pleased that she was seeing Arthur and working in the clinic with him.

On the other hand, she just could not visualize a future with him, even though it might be the most sensible thing she could do. Perhaps she was a foolish romantic . . . or perhaps she would have been better off if she had never met Joe Spencer.

As winter set in across Dawson, Ruth spent more time helping Arthur in the clinic. Colds, pneumonia, and influenza were common, and then an outbreak of measles brought on another swell of patients. Ruth walked home in late afternoon exhausted, and as she looked around the town, she saw the sad effects of people struggling to stay warm and fed. Prices had begun to soar, from lots for building sites to groceries and hardware. The supplies on board the last boat were drastically short of food and heavy in liquor, which added to the problems of the town. More fights broke out in the saloons, more crime was present. She no longer ventured out beyond the hours of daylight.

"Ruth, I want to speak seriously to you." Arthur had detained her one evening in December as she tugged on her warm gloves and tightened the chin strings of her cloak.

"What is it?" she asked, studying his somber expression.

"I'm very concerned for your welfare," he said, his green eyes mirroring his concern.

"I feel responsible for you, Ruth. And I know your father would have wanted me to take care of you. In view of that—"

"Arthur," Ruth put up a hand, "I'm perfectly capable of taking care of myself. You needn't trouble yourself. You have enough to worry about with all the patients you're seeing now."

Arthur shoved his hands into his pants pockets and studied the thin rag rug. "I'm not saying this well. I didn't mean to imply that you aren't capable. You're the most responsible woman I've ever known." Slowly, his eyes rose to meet hers. "Perhaps I have the cart before the horse, so to speak. I'm the one who needs you."

Ruth paused at the door, her hand on the knob. She turned and looked at him, realizing that the question she had been expecting for weeks was on the tip of his tongue, and she was not prepared to answer it.

"I think it's best if I just speak plainly," he said, abandoning all efforts at romance. Ruth had already decided Arthur was not the romantic type and she was disappointed by that realization, but she tried to tell herself other things were more important, given their situation.

"Arthur, it will soon be dark," she said in a rush. "I need to get home. Could we talk about this tomorrow?"

"I need to say it now. Will you marry me?"

The question fell into the tense silence as he stared bleakly at Ruth. She stared back, unable to respond.

"I wish our circumstances were different. If we were in Victoria, I would take you to the gardens, we would have tea and a lovely meal. But we aren't in Victoria," he sighed, "we're in a rough mining town where half the town may starve before the winter is out. The other half may freeze to death. I want to protect you. I think it only makes sense for us to be together through this, don't you agree?"

Ruth sighed, dropping her gaze to the floor. She had considered, more than once, accepting his proposal when it came; but now that it had, she felt no excitement, not even a tiny spark of pleasure over the prospect of marrying him.

"Arthur," she said, choosing her words carefully, "I'm afraid I cannot commit to marriage just because it makes sense." Slowly, she lifted her eyes and looked at him, pleading with him to understand. "I would like to think that if we were in Victoria, enjoying the beauty, cast in a different mood, a different atmosphere, I might be more inclined to accept your proposal. But . . ." She couldn't bring herself to reject his proposal; the words were too difficult. Yet she didn't need to say more for he seemed to understand. She watched the disappointment slip over his features. "I want you to know I have the highest respect for you," she quickly added. "I admire your work, and I like being your nurse."

He sighed heavily and looked at her with sadness. "So what is the problem, aside from our having to be practical? And we do have to be practical, Ruth. We are in a very difficult situation here, one that is not likely to improve until the winter ends. People are marrying for less important reasons—to have a roof over their head, for example, or the assurance of food for the winter."

She nodded. "I know that. But you see, Arthur, I already have a roof over my head and food for the winter. For that reason, I do not feel compelled to rush into a lifelong commitment simply because it seems the logical thing to do." She took a deep breath. "I need something more than that, Arthur. And I'm not saying I won't find it with you. It's just that the timing is wrong."

His expression brightened. "I see what you're saying, and I think you have a valid point. We do not want to make a decision in haste. You owe that to your father, and I owe it to Katherine's memory, as well."

Ruth nodded, aware that Arthur still grieved over Katherine. That was the other thing. She did not want to be a rebound romance, someone who was grabbed in desperation to fill a lonely void in a man's heart. She wanted to be loved based on who she was as a person. She wanted the kind of love that was built on Christian principles and based on respect and need, but she also wanted to feel a glow in her heart. Furthermore, she wanted to look in the mirror and see joy in her eyes, the joy that she had seen on her mother's face. Perhaps it was an unlikely dream, given her circumstances; perhaps that kind of love didn't come to everyone. Perhaps her parents got lucky.

"We'll talk about this at another time," Arthur said tactfully. "Now shall I walk you home?"

Ruth looked out. It was almost seven o'clock and completely dark. The hours had flown by during the afternoon, as the clinic had been overflowing with patients and she couldn't abandon Arthur. But now, looking out, she knew better than to venture down the streets alone, with so many miners and drifters overflowing the saloons, hungry for a woman—any woman.

"Yes, Arthur, I would appreciate your walking me home."

He seemed grateful to be awarded the opportunity.

"Bear in mind," he said as they trudged back in the cold, "that I have the funds to buy your house, and we could set up a better clinic there. There wouldn't be any major adjustments for you. You would be working in the same surroundings as with your father. It could be very simple, Ruth. Very uncomplicated."

"And very practical," she said, trying to see his face through the cold darkness. "Maybe it's absurd, Arthur, but it just seems a bit too practical." She sighed. "I suppose I'm a foolish romantic who has read too many Dickens' novels. I'll take into consideration what you have said to me this evening. And I want you to know that I am flattered that you care enough for me to marry me."

"Thank you," he said, pressing her arm gently as they climbed the steps to her front porch.

Arthur had never touched her, other than linking his arm through hers to assist her in maneuvering her way over the uneven boards of the sidewalk, to ascend the steps. This time it was different. As he took her key and unlocked the door, he reached out for her, impulsively it seemed, and planted a cold kiss on her lips.

Ruth tried to respond but found it impossible. She merely smiled and touched his cheek with her gloved hand. "Good night," she said as she stepped inside and closed the door. Quickly, she lit the lantern in the hall, trying to ward off the terrible thought that had rushed to the foreground of her confused mind.

Arthur had kissed her and she felt nothing. Joe Spencer had merely looked at her and her heart had started to beat faster. Furthermore, when she was with Joe, something stirred in her soul, something responded in a way she could neither understand nor rationalize. Feelings; how strange and deceptive they were. How could she pass up a man who cared for her, who had so much to offer her for the hope of a man who had offered nothing, not even proof that he had any feelings for her beyond a polite friendship?

7

*J*oe and Ivan had worked together for weeks in the bitter cold, the only sound between them the creak of the windlass that passed from beneath the frozen ground to the top. Their hard labor had begun to pay off, however, for on the snow-covered ground there had been piles of gold-filled gravel days before. Now the gold had been filtered out, sacked up in bags, waiting to be taken into Dawson. At last there would be money to reward them for their efforts.

"Don't you want to go into town with me tomorrow?" Joe asked Ivan as they wearily spooned up their beans that evening.

Ivan shook his head. "I do not like people."

Joe chewed his food, staring across at the big man whose bald head gleamed in the glow of the lantern. "Then I'll collect the money and return."

Ivan looked across at him, saying nothing.

"Do you trust me?" Joe asked.

Ivan nodded, turning back to his beans.

❧

The next day as Joe rode into Dawson loaded down with a bulky pack of laundry and his rifle, he was shocked by the mood of melancholy that enveloped the town. The sight of thin dogs and slab-ribbed mules first greeted him. Then he noticed the grim-faced men moving briskly toward their tents. Scraping the mud and sand of the Yukon from his boots, he opened the door of the Alaska Commercial Company, where the tension of the town was being verbalized.

"It's the truth!" a voice bellowed as Joe entered.

The clerk behind the board counter had the gathering of men around the potbellied stove captivated.

"Ya mean to tell us," an older gentleman spoke up, "that if we'd taken free passage to Fort Yukon, the same thing could have happened to us?"

"Sure could of," the clerk answered.

"Hello." A female voice spoke up behind him.

Joe turned and looked down at Ruth Wright, standing directly behind him. Removing his hat, he smoothed down his hair and wondered about the rugged state of his appearance.

"Hello. How are you?" He smiled at her.

She looked as though she had lost more weight, although it was difficult to tell, for she was bundled in a black woolen cloak. Still, her cheeks were hollow and the shine was gone from her wide-set hazel eyes.

"I'm okay," she answered in a firm voice. "And you?"

The raucous conversation practically drowned out their words. Glancing back at the men then at Ruth, he took her elbow and they walked toward a quiet area in the rear of the store.

"I just got to town," he said, glancing at the men whose faces were flushed with emotion. "Could you tell me what they're discussing? Everyone seems to be upset."

Ruth nodded, glancing back at the group. "This fall the *Weare* dropped its fare to fifty dollars per person with the hope of encouraging some of the residents here to leave for the winter. We're already short of everything from food to supplies. When only a small number of people left on the *Weare*, the government offered free passage on the *Bella* to anyone who would leave Dawson and winter in Fort Yukon."

Her eyes returned to him, and she looked even sadder than before. "Unfortunately, the *Weare* couldn't get through the ice blocks near Fort Yukon. Passengers were loaded into small boats, but even those were blocked by the ice. Finally, the people anchored the boats at the edge of the forest, got out, and walked for three days to reach

Fort Yukon. When they arrived, frozen and starved, they discovered a shortage of food there, just as here."

Joe shook his head. "That's terrible." He glanced back at the group of men who had become silent, staring glumly into space.

"What Mr. Carson was saying when you walked in was that some of those people who reached Fort Yukon pulled guns on the clerks at the Alaska Commercial Company there and demanded clothes and food. I guess they were desperate."

Joe had been listening to her words, while mentally sighing with relief that he now had gold to outfit himself and Ivan.

"What about you?" he asked suddenly. "Are you okay? Do you need anything?"

She looked startled by his question for a moment; then she shook her head and tried to smile at him. "No, I have enough. What about you?"

"I'm fine," he answered, looking into her troubled eyes. Her question and the concern in her eyes melted his heart. He forgot everything he had told himself about why he wouldn't bother to see her on this trip. She was standing before him, speaking to him in that kind voice that seemed to reach to the depths of his soul. A surge of tenderness for her rushed back.

"Look, I believe I owe you a meal or two. Is there any place in town that serves decent food?"

She smiled, a bit more cheerfully this time. "I do."

"I agree. You serve the best. What I had in mind was treating *you* this time—unless there's some reason you can't join me," he added, remembering Dr. Bradley.

She shook her head, and the hood toppled back onto her shoulders. He couldn't resist staring at her lush auburn hair.

"No, as it happens, I left the clinic early. I'm helping Dr. Bradley," she explained quickly.

Joe did not respond to the reference to her work. He wanted to keep the conversation away from his competition.

❦

Ruth bathed and dressed for her date with Joe—*date?* she wondered. Her hand hesitated on her black silk dress as she pondered the question. Was this really a date? They were simply having a meal together, the voice of logic argued. Nevertheless, Joe had invited her out for a meal. In Seattle, that would be considered a date.

Humming softly to herself, she finished dressing then turned before the mirror, surveying her reflection. She was still grieving for her father, of course, and wore black; but she decided to forgo the usual dress of flannel, which most women in Dawson now wore for warmth, and chose instead a black woolen dress that was tucked at the bodice and hugged her narrow waist, showing off her good figure. She had lost weight and the dress was a bit loose through the shoulders, but it didn't matter.

Tilting her head, she studied her face. The loss of weight made her hazel eyes seem larger than ever; and although her complexion was quite pale, when she pinched her cheeks and bit her lips, a faint pink touched her skin.

Suddenly, she thought of her mother, and she knew her father had been right. With the unusual heart shape of her face and the thick auburn hair, she knew she very much resembled her mother when she was young.

She opened her small jewelry box and withdrew the cameo that had belonged to her mother. As it lay in the palm of her hand, she thought of how she and her father had both been cheated by the loss of such a lovely woman. Yet, the memories of her parents would always live in her heart.

Opening the clasp of the cameo, she placed the pin at the neck of her dress. It was the perfect complement to offset the stark black of the dress. Smoothing back the strands of her hair into its thick chignon, she turned from the mirror and began to speculate about her evening with Joe.

❧

The dining room of Mrs. Taylor's restaurant was a large, square room with six tables, four chairs to a table. The plain wooden tables were overlaid with tan linen cloths, and the bone china and silver cutlery were nice reminders of the homes so many people had left behind.

Joe pulled back a chair for her and she spread her skirts as she took a seat. He was wearing a fresh white shirt and dark trousers.

"Everything else that I own has been left at the laundry." He smiled across at her.

She nodded. A Tlingit family ran the local laundry, and she was always amazed at the enormous amount of work they managed. "They're very particular with the clothes," she said.

But she was not thinking of the people or the laundry as she looked across the candlelit table to him. His blond hair was slicked back from his bronzed face, and tonight his blue eyes seemed larger than ever and were the nicest shade of blue she had ever seen.

"Please excuse the length of my hair," he spoke up, as though her staring might be due to some fault on his part. "I haven't had time to visit a barber."

"There's only one good one that I know about here," she said, folding her hands in her lap. She gave the man's name and the location of his small log cabin. Many of the inhabitants of Dawson operated businesses out of their homes.

Mrs. Taylor appeared at their table, announcing that tonight's menu would be baked salmon, rice, dried apricots, canned tomatoes, and tapioca pudding. While she varied her menu each evening, she served family style to everyone.

"That sounds fine." Joe looked across at Ruth.

"Yes, it does," she agreed.

After Mrs. Taylor had left the table, the two sat staring for a moment, then Ruth cleared her throat.

"How are you doing with your claim?" she asked.

"It's going well," he said.

❧

Joe stared at her for a moment, thinking. Should he tell her? He hadn't been to the assayer yet, but he knew the claim would probably make him rich. Ivan had said that gold salted with black sand was worth eleven dollars an ounce. "We completed our shaft and have been windlassing a ton of mud and gravel." He paused, glancing around the small dining room. "I brought in a sample," he said quietly.

"I hope it proves to be profitable."

"Thank you." As he looked at her, he kept wondering about what she was going to do. "How are you doing? I know I asked you that earlier, but I mean . . . how are you really doing? I've been worried about you."

She sighed. "Yes, it has been difficult."

"You must miss your father very much."

"I do." Then she took a deep breath and looked at him. "How is Kenai?"

He grinned. "Hungry. Do you have any idea how much malamutes eat?"

"No," she laughed.

"Actually, Kenai has been a great deal of company to me and to Ivan. In fact, Ivan needs him more than I do, I think. Ivan's a loner who doesn't trust people very much. Kenai is exactly the kind of companion he prefers."

Their food was delivered on pretty plates, served attractively, and Joe cast a longing glance at the crusty hot bread placed before them.

"I'm glad you invited me to eat with you," Ruth said.

Joe glanced across at her and saw that her hazel eyes held a glow again, and he was glad.

"I'm glad you could join me," he answered, picking up his fork. When he looked back at her, he saw that her eyes were closed for a moment before she reached for and unfolded her napkin.

"I must seem very rude," he said, "digging into my food without saying grace."

"No," she said with a smile. "You just seem like a hungry man."

"I am that," he answered, and they both laughed.

They were silent for a few minutes as they both enjoyed the food, then Joe put down his fork and looked at her. "You were right. The food here is very good, but I think you're the best cook in Dawson."

"Thank you," she answered. "When are you returning to camp?"

He sighed. "Tomorrow. Wish it were not so soon, but we're almost out of food, and we needed some mining supplies."

"Were you able to get what you needed at the mercantile today?" she asked.

"Not everything. There will be no more canned fruit until the boat comes in next spring. They're rationing sugar and coffee, as well. We can do without sugar, but we need the coffee to keep us alert." A sigh escaped him as he recalled the long, hard hours of work. Kerosene could no longer be obtained in Dawson, and now they would be working by the light of candles.

"Do you plan to stay in Dawson?" she asked. "I mean, after you strike it rich."

"I guess that depends on if I strike it rich," he said then laughed.

She tilted her head and looked at him thoughtfully, then she nodded slowly. "I think you will. You have the intelligence and determination."

"What about you?" he asked, watching her carefully. "You said you would probably leave, but that you might not return to Seattle." He was testing her, wondering if she would tell him about Arthur Bradley now. He had an almost overwhelming desire to know her plans, for he could no longer deny his feelings, although he had desperately tried.

"Why, Ruth!" A high-pitched voice turned his attention to the plump woman standing at their table, staring at him rather than Ruth. "How are you?"

Joe looked at Ruth and saw that her mouth had tightened, and her eyes seemed to have narrowed a bit. Something about this woman put Ruth's nerves on edge; that was obvious. As he looked back at the woman, he could see why. She was rudely gawking at both of them, and he wondered who she was. He didn't have to wonder long, for Ruth spoke up.

"Mrs. Greenwood, do you know Joe Spencer?"

Joe stood up and forced a smile. "I don't believe I've had the pleasure."

Her mouth dropped open as though taken aback by his response.

He had noticed that not too many men here had manners; she seemed to be shocked by his response.

"This is Mrs. Greenwood," Ruth said as Mrs. Greenwood took in every inch of his clothing and even his boots, which he was glad he had just cleaned.

"Hello," she said.

"How do you do?" He tried to force a smile, although she wasn't smiling; she was merely gawking at him.

Then the woman's large eyes shot back to Ruth. "How are you doing, dear?" The tone of her question made Joe suspect that she was probing for more than Ruth's health.

"I am well, thank you," Ruth said, looking uncomfortable as Mrs. Greenwood lingered at their table.

A silence followed, which Ruth did not bother to fill, so Joe sat back down in his chair.

"Well . . ." Mrs. Greenwood folded and unfolded her hands. "I'll be going. I just came to pick up a plate to take home to Mr. Greenwood. Nice meeting you." Her protruding eyes returned to Joe, boring through him once more before she turned around and pressed down her wide skirts to make the distance between two tables.

Joe looked across at Ruth and saw that her eyes were lowered. He wanted to ask about the woman, but Ruth didn't seem inclined to talk about her. He picked up his fork again, trying to remember where he had heard the name. Then it came to him. Miss Mattie at the boardinghouse had said that a Mrs. Greenwood had entertained Ruth and Bradley at her home for Thanksgiving.

As he pretended to concentrate on his food, he realized that what he had seen on Ruth's face now was embarrassment. If she were seeing Bradley, maybe she was embarrassed to be seen here with him. And yet, nothing about Ruth suggested that she would be dishonest or unfaithful once she was committed to someone.

Her heavy sigh caught his attention. "I'm afraid that by breakfast tomorrow everyone in Dawson will know that we had dinner together."

"Oh? And is that so bad?" he asked, his tone guarded.

She shook her head. "No, of course not. This is the first evening I've truly enjoyed." She sighed. "It's just that Mrs. Greenwood is a bit of a busybody, and she seems to have taken me under her wing since Father died."

"So how does taking you under her wing affect my having dinner with you?" Suddenly, he was thinking about his past, wondering if Mrs. Greenwood would start asking questions. The very idea of that made him nervous, and his appetite began to wane.

She looked thoughtful for a moment. When her eyes returned to his face, the glow in her eyes was gone. "She thinks I should accept Bradley's proposal."

Her honesty caught him off guard, and for a moment he could only stare at her. What he saw in her eyes, however, lifted his spirits. At the mention of Bradley's name, there was no enthusiasm in her voice or in her eyes. At last, he had the opportunity to ask the question that had been troubling him.

"And how do you feel? Do you think you should accept his proposal?" His throat tightened on those words, and he found them difficult to speak, but he had to find out.

She shook her head. "No, I don't. In fact, I've already turned him down."

"You have?" His voice betrayed him again, and his eyes, too, he imagined. It was the best news he had heard since he had been in Dawson. To his surprise, he felt, at that very moment, Ruth Wright mattered even more to him than the gold. That frightened him.

She looked down at the bread in her hand. "I don't love him. In the Yukon, that doesn't seem to be a logical reason to decline a proposal. Widows are marrying the first respectable man who asks, some women are coming here from advertisements in newspapers, others are simply fortune hunters drifting in. . . ." Her words trailed as her cheeks colored.

The latter description was obviously a referral to the women who had set up shop on the back street in the world's oldest profession. He leaned back in the chair and looked at her.

"But you aren't like any of those women. You are a very special woman and you have a lot to offer. Don't settle for less than you want, Ruth. Don't let loneliness or hard times force you into a commitment that would not make you happy."

She looked up at him. Her eyes softened and she began to smile. "Thank you for speaking words I very much needed to hear. You see, I feel I would be cheating the other person as much as myself. Maybe I'm just a romantic at heart, but if I can't enter into a commitment that brings me happiness and joy, I'd prefer to remain single. I'm speaking very personally," she added, looking away. "It's just that Mrs. Greenwood and—"

"And Arthur Bradley, I imagine—"

"Yes. They think I should be considering my security and safety. I am constantly reminded that it is unsafe for a single woman to live in a large house, as I do, where medicine has been kept and where so many desperate people have come to our door. Some of those men have been out in the bush and don't know my father has died."

He leaned forward, pushing his plate away, concerned for her now. He hadn't considered the importance of what she was saying, and he felt like a fool for not having thought of it.

"That does make sense," he said. "I mean, about your safety. But you don't have to marry someone just to insure your safety. Why don't you take in boarders? Some of these other widows you just mentioned. It seems to me they should be banding together with each other rather than jumping at the first offer to marry a man, when many of those men will be out in the bush half the time, anyway. Unless they're merchants," he added, "which would make more sense."

"I thought about it," she said, nodding slowly. "But the truth is, I enjoy being alone. I suppose that's a selfish attitude, but I can last until spring on my own, and I do know how to use a gun," she added with a little smile. "I'm quite certain I could never bring myself to use that gun, but it poses a threat."

His mind was still lodged on the knowledge that there was some merit to Mrs. Greenwood and Bradley's argument about her being alone in her particular situation. "It's a large house for Dawson. Surely you could find one or two respectable women who could live with you, and there should be enough room."

"There is," she said, touching the linen napkin to her lips. She, too, had lost interest in the meal. "And you have a very good idea. I'll give that some serious thought tomorrow."

He was pleased to see that her eyes looked more hopeful now. For a moment, he feared Mrs. Greenwood had destroyed their evening.

"Good." He couldn't resist thinking about how it would be to come in from the mines to her home, to be there with her, enjoy her companionship as he was doing now. Just as quickly, he pushed the thought aside. What was wrong with him? He couldn't allow himself to fall in love with Ruth Wright. He was here on a mission, and he couldn't for one moment forget it.

"Thank you for inviting me to dinner," she said as a waiter came to clear away their dishes.

"It's been my pleasure, I assure you. Ivan doesn't make a very good dinner companion," he added, wanting to change the subject.

"Christmas Day is only two weeks away," she said, looking around the restaurant. The sparse decorations in town practically ignored the season, but Ruth was determined to celebrate it as always. "Will you be returning to Dawson over the holidays?"

He frowned. "I'm ashamed to admit that I hadn't even thought about it."

"You have a lot on your mind," she acknowledged. "I just wanted to say that if you do, I'd be happy to share my Christmas meal with you."

"That's very nice of you," he said, genuinely touched. "Are you saying you'll be alone?"

She sighed. "I imagine Mrs. Greenwood will invite me to her house."

He grinned at her. "You don't seem too enthused by that."

She said nothing; she merely smiled at him, but her eyes said it all.

"In that case, I'll make it a point to return to town to spend Christmas Day with you. In fact, I'll look forward to it."

Her eyes brightened. "I can't promise turkey, but I will do my best to have a meal comparable to the traditional feast."

"Just being with you will be special enough," he said, and for a moment their eyes locked.

She blinked and glanced down at her plate then back at him. "There'll be a special church service that evening. Would you like to accompany me?"

He hesitated. In all honesty, he had to admit he had enjoyed the last service, and he knew some spiritual growth was needed in his life. "Yes, I would be happy to attend."

She smiled and suddenly looked relieved. "Good."

He glanced around and realized the dining room was emptying.

"Does Mrs. Taylor have a designated hour for closing?" he asked.

Ruth glanced around the room. "About now, I think." She looked back at him and they both laughed. The time had flown by.

"Shall we go?" He stood up and came around to hold her chair. His eyes moved from her narrow shoulders to her tiny waist. She had lost quite a bit of weight since he first met her. Was it from lack of food, or did she miss her father that much?

A new resolve settled over him. If he could make this woman happy, he was certainly going to try. He might not ever meet anyone like her again. He was glad he had accepted her invitation to return for Christmas and attend church services.

He paid the ticket, six dollars for two meals, which might have been considered steep to some, but to him it had been a bargain. He decided to at least share that thought with her.

"This is the first meal I've enjoyed since my last one at your home." He took her elbow and steered her back to the coat tree beside the door. As he helped her into her heavy cloak, his hands lingered on her shoulders for a second, and he found himself desperately wanting to put his arms around her, shield her from the night cold they were about to face. Instead, he forced himself to reach for his coat and hat.

"Then you should eat here again," she said as he opened the door for her and they stepped onto the boardwalk.

"I think the company increased my enjoyment of the meal. So if I eat here again, I would need for you to join me."

Her laughter flowed into the soft darkness. "I think I could manage to do that."

They sauntered along, following the dim patches of light from the candles in windows decorated with pine cones and colorful bows. Joe was grateful for the short walk to her house, for he found himself thinking of her safety again as his eyes darted to open alleyways and the shadows of men leaning against a building farther down the street.

"Do you go out much?" he asked, tightening his grip on her arm.

"I only go out alone during the four to five hours of daylight."

"What about to and from the clinic?" he asked, frowning.

"Arthur walks with me," she said in a quiet voice.

"I see." He was sure Bradley was more than happy for a chance to be with her, and he was suddenly fighting jealousy; but he told himself to stop behaving like an idiot and be glad for Ruth's safety. He was glad there was a man to see her home.

"One really has to adjust to daylight and darkness here," she said in a pleasant tone, as though she had long since conquered the problem. "At first the long daylight hours were such a novelty," she said and leaned against his arm. "When we arrived in midsummer, we had twenty hours of daylight, and the days seemed to go on forever. I had difficulty going to bed when it was still light outside, but I solved the problem by covering my bedroom window with dark flannel." She laughed softly, and her breath made a tiny circle of fog before her mouth as the cold air pierced their faces. "Now, I move around the house with a lantern in my hand most of the time."

"Do you still have a supply of kerosene?"

"Yes, I'm fortunate there. Father was wise enough to stock us up on the most important basics. I'm grateful for that. I'm afraid I was quite ignorant about what we needed here."

They had reached her front porch, but she seemed inclined to continue the conversation. "The editor of the Seattle paper published a letter for all people heading for the Klondike. The letter was a real blessing. The letter was from a woman in Skagway and listed the provisions a person should have before even considering a trip here. We followed her list precisely, even to my purchase of knickers to wear under skirts. It was a wise suggestion," she added, laughing softly as they climbed the steps.

Joe remembered noticing the things most people referred to as bloomers peeking from under women's dresses, and he saw the practicality of those in such cold country.

"I suppose you were accustomed to fancy petticoats and such," he said, grinning at her.

She laughed at that. They were standing at the door, and she hesitated.

"You don't need to feel compelled to invite me in for a cup of tea," he said quickly. "Not that you would," he added, hoping he hadn't sounded too presumptuous.

"Take care of yourself, Joe Spencer," she said, reaching for his hand.

Through their gloves, he could feel her firm grip and marveled at the courage of this remarkable woman. That thought prompted him to squeeze her hand gently.

"Thank you, Ruth. Please be careful," he added, feeling more protective of her than ever. "In fact," he looked at the dim light through the front window, "if you will allow me, I'd like to come in and check out the house for you. I'll wait until you've lit more candles."

"All right," she said, turning to unlock the door. "That's a very considerate thing for you to do, Joe."

As he entered the quiet, dim house, he found himself suddenly thinking of Mrs. Greenwood and he glanced over his shoulder. He felt certain that at the moment she was probably peering through a window somewhere, wondering if Ruth was safe with him tonight.

The hallway echoed the hollow steps of his boots as he walked to the clinic, checking the locked door. He turned and looked up and down the hall, and as he did, he realized how quiet and lonely the house felt. He turned to Ruth, who was removing her cloak and placing it on the coat tree.

"You know, you are a very brave woman," he said, voicing the thought that had been uppermost in his mind. "I'm afraid I hadn't given much thought to your situation here. It's good that you have friends who do think of that and are concerned for you."

She shook her hair back and he stared at the rich auburn color highlighted by the glow of the lantern on the table. "I'm afraid Mrs. Greenwood is more concerned than I'd like her to be," she said, looking perplexed. "But I know she means well, and I must continue to remind myself of that."

"Let me check the upstairs for you," he said, glancing at the stairs that rose into darkness. "You can wait here, if you like."

Ruth looked at him and felt a bit of relief in having someone other than Arthur looking out for her. "All you'll find is a few tumbled rooms," she called after him.

She still kept the house immaculate, for she had little else to do to occupy her time, but she hadn't been able to force herself to go through her father's things to sort through and select what should be kept and what should be donated. She had begun the process but then stopped halfway, and now there were books stacked in little piles all over the living room floor.

She could hear his footsteps overhead, slow and deliberate, as he moved from room to room. He was a kind and caring man, she decided, and this made her feel better about her undeniable attraction toward him. Her father had said they didn't know him very well, and that had been true at the time. Now, however, she felt she knew him as well as anyone else in Dawson. Or rather, she knew him well enough to allow her heart to take the chance.

Hugging her arms against her, trying to offset the chill of the downstairs, she watched as his long legs descended the stairs; then her eyes moved upward to the broad chest in the white shirt and lingered on the gold sheen of his hair. As she met the deep blue eyes, her heart beat faster, and she turned to adjust the wick on the lantern.

"Everything looks fine," he said, as he reached her side again. "Do me the favor of inviting a lady to share the house with you, please. Otherwise, I'm going to worry about you."

She turned from the lantern and looked into his eyes. "Thank you. It's comforting to know that you care."

"I do care," he said quickly.

She must have taken a step closer to him without realizing it, for he was suddenly standing very near to her. Or had he moved when she did?

He reached for her hand, and as her palms touched the thickness of his fur gloves, she could sense the strong masculinity of him, and for a moment, her thoughts flew wildly. She found herself wondering what it would be like to take shelter in his arms, rest her head against his broad chest, and feel the safety everyone felt she needed. More important to her was the opportunity to offset the terrible loneliness that engulfed her at times.

Had her thoughts brought the action about, or had he read something in her face and reached for her? Suddenly, she was standing with her head against his chest. She could feel the strength in his arms, and yet he was a gentle man. She sighed, unable to resist the pleasure of just having someone hold her. No, not just *someone*. It was Joe Spencer she wanted.

"I'd better go," he said, breaking into her thoughts.

She looked up into his face, half in shadow now with his back to the lantern. She tried to read the expression in his blue eyes for she longed to know how he really felt for her. As she stood looking up into his face, his lips brushed hers in a sweet gentle kiss. And for the first time in her life, she had an inkling of what real romance was . . . a friendship then a kiss, a kiss that brought a feeling of joy and longing to be near that person. Always.

But already he was withdrawing from her, stepping back, looking deep into her eyes. For a moment, neither of them spoke, then he took a deep breath. "I must go," he said.

"Thank you for a lovely evening," she said, amazed that her voice was calm despite the rapid beat of her heart. "And I hope you'll stop in the next time you come to Dawson," she added.

"Yes, I will." He headed for the door, and her eyes followed him, watching as he replaced the felt hat on his golden head. "Ruth . . ." He turned slowly and looked at her.

"Yes?" She waited anxiously, desperately wanting him to speak words of reassurance, words that would let her know he felt the same way she did.

"Take care of yourself," he finally replied.

"Thanks. You, too." She smiled, following him to the door. Her hopes were already sinking, but she tried to cover her disappointment. During the ten minutes he had been inside the house, he could have been any other well-meaning friend or neighbor. Except for the kiss. Surely, he realized she didn't allow just anyone to kiss her; it had been a very personal thing for her. How did he feel?

He smiled at her then stepped out, closing the door softly. She turned the key in the latch then leaned against the door, pressing her head against the cold wood.

What if he didn't feel the way she did? What if his heart wasn't beating in the same crazy rhythm as hers? She couldn't bear to think he didn't share her feelings. She hugged her arms around her, feeling cold and lonely again as she climbed the stairs. Maybe there was no future with Joe Spencer, but she would prefer one sweet memorable evening with him to a lifetime with Arthur Bradley, bless his heart.

❧

As Joe walked back to Miss Mattie's Roadhouse in the cold darkness, thoughts flew about his brain like pesky mosquitoes in summer. It had taken every ounce of self-discipline not to take her in his arms and kiss her again and again. Still, she was a lady and a very good one at that. A Christian lady, he added, recalling their hour in the prayer service.

Shoving his hands into his coat pockets, trying to absorb some warmth, he tried to sort through his feelings. He cared for her more than any woman he had ever met in his life, and he knew that now. She was a strong woman, yet kind and gentle; she was not a whiner or a complainer, even though she had reason to complain. Life had not been fair to her; that much was obvious to him. She had lost her mother when she was young. Then she had obviously passed up a comfortable life in Seattle and many suitors, no doubt, to come to Dawson with her father. She had said it was his dream. Or maybe he said that. In any case, he knew Ruth Wright had come here for her father's benefit rather than her own.

He recalled his first conversation with the two of them. "We didn't come here to get rich," she had said in a quiet yet firm voice. "We came to help those who would obviously be in need of medical care."

And they had. It seemed a cruel twist of fate that her father had been taken at a crucial time, leaving her alone to survive the winter. But even at that, she seemed to be attempting to hide her tears, and she was obviously determined to cope.

He had reached the boardinghouse, but he felt inclined to linger outside for a moment and stare up at the stars. The sky was a dark canvas with bright glittering stars and only a half moon. The air was very clear here in the north, and it did him good to look up at the vast sky and study the handiwork of God.

The handiwork of God. That kind of thought had not crossed his mind in a long time.

He sighed and turned for the door. Ruth was good for him in many ways. He longed to stay on for a few days, spend more time with her, follow the strong pull of his heart toward Ruth Wright and see where it led.

A deep sigh wrenched his body as reality pushed through his fogged brain. There was gold waiting to be assayed, and supplies to be bought, and a claim to be worked. He couldn't get soft now; the timing was all wrong.

With that in mind, he entered the boardinghouse and forced himself to think of tomorrow and what must be done.

8

*R*uth had taken Joe's concern more seriously than that of Mrs. Greenwood and Arthur Bradley. Before going to sleep, she had prayed for the right person with whom to share her home.

Her answer came the first of the week, when a woman appeared at her front door, with a thin pale face peering from beneath a thick, black hooded cape.

"Good morning," she said. "My name is Dorie Farmer. Miss Mattie at the boardinghouse said one of her guests suggested you might be interested in taking in a lady boarder."

The *boarder* who had suggested this to Miss Mattie, of course, was Joe, and Ruth smiled at that, as she looked at the woman before her. She was a tall woman who appeared to be in her mid-thirties. Her face was plain with the exception of keen brown eyes that reflected intelligence and curiosity as she looked at Ruth. Beneath the thick cloak, Ruth could see this woman was dressed in the most liberal fashion of the day—a shorter skirt, ankle length, that revealed thick flannel bloomers above rubber boots, crusted with mud. As Ruth's eyes swept back up the dark, serviceable cape, she saw the dirt stains on it as well.

"I know I must look a sight," the woman said, glancing down at her clothing. "But if you understand that I walked over Chilkoot Pass—"

"Chilkoot Pass?" Ruth gasped.

It was one of the worst journeys a man could make to Dawson; Ruth couldn't imagine a woman making this tortuous journey, even though some had arrived by that route during milder weather.

Ruth opened the door wider. "Come in. You must be half-frozen."

"Thank you. First, I'll remove these filthy boots." Dorie Farmer stepped out of her boots, and Ruth glimpsed a pair of moccasins underneath as the woman stepped inside and looked around. "I hear you have the nicest home in Dawson, and I can see this is true."

"Thank you," Ruth said. "May I take your cloak?"

"Yes, please." The woman removed her fur gloves and stuffed them in the pockets of the cloak. Then she removed the cloak as her eyes slowly moved over the interior of the house. "I understand this was a clinic," she said, carelessly patting down her thin brown hair, streaked with gray on the sides and worn in a loose chignon.

"It was," Ruth nodded, hanging the cloak on the coat tree. "My father and I came to Dawson back in the summer. He passed away recently."

Dorie Farmer nodded. "I heard that," she said, speaking gently. "I'm so sorry. Are you still running the clinic?"

The question took Ruth by surprise. Unlike everyone else who expected her to shut down, which indeed she had, this woman seemed to think it was possible for Ruth to run the clinic on her own.

"No," she replied, shaking her head. "I'm a nurse, not a doctor. I do assist the other doctor here in his clinic."

"I see. Well, you'll find that I am curious by nature. It accompanies my profession."

"Which is?" Ruth asked with a smile. It was easy to be frank with this woman.

"I'm a correspondent for the San Francisco *Examiner*," she answered. "I'll probably write a few articles for the Klondike *Nugget* here, as well."

"How fascinating!" All sorts of questions were rushing into Ruth's mind, but then she remembered her manners. "Come upstairs and I'll make tea."

"Thank you very much. I haven't had a decent cup of tea since . . . well, I can't remember when. On the Pass, we were lucky to get enough snow melt for drinking water."

Ruth glanced back at her, still amazed that this woman had survived such a tortuous journey.

"Oh, this feels like home," Dorie said upon following Ruth through the living room to the kitchen. "May I wash my hands?"

Ruth pointed her toward the wash basin as she checked the water in the teakettle, relieved to see that there was enough and that it was still hot. She went to the cabinet for tea and cups.

"I'm in desperate need of a wash house. Can you refer me to one?"

Ruth considered offering the use of her tin tub, but remembering hygiene, forced herself to limit her generosity until she got to know Dorie Farmer better.

"There are two bath houses here," she said. "One offers spruce steam baths, and that is the one I would recommend. It's run by a Tlingit couple—"

"Oh, yes, the Tlingit," Dorie nodded. "They are so wise and practical. We had Tlingit guides leading us over the Pass. I'm certain we would never have survived without them."

Ruth nodded. "They know the area well, since they were the first inhabitants. The people who run the bath house I mentioned learned about the proper bath system from an American living in Skagway. Like the people who run the laundry, they are very clean and take pride in their equipment. I think you'll be as comfortable as you can be, given the choices." Then she tilted her head and looked at Dorie with the eye of a nurse. "Are you feeling all right? Malnutrition and scurvy are common maladies of the journey here."

"I've been fortunate, thank you," Dorie smiled. "I brought my own cache of herbs and dried fruits, which have saved my life more than once since leaving San Francisco a year ago—"

"A year ago?" Ruth asked, surprised by this.

"Yes, I've spent the past year interviewing miners, travelers, anyone and everyone who could tell me something about this country— those who had lived here and those who wanted to get rich here. I first disembarked at Juneau and spent some time there. Then I caught a boat to Skagway and got stranded there for the winter. At spring breakup I went the ten miles to Dyea. My ultimate goal was Dawson, and to get here I knew the most entertaining route would be over Chilkoot or White Pass, but I chose Chilkoot, since there seemed to be more stories circulating about that one."

"So you climbed over that steep pass to get stories for your paper?"

"That's right. I guess I sound pretty crazy, but then I had to wonder about my sanity when I ended up wintering in Skagway. It's a disorderly little place but not really as notorious as it's made out to be. Grant you, there are shootings day and night, but I'm afraid I've used that to my advantage. My job is entertaining people back in San Francisco. Shameful, isn't it?"

Ruth looked at her. In a way, she thought it was; but this woman was so honest about herself and her job that she couldn't help liking her.

"Well, I'm sure you've met lots of interesting people in your travels."

"I have. And I've been greatly inspired by those who left everything behind to follow their dream of striking it rich. So many have died in the process," she said on a heavy sigh. "But there *are* many interesting stories. And you'd be amazed at the number of enterprising women who have followed their husbands and ended up getting rich through their own ingenuity in supplying what was needed in camps and tent towns."

Ruth nodded. "There's a woman here in Dawson who's making a nice income simply by selling hot water bottles to miners and silk cloth to the women who were desperately homesick for the nice things they left behind."

"That's the kind of ingenuity I mean. This woman was smart enough to think of that, you see. Maybe I'll interview her for a story!" Dorie's brown eyes brightened as she shook the dripping water from her hands into the basin.

Ruth handed her a cup towel. "I can see that you're going to liven up my lonely house," Ruth said. "I can't wait to talk with you. You must have lots of stories to tell."

Dorie dried her hands and studied Ruth with an amused grin. "You've decided to take me on as a boarder, then?"

"Of course," Ruth smiled, motioning her to a chair. On an impulse, she went to the cabinet and got down a tin of tea cakes that she reserved for special occasions, now that she was having to ration herself on everything she ate.

"Tea cakes!" Dorie clasped her hands together before her gallused shirt, looking as delighted as a child on Christmas morning. "Do you have any idea how long it's been since I had anything resembling a delicacy? Beans and hardtack, and the occasional smoked fish. I may never eat those three items again," she said, taking a seat.

Ruth laughed, delighted by her new boarder. She knew that Dorie was an answer to her prayers. Suddenly the long winter stretching before her didn't seem so bad. Then she had another thought. "How long did you want to stay?"

Dorie shrugged, lifting her teacup. "Hard to say. Everyone's telling me we're frozen in here for the winter, but I don't know if I can stay in one place that long."

"I'm afraid your destinations are limited, unless you want to go out to the mining camps to interview the miners."

"Oh, I already spent some time at one camp, and I plan to go to others," Dorie said after a generous sip of tea.

Ruth's eyebrows rose. She had merely been teasing, but she saw that Dorie was perfectly serious.

"Makes for the kind of reading folks back in San Francisco want," she explained, reaching for a tea cake.

Ruth sipped her tea, recalling the mood of her hometown before she left. "Yes, I remember that everyone in Seattle was wild to hear news of the Klondike."

"So you and your father just arrived this summer?"

"In the height of mosquito season," Ruth said, shaking her head. "I will be forever grateful to an article in our newspaper about the importance of taking mosquito netting for hats and gloves to protect the hands."

"I wrote a similar article for my newspaper, only I'm afraid I did more complaining than warning. I've had some unpleasant run-ins with those varmints," Dorie said, then looked at Ruth with a blissful smile. "This tea cake is manna from heaven. But speaking of mosquitoes, I don't remember them being as much a challenge as trying to survive the Chilkoot."

Ruth leaned forward. "How on earth did you survive that awful journey at this time of year? In fact, I thought the Pass was already closed down."

"We were the last people over it." She sighed. "I hope I can blot from my memory some of the terrible things that happened along the way. Dogs and horses dropping dead from exhaustion, people lying down in the snow, begging God to let them go on and freeze. It was awful," she said, looking seriously at Ruth.

Ruth's mouth fell open, and for a moment she couldn't even visualize such horror. "I've been spared those atrocities," she said. "We've had lots of patients as a result of climbing one of the passes. They've come in with pneumonia, rheumatism, or scurvy, and in one case all three. However, most of those people were so sick and weary that they wanted to forget their experiences rather than discuss them."

"Which is what I should do," Dorie said, staring at Ruth's tablecloth.

Then with a chapped hand, she touched the tablecloth, trailing the balls of her fingers over the smooth linen. "You have no idea what a pleasure it is just to touch a nice tablecloth or press a cloth napkin to my mouth." Her brown eyes roamed over the kitchen. "Or to sit in the warmth and comfort of your kitchen. It seems as grand as a ballroom compared to the frozen campfire suppers or windblown tent kitchens."

Ruth smiled sadly. "I don't see how you did it. I imagine a soft bed will feel even better to you."

Dorie groaned. "There's nothing I can think of that appeals to me more. The softest thing I've put to my back is a board covered with clothing for a mattress."

"Is all that really worth the story?" Ruth asked, amazed that this woman had endured so much, having come from a nice city like San Francisco.

Dorie laughed. "I'm afraid being a correspondent is my obsession in life. Actually, it is my life. I've never been married, never even wanted to be. My work has meant everything to me."

"I've never been that enamored with nursing," Ruth sighed. "I enjoy helping sick people, and the satisfaction of seeing them restored to good health is a reward, but . . ." Her voice trailed. What she really wanted was to have a family, to be a wife and mother.

"Now tell me," Dorie said matter-of-factly, "will I be putting you out here? I'll be delighted to sleep on that sofa I saw in there." She indicated the living room with a wag of her head.

"I can put you up in my father's room, although I'll have to do some straightening up."

"Please don't trouble yourself," Dorie said. "If this is a painful task for you—after so recently losing your father, I mean—I will be more than happy to take care of that myself, if you instruct me how you want things done."

Ruth shook her head. "No, I can manage. In fact, I'll probably thank you later for giving me the incentive I needed to assemble those piles of books into some kind of order."

Dorie nodded then pressed her hands against the table and stood up slowly.

"Are you aching in your muscles or joints?" Ruth asked, suddenly feeling like a nurse again.

"Just a bit stiff. I'll get over it. May I call you Ruth? And of course I'm Dorie."

"Of course," Ruth smiled.

"Now, Ruth, I want to make it clear that I'll pull my share of the load. I'm accustomed to doing things that way. We can take turns washing dishes and cooking, if you like."

Ruth considered her suggestion. "For now, why don't you just take care of any business you have in town and let me handle the house?"

Dorie gave her a grateful smile. "I'm so appreciative of your kindness. I think God sent me directly to your door."

"Oh, I'm sure He did," Ruth answered quickly. "And I must remember to thank Joe for passing the word on."

"Who?"

"Joe Spencer. He's a friend who suggested I take in a boarder, although I didn't think I needed one."

Dorie nodded. "By the way, I haven't asked how much you charge."

Ruth hadn't even thought about it. "Having someone in the house with me is payment enough."

"Oh no." Dorie frowned, thoroughly rumpling her forehead again. "That's no way to do business, friend. I can pay you a dollar a day if that sounds fair."

"That's too much," Ruth said, even though she knew it was lower than Dorie would pay anywhere else in Dawson. Still, as she had said to Joe, she and her father had not come here to get rich.

"It's only fair," Dorie insisted. "I'm going to be eating with you, and I've already heard about the scarcity of groceries, so we have to be practical here."

Ruth hesitated. "All right. I will need boat passage in the spring, so I can use the money to start saving up for my fare."

"You're leaving then?"

For a fleeting moment, the image of Joe Spencer flashed through Ruth's mind. Still, she knew she could not plan her life around him unless there was reason to do so. "I'm planning to leave, yes."

"Don't blame you," Dorie said. "I'll probably be on the boat as well. When do they think the earliest passage might come about?"

Ruth thought of the conversations she had heard around town. "Most people think it will be late May before the Yukon thaws out enough for a boat to get through."

Dorie groaned. "And this is December. Sounds like forever. Well, I'm off to run some errands. Can I pick up anything for you?"

"No thanks." Ruth smiled. She was already feeling the relief of having someone to endure the winter with her, to help with food and errands, and offset the long, dark days and nights.

"Then I'm gone." At that, Dorie hurried out of the kitchen.

Ruth lingered at the table, listening to her footsteps flying down the stairs. She marveled that she had the energy to move after such a grueling journey.

As she took the cups and plates to the sink, she thanked God for sending Dorie Farmer to her door. And she added a word of thanks for Joe Spencer, as well. He was proving to be a blessing in her life, and she was grateful for that.

❧

Joe had ridden back to camp with the good news that their claim was going to be a rich one. He had deposited almost three thousand dollars in their joint account and had given Ivan the deposit slip to prove the money had been deposited.

"Our supplies came to almost seven hundred dollars, doing the best I could to save us money," he explained.

"Robbers," Ivan grumbled. "The shopkeepers are robbers."

Joe sighed. "True, but without them, we couldn't mine and we'd starve to death, so we have to pay their prices."

"And they know it," Ivan fussed. He looked Joe over. "You are tired. I will unload," he said in his matter-of-fact way.

Kenai trotted up to lick Joe's hand, and he knelt, stroking the thick fur and looking into the dog's soulful eyes. "Someone asked about you, Kenai," Joe said softly. "A very pretty someone."

He petted Kenai for a few more minutes then dragged himself inside the cabin and collapsed on his cot. Every bone in his body ached from the hurried trip into Dawson and back and all the errands and business he had tried to cram into his short stay there.

Ruth slipped across his mind, a warm comfort as the wind howled about the eaves of the cabin. Stretching his aching legs, he closed his eyes. To offset the cold and the weariness in his bones, he allowed himself the pleasure of imagining her hazel eyes shining up into his and feeling the soft touch of her hand. He had practically fought himself to keep from touching her thick hair, and it had been an even greater struggle to keep from kissing her more than once.

He heaved a sigh. She was a fine wonderful woman but one he couldn't have. Or could he? First, he must come to grips with his personal life before he allowed himself to think about Ruth.

For the hundredth time, he longed to go back in time to that fateful night in Skagway. If only he had not been so stupid, so impulsive. The pain of regret stabbed him unmercifully, worse than any physical pain he had ever experienced. If only there was some way to change his past, to make amends. Then he could begin a new future with Ruth . . . well, at least he would be in a position to ask her . . . what? To marry him? Was that what he wanted? A future with Ruth?

Throughout the night, he tossed and turned, trying to sleep; but for most of the night, sleep eluded him. When he heard Ivan stumbling around, lighting candles, signaling it was time for their work day to begin, he regretted wasting precious rest time, trying to make sense of his life.

～❧

Ruth had worked side by side with Arthur, busily caring for one patient after another until the day finally ended. They hadn't even stopped for lunch, only a quick cup of tea here and there throughout the day. When the last patient left, Ruth sank into a chair, exhausted.

"Ruth, it isn't fair to ask you to work these long, grueling hours," Arthur said.

"It isn't as though either of us has a choice, Arthur. Who else will tend these sick people? And they seem to be multiplying," she said, shaking her head as she stared into space.

He sighed, dropping his thin frame into the chair opposite her. "I wish I had never come here," he said dully.

She frowned, focusing on him through eyes that ached with the need for sleep. "I know you have regrets about losing your wife, but are you saying you regret being a doctor here?"

He nodded. "I'm not cut out for this kind of work. Perhaps I would be happier in a hospital setting. I know for sure I can't bear this awful town."

Ruth listened to him and compared her own feelings with his as he spoke. "I don't mind Dawson that much, and I feel truly rewarded from caring for these people. I don't understand why you don't."

He shook his head. "I don't know, either. But I don't."

His mouth sagged with defeat, and his thin face looked pale and drawn.

"Arthur, I recall Father suggesting that you read Paul's epistles. Do you read your Bible at all now?"

He stared at the floor and shook his head. "No, I don't."

"I believe you would find comfort by reading the Bible. God will help you, Arthur, if only you'll turn to Him."

He lifted his face and looked at her. "He hasn't helped me much so far."

The bitterness in his voice shocked her. She was trying to find the right words to respond when he answered her thoughts.

"I lost my wife, and then when I met you, I hoped I might find happiness again. However," he sighed, returning his gaze to the floor, "you've made it quite clear that you have no interest in me whatsoever."

"That's not true. I *am* interested in you as a friend, Arthur. Can't we be friends?"

For several seconds he didn't answer. Then when he lifted his eyes to her, she saw the pain in his face.

"No, we can't be. You don't know what it's like," he said miserably, "working side by side with someone who can never belong to you. It's like looking through a shop window, seeing something bright and lovely, and wanting it with all of your heart. Then the truth cuts like a knife: You can never have what you want. Why, Ruth?" he said, his voice rising. "Why do you have to be so unreasonable? Can't you see that we should be together? That we could make each other happy?"

"No, I can't see that. And in time, I think you will find someone with whom you will be happy. But I'm not that someone."

"I think you are."

She thought he was being stubborn, but she was too weary to argue. She pushed herself out of the chair and walked to the coat tree. "I'm going home for the night. I think you need to get some rest, as well."

He stood and walked over to help her with her cloak, but then his arms lingered on her shoulder. "Ruth, please give me a chance," he said, turning her to face him.

"Arthur, there's no point in talking about this," she said, beginning to feel angry now that he was being so persistent.

Then he surprised her by pulling her against his chest and pressing his lips to hers.

Shocked, then angered even more, she put her hands on his chest and pushed him away.

"Don't ever touch me again," she said, glaring at him. "Until now, I have considered you a friend. But I'm not sure I think of you that way anymore."

She was out the door before he could say anything more. She

started trudging home, not caring about the cold and the darkness or the fact that she was alone. Soon she heard footsteps racing up behind her, and Arthur had caught up.

"You shouldn't walk home alone," he said, stuffing his hands into the pockets of his overcoat.

She did not reply; she was still too angry. Quickening her steps, she said nothing to him until they reached her front porch. Looking up and seeing the lights in the window, she was more grateful than ever that Dorie Farmer was boarding with her.

"Good night," he said. "And again, I am sorry."

She turned back to him, having made a decision during the cold walk home. "Arthur, I've been thinking about what you said about the . . . difficulty of our working together. I think it's best if I resign from being your nurse. Mrs. Westhoover can help you. I believe she was a nurse a number of years ago in Toronto."

"But Ruth, I've apologized!"

She took a deep breath, feeling the cold air sting her lungs. "And I accept your apology. If you will be gracious about my resignation, I'm willing to keep what happened tonight between us. I see no point in discussing it further—with you or anyone else." She turned and walked up the steps to her front door. "And I hope you'll start reading your Bible."

She left him standing at the foot of the porch steps, staring after her with tears in his eyes.

The next morning, bright and early, Mrs. Greenwood was pounding on her door. Dorie had already left to visit the local newspaper and Ruth was having a second cup of tea.

"Good morning, Mrs. Greenwood," Ruth said as she opened the door.

Mrs. Greenwood rushed inside, bringing with her the icy chill of December. She was bundled in heavy scarf and mittens, and the tip of her nose and her round cheeks were red from the cold.

"Ruth," she said, peering at her with watery blue eyes, "I just heard from Arthur that you've resigned from the clinic. Why did you do that? Don't you realize how much you are needed there?"

Ruth tried to suppress a deep sigh. "Mrs. Greenwood, would you like to come up for a cup of tea?" she asked in a voice that sounded more calm than she felt, in comparison to Mrs. Greenwood's breathless chatter.

"No, I haven't time. Why, Ruth? Why did you quit?"

Ruth sidestepped the question. "I'm not the only nurse in Dawson, Mrs. Greenwood. Arthur can get someone else to assist him at the clinic. Frankly, I'm worn out. We've worked long, tedious hours, and I really haven't had a chance to rest since losing my father."

Mrs. Greenwood tilted her head as she listened, thoughtfully taking in this bit of information.

"Well, yes. I know it's been difficult. But . . ." Her voice trailed as she seemed to have bogged down in her argument in Arthur's defense.

"Please don't concern yourself," Ruth said, her voice a bit firmer now. "I'm sure Dr. Bradley will manage without me."

A frown rumpled Mrs. Greenwood's brow as her watery blue eyes searched Ruth's face again. "He really cares for you, Ruth."

Ruth arched an eyebrow. "What does that have to do with my being a nurse?"

Mrs. Greenwood shifted from one foot to the other, and for a moment her eyes darted over the hallway. "I just wouldn't want to see Dr. Bradley get hurt. He's such a nice guy."

Ruth's mouth fell open. "What about my feelings, Mrs. Greenwood? Or is that not important? Are we only thinking of Dr. Bradley here?"

For a moment, Mrs. Greenwood was at a loss for words. Then she found her voice, and her tone was edged with anger. "Mr. Greenwood and I feel it only fair to mention something, considering your father is no longer here to look out for you."

Ruth felt her back stiffen, and she knew they were about to get to the real purpose for Mrs. Greenwood's visit.

"That stranger you were with the other night—"

"His name is Joe Spencer, and he isn't a stranger to me. He visited the house when my father was alive; he even accompanied us to the midweek prayer service."

Mrs. Greenwood cleared her throat. "Well, the point is, he's collecting money on a claim that isn't even registered in his name."

Ruth gasped. "You mean you've already checked up on him?"

Mrs. Greenwood's face, already flushed from the cold, grew even redder. "Well, Mr. Greenwood was waiting for me at the door of the restaurant when I saw you two together. He said the next day he came in and collected money—quite a bit of it—on a claim that is registered to an Ivan Bertoff. He made no explanation of—"

"Did Mr. Greenwood inquire about this?" Ruth asked, unable to control her anger. She'd had quite enough of this woman's prattle, which extended beyond concern. She was being rude and critical of someone she knew nothing about.

"No, he—"

"Then perhaps I should remind you of what I told you during our Thanksgiving meal. Mr. Spencer has a partner in the claim, Ivan Bertoff. Since Mr. Greenwood has already checked, I'm sure he knows the claim is filed under Mr. Bertoff's name. Mr. Spencer takes care of the business end of their partnership. I see nothing sinister about that. If Mr. Bertoff has no objections, I can't see why anyone else should."

Mrs. Greenwood's eyebrows hiked at those words, and an ugly sneer contorted her features.

"Well, the way you are rushing to his defense obviously betrays your feelings, Ruth. I'm shocked that you would take up with someone you know so little about. A miner, as compared to a man like Dr. Bradley."

"Mrs. Greenwood, I am not 'taking up,' as you put it, with anyone who is disreputable. Even so, I think I am the one to judge my friends, rather than you and Mr. Greenwood. I know you mean well, but I have begun to feel pressured to encourage Dr. Bradley's attention. I won't do that. While I respect his profession, I have no interest in him as a suitor. So maybe we can put that matter to rest, once and for all."

Mrs. Greenwood turned for the door. "In that case, I'll be leaving. You obviously resent my concern. I was mistaken to think you appreciated the fact that we cared about you, but I see that I have misjudged you. You are far too headstrong for your own good, young lady." Flinging that parting shot over her shoulder, she stormed out, slamming the door behind her.

Ruth glared at the door, seething with anger. She fought an urge to yank the door open and tell her if she cared about her, she should be checking on Arthur Bradley rather than Joe Spencer. At least she hadn't had to wrestle herself out of Joe's embrace, whereas Arthur had made a grab for her, practically forcing himself on her.

At the same time, she knew it would be unfair to speak her mind when she was angry, particularly after she had promised Arthur to say nothing of what had happened.

Turning, she rushed back up the stairs to the kitchen, trying to regain her composure. It took another cup of tea and a few minutes of introspection before she finally came to the conclusion that perhaps she had saved all of them time and trouble by stating her case. She did not want to be invited to any more of Mrs. Greenwood's dinners and have her trying to play Cupid. Furthermore, it would be a relief not to have the Greenwoods breathing down her neck. It was time someone let Mrs. Greenwood know that her busybody antics were not appreciated.

Despite her argument with herself, she was still feeling frustrated and listless when Dorie sailed in an hour later.

"I just met Kate Carmack!" Dorie said, grabbing a teacup and helping herself to tea. "Do you know her?"

Ruth was relieved to have a pleasant diversion from her conversation with Mrs. Greenwood.

"Yes. Her husband George and her brother Skookum Jim came to the clinic when we first opened. Both men were suffering from influenza."

"They're the ones who first discovered gold here, isn't that right?"

"So far as I know, yes, they were the first ones. Skookum Jim and Tagish Charlie are of the Tagish tribe, you know. They teamed up with George Carmack and discovered the first gold on Rabbit Creek. It's now called Bonanza Creek."

"I'm fascinated with Kate," Dorie said, propping her chin in her hand and staring into space.

"I want to do an article on her—the first woman in the Klondike gold fields. The people at home will be fascinated. What's even more interesting is her background. She was raised in the south central region here. She lost her first husband and their infant daughter, she told me."

"That's right," Ruth nodded. "They died of influenza, which is why she insisted on George and Skookum Jim seeing a doctor. Kate's a remarkable woman who kept the men in supplies by taking in laundry and sewing and selling moccasins to the miners. She also picked berries and set traps for rabbits. I've heard from several people that without her, her husband and brother could not have survived the first desperate winter here."

Dorie shook her head. "It's amazing what women will do for their men."

Ruth sipped her tea, thinking about that. Until Joe Spencer, she had never met anyone who would inspire her to take in laundry or sew or do any of the grueling tasks that were common to so many of the women whose husbands were miners. Still, when a woman really cared for a man, she could see that the tasks that seemed so difficult at least had purpose.

"I should add that it's also very amazing what doctors and nurses do for people," Dorie added, smiling across at Ruth. "I admire you so much, Ruth."

"Do you?" Ruth asked, surprised.

"Why, of course. You've shown real courage and stamina by coming here and then by treating all the sick people."

Ruth dropped her head, aware that she no longer had that purpose.

"Now what did I say wrong?" Dorie inquired, leaning forward.

Ruth began to tell her what had happened with Arthur Bradley and then Mrs. Greenwood.

"And you've let a narrow-minded person like that ruin your day?"

Ruth sighed. "The Greenwoods have been good to me." She went on to tell about the Sunday dinners and the fact that Mrs. Greenwood had come to the house when her father died, had held her in her arms as though she were her daughter.

"I'm already feeling guilty for what I said to her." Ruth frowned into her teacup, wishing she had not lost her temper.

"Well, a person can't go around poking their nose in other people's business and expect to be complimented for it. I'm sure you'll have a chance to make amends, if that's what you want. Tell me more about this Joe Spencer. You probably don't know it, but your eyes light up when you mention his name. I'd say you're smitten," she said, teasing her.

Ruth got up and went to the stove for the teakettle, needing the action to cover her sudden nervousness at Dorie's frank observation.

"He's a nice man. Mrs. Greenwood wants to insinuate that I should be wary of him, but I know she's trying to shove me into Arthur Bradley's arms."

"Hmmph. I would have difficulty dealing with someone who wanted to choose a man for me. If I wanted a man, I would choose one myself, which I did once." She sighed. "It didn't work out, which is one reason I jumped at the opportunity to come up here."

Ruth refilled Dorie's teacup and glanced at her new friend. For a moment, an expression of sadness crossed Dorie's face, and Ruth couldn't help wondering what went wrong with the man she had chosen, but she didn't ask. She knew, in time, if Dorie wanted to tell her, she would.

"I want you to know I'm so happy to have you living here," Ruth said to her. "Just being able to talk out my frustrations means a lot. You've made me feel a lot better."

"Good! Try not to worry over things that cannot be helped. My theory is just do your best and let God do the rest."

Ruth's smile widened. "That's a wonderful theory. I'll try to practice it more."

"Well," Dorie came to her feet, "now that I've enjoyed your good tea, I'm going to my room to do some writing while I'm still fired up about Kate Carmack."

"And I'll put something on the stove for lunch. Are you very hungry?"

"No, I'm not accustomed to eating a lot. So just yell whenever you want me to come help."

"Thanks," Ruth said, quietly thanking God for sending Dorie to her.

❧

Two days later, a handsome man dressed in parka and jeans appeared at her door. He had brown hair, deep thoughtful eyes, and an engaging smile. "Are you Miss Wright?" he asked politely.

"Yes, I am," she replied, studying him curiously.

"Hi, I'm Jack London," he said. "I have a little cabin near Joe and Ivan. When Joe heard I was coming into town for supplies, he asked me to drop this off to you."

He handed her a sheet of paper, folded into a neat square, with her name on it.

"Thank you," she said, accepting the note. She looked back at the man, who was regarding her with curious yet friendly eyes.

"How is Joe?" she asked.

"He's working very hard, but generally he seems to be okay." He smiled briefly. "Well, I must go. It was nice meeting you."

"You, too," she replied then stepped back inside. She hurried up to her bedroom and sat down to read the note, written in bold yet neat handwriting.

Dear Ruth,

I wanted to thank you for a wonderful evening. Also, I want you to know how much I appreciate the invitation to Christmas dinner. I will look very forward to sharing that special day with you as I battle the cold and the drudgery that is my life here. I have not looked forward to Christmas very much for several years. This year is different. I can hardly wait to see you again and enjoy the pleasure of your company.

Until then, take very good care of yourself.

Your friend,
Joe

She smiled, traced a finger over the paper, and tried to imagine him sitting down in the small cabin he had described to her, thoughtfully writing out the letter. She sighed, pressing the letter against her heart.

Thank you, God, she silently prayed. How could Mrs. Greenwood or anyone doubt the sincerity of this wonderful man?

Singing a Christmas carol, she got up and went to her room, wondering what she would wear when he came to see her.

9

As the Christmas season approached, some of the merchants made noble attempts to honor the birth of Christ. Wreaths and candles dominated the shop windows and a few of the log homes. However, it was common knowledge to all that there would be no bountiful feasts on anyone's table on Christmas Day, for now even the merchants were worrying about what they would eat. Many of the staples on which people depended were completely gone from the shelves, except for the few hidden away for the merchants and their families. Most people would gladly have paid the asking price of a dollar per orange back in the fall, but now there were no oranges or fruit of any kind, except for the dried variety.

Ruth tried to keep her spirits up, despite the absence of so many things. She had spent many hours with her needle and thread, making little white angels from used white petticoats, using buttons for eyes and making hair from yarn. Noticing the angels, one of the merchants had begged her to make more to sell in shops, but Ruth was out of yarn and buttons, and couldn't make more without cutting up clothes, and she didn't want to do that. The red silk petticoat she had brought to Dawson had seemed absurdly out of place once she arrived. Now, however, it was about to serve a purpose. Working adeptly with scissors, needle, and thread, she cut and shaped it into a tablecloth for the holidays while thinking of the meal she would prepare for Joe Spencer. During the drab season, the reminder that he was eating Christmas dinner with her kept her going when she might have been moping like so many others.

Lucky, her father's devoted patient, had brought a small spruce tree to her for a Christmas present; and in return, she had gone through her father's medicine cabinet, selecting liniments and cough syrups for Lucky.

She had sewn a few ornaments for the tree and strung popcorn and holly for decorations. She removed one branch, already decorated, from the back side of the tree and took it to the cemetery. There, she thrust it into the hard-packed snow as a tribute to her father for the happy Christmases they had shared.

Two days before Christmas, she braved the subzero weather by bundling up in her warmest clothes, wearing three pair of socks, and her sturdiest rubber boots to make a trek through the snow to the mercantile.

She was half-frozen by the time she arrived. Opening the door and expecting to be warmed by the potbellied stove inside, she was surprised to see the clerks bundled up in coats and mittens and the patrons huddling as close as possible to the stove. Although the store was warmer than outside, it was a startling contrast to the once-cozy, warm store of two weeks before.

As she approached the clerk, he greeted her and offered an apology. "We are having to ration our wood," he said, nodding toward the stove. "I apologize. Why don't you warm yourself while I get your items for you, Miss Wright?"

"Thank you." Shivering from the cold, she glanced at the stove, grateful for the supply of wood her father had accumulated. She removed her mittens and with stiff fingers opened her string purse and removed the list.

The clerk hurried off with the list. Ruth felt as though her legs had become wooden posts as she edged toward the stove where everyone huddled.

"Miss Wright," a familiar voice called to her.

She turned to see Arthur Bradley. Noting the *Miss Wright*, she appreciated the fact that he was being more formal now that she had broken her friendship with him.

"Hello," she said, trying to move her cold lips into a smile.

"I'm sorry to see you out in the cold," he said, looking concerned. He had lost more weight and was now pitifully thin. His cheeks were gaunt and there were dark circles under his eyes.

"I needed the fresh air. Are you well?" she asked, looking him over with concern.

"Not very, but I will manage."

"What's wrong?" she asked worriedly, for she did care about him as a friend, after all.

He shrugged. "Just a bout of influenza that I was able to conquer. I have worried about you," he added, his pale green eyes staring into her face.

"I have taken in a boarder," she said on a more cheerful note. "A nice lady named Dorie Farmer. She is a correspondent for the San Francisco *Examiner*."

He did not react with the relief she would have expected, and then she realized why. He wanted to be the one she turned to for help. He didn't want her to survive on her own without him.

"I hope the arrangement is working out," he said, his voice as doubtful as Mrs. Greenwood's had been.

Remembering their argument, Ruth lifted her chin and took on a more firm stance. "The arrangement is working out just fine, thank you."

"Here are the items you needed, Miss Wright."

To her relief, the clerk had returned with two large bundles, heavily wrapped. "We are out of coffee, sugar, and salt." He pointed to the list. "I'm sorry."

She turned to the clerk, hovering nearby, looking distressed. "But . . ." Her voice trailed as she glanced at the men knotted around the stove. Her father had said the merchants would retain a stash of items for themselves and the doctors.

But her father was dead and she was no longer a nurse, she reminded herself.

"Maybe I can help you." Arthur lowered his voice.

Pride surged back as she looked from the clerk to Arthur. "Thank you, but I can manage just fine. I have enough in my pantry to make do." She turned and followed the clerk to the counter, opening her string purse to pay for her purchases. To her surprise, it took almost all of the money she had.

After she had paid, Arthur trailed her to the door, opening it for her. "Won't you join me at the Greenwoods' home for Christmas dinner?" he asked suddenly.

"I have made plans for Christmas," she answered as they stepped out onto the snow-covered boards. When she looked at him, she saw the pain on his face. She felt desperately sorry to have hurt him and wished she could make amends. "Arthur, I want you to understand that I am no longer upset with you. I have forgotten our . . . differences."

"Then what is it?" he asked miserably.

She hesitated for a moment as she pulled her scarf over her head and about her face, tucking it into her collar. She decided she might as well be honest with him. "I have met someone," she answered.

His pale brows arched suddenly. "Are you talking about that drifter?"

"I don't know to whom you are referring, but I can assure you I haven't taken up with a drifter, Arthur."

He frowned, obviously trying to remember a name. Then his eyes snapped as though something had dawned on him. "The miner, Spencer, whom no one knows anything about."

She sighed. "I see you and Mrs. Greenwood have been talking. Well, I can assure you that Mr. Spencer is a gentleman. Furthermore, Dorie will be joining us, so it isn't as though we will be unchaperoned. Merry Christmas, Arthur."

She turned and left him staring after her on the snowy boards in front of the mercantile. As she hurried home, gripping her packages tightly against her chest for warmth, anger churned through her, warming her and quickening her steps. By the time she reached the porch steps, gripping the post as she raked the caked snow from her boots, her temper was boiling.

She was sick and tired of Arthur and the Greenwoods trying to run her life. They seemed determined to conspire in an arranged marriage between Arthur and her, which made her more determined than ever to avoid them. Furthermore, she thought with a smile, it made Joe Spencer even more appealing.

❧

On Christmas Day, she and Dorie were in the kitchen early. While she, too, had been forced to ration her wood, the kitchen was warm and cozy. Dorie had volunteered to make a berry pie from some huckleberries she had been hoarding in a leather pouch since early fall.

"I kept these against starvation on Chilkoot Pass then forgot about them until I unpacked my belongings. I will make us a berry pie."

"Can you stretch the sugar?" Ruth teased.

"That I can do," Dorie laughed as they worked side by side, putting together the meal.

Lucky had brought a duck to Ruth in late fall, and she had wrapped it in a thickness of cheesecloth and buried it in the snow to freeze it. Two days ago, she had retrieved it, thawed it on the stove, and last night she had put it in to bake.

"We may be the only people in Dawson who are having meat for our meal," Dorie said, suddenly looking sad. "Some of my friends at the *Nugget* were complaining that their Christmas meal would be drastically different this year. Unless one is a hunter willing to brave the elements, there is no meat left in Dawson, I hear."

Ruth nodded. "God has been good to us."

"And you certainly know how to conserve your food supply. I've been amazed at the way you do that."

Ruth laughed as she placed the bread on its baking pan. "I had a very comfortable upbringing in Seattle, and yet my mother came from a family with nine children. She was always very practical in the kitchen, and I learned many tricks from her."

Dorie smiled. "I've watched you pick up half a leftover biscuit and dump it in that tin." She nodded toward the large tin that was a familiar object in Ruth's kitchen.

"And now I have enough corn bread and biscuit to put together my dressing for today," Ruth said, feeling a bit of satisfaction at how she was managing her supplies.

"So I see," Dorie laughed. "And what time is our guest arriving?"

Automatically, Ruth's eyes drifted toward the kitchen window. "I should think any time now."

Then she glanced down at her dress. Beneath the muslin apron, she wore her green woolen dress, and she had styled her hair in a softer chignon today. Deep waves on the sides of her face softened her eyes, and she knew the happiness along with the heat of the oven would color her lips and cheeks.

Almost as soon as Dorie had posed the question of their guest, she heard the neigh of a horse.

She clapped her hands together, dusting off the loose flour. Picking up a cup towel, she wiped her fingers as she walked to the window and peered out.

Joe had arrived and was steering his horse toward the hitching post. He was carrying a bundle of something in a tote sack in his arms, while one gloved hand gripped the reins. Balancing the load, he dismounted his horse. Both man and horse were covered with snow. He wore a heavy parka with hood, and his face was red with cold. Before he could look up and catch her gawking, she quickly stepped back from the window.

"He's here," she said and beamed across at Dorie.

"So I gathered," Dorie chuckled. "Look, you've done everything other than bake the bread. Why don't you let me finish up the meal while you visit with him in the living room?"

Ruth hesitated then quickly consented. "If you don't mind," she said, hurrying from the kitchen.

She left the door open to admit more heat into the living room. Removing her apron and laying it over the back of a chair, she began to punch up the goose down feathers on the sofa. She moved to the bookcase, straightening a few toppled books and wiping a fleck of dust away. Then she turned back to her tree, staring at it for a moment with pride.

In spite of her meager circumstances, she had managed to obtain a cheerful mood both in her home and within herself. She had spent a few hours crying over the fact that her father would not be sharing Christmas with them, but then she had counted her blessings of Dorie and Joe, which always lifted her spirits.

As soon as she heard his knock on the door, she rushed down the stairs into the cold hall and quickly opened the door.

He looked taller and leaner than ever, and this time he had grown a blond-brown beard, neatly trimmed. The blue eyes looked even larger in his bronze face, and she realized that he had indeed lost weight. Her eyes ran down his lean body and she saw, from the horse-hair mat, that he had done his best to remove the snow from his shoes.

"Hello." She smiled at him.

"Merry Christmas," he said, still holding the mysterious bundle. "I've brought along some firewood that I thought you might use."

"Wonderful," she said with delight, for wood was a major problem for everyone in Dawson. "I can't tell you how much I appreciate that. Why don't you just put it down here in the hall by the coat tree?"

He entered the hall, placing the sack on the floor with a thud. Then carefully he began to remove his snow-dusted parka. From the pocket he retrieved a small package, and Ruth hoped it was not a gift for she had nothing for him. He turned to face her, looking more handsome than ever in his white dress shirt and dark trousers.

"Was it rough traveling over the road?"

"Not too bad," he replied, his eyes barely leaving hers. "This is for you," he said, extending the small brown-wrapped package to her.

She swallowed, feeling embarrassed. "I . . . I have nothing for you."

He had closed the door, but still the frigid air that had rushed in surrounded them.

"I beg to differ. You have given me one of the best gifts I've ever received—the joy of your company on Christmas Day."

Her eyes locked with his for a moment, and she finally admitted to herself what she had secretly known all along. She was in love with Joe Spencer.

The bump of something overhead shook her back to her senses. "Please come upstairs," she said, smiling into his deep blue eyes.

"I'll remove my boots and leave them here by the door," he said, preparing to remove the heavy work boots.

Upon removing his boots, she saw that he had also brought along an extra pair of clean leather boots, and he was putting those on now. *What a kind, considerate man he is*, she thought as her heart beat faster.

Turning for the stairs, she lifted her skirts and walked ahead of him, holding his present as though it were a precious treasure, which it was. When they entered the living room, she saw that Dorie had emerged from the kitchen and stood eagerly waiting to meet Joe. As Joe and Dorie faced one another for the first time, Dorie's eyes widened for a moment and she tilted her head thoughtfully.

As Ruth made the introductions and both responded, Dorie retained that same thoughtful expression. "I have the feeling we've met before, Mr. Spencer," she said, eyeing him up and down.

He stroked his whiskered chin. "I'm sure I would have remembered, Miss Farmer," he said in his smooth southern drawl.

"Dorie is a correspondent for the San Francisco *Examiner*."

"I see," he said, shifting his eyes back to Ruth. "Then it's possible we may have passed one another on a street in San Francisco," he said.

Ruth thought he seemed to be explaining the fact more to Ruth than Dorie, so she turned back for Dorie's reaction.

"Yes, that's possible," Dorie nodded. "Anyway, being a journalist, I don't usually forget a face. Particularly a handsome one," she added boldly.

Ruth laughed and Joe joined in rather self-consciously. "Thank you. Nor am I inclined to forget a pretty woman like yourself."

Dorie ducked her head and blushed, obviously unaccustomed to such a compliment. Ruth smiled at Joe, knowing he was being kind. Dorie was many wonderful things, but pretty was not an adjective she would use to describe her.

"How can I help in the preparations?" he asked as Ruth went to put his package under the tree.

"If you'd like to wash up in the kitchen, I'll give you a job," she said. She had decided to let him join in the preparations so that he would feel more like he had a part in their celebration. "I haven't had time to sweep the hall steps or the hall. If you wouldn't mind the task, I'll give that to you while Dorie and I finish with the meal."

"I'll be happy to do that," he said, accepting the homemade broom Dorie handed him.

When the two women were alone in the kitchen, Dorie rolled her eyes. "You didn't tell me he was so good-looking or so charming."

"I'm keeping that secret to myself," Ruth teased back.

While their meal was scant if compared to the other Christmas dinners Ruth had enjoyed throughout her life, Dorie and Joe complimented her and she, too, enjoyed the food. Afterwards, they settled down around the tree to open presents.

At Ruth's suggestion, Dorie opened her present first. Ruth had made a cloth cover for the journal that Dorie carried everywhere. When Dorie opened it, she was ecstatic.

"I'm so grateful that my journal will be protected from the elements," she said, beaming proudly. "Thank you, Ruth. Now you open yours."

Dorie had given Ruth a collection of recipes that she had organized into a neat little book. Ruth was delighted.

"The recipes came from the Tlingit woman who accompanied her husband, guiding us over the Chilkoot. She was our cook, and I found some of her native dishes quite wonderful. Also, she had a very ingenuous way of preparing things. I copied down her methods, but not being a cook, I doubt that I will ever have use for them." She laughed self-consciously as she looked at Joe, who smiled back at her.

"Thank you so much, Dorie," Ruth replied. "How thoughtful of you."

The remaining gift to be opened was from Joe, and Ruth hesitated. She had thought it improper to buy a gift for Joe, and now she felt a bit awkward in accepting one from him.

"The gift is merely an acknowledgment of your kindness and that of your father," he added. "They treated me with a back injury," he explained to Dorie, "and I felt Doc never charged enough for his services."

Ruth smiled, grateful that he could explain away any improprieties of the gift. When she opened the paper, she found, wrapped in delicate tissue, a small pin fashioned from a gold nugget.

She gasped, holding the tiny gleaming gold in the palm of her hand. "This is gorgeous."

Joe smiled, looking pleased that she liked his gift. "We are doing fairly well with our claim. The last time I was in Dawson, I stopped in at Mr. Bromberg's little house, having heard he had been a jeweler in New York. He agreed to design the pin for me, and he did it rather quickly."

"But . . . ," Ruth looked from Dorie to Joe, "I can't accept anything this expensive. What about . . ." She had been about to suggest he send it to his mother, but she was dead. "Do you have any sisters?"

Joe shook his head. "No, I don't. You really shouldn't be self-conscious about it. I've explained my motives. This is just a meager show of appreciation for what you and your father did for me."

"He's right," Dorie jumped in, eager to encourage Ruth. "There's no reason you shouldn't keep such a thoughtful gift." She looked at Joe. "You must be one of the few who is doing well with your claim."

"I suppose I am," he answered. As he spoke, Ruth thought his words held just a hint of formality. "I have a partner, Ivan Bertoff, a Russian gentleman who originally filed the claim. I think I've been lucky to join up with him."

Ruth sighed deeply, then covered the sigh with a smile when both Dorie and Joe looked at her. After Mrs. Greenwood and Arthur's badgering, it was wonderful to hear the truth about his claim spoken in the presence of Dorie, who was sure to back her up or even spread the word herself.

"I'm happy for you." She was staring at him again, and both Ruth and Joe noticed. "I still have the odd feeling we have met. When did you arrive in the territory?"

There was a moment's hesitation. "The boat pulled into Dawson the first of August. I'm originally from San Francisco, but we already agreed that we must have passed one another in a shop somewhere and not realized it until now."

Dorie nodded, apparently satisfied by the answer. "I'm rather nondescript, let's face facts. So it's quite possible you wouldn't remember me. Well," she said, looking from Joe to Ruth, "I did promise the Fairhopes that I would drop in on them this afternoon for tea and spice cake."

She came to her feet, clutching Ruth's gift to her chest. "It has been a wonderful Christmas."

Joe stood, then Ruth did, as well. For a moment, she felt a bit awkward. She hoped Dorie wasn't inventing an excuse for her to be alone with Joe. She opened her mouth to say something, but there seemed to be no adequate response. She had no doubt the Fairhopes had invited Dorie for tea. Since the Fairhopes owned the local newspaper, it was quite logical they would invite Dorie to drop by on Christmas Day.

"I've enjoyed spending part of the day with you," Joe said to her.

"Thank you." That self-conscious look that often slipped over Dorie's face in Joe's presence returned as she hurried into her bedroom and began to rummage around.

"I believe I'll go down and bring up some of that firewood," he said, turning for the door.

"I'll help," Ruth offered.

"It isn't necessary," Dorie called back, already busy in the kitchen.

For the brief time she was alone in the living room, she admired her pin again. Then, to show her appreciation, she decided to wear it. She fastened the delicate clasp at the neck of her dress, and the little pin gleamed brilliantly against her white collar. She was literally soaring with joy over the wonderful day they had spent together. Thinking back, it was one of the finest Christmas Days ever.

Dorie entered the room again, a box in her hand. "I save all of my newspaper articles," she said, indicating the box. "I hope that doesn't seem too vain, but I thought I'd take over some of the articles I wrote about Skagway. Mr. Fairhope thought we might be able to use something in the paper here, since everyone is hungry for news of other areas, how they've done with gold mining, that sort of thing. Skagway had a rough time surviving last year, so perhaps seeing how those courageous people made do just may help the people here."

Joe's footsteps sounded on the stairs, and Dorie glanced toward the open door.

"He brought firewood," Ruth explained, smiling.

"He's a gift from above." The words formed on Dorie's lips, though she did not voice them for Joe was entering the living room. He glanced at Dorie, who stood with her cloak on, preparing to leave. "I'll just stoke up your fire in the stove," he said to Ruth.

"Good day, Mr. Spencer. I'll be out for a while. I trust you'll be here when I return and join us at the Christmas service?"

A look of regret crossed his face. "I have to leave to return to the mine today. It will be getting dark soon. Will you be all right alone?" he asked with concern, looking at Dorie.

"The Fairhopes will see me home, thank you."

There was only four hours of daylight now, and Ruth had begun to dread the darkness that seemed so interminable. She knew it was a long journey for him, and yet she wished he could stay.

"You aren't staying at Miss Mattie's this time?" she asked, trying to keep a cheerful note to her voice.

"No. With the bad weather, we're very limited on our working hours. We have to take advantage of the short daylight and the fact that there's no more snow right now."

"But how do you work with so much snow?"

"We just have to keep fires going, dig, and windlass, but we are very limited in that and can only do so during the middle of the day, when the temperature is not as brutal."

"But it's still brutal, isn't it?" she asked, following him to the kitchen and watching as he put more wood into the stove. "I walked to the mercantile a few days ago and it was agony. I really don't see how you do it."

He finished with the fire, closed the stove door, and wiped his hands on the old towel she handed him. "Ambition, I guess. And truthfully, I enjoy mining."

"Do you?" she asked, surprised to hear that. "So many consider it a drudgery and are in it only with the hope of getting rich quick."

He grinned as they walked back to the living room. "Well, that's part of the reason I enjoy it, I suppose."

As they took their seats, Ruth studied his face, noting he was the only man with a beard whom she regarded as handsome. It seemed despite good barbers and conveniences of the city, Joe always managed to look good. His shoulder-length hair and thick beard, though neatly trimmed, did not make him less appealing to her.

"You've asked if I plan to stay on in Dawson. What are your plans?" She had been so curious about him, wanting to know everything, yet reluctant to ask.

"I want to return to San Francisco," he said matter-of-factly.

"You do?" She was surprised by the answer, even though she knew she shouldn't be. He had lived in San Francisco before.

He nodded, looking across at the little Christmas tree. "I enjoyed ranch life and have ridiculous aspirations of someday owning a ranch." He turned back to her with a grin. "I suppose it's the love of land in my blood from generations of plantation owners. When my ancestors lost their land after the Civil War, they were never quite the same, or so I've been told. Anyway, there must be that need to own my own spot of ground." He paused, looking toward the window where darkness was already beginning to gather. "If I can't buy a small ranch, I hope to at least homestead a few acres and build a cabin. I think Ivan and I will make enough money for that."

She nodded, thinking of what he was saying. "That's a realistic dream." And it was his dream that turned her thoughts back to her own future. She had been worried sick about what she was going to do. She could sell the house here and the funds would sustain her for a while back in Seattle, but then what? She still had the house there, but it would need repairs, and there were her future needs to consider. She was trained for nursing, but now that held no appeal, either. What she really wanted was a husband and a family. She hadn't realized she was staring at Joe until he spoke.

"Is something wrong?" he asked gently. "Food in my beard?" he teased.

She flushed and laughed softly. "I'm sorry. I was miles away, thinking of my future."

"And what is your future, may I ask?"

She shook her head. "I'm not sure. Since I can't depend on a bonanza from mining—" She broke off, suddenly remembering the claim her father had taken from a patient. It was tucked away in a bureau drawer; in fact, she had almost forgotten about it. Automatically, her eyes drifted toward her bedroom as her mind seized upon a plan. If Joe knew mining, was willing to work so hard to succeed at it, perhaps he was the person to consult. Of course he was!

"Excuse me for a moment," she said, getting up and hurrying into the bedroom. Opening the middle drawer of her chest, she moved aside a layer of undergarments and retrieved the piece of paper that neither she nor even her father had taken very seriously.

Gripping it in her hands, glancing over it, she walked back into the living room. "Would you please take a look at this?"

His brows lifted as she handed the paper to him. He scanned it then looked at her in surprise. "It's a claim that's located not far from ours. I believe that should be a good area."

Ruth smiled, pleased with that news. "A miner with tuberculosis gave it to my father in payment for treating him for a week before he departed, saying he never wanted to see this area again. He was a very sick man, and my father gave him money for boat passage back to the States. That's when he gave us the claim."

She went back to her seat. "I don't think my father thought much of it. He had probably even forgotten about it when you asked if he had any aspirations to be a miner. He had heard so many stories of men about to strike it rich, only to watch them come back empty-handed and terribly ill."

She touched the gold nugget at her neck. "You obviously know what you're doing. Would you be interested in taking me on as a partner?"

He stared at her for a moment as though he couldn't believe what she had asked. Then his eyes dropped to the claim, and he read it again. "I don't know what to say," he finally replied. "I would be honored to be your partner. And I will do my best with this." He indicated the paper. "Are you sure there isn't anyone else you want to do business with?"

She laughed. "Not unless Clarence Berry is interested, and I believe he is currently enjoying his wealth in another area." Her laughter died away as she looked at him seriously. "No one else has brought me firewood, or a present on Christmas Day, or been the gentleman that you have been. I'm certain that you're the one I want to entrust my claim to, although it may be worthless. I don't want to waste your time."

Joe stared at the claim again. The location was prime, although these things were always a gamble. The emotion he had felt for Ruth was brimming up inside him now. If she were that honest with him, how could he be less with her? He had to tell her about the incident in Skagway.

He drew a deep breath, wondering how to begin.

"Why don't I make us some coffee?" she suggested.

He shook his head. "I'm learning to enjoy plain tea."

"Good. I have more tea than coffee. There's very little coffee left, and Dorie and I limit ourselves to half a cup of very weak coffee each morning in order to wake up."

"And I'll not deprive you of that," he said, standing. "I'll join you in the kitchen."

As he walked behind her, his eyes roamed over her shining auburn hair, the straight back and tiny waist, the slim hips in her flowing skirt. He had to tell her, he had to. *But how?* How could he make her understand? And if she knew, it would be her duty to contact the Mounties. Would she do that? He suspected that she would not; on the other hand, she wouldn't go through with their partnership on the mining claim.

Looking down, his mind weighed the alternatives. If she were willing to trust him with the claim, he might be the only one who would deal honestly with her. And if the claim made them rich, he could go back to Skagway, hire a decent attorney, face the truth. Or he could get on the boat with her and return to the States. Given those choices, he could not bring himself to be honest enough, or reckless enough, to throw away a bright future.

By the time they took their seats at the table and sipped tea, he had carefully folded the claim and put it in his breast pocket, buttoning down the flap.

"I promise you I will work hard on this claim—"

"It isn't necessary to make any promises. You've proven you are a hard worker. Just don't make yourself ill like the last man who owned it. And really, Joe, I have nothing to lose. That claim has just been occupying space in the drawer. When I leave next spring, I doubt that I would be able to get a fair price for it." She sighed. "I've heard how people take advantage of widows with mining claims, and in some ways I'm very much like those widows."

He reached across, covering her soft hand with his. "But you are not a widow. And to my enormous good fortune, you are not betrothed."

He looked into her eyes and felt his love for her filling every corner of his heart. Maybe he couldn't tell her about Skagway just yet, but he could share his feelings for her and he would be honest in what he said.

"Ruth, this has been the most special Christmas of my life."

She gasped, and her eyes widened. "Surely as a boy with your family—"

"No." He shook his head. "I was not with the woman I loved. And I do love you, Ruth."

As her cheeks colored at those words, he rushed on. "I want you to know I'm not speaking impulsively or dishonestly. I've had many long nights to think about this, to think of you and nothing else. Please forgive me if I'm being too forward. I don't want to embarrass or offend you."

Her eyes were glowing as she squeezed his hand, and he breathed a sigh of relief as she answered him. "Your words neither embarrass nor offend me. I am filled with joy that you feel this way because . . ." She faltered, dropped her eyes to their clasped hands for a moment. Then, as though she had gathered her courage, she lifted her hazel eyes to him and spoke in a firm voice. "Because I feel the same way. I love you, too, Joe."

His breath caught. A joy too sweet to believe filled his being. He had never in his life felt such happiness, such hope. He stood, lifting her hand to his chest, drawing her gently from her chair.

"I love you," he repeated, his hands cupping the sides of her heart-shaped face as he kissed her with all the fervor of a man deeply in love. She returned his kiss, and as their lips expressed their joy, she pulled back from him, breathlessly. The light flushed her cheeks and the radiance in her eyes told him she would be a wonderful wife, eager to accept his affections and return them. She would not be cold or impassive, as he had heard some men complain.

"Ruth, would you—" He stopped himself. How could he propose to her without telling her everything? And if he did, he would lose her.

Her face was tilted slightly, and she seemed to be holding her breath, waiting.

"I don't want to rush you," he said, gently backing himself out of the situation. "I just want you to be certain about how you feel. We'll talk more seriously when I return."

At that, he glanced over his shoulder and saw complete darkness through the window. He sighed, releasing her. "I have to go."

"I don't want you to," she said suddenly then bit her lip. "But of course you must. I hear of accidents on the trail, and there is always the danger of frostbite from exposure. Please be careful." Her voice was low and plaintive, drawing him back to her.

He kissed her again, quickly this time, and then he forced himself to head for the door. He knew that with each minute he spent with her, the opportunity to leave was becoming more difficult. He longed to stay with her . . . forever. But he must earn her love and their future, and that meant returning to the freezing, torturous work that lay ahead of him.

She followed him down the stairs, crossing her arms over her chest, watching silently as he removed his boots and pulled on the heavier ones, then bundled himself back into the parka.

"Could I give you an extra blanket?" she asked suddenly.

"I carry one in my saddlebag," he said. "Merry Christmas, Ruth." He hesitated at the doorway, again hating to leave.

"Merry Christmas, Joe." This time it was she who leaned forward and brushed his lips with a kiss.

The kiss warmed his lips against the freezing night that enveloped him, and the memory of the glow in her eyes, the words she had spoken—*she loved him!*—gave him the endurance he needed to return through the bleak winter night to the drafty cabin he shared with Ivan.

$\mathcal{T}$he cold darkness of January seemed interminable. Only a few hours of daylight broke the monotony, and during those hours Ruth and Dorie tried to maintain their chores. Dorie worked long hours at the newspaper office, for the small newspaper was a major source of entertainment for the residents of Dawson.

Ruth spent much of her time planning the best way to convert their dwindling supply of food into nutritional meals. More and more she turned to God for strength. She read her mother's Bible often, and many days she was tempted to sink into grief. It was the memory of Joe Spencer, however, that always gave her hope and joy.

She had not heard from him since Christmas Day, when he left the house. They had been enveloped in a glow of love that day, a glow that warmed her during the fiercely cold nights when the wind howled around the eaves of her house. Then she longed for Joe's strong arms, and she worried that he was cold or hungry or sick. When worry burdened her heart, she prayed. Many nights, the wee hours found her on her knees by her bed, a blanket wrapped around her shoulders to warm her as she asked God to protect her beloved. She had lost both parents, and now she agonized about losing Joe.

During the first week of February, a heavily bundled Arthur Bradley appeared at her door, hugging a sack against his chest. Although surprised to see him, Ruth found herself glad that he had come, and she quickly invited him inside, for there was only a thin sliver of daylight and it was freezing cold outside.

"Ruth, I have more food than I need," he said, following her up the stairs to the living area. "I wanted to share a few items with you. I've been worrying about you."

"I'm fine, Arthur," she answered with a smile.

He waved aside her reply as they entered the kitchen and he placed the sack on the counter. "I'm sure you are. However, with very little daylight and the weather so terribly cold, I don't like the thought of you trying to walk to the mercantile. And if you did," he said, shaking his head, "you wouldn't find much to purchase."

She sighed. "It's really bad, isn't it?"

He was removing his parka, his scarf, and then his gloves. "Yes, I'm afraid the lack of food is getting quite serious. However, everyone seems to be making do, although I can tell you the faces are getting thinner and thinner."

She shook her head, turning for the stove. "Then let's have a cup of hot tea and be grateful for our blessings."

"A splendid idea," he said, taking a seat at the table.

When she asked about his work, he began to relate stories from the clinic. As they sat at the kitchen table sipping weak tea and discussing medicine, she felt relieved that he had come. In an odd way, it brought back conversations with her father. She had missed Arthur. When finally he lapsed into silence and looked deeply into her eyes, Ruth sensed that he still cared for her.

She got up to refill their teacups, wanting to escape the look of sadness in his eyes.

"Arthur, Dorie told me there is word of a missionary hospital to be established here later in the year. Is this true?" she asked, eager to divert his thoughts.

He blinked, as though clearing his head, and nodded. "Yes, I expect there will be a hospital, although it will be small and sparsely furnished in the beginning. Still, it is much needed, and I will not feel so guilty when I leave."

She sat down in the chair and looked across at him. "You are leaving, then?"

He nodded, staring at his cup. "As soon as I can. Of course, I will wait until some of the medical missionaries arrive, but I hope they will be on the first boat this spring. I hate it here, Ruth." He sighed. "I am not cut out for this type of life."

"Is anyone?" She smiled sadly.

"It doesn't seem to have bothered you as badly as most."

She considered the thought and shrugged. "Perhaps it is because I know there is nothing I can do to change my circumstances during this time. I just have to try and be patient."

"Patient for what?" he asked, frowning. "For travel to commence again so you can go home?"

She hesitated. For a moment, she longed to tell him about Joe, but then she knew it would only hurt him. She could no longer speak to him as a friend, for his feelings for her exceeded friendship, and she regretted that.

Noticing her hesitation, he continued. "Are you still seeing Mr. Spencer?"

"Yes," she replied and smiled in spite of herself. "I care for him, Arthur. And he cares for me. I don't know what the future holds, but I am happy for now."

"I see," he said, speaking more formally. "What news did he bring of his claim last week? Mr. Greenwood says he is the only miner making money. Maybe you didn't do so badly in choosing him," he said with a wry grin, "although it pains me to say so."

She stared at him, her mind closing over the other words he had spoken. "Last week?" she repeated, still wondering if she had heard him correctly. "You saw him last week?"

"Actually, I didn't. Mrs. Greenwood just remarked that her husband had measured out nuggets from one of Spencer's claims, and that the nuggets were quite promising. Perhaps he has struck a bonanza after all, although I'm sure it will be months before he can work in earnest, considering the weather conditions."

She heard the wind rattling a loose board at the corner of the house, and at the same time, something cold crept through her heart. If Joe had been in town, why hadn't he come to see her?

She lifted her teacup and took a sip, oblivious to the weak taste, to whatever else Arthur was saying. Why would Joe come to town and not visit her? She tried to ignore the sting of hurt, rationalizing that he might have come and knocked; perhaps she had been in the back of the house and not heard him. So often the boards rattled and she had learned to ignore the occasional bump. If she had not been looking out the window as Arthur arrived, she might not have gone to the door.

Arthur took out his pocket watch and sighed. "Amazing how the hours drag during the lonely darkness. I've spent an hour here with you, and yet it seems that only a few minutes have passed."

Ruth forced a smile as she put down her teacup. "I hope you aren't working too hard," she said, her voice sounding odd in her own ears.

"I am, but I prefer to stay busy. Frostbite is rampant. And scurvy. Miss Mattie's boardinghouse is full. Many of the miners have given up and come in for the duration of the winter. It was a wise decision. Some would have died, otherwise." He stood. "Thank you for your hospitality. You have brightened my day."

"Thank you for coming, Arthur." She glanced at the items on the kitchen counter that he had brought to her.

"You were kind to bring food. Dorie will be appreciative, too. Have you met her?"

He nodded, looking pleased. "I am so relieved that she is living with you, Ruth. She seems like a nice woman, and I don't think you need to be here alone," he said, his eyes trailing over the kitchen.

"She's an answer to prayer. It has proven to be a most satisfactory arrangement for both of us," she said, following him back through the living room. She hugged her arms around her, almost hating to see him go. She thought of the night he had kissed her and the anger she had felt. All that was in the past now. He was still concerned for her, despite her rebuking him, concerned enough to bring food.

Why hadn't Joe done that?

She followed him down to the front door, bracing herself for the icy blast of cold that would hit her once the door was opened.

"Good-bye, Arthur. Take care," she said, watching him as he huddled into his parka and drew the woolen scarf about his chin.

"You, too," he said, his words muffled by the scarf.

"Good-bye," she said, closing the door. The cold quickly penetrated her woolen dress, following her as she hurried back upstairs.

She wondered why people didn't drop dead in the streets. To live in Dawson, one had to be a survivor; lack of knowledge could take a life in minutes. Most people knew exactly how long it would take for exposed skin to freeze. They also knew it was committing suicide to try and challenge the elements. As she hurried back to the warmth of the kitchen, she thought about what the past year had brought to her.

Never a patient person, she had learned patience, and she had learned to trust God. She had no choice. It was comforting to know that God was watching over her. Even today. He had sent Arthur with food when she had prayed yesterday for knowledge of how to best stretch the meager items left in her pantry.

She opened the sack and examined the tinned goods . . . and the small pouch of coffee.

"Oh, Arthur," she sighed, lifting the pouch and relishing the smell of coffee beans. It had been weeks since she and Dorie had tasted coffee. Now they were in for a treat.

Joe, she thought miserably, *why didn't you come? Why didn't you bring me coffee and food?*

Closing her eyes and pressing the leather pouch against her cheek, she tried to fight off the tears that welled in her eyes.

"You came," she spoke into the silence of the kitchen. "I know you came to my door and I didn't hear you. And the door was locked. Oh, Joe, I'm sorry. Why didn't you yell to me? You must have known I was here."

Only the silence of the kitchen answered back.

❧

"Oh, Ruth! Fresh coffee! I think I must have died and gone to heaven," Dorie exclaimed the next morning as she sipped the steaming coffee while both women luxuriated in the smell and taste of it.

They were sitting at the table dawdling over a piece of sourdough bread, one piece each, without the butter or jam that had been their fare weeks before.

"Isn't it wonderful?" Ruth asked, smiling across at Dorie.

As usual, Dorie's hair was a bit mussed and her plain face was thinner than before, but Ruth knew that her own face was thinner, as well. "I'm so grateful you are living with me, Dorie," she said, smiling at her friend.

"I'm the grateful one. Perish the thought of trying to survive in a boardinghouse filled with men. Isn't it amazing how everyone is opening their tiny cabins to take in a boarder in order to make an extra dollar?"

Ruth nodded. Her father had provided well for her, and for the first time she could truly appreciate what she had taken for granted most of her life.

"Speaking of boarders, have you met Jack London?" Dorie asked, her eyes bright.

Ruth thought back to the man who had come to her door with a note from Joe. "As a matter of fact, I have. Do you know him?"

"He dropped in at the newspaper office yesterday. He's a writer, you know. He left us a very good article he had written about life here in the territory. He's quite talented."

"Is he staying in town now?" she asked, thinking of Joe.

"Yes. As a matter of fact, I'll be seeing him again today or tomorrow. We'll have a small payment for him for his article."

"Dorie, would you ask him about Joe? His cabin is not far from Joe and Ivan's place."

"I'll be glad to," Dorie said, smiling at Ruth. "You've missed him, haven't you?"

Ruth nodded, averting her eyes. She was still haunted by the words Arthur had spoken. The Greenwoods were gossips. No doubt Mrs. Greenwood was confused about when the nuggets had been brought in to be assayed. Taking a deep breath, she looked back at Dorie. "I'm anxious to hear from him, but with the weather conditions, I don't expect that to happen anytime soon."

Dorie nodded, falling silent. Suddenly it occurred to Ruth what Dorie must be thinking. If so many other miners managed to get to Dawson, why couldn't Joe?

"Well, I must get busy," Dorie said, getting up from the table. "I'm spending the morning in my room. With the wind so brutal, I thought I would go through my box of clippings from Skagway. I never did do that article on survival. On Christmas Day, when I took the clippings over to the Fairhopes for my visit with them, we got sidetracked discussing London—they were there last year, you know. I confessed that I long to go some day, and the first thing I knew we were into a lengthy discussion of Europe. Well, in any case, this is the best time to write my article on survival. It was brutal in Skagway last winter. Many people died, but the important thing to remember is how many survived. That's what I want to cover in my article."

Ruth nodded. "Good idea. I'll try not to drop a dish to break your concentration."

They laughed and Dorie hurried out. Ruth smiled after her, thinking how she always moved at a rush. If ever there was a reason to be in no hurry now, the lifestyle in Dawson provided one.

An hour later, Ruth was kneading a fresh batch of sourdough when Dorie appeared in the kitchen door, an expression of horror on her face.

"Dorie, what is it?" Ruth asked, immediately sensing that something was terribly wrong.

For a moment, Dorie said nothing. She merely stared at Ruth. Then she looked down at the box of clippings she was holding, and Ruth realized that her stricken look was somehow connected to something she had read.

Reaching for a cup towel, Ruth wiped her hands and poured two cups of tea. "I can see that whatever is troubling you will require some tea and conversation."

Dorie walked slowly to the kitchen table and sat down, carefully placing the box on the table. As Ruth joined her, she glanced over the neatly clipped articles, wondering what Dorie had seen in those clippings that had upset her so badly.

"Ruth, I don't know how to tell you this," Dorie said, looking distressed.

"Tell me what?"

Dorie reached into the small pile of clippings and extracted one. Carefully, she laid it and a "Wanted" poster on the table, and what Ruth saw brought a gasp to her throat. She was looking into Joe's face.

While he was heavily bearded, there was no mistaking the eyes or the hair or anything else about him. Except the name. Joe Whitworth.

"I . . . felt that I had seen him before when we met on Christmas Day," Dorie said slowly, her tone of voice heavy with regret. "What I didn't realize was that I had not actually seen him, only this. . . ."

Ruth was staring at the article, her heart beating wildly, her fingers trembling on the handle of the cup. It read:

Joe Whitworth was arrested this morning and charged with the shooting of Austin Hankins after an argument erupted in the Dollarhide Saloon. . . .

The tears that glazed Ruth's eyes made the print swim before her, so she stopped reading and looked at the picture of the other man, Austin Hankins. He had the kind of face one would not forget, an ugly face with long, hooked nose and narrow-set, angry eyes. She put a hand to her forehead, unable to read more, think more, feel more. One thought, however, was uppermost in her mind; and in the coming weeks, it never left her. It was something her father had said shortly before his death.

"Ruth, we don't really know Joe Spencer. . . ."

11

*R*uth had not touched the food Arthur had brought or the soup Dorie had prepared the evening before, when Ruth had been unable to cook. Sick at heart, Ruth had gone to bed, trying to sort through her muddled thoughts. She so wanted to defend Joe because she had loved him, but now she had to face the fact that her father had spoken the truth: She did not know him, not really. And if she did not know the real man, how could she love the man he pretended to be? She couldn't, she told herself. Yet, that did nothing to erase the terrible ache that filled her heart.

If he was innocent of the crime, why had he escaped Skagway, as the article went on to detail? And if there was some mistake, why had he not confided the story to her? Apparently Hankins had been a "colorful" local with dubious connections, but still . . .

Another thought had taken root sometime during her sleepless night. She had given him the mining claim in good faith, and she couldn't push aside the memory of Arthur's report: that Joe had been into town with some promising nuggets from one of his claims. Plural. What if that rich nugget was from her claim? If so, it would explain why he had not come to see her while he was in town. If he was a thief and a murderer, he would not hesitate to take advantage of her. This brought on more bitter tears.

Dorie had come home to see about her at noon. Ruth sat on the sofa in the living room, staring into space, trying to put herself back together. The sight of Dorie's face, however, did nothing to cheer her. She looked even more downhearted than when she left this morning, offering a few cheerful words for Ruth in parting.

"Oh, Ruth," Dorie sighed as she entered the living room and took a seat opposite her. "I'm afraid I have more bad news."

"More?" Ruth echoed, wondering what could possibly be worse than what she had already heard. Her heart had been broken in half. Could she even feel anything now? Then she looked at her friend and her eyes widened as another fear took root. "Is something wrong with you, Dorie?" she asked suddenly.

"No, it isn't me," Dorie answered quickly. "Other than feeling a deep sadness for you, I am okay. It's just that . . . well, Jack London came into the newspaper office to pick up the payment for his article, and I asked him about Joe Spencer or Whitworth . . . or whoever he is. I remembered you mentioned he had a cabin nearby."

Ruth was torn with conflict. She wanted to hear about him and yet she could tell from Dorie's face that whatever she was about to tell her would only make matters worse.

"Go on," she said dully.

"Mr. London said Joe and his partner packed up and moved on. He didn't seem to know where or why."

"Where would they go?" Ruth asked incredulously. "I thought we were locked into the territory. No one can travel over the Pass now; there are no boats coming or going. . . ." Ruth's logic bogged down in the face of this latest news.

"Well," Dorie sighed, "it seems that a few miners—idiots it would appear—have taken another route out. Mr. London didn't seem to know much about it. All he knew was that the men were gone."

Ruth studied her hands, folded tightly in her lap. "I guess maybe he had reason to go," she said, taking a deep breath. "Dorie, there's no point in trying to pretend it doesn't hurt, but I can see that I was completely taken in by this man. I always prided myself in being a good judge of character, but what is the saying? Pride goes before a fall."

Dorie reached out, gently touching Ruth's shoulder. "He was a charming man. I, too, was fooled by him. I wish there was something I could say or do to make matters better."

Ruth shook her head. "I'll get over it. But thanks for caring," she said, lifting her eyes to Dorie and hating the fact that she could no longer restrain the tears.

"There now," Dorie said comfortingly. "You'll get over it. I did," she said miserably as her eyes drifted thoughtfully. "I got my heart broken once, but in time one heals."

As tears poured down Ruth's cheeks, she looked at her friend and felt a fresh stab of pain. She hadn't known it was possible to feel this way about a man; now, she was learning what it was like to be hurt by that man. She swallowed hard, reaching into her pocket for a handkerchief. "You're right about one thing, Dorie. I will get over this."

But as the days dragged into weeks, Ruth began to wonder. It no longer mattered to her that there was little food in their pantry, for her appetite had vanished. She found that she was forcing herself to read the Bible, and she realized late one evening that she was mad at God, as well.

How could You let me hurt this way? her heart cried out.

And strangely, an answer whispered through her thoughts. *My child, I love you. I will never leave you nor forsake you.*

Huddled into her blankets to offset the cold of the house, for even the wood supply was getting low, Ruth took comfort from those words. She began to feel better because in her heart she felt the deep assurance that she was not alone. God had promised never to leave her alone or put on her heart more than she could bear.

❧

The snow fell in large flakes around him, quickly covering him. He had picked the warmest day of the month to ride into Dawson, and yet that day was brutal. By the time he reached the outskirts of town, he was frozen to the bone. Though he had been careful to keep himself well insulated with clothing, he knew it would take hours to feel warm again. That didn't matter to him. All that mattered was that he was on his way to see Ruth. And he had something very important to tell her.

He rode straight to her house, his heart hammering in his chest. It had been almost three months since he had seen her. During that time, life had been difficult. He and Ivan had worked in the brutal cold, enduring illness, suffering numbness in every joint, and once he had almost frozen to death by staying too long in the cold. Ivan had found him, dozing off against a tree, seeking the warmth that had begun to steal over him. Ivan had saved his life that night, and it had taken two weeks to recover, suffering a bout of influenza that had almost cost him his life a second time. Now he had recovered, and ever since moving up the creek to an abandoned shack near Ruth's claim, his heart had been filled to the bursting point. The claim was rich; he had been certain of it when Ivan brought in some nuggets for assaying while Joe lay sick on his cot. The news had helped to heal him, and now that he was stronger, he couldn't wait to share this good news with Ruth.

The sight of her log home brought a surge of joy as he turned his horse in at the hitching rail. Slowly, he climbed down, feeling as though his body was made of wood. Looping the leather reins over the post, he walked stiffly up the steps, eager to see the woman he loved. He had knocked several times before the door opened. Instead of facing Ruth, however, he was looking into Dorie Farmer's shocked face.

"Hello," he began, trying to force a stiff smile onto his frozen lips. "Is Ruth home?"

Dorie stared at him for a moment, saying nothing, and he wondered if she had forgotten who he was. "I'm Joe Spencer and we met—"

"I remember our meeting," she answered coldly, "and I don't think Ruth will want to see you, but I will ask."

Her words stunned him, and he leaned against the door jamb when the door was suddenly closed in his face. What was wrong with this woman? Had she taken leave of her senses? Did she have him confused with someone else?

If he hadn't heard the key turn in the lock, he would have rudely thrust the door open and walked inside, calling out for Ruth. His mind was a fog of confusion as he waited anxiously for Ruth to come to the door. *Surely there must be some mistake. Surely—*

He heard the key turn in the lock and he straightened, eager to face the woman he loved. Again, it was Dorie Farmer who glared at him, and this time she shoved a newspaper clipping in his face. A quick glance told him more than he wanted to know. His heart sank. Slowly, his eyes moved back to Dorie's face, now contorted with anger.

"How dare you take advantage of a sweet, wonderful woman like Ruth. You've hurt her terribly. Don't ever come back to this house!" She slammed the door in his face, and this time he did not linger as the key turned in the lock.

There was nothing he could say or do, or if there was, he was too stunned to react. The moment he had feared and dreaded had finally come. The truth was out. And if Ruth and Dorie knew, it was only a matter of time until everyone in Dawson knew.

He felt as though he had aged ten years in a matter of minutes as he pulled himself wearily into the saddle and turned his horse toward the tiny log hut that served as the Dawson jail. He was tired of running, tired of hiding and pretending, tired of living. He had lost Ruth, and now nothing else mattered to him.

❧

Within the hour, Dawson was buzzing with the news: A notorious criminal had turned himself in; he would be returned to the authorities in Skagway as soon as weather permitted travel. The news was met with a mixture of feelings. The Greenwoods were smug with their conviction that the stranger had always acted a bit suspicious. Arthur Bradley was sorry for Ruth but dared hope she would take him seriously now. Miss Mattie and some of the men at the boardinghouse were shocked and saddened by the news, for those who had come to know him liked him.

It was Ruth who was troubled most by his surrender. She wondered why he had not kept on running, why he had bothered to surrender at this time. He had money, freedom, a chance at a new life. What had made him turn and do the right thing? Did she have anything to do with it? Did God? At one point, she would have swallowed her pride and gone to the jail to see him, if not for Dorie. Dorie was on a self-appointed mission to take care of Ruth until the boat pulled in, at which time Ruth was leaving Dawson. She had guarded the door, admitting only those Ruth wanted to see; she had even taken over some of the cooking, since Ruth had no interest in food. Most of all, she had warned Ruth that she would only make matters worse by showing up at the jail. There was nothing she could do for Joe Whitworth; and speaking from personal experience, she promised Ruth that the quicker she got over him, the better she would feel. Seeing him again would only open up the wound in her heart.

Listlessly, she packed up her possessions, eager to be ready when the Yukon thawed and the first boat came to Dawson. Arthur Bradley frequently came to call, and she was glad to see him. If only she had not met Joe, she might have taken Arthur more seriously, she told herself. Perhaps she would have even fallen in love with him; then she would be accompanying him to lovely Victoria rather than going back to Seattle alone. Arthur had even broached the subject, but she had told him again, as gently as possible, that she felt only friendship. She knew this was true and that she could not have loved him, even if she had never met Joe.

As Joe sat in the jail cell day after day, feeling only misery and torment, he dared hope that Ruth would visit him. His only wish now was to tell her the truth, to try and explain things to her. He would take what was coming to him; he was willing to do that. He just couldn't bear for Ruth not to know his side of the story. In the long, dark hours of night, as he lay on the hard cot with the cold seeping through cracks in the walls, his soul ached even more than his body. He had gone to church with Ruth and felt again the stirring of God's love and the need to renew his spiritual life. He had even fought tears during the invitational hymn, but he had hardened his heart and ridden out of town. Now there was no place left to ride, no way out.

God, if You'll have me, I want to come back to You, he silently prayed. *Please forgive me for what I've done, and please help me to make amends to everyone I've hurt.*

Tears slipped down his thin, bearded cheeks, and soon his body shook with restrained sobs. The years of hurt that had built in his heart seemed to wash away with his tears, with the gentle cleansing power of God's healing love. The jail cell no longer seemed so lonely or so cold, and for the first time since his mother died, he felt a sense of peace take root in his heart.

❧

Ruth stood at the wharf, waiting to board the *Bella* as it slowly nudged its way into the dock. Shouts erupted throughout the crowd around her as the gangplank was lowered. At long last, the famine was over. Food, supplies, mail from home, and dozens of other delights awaited those in Dawson. For at least forty other people, eagerly gripping their tickets, the boat represented an escape out of the territory that had imprisoned them for the winter.

"Looks as though we'll have a bit of a wait," Arthur said, standing close beside Ruth. They were traveling together as far as Skagway, where they would each change boats again and head in opposite directions.

"Yes," Ruth agreed, recalling how Arthur had told her she had until Skagway to change her mind and go to Victoria to marry him. Feeling a sense of loneliness overtake her, she was tempted to accept his proposal. With mixed emotions, she turned and cast one last glance over the town where hammers pounded lumber once again, as tents were replaced by more log cabins. Briefly her eyes lingered on the tiny hut that served as the jail, and she thought of Joe.

A lump filled her throat. She still couldn't understand the pull she felt toward him, knowing what he had done. Dorie was right; it would take time to heal. She and Dorie had said tearful good-byes, for Dorie was remaining another week to complete a story on the reopening of Dawson. She would live in Ruth's house until then, at which time the missionaries coming to open the hospital would stay there. She had decided to donate the house to them for as long as they could use it. God had led her in this direction, and she had felt a sense of peace as soon as she made the decision.

Her eyes moved on to the cemetery on the hill, and the lump in her throat grew. She hated leaving her father here, but of course his soul had gone on to heaven, so she wasn't leaving him. She would join him some day.

Drawing a deep shaky breath, she turned her attention toward the arriving passengers, and suddenly one in particular caught her attention as he moved through the crowd. Directly in her line of vision, she studied him intently and then her breath caught. *It was him!*

She began to move toward him, scarcely aware of what she was doing, gawking at him like one who has never seen another human being. She was only vaguely aware of Arthur calling to her as she approached the thin, ugly man with long hair and beard, sharp hook nose, and narrow-set eyes.

"Excuse me," she said, stepping directly into his path to stop him. "Aren't you Austin Hankins?"

The narrow-set eyes widened momentarily as he looked her over. Then slowly he nodded. "Am I supposed to know you?" he asked.

"You aren't dead!" she exclaimed.

He stared at her as though she had lost her senses, and now Arthur stood beside her, staring at the man. "Ruth, what is it?"

"This man," she glanced at Arthur, "was not killed in Skagway. Joe didn't kill him, but he's being held for murder."

"He's here?" Hankins took a step back from her.

"In jail," Arthur was proud to volunteer.

"For your murder," Ruth repeated. "For some reason, you were assumed dead."

Hankins nodded. "I had my reasons for disappearing."

"But Spencer . . . or Whitworth . . . whoever he is . . . ran out," Arthur said, explaining this to Ruth rather than to the man.

"Never had to pay for what he did to me. And he should of paid!"

"He is paying now," Ruth said. "He has surrendered."

Hankins was the one to gawk now. "Why'd he do that? Surrender, I mean."

"Maybe he wanted to do the right thing. Don't you think it's time you did?"

Hankins snorted. "I ain't gettin' involved."

"You're already involved," she said, glaring at him.

He glanced toward the boat, as though considering heading back up the gangplank.

She spotted Lucky and a friend milling through the crowd, studying the boat and its passengers. He had turned in her direction and she waved to him.

"What is it, Miss Wright?" he asked, quickly approaching.

"This man," she indicated Hankins. "He's the one Joe is supposed to have killed. But as you can see, he's very much alive."

Hankins shifted from one foot to the other, his discomfort apparent as Lucky and his burly friend closed in on either side of him.

"Reckon we better mosey on down to the jail," Lucky said, taking his arm.

"Whitworth owes me for medical bills," he complained.

"Ruth, that is a matter between this man and the authorities." Arthur was tugging at her sleeve. "Come on, we can board the ship now."

Ruth yanked her arm free. "You go right ahead, Arthur. I'm going with these men to the jail. I think Mr. Hankins will want to give Joe Whitworth an opportunity to take care of his . . . *medical bills.*"

"Ruth—"

"Arthur, please mind your own business," Ruth snapped, glaring at him.

This time he backed away from her, drew himself into a rigid stance, and looked at her with contempt. "I am through trying to reason with you. Good-bye, Ruth." He turned and stomped off, but Ruth didn't care. She was oblivious to everything except the man beside her. He was the type of man she would have avoided under other circumstances, but today he was the most special person in Dawson.

"Let's go." Lucky tugged the man's arm.

Sergeant Underwood bolted from his desk when they entered with Hankins in tow. His eyes widened as he looked at Hankins, as recognition flashed in his eyes.

Ruth was about to make the explanation when Hankins suddenly found his courage, which had been prompted, no doubt, by the fact that he wanted to exonerate himself of any charges.

"I hear you got a prisoner here, sir. There was a, er . . . a little misunderstanding in Skagway. I'm willing to drop charges against him under certain conditions."

The door was ajar that led to the cells, and Ruth's eyes locked on Joe's haggard face. He looked stunned for a moment, unable to believe what was happening. To her surprise, the anger she had felt for him began to fade. She was not ready to dismiss what he had done, but she felt a sense of relief in bringing the two men together.

The sound of the boat whistle jolted her back to her senses, and she turned to go.

"Ruth . . . wait," Joe called out.

She hesitated, her hand on her skirt. Slowly, she turned and looked at him again.

"Please give me a chance to explain. You owe me that." His eyes pleaded with her, and she felt powerless to walk out now, even though the boat's whistle sounded again, a warning for departing passengers to get on board.

Sergeant Underwood and Hankins were walking toward the cell, blocking Ruth's vision. "Is this the man?" he asked Hankins.

"Yep, he's the one."

"They said you were dead!" Joe said, gaping at him.

"And you were gonna swing from a rope," Hankins snorted.

Ruth could not stay out of it for another second, even though she tried. One question burned through her brain, and she had to know the answer. Then she would rush out, board the boat, and leave Dawson.

"Joe, why did you run?" Ruth asked, approaching the cell.

He looked into her eyes and shook his head. "I was weak and scared. I had been beating all those men in poker for over a week. They hated me. I knew everyone would back up his story. Hankins pulled a gun first," he said, turning to Sergeant Underwood. "I fired back in self-defense, but no one would believe that, either. Then he disappeared, and one of his buddies said he died as a result of the gunshot after he was taken back to camp. They said they buried him there," he added bitterly, "and everyone believed them. Even I believed them," he added on a heavy sigh. "Then when the deputy fell asleep with my cell unlocked, I couldn't help myself."

itworth, this fella is willing to drop charges against you." Underwood took over again. "The provision is that you pay for his medical expenses."

"Medical expenses?" Joe asked bitterly.

"Yep. I had some big medical expenses," Hankins crowed.

"I'm going to wire the authorities in Skagway," Underwood stated. "They may still request a trial."

"Why?" Hankins looked disappointed. "I'm alive. I ain't pressing charges if he pays for my medical expenses."

"I'll do that," Joe said, looking at Ruth.

The sound of the boat whistle was more vague now, and Ruth heard it with less concern. It wouldn't hurt to wait another week and leave with Dorie, she decided. Then she remembered her trunk, abandoned at the dock.

"I must go," she said.

"Ruth!" Joe was staring at her cranberry woolen dress and matching hat. "Are you leaving Dawson?"

She took a deep breath. "Not today. I'll wait a week to see what is going to happen to you."

She started to say more but restrained herself. She would give him a week; somehow, she felt she owed him that. She had been taught by her parents to always be fair, and as a Christian, she tried to be a forgiving person. In good faith, she felt she had to give him one last chance. One more week in Dawson would not change her life, whereas if she left now, never to see him again, she knew her life would drastically change. For in that ten minutes that she had stood in the jail, looking into his pleading eyes, she knew she still cared for him.

❧

On Sunday, after the church service, Ruth and Joe sat in the living room of her house. Dorie had tactfully disappeared to her room to work on her newspaper article. So much had happened in the past few days that Ruth's head was still spinning. Still, she forced herself to listen to Joe as he spoke calmly and looked at her with eyes that begged forgiveness.

"I know it will take a while to regain your trust, but I'm coming to you now as a different man. God finally got my attention," he said, with a wry grin.

"And you rededicated your life this morning at church," she said, smiling at him. "Even the pastor thinks I should forgive you, so what choice do I have?"

"Don't tease me, Ruth," he said earnestly.

She took his hand. "I'm sorry. You've been through enough. I think it's time to put the past behind us and get on with our lives."

"Now that I've made my settlement with Hankins, I'd like permission from you to continue working your claim this summer, Ruth. It's a rich one, and by the time the boat leaves at the end of the summer, we could have a real nest egg for that ranch." He dropped his head. "I'm sorry. I'm assuming too much. It's your money."

"Excuse me, but I believe we had a deal."

He looked up, startled.

"We're partners, remember? Half of the proceeds of that claim belong to you. You could have your own nest egg."

He took her hand in his and moved closer. "Ruth, I've dreamed of a ranch for years. How do you feel about that?"

She smiled. "I could feel good about that . . . if I were with the man I love."

Joe took her into his arms, tilting her chin back and smiling into her face. "I don't know what I ever did to deserve a person like you, but I promise you, as God is our witness, I will be the best Christian I can possibly be. And the best husband," he added.

Tears filled her eyes. "Joe, I've always prayed to have the kind of relationship my parents had. I know God blessed their marriage because their lives were dedicated to pleasing Him. I do love you, and now that you have come back to God, I feel we have a chance for real happiness." She put her hand to his cheek, gently stroking his clean-shaven face. "Must I wait until the end of the summer to put you to the test? About being a good husband?"

He laughed. "Of course not. Nothing would make me happier than to get married right away. If you're planning to stay on here and help get the missionary hospital going, then I can be a weekend guest, if that's okay with you."

"That's fine with me," she said, smiling into his eyes as he lowered his lips to kiss her.

❧

Peering through a crack in the door, Dorie felt like a mischievous child, and yet seeing the two together again, happy and so in love, warmed her heart. And it gave her new hope. Ruth and Joe had been given a second chance at happiness.

Dorie smiled, quietly closing the door. Maybe someday it would happen to her.

$\mathcal{I}$F THE
$\mathcal{P}$ROSPECT $\mathcal{P}$LEASES

BY SALLY LAITY

To Randie, my sweet daughter-in-law. I'm so glad the
Lord brought you into our lives.

Many thanks to Andrea Boeshaar, Gloria Brandt, and
Dianna Crawford, for their patient shredding and
tireless encouragement. May God bless all your
writing efforts.

$\mathscr{P}$ROLOGUE

Philadelphia, 1875

$\mathscr{N}$othing would ever be the same. Ever. Annora Nolan yearned with all her heart to awaken from the nightmare . . . but the smell of the moist ground in the fenced area behind the church more than proved it was all very real.

Last week it had been Papa, her copper-haired hero, who had succumbed to the dreaded typhoid. Now folks had gathered to lay away her soft-spoken mama as well. Clutching her damp woolen cloak closer against the chill, Annora scarcely heard the minister's voice droning through the funeral scriptures. She was too busy praying she would die, too . . . though in her heart she doubted the plea would be granted.

Adding to her misery, the relentless October drizzle falling from the leaden sky had fused the brilliant hues of autumn into sodden clumps of burgundy, gold, and brown, heavy masses never to be separated again. To Annora, the pathetic sight seemed a symbol of her own future, and the thought sent a desolate shiver through her as the wind plastered her wet skirt to her legs.

Gazing at the closed coffin through a blur of tears, Annora lowered her eyelids against the ache in her heart. What would become of her now?

"Come along, child."

The service must have ended. Realizing that someone had addressed her, Annora turned and looked up into the face of the Reverend Baxter's wife, Millicent. The hazel eyes in the woman's plump but refined features expressed abundant sympathy. "You'll be coming home with us for the night," she explained gently, extending a gloved hand.

"But . . . my things. I—I need—"

"I'll send our housekeeper for them presently. It's all right. Come along now."

Annora swept an uneasy glance from the black-clad figure to the woman's other side, where the couple's daughter, Mirah, stared with brown-eyed coolness at Annora from beneath the brim of her velvet and satin bonnet. An exquisitely beautiful girl two years younger than Annora, not a muscle in her perfect oval face moved, even when a sharp gust splayed a brunette ringlet across her cheek. Annora had never been fond of the overly pampered girl, but she knew she had no other recourse. After all, it was just for one night.

❧

Alone in Mirah's second-story bedroom while the younger girl visited the privy outside before turning in, Annora could hear the Reverend Baxter's words drifting up from the room directly below. She shifted uncomfortably on the pallet that had been laid out for her on the floor.

"Fourteen is rather old to be relegated to the Children's Home, Millicent, my dear."

"I'm fully aware of that, Phineas," his wife replied, normally the dominant voice of the household. "But I fail to see what else is to be done—short of trying to place her ourselves where she might be useful."

"We could assume guardianship," the reverend went on in his familiar nasal tone. "We've known her since she was a young girl, and there's hardly a more mannerly or more respectful young person in our entire flock. Besides, she has no other living relatives, and her parents numbered among the founding families of this church. It would deem us well not to overlook their support of our parish over the years."

"Quite. However—"

"The matter needn't be decided this very instant," he interrupted, and Annora could envision any number of typical gestures he might have used to cut in. His slight frame a mere shadow in comparison to his wife's more fleshy presence, he sounded uncharacteristically firm in his resolve. "Do not forget the influential families among our congregation who look favorably upon such acts of benevolence—who might even consider it our Christian duty to take in the girl as our ward. And it very well may be."

After a brief lapse, he started in again. "I shudder to imagine how tongues would wag should we turn their daughter out in her hour of need."

Annora held her breath in the ensuing pregnant silence while her fate was being decided downstairs.

"Bear in mind," the pastor continued, "the girl would be a help to Nellie, to say nothing of being company for our dear Mirah. We've always wished God had blessed us with another child. Perhaps this is His way of granting that wish."

"I hadn't thought of that." A note of optimism rang in his wife's tone. "The idea might have merit after all."

"What idea?" Mirah asked sweetly, obviously having come back inside.

"Mirah, dear, your father and I were relating how wonderful it might be for you if we were to have another young girl living with us. Someone near your own age to keep you company."

"Oh."

The tightly contained emotion in the answer made Annora cringe, and tears stung her eyes. It was no secret among the young people at church that Mirah Baxter reveled in her lofty position as only child, daughter of the pastor. Her gifts went beyond mere exotic beauty to exceptional musical talent as well. And when Annora had been chosen over her as soloist in the last two recitals, she had pouted for days . . . but never in the presence of her parents, before whom she maintained guileless behavior at all times.

No, Mirah would not welcome having to share her life of privilege, especially with a foundling who happened to be a little older than herself and who might be given extra privileges for that reason. Annora drew the quilts more snugly around her, trying to squelch feelings of mortification threatening to overwhelm even her unspeakable grief.

"We've not as yet undertaken permanent arrangements," the minister explained. "We're merely considering possibilities."

"Then permit me to voice my feelings, Father," Mirah pleaded. "I far prefer things as they have always been—you, Mother, and me. Pray, let's keep it that way. Please?"

"I'll give your wishes proper consideration, Daughter," the Reverend Baxter replied. "But I must weigh this matter very carefully. And be assured that my decision will be final. Now, be a good girl and go to bed. Tomorrow is another day."

"Yes, of course, Father," she returned, all sweetness again. "Good night. Good night, Mother."

"Good night, angel."

As the younger girl's slippers padded up the open staircase, Annora turned her face to the wall and feigned sleep. She was careful not to move even the slightest bit as the door swung closed—though she could almost feel Mirah's dark eyes stabbing her like ice picks. When the rustle of embroidered silk indicated the daughter of the household had removed her wrap and slipped into the warmth of her canopied feather bed, Annora slowly released a pent-up breath. But not until Mirah's disgruntled huffs settled into the even rhythm of sleep did Annora give in to her sorrow.

⤸

To her amazement, Annora found life with the Baxters quite bearable. The minister and his wife went out of their way to make her feel welcome and a part of the family, which helped immensely to get her through the initial crushing sadness over the loss of her parents. And—even more surprising—Mirah, too, seemed to accept her.

Or so she thought.

But when an heirloom timepiece unaccountably disappeared from Mrs. Baxter's jewelry chest, only to turn up in the drawer designated for Annora's belongings, things took a decided turn. Annora, her cheeks aflame as she stammered her denial of guilt, would remember until her dying day the shock and disappointment on her guardians' faces . . . and the unabashed innocence on Mirah's. That was when Annora sensed that despite all the Baxters' well-meaning gestures toward her, she would forever remain an outsider in this home.

And that was just the beginning.

A spattering of other rather minor infractions pointing to Annora occurred over the next few months. But not until Mirah's handmade quilt met its ruin did things finally come to a head.

"I truly regret that my husband and I found it necessary to take this step, Annora," Mrs. Baxter said, standing in the doorway of the chilly attic room. She had the grace to look ill at ease as she flicked a glance around the stark quarters. "But since it appears the fate of your very soul is in question, you leave us no choice but to take drastic measures. One must learn there are consequences for one's actions.

"Hereafter, except for those periods when you are performing your duties, you will remain here by yourself until such time as we feel you are once again deserving of our trust. I suggest you use the solitude to reflect on what lies ahead of you if you do not mend your ways."

"Yes, ma'am." Annora gave a dutiful nod as the minister's wife departed without further word, the sound of her button-top shoes fading to silence as she returned downstairs.

Gloating in this, her most recent victory, Mirah leaned against the doorjamb and crossed her arms. "This should do quite nicely . . . for you."

Refusing to acknowledge the satisfied smirk on the younger girl's face, Annora breezed past her with an airy smile and came the rest of the way into the tiny room graced only by the hazy light from a small dormer window. She set the belongings she'd carried up the stairs onto the narrow bedstead abutting the jointure of low wall and sloped ceiling. "Yes. It's quite an improvement, actually. I rather like it." Hands on her hips, she hiked her chin and looked about as if admiring the most splendid of accommodations in all of Philadelphia.

Mirah's jaw gaped. "Indeed. Well, now that I've managed to oust you from my room, I'll concentrate on the next step—getting you out of this house. It should be a simple enough feat, I'm sure." A vicious sneer moved across her proud lips.

Unable to come up with a suitable retort, Annora presented her back.

The Baxter's stout housekeeper, Nellie Henderson, trudged in from the landing just then, her arms filled with bedding. She dumped the burden on the cot. "La, such a climb," she panted, placing one hand over her cushiony bosom, which rose and fell in time with her labored breathing. Her fair cheeks remained a bright rosy pink beneath her faded blond coronet until the short gasps lengthened to more normal intervals.

"Sorry you've gone to so much trouble," Annora said with true concern, ignoring Mirah's blatant look of contempt as the younger girl turned on her heel and traipsed back downstairs.

Mrs. Henderson glanced after her, then met Annora's gaze with a shake of her frazzled head. "This is a fair disgrace, miss, that's what it is," she said in a near whisper. "Puttin' a young thing like you way up here by yourself, with us still in the throes of winter. You'll not have a lick of heat, except what might waft up from below. Don't know what madam is thinkin'. She and the reverend have always been such soft-hearted folks, up till now."

"Oh, well, no matter how cold the attic gets, it'll be nothing compared to what I had to endure sharing their only daughter's room," Annora muttered. Then she flushed with embarrassment. "Forgive me. That must sound ungrateful. It was more than unselfish of the reverend and his wife to become my guardians. They've been nothing but generous and loving to me."

"Yes, well, nobody except the two of us knows who really rules this household," the older woman continued with an understanding nod. "Let me tell you, things changed around here once that little dickens made her appearance in the world. And not for the better, I don't mind sayin'. The way her parents dote on her . . . *tsk tsk*. Of course, she acts the perfect angel around them. But to think they actually believed you would deliberately pour a bottle of ink over the counterpane her grandmother finished mere weeks before she died!"

Slowly wagging her head, the woman bent over and began unfolding the topmost quilt on the pile she'd brought upstairs.

"Please, you needn't do this," Annora said, gathering the heavy folds the housekeeper was in the process of shaking out. "I'll make my own bed, then I'll come and help with dinner."

"Well," came the hesitant response, "if you're sure. I must say, it's been a blessing havin' an extra pair of hands since you arrived, what with lookin' after the parsonage *and* the church by myself since old Mr. Baldwin crossed over."

Annora smiled. "I don't mind daily chores. I'd rather keep busy than sit around reading dime novels and eating bonbons."

"Like Her Highness, you mean. Well, one of these days the little miss is sure to get her comeuppance. See if she don't. The Lord will see to that in His time." With a conspiratorial wink, the housekeeper nodded and moved toward the doorway but paused briefly before departing. "Now that you've got a room to yourself," she began, grimacing as her glance swept the dismal quarters, "there's somethin' you should know. I managed to rescue a few of your mama's special things for you . . . kept them out of the auction that was held to pay your father's creditors."

"You didn't!" Filled with the first real comfort she'd felt since her parents had passed away, Annora flew to give her a hug.

"Now, now," the amiable woman murmured, patting Annora's back before easing away. "I couldn't see how a few baubles would make a lick of difference one way or the other. Anyways, a gal should have somethin' to remind her of her family. I was waitin' for a time when Miss Uppity wouldn't be stickin' her royal nose into your business. We can tote them up after while, when you and me fetch the rest of your clothes and things."

"Thank you. Oh, thank you, Mrs. Henderson."

" 'Twas the least I could do, miss. Only right you should have them. Oh, and I'm sure I can rummage up some extra curtains and a rug to help brighten this place up a little. We'll get it set to rights soon enough."

As the housekeeper took her leave, Annora couldn't hold back a smile at the joyous thought of having some of Mama's precious possessions to hold in her hands again, but it quickly wilted as she settled back and took a closer look at her bleak surroundings. Bare and harsh in its grim simplicity—to cause her to consider the consequences of her *wicked ways*—the place contained nothing besides the cot and a wardrobe with warped doors, but at least it was her own room. She was glad it wasn't so cluttered with useless discarded items that she'd bump into something every time she turned around.

Well, she told herself on a sigh, it wouldn't help matters to sit and bawl over life's injustices. Papa always said it was prayer that changed things. Of course, when it came to Mirah Baxter, one had to wonder if any amount of prayer could change her!

Drawing a fortifying breath, Annora rummaged about for a sheet and flicked it out over the hard mattress. Maybe once there were curtains and a rug it would look somewhat more cheery. This haven might not be so bad after all.

Philadelphia, Summer 1878

*A*nnora, wait." As the departing crowd exited the dark wooden pews and milled toward the church doors after the Sunday service, Lesley Clark leaned around Michael Porter's tall frame, her expressive face aglow. "Will you come to the picnic at Franklin Square next Saturday?"

Just about to vacate the bench where she'd sat with Lesley and several other young people, Annora met her best friend's hopeful smile and hiked a shoulder. "I'm afraid I really can't say just yet."

"Why not?" Michael asked, a merry gleam in his dark brown eyes. "Cousin Jason plans to be there."

Annora fought to quell the stubborn blush that insisted on making an appearance whenever someone made mention of Dr. Markwell's eldest son. Easily the handsomest and most eligible young man among the younger set of Arch Street Church's congregation, his presence within the slightest proximity of hers always caused her pulse to increase—especially since he made no secret of the fact that he sought out her company at gatherings. "Because," she explained for the dozenth time, "you know I have extra duties to tend to at the week's end. I'll have to wait and see if I'm free."

"Oh." Crestfallen, Lesley absently fingered a fold of her striped taffeta skirt.

Annora reached to give her an encouraging pat, noticing as always how much bluer her friend's eyes appeared whenever she wore an ensemble that matched their hue. "Don't despair. I'm quite a fast worker. I'll do my best."

"Splendid. Then we'll pray you make it." With a toss of her

honey-blond waves, Lesley took her beau's arm, and the pair headed for the vestibule.

Thoughts of the picnic a few days hence made Annora smile as she started toward the back door for home.

❧

Mirah Baxter, peering into the sanctuary from a slim crack in her father's office door, narrowed her eyes and closed the latch without a sound. For two and a half unbearable years, she'd had to put up with that redheaded goody-goody with the unflinching green cat eyes. So she was counting on a picnic, was she? To flaunt herself around Jason Markwell. Well, more's the pity. Mirah had designs on that young man herself. Even if he did happen to be a few years older than she might have preferred. And even if nature did seem to be taking an inordinate amount of time to endow her with measurable charms! She looked scathingly at her girlish body and frowned.

Still, Jason met all of Mother's criteria for a suitable match. All one had to do was get him interested. He seemed partial to sickening sweetness . . . and Mirah knew she was more than accomplished in presenting that sort of face to the world. She would just have to see to it that Annora couldn't quite make this particular outing.

A slow smile teased her lips as her active mind toyed with a few possibilities.

❧

"Phin—e—as!"

Even in the attic with her door closed, Annora heard the blood-chilling shriek clearly. She rolled her eyes and expelled a frustrated breath, incapable of imagining what Mirah had done *this time* that would ultimately be blamed on her. Hardly a fortnight passed without at least one incident of a destructive nature. As it was, Annora had long ago been deprived of even the smallest privilege. When she wasn't helping the housekeeper with the housework or the cooking, or attending service, she was banished to her room. Very seldom was she permitted to leave the grounds unless sent on an errand. anyone could surmise she somehow managed to find time for mischief despite that fact was beyond her.

Bolstering her courage, she opened the door and tiptoed to the landing in order to ascertain the problem. She could already detect the light pattering of Mirah's footsteps as the younger girl all but flew out of her bedroom and down the stairs. Annora knew she would have to follow soon enough, so she quietly began descending.

"Whatever is amiss, Mother?"

"Look!" Mrs. Baxter wailed. "Just look! Six months of painstaking needlework, all for naught. Why, the entire piece is in tatters. Ruined. Completely ruined. That wretched, ungrateful girl . . ."

"Oh, Mother," Mirah crooned in utmost sympathy, her tone absolutely dripping with honey. "How perfectly awful. Your poor, poor scene . . . and after all your labor every evening."

Annora could just picture the brat's innocent face. No doubt the halo above her head must be dazzling in its brilliance. Why, the dear young thing could do no wrong. Almost choking on the ludicrous farce of it all, Annora held her breath, anticipating how long it would take before she was summoned to face up to this latest alleged infraction.

Barely a heartbeat.

"Annora! Annora Nolan!" the older woman called out. "Come down here this instant!"

"What's happened, Millicent?" the minister inquired, finally arriving at the parlor. "I heard you all the way out in my office."

Descending the main stairs to her certain doom, Annora could see his wife holding forth the tattered embroidery—its myriad strands of colored threads dangling. Obviously it had been savagely hacked to shreds with scissors. She felt a huge lump clog her throat at the horrific sight and swung her attention to Mirah.

The most minuscule gleam of triumph sparked in the frigid brown eyes, then immediately softened with an affected shimmer of moisture as she turned to fawn over her mother.

As Annora proceeded into the parlor, the threesome seared her with the heat of their gazes.

Mrs. Baxter broke the weighty silence. "It positively astounds me, young lady," she said, her clipped words masterfully controlled by what she termed her good breeding, "that you could find it in yourself to be such a constant source of malicious harm to this household."

"I did not do it, madam," Annora whispered.

"Hush!" She shot a glance toward her far-too-meek husband, then directed it at Annora again with a disbelieving shake of her head. "I might have surmised you would resort to falsehood *again*, as you've done so often in the past. In fact, I've come to expect your lies by now. And that, despite all our prayers on your behalf."

"But I did not do it," Annora repeated. "Why would I want to—"

"Precisely!" The control began to wane. "Why *would* you be so ungrateful—so unbelievably *hateful* to people kind enough to take you in when you were homeless and alone in the world? And penniless, I might add, after those less than wise investments your late father made. I must confess, the thought quite boggles my mind. I had hoped, after these tendencies of yours had surfaced when we first took you in, that our dear little Mirah might be a good influence on you. But I see now that I was wrong."

Seeking support from the minister but finding none, Annora felt her last hope fizzle away. She could not bring herself to look at *dear little* Mirah.

"Well, Phineas," the woman continued, her tone one of both resignation and utter defeat, "it should be obvious by now that this . . . ward you insisted we take into our home has far too much idle time on her hands. Some additional labor might be what it will take to cause her to mend her ways. It's high time she assumes the upkeep of the church along with her other duties. Nellie has been feeling overly tired of late. This should serve to alleviate both problems."

Annora could barely swallow.

"Mother," Mirah broke in, cloyingly gracious in her manner. "Perhaps I could help out somehow."

Mrs. Baxter's eyebrows arched high in surprise. "Why, that's very generous of you, darling," she gushed. "But there's no reason why you should trouble yourself over any of this. And I'm afraid your music lessons would suffer were your hands to become roughened by harsh soaps." Her demeanor turned to stone as she regarded Annora once more. "The matter has already been settled."

"Yes. Settled. Ahem." Rocking forward on his toes, then back on his heels, the minister peered through the reading glasses still centered on his nose, his color heightening by the minute. "Well, Miss Nolan, it seems my wife has been gracious enough to extend you yet another chance. I trust you will not waste it. I should hate to be forced to take any more . . . drastic measures. Kindly return to your room. And on the morrow, I shall see you in the sanctuary."

"Yes, sir," Annora all but croaked. "Madam."

On her way to the staircase, she met the housekeeper's expression of understanding as Mrs. Henderson hovered nearby in the hallway. But the level of Annora's misery precluded any comfort from the woman who had grown to be a dear friend. She willed her legs to carry her up to the attic.

Once in her refuge, she lay back on her bed and stared at the rough beams above her head. Only the deep, abiding faith she had in the Lord kept her from hating Mirah Baxter. It would have been an easy enough thing to do, but then the younger girl would have had even more to gloat about if she knew she had turned Annora into a person similar to herself. No, it wouldn't be worth it, when Annora had ammunition of a far superior kind.

She rolled off the bed and onto her knees. *Dearest Father in Heaven, I am supremely thankful for Your presence in my life. If it had not been for You, Mrs. Henderson, and the comfort I find in Mama's Bible every morning, there's no way of knowing what would have become of me. I cannot say I feel any love for Mirah—but I know Your great love extends even to her. Her parents have tried to keep my welfare uppermost in their minds, and I know they've meant well each time they inflicted a new punishment on me. After all, they truly believe I am in the wrong. Who wouldn't fall for that angelic act their spoiled daughter plays to perfection?*

She expelled a slow breath, then continued. *I know Your dear Son faced even more painful betrayal when He walked this earth, and I pray that You will help me to remember how He suffered in silence and how His very life radiated Your infinite love. Please help me to be faithful in following His example.*

Rising to her feet, Annora moved to the window to gaze out upon the rows and rows of rooftops whose varied hues changed colors as the sun moved across the sky. The view was speckled liberally with patches of green grass where laughing, carefree children played. The pleasant scene added to the indescribable peace flooding her being, and Annora smiled. Somehow, some way, even this would work out for her good.

⁓

"The cleanin' things are stored in the closet at the end of the hall," Mrs. Henderson explained, escorting Annora about the church building the next day. "I usually look after the reverend's study on Monday mornings, when he goes to visit our shut-ins. Sweepin' and dustin', mostly. Sometimes after a rainy spell you might need to mop. But he don't like anything on his desk disturbed."

"I understand."

The housekeeper exhaled in a huff. "I know I don't have to tell you that the reverend and his wife are good folks at heart," she said gently, placing a hand on Annora's arm. "They made a home for me when my husband passed on and have paid good wages all these years. I wouldn't think of turnin' my back on them. Not even when I'm bone-weary of Mirah and her tempers."

"I know," Annora sighed. "I keep hoping that if I stay long enough, I'll be vindicated, possibly even repay them for their kindnesses. Otherwise, I'd have sought employment with some other family before now."

The older woman appeared to mull over that thought for a moment, then tipped her head. "Still, this is just too much, them pushin' all this work onto those slight shoulders of yours. Why, a good gust of wind could up and whisk you clear into the next county."

"I'm stronger than I look, dear friend," Annora said with a wry smile. She patted the woman's gnarled hand. "And I'm sure I'll catch onto all of this soon enough. What's next?"

Mrs. Henderson continued to regard her for a moment. "I sometimes think you must've been born all growed up. Or else you just had to grow up quicker than most other gals your age—and a far sight more than Little Miss Uppity ever will, I expect!"

Annora could not help but laugh. "I'm just following the example my mother left me. She loved helping people. And now I know why. It brings joy."

"Could be, missy. Could be." Nodding, she started forward again, gesturing toward various rooms as they came to them. "Well, on Tuesdays the ladies get together in this side room and make quilts for the hospital or roll bandages . . . whatever's needed. There's a remnant box in the closet they'll root through. Mostly they bring spare goods from home. After they finish up, around noon, I come back and straighten things a bit. I do whatever other extra rooms look like they need attention through the week."

Annora made a mental note as she listened.

"Of course, the sanctuary gets swept through and dusted toward the end of every week without fail. Mopped at least once a month—sometimes more often near the doors in rainy or snowy weather. On occasion there might be a weddin' or funeral, too. That makes extra work for sure. I'll come help out then. And now and again the reverend likes to have the pews polished. I leave it up to him to say when. Only other thing is the board."

"Board?"

"The public board in the vestibule. A fellow brings by notices to post as they come in from the territories. Sometimes somebody in the congregation wants to rent out a room or sell something. They'll drop a bulletin in the basket for you to pin up. Just keep it lookin' neat, take down the old ones . . . that sort of thing."

"Doesn't sound too awfully hard, really," Annora commented with no little relief. "Spread out through the week the way you've done it."

"Well, all the same, you give a holler if it gets too much for you. I don't mind a'tall lendin' a hand. You've been such a help since you've been here. But . . . be watchful, if you catch my meanin'. Maybe some of the shenanigans will stop now that you'll be so busy. Then again . . ."

Annora gave the housekeeper a hug. "I'll be very, very careful. I promise."

2

*A*fter helping the housekeeper bring supper in from the kitchen a few endless days later, Annora took her place opposite Mirah at the table and bowed her head for grace. It never ceased to amaze her that, despite her many alleged offenses, she was expected to dine with the Baxters every evening. But then, she supposed it presented the illusion of family unity, should the odd church member happen by.

". . . in the name of Thy Son, we pray. Amen."

The others echoed the minister's last word, bringing Annora back to the moment at hand, and with supreme effort she opened her eyes.

"It's been the grandest day," Mirah declared, helping herself to a small portion of roasted chicken breast from the platter her father passed her. "But tomorrow will be even better. Just everyone will be at the picnic."

Picnic! Annora had been so busy with her duties, she had completely forgotten about Saturday. And with all that remained to be done to ready the church for Sunday service, she knew she could not even dream of an outing. She seriously doubted she would receive permission anyway, considering the gravity of her latest *transgression*.

"We'll have Annora and Nellie prepare an extra special basket for you, darling," Mrs. Baxter said, subtly quashing Annora's hopes. "There should be plenty of food left over from this evening. Nothing is quite as tasty in a picnic lunch as cold chicken."

"Thank you, Mother. If the weather remains pleasant, I'll wear my new dimity frock." She nibbled delicately at the tender meat on her plate.

Annora well knew that the look of relish on the younger girl's face had nothing to do with food, but she maintained her composure, even as her own spirit sank to its lowest ebb. She forced herself to eat as if nothing in the world was wrong, as if her appetite hadn't vanished the instant Mirah opened her mouth. After all, summer wasn't half over, she assured herself. There would be plenty of other social gatherings with Lesley and the other church young people. With Jason. Avoiding the haughty brown eyes across the table, Annora somehow endured the remainder of the interminable meal.

Just as everyone was finishing, the housekeeper entered the room and handed a note to the Reverend Baxter. "This just came for you, sir."

The minister's wife smiled at her. "I must compliment you, Nellie, on this excellent spread. And were those huckleberry tarts I smelled earlier, perchance?"

"Yes, madam."

"Wonderful. I shall have sweet cream on mine, please."

"Well," the reverend cut in, directing his attention to his wife as he laid aside the folded stationery and came to his feet. "I'm afraid I'll have to decline, my dear. I am needed at the Thornby residence right away. It's unlikely I'll be back for several hours. You needn't wait up."

"As you wish." She nodded to Annora. "You may help Nellie serve dessert."

"Yes, ma'am." Blotting her lips on her linen napkin, Annora rose and began clearing the supper plates, glad for the opportunity to leave the room for even a few moments. She was so weary it would be a chore to stay awake until the dishes were done, but no amount of fatigue would stay her tears over the missed outing with her friends.

❧

The interior of the church had never seemed so huge before. Pausing to catch her breath, Annora rested her palms atop the broom handle and gazed at the play of sunlight streaming through the stained glass windows. She had never noticed before how it sparkled over the dust motes in the air, then fell in glowing rainbow patches on the dark polished floor. The gentle peace and reverence of the sanctuary was a balm to her wounded soul as she comforted herself about not seeing Jason Markwell.

She blew a few damp hairs from her eyes and adjusted her kerchief before continuing with the sweeping. Even though the doctor's raven-haired son had never openly declared any special feelings he might have for her, Annora always sensed he enjoyed her presence as much as she did his. Had her absence at today's picnic disappointed him also? Well, she'd probably find out soon enough, when she was forced to suffer through Mirah's embellishments of the occasion over supper. Clenching her teeth, she propped the broom in a corner and pulled a dust rag from the waistband of her apron, then returned to the front.

As she moved between the pulpit and the pump organ in the high-ceilinged room, she heard a woman's muted voice, obviously distressed, drifting from the minister's office.

". . . and he now fears Bertram may not last the night. I don't know what we shall do if he should actually . . . if he—"

"I cannot tell you how sorry I am, my dear Mrs. Thornby," the Reverend Baxter said in his most consoling tone. "He seemed to rally last evening. Of course I will join you and your son as you keep vigil at the bedside."

Feeling the intruder as she eavesdropped on someone's troubles, Annora tiptoed to the opposite end of the large paneled room. She still needed to set the vestibule in order for the morning service, so she made short work of sweeping the enclosed entry.

The sills of the windows flanking either side of the door needed her attention next, she noticed, brushing the rag across their smooth length.

The pastor's door squeaked open just then.

Annora started, and her elbow bumped the small basket off the shelf beneath the public board. Little pieces of paper scattered everywhere even as the Reverend Baxter and his visitor headed toward the vestibule. Quickly gathering the notices within her reach, Annora stuffed them into her apron pockets out of sight, restoring order.

"I'll be along very shortly, Mrs. Thornby," the reverend assured his guest as they reached the exit.

The large-boned woman drew a handkerchief from the wristband of her long sleeve, then pressed it to her nose. "Thank you. Percy and I, we appreciate your prayers and your presence in this hard time. Hester will let you in when you arrive."

Pinning up the new notices during the exchange, Annora saw the pastor nod and close the door behind Mrs. Thornby. Then with little more than a cursory glance at Annora, he went back to his study.

She breathed a sigh of relief. Finished with the last bulletin, she took a last look around, then went to put away her cleaning things. She might be done here, but there was still supper to get.

❧

"And, oh, it was ever so pleasant to stroll in the shade," Mirah gushed as she, her mother, and Annora partook of the evening meal without the reverend. "But best of all was when we paired up for croquet."

"Always a delightful endeavor," Mrs. Baxter said, forking a thin chunk of the roast beef on her plate. "Did you choose a partner, dear?" She raised the meat into her mouth.

Annora toyed with her own food, bracing herself for what she knew would follow.

"I didn't have to, I was chosen. You'll never guess by whom, Mother. It was Dr. Markwell's son, Jason—"

Although Annora thought she was prepared for the news, it still hurt. Little parts of her heart began to shrivel around the edges.

"—and he was ever so gallant, carrying my mallet for me, seeing to it that I never lacked for lemonade. He was easily the handsomest young man there. And he's quite the wit, as well. I thought I might never stop laughing."

Mrs. Baxter positively glowed. "I couldn't be more pleased, darling. You must do all you can to encourage his attentions. That boy has a splendid future ahead of him, and by the time he finishes studying the practice of medicine, you'll be almost the perfect age to marry. I couldn't think of anyone who would make a finer son-in-law."

It was all Annora could do to force food past the huge lump in her throat.

Later that evening, she couldn't even remember how she had gotten through the remainder of the meal. In the solace of her room at last, while changing into her nightgown, her gaze fell upon her mother's Bible. It was Annora's most treasured possession now—even more dear than the few prized pieces of jewelry Mrs. Henderson had saved from Mama's things. She opened the worn volume to the marker for her habitual daily reading, today in the Thirty-seventh Psalm:

> Fret not thyself because of evildoers, neither be thou envious against the workers of iniquity. For they shall soon be cut down like the grass, and whither as the green herb. Trust in the Lord, and do good; so shalt thou dwell in the land, and verily thou shalt be fed. Delight thyself also in the Lord; and he shall give thee the desires of thine heart. Commit thy way unto the Lord; trust also in him; and he shall bring it to pass.

Her eyes shifted to the window above her bed as she reflected on the passage she had read. It certainly seemed as if at least one evildoer resided at the parsonage, and though Annora didn't exactly wish Mirah *cut down*, it would be rather gratifying to have her be caught in a falsehood once or twice. Then, chagrined at wishing something so bold, Annora returned to the psalm:

> And he shall bring forth thy righteousness as the light, and thy judgment as the noonday. Rest in the Lord, and wait patiently for him: fret not thyself because of him who prospereth in his way, because of the man who bringeth wicked devices to pass. Cease from anger, and forsake wrath: fret not thyself in any wise to do evil. For evildoers shall be cut off: but those that wait upon the Lord, they shall inherit the earth.

I wonder if that could be true for me, Annora mused. *Just wait patiently, and be exonerated. It's my deepest hope, yet it seems so unattainable a dream.* Exhaling a ragged breath, she stood to fold her work clothes for tomorrow.

When she shook out her apron, a small piece of paper floated to the floor. Curious, Annora picked it up, then recognized it at once as a notice that should have gone up on the public board:

In desperate need. Widower with two small children seeks woman to care for same. Duties to include cooking and upkeep of home. If the prospect pleases, position may lead to matrimony. Travel expenses paid. Reply to Lucas Brent, General Delivery, Cheyenne, Wyoming.

A profound sadness crept over Annora as she read the announcement over again. Here she was, living in a large city, where one could easily obtain whatever one required . . . and feeling sorry for herself! She so seldom gave even the slightest thought to those out in the wild territories who had left home and family far behind to begin new lives where few conveniences were available.

With a shake of her head, she breathed a swift prayer of forgiveness, tacking on a fervent petition for Widower Brent and his little ones. She'd be sure to pin that notice up on the board tomorrow.

But the burden for the needful little family remained on her heart for a good part of the night.

3

Cheyenne, Wyoming

"Come on, Noah. Put some muscle into it, will you?" Lucas Brent rasped at his dark-haired kid brother as the two of them rocked the stubborn post back and forth. Widening the gate to the corral had been a harder job than he'd anticipated.

"Can't see why we have to get rid of this fool thing any-ways," Noah grumbled, swiping his shirt sleeve across his sweaty forehead. He flicked a lock of damp brown hair out of his eyes, then heaved against the wood with all his might. After an almost audible groan, it finally gave, throwing him headlong to the dirt. "Aaaah!"

Lucas had sidestepped just in time. He smirked and offered a hand to his sibling, then tugged him to his feet. "I didn't want it there, that's why."

"Don't know what difference it makes," Noah groused, sweeping a scathing glance down his now-dusty shirtfront. He brushed himself off and wiped his hands on his jeans. "Can we call it quits now?"

"There's lots of daylight left."

"Man, all you want to do anymore is work! I'm tired. It's hot. And it's been a long day."

"Well," Lucas said with a shrug, "looks like there might be a storm coming. Go on. I'm gonna keep at it for a bit."

Noah's youthful features relaxed, and his blue eyes shone with re-lief as he turned and strode past the barn.

"Hey, check on the girls," Lucas called after him. "Make sure they aren't into something they shouldn't be. I'll be along soon."

"Sure." Whistling now, the young man lengthened his strides to-ward the four-room clapboard dwelling a short distance away.

Lucas watched him go, noting how his brother's once-skinny

frame was muscling out since he'd come out to Wyoming in hopes of finding adventure. Seemed to be mellowing a little, too. The hard work was curbing some of the mischievous bent he'd acquired growing up in Denver. But would the kid ever settle down? Contemplating the unlikely possibility, Lucas inflated his lungs and slowly let the air out as he began filling the hole the extracted post had left behind.

Oh, well, he should be thankful to get *any* help out of that daydreaming nineteen-year-old. Noah showed little regard for the never-ending amount of chores that needed doing on a farm. One of these days somebody should give him a good—

A joyous, high-pitched shriek cut into his musings. Straightening to ease a kink in his back, Lucas swung a glance in the direction of the house just as his little daughters, Melinda and Amy, scampered out onto the weathered front porch. He smiled to himself. It was good to hear them starting to act like youngsters again. They'd been far too withdrawn since the funeral, hardly ever giggling like they used to.

But dwelling on the relentless ache inside him since Francie's death would only worsen it. With a sigh, he turned his focus to the task at hand and tamped the loose earth into place.

"Papa! I'm hungry," towheaded Amy hollered from the yard.

"Isn't it getting suppertime? The sun is low," her big sister pointed out with six-year-old logic.

"Yeah, I'm coming." Gathering his tools, Lucas headed for the barn.

The pair met him halfway and skipped hand in hand along-side, Amy's long blond hair feathering in the breeze. Lucas noticed it wasn't nearly as shiny as it had been when their mama had kept after it. But the braids he'd put in Melinda's deep brown locks were holding up pretty well, if he did say so himself.

"Melinda found a hurt birdie," Amy said, eyes the same azure shade as Francie's shining up at him. "Uncle Noah says it's gonna die. Is it, Papa?"

"I don't know, pumpkin. I'll have to see how bad it's been hurt."

"I hope it doesn't die," Melinda said on a sad sigh, her lips turning down at the corners. She fingered a new tear in her dress.

"Did God put birdies in Heaven?" Amy asked.

Lucas grimaced. He had stopped giving much thought to heavenly affairs the day Francie had been laid to rest . . . when it dawned on him that the Almighty didn't seem overly concerned about two innocent little ones who now had to grow up without their mother. But he smiled gently and squeezed her little shoulder with his free hand. "Well—"

"Course there's birds in Heaven, silly," her sibling announced. "Birds are pretty. And Heaven has all pretty things. Mama told us that, remember? When we looked in the picture book."

The sweet remembrance crimped Lucas's midsection, and he found it hard to respond. But they had reached the barn entrance, and as usual, the girls made a beeline for the stall housing Chesapeake, his sorrel-colored stallion. Parking his gear with the rest of the tools, Lucas watched them petting and cooing over the sorrel-colored bay while he checked to be sure Noah had fed the animal.

"Come on, you two," he said, offering each a hand. "Let's go get supper going."

"Hooray!" the girls chorused, each trying to be first to grab hold.

Their sweet smiles were a pleasure to see . . . even against those dirt-streaked faces. A person didn't have to look too close to concede that both girls could use a decent bath tonight. And once they were tucked into bed, he'd make good use of the water himself. If he hunted hard enough, he might even find some clean clothes somewhere, too. If not, reasonably clean would have to do.

"What're we gonna eat?" Melinda asked.

Lucas had been wondering the same thing himself. The long hours of work it took to keep his mind too occupied to feel sorry for himself precluded any kind of involved meal. "Did you two bring in the eggs today?"

"Uh huh." Amy scrunched up her face. "But we had eggs last night. And yesterday at dinner."

"And beans and ham almost every other day," his older daughter reminded him.

"Well, how about pancakes?" Lucas offered. "You like those."

"You mean, every day?" Melinda challenged.

"No, sweetheart. Just tonight. For special."

She nodded. "All right. Pancakes."

"All right," he said as they neared the house. "Wash up, then, while I get them going." He gave one of Melinda's braids a gentle tug. "Help Amy do a good job, huh?"

"Sure, Papa. Come on, Sissy. You can be first."

The girls went to dip water from the rain barrel into the wash basin that sat on the low table next to it, and Lucas continued on into the house.

Barely through the open doorway, he shook his head and turned his eyes upward. Only four rooms, and nothing but clutter from one to the next—while Noah, oblivious to it all, lounged on the sofa in the front room, one leg hooked over the arm, his bare foot dangling.

Lucas glared at him on the way to the stove. "Wouldn't hurt you to pick up a little once in awhile, you know."

Noah snorted and closed the Sears Roebuck catalog he'd been flipping through. "Why? It'll only get messed up again. Besides, nobody sees it but us."

"No excuse. This isn't how you were raised."

"Yeah, well, Ma and Pa ain't gonna swoop down here with their harps to yell at me no more, are they? It ain't my idea to work my head off all day every day, like you're so set on doing since Francie died. I put in my share outside. I shouldn't have to keep it up when the day's done."

"Is that right?" Lucas replied, looking askance at him.

"Yep. That's the way I see it."

"Well, the way *I* see it, it's time you grew up and took on some responsibility. Show some appreciation for having a roof over your head."

"Plenty of time for that." Noah came to his feet. "Right now, I think I'll ride on into town."

"I told you a storm's on the way."

"So? A few drops of rain never hurt anybody. I need to see a cheerful face for a change. Might even run into Postmaster Cummings while I'm there. He'd know if there's been an answer to the notice you sent east with the circuit rider." He jammed his bare feet into his boots and tromped out the door. But Lucas knew it was way too soon to hope for answers.

❧

Almost every member of Arch Street Church must have come to Mr. Thornby's funeral yesterday, Annora deduced. At least that's how the floor looked, tramped from front to back with mud from the heavy rain. And with this being Mrs. Henderson's baking and laundry day, Annora knew she would have to handle this task on her own. She blew some stray hairs out of her eyes with a disgusted huff, then went to get the bucket and scrub brush.

Knowing she was going to be at it for hours, she decided to start back at the door, where it looked the worst, then work her way toward the front. She rolled up her sleeves and began the tedious chore.

Annora had finished the length of one side and had gotten to the middle of the other when she first detected faint voices coming from the pastor's office, its door typically ajar during the warmer months. Not particularly prone to eavesdropping on matters that didn't concern her, Annora was rather glad the conversation could not be heard over the noise of the scrub brush. But when she switched to the rinse rag, short snatches could be heard quite distinctly, so she tried to concentrate on her work rather than listening.

". . . but for that will. I had no idea it existed."

"He might not have been thinking clearly, my dear Mrs. Thornby. The stipulation was likely due to his illness, I'm sure."

"That's not what Lawyer Sherman tells me. He is convinced Bertram was in his right mind to the end."

Dipping the brush into the suds once more, Annora scrubbed another portion of the floor around her, then wrung out the rinse rag to wipe up the soap and dirty water.

"But marriage!" The woman cried. "To attach such a condition to Percy's inheritance. Bad enough for us to be left alone so suddenly— but that!"

Annora couldn't resist chuckling inwardly. Percival Thornby? Get married? A picture of the paunchy young man with sallow skin flashed in her mind. His forehead had already laid claim to all the territory up to the middle of his scalp—and him no more than twenty-five. Worse yet, he mirrored many of his mother's irritating gestures and voice inflections. He had turned his simpering affections in the direction of nearly every unmarried girl at church at one time or another, without getting a single taker. In fact, it was rather a joke among them that such a sissy would never find gumption enough to leave his doting mother in the first place!

Nevertheless, she couldn't help but remember how sad it felt to part with a member of one's family. Whispering a prayer of comfort for the newly bereaved church folk, Annora took the brush again and began the next section. Rinsing it, she let her thoughts drift to Jason Markwell and his enticing manliness.

"Now, now, my good woman," the minister said soothingly. "Your concern might be premature. Let's pray about the matter and leave it in God's hands. Meanwhile, put your mind at rest. I'll see what I can find out about it from your lawyer and call on you the moment I have anything to report."

"If you think there's hope," she said hesitantly, her own tone evidence of her doubt.

Standing to her feet, Annora picked up the heavy water bucket and moved to the next area.

The voices grew fainter momentarily, an indication that Reverend Baxter had shown the widow out the side exit. Expecting complete silence after that, Annora was startled to hear the minister's wife speak directly after the report of his footsteps indicated his return.

"Well. I must say, that is about the strangest thing I have ever heard. Didn't it strike you as such, Phineas?"

He grunted in response. "Just remember, it was related in strictest confidence. It is not to go beyond these walls."

"Of course. But my heart goes out to the poor woman. She's beside herself. There must be something we can do to help."

Annora picked up the brush to rewet it.

"Well," she heard the minister say, "there are a number of young women in our congregation who are of marriageable age. Edna Morris, for one. Violet Biddle and her sister Iris." He paused. "And do not discount the younger set—Lesley Clark and her circle."

The brush slipped from Annora's grasp and plunged into the murky scrub water. Retrieving it, she resumed her chore.

"Phineas . . ."

Something in Mrs. Baxter's tone made Annora freeze in place, sudsy droplets plopping from the bristles to the floor. She sat back on her heels, a deep foreboding pressing upon her chest.

"You know," the woman went on in a confidential tone, "this might just be an answer to our prayers."

4

n answer to prayer? Mrs. Baxter's remark sank like a rock to the bottom of Annora's heart. She had a dreadful suspicion what the answer to those prayers might be . . . or rather, *whom.* A ward was, after all, expendable.

More rational thoughts took over. No sense jumping to conclusions when her fears might be entirely ungrounded. With her pulse throbbing in her ears, she kept absolutely still, straining to hear more.

"What do you mean, Millicent?" came the pastor's voice.

"Well," his wife explained quietly, "think of our dilemma. Of the *incidences* that have occurred in our own home over the past two years."

A short pause. "You're referring to Annora."

"Of course."

The slender thread of hope to which Annora had clung snapped, and a heaviness like nothing she had ever experienced pressed the very breath from her. Fearing that her guardians might inadvertently glance into the sanctuary and discover their conversation was anything but private, she crept silently out of the line of view. She stooped down behind a plant table near the front corner, longing desperately for the discussion to end.

"Much as I rue having to admit failure with that girl," the older woman went on, "I fear we've no other choice. Rather than showing common gratitude for the refuge provided her in time of dire need, she has chosen to inflict us with malicious harm. Time and again. And I, for one, have reached my limit with her."

"Still," the pastor reasoned, "there's much to consider here. I shouldn't want to make a decision in haste."

"Haste! Is that what you deem it—when what we must consider above all else is our own daughter's welfare? I dare say, while we sit by waiting for Mirah's excellent character to make even the slightest impression on the girl, the very opposite could be happening. I could not bear it if our own darling child were to be corrupted by the likes of her."

"Hm. I see your point—however unlikely it is. I'll mention the possible solution to the Widow Thornby when next I call on her."

"This opportunity comes straight from God's hand, Phineas," Mrs. Baxter murmured. "I truly feel it."

"Yes, well, unless the widow and her son are receptive to the suggestion, there's no point in mentioning it to anyone just yet. Most especially not Annora."

"I agree. I'll not say a word."

"Good. Well, I have some calls to make, my dear. I'll escort you over to the parsonage."

Seconds later, the closing of the side door echoed hollowly through the building.

Annora felt utterly empty, utterly alone. She sank slowly to the floor in silent misery, the tears inside her trapped somewhere between anguish and despair. What had she done to deserve such punishment? Would the Lord truly allow such a fate to befall her?

Even hours later, the ache remained. The church had once again been set to rights, ready for the next service. Annora had beaten the Persian rug from the parlor free of dust and polished Mrs. Baxter's silver tea service to a satin sheen. As she replaced her soiled work apron with a fresher one up in her attic room, her wrist brushed against the pocket, bringing a faint crackle of paper. *The unposted notice*—still awaiting a prominent place on the public board! If it weren't for her forgetfulness, someone might have seen it and applied for the position by now!

Annora gave fleeting thought to the possibility of writing to the widower herself, then just as quickly rejected the idea. After all, if a man were desperate enough to advertise for a wife, he must be even worse than Percival Thornby!

The uncharitable thoughts pricked her conscience. She really must remember to take that bulletin with her next time she went to the church! Tossing it on the stand beside the bed, she hastened downstairs to help with supper.

"You seem a little off today," Mrs. Henderson remarked a short while later, quartering the potato Annora had just peeled. She dropped the cut vegetable into the pot of stew bubbling atop the coal range. "Something troubling you, honey?"

Annora manufactured a smile. "I'm a little tired." It was by no means a lie, but neither was it the whole truth. She just didn't trust herself to elaborate on something which—hopefully—might turn out to be of no consequence. Time enough for that if her worst fears were confirmed. Percival Thornby might not accept the Baxters' proposition.

"I'm sure you are," the kind woman crooned. "And sorry I was that you were left with the whole sanctuary to do after that big funeral."

"No matter. It's finished now." She rinsed another potato in the bowl of water and handed it to the housekeeper, then started on the carrots. But having been reminded of Lucas Brent and his troubles, mere moments before, her mind drifted to the matter several times as she continued supper preparations. Perhaps someone in another church had responded to the widower's plea, and soon he would have the help he so desperately needed. She prayed so.

❧

". . . and Mr. Montclair said I'd played a wonderful rendition of the piece," Mirah boasted proudly, taking a second warm roll from the basket and breaking off a small section. She dipped it in her stew, then popped it into her mouth.

"Why, that's splendid, darling," her mother gushed. "I'm gratified that your talents merit the dear price we pay for the man's instruction."

Only vaguely listening to the chatter over the mealtime tinkle of silverware and china, Annora took a sip of water from her goblet. As she did, she caught a peculiar look pass between the minister and his wife, and a sickening dread erased the limited appetite she had brought to the supper table.

Mirah, however, seemed blissfully unaware of the underlying current of tension Annora felt as keenly as a toothache. "He has ordered a new collection of minuets and concertos for me to master," the younger girl went on, her brown eyes sparkling. "If I learn them well enough, he says I might be invited to play in the next recital at the conservatory! And only a select few of his outside students are extended that honor, Mother." Her long, tapered finger flicked a shining ringlet behind her shoulder.

"How wonderful, my dear," her father commented. "However, do rest assured that whether or not an invitation to play at the conservatory ensues, your mother and I are very proud of you."

"Indeed." Giving her daughter's hand a few loving pats, Mrs. Baxter then rang a tiny silver bell, signaling for dessert.

Annora stood at once and began collecting dinner plates and bowls. Rounding the head of the table, she reached to remove the pastor's dishes.

"Thank you," he said in customary politeness, but his demeanor appeared troubled. He cleared his throat. "Later this eve, after you've finished helping Nellie, Mrs. Baxter and I would like a word with you, Annora. In my study."

"Yes, sir," she managed, purposely refraining from meeting Mirah's curious expression. And worse, his wife averted her gaze entirely. Annora's insides began to quiver. *Please, Heavenly Father, don't let it be what I think it is. I could not bear that.* But inside, she knew the plea was in vain.

❧

Annora found the older couple waiting for her when she finally succeeded in forcing her legs to carry her to the study. The room, with its rich assortment of books lining the built-in shelves, had grown quite familiar to her since she'd begun dusting and sweeping it regularly. But on this visit the scent of the leather bindings she had once found so pleasant seemed cold and acrid. The very atmosphere was heavy and unwelcoming.

"Come in, child," the reverend said calmly. "And close the door, if you will." His small frame seemed dwarfed behind his massive carved desk.

Noting Mrs. Baxter's rigid posture in a Queen Anne side chair, hands folded in the lap of her somber afternoon ensemble, Annora could scarcely will her trembling fingers to make the latch function. But as the click echoed in the room, she drew a ragged breath and straightened her spine, then turned to face her guardians.

"Sit down, please," the minister said, gesturing toward a vacant chair near the desk.

As always, she obeyed.

"I'll come right to the point," he continued. "You are aware, of course, that a prominent member of our congregation has passed away."

"Yes," she whispered.

"Well, it seems the late Mr. Thornby left his loved ones in somewhat of a quandary. Through an unusual stipulation inserted in his most recent will, it seems his only son and heir, Percival, is prohibited from claiming his rightful inheritance for many years unless he marries before his next birthday . . . which, as it happens, is less than a month away."

Only with supreme effort was Annora able to remain dutifully in her seat. The compulsion to flee the room, her guardians, and the house was all she could imagine as a way out of this horrible predicament. Her throat tightened. "I–I fail to see what that has to do with me," she stammered.

"On the contrary, my dear," Mrs. Baxter said evenly, her aloof hazel eyes suddenly focused directly on Annora, "it would quite surprise me if you did not have some inkling regarding the decision my husband and I have made, as well as your personal involvement in the matter."

A huge mass of fear clogged Annora's throat.

"We have approached Percival Thornby and his mother with what we feel is a solution to a number of problems. Ours and theirs," the Reverend Baxter announced.

"Please," Annora begged, looking from the man to his wife, then back again. "Please, don't tell me I—"

"Oh, do not resort to useless entreaties," his wife piped in. "It has been obvious to us from the very first that you have been anything but grateful we took you into our home."

"But that's not true—"

Mrs. Baxter raised a hand to silence her. "Regardless of your denials, I fear your actions have spoken far more blatantly than anything you might try to say now. Let me assure you that for some time I have been on the verge of complete and utter despair over your spiteful deeds. For such an opportunity to arise now in order to benefit the lot of us, it can only have come from the Almighty's own hand."

"You do happen to be of marriageable age," the reverend explained before Annora could respond. "And for us, your legal guardians, to be able to arrange such an advantageous match for you is an answer to prayer. We can rest in knowing you will be comfortably taken care of. The Thornby wealth is considerable. If our Mirah wasn't so young, we would not hesitate a bit in securing such a splendid match for her."

"But . . . but I . . . can't—"

The older woman's obvious impatience began to assert itself. "We did not call you in here to ask your opinion of the matter," she stated firmly. "Only to inform you that your marriage to young Mr. Thornby has been agreed upon and will proceed as swiftly as we are able to arrange it. Naturally, as our ward, we desire you to have a beautiful wedding not unlike we intend for our dear Mirah one day. These plans, of course, will take some doing, on such short notice. But that is our concern, not yours."

"I shall post the banns at once," her husband went on.

"And I shall schedule your first fitting for your bridal gown and trousseau on the morrow," Mrs. Baxter added.

Annora could only stare in mute defeat. They weren't interested in her opinion. They didn't care how she might feel about having her whole future handed to someone she loathed. And their dear sweet Mirah . . . Annora could just imagine the triumphant gloating she'd have to endure from that one!

"In view of the nearness of your upcoming nuptials, Annora,"

Mrs. Baxter said, cutting into her bitter musings, "we shall, of course, relieve you of some of your duties. We wouldn't want you to appear taxed when the day of your wedding arrives."

Stunned and shocked as she was over the fate awaiting her, the pronouncement of less work carried not even the slightest comfort. Annora could not manage any kind of utterance. The older couple regarded her steadily as if she should consider this the happiest news ever delivered.

"You may go to your room now," the minister finally said. "I'm sure you need time to thank our blessed Lord for this most fortunate turn of events. And tomorrow evening, we will invite your betrothed to supper. It's only proper that the two of you become better acquainted in the scant time remaining before you two are united in marriage."

"Our Mirah will be so pleased for you," her mother breathed.

With that understatement ringing in her ears, Annora rose with as much dignity as she could muster, her quaking legs barely able to support her as she stumbled to the door and mounted the stairs to her sanctuary in the attic.

And all the way up, she hoped she would die in her sleep.

Collapsing on her bed, she drew her knees to her chest and lay shivering in her misery, her glance drifting idly about the small quarters. Her gaze came to a dead halt when it fell upon the forgotten notice still awaiting its prominent position on the public board.

Annora bolted upright and snatched it from her bedside table. Heart pounding, she unfolded the handwritten bulletin and read it over again.

A housekeeper. She'd had sufficient qualifications there.

Someone to care for two small children. Well, no actual experience, but Mama had often remarked that a child who was kept clean and fed was a happy child.

If the prospect pleases, position could lead to matrimony.

In this case, she would at least be given a choice. And surely, whoever this Lucas Brent was, he couldn't be any worse than that mama's boy, Percival Thornby. Could he?

Annora rooted through a discarded lap desk she'd discovered some weeks ago and removed paper and a quill, praying that her letter and Mr. Brent's returning answer would reach their destinations before the dreaded day.

5

*I*n her newest, most fashionable jade taffeta gown, her red-gold tresses a mass of ringlets intertwined with ribbons, Annora grudgingly answered the summons to join the Baxters and her intended in the parsonage's luxurious parlor.

Percival Thornby rose and met her in the doorway as she approached. "Ah. Miss Nolan," he wheezed. "I've been anticipating the opportunity to dine with you this evening."

"Mr. Thornby," she managed, with a slight dip of her head as she smothered her displeasure.

He reached for her hand and bowed ceremoniously over it. Thankfully, however, he did not kiss it but escorted her to the indigo brocade settee and seated her. He took the opposite side.

A brief uncomfortable period followed, during which no one looked at anyone for more than a split second. Finally the Reverend Baxter resumed the polite conversation Annora's arrival had obviously interrupted.

Tongue-tied amid the drone of voices, she disregarded them completely, maintaining her composure by sheer determination. She could not help noticing how the waistcoat of Percival's black silk suit strained across the broad expanse of his belly as he leaned back against the cushions. And the collar of his shirt had been starched so crisply he appeared to have no neck at all.

Annora shifted her position and tried to focus on the contrast between the heavy furnishings and some of the exquisite porcelain figurines adorning the room. Anything to keep her mind and eyes elsewhere. From time to time she would become aware of Percival

Thornby's admiring glances, and her color heightened along with her discomfort. This evening was destined to last forever.

But she could not dismiss the expression on her intended's flushed face . . . a mixture of incredulity and satisfaction at having been granted a hitherto unattainable prize. And something about the way he looked at Annora made her feel undressed. She studied her hands, tightly clasped in her lap to keep them still.

"I'm ready to serve supper, madam," Mrs. Henderson finally announced from the doorway.

Everyone rose. But before Annora could take a step, Percival tipped his head politely and offered his arm. She forced a smile and placed her fingers lightly atop his smooth sleeve. At least in the dining room, eating would consume part of the time, and she would have a valid excuse not to join the inane chatter.

"And what are your future goals, Percival?" the Reverend Baxter asked, after everyone had been seated and the blessing pronounced. He handed the platter of roast pork to their guest.

The fleshy young man altered his position self-consciously on the chair. "Goals. Ahem." He helped himself to several generous slices of meat. "I suppose," he announced in his high-pitched lisp, "I'll be doing my utmost to look after the two women in my life. I haven't thought beyond that."

Two women. Annora cringed inwardly at having been thrown upon the Thornby household merely as a means to save the inheritance. She could only surmise how the recently widowed matriarch would view the presence of a usurper to her son's attention.

Detecting Mirah's barely visible smirk as the dark-haired girl took a sip of water from her goblet, Annora felt the last remnants of hunger vanish. Normally she would have devoured the sumptuous fare, but tonight the sight and smell of serving dishes heaped high with the housekeeper's fine cooking only made her stomach churn. She accepted the platter Percy was passing to her and took the smallest slice possible. He, however, scooped a veritable mountain of mashed potatoes onto his plate and sampled a forkful.

"Are you planning a wedding trip?" Mirah asked him, her lips twitching with restrained mirth.

"Trip. Ah." Percy swallowed and blotted his mouth on his napkin. "Actually, Miss Nolan and I have not yet discussed her wishes along that line. Mother and I are making arrangements to set aside a six-week period for travel. Naturally, we will be only too happy to escort my new bride anywhere she desires."

Annora's heart plummeted as everyone turned to her, awaiting a response. All she could think of was how very little effort it would take to be sick, right here, in front of them all.

∽❧

Lucas listened idly to the jingle of the harness as Jethro and Rex, his workhorses, plodded homeward from town in the growing dusk.

"How much farther, Papa?" Melinda asked, standing up in the bed of the wagon and clutching the seat back. "I have to go."

"Me, too," Amy piped in at her side.

"Didn't you go with Miss Rosemary to the outhouse, like I told you, while I was getting the supplies?" he chided his older daughter gently.

"Yes, Pa, but then she took us to the well and let us turn the crank. She let us have a big drink of cold water from the bucket. Now we have to go again."

"Okay, okay." Rolling his eyes, Lucas released a long, slow breath and drew in on the reins. "There are some bushes over there," he indicated with his head. "Be quick about it."

"Yes, Papa," the youngsters chorused. Hopping down from the wagon, they bolted happily out of sight.

Waiting for the girls to return, Lucas reached for the mail he'd picked up in town and sifted through it one more time, carefully, just in case there had been a letter from back East that he hadn't noticed. But no such luck. Maybe there'd never be an answer.

He set aside the items from the post office and let his thoughts drift to Rosemary Evans, the comely milliner whose small bonnet shop was becoming more and more a lucrative enterprise with the growth of Cheyenne. Though fetching enough to turn any number of heads, the hatmaker showed no inclination to marry at the moment . . . at least, not a widower who'd been "saddled," as she'd termed it, with two children.

Lucas suspected that if he'd been left completely alone, however, flaxen-haired Rosemary would have been first in line to pick up the pieces of his life. She'd all but come right out and said it over refreshments she'd served when he'd gone by her place to pick up the badly needed mending she'd been kind enough to do for him. No, best not to entertain fantasies about a lady who was more interested in making her fortune than she was in being mama to a pair of little girls that weren't hers.

His musings came to an abrupt end with the sound of giggles and pattering footsteps as his daughters scrambled aboard the wagon again. Flicking the reins over the horses' backs, Lucas clucked his tongue. "Come on, boys. Let's get on home."

∽

Annora stepped behind the folding screen to dress. Tired after standing motionless on the dressmaker's fitting stool for most of the afternoon, she circled her head slowly, trying to relieve her stiff neck. Then she removed her petticoats from the wall pegs and began pulling them on.

"Let me know when you need help fastening buttons," Gertie Simms, the bubbly assistant called out.

"Thank you, I will." But less than anxious to return to the parsonage just yet, Annora continued her leisurely movements. The Baxters had spared no expense in providing her with a lovely trousseau. Indeed, under any other circumstances, Annora would have been in seventh heaven at the very thought of possessing such a glorious wardrobe. But although her guardians truly believed they were acting in her best interest, such an unwanted marriage made Annora's very skin crawl. She was taxed to maintain a pleasant demeanor in their presence. There had to be some way of forestalling her union with the heir to the Thornby estate. A miraculous intervention by God. *Please, Dear Father, don't let this happen to me.*

"Ready?" Gertie asked, peeking around the screen, her bright blue eyes alight with friendliness.

"Yes." With a thin smile, Annora turned her back to the nimble-fingered brunette who appeared only a couple years older than herself.

"La, what a pretty wardrobe you'll be wearin'," Gertie said breathlessly, slipping each pearl button on Annora's dress through its corresponding loop. "Your missus chose all the newest fabrics from France and laces from Belgium. So elegant, they are, to work on."

"Yes. And I'm surprised at how quickly you're finishing everything," Annora said with fatal acceptance. No one seemed to care that her whole future was spinning out of control.

"Well, my mistress has all us girls sewin' past closin' to fill the order. She'd have our heads if it was our fault that a grand weddin' got held up!" Chuckling to herself, the slim girl straightened and stepped away. "There. Now, a few more fittin's an' you'll not be seein' the likes of us again for awhile."

"I've enjoyed getting to know you and the others," Annora admitted truthfully. "Especially you, Gertie. I hope your mother continues to gain strength."

"Thanks, miss. It's been a help, my earnin' good money here. Little by little, the Good Lord supplies what she needs."

"Yes. Well, I'll see you tomorrow afternoon, then. Do have a pleasant day." Smiling, Annora crossed through the cluttered workroom. The small silver bell jangled in its bracket above the entrance as she exited.

Late afternoon sunshine cast long shadows between the red brick buildings lining either side of Market Street. The coolness of the shady spots felt welcome to Annora's feet as she traipsed along the edge of the cobbled road. Grateful that no one had accompanied her today, she gave in to the impulse to pop in on her best friend from church. The bakery Lesley's parents owned was barely two blocks out of her way.

As she neared the squat one-story building tucked between a leather shop and a printing business, the tantalizing aroma of fresh baked goods grew stronger. The overhead bell sounded as she opened the door and went inside.

л," Lesley said, looking up from behind the wide
rosy lips widening with a smile. "A friendly face. Always
sight." She wiped her hands on the long apron covering
her dress and came to hug Annora. "What brings you by?"

"Mostly I needed to see a friendly face myself," Annora admitted
glumly as the embrace ended and they parted.

"Why? Whatever is wrong? Are the Baxters working you too
hard—as usual?"

"You haven't heard?"

"Heard what? I've been up at Wind Gap at my auntie Edna's for
the past ten days, remember? I just got home last evening."

At the look of puzzled concern on Lesley's expressive features,
Annora felt her own eyes fill with tears. "Oh, Les. You have no idea
what's happened. It's just dreadful."

"What is?" Reaching for Annora's hand, Lesley clutched it in both
of hers, her delicate brows dipping into a vee above her clear blue
eyes. "Oh, do tell me what has you in such a state."

Still struggling to contain her emotions, Annora drew a stabilizing
breath. "I—I'm to be . . . married." Then the floodgates let loose, and
she collapsed, weeping, into her dear friend's comforting arms.

The slender honey-blond crooned softly as she patted Annora's
back. "I don't understand. How can that be?"

"They—they want to . . . get rid of m-me," Annora sobbed.

"Why, I've never heard anything so horrid," Lesley said consolingly. "But—whom will you marry?"

Annora couldn't bring herself to answer. Inside, a part of her still
clung to the hope that she'd awaken from this nightmare . . . that unless she actually uttered the truth aloud, it wouldn't be real.

"Who is it, Annora?" her friend probed gently.

"I—I don't even w-want to say his n-name." It took two tries before she managed to force it past her lips. "It's—it's *Percival Thornby!*"
The announcement spewed forth on a croaking whisper.

Lesley's breath caught in her throat, and she clutched Annora all
the more tightly, stroking her hair as the sobs continued.

How much time passed, Annora could not even guess. But when
her tears began to subside, she sniffed and eased away, drying her

cheeks on a handkerchief from her pocket. She had only a fragile hold on her control, and she knew if she dared to meet her friend's sympathetic gaze, she would break down again.

"There's only one thing to do. You must run away," Lesley declared adamantly.

"Where could I go?"

"I don't know yet. But I'll think of someplace, I promise."

Annora finally raised her lashes and searched Lesley's face. The sight of the determination displayed there bolstered her courage. "Well, the truth is, I've applied for a position out in the Wyoming Territory . . . a housekeeper and nursemaid."

"Are you serious?"

With a nod, Annora sighed. "I haven't told anyone. But there hasn't been time to hear if I've been accepted for the post. Someone else may have already been selected."

Lesley did not respond.

"That position might also involve marriage."

The look that passed between them held a raft of unspoken implications, but Lesley was considerate enough not to press the matter. "When is the, um, wedding here supposed to take place?"

Annora grimaced. "Sometime before Percy's next birthday, two weeks away . . . the very moment all the plans have been finalized. I'm returning now from a fitting for my gown and trousseau," she continued in a rush before another wave of tears swamped her. "I've never possessed such lovely, elegant things. The Baxters truly think they're doing me a favor—and, of course, Mirah's absolutely jumping with glee. You cannot imagine."

"This is all pretty grim," Lesley agreed. "But perhaps you'll hear from Wyoming before then . . . not that I wish to part with my bosom friend, you understand."

"I hardly think there's time, Les. Everything is progressing so quickly."

"That may very well be," Lesley said with conviction. "But I'm not about to stand by and do nothing while your whole life is thrown to the vultures. This wedding will not take place. You'll see. Somehow, some way, we'll come up with something. Some way out."

6

*I*n her room, early that evening, Annora heard the bell pull announce the arrival of a visitor downstairs. Shortly afterward, light footsteps sounded on the steps, pausing briefly on the second floor before continuing on to the attic.

Annora sat up on her bed, and her questioning glance caught her best friend's pretty smile at the door.

"May I come in?" Lesley asked breathlessly.

"Of course." Annora patted the coverlet beside herself.

Lesley stepped inside and crossed the room, a small wrapped package in her hands. "I brought you something . . . so Mrs. Baxter wouldn't feel it odd that I came."

"You've always been clever," Annora teased as she accepted the gift. Smiling, she unwrapped the brown paper. Her heart contracted at the sight of a pair of fine batiste pillow slips. "Oh, Les," she murmured, fingering the embroidered hems edged with handmade lace. "How beautiful. But these are things you've made for yourself, for the day you become a bride."

"Well, yes. But I wanted to give you something special, so when you're an old married lady you won't forget the girl who was once your dearest friend."

"You'll always be my dearest friend," Annora assured her with a hug. "Married or not." Then, drawing away, she grew serious. "But if the gift was only a pretext, what is the real reason for your visit?"

Lesley rose and tiptoed to close the door. "I don't want anyone to overhear us," she whispered, returning to her seat.

"Why? What's happened?"

"Nothing. I've just been so consumed with worry for you, I wanted to find out if there'd been any word from Wyoming yet."

Annora shook her head soberly. "And I'd hate to surmise what would happen if something should arrive on a day when I'm not the one who picks up the household mail. I'd be called to account for such a scandalous act. Besides, in truth, I'm not completely sure that's a better fate than what awaits me here."

"Well, I dare say, it can hardly be worse!" Lesley exclaimed.

Annora conceded inwardly that her friend was likely right.

"What will you do if there's no response?"

"I'm trying not to dwell on that."

A conspiratorial expression drew Lesley's fine brows together. "Well, I'll tell you what I would do, were I in your shoes."

"Oh? And what might that be, if I dare ask?"

"I would go anyway."

The announcement hung suspended between them for a timeless moment. Then Annora shook her head. "How could I, Les? How? It's possible that Mr. Brent has already hired someone else, you know. But even if he hasn't, I've no idea of the price of a fare west, much less where I'd obtain traveling funds for such a journey. Then there's the small matter of sneaking a trunk packed with clothes out of the house, to say nothing of lugging it all those blocks to the railroad station without anyone noticing." She paused to take a breath, trying to convince herself a single one of those thoughts she had entertained was even feasible. "And even if by some miracle I could somehow manage all those things, the very idea of going so far by myself is—is . . ."

"Shh." Lesley put a comforting hand on Annora's shoulder. "All of that, as my mother is so fond of saying, 'is difficult, but not impossible.' First things first. The money."

Her curiosity sparked, Annora met the confident gaze.

"Didn't you tell me that Mrs. Henderson salvaged a few pieces of your mother's jewelry?"

"Well, yesss . . ." Annora hedged. "But how could I part with those? It's all I have left of Mama's."

Lesley nodded in understanding as she toyed with one of her

shiny blond curls. "But consider the alternative, Nora. Would you rather have the jewelry and go through with your wedding to Percy? Or could you put those sentiments aside and accept your mother's help? I'm sure she wouldn't want you to settle for a lifetime of unhappiness. Would she?"

Annora could not even respond. What she needed most was time to reason things out. Time to pray.

"Come by the shop again after tomorrow's fitting. We'll go together to inquire about a railroad ticket."

"I can't promise," Annora confessed. "But I will try."

"It doesn't cost anything to ask, you know," her friend urged softly.

At the sound of approaching footsteps, Annora placed a finger to her lips.

Three soft taps on the door, and Mrs. Baxter raised the latch and entered.

Mirah, like an ever-present shadow, came in behind her mother, a gloating sneer curling one side of her lips.

"We don't mean to interrupt your visit," the older woman began hesitantly, but something in her demeanor indicated she had news to impart.

"We don't mind," Annora said, deliberately quenching an ominous premonition she had sensed on the pair's arrival. "I've just been admiring these lovely pillow covers. Lesley made them herself." Annora held them up for her guardian to see.

"Why, they're exquisite." Mrs. Baxter beamed at the guest. "You do exceptional stitchery, dear."

"Thank you." A faint blush pinkened Lesley's fair cheeks.

Then the minister's wife returned her attention to Annora. "I thought you might be pleased to know we've set a day for your nuptials."

Annora's mouth went dry, and her fingers clutched a handful of the coverlet beneath her to steady herself. She felt, more than saw, Mirah's satisfied smirk.

"Yes," her guardian went on. "I probably should have waited to announce this tomorrow eve, when young Percival comes to dine with us again. But I just couldn't contain it another moment. Mirah suggested Lesley might like to share in your happy news."

Trembling inwardly, Annora struggled for composure as a sickening dread turned her blood to ice.

"Mistress Fitzpatrick assures me that after tomorrow's final fitting, your trousseau will be delivered the very next day. So we shall schedule the glorious occasion for the week's end. Mid-afternoon on Saturday." The matron glowed with anticipation.

The triumphant set of Mirah's proud shoulders indicated in eloquent silence her own unbridled glee.

It was all Annora could do to muster a polite smile. She met Lesley's wide blue eyes in wordless misery.

"How exciting!" That her friend's enthusiasm was a sham was obvious to Annora as Lesley grasped her shoulder in a hug. "That is delightful news. I'm so happy for you." But as she leaned close, she put her lips up to Annora's ear. "Remember what I said," she whispered.

"Yes," Mrs. Baxter gushed. "We're thankful the Lord has enabled us to secure such a prosperous union for our Annora."

Lesley cleared her throat and rose to her feet. "Indeed. Well, I'd truly like to stay longer and hear more about the arrangements, but Mother insisted I come directly home. I just had to deliver my bridal gift. Perhaps another time." With a last hug, she gave Annora a pointed stare, then turned with a smile. "I'll be off, then. Good evening, Mrs. Baxter, Mirah."

"Good evening, dear," the minister's wife replied. "I'll show you out." Still smiling from her earlier pronouncement, she nodded to Annora, then ushered the willowy younger woman toward the stairs.

The daughter of the household swung a furtive glance from Annora to Lesley, then back. "I'm just thrilled for you," she gushed in syrupy sweetness. "Positively ecstatic."

You would be, Annora railed silently but held onto her composure as Mirah turned and fairly danced downstairs after the others.

As the sound of their footsteps faded, Annora sank to her

knees . . . but the fervent plea of her heart could find no expression. Three days. *Three days!*

❧

Annora slept fitfully and awakened in the chill blue of dawn to hear the ice wagon rumbling up the cobbles on the street below, its vast store of crystal blocks leaving a trail of droplets in its wake. The bearded driver, so tall and lean he appeared to be all bone and gristle, was as regular as morning itself . . . he and the new day both reminders of God's faithfulness.

Her quiet time of prayer and Bible reading also instilled peace within her, and Annora had wrapped her mother's treasures in handkerchiefs and tucked them into the bottom of her drawstring handbag. The moment the opportunity presented itself, she would steal away to Lesley's. With that hope uppermost in her heart, she raced downstairs.

Mrs. Baxter and her daughter were on the bottom landing. "Mirah will be going with you today," the woman informed her.

Annora's spirit drooped low. Detaching herself from the younger girl's overbearing presence would prove difficult now.

The bleak thought only grew stronger as the two of them stood motionless on the dressmaker stools a little over an hour later.

"This is so tiresome!" Mirah fidgeted as the hem was being pinned in her gown. "I can't see why Mother insisted I have a new frock for this silly affair."

Annora could conjure up a few more descriptive terms for the occasion herself but held her tongue and made a quarter turn on her own perch so Gertie could continue around the rich satin skirt of the bridal gown.

"How much longer?" Mirah groused. "My feet hurt. Father should have driven us here in the carriage. And I'm hungry."

"If ye'd be holdin' still, miss," shy, mobcapped Annabelle announced with surprising fervor, "I'd have ye done in two shakes of a lamb's tail."

Mirah folded her arms and huffed but finally relented.

Annora glanced across the workroom at the clock. Almost noon, and not a moment of it without Mirah, whose pouty presence had put a damper on the usual good-natured chatter among the seamstresses. The significant glances passing between them, however, bespoke far more than words. Annora released an unbidden sigh from deep inside.

Just then, the resident cat ambled through the curtained doorway separating the workroom from the main part of the shop. After an elaborate stretch, it sought the soft comfort of its pillowed basket in the corner and curled up with a contented, almost inaudible, purr.

With her back to the animal, Mirah sneezed. "Excuse me," she said, frowning. Then she sneezed again. "I—" Another sneeze followed. "This is just horrid. I don't know what—"

Annora smothered a giggle.

"There." Annabelle rose from her knees. "All done, Miss Baxter."

Mirah all but jumped off the stool and turned to allow the worker to help her off with the gown. She stiffened and her eyes widened. "A cat! No wonder I'm—" A succession of undignified sneezes brought tears. "And I've forgotten to bring a handkerchief." In her camisole and drawers, she scrambled out of the pooled skirts at her ankles and made a dive for Annora's reticule.

Mama's jewelry! Annora's heart all but stopped instantly. "Here, let me help you," she blurted, springing out of Gertie's reach to reclaim her bag from Mirah's fingers.

But the younger girl was already rooting through it. Racked by yet another sneeze, Mirah yanked a lace-trimmed cloth from the bag.

A cameo brooch dropped to the floor between them. Annora cringed and held her breath as Mirah dabbed at her eyes.

"Not to worry, miss," Annabelle said consolingly. "I've whisked Dimples right out of here. He'll not be botherin' ye now."

"The damage has already been done," Mirah said despairingly. She clutched her stomach. "I feel rather ill."

Sliding the brooch out of sight with the toe of her slipper, Annora put an arm about the younger girl. "We need to get you home as quickly as possible."

"The mistress's carriage is out back," Gertie told them. "I'm sure she won't be mindin' if Annabelle borrows it to drive the young miss. Come on, dear. I'll help you dress while Annie checks with Mrs. Fitzpatrick."

Mirah sniffed and nodded and allowed Gertie to lead her away.

Just before they moved behind the dressing screen, Gertie glanced over her shoulder at Annora. "Hope you don't mind stayin' behind. We still have two gowns with hems to mark."

Limp with relief, Annora stooped down and deftly plucked the cameo up and returned it to the safety of her handbag.

Her smile of victory made the whole day brighter.

7

"ould you tell us a story, Pa?" Amy begged, turning soulful eyes up to Lucas. "Please? Please?"

Her sister's fervent nod gave the request even more weight.

Looking from one sweet face to the other, Lucas was a goner. He straightened from tucking the pair into bed and swiped his shirt sleeve across his forehead. He had so much more to do before dark—but would there ever come a time when that wouldn't be true? Exhaling a weary breath, he cocked one side of his mouth into a smile. "What kind of story?"

"You know, about Baby Moses, like Mama used to tell us."

"No," Melinda corrected. "About the little slave girl who helped her master with lep—lepro—Oh, you know."

"Leprosy. Well, tell you what," Lucas suggested, reluctant to pass on tales he was trying to put out of his mind. "How about I make one up, instead."

"Oh, goody!" Golden-haired Amy sprang to a sitting position and clapped. Then, catching the frown her father leveled at her, she just as quickly lay back down.

He winked, then rubbed his jaw in thought and squatted on one knee beside the bed the little ones shared. "Well, let's see . . ."

"No, Pa. 'Once upon a time,'" Amy said in all seriousness.

"Right. Once upon a time, there was . . . a pony named Star. He was named that because he had this patch of white right about—here." He tapped his youngest daughter's forehead, and she grinned. "Only Star wasn't a very happy little pony."

The two young faces scrunched up.

"Why?" Melinda asked.

"Because he heard his owner tell a stranger that he could buy Star. And Star didn't want to leave his pasture. He was happy there, prancing around with the other ponies. He wanted to stay where he was for a very long time. Maybe forever."

"Ohhh," the girls moaned.

"But what he didn't know," Lucas went on, "was that the strange man had two little girls at his house, who would love Star and take very good care of him."

"So he was really going to a happy place," Melinda chimed in.

"And the little girls would love him lots and lots," Amy added, her blue eyes shining.

"Right." Lucas ruffled their hair, then winced at how stringy it felt. Why were the days so blasted short all the time? He needed extra hours to see to the farm and take care of little ones besides. There was no end to the constant chores.

"Will you buy us a pony someday, Pa?" his older child asked hopefully, cutting into his musings and ending the story.

"I'd love nothing more, pumpkin . . . if the crops sell and the day comes when I can buy that string of good horses I'd like. That won't be for awhile, though."

"It's all right," she said quietly. "Mama told us you always do what you say . . . when the time is right."

Francie had said a lot of things, he recalled. She had set such store by all his grand dreams. But many of those dreams had died with her, and what the girls didn't know was he hardly cared one way or the other about the old plans now. He was just going through the motions . . . and not doing such a good job, judging by the less-than-spotless appearance of these two motherless angels. Their bed sheets didn't look a whole lot better than they did. He rose. "Well, time to sleep now. I'll be right outside, so no whispering."

"But—won't you hear my prayers first?" Melinda asked.

He inhaled slowly. "Sure. Go ahead."

The youngsters steepled their tiny hands and solemnly closed their eyes. "Dear God, thank You for the happy day and the nice story

Pa told us. Please give Mama a hug and kiss and tell her we love her. Good night, God. Amen."

"Amen!" Amy echoed.

Lucas had to swallow hard. " 'Night, you two. No whispering, remember." A last smile, and he exited the little room—and promptly tripped over a pile of dirty clothes Melinda had dutifully gathered together.

Man, if that lazy brother of mine deigned to spend half as much time lending a hand around the place as he did gallivanting off to town, maybe the place wouldn't be such a shambles, Lucas groused, picking himself up. He bent to retrieve the soiled laundry to be added to his own stack for wash day tomorrow. He just hoped somebody would soon reply to the notice he'd sent east. And right now, he'd settle for just about *anybody*, no matter how old or decrepit she might turn out to be.

❧

In a changing room in the church basement, Annora gazed in the full-length looking glass, not even recognizing the person staring back at her. Having stood still as a statue in Mistress Fitzpatrick's Fashion Salon while the exquisite satin bridal gown was pinned and tucked and fitted to perfection, she had never once caught sight of how she actually looked. But here, now, observing the play of light over the folds of rich fabric, the pearls and white sequins shimmering with her slightest movement, her hair in a glorious cluster of ringlets, the enormity of what she was about to do settled oppressively over her spirit.

"I could very nearly cry," Mrs. Baxter said softly, fussing with the fragile veil of tulle and lace, arranging it just so over Annora's red-gold curls. "This is one of the happiest moments of my life." Leaning to bestow a hug, she smiled in the mirror at Annora's reflection. "Pray, do not be nervous. On this most special of all days, you'll be embarking on one of life's wonderful adventures."

"I . . . I don't know how to thank you," Annora said around the thickness in her throat. "You and the Reverend Baxter. You've been very good to me. And I—I'm very—"

"Pshaw!" her guardian exclaimed, obviously taking the incomplete statement as an apology for past wrongs. "All is forgotten. You're going off on your own now. Be happy, that's all we could ask. Now I must go next door and see that Mirah is dressing, then check on a few other details. Nothing to worry yourself over. You've finished so early, you can just relax and think calm thoughts. When everyone has assembled upstairs in the sanctuary, and we're ready for you, I'll send Mirah."

"Thank you." Unable to meet the older woman's gaze, Annora smiled thinly and pretended to be entranced by her own reflected image. And all the while she listened to her guardian's diminishing footsteps, her pulse throbbed with increasing intensity.

At last the door at the top of the stairs clicked shut. Reminding herself to breathe, Annora waited a full two minutes, then crept up the steps, straining to listen for an indication of anyone else's presence in the building. Hearing none, she let herself out the side door.

Then she grasped her skirts and ran for all she was worth.

ᵔᴥᵔ

The Southern and Western Railroad Station in Philadelphia occupied a significant portion of South Broad Street. Annora tamped down her nervousness as she, Lesley, and Lesley's beau, Michael Porter, joined the noisy throng of eager, excited people surging into the great arched hall. Once inside the vast interior, all sounds magnified accordingly, competing with the hisses and bursts of steam from the waiting locomotives, the chugging coughs of the departing ones. Annora eyed the flaring stacks with alarm, already having second thoughts about her impetuous act.

"Are you positive you've got everything?" Lesley asked, straightening the collar of the apple green linen traveling suit she had loaned Annora. "Michael has already seen to your luggage, and I've packed a feast for you in the basket." At Annora's bleak look, she gave her a reassuring hug.

"You're doing the right thing," the brown-eyed young man said confidently, clamping her shoulder. "It will all work out in the end, you'll see."

"Yes. Do stop worrying," Lesley gently scolded her. "You look divine."

"Then why do I feel like a louse?" Annora asked miserably. "You should have seen Mrs. Baxter's face, Les. She almost *loved* me."

"Yes. Almost. That about says it. What she loved most was this chance to pass you off to the first available taker."

"Perhaps." Annora swallowed. "Well, I don't know how I'll repay you both for all your help. I'll never forget it."

"I should hope not." Even though said in a teasing tone, Lesley quickly blinked away sudden moisture in her eyes. "You must promise to write the very minute you get settled. So *I* can stop worrying. You hear?"

Nodding and fighting her own tears, Annora tried to smile.

"All abo—arrr—d," a deep voice called above the hubbub.

Annora's feet refused to move until her friends propelled her from behind. Nearing the portable steps to the huge passenger car, she felt herself being swamped with hugs.

"Take care, Nora. God be with you," Lesley breathed.

The sight of her friends' faces blurred behind a sheen of tears, and Annora could not speak. She touched her fingers to her lips and pressed them to Lesley's, braved as much smile as she could to Michael, and mounted the steps. Turning on the landing, she lifted a hand in final farewell, then before her last shred of composure dissolved, she stumbled, unseeing, into the paneled car.

❧

Someone gently nudged Annora's shoulder.

"Ticket, miss."

Opening her swollen eyes and lifting her head from where it rested against the sooty window, she beheld the portly conductor, resplendent in his crisp navy blue uniform. "I—I must have dozed off," she responded inanely. Exhausted from the sleepless nights leading up to her almost-wedding, the steady rhythm of the steel rails had lulled her into oblivion. Her head throbbed as she rummaged through her reticule and placed her ticket in his extended hand.

A quick perusal, and he punched it with a small silver tool, then returned it to her and continued up the aisle.

Annora averted her gaze, chagrined that strangers might have been staring at her as she slept—a possibility she found less than comforting. But many of the remaining seats were unoccupied, and of the handful of passengers ahead, no one seemed to be paying her any mind. She exhaled slowly and relaxed a bit as the gently swaying car clacked along the rails.

"Well, I see you've returned to the land of the living," a woman's voice said from nearby.

Turning, Annora met the face of an elegantly attired young woman across the aisle and one row back. With dark hair and olive skin, she appeared only a few years older than Annora and held a small babe in her arms. Annora remembered having caught a brief glimpse of the woman through the blur of tears as she'd made her way to her own seat some hours ago.

"I hope I didn't make any embarrassing sounds," Annora said, feeling the warmth of a blush. She noted the classic beauty of the mother's face, framed as it was by its fashionable bonnet, and suspected her own appearance must surely show the effects of anxiety and the sad Philadelphia parting. Unconsciously, she reached up to touch her bonnet.

The woman smiled kindly. "Not at all. I was only concerned that you might awaken with a stiff neck. I'm afraid these seats aren't conducive to restful sleep. I'm Hope Johnston."

"Annora Nolan. Pleased to meet you." Her gaze dropped to the child. "How old is your baby?"

"Four months, already, and growing like a veritable weed. The time flies so quickly." She paused. "I . . . couldn't help noticing you're alone. Are you journeying far?" the narrow-shouldered mother asked.

"Quite far. Wyoming, actually. Cheyenne."

"Why, what a splendid coincidence! Little Rachel and I are on our way to join my husband at Fort Russell! We'll practically be neighbors—for out west, anyway. I was afraid there wouldn't be a living soul with whom to pass the long, dreary journey we have ahead of us . . . that is, if you don't mind listening to a chatterbox. I do tend to get carried away—or so I've been told."

Drawing indescribable comfort from the very concept, Annora grinned. "I think that is what I need the most just now." She gathered her basket and handbag and moved to the empty seat just behind the one she now occupied to make conversation easier. "Chatter away."

By the time the western sky was displaying bands of deepening colors, Annora had acquired a new friend. *How like the Lord*, she decided, *to send along one of His angels—and a knowledgeable one at that*. She took it as a sign of God's approval.

After having come east for the birth of her first child, Hope was now leaving her parents' home in the Philadelphia suburb of Doylestown and making the return trip to her husband's side. She had not only made the westward journey once before, but she knew the intricacies of changing from one train to the next all along the route. Annora breathed a prayer of humble thankfulness, and the greatest sense of peace she had known in a very long time flowed through her being. It made the poignant memory of the bosom friend she'd left behind a little less sad.

Her trepidation at what lay ahead never quite left her, however. What if this Lucas Brent had already hired another housekeeper? What would she do then?

8

The hiss of steam and the clanging bell were deafening as Annora finally stepped off the train in Wyoming several endless days later. She moved as far from the noise as possible, staying out of the way of the clusters of people greeting arriving individuals or bidding farewell to those about to depart.

Her head buzzed with the information Hope Johnston had passed on regarding the territory in general and Cheyenne in particular. But despite all the preparation, Annora's heart plummeted when she took her first actual look at the bustling frontier town.

It was even worse than her imaginings. No cobbled, treelined streets here nor tidy rows of impressive business establishments. No huge river upon whose tides ocean vessels came and went. Instead, wooden sidewalks teemed with vagabond strollers, savage-looking miners, high-booted and shaggy-haired roughs, scouts in buckskins, young men wearing military blue, and rambunctious children. And there was no lack of saloons or gaming places. The loud ruckus spilling out of some buildings in the vicinity made that very obvious, as did the appearance of some rather scraggly-looking individuals loitering near them.

As Annora waited on the wide, level platform for her luggage to be unloaded, the hot afternoon wind whipped a sheet of dust over her. She brushed futilely at her already sooty and wrinkled traveling suit. Some grand impression she would make if Mr. Brent lived in town . . . and if he didn't, that presented problems of a whole different nature.

"There you go, Miss Nolan," a railroad man said, setting her trunk down next to the valise she had kept with her.

She smiled her thanks, wondering if there could possibly be a single article of clothing inside her luggage that would be less wrinkled than what she had on. During her final three days in Philadelphia, she had sneaked all the clothing she could manage over to Lesley's, and her friend had taken over, packing as much as would fit into an old trunk in her parents' attic. Annora wasn't even sure what all she had with her, and the best she'd been able to do during the journey was sponge her face and hands clean from time to time and brush as much soot from her ensemble as possible.

"Well, Annora," Hope said, approaching her from behind, "I wish you every happiness in your new venture."

Annora turned to step into a parting hug that included the two of them and tiny Rachel as well. "Thank you. I was so glad to find a friend on that tiresome trip, Hope. I'm convinced the Lord put you there just for me."

Easing away, the brunette smiled, cuddling her sleeping baby daughter closer. "Actually, I thought it was the other way around. But in any case, I, too, am glad to know I have a friend in Cheyenne. Our paths may cross again one of these days."

"Now, wouldn't that be a treat!"

"Indeed. Well, I must go and check to see what the departure time is for the stage to the fort. I'll be keeping you in my prayers."

"And I, you. Take care of that sweet little angel." Watching her new friend walk away, Annora felt greatly comforted just knowing that at least one familiar face lived in this wild, unknown territory. But she wasn't completely at ease after Hope strolled off. She was all on her own, now—and hadn't the slightest idea where to go.

Well, she affirmed silently, *I can start with the clerk at the ticket window.* "Excuse me, sir," she said, nearing him.

The short, small-featured man standing inside the cutout window of the station peered at her between the brim of his visor and a pair of spectacles perched halfway down his nose.

"I was wondering if you might be able to tell me where Mr. Lucas Brent lives or how I might contact him."

"Brent," he repeated, squinting his eyes in thought. "His place is half a dozen miles or so outside of town. But—" he pointed to someone loading a pair of barrels onto a wagon—"I reckon that young fellow over yonder should be able to take you right to the man's door. That's where he's goin'."

"Splendid!" Annora exclaimed, wondering over yet another miracle. Her parents had instilled in her long ago the fact that God cares for His own, and she was finding that to be very true. Had He arranged for this individual to be here at the very moment she needed transportation? She dared not consider what she'd do if he happened to refuse. Hope had reported that people in the territory were quite helpful and friendly, especially to newcomers, common as they were. Praying that was the case, Annora made her way to the young man's rig, glancing over his muscular frame and sable hair as she got closer. "I beg your pardon?"

Blue eyes glanced in her direction as he straightened. "Talking to me, miss?"

"Yes. I—I'm trying to get to Mr. Lucas Brent's place. Do you know where it is?" She nibbled her lip hopefully.

He eyed her boldly, a smile twitching a corner of his mouth. "Matter of fact, I do. You have business with him?"

"Yes. Well, no. That is . . . I'm hoping the position he advertised is still open. I've come to apply for it. I wrote him a letter—" Afraid to confess it had been barely two weeks past, Annora cut the explanation short. "I'd be willing to pay for a ride, if you see fit to take me there."

"You don't say." A spark of humor shone in his eyes as he appeared to consider the request, and for some reason it prickled Annora. "Have any luggage?"

"One trunk, plus a small valise."

"That's it?"

She nodded.

"Well, point me to them, miss. Looks like I'm your man."

Within moments, she found herself aboard the wagon seat, her baggage loaded into the bed of the rig. From this perspective she had an opportunity to get a closer look at the town she expected would be her new home.

Cheyenne did offer some respectability—at least for a span of two or three blocks—with neat brick buildings, an attractive show of shop windows, and even a three-story hotel. But beyond that it relapsed into a bold disregard of architectural style. Almost every ten paces along the dusty streets sat a saloon or barroom offering games of chance.

Annora was greatly relieved to count a few churches and a decent schoolhouse in passing as the driver guided the team out of town, heading westward. "I'm Annora Nolan," she finally remembered to say, her voice wavering as the wheels lurched over the uneven rats.

"Just call me Noah."

"That would be somewhat forward, I dare say."

He shrugged. "Not in these parts, it ain't."

Not entirely certain he wasn't toying with her, Annora felt a little ill at ease and shifted on the seat. But the smile he turned on her didn't seem particularly threatening, only—peculiar. She tried to relax, taking in the openness of the landscape in comparison to Pennsylvania's thickly forested hills. A liberal sprinkling of sagebrush and other strange-looking scrubby bushes dotted the parched grassland for miles. "Do you know Mr. Brent personally?" she asked after a short silence.

"You might say that."

"Oh, I suppose everyone knows everyone else around here."

He merely grinned.

Really! Annora thought. *I'm simply trying to make polite conversation.* Releasing a small sigh, she crossed her ankles and hands and straightened her spine. She directed her attention to the scenery again, wondering exactly how much farther it was to Mr. Brent's.

After an interminable amount of time, the wagon pulled off the main road and onto a lane. Once they had crested a small knoll, a group of farm buildings came into view. There was a rather dismal frame house with a porch across its front, a fairly large barn, and several outbuildings.

A wide section of land beyond had been plowed and planted with what appeared to have been corn, recently harvested. The leftover shocks had been cut and stacked about the field. Rows of other crops were also visible. The varied greens contrasted sharply to the surrounding arid land. "Is—is that—"

"Yep."

Annora waited for additional information, but none followed. She tamped down nervous flutterings in the pit of her stomach, wishing she had thought to prepare a speech during the oppressively silent drive from town. Only a few moments now remained to come up with one. She frowned in concentration. *Good day, Mr. Brent. I've come in answer to your notice.* At that inadequate try, she cringed. *Why, it's a pleasure to meet you, Mr. Brent. I do hope you received my letter.* She rolled her eyes, finally settling on a frantic silent prayer instead.

The petition was interrupted by girlish squeals. "Noah! Noah's coming!"

Annora followed the sound of the voices to two little urchins jumping up and down on the porch. And the nearer the rig drew to the place, the greater Annora's disquiet. The poor things were so thin. Thin and filthy, their little dresses soiled and torn.

As the children spied her, they turned silent and stood still, the older, one sliding an arm around the younger. Even as the assurance flowed through Annora that the position must still be open, doubts about her foolhardiness drained it away. Perhaps Mr. Brent was riffraff, the ungodly sort, impossible to work for. He might have even driven three or four applicants away already. And who knows what his temperament would be like? Her hands began to tremble.

Noah stopped the wagon near the edge of the yard and hopped down. Still staring at the unkempt children, Annora suddenly realized he was waiting to assist her. She gathered her courage and stood, then leaned into his upraised hands.

He set her on her feet. Then without a word, he went to unload her things before climbing aboard the rig and driving it toward the barn, whistling as he went.

Assuming that was where the goods from town needed to go, Annora smiled at the girls, who scarcely moved a muscle as they stared mutely at her. She shifted from one foot to the other, keenly aware that in all likelihood, she didn't look so good herself. "I've come to see your father," she finally said in what she hoped was a pleasant tone. "Is he here?"

The two exchanged wary glances, then the older one nodded.

"Would you please go and get him for me?"

After a split-second's hesitation, the pair took one another's hands and jumped off the porch, running past the barn.

❧

"Pa! Pa!"

Discerning an unusual note of alarm in his older daughter's voice, Lucas paused in replacing the chicken wire and turned so he could scoop the two children up in his arms the minute they reached him. He'd heard the wagon rumbling over the lane and concluded that Noah must have finally arrived with the supplies. But what could be upsetting the girls?

Melinda got to him first, and he wrapped one arm around her and the other around Amy, a step behind. "It's a lady, Pa. Come to see you."

A lady? The only one of those he knew was Rosemary, and the youngsters would surely recognize her. He scratched the few days' growth of stubble on his face. *Must be someone else from town.* With a shrug and a cheery grin at his daughters, he took each by the hand and allowed them to lead him to the house, wishing he could clean up a bit for *company*.

Coming within sight of the visitor waiting just shy of the porch, he stopped short. She was turned away slightly, her petite form as slim as a quill. Lucas had no idea what someone so young could want with him. Especially someone whose appearance was that of one who'd been traveling for a long time. He squeezed his daughters' hands and smiled down at them. "How about checking for any new eggs while I tend to the *lady*?"

"Yes, Pa." They skipped happily off, and Lucas continued up the path to the yard.

She swung to look at him as he approached.

Lucas had never seen eyes such a light green before—or did they just seem so?—set above fine, high cheekbones in that guileless face and crowned with slender tapered brows. He gave himself a mental shake. "My daughters said you were asking for me? I'm Lucas Brent. What can I do for you, miss?"

A tentative smile curved her rosy lips at the edges, and she extended a gloved hand. "Pleased to make your acquaintance. I'm Annora Nolan."

She'd said it like an announcement, but her name meant absolutely nothing to Lucas. He maintained a blank stare and watched her confidence fall a few notches.

"I–I wrote you a letter. Hasn't it arrived yet?"

"You mean—"

"Yes!" she gasped in relief, obviously assuming he knew what she was talking about. "I've come to apply for the position you advertised."

With a quick glance that took her in from head to toe, Lucas fought the urge to laugh in derision. A fragile, refined gal like her wasn't even old enough to have developed any of the qualifications a more mature woman would have arrived with. She was no more a housekeeper than he was a sawbones! And worse yet, even with that red hair of hers twisted into the semblance of a knot beneath that prim bonnet, she was hardly more than a baby herself! He needed help, sure—but this little filly would be just one more little girl to look after! The whole idea was absurd. He opened his mouth to tell her just that.

Noah chose just that moment to stroll up from the barn. "See you've met our new housekeeper," he said, grinning like a barn cat by a pail of spilled milk.

Lucas branded his kid brother with a sizzling glare. "And just what part did you play in this?"

Shoulders and brows rose as one in supreme innocence. "She asked me to drive her here. That's as much as I know."

Returning his attention to the visitor, Lucas saw shock tinged with mortification paint two rosy circles on her fair cheeks. Lips pressed into a thin line, she gaped from Noah to him, then back, looking from all appearances as if she was on the verge of bolting and running the whole seven miles back to town.

He held up a calming hand. "All right. Let's stop this whole thing here and now. I need to get a few little details straight. First of all, Miss—Nolan, did you say?"

She nodded, a frown still crinkling her brows.

"I take it you've met my brother, Noah."

Her eyes hardened. "He only gave his first name. I assumed he was a delivery man."

Noah averted his gaze and tried to appear guiltless, even with his tongue teasing his cheek.

"Figures," Lucas grated in disgust. He switched back to the redhead. "And you say you wrote me a letter."

She swallowed. "Yes. From Philadelphia. I saw your notice on the public board at my church and applied for the position some weeks ago."

Noah drew a crumpled blue-gray envelope from the inside pocket of his vest. "Postmaster gave this to me today. Says he found it wedged between the wall and his desk. Didn't know how long it'd been there."

At the sight of the stationery she had found in Mrs. Baxter's old lap desk, Annora realized he had never even gotten it! She wanted to crawl into the nearest hole. And die.

Lucas kneaded his jaw. Reaching for the missive, he opened it and scanned through the single page she had written. Then he released a whoosh of breath. He'd been stupid enough to think every unimaginable thing that could possibly happen to a man had already come his way. But now this!

He turned to his brother. "Hitch the wagon back up," he ordered sternly, avoiding the girl's widening green eyes. "Miss Nolan needs a ride to town."

9

No!" Realizing she had actually stomped her foot, Annora felt her face turn a vivid shade of crimson as Noah halted in his tracks and turned.

Both men's astonished blue eyes leveled straight on her.

Annora centered on the most penetrating ones, those in dark-haired Lucas Brent's unsmiling face, and spoke much more softly to regain her composure. "I can't go back. Please, don't send me away."

The brothers swapped incredulous glances, and the elder of the two shook his head. "Look, miss, I'm sure you meant well by taking it upon yourself to come here unannounced—"

"I sent a letter," Annora reiterated slowly, distinctly.

He turned his gaze skyward and shrugged, palms up.

Annora had no choice but to plead her case. "The notice said 'In desperate need.' Has that changed? Has anyone else come to help out? Or even offered?"

"No," Mr. Brent admitted.

"Then, give me a chance. That's all I ask. I've come all this way, and—"

"She's right." Noah, who had only watched the exchange up until this point, finally spoke up.

The farmer cut him a glower. "Don't be ridiculous." Switching his attention to Annora once more, he shifted his stance and raised a callused hand as if he was about to shake a finger in her face. But with an exasperated huff, he lowered his arm instead. "Miss Nolan."

She bristled at his placating tone.

"I appreciate your generous offer," he went on. "I really do. But as you can see, I already have two little girls to look after. I do not—I repeat, *not*—need a third. If you really want to help me out, go back home. I'm sure your parents are worried about you."

Annora hiked her chin. "My parents are dead. I have no home."

"About figures," he mumbled under his breath.

Spying the children heading toward them, the egg basket looped over the older one's arm, Annora moved a little farther out on the limb. "And it appears to me your daughters could stand a little more 'looking after.'"

Noah snickered.

Lucas Brent's head drooped, and he rubbed at his temples. He did not say a word.

"A month." Annora urged in her most businesslike manner. "Give me a month's trial. Let me prove I can cook, clean, and care for your daughters. Then if you feel I'm not doing a good job, or if another woman comes along whom you feel is better qualified, you . . . you can ask me to leave."

"Sounds fair enough," Noah piped in.

His older brother opened his mouth to reply, but one of the children sidled up to him, shyly taking stock of the stranger. "I'm hungry, Pa. When's supper?"

Annora thought she discerned an easing of the man's determination, a slight resignation in the sag of one broad shoulder. He gazed down at his girls, then up at her. "You say you can cook?"

"That's right."

"Well, then, there's the house. Let's see what you can do." He turned on his heel and strode back in the direction from which he'd come.

A fraction of Annora's fear subsided. He was giving her a chance!

"Whoo-eee!"Noah smacked one knee with his open palm and sauntered to the barn.

The girls, peering hesitantly after both of them, lifted their dirty faces to Annora. "What's your name, lady?"

❧

Annora's spirit had hit rock bottom at her first disheartening glimpse of the chaos greeting her inside the dwelling. But after unearthing some dried fruit for the girls to nibble on while they went back outside to play, she slipped off the jacket of Lesley's once-spotless suit, rolled up her sleeves, and filled a big kettle with water to heat on the cookstove. She turned and faced the disaster behind her and took a deep breath. She would set the living quarters to rights or die trying . . . and for the first time ever, she thanked her Heavenly Father for all those months she'd been forced into drudgery at the Baxters'.

Melinda and Amy had shown her to the smokehouse, so Annora put some meat on to stew while she labored with broom, scrub brush, and dust cloth. Before long the hidden charm of the little house began to make its appearance. Annora tried to envision a young wife and mother bustling about, tidying up, rubbing oil into the mantel, shining the glass chimneys of the lamps . . . typical duties that maintained a proper home. And there were a few inexpensive pieces of bric-a-brac and framed embroidered samplers on the walls, niceties that a woman takes pleasure in displaying. She wondered what sort of woman the late mistress of the house had been.

Then Annora's thoughts drifted to the tall, lean-faced man who at present was her employer. She estimated he was at least ten years her senior. His bluish-gray eyes were shaded by straight brows the identical black-brown of his hair . . . and held more than a trace of sadness. But it wasn't hard to imagine that tanned face without its set jaw, without the creases the obvious intense pain of bereavement had wrought.

In fact, she decided, he could actually be considered quite . . . handsome, under all that stubble. She had caught tiny glimpses of his softer side when he looked at his daughters. Surely even someone as gruff as he could not be all bad. But considering how intimidated she had felt in his presence, Annora blushed at the shameless way she had stood up to him. She had even surprised herself, if the truth were told—but she chalked it up to desperation bringing previously unknown qualities to the fore.

Chopping fresh vegetables and adding them to the stew, she inhaled the rich broth simmering on the stove and concluded it would turn out as tasty as Mrs. Henderson's. The woman had been a wonderful teacher. Now, to stir up some biscuits.

It was dusk by the time Annora finished the living room and kitchen. Way past the normal supper hour. But stepping out onto the porch to ring the dinner bell, she knew it could have been much worse. She willed aside the aching of her entire body and clanged the iron rod against the triangle, fighting an impulse to laugh as a veritable stampede of feet followed immediately.

"Hey, you two. Wash up for supper," Lucas ordered, snagging his little girls midstep in their mad dash to the porch. He steered them to the rain barrel and dipped a liberal amount into the basin on the stand beside it. While they soaped their hands, he took a towel and scrubbed the childish faces. Then they scampered off. He splashed some of the cold liquid over his face and neck, dried off, and followed the tantalizing and almost forgotten smell of good cooking into his house.

He could not believe his eyes. For the first time since Francie's passing, the place—at least what he could see of it from the doorway—was clean and orderly. The table sported a fresh tablecloth, something he never bothered with. And Miss Nolan had even cut some roses from the scraggly bush outside for the middle of the table.

"These are my mama's Sunday dishes," Melinda said accusingly, as she and her sister climbed onto their chairs. "We're not supposed to use the Sunday dishes unless there's company."

"Company," Amy echoed with a decided nod.

Carrying a serving bowl of stew over from the sideboard, Annora Nolan blanched, making the sprinkling of freckles across the bridge of her pert nose more distinct.

Lucas knew only a blind man would fail to see how spent the young woman was when she set the burden down. A twinge of remorse shot through him at the thought of how he'd taken advantage of her . . . dumping the whole sorry mess on those slender shoulders, and after that exhausting journey, yet! He ruffled his older daughter's hair. "It's all right, pumpkin. Miss Nolan *is* company tonight."

The explanation seemed to satisfy the girls.

Noah clomped across the porch and entered then, his face aglow from a vigorous washing. A grin broadened his boyish features, sending a twinkle to his eyes as he pulled out a chair and sat down. "I'd say you've got yourself a job, little lady. I won't need to be traipsin' off to town to get a decent meal anymore, with you around."

She almost smiled as she set a plate of hot biscuits next to the stew, then turned away.

"Aren't you eating?" Lucas asked with a frown.

"I'll wait until the family is finished," she said, casting her gaze to the floor. "I'm only the housekeeper."

"Hmph. That might be the way things are done back East," he replied. "But out here, folks eat together. Set yourself a place."

"Yes, sir."

"And don't call me sir."

She caught her bottom lip in her teeth and did as told. After easing to her seat, she bowed her head.

Lucas stared for a second or two, and warmth climbed his neck. He cleared his throat. "We quit wasting time on grace here . . . but if you're set on it, we won't stop you." He lowered his head but did not close his eyes.

"Dear Heavenly Father," she began, "thank You for bringing me safely to Wyoming. We thank You for these provisions and ask Your blessing on them. And thank You that Mr. Brent has given me this chance. Please help me do my best for him. I ask these things in Your Son's name. Amen."

An uncomfortable knot formed in Lucas's throat. The simple way she talked to the Almighty brought a remembrance of Francie's intimate friendship with God—one he had shared—and another wave of guilt washed over him. He couldn't even remember the last time he had prayed. Collecting his thoughts, he ladled stew into his daughters' bowls and took some himself, savoring every mouthful as he ate . . . but never once meeting those arresting green eyes farther down the table.

"Mmm. This is real good," Amy proclaimed.

Melinda, downing her entire glass of milk in a quick succession of gulps, only nodded.

Noah, occupying the foot of the table, was already helping himself to seconds. "Best I've had in a dog's age," he said with a broad grin and reached for a couple more biscuits.

The delicious meal was already more than Lucas would have expected. But the warm apple pandowdy topped with rich cream earned applause from the little ones. He had to admit, it went perfectly with the fresh coffee in his mug.

Noting absently that there seemed a bit less conversation during dessert, Lucas chalked it up to the lateness of the hour, or the fact that everyone had been so hungry to start with. But suddenly even the girls stopped chattering. Looking up, he saw their attention was centered on Miss Nolan, sitting straight as a poker, her hands folded in her lap . . . sound asleep.

"Would you look at that," Noah murmured. "She's plumb wore out."

Feeling a new onslaught of reproach, Lucas quietly eased his chair back and got up, skirting the table. He swept the new housekeeper up into his arms and carried her to his bedroom, where he laid her gently on the bed and flicked a light blanket over her sleeping form.

The glow of the lamplight from the other room illuminated that classic, heart-shaped face of hers, now as innocent and trusting as a child's. Lucas caught himself staring, then shook his head and left the room, closing the door behind him without a sound.

Annora. He mulled it over in his mind. *Suits her.* She'd weighed less than a feather in his arms.

Then, before he let himself get caught up in thoughts he didn't need to be having, he strode purposely to the kitchen. The least he could do was get the dishes out of the way and dunk the girls in the tub. It would give the little gal from Philadelphia a bit less to wake up to.

But he couldn't help smiling at the remembered sight of the fiery young redhead asleep at the table.

*A*nnora sensed someone's presence as she slowly came to consciousness. She raised her lashes to find two sets of solemn blue eyes studying her.

The children were leaning over on the bed, elbows resting on it, chins cupped in their hands.

"She's waking up," Amy whispered.

Her big sister nudged her. "She's already awake, silly. See?"

With sudden awareness, Annora flew to a sitting position. It was morning! She was in someone's bed! Worse yet, she had no idea how she had gotten there. Even in her muddled state she absorbed the room's simple furnishings . . . a plain double bed, a washstand, and an armoire. Her trunk and valise had been set on the floor against one wall. But how had she come to be here?

"This is our mama's bed," Melinda announced.

"Pa had to sleep outside," the little one added.

"In the barn."

Trying to process that humiliating information, Annora went back in her mind over the previous evening. The last she could recall, she had just served dessert and was listening to the pleasant chatter between the young sisters about a special new litter of barn kittens. There was a tiny fragment of a dream, however, of being held in someone's arms . . . She swallowed. "I—I must make breakfast!"

"Huh-uh," they chorused, heads wagging slowly back and forth.

"You've already eaten?

They nodded.

Annora's heart sank. The very first day in this household, trying to prove she could take care of all the necessary duties, and she'd overslept! Disgusted with herself, she cast her gaze toward the ceiling, then swung her legs over the side of the mattress and stood. "Well, then, I'll have to find something else to do, won't I?" She smiled at the urchins, noticing that even though they were wearing the same clothes as yesterday, they themselves appeared cleaner.

"You prob'ly have to go to the privy," Melinda informed her in six-year-old importance.

"You can use the pot under the bed," Amy suggested.

Despite her disquiet, Annora barely stifled a giggle. She was going to like these two. Looking from one to the other, she affirmed their opposite coloring, something she had noticed only subconsciously in the busyness of yesterday. Melinda, the older one, had her father's olive complexion and brunette hair, whereas four-year-old Amy was fair and golden blond. But they were equally engaging. She smiled at them both, then focused on Melinda. "After I've been to the privy, I'll need to find the washtub and soap so I can start on the laundry."

"Come on. I'll show you." The dark-haired youngster slid a small hand into Annora's and began leading her toward the kitchen door. "Pa already filled the big kettle. It's on the stove."

Chagrined, Annora had to be thankful that she wouldn't be wasting still more of this morning waiting for the water to heat. But how would she ever face Mr. Brent after this blunder? As it was, the very sight of those blue eyes of his sent feelings through her that she had never before experienced. And something about his presence made her knees feel a little weak. But whatever low opinion he must surely have of her now, she would, at the very least, see to it that he and his brother had a decent dinner, come noon.

Thanks to the helpful little guides, Annora soon found herself up to her elbows in sudsy water. Within a couple hours, the two long clotheslines were filled with newly washed items billowing in the ever-present breeze. The sight was gratifying, as was the amazing speed at which they dried. She even felt better herself, having freshened up in the privacy of the bedroom and changed into a navy cotton skirt and plain white shirtwaist.

Returning to the kitchen, she raised the towel covering the rising bread to check its progress, then smiled. The loaves would be done for supper. Right now, everyone would have to settle for more biscuits. She gave the big pot of beans and bacon a stir, then removed a double batch of golden biscuits from the oven. With a quick glance at the table, she smiled her approval and went to ring the bell.

❧

Lucas wiped his mouth on the cloth napkin and got up, shoving the chair away with the backs of his knees. "That was one fine meal, Miss Nolan. Thank you."

"I'm glad you enjoyed it," she said softly.

"That's puttin' it mildly," Noah declared. "I was starved without even knowin' it!" Snatching one more biscuit from the diminished stack, he pocketed it in his jeans and gave a satisfied nod as he headed outside.

Noting that his brother had spent the better portion of the meal gawking at *the help*, Lucas quickly followed after him. He'd better remind the kid that this arrangement was only temporary.

"Mr. Brent?"

One foot already over the threshold, Lucas paused and turned, a hand braced on the doorjamb.

"I—I must apologize," Annora stammered. "About last night, I mean. Falling asleep, and all."

"Happens to the best of us, one time or another," he said gently. Unable to put out of his mind how young and vulnerable she had appeared when he'd placed her on the bed, he had purposely refrained from looking directly at her during the meal. Now, however, he could no longer avoid it.

In everyday clothes, her hair brushed and pinned in an intricate coil at the nape of her neck, she seemed more delicate than ever. And who could miss the way the waistband of Francie's long apron met in the middle of her back, with the ties dangling almost to her ankles? She seemed like a little girl playing at being grown up.

All the more reason not to saddle her with the endless chores running this house entailed. He really wanted someone older. Someone . . . substantial. But he'd as much as agreed to this trial, so no sense putting a damper on things. She was trying real hard to please . . . and this would only be for a couple weeks. What could happen? He winced. Better have that talk with Noah. Today.

~❧

Once the dishes had been taken care of and the kitchen restored to order, Annora retrieved a bar of rose-scented soap from her valise and took the remains of the heated water in the kettle outside near the rain barrel. She knew the men were occupied, and this was a perfect opportunity to tend to another desperately needed chore.

"What 'cha doin'?"

Annora smiled at the girls as they gravitated to her from the porch step, where they'd been standing all the extra clothes-pins in a row. "I need to wash my hair."

"In the daytime?" Melinda's tone indicated the concept was completely unheard of.

"Well, I got kind of dirty on my long train ride, and this is the first chance I've had to wash some of that off."

"Oh."

Unpinning her chignon, Annora bent over at the waist and poured warm water over her head. Even just that felt wonderful. She had never before gone an extended period without having a chance to bathe properly. Application of the soap made leftover soot from the tiring journey feel like grit under her fingertips, but at least it was coming out.

"Mama had long hair like yours," Amy said wistfully.

"Only it wasn't red," Melinda supplied. "It was blond like Amy's."

"You must miss her a lot." Reaching for the pitcher again, Annora dipped it into the rain barrel, then squeezed her eyes closed as she rinsed with the cool, clean water.

"Why did God take our mama away?" Melinda asked.

The poignant question tore at Annora's heart. She knew exactly how the little ones felt. Wrapping her hair in one of the clean towels, she flipped it behind her back and stooped down to their level. "I'm afraid only God knows that for sure, sweetheart."

"Miss Rosemary, in town, says God needed Mama to help Him in Heaven. But we need her, too."

Annora wondered who Rosemary was and what her relationship to this little family might be, then decided that the matter would probably become clear during the month ahead. Turning her attention to the children again, she gathered them close. "Well, whatever the Lord's reasons for taking her, that doesn't mean He doesn't still love you. Your mama still loves you, too, and she'll always be with you in your heart. She probably asked God to send extra angels to watch over you, since she can't do it herself."

"Do you think so?"

"Mm-hm. Know what else?"

"What?"

"My mommy and daddy live up there, too. I'll wager they were real happy to have your mama for their new neighbor. They've probably been showing her all around those golden streets and introducing her to Ruth and Jonah and the apostle Paul."

Amy's azure eyes grew soft as she appeared to ponder the thought. Then she brightened. "Wanna come see the new baby kitties in the barn?"

"Their eyes aren't open yet," Melinda added. "They're so cute."

"I'd really like that—if you'll help me for a little while in the garden afterward."

The pair traded glances and nodded.

❧

Grooming Chesapeake in the end stall, Lucas heard the patter of skipping feet approaching. He glanced up at the cheerful threesome—his two little ones and a gal who could easily pass for their older sister. Especially with that red-gold hair of hers loose and splayed over her shoulders. It didn't seem fair for someone so fragile as she to have so much responsibility laid on her all at once. Obviously she was an efficient worker, but he couldn't get past the conviction that she should still be at home, helping her own mother or aunt or other relative. Even having some fun.

He wasn't purposely trying to hide his presence, but as they clustered around the box of sleeping kittens, they were obviously unaware that he was there. Muted oohs drifted to his ears as they fawned over the tiny creatures. Not wanting to intrude, Lucas kept stroking the brush over the sorrel back.

"Pa says we can't pick them up yet," Melinda said.

Amy nodded. "It makes Wilhelmina nervous."

Miss Nolan had an arm on each of the girls' shoulders, and she drew them a little closer to herself. "Well, thank you for showing me your special kitties. Wilhelmina doesn't know who I am yet, though, so I'd better get back to work now."

"Didn't you say we could help?" Melinda asked.

"If you want to."

Watching after them as they exited the barn, Lucas reminded himself to concentrate on what he was doing. But the animal's reddish hide reminded him of Annora Nolan's shiny hair. Stifling any further thoughts, he patted the stallion's muscled neck and put down the brush. This was as good a time as any to talk to Noah.

He found his brother just outside, lounging against the fence, still grasping the hoe he was returning to the shed.

"She's some looker, ain't she?" Noah remarked. "Can't be more'n two or three years younger than me, either. Maybe I'll—"

"No, you won't. She's here for that month she talked her way into. No more. You leave her be."

A corner of Noah's mouth rose sardonically. "What I do is my business."

"As long as you're on my place, it's not." Lucas wrapped his fingers around the handle of Noah's hoe, his gaze unrelenting in a silent challenge.

"We'll have to see about that, won't we?" With a snide grimace, the kid jerked the tool free and stalked off toward the shed.

Lucas released a pent-up breath. Maybe he should rethink this whole matter of her staying, before things got too sticky.

❧

Annora picked up on a subtle tension between the brothers that evening as they ate their ham slices and mashed potatoes in stony silence.

Feeling the outsider, she pretended not to notice and did her best to respond to the girls' remarks whenever necessary. But she was relieved when dessert was over and everyone started to go their separate ways.

She snagged her employer again as he was about to leave the house. "Mr. Brent?"

He glanced over his shoulder, then turned to face her.

"I've been thinking," she began. "About the sleeping arrangements."

"We'll just keep them as they are, for now."

"But that's not necessary, really. I shouldn't be putting you out of your own bed. Your daughters need you to be near if they wake up in the middle of the night."

"So what are you suggesting? The barn, maybe? Noah sleeps in the loft."

Annora took no offense at his slightly suggestive tone but held her ground. "There are plenty of blankets. I'll make a pallet in the girls' room, and—"

A raising of his hand cut her off. "Nice of you to offer, miss, but there's no extra floor space in there."

"Well, perhaps—"

Mr. Brent gave a weary shake of his dark head and grew serious. "Look, the truth is, you should have a place to call your own. Tomorrow I'll see about clearing out the lean-to on the side of the house. It's not big or fancy, but it'll take a narrow bed, and it's private. You can use that as long as you're here."

The last statement sounded a touch unsettling, but Annora didn't want to make any more waves than she had already. She gave a consenting nod. "Whatever you say. I'm only sorry I'm making extra work when I came with the intention of being a help."

When his compelling eyes turned straight on her, she realized how seldom an occurrence that was—how he seemed to put a lot of effort into never quite looking at her. Annora pondered that knowledge in the brief pause before he spoke.

"You know," he admitted, "even though I'd sent all those notices east and was hoping somebody'd show up—I didn't expect anyone actually would, especially without giving me time to prepare. I should have been ready in case." The hint of a smile emerged. "And you are a help, I can't deny that. A man almost forgets what it's like to have a . . . to have—someone—looking after his house."

Taking the comment as a compliment, she warmed under it.

"So, for the rest of the month, the lean-to will have your name on it." With a decided nod, he turned and left.

The warmth she'd felt quickly evaporated, and she stood where she was, staring after him. *You must be extremely sure I'm not going to work out, aren't you? Well, you must never have met a determined woman before.*

Throwing back her shoulders, Annora moved to clear the table.

11

*C*lose your eyes," Melinda said, taking Annora's hand.

"It's a surprise." Amy slipped her tiny fingers into Annora's other hand, and the two girls led her away from the well where she had gone to draw water for cooking.

"How can I see anything with my eyes closed?" Annora teased as she gingerly navigated the unseen, uneven ground under the warm Wyoming sunshine.

"I'll tell you when you can look," Melinda replied.

Annora did her best to retain a puzzled expression but surmised they were taking her to the lean-to, which had been the source of a considerable amount of hammering, sawing, and muffled mutterings throughout the morning. Her suspicions proved correct when the girls stopped a short distance later and a door squeaked open.

"Surprise!" the little ones chorused.

Opening her eyes, Annora saw that the simple structure abutting the house had, indeed, been turned into a room for her. It appeared a mite cramped, and its dirt floor rendered it even less elegant than her attic quarters in Philadelphia, but at least it was private.

She surveyed the plain narrow cot with the washstand next to it, noting a newly cut window in the side wall that would provide her with light. The interior was fragrant with the scent of the new wood Mr. Brent had used to make shutters. Surely her presence here would no longer seem such an imposition on everyone now that she had a place of her own!

"Like it?" towheaded Amy asked.

Annora ruffled the child's golden hair. "It's fine. Just fine. It'll do quite nicely, I'm sure."

"There's extra blankets in the trunk in Pa's room," Melinda announced.

"Good. I'll get my bed made up for later. Want to help bring out my things?"

The better part of the next half-hour saw the three parading back and forth between there and the house, readying the new quarters for occupancy. When the last of her possessions had been transferred, Annora excused the girls to run and play while she made up her bed.

Just as she finished, a shadow fell across the room's interior. She had not heard approaching footsteps but looked up to see Noah leaning against the doorjamb, his expression unreadable.

"Probably not quite what you're used to," he said.

Choosing to ignore the quality of familiarity in the young man's gaze, Annora smiled. "Oh, it's more than adequate. I appreciate all the trouble this caused you and Mr. Brent."

He shrugged offhandedly. "Actually, it—"

"Don't you have some chores to finish up?" his brother's voice interrupted from behind him.

One side of Noah's mouth tightened, and he turned his eyes upward. "Yes, sir," he said, snapping around with overplayed compliance. He wheeled about and strode away in a huff.

Mr. Brent came closer and peered inside. "We'll try to get a proper floor in here in the next couple days," he said, his tone apologetic, "plus make sure it won't be drafty at night."

Annora gave a cursory nod as she watched his glance roam the limited space. He had taken to shaving every morning, and she couldn't help but notice how much younger he appeared, despite a persistent five o'clock shadow that resurfaced by midday. Still, she was far from comfortable in his commanding presence, and she switched her attention to the immediate area around her before her thoughts wandered any further.

"Have to make a trip into town tomorrow," her employer said after a short lapse of silence, "to take another load of potatoes to the store and pick up a couple of mares due to come in on the train. You're welcome to tag along and pick out some yard goods for a curtain."

"Thank you. I'd like that very much." Her subdued answer belied the sheer delight caused by the opportunity of going to some actual shops.

"We'll make a day of it, then. It'll be a treat for the girls."

"Shall I make a basket lunch?"

Mr. Brent shook his head. "We'll leave after breakfast and pick up something while we're there."

~❧~

After a surprisingly restful night in her new bed, Annora rose early and dressed, then enjoyed some quiet moments in prayer before starting breakfast. She had heard the farmer exit the kitchen door a short time ago and assumed he was seeing to his morning routine, which included taking the stallion for his usual daily workout.

The girls were still in bed when she went inside, but their quiet whispers and darling giggles carried easily to Annora's ears. She knew the little ones had to be excited about the planned outing. Tiptoeing to their open doorway, she peeked in at them, catching their bright smiles. "Good morning, sweethearts."

Melinda sprang to a sitting position. "We're goin' to town today."

"All of us," her sister added. "You, too, Pa says."

"That's right. So how about washing up and putting on your prettiest dresses," Annora suggested. "And don't forget to make your bed."

"Aw . . . are we gonna haveta do that every day?" the older child asked. "Pa never made us."

"Well, that's because you were just little girls up until now. But since you've been helping with chores so nicely, you're starting to become young ladies."

"Ladies?" Amy sputtered into a giggle. "Like Miss Rosemary?"

Melinda poked her in the ribs. "No, silly. She said *young ladies*. That means—" She thought for a second. "—big girls. Right?" The questioning expression she raised to Annora was almost comical.

"Right." Annora was hard pressed to contain a smile. "And even better, it shows you have love in your heart. That's what families do. Each person helps the other, then everybody is happy."

A dubious glance passed between them, then the older sibling nodded. "Happy is nice. We'll make the bed. Come on, Sissy."

As the two settled to their task, Annora returned to the kitchen to strain the pail of fresh milk on the sideboard and prepare breakfast. But reminded again of the elusive Miss Rosemary, her curiosity was piqued.

After the family finished eating and the kitchen had been set to rights, Lucas Brent went to hitch up the wagon. The girls wasted no time in jumping aboard. Annora climbed up with proper decorum, only to discover she would either have to sit between the two Brent brothers or ride in back with the girls. When she chose the latter, her employer clucked the workhorses forward.

The Indian summer day added gentle beauty to the open countryside, and soft breezes stirred the drying grasses and fading vegetation as the wheels crunched along the rutted road.

While Melinda and Amy giggled over the excitement of going to town, Annora watched the play of sunlight against Mr. Brent's muscular shoulders as he and Noah chatted quietly up front. In his form-fitting jeans, work shirt, and Stetson, the farmer fit in naturally with this open, untamed country. She could not even imagine him in a proper dark suit, confined behind a desk in some city office.

Nevertheless, Annora had dismissed immediately upon arriving at the Brent farm the farfetched notion of this position ever leading to marriage. Truth was, she was in no hurry to wed anyone—ever—especially a man much older than she. All she wanted was for this trial period to work out so she could stay until a better opportunity presented itself. She was determined never to return to Philadelphia as long as she lived! Pressing her lips together in confirmation, she diverted her attention to the passing landscape, catching an over-the-shoulder glance from Noah as she did so. It was not the first she'd noticed in the last couple days, but she paid him no mind.

Cheyenne, never peaceful or idyllic even at the best moments, was its normal bustling self, with a liberal assortment of humanity thronging the dusty streets between business establishments. Reading the hand-painted signs identifying those the wagon passed, Annora was mildly surprised when Mr. Brent halted the team before, of all places, a millinery.

He turned to her. "I have to pick up some mending we left here last time. You might as well come in. After that, I'd appreciate it if you'd ride herd on the girls while Noah and I take care of business."

"Of course."

"Think I'll check with the postmaster while the rest of you go in there," Noah announced, helping Melinda down while Annora handed Amy to her father.

Wondering if word would come soon from another applicant for her position, Annora quashed her uneasiness, then allowed Mr. Brent to lower her to her feet. She purposely did not permit herself to reflect upon how strong his touch had felt upon her waist but joined him and his daughters as they clomped over the wooden walkway to the store's entrance.

A small bell above the door tinkled as they went inside, the sound bringing a slim young woman from the back room. Petite in stature, she was scarcely an inch taller than Annora and was impeccably attired in a rich shade of sapphire that accented the flawless, fair complexion beneath her coronet of golden braids. The few wispy hairs that formed curls alongside her face only added to the delicacy of her feminine features.

"Good day, Miss Rosemary," the little ones singsonged.

"Girls." The polite smile curving the lady's lips split into a warm grin as her shrewd hazel eyes settled on Mr. Brent. "Lucas." They narrowed almost imperceptibly when they came to Annora.

"Rosemary," the farmer said, tipping his hat. "Thought I'd stop by for the mending."

"I see. It's in back. I'll just be a moment." Flicking another glance in Annora's direction, she went through the curtain panels separating the main room from the work area and returned seconds later. "You have company?" she asked pointedly, handing him a wrapped parcel.

"Miss Annora's our new housekeeper," Melinda said proudly.

"*Housekeeper.*" The bonnetmaker's tone fairly dripped with incredulity.

"She's been sleepin' in Pa's room," Amy elaborated. "But Uncle Noah helped him build a new one for her."

Annora felt her face flush with the implication that could be taken from Amy's innocent comment and thought she detected a noticeable ruddiness about Mr. Brent's neck as he shifted his weight from one foot to the other.

He cleared his throat. "I'd like you to meet Annora Nolan, Rosemary. She's from the East. Came in answer to my notice. Annora, this is Rosemary Evans, a friend of ours."

"I'm pleased to make your acquaintance, ma'am," Annora said, mustering her friendliest smile.

The woman stared in cool appraisal momentarily, then she gave a perfunctory nod. "*Housekeeper,*" she repeated in disbelief. "Now I've heard everything."

Trying very hard not to be offended by the less-than-enthusiastic greeting or the insinuation behind it, Annora chewed the inside corner of her lip and averted her attention to some of the fashionable hats on display stands about the room.

Mr. Brent finally responded. "Yes, well," he said with a shrug, "thanks for taking care of these. I'll settle up with you when I get back from the bank."

Mildly annoyed that he hadn't bothered to explain, Annora stole a quick glance through her lashes at the store's owner.

If Rosemary Evans was put off by his obvious omission, she concealed the fact. "No hurry. I trust you, Lucas. You should know that by now."

He nodded, then offered his free hand to his younger daughter. "Come on, pumpkin. We'll let Miss Rosemary get back to work. How about you and Melinda showing Annora around while your uncle and I see to business?"

"Oh, goodie," Amy said, raising her adoring gaze to him.

Claiming Melinda, Annora followed her employer to the door, aware of those icy eyes watching her departure. She was relieved to step back out into the sunshine once more. But the chilly reception she had received from the bonnetmaker stole some of the enjoyment from Annora's day—especially when a passing glance or two at the millinery during the next hour or so revealed the Evans woman staring out at her. Realizing the lady must actually view her as a rival for Mr. Brent's attentions, Annora shook her head, sloughing off the ludicrous possibility.

❧

Later that night, after the weary girls had been tucked into bed, and the men had gone to the barn to look after the new horses, Annora sought the sanctuary of the lean-to.

Neatly folded atop her coverlet lay the yard goods she'd chosen. She picked up the material and shook it out, then held the fabric up to the window. The bright yellow calico would definitely add cheer to the dismal room, she decided with satisfaction. Setting it aside, she gazed at her other purchase, one which a small amount of her remaining traveling funds had provided—a supply of writing paper. She had only begun to realize how much she missed Lesley.

After lighting the bedside lamp, Annora sat cross-legged on her cot and smoothed a sheet of paper over the lap desk she had borrowed from the house. She thought for a moment, then began writing:

Dear Lesley,

It seems ages since I last set eyes upon that smiling face of yours. I missed you from the onset and thought of you throughout my long, exhausting rail journey. The Lord did provide me with a rather nice woman friend on the train, but I will elaborate on her another time. There is far too much other news to tell you just now.

I pray you and Michael did not suffer undue consequences for my fleeing Philadelphia. My conscience still pricks over having deceived my guardians, as I know they truly meant well. Nevertheless, I am convinced I made the right choice in coming to Wyoming.

This farm is several miles outside Cheyenne, so I had to get used to being somewhat apart from even that limited amount of civilization. I do like the open country, especially at sunset, when the whole sky is ablaze with vivid color.

I must admit, my sudden appearance here caught everyone off guard. Somehow my letter had gotten waylaid, so I actually arrived before my missive. It made things a bit awkward at first, but I pleaded for Mr. Brent to give me a month in which to prove myself. If that works out, I shall be satisfied to remain here indefinitely. I am not entertaining the slightest notion of someday marrying the man. He seems a decent sort but is somewhat older. I also believe there is a woman in town who has designs on him.

I do love his little girls, however. Melinda and Amy are adorable. They seem to enjoy having someone around to read to them and spend time with them, but at the same time, they show a natural possessiveness about their late mother's things. Once their father assured them I am here only temporarily, they were more able to accept my presence.

Tapping her pencil against her teeth in thought, Annora debated whether to mention Noah, then continued:

Mr. Brent's younger brother, Noah, also lives here on the farm. He does not impress me as much more than a shiftless prankster, but he is quite handsome. No doubt he turns a few heads among the eligible young women in town, but he has not spoken of any in particular.

We have not as yet attended Sunday services. That does feel strange, after having almost lived at church during the past three years. I shall inquire about going this week's end. Surely my employer is concerned about the eternal fate of his daughters' souls.

In case you have no time to spend reading overlong letters, I shall close for now. But please know, dear Lesley, that I shall

perish unless I hear from you soon. Until then, do take care. Give
Michael my warmest regards, and may the Lord bless you always.
With deepest affection,
I remain your friend,
Annora

Scanning the entire letter through, Annora folded it and tucked it into an envelope to be ready for delivery on the next trip to town. But it took awhile for the pang of homesickness for her best friend to subside.

Annora could not help wondering if she would ever feel at home anywhere, ever again.

(12)

*A*nnora's immersion into the backlog of household duties made the next week pass quickly for her. Harvest and its related field work had all but come to an end, along with the long laborious hours of backbreaking toil that normally occupied the men during the warm weather. Mr. Brent was free to turn his attention to other matters—and with the acquisition of the two mares he'd sent for, his high spirits lent a more buoyant air to the atmosphere around the farm.

His optimism spilled over onto his daughters, who now helped willingly with daily household chores in return for horseback rides with their father. Annora decided not to let the girls' cheerfulness go to waste. Concluding that her employer wouldn't deem it a proper use of time to drive to the school in Cheyenne every day until both children were old enough to enroll, she planned to start spending part of their story-reading sessions teaching them the alphabet.

One afternoon, while taking down some wash, Annora caught a glimpse of Mr. Brent putting Chesapeake through his paces. Curious, she went to the corral fence and climbed up on a low rung to watch, fascinated by his skill and his obvious love for the spirited mount. She couldn't help but admire the beautiful reddish-brown horse with its black mane, tail, and points.

"They're something, ain't they?" Noah, just back from town, took the spot next to her, chewing absently on the stem of a long weed he had quirked in one corner of his mouth. His shirt sleeve rested against Annora's bare arm.

Uncomfortable at his nearness, she shifted her weight slightly away from him. "I've never seen prettier horses," she answered casually, her sweeping glance including the mares serenely exploring an adjacent section of the corral. One was a black color with a silky mane and tail, and the other, gray with speckled hindquarters. Even the workhorses were fine-looking creatures and had temperaments almost as pleasant as the milk cow grazing in the pasture.

"Well, if there's one thing that brother of mine is a good judge of, it's horseflesh. This is the beginning of his grand dream, you know."

"Oh?" Annora turned toward the young man.

"Yep. All this farmin', it's just been a means to an end. Sale of the excess crops to the local stores has provided capital he's been needin' to buy stock. With all the big cattle spreads in the territory, he figures there'll be a steady market for good, trained mounts in the future. He wants to raise 'em."

Annora returned her attention to the working pair. "Is that your dream, too?"

Noah gave a derisive snort. "Nah. If I ever get wind of a new gold strike anywhere, I'm off to parts unknown. Don't have the patience Lucas has, to spend years and years developing a herd of prize stock." Removing his wide-brimmed hat, he used it to point with as he blotted his forehead on his other sleeve. "Take old Ches, now. He has enough thoroughbred in him to make him fast. Real fast. Meanwhile, his pacer blood makes him agile. And the mares, they're strong and sturdy. Should make a good combination of qualities for cattle ponies. Course, Lucas'll keep adding to his breeding stock, too, as his finances allow."

Contemplating the information while Noah replaced his hat, Annora admired the sorrel's fluid movements—to say nothing of those of his owner. They moved and worked as one, the beautiful animal responding to the slightest flick of the rein from his master.

"Do you ride?" Noah asked suddenly.

"Me?" she asked with a light laugh. "No. I've never been around horses much."

"I'd be glad to teach you sometime." A provocative smirk tugged at his mouth.

Somehow, surmising he had other things in mind besides mere riding lessons, Annora heard an alarm bell go off in her head. She hopped down from the fence rail. "Thanks." She brushed the fence dust from her hands. "But I doubt there'll be a chance for anything like that in the near future. I don't have much time left, you know, before my trial month is up."

He slanted her a lopsided grin, his blue eyes gleaming. "What makes you think you won't get the job permanent?"

"I haven't heard anything that would make me think so."

"Well, now, you just never know, do you?" He cast a glance in his brother's direction, did a double-take, and sobered.

Annora noticed Mr. Brent eyeing the two of them.

Noah turned and started for the barn, then stopped. "Oh. By the way. Almost forgot. Postmaster gave me this for you." He reached inside his vest pocket and held a letter out to her.

"Truly?" Her heartbeat quickened as she unceremoniously grabbed the envelope. Recognizing Lesley's handwriting, she concluded that her own letter and Lesley's had probably crossed somewhere en route. She dashed to her private quarters and tore open the treasure, scanning its contents.

Dear Annora,

I am sending this in care of Mr. Brent in the hope that it will find you. I knew I would miss you, but I had no idea exactly how empty this great city would seem after you left. I do pray you are faring well out in the wilds, but never forget that you do have a home back here among your friends, should you find yourself in dire straits.

You must be wondering what happened at the church after your hasty departure. From what I heard, the sanctuary was absolutely packed with an expectant audience as the flustered, perspiring groom came to wait for his nonexistent bride to walk down the aisle. When you did not appear, the Baxters were beside themselves. After dismissing the crowd, they set up an immediate meeting with Percy's solicitors to see what could be done to forestall having his inheritance tied up in a trust fund for the next twenty-five years. Finally, in an effort to save face, it was decided that Mirah would marry Percival when she turns sixteen. How I *would have loved to have seen the brat's face when the news was presented to her! She's always had such high and lofty intentions.*

At this unforeseen turn of events, Annora was overcome by giggles and laughed until she had to hold her sides. So Mirah Baxter had gotten her *comeuppance* after all, just as Mrs. Henderson had predicted! When her mirth subsided, she shook her head and continued reading:

I do hope things have worked out in your favor regarding your position in Wyoming. The moment you have time to take pen in hand, I hope you will go into great detail about your new home, your employer, and his children. Until then, know that you are constantly in my prayers. Michael joins me in wishing you every happiness.

Your friend always,
Lesley

Blinking unexpected moisture from her eyes, Annora hugged the missive to her heart, then reread it through from the beginning. Lesley had given no indication of having been implicated in Annora's flight to the West. With a great sigh of relief, she lay back on her bed and smiled.

Her reverie met a swift end with a knock on her door.

"Miss Annora?" Melinda asked. "When's supper?"

"I was just about to start on it, sweetheart." Rising, Annora folded Lesley's letter and tucked it inside the envelope once more, then put it under her pillow for later readings.

❧

Annora ladled portions of rich venison stew into everyone's bowls, then lowered herself to the chair and bowed her head. "We thank You, dear Lord, for Your wondrous provision and bounty. Please bless this meal and use it to our sustenance and us to Your service. Amen."

Gratified that her custom of saying grace at mealtimes had so easily become an accepted practice here, she slathered butter onto a thick slice of bread and bit off a chunk as she worked up courage to broach yet another questionable topic.

Mr. Brent and Noah, apparently more hungry than talkative this evening, made quick work of their first helpings, then refilled their bowls and dug in again.

Annora swallowed. "Tomorrow's Sunday."

The silence bracketing that pronouncement was so profound, her words seemed to ring in the air.

Melinda and Amy looked at her, then at their father, whose face registered nothing whatever.

"And I was wondering," Annora plunged on, "if we could start attending services."

Her employer filled his lungs and slowly exhaled. "Not much point in that," he said flatly with barely a pause in his eating.

Refusing to be cowed by his attitude, she pressed on. "No point in worshipping God?"

Lucas Brent set down his spoon and met her gaze straight on. "Look, miss. We used to put a lot of store in that truck. Now we get along just fine without it. Besides, there's work that needs doing. We can't be traipsing off to town all the time."

"But it would be good for the girls to—"

His demeanor hardened, as did the steel blue of his eyes. He opened his mouth to speak, but his brother beat him to it.

"I could drive 'em in on Sundays," Noah piped up.

"Forget it. If we go someplace like church, it's either all of us or none."

Annora didn't quite know what to make of that statement.

"We used to go to meetin' every Sunday," Amy said in a tiny voice, "when Mama was here. She said it was 'portant."

Some of the resolve tightening Lucas Brent's lips appeared to lessen. "I don't want to talk about this right now." He rose and shoved his chair back with his legs, but before he could take his leave, the child's rounded azure eyes shimmered with tears. "I'll . . . think on it," he muttered. "But don't count on tomorrow." With that, he crossed the room and stomped out.

Annora flinched as the door banged shut behind him.

Noah just grinned. "Well, well. It would appear somebody's startin' to get through to Big Brother."

But it was much too soon to count her employer's weakening stance a victory, Annora knew. As she cleaned up after the meal and readied the girls for their bedtime, she felt far from easy about having confronted the man right under the noses of his children. The least she could do was apologize.

She had been around long enough to perceive that whenever the farmer seemed particularly tense, he spent extra time with his beloved Chesapeake. The bond between the horse and the man was almost tangible, even to a casual observer. So when the opportunity at last presented itself, she made her way to the barn.

"He's very beautiful," she said quietly, approaching the stall. Tentatively, shyly, she reached to touch the velvety face, surprised at how soft and warm it was as the animal nuzzled against her palm.

Her employer's dark head turned, and he looked at her but did not speak.

Lowering her hand, she settled back onto her heels and fidgeted a little, toying nervously with the edge of her apron. "I came to say I'm sorry, Mr. Brent. I didn't mean to cause a scene at the supper table."

He leaned his forearms on the horse's rump and cocked his head, regarding her with those penetrating eyes of his. "Don't you think it's about time you dropped the 'mister' bit?" he asked simply. "Makes me feel like I'm my dad. My friends call me Lucas."

It was the last thing Annora would have expected him to say. Not sure of how to respond, she drew her lips inward and lightly bit down on them.

"After all that grace saying, I should have known it was only a matter of time till you brought up going to church. Must be a woman thing."

Annora tucked her chin. "You don't mean that."

"No . . . I guess I don't," he admitted reluctantly.

Something about the way he'd said it—or was it the honesty behind it?—gave Annora hope, and she felt herself relax a notch as he went back to brushing the reddish-brown hide.

"It was pretty important to my wife," Lucas went on. "To both of us, actually. But when she died, I . . ." Though his words trailed off, the pain they etched into his tanned features quite eloquently finished the thought.

Annora nodded with understanding and silently prayed for wisdom before she replied. "It's . . . hard to part with someone you love. Hard to understand the whys . . . especially when they don't make a lick of sense."

He appeared to consider the comment as he kept working, and a corner of his mouth twitched, but he didn't quite smile. His gaze sought hers again, as if reading her innermost thoughts. "Yeah, I guess if anybody knows what it's like to be left alone, it'd be someone like you."

"You get used to it," she said softly. "Anyway, I have never been completely alone. The Lord has always been there for me."

His movements stopped. "Then, why do you suppose He delights in snatching a mama away from young'uns who need her?"

Annora thought for a minute. "I don't think He *delights* in it. At least, not in the way you mean. The Bible says the death of His saints is a very precious thing to Him . . . a reward, if you will, to His faithful ones. And it says that all our days are numbered before we are even born. We're the ones who think everybody is entitled to that three-score years and ten it talks about."

A wry smile played across Lucas's mouth as he shook his head in contemplation, the lantern's glow making silver highlights against his brown-black hair. "Never thought about it quite that way." Hanging the brush on a hook, he patted Chesapeake's muscular neck and exited the stall, latching it after him. "Don't suppose there's any more of that good coffee we had at supper."

"Sure is. And it goes perfectly with the apple pie."

He grinned unabashedly. "One thing's for sure, Annora. You know your way around a kitchen."

"It's something else I got used to, awhile back."

"Well then, maybe I'll trouble you for some pie and coffee . . . if it won't make us oversleep for church tomorrow."

The surprising words all but sang across Annora's heart-strings. This truly was a victory . . . and a joyous one, at that. A smile broke forth. "Not at all . . . Lucas."

$\mathcal{L}$ucas hadn't intended ever to darken church doors again after Francie's funeral. How on earth he had allowed his little red-headed housekeeper to coerce him into coming to service today would forever remain a mystery. But here he was.

He had dawdled about, taking his good-natured time parking the wagon while the rest of the family went inside. Now through the partially open windows the first wheezy notes from the pump organ drifted to his ears.

Might as well get this over with. Filling his lungs, Lucas wiped his sweaty palms on his pant legs, trudged up the familiar steps, then before he changed his mind, strode purposely through the vestibule.

The very second his boot heels echoed on the plank floor, every individual present turned to gawk. Lucas shut out the volley of hushed whispers and the amazed expressions making the rounds. They were the least of his woes. . . . Noah had led the family to the first pew, clear up front! Grinding his teeth in consternation, he made a solemn vow. *That kid brother of mine better be on speaking terms with his Maker. When I get him home, I'm gonna wring his scrawny neck!*

Feigning nonchalance, Lucas marched the length of the center aisle to join his kin. And all the way, he tried to convince himself it was his imagination that the tempo of the prelude matched the rhythm of his steps.

He crossed in front of Noah—who purposely avoided the look intended to sear him to his bones—crossed in front of the girls, then Annora, taking the next spot on the hard bench. He was still seething when Rosemary Evans came from the opposite aisle and plunked herself down beside him, a brilliant smile on her face as she settled her yellow taffeta skirts about her.

The musical piece ended on a sustained final note, and the Reverend Miles Gardner stepped to the pulpit. The gray-haired minister's round face fairly beamed as his gaze finally moved from Lucas to include the other worshipers. "My dear brothers and sisters," he began. "This is a day of great celebration. Let us bow our hearts before our Holy God."

Lucas was so busy plotting his brother's demise, he missed all but the closing "Amen." But since he'd made that drive into town expressly for the worship service, he'd see it through. He crossed his arms and focused his attention on the minister even as Rosemary inched closer.

There weren't many similarities between this small clapboard church and the grand brick one where the Reverend Baxter served, Annora decided. Clear windows rather than stained glass, plain pulpit instead of one ornately carved, and many of the folks who had come this morning were dressed quite simply. A few men even wore what appeared to be work clothes. But everyone's smiles had seemed genuine when she and the girls had traipsed down the aisle behind Noah.

Drawing comfort from the familiar hymns and the friendly atmosphere of the rustic frontier church, Annora purposely avoided returning any of the pointed looks the bonnetmaker occasionally threw her way. It had been weeks since she'd last had the privilege of being in Sunday services, and Annora looked forward to feasting again on the Word of God. When the minister stepped to the pulpit, something about his demeanor assured her that her spirit would not go away unsatisfied.

The pastor's kindly brown eyes surveyed the small congregation, and he smiled. "Brothers and sisters, this will be the third and final message in our series, 'Restoring a Broken Fellowship with God.'"

Beside her, Annora felt Lucas stiffen slightly. She breathed a desperate prayer that he would stay and listen to what the Lord laid upon the minister's heart and that everyone present would benefit from the truths presented.

"You will recall," the pastor went on, "that two weeks ago we learned some of the marks of a backslider—including, among other things, no interest in attending church, no desire for Christian fellowship, and no personal time alone with the Lord."

Referring to his notes again, he continued. "And last week we studied some of the reasons why a Christian falls away from his faith—whether it be because of a particular weakness, the result of deep sorrow, or just a gradual cooling toward spiritual matters. But this morning, dear friends, we have not come to focus on the negatives but rather on the glorious positives. I've entitled this sermon 'Coming Home.' Turn with me, if you will, to our text for today, found in the second chapter of Revelation."

The flutter of pages sounded from the few Bibles among the folk present. Annora opened hers and let it rest on her lap.

"This passage," the Reverend Gardner explained as he scanned the audience, "speaks of the church at Ephesus, reminding them that they had left their first love. For whatever reason, they had forgotten the joy of their former days. They had ceased working for the Lord and their zeal had grown cold. But did the Lord give up on them? Not at all. Just look at what the risen Christ tells them to do in verse five: 'Remember therefore from whence thou art fallen, and repent, and do the first works.' We'll look at what those 'first works' entailed—but before we do, let's consider what had to take place beforehand—repentance. . . ."

Annora lost herself in the stirring message, noting how a few of the pastor's gestures and voice inflections reminded her of the Reverend Baxter's manner of preaching. For a few seconds she mentally transported herself back to Philadelphia, imagining she was sharing a pew with Lesley and her other friends. But that fantasy vanished with the realization that if she'd remained in the East, she'd have been sitting with her husband and mother-in-law. A shudder crept up her spine, bringing her attention back to the sermon, which had wound down to the points of application.

When the singing of "Blest Be the Tie That Binds" and a closing

prayer brought the service to an end, Noah beat ever̶y̶
in his rush to spend the remainder of the day in town
The rest of the worshipers filed out of the pews toward the d̶
ble door, where the Reverend Gardner waited to shake hands w̶
flock.

As a few of the departing folks stopped to chat with Lucas and
the girls, Rosemary sidled up to Annora. "So, how's our little housekeeper today?" she asked with a twinge of scorn. "Keeping up with
your duties?"

Annora matched the milliner's cool tone. "Yes, as a matter of fact,
and discovering what good helpers little girls can be."

"I would imagine." Rosemary's gaze slid to the children, who were
absorbed in the chatter going on around them. "Well, perhaps in another year or so, Lucas will take my advice and send them East to be
educated. Frontier schools leave much to be desired."

"Personally," Annora countered, "I feel that children need to be
with the people who love them. That's far more beneficial than learning needlepoint and Latin."

Rosemary's eyebrows arched higher, then quickly resumed their
normal position when she spied Lucas's daughters coming her way.

"Morning, Miss Rosemary," Amy breathed, an angelic smile lighting her face.

"Hello, precious," the milliner cooed, fawning over the young
pair. "I've been working on a surprise for both of you."

"For us?" Melinda asked. "A surprise?"

"Mm-hm. It'll be finished real soon."

"Oh, goodie!" Amy hugged the slender woman's waist.

"What's all this?" Lucas asked, coming to join the group.

"Miss Rosemary's making us a surprise," Melinda told him. "She
says it's almost finished."

"Well, that's nice, pumpkin." He tousled his daughter's hair and
smiled at Rosemary. "I'm amazed you have time to devote to a special
treat for the girls, busy as you are with your shop."

"I always have time for the people who matter to me," she replied
with a dazzling smile.

"Excuse me, please," Annora murmured, withdrawing from the

e woman was nowhere near as accom-
igning sweetness. Besides, all that claw-
e. Annora's relationship with the farmer

astor's hand, Annora fought to forget the
n her heart that the Lord had someone
store for Lucas and his little darlings.

(Fragmentary text in torn corner: one to the exit / with friends. / pen dou- / with his)

❧

After dining on succulent roast beef and mashed potatoes at the Brass Kettle Restaurant, Lucas steered the girls to the waiting rig. Noah had dined with friends of his and would hitch a ride home with them later.

"You might as well ride in comfort," Lucas quipped, assisting Annora up to the seat while his daughters climbed into the wagon bed. Then he loosened the reins from the hitching post and hopped aboard.

Melinda and Amy, who had dominated the conversation in the restaurant by keeping up a lively string of talk during the meal, resumed their girlish chatter and giggling in back. But before the team had covered half the homeward miles, Annora noticed that the pair had grown unaccountably quiet. She peered over her shoulder and discovered they had fallen asleep.

Lucas followed her gaze, then turned his head forward.

Annora studied her nails momentarily, then let out a breath of resignation as the countryside rolled by.

Finally he looked at her, his eyes shadowed by the brim of his Stetson. "Would you call me a backslider?"

"I beg your pardon?"

"You heard me. That was some sermon the reverend lambasted me with."

Annora wanted to smile but knew better. She assumed what she hoped was a pleasant look as she silently sought wisdom from the Lord. "He wasn't lambasting you, Lucas. He didn't even know you'd be there. His message was part of a series he started weeks ago."

"Sure sounded like he aimed it right at me."

"Well, perhaps it wasn't the—" Flushing over almost speaking her mind, Annora tried again. "I mean . . ." In despair, she closed her mouth and averted her gaze.

"Go on and finish what you were saying," he grated. "Couldn't be any worse than what was hurled at me from the pulpit."

After a slight hesitation, Annora moistened her lips and began over. "I was going to say, if it seemed all that personal, perhaps it was the Lord, not the pastor, trying to get your attention."

He stared straight ahead and didn't respond right away. A muscle worked in his jaw. "The Lord got my attention real good not too long ago when he took my wife away from me."

"Had she . . . been sick?" Having actually voiced the question, Annora caught her lip between her teeth. Had she pried into something too deeply personal?

Lucas shook his head. "Francie was . . . in the family way. She was so happy, thinking maybe the Lord was going to give us a son this time. The girls didn't even know about it yet, but we were on the verge of telling them." The beginnings of a bittersweet smile appeared, only to disappear on a ragged breath.

Knowing it must be intensely painful to talk about it, Annora wanted to say she was sorry for asking and that he didn't have to tell her more. But he didn't give her the chance.

"One hot afternoon when I was working out in the field, she took it upon herself to bring me some lemonade. To this day, I don't really know what happened—whether she caught her heel somehow, or stepped in a hole, or just plain tripped. But she fell. Hard. And then the bleeding started. When I heard her cry out, I carried her to the bed and rode for the doc. But by the time we got back, she was—" His voice broke. "She . . ."

It was more than Annora could bear. Without thinking, she took his big, callused hand in her much smaller one and squeezed it in wordless comfort. There was nothing she could say anyway.

A moment or two passed before Lucas withdrew his hand from her grasp. Then before she knew what was happening, his fingers brushed across her cheek, wiping away a tear.

Annora had no idea it had been there until the breeze whispered over the damp streak left behind. That he would be concerned for her despite his own pain provided a small glimpse into the depth of the man's compassion. And the fact that her face still tingled where his fingers had brushed against it sent a surge of indescribable flutterings through her being. Confused over the tangle of emotions within her, she fought the maddening tendency to blush as she looked away.

They rode onward in silence, the jangle of the harness, the clomping of the horses' hooves, and the rattle of the wagon the only sounds.

Lucas was first to speak. "You never answered my question, you know." The lopsided grin he flashed appeared a touch forced, but it helped lighten the moment. "Do you think I'm a backslider?"

Annora, exceedingly grateful for the change of mood, dared to jump in. "Did the shoe fit?"

"Like it was made to order."

She smiled back. "Well, if it's any comfort, there was something in that sermon for all of us, Lucas. Me included."

"Is that so?"

"Mm-hm. For example, that God is sovereign. That the things that happen in our lives don't have to make sense to us, only to Him. And that what matters is how we respond to those circumstances. After all, He has promised to work all things out for our good."

Lucas thought for a few seconds. "For such a young person, you sure sound like a preacher sometimes."

"Maybe because I lived with one after my parents died."

"They die sudden?"

"Barely two weeks apart. Typhoid." Surprisingly, the memory had lost some of its old sting.

He shook his head. "I guess you know about death's cruel blows yourself." And with a smile, he reached for Annora's hand and enveloped it tightly in empathy, holding it for a second timeless moment as they rode along.

Annora derived immense comfort from that tender gesture. But in spite of the way his touch seemed to do strange things to her insides, she reminded herself that nothing was different. Lucas was still her employer and she merely his hired help. But as they came within sight of the farm, she felt that some inner healing had taken place this day . . . in both their hearts.

*P*astor Gardner's sermon nagged at Lucas for days. He tried to keep busy, but no amount of work could completely erase the things that had been said during—or after—the Sunday service.

A few nights later, after everyone else had gone to bed, he lay in the stillness with his fingers laced together behind his head, staring at the ceiling. Echoes of the minister's words buzzed around in his mind like a persistent insect.

Backslider. What a disagreeable word that was! Rude, even insulting . . . yet excruciatingly true. The term aptly fit a believer who had strayed from the Lord. Whether or not his reasons for turning his back on God had appeared justifiable at the time, Lucas knew there was no excuse for willfully slamming shut the door of his life in the very face of God.

God is sovereign.

The things that happen in our lives don't have to make sense to us, only to Him.

What matters is how we respond to those circumstances.

Annora's quiet melodious voice had given those concepts a gentle logic Lucas could not fault. Odd, the depth of spiritual wisdom that came "out of the mouths of babes," as the Bible said. First, that tiny reminder from Amy about the importance of worshipping the Lord, then the guileless remarks that fell so incredibly easily from Annora's tongue at just the right moment. Reflecting upon the inherent sincerity that seemed so much a part of her, he mulled her comments over in his unrest, examining them from every possible angle.

He contemplated the selfless, giving personality his housekeeper had displayed since arriving on the farm. For someone of her tender age, she had reached a level of maturity far beyond her years. She'd been through a great deal—enough to make a lot of folks bitter. Yet any trace of sadness in those emerald eyes paled behind the glow of her inner peace . . . the same peace that had once been a precious part of his own life.

Lucas rolled onto his side and punched his pillow, trying to find comfort as his conscience and his reason struggled against each other.

Maybe it's too late for me, he mused. *Maybe I've gone too far and could never find my way back . . . even if I wanted to.*

The instant those bleak theories reared their heads, Lucas flatly rejected them. What was that saying his godly parents had tried to instill in his and Noah's hearts all those years? Oh, yes. *God does not forsake His own.* It might even be possible that although he'd tried to run from the Lord, God had kept him in sight the whole time. The possibility was strangely comforting.

Having had a taste of life without God, Lucas was ready to admit it offered nothing but empty hopelessness. Perhaps the Almighty had brought Annora all the way out here just to remind him that God's faithfulness would forever remain constant. Since she had arrived, Lucas's insides felt like a glacier under the summer sun, beginning to warm, slowly melting around the perimeter. Lately he'd even found himself longing for what he'd once taken for granted, to yearn for the "former things" the pastor had mentioned.

A lot of that was because of her.

Too bad her trial month was almost over.

Too bad she had to be so . . . captivating.

What are you thinking, you addlebrain? He railed inwardly. *You're starting to sound like Noah. She's scarcely more than a child. Best to let her go back where she came from before one of us makes a fool of himself.* Lucas was surer now than ever that he shouldn't extend her stay. That would be the wisest course for all concerned.

Grimly he rolled onto his back again and shut his eyes. He dared not think about how he looked forward to every new day again. Or that it was getting hard to focus on something other than that coppery hair, those soft jade eyes. Or about how empty the place would seem if she went away. He only knew he was getting a little too used to having her around, and that was not good. Not good at all.

❧

The dried apple scones smelled luscious as Annora slid the hot, golden-brown mounds onto a cooling rack. They were sure to complement the cinnamon applesauce at the end of supper. As she placed the hot baking tray into the sudsy water, she heard the girls clatter down the porch steps.

"Somebody's comin', Miss Annora," Melinda called out. "Looks like company!"

Annora moved to the open door.

A visitor was indeed approaching. The classy red wheels of a canopied buggy rolled smoothly down the lane—and driving a splendid chestnut horse was none other than Rosemary Evans.

Annora tightened her lips. "Go get your pa, girls," she told them, retreating back into the kitchen.

A cheery hubbub soon carried to her ears. Determined not to give in to her curiosity, Annora kept at her chores. But before long Amy burst into the house, her childish face alight.

"Look, Miss Annora. Isn't it pretty?" She held out a lovely frock of sky blue organdy. "Miss Rosemary made new dresses for Sissy and me. For church. Sissy's is pink."

Annora stooped down and drew the child close, admiring the flounced hem and ruffled sleeves, the abundance of lace trim. A dress elegant enough to grace even a big city church back East. "Why, it's just beautiful, sweetheart. You're sure to look real pretty next Sunday."

"Pa said Miss Rosemary could stay for supper, too. He said to tell you to set an extra place. He's takin' her to see the new horses." Without waiting for a response, she tugged free and darted outside again, the new frock left behind on a kitchen chair.

Annora's spirit sank. For a full minute she remained where she was. Then slowly she rose and surveyed the tidy house. She had mopped and dusted earlier, so everything looked about as good as it could. It was her own appearance that left much to be desired. Why had she chosen this day to beat the big rug out on the clothesline and polish that big black stove? Those chores had left her feeling grubby to the bone, and she longed for nothing more than to soak in a big luxurious tub like the one the Baxters had—which, of course, did not exist here on the Brent farm.

With a resigned sigh, she untied her soiled work apron and took a basin of warm water out to her room to make what repairs she could in the few private moments before Lucas and his guest would descend upon her for supper.

Within the hour, everyone gathered around the table. Lucas, as always, occupied the head and Noah the foot, leaving one side for the girls, and the other for Annora and Rosemary. As discomfiting as it was for Annora to sit beside the bonnetmaker after bringing the fried chicken and roasted potatoes to the table, the reprieve serving the food provided was a consolation. At least Rosemary wouldn't be eyeing her throughout the meal.

Absorbed in her thoughts, Annora finally realized that everyone was waiting for her to ask the blessing. She moistened her lips and bowed her head. "Thank You, most gracious Heavenly Father, for giving us these rich stores from Your bounty. Please bless this food and allow us another day to serve You. Amen."

"My," Rosemary gushed as she looked up, "you must have been in the kitchen all day, Amanda."

"Annora," she corrected.

"Oh. Of course. My mistake."

"Actually, we've been eatin' real good since Annora got here," Noah piped up.

"She even makes cookies and pies," Melinda added.

"You don't say." The milliner helped herself to a steaming potato from the bowl Lucas passed to her.

"And," Lucas said, "she keeps a neat house. Our little Annora has been a real asset around the place."

Hearing herself all but lumped in the children's category, Annora swallowed her bite of chicken without chewing it. She toyed with the remainder of her food, pushing buttered string beans around her plate while the family chatted with their guest. Thankfully, she reminded herself, she had Lesley to pour her heart out to whenever she felt particularly depressed about anything. It took awhile for letters to go back and forth, but somehow just the writing out of her innermost feelings made dealing with things easier.

". . . and Sissy and me can wear our new dresses."

Amy's voice drew Annora back to reality.

"They're so pretty," the little one went on as she reached for her glass of milk. Halfway to her mouth it slipped from her greasy fingers and tumbled onto the table, flooding the tablecloth and spilling over onto Rosemary's lavender skirts.

"Oh!" the milliner gasped. "My dress!" She sprang to her feet, using her napkin to mop uselessly at the creamy blotches as the girls' mouths gaped in horror.

Lucas rose also but stood helplessly looking on.

"I'll get you a damp cloth," Annora offered. In seconds she returned and handed the clean rag to the disgruntled guest, who was almost in tears over the ruination of her lovely ensemble.

"Sorry, Miss Rosemary," Amy said weakly.

With scarcely more than a pointed glare at the child, the woman continued sponging her skirt.

"Accidents happen," Lucas told his daughter in a consoling tone. He touched Rosemary's shoulder. "Come on, I'll drive you back to town before the stain sets."

"I—I wouldn't want to put you out," she hedged.

"No problem. I'd feel better about it if I at least knew you got home safe. I'll go saddle Chesapeake and tie him behind your buggy."

"Well, I really would appreciate that," she said, warming immediately to the suggestion. "We could continue the conversation we started a little while ago."

He nodded and took her elbow to assist her outside but glanced over his shoulder at his brother. "Make sure the stock is looked after before I get back, will you? I shouldn't be too long."

"Right." Claiming another drumstick from the platter, Noah continued eating as though nothing untoward had happened.

Thoughts of Lucas sharing seven cozy miles with Rosemary Evans was not exactly comforting to Annora, but she knew she had no claims on the farmer herself. He was a grown man and more than able to make his own choices—no matter how unsuitable she might deem them personally. Returning her attention to Melinda and Amy, she noticed they appeared a bit subdued. Annora smiled at them. "Here, let me take your plates, girls. Ready for some applesauce and warm scones?"

They dragged their worried gazes from the doorway their father and his guest had so recently exited.

"Everything will be fine," she said gently. "Miss Evans will wash and iron her dress and it will be good as new. I promise."

Their troubled frowns disappeared, and Amy gave a huge sigh. "I really didn't mean to spill my milk."

"I know, sweetheart. Now, stop fretting. I'll get some dessert, and we'll finish our meal."

Noah chuckled. "Sure can get mad, that one," he said with a tip of his dark head in the direction of the door. "Least little thing, and she's like a chicken that got dunked in the crick."

Melinda sputtered into a giggle, but Annora shot the young man a scathing glower. "Now, now."

"Yes, ma'am," he said in acquiescence. "Must remember not to gloat over somebody else's misfortune, and all that rot." But his mischievous gaze held hers and wouldn't release.

Annora finally looked away. "I'd better clear the table." Telling herself he was naturally forward and didn't mean anything by his ungentlemanly ogling, she hastened to make room for the end-of-meal sweets.

But as the sound of the departing buggy drifted in from the lane, she realized the scones and applesauce no longer held any appeal for her.

～●

The sun sank below the horizon, spilling the sky's pastel hues in a muted glow over rocks and bushes in the gathering dusk. Lucas drove the rented buggy toward Cheyenne at an unhurried pace, his spirited sorrel plodding patiently behind.

Rosemary turned toward him. "It was very sweet of you to insist upon seeing me back to town, Lucas."

He shrugged one shoulder but felt no need to comment.

"And I appreciated the supper invitation," she continued. "A pity the evening came to such an abrupt end." Her wistful expression brightened with a glorious smile. "Or perhaps one might term it a blessing, since it provided a chance to spend some extra time alone." She shifted her position slightly, bringing herself a little closer to him.

"You've always been good company," Lucas admitted. "And the girls think the world of you."

"Yes, well, the little darlings are at such an adorable age," she gushed a little too brightly. "Who can resist those girlish . . . charms?"

He grinned appreciatively. "Thanks for the dresses you made them, by the way. They'll count the hours till Sunday."

"Young ladies need to have new pretty things from time to time— especially when they're growing so quickly." She paused, toying with one of the fine curls framing her face. "I must say, I was pleasantly surprised to see you at church last week."

"It was . . . time." But even as he admitted that truth, Lucas had to wonder if he'd ever have gotten around to attending services if it hadn't been for Annora's gentle prodding. The housekeeper had a way about her that made it hard for a man to refuse whatever she asked . . . considering how little she actually did ask.

"You've done an amazing amount of work on your place since my last visit," Rosemary said, cutting into his reverie. "It really looks nice."

"Thanks." Lucas knew that most of his accomplishments were a direct result of having Annora there to look after the domestic end of things. He hadn't known that kind of freedom since Francie's death. Amazingly, rather than the customary tumult caused by thoughts of his loss, an unusual peace settled over him instead.

A sudden breeze rifled the buggy's framework, and Rosemary snuggled nearer. She laid a hand on his sleeve. "Since you've decided to fit church services into your busy life again, why don't we plan a picnic afterward this Sunday, before all the pleasant weather has passed?"

Lucas feasted his eyes on her delicate beauty. The notion did have some merits.

Then she added specifics.

"The four of us, I mean. You, the girls, and me. After all, it's obvious that Noah is completely enamored by your little housekeeper. I'm sure the two of them would appreciate an opportunity for some time together without so many chaperons around."

Lucas turned his attention forward again. A month ago a picnic with Rosemary might have been a trifle more tempting. But at the moment, he wasn't all that sure he was ready to encourage the bonnetmaker's attentions . . . to say nothing of the hazards of giving his younger brother liberties with Annora that had purposely been withheld until now. "Oh, I don't know, Rosemary," he hedged. "A lot depends on the weather and other things."

"But will you at least think about it?" She swept a yearning look at him through her lashes. "For the sake of the girls? They're getting a little too attached to your maid—whose time there, as I understand it, is almost over."

Rosemary was trying to shove him into a corner, he realized as he made an effort to retain his casual demeanor. "I'll think about it," he mumbled, then clammed up so she'd quit talking.

Lucas needed no reminder of the passage of Annora's trial period. But somehow, hearing those words from someone else sent a cold jolt of reality through him. How could a month have flown by so fast?

$\mathcal{A}$ fter Annora read the girls a story and tucked them in bed, she finished straightening the kitchen and went out to her quarters. Lucas had not returned from town as yet, which disturbed her more than she cared to admit. But keeping in mind that her employer was old enough to choose his own special friends, she lectured herself on the hazards of becoming overly concerned with the man's personal affairs.

But does it have to be Rosemary? Recalling the vexatious glare the bonnetmaker had leveled on poor Amy after the unfortunate accident with the milk, Annora had to wonder what sort of a stepmother the woman would make—assuming Lucas was considering establishing a permanent relationship with her. Surely other far more suitably eligible females were in town. Perhaps now that he had taken the first step in attending church again, someone more pleasant might catch his eye.

You have no right to be jealous of her, an inner voice pointed out.

Jealous! Annora gave a disdainful huff. *Why, I have never been jealous of anyone in my entire life.*

Not even Mirah? On the day of the picnic? her conscience persisted.

"Well, that was different," she muttered under her breath. "Mirah was after Jason." The remembrance of that past disappointment appeared trivial in the light of her current circumstances. Annora shook her head in astonishment; she had severed so many emotional ties upon leaving Philadelphia, the doctor's son had scarcely entered her mind since the day of her departure. After all, she assured herself, Jason was nowhere near as mature or compelling as . . . Lucas Brent.

What are you thinking? Annora felt her cheeks flame with guilt. All those fluttery sensations that teased her insides in his presence, the peculiar need she felt to restore what he'd lost, the simple joy she found in watching the care lines softening around his eyes whenever he spent time with Melinda and Amy . . . were those proper feelings for a mere housekeeper?

Taking a closer look at them in the quiet solitude of her room, Annora had to admit that no, they were not. In fact, if anything, they were quite the opposite.

She could no longer avoid the truth. The impossible had happened. Somewhere along the way, she had grown to love Lucas Brent. With the inward admission of that surprising truth, Annora's heart soared into the darkening sky . . . only to plunge immediately back to earth like a falling star. It was all for naught. Lucas thought of her as one more little girl.

Well, there was nothing she could do to alter her age. Or his. But one thing she could do was keep these newfound feelings to herself for the remainder of her time here—which she now realized she must terminate on her own when the final day arrived. No use in setting herself up for real heartache.

As always, when beset by things beyond her control, Annora reached for her Bible and opened it to the Psalms. A sound interrupted her, and she glanced up at her door just as someone rapped.

"Annora?" Noah asked.

Wondering what might have brought the young man to her lean-to, she lay the Scriptures aside and got up to open the latch. "What is it?"

The expression he wore seemed a curious blend of mystery and mischief as his lips slid into a lazy smile. "I, er, need you to sew a button on this for Sunday. That is, if you would be so kind." He held out a striped shirt.

"Oh. Of course. I'd be happy to take care of it, Noah. I don't suppose you saved the button, by any chance?"

He shook his head, his eyes imprisoning hers.

"Oh, well, I'm sure Mrs. Brent must have had a button tin. I'll check with the girls tomorrow." Smiling, she turned to set the garment down while Noah took his leave.

He didn't leave.

He followed her inside, giving the door a slight kick with his boot. It clicked shut.

Slanting him a glance, Annora felt little prickles of alarm skitter up her arms. "Is there something else?"

"You might say that."

She gave a perfunctory nod. "Well, tell me what it is. I'm rather busy just now."

"Are you?"

Annora leveled a stare on him, hoping she appeared more confident than she actually was. She opened her mouth to rattle off a list of duties needing her attention, then thought better of it. She didn't have to answer to her employer's younger brother. When he took a bold step closer, she inched backward, knowing she was quickly running out of room in the tiny lean-to.

Still regarding her with that too-penetrating gaze of his, Noah reached out and took a tendril of Annora's long hair, toying with it in his fingers, feathering it past his nostrils. "Nice," he murmured. "Soft, like you. Smells real pretty."

Annora pulled free and set her shoulders. "Stop it, Noah. You've brought me the shirt. Fine. I'll fix it for you. Now, please go."

"Why?" he crooned suggestively, cocking his head to one side. "For once in our lives, nobody is around to order us to go here, do this, do that. Why don't you and me get to know each other a bit?"

"No. It's not proper," Annora retorted.

"But I'm sure a city gal like you must know your way around." He leaned so close his warm breath feathered her neck.

Startled, shocked at his brazen attitude, she placed her hands on his chest and shoved with all her might.

Noah yelped in reflex as he toppled over the corner of her cot. He scrambled to his feet again, rubbing his backside. A lopsided grin added a dangerous gleam to his eyes. "So, that's how you wanna play it . . ."

"Noah!" she scolded forcefully, her arms out in front of her like a shield. "Stop this. You're scaring me. Think about what you're doing."

"What I'm doing," he drawled, "is just—"

The door burst open. Lucas towered in the portal's space.

Annora had not heard her employer return, but she was never so relieved to see anyone in her entire life. Completely unaware of how frightened she had actually been, she felt her knees give way, and she sank onto her bed.

"I told you to keep your hands off her!" she heard Lucas bellow as he yanked his brother bodily outside. "But no, the minute I turn my back, you're all over her like fleas on a dog."

"So what?" Noah returned defensively. "You expect us to believe you didn't just get done smoochin' with Rosie? I figure I'm entitled to—"

One well-directed blow sent the younger man sprawling.

Annora, utterly stunned by the unexpected altercation, could only gawk in horror as Noah crawled to his unsteady feet, rubbing his jaw. He shot a sizzling glower at Lucas, then without further word, he spun on his heel and stalked away in the direction of the barn.

Lucas watched him for a few seconds, then turned and entered the lean-to.

Still shaken, Annora didn't quite know how to react. "I—I'm . . . sorry," she stammered.

"There's nothing you need to be sorry about," he said gently, concern making his straight brows all but meet. "If anybody should apologize, it's me—for that dunderhead brother of mine. I can't let him out of my sight for two minutes." He grimaced. "You all right? Did he hurt you?"

Annora shook her head and smiled thinly as she rose. "I'm fine." But her wobbly knees belied her words.

Lucas reached out and clamped his strong fingers around her upper arms, steadying her. "You're fine. Right. Look at you—you're shaking like a leaf." Without further word, he swept her up into his arms and turned for the door.

The fluid motion rendered Annora speechless as a fragment of memory brought another similar moment to her mind . . . one so faint that she wondered if she had only dreamed it on her first night in Lucas's house.

"Come on," he was saying as his long strides carried them to the house, "I'll fix you a cup of tea. It's gonna be all right, Annora. I'll never let him—"

Before he finished the statement—before the fact registered that his heart was hammering every bit as erratically as hers—the clatter of horse hooves broke in on them.

Lucas relaxed his hold a measure and whirled around. "Chesapeake!" he gasped, going rigid with fury. "Noah! You! Noah!" he hollered. "Get back here! Now!"

But the younger man did not so much as slow down as he galloped away.

Annora felt Lucas's shoulders sag, and he mumbled something under his breath as he set her on her feet. She didn't know whether or not to say anything. Besides, even if she could come up with some profound reply, her emotions were so jumbled she couldn't trust her voice. The events of the last several minutes were beyond anything she would ever have dreamed.

"If he harms Ches, I'll tear him limb from limb," Lucas muttered. Staring uselessly up the now-empty lane for a few seconds, he exhaled a whoosh of defeat. Then, as if coming back to his senses, he took Annora's hand and led her through the door and to the table, where he drew out a chair for her.

"Thank you," she breathed.

Neither spoke as Lucas dumped some tea leaves into the pot and added hot water from the kettle atop the stove. His posture and impatient motions more than revealed his controlled agitation—as did the set of his jaw.

A short time later when he crossed the room with two cups of the rich brew, Annora smiled tentatively as she accepted one and watched him sink heavily onto the seat opposite her.

"I . . . I didn't mean to cause trouble for you," she finally managed in the uncomfortable silence.

"You're not the cause of the trouble," he grated. He took a gulp of tea, then set down his mug with a clunk and got up to pace to the door.

Annora felt his worry as she watched him standing there with his fingers in the back pockets of his jeans, gazing helplessly at the darkened lane. "Can't you go after him on one of the mares?"

He shook his head. "They're not saddle-broke. The hothead will mosey home eventually . . . and when he does, I'll be waiting for him."

Not even daring to imagine yet another confrontation between the two men, Annora nibbled her bottom lip. She could only pray that the Lord would take control of the whole mixed-up situation and keep everyone from getting hurt.

Lucas, a decided droop to his bearing, finally went outside, his steps fading as he trudged away.

Annora stood and took the cups to the sideboard before returning to her haven. Aware of her employer's misery and concern for his fine mount, she was too agitated to sleep, but she changed into her night shift and got out the lap desk. Perhaps a visit with Lesley would calm her spirit.

How long she sat cross-legged on her bed, tapping her pencil on that blank sheet of writing paper, Annora couldn't estimate. But after a time, she put away the writing equipment and blew out the lamp, then crawled between the sheet and light blanket on her bed. There she lay with nothing to do but pray.

Another hour or more dragged by. And one more after that one. Finally, the faint sound of horse hooves drifted from far away. Annora thought at first the noise was her imagination, until the hoof falls grew louder. Something about the pattern did not quite seem right, she realized, and she strained to listen more closely.

There it was again . . . that uneven, halting sound. Her heart thudded to a stop.

Apparently Lucas, too, had detected Chesapeake's return. She heard him come running from the barn.

Hoping against hope that nothing was amiss, Annora swung her legs over the side of her cot and slipped into her silk wrapper, tying it hastily about her waist. Then she padded outside barefooted, anxious to put her mind at ease.

But coming within sight of the lane, she saw Lucas was already kneeling at one of Chesapeake's forelegs, and a jolt of alarm shot up her spine. She picked up her pace, realizing that the horse had no rider. Noah was not to be seen.

"What is it, Lucas?" she whispered when she reached his side.

"If I ever set eyes on that no-account brother of mine again, I'll—"

At the flatness of his tone, Annora laid a comforting hand on his shoulder and sank down next to him. *Please, don't let it be bad*, her heart pleaded. *Not that.*

All the breath seemed to leave the farmer's lungs as he stood to his feet and brushed off his pant legs. "He's hurt. It's his front leg."

Deep despair settled over Annora as she rose and moved to one side so that Lucas could accompany his beautiful bay the rest of the remaining distance to the stall. The sight of the horse's ungainly limp brought tears to her eyes, and she swallowed back a sob. "What can I do to help?" she asked around the tightness in her throat.

"An old blanket. Some cold water," Lucas replied over his shoulder. "I doubt there's any ice left in the root cellar."

"W—will he . . . be all right?"

Lucas did not answer.

16

As lantern light revealed Chesapeake's condition, Lucas groaned internally. Along with the swollen and bruised foreleg, numerous scrapes and scratches marred the horse's right side. The sorrel must have taken a spill. *Well*, he thought with a rueful grimace, *it's probably too much to hope that Ches rolled over my stupid brother when he fell.* Decidedly lacking in charity at the moment, Lucas could not overlook Noah's irresponsibility—which to him seemed the mark of the kid's whole worthless existence. "Galloping out of here in the dark on a horse that's already tired," he grated under his breath, then expelled a lungful of air in disgust.

At the approach of Annora's soft footsteps, he glanced up.

"How's he look?" she asked shyly, holding out a basin of water to him, along with the pathetic remnant of ice she'd uncovered in the root cellar.

Accepting them gratefully, Lucas gave her a thankful nod and set the containers on the ground. "Bad enough to make me want to spit nails . . . but at least he won't need to be put down. No way I could stomach that." He wet a rag and wrung it out, then began gently dabbing at the misshapen injury.

With a small relieved sigh, Annora slid the worn blanket from her shoulders. "Shall I tear some strips?"

He nodded. "Thanks. No reason for you to lose sleep over this, though. You might as well go get some shut-eye."

Annora regarded him with a steady gaze. "I'd just as soon stay, if you don't mind. I was worried about Ches, too."

The comment came as no surprise. Annora's actions since she'd come west more than demonstrated her sincere care for the people she knew . . . and the knowledge made Lucas feel privileged. And very aware of her presence. He swallowed.

"What will you do for his leg?" she asked.

"Rub liniment on it, apply cold compresses, keep it wrapped, keep him quiet till the swelling goes down. I just hope and pray he didn't pull a ligament." The mention of prayer had come of its own accord, and as Lucas flicked a glance at Annora, he caught her smile.

"I'll pray, too. Would you like some coffee?"

"Sounds great. It's likely I'll be at this for some time." *And I'd just as soon not be alone*, he nearly added as she went back to the house. But with all the conflicting feelings assaulting his insides right now, he was real glad he'd been smart enough to keep his mouth shut.

Chesapeake was safe at home now, where Lucas could look after him. And Annora, too, was safe. Noah had not done her any serious harm. *This time*. Reminding himself to relax his jaw, Lucas went back to his task. *There would be no next time.*

❧

Once the coffee was ready, Annora set the pot on a tray, added two mugs and a pitcher of cream, and returned to the barn. She wondered where Noah was, but she knew better than to bring up that sore subject. For now it was enough that the horse had come back. She'd noticed an easing of Lucas's agitation right away. True, he had a long night ahead, but his steely determination and love for the spirited animal would get him through.

Reaching the stall, she set down the tray, filled the mugs, and added cream. She handed one to her employer before sitting down on the straw nearby to sip her own while she tore up the old blanket.

He nodded gratefully, drained the rich coffee in a few successive gulps, then took up swabbing the horse's numerous scratches with clean water and antiseptic.

Watching him work, Annora was fascinated by his hands. Strong, square, callused, they nevertheless possessed a softness, a gentleness Lucas brought forth whenever needed. She had experienced some of that herself, when he had carried her inside. He'd been every bit as considerate of her as he'd have been of his own daughters. Of course, realizing that another father was about the last thing she wanted right now, she quickly steered her wayward thoughts to another subject. The horse.

Annora saw that the sorrel's huge velvet eyes had lost the confused, frightened glaze she had glimpsed awhile ago. Now in the presence of his master, submitting to those kind ministrations, a quiet acceptance—an infinite trust—seemed to shine in its place. Lucas Brent, Annora conceded, was a man worthy of that depth of trust.

Of their own volition, her eyes sought the farmer again, and she noted that the care lines that earlier had creased his forehead had vanished. His mouth had lost its rigidity, too, giving a softer quality to his lips. She wondered how they would feel if—*You goose!* she railed inwardly. *You've no call to be entertaining such wanton thoughts about Lucas Brent!* In an effort to gather her emotions, she quickly rolled the remaining strips and stacked them in a neat bundle.

She could not help but think back on the events of the evening—the absolute hopelessness and fear that had torn at her when Noah had made his unwelcome advances. If Lucas had not come back when he had, heaven only knows what might have happened. The mere memory made her insides quake.

And yet, she felt nothing but safe around Lucas. He displayed only the utmost courtesy and respect toward her, and despite the difference in their ages, he spoke to her as an equal. Quite a contrast, those two men.

Even as she measured the one against the other, though, she could not escape the knowledge that they were, in fact, brothers. And she had come between them. Painfully so. With her trial period winding down to its final days, she resolved not to do anything to prolong her stay. Sad as she would be to part with Melinda and Amy, who had become incredibly dear to her from the first . . . it would be sadder still never to see Lucas again. But family relationships were important, and she needed to give this one room and time to mend.

With that conviction taking firm root in her heart, she let out a shallow breath and leaned to refill both their cups.

Time went by quietly. No words passed between them, yet she didn't sense he wished her to go, so she stayed. After about an hour, she watched Lucas unroll the bandage wrapping Chesapeake's foreleg and assess it critically. "How's it doing?"

He cocked his head back and forth in thought. "About as well as could be expected, considering." Then he reapplied liniment and a fresh strip of chilled blanket. "Think that's about all we can do to-night," he finally admitted as he finished up. "We'll have a hard enough time functioning tomorrow if we don't catch a few winks." Exiting the stall with the lantern in one hand, he secured the door, then offered his free hand to Annora.

"Thank the Lord he's going to be all right," she breathed, placing her fingers in Lucas's strong grasp and allowing him to assist her up. She was sure it was her imagination that he held on slightly longer than necessary. And she ignored a flurry of heartbeats as they left the barn side by side in that same pleasant, companionable silence.

"Thanks for keeping me company," Lucas said when they reached the door of the lean-to. "Don't mind admitting that would have been a lonely job, if . . ." His words trailed off, and he brushed the backs of his fingertips over her cheek, a weary smile curving his lips.

"I'm . . . just glad Ches will soon be his old self," she managed. She wanted to say more, wanted to respond to that tender gesture . . . but she knew that if she did, it would only make her last days here harder than ever. "Good night, Lucas."

" 'Night, yourself. You're safe now, you know."

"Yes. I know." With a small smile, she took the lantern he held out to her and went inside, her pulse pounding so hard she wondered if he could hear it, too. Without courage enough to meet his gaze, she softly closed the door, then sagged against it as she listened to him striding away.

She was going to need a lot of prayer to bolster her decision to leave this place willingly . . . especially without even hint of an alter-nate plan. Where could she go? What would she do? The first thing she would do, she decided as she undid the buttons on her shirtwaist, was pour her heart out to her Heavenly Father and seek the wisdom. He promised to those who asked.

❧

Bone weary, Lucas could barely keep his eyes open long enough to strip off his outer clothes and hit the sack. He hadn't formulated an actual prayer of thanks when he'd heard Chesapeake's return, but a steady stream of wordless praise had more than expressed his deepest feelings, and he didn't feel he could improve on that. The animal could have fared far worse. Noah, however, he would deal with later.

His mind went over the evening's events beginning with Rosemary's arrival, and he smiled. Melinda and Amy hadn't been the only ones who'd been surprised by the golden-haired milliner's unexpected visit. She had been a staunch friend to him since Francie's passing. Never pushy or intrusive but always available in the background whenever he needed to talk or have some sewing done. And she had a pleasant nature. For someone who had hinted strongly that she wasn't ready to tackle child-rearing, she sure had gone to considerable trouble making those new dresses for Melinda and Amy. The girls had been thrilled.

Too bad Amy had to have that accident. A woman accustomed to being around youngsters wouldn't have been put off in the least by a little spilled milk. But obviously to someone like Rosemary, it was a catastrophe. Probably in time she would get over the tendency to think that way.

Would she welcome the chance? Lucas wondered. *Was this the reason she'd come all the way out here today—just to let me know she's open to the suggestion?*

He'd never been really sure that Rosemary liked his daughters. She did try to converse with them—tried real hard—but somehow it didn't come off natural-like.

With Annora, things were different. From the first day she set foot on the farm, she took the girls right into her heart . . . and the reverse was equally true. Annora just fit in. Fit in fine.

Recollecting her genuine concern for Chesapeake, her willingness to help in whatever way she could, Lucas realized how he was coming to depend on her. The two of them hadn't started out on the right foot, exactly, and Lucas had to admit he had taken advantage of her in the beginning—mostly in the hope of driving her away. But now, she was such a part of the place he could barely picture the farm without her there.

In fact, Lucas wasn't sure he wanted to. With an involuntary yawn, he turned over.

❧

Lucas was in the middle of his chores the next morning when he sensed someone's presence in the barn. He turned.

"Leave it to old Ches to get home all right," Noah said nonchalantly, sauntering toward the end stall, his hands in his pockets.

The sight of that cocky smirk sent a surge of white heat through Lucas, exploding the rage inside him. "Yep," he replied offhandedly, as if they were discussing the weather. "Thanks to you, he *limped* back a few hours later!" The handle of the rake banged to the floor as Lucas lunged at his brother, slamming him against the boards of the next stall.

Noah landed on the floor. Winded, surprised, he lumbered to his feet.

The second he was upright, Lucas lit into him again. "This is for Ches," he said with a hard punch to the gut, "and this is for Annora." His knuckles connected with Noah's jaw, knocking him to the dirt. Hard. Blood trickled from the corner of his mouth. The sight of it gave Lucas a perverse sort of satisfaction. He'd wanted to catch the kid off his guard, make him feel some of the shock Annora had experienced. For some reason that was very important.

Noah's own anger came to the fore. He scrambled up, fists raised in front of him. "You always were an overbearing lout," he hissed, "thinkin' you're better 'n everybody else." He jabbed at Lucas.

The blow caught Lucas in the eye. Stumbling backward a step, he regained his balance. "Better that than a good-for-nothing, lazy—" His words were cut off when Noah threw himself at him. They crashed to the ground again in a flurry of punches and grunts, rolling over and over in the dust.

The patter of small feet sounded above the melee. "Pa! Uncle Noah!"

Lucas jerked up his head and caught Melinda and Amy gawking in horrified shock. Then the two of them burst into tears.

❧

Annora was busy getting breakfast when she heard a commotion from the barn. Glancing in that direction, she saw Amy coming at a dead run, screaming. She dropped what she was doing and flew to the door, her arms outstretched to the little girl. "What is it?"

"Miss Annora!" the child cried, flinging her arms about Annora's waist. "They're fightin'! Pa and Uncle Noah. And Sissy's cryin'. I'm afraid!"

"Oh, dear!" Annora hugged her tight.

"They . . . they're hittin'! Punchin'!" the child sobbed. "Like they don't ev—even l—love each other anymore."

Knowing how upsetting the small scuffle she'd witnessed outside the lean-to had seemed, Annora could think only of Melinda—and of sparing her from further distress or possibly even hurt. Taking Amy's hand, she drew her to the sofa. "You sit here, sweetheart. I'll go get Sissy. Everything will be all right." But inside her heart, she had more than a few doubts.

On winged feet, she ran to the barn, where she found the men still at it, arms and legs flailing amid thuds and grunts. Moving immediately to Melinda, who cowered in a corner with her hands covering her face, Annora swept the child up into her arms. The thought that two grown men would carry on with apparently no concern for how their conduct might affect innocent children made Annora furious.

"Would you look at yourselves!" she hollered. "Carrying on like common ruffians—and in front of babies, yet! It's the most disgraceful, despicable thing I have ever seen in my life!" Branding the pair with every ounce of scorn she possessed, she stomped toward the exit but turned around in the doorway. "And don't you dare come to my table with blood and dirt all over you. *Either of you!*" And with that, she flounced away.

By the time she reached the house, she cringed, remembering the remarks she had so rashly blurted out in the barn. But the fact was, her only concern had been six-year-old Melinda.

Once in the sanctity of the home, both girls began to calm down. "Why did our Pa fight with Uncle Noah?" Amy asked.

Wrapping an arm around each of them, Annora formulated her reply. "I suppose even grown-ups get mad sometimes, when things hurt them very badly inside. But when it's all over, they kind of forget about what bothered them, and then things go back the way they were before."

"Promise?"

"I promise. Now, let's wash those tears away. There are two men who are sure to be pretty hungry by the time breakfast is ready." But the truth was, her own confident words rang hollow as she sliced off more bacon and broke some extra eggs into the bowl.

Sure enough, though, when Annora clanged the metal triangle a short while later to signal breakfast, she saw Lucas trudging toward the house. Not too many yards behind him, Noah followed. A short stop at the barrel to scrub up and comb their hair, and they tramped into the kitchen.

Melinda and Amy, their eyes huge as saucers, snuggled a trifle closer to each other in mute silence as their subdued father and equally collected uncle pulled out a couple of chairs.

Annora, trying to act as if it were the most natural thing in the world to show up for breakfast bruised, with black eyes and bloodied noses, quickly bowed her head. "Dear Father, we thank You for this new day and for Your goodness to us. Please bless this food to our bodies and us to Your service. Amen."

The heavy silence that followed only magnified every crunch of crisp bacon and every swallow. Feeling more than ever responsible for the great chasm that had torn the two brothers apart, the tension underscored Annora's conviction that, regardless of Lucas's decision, she would not stay on at the Brent farm.

She would pack her things today. And at the first possible opportunity, she would ask Lucas to drive her to town.

(**17**)

*A*fter cleaning up the breakfast clutter, Annora made certain the girls were occupied before going in search of Lucas. She found him alone in the barn, kneeling as he undid the wrap on Chesapeake's injury.

"How's the leg doing this morning?" she asked, squelching a wince at the sight of her employer's shiner and swollen knuckles. Not a word had been said regarding the confrontation between him and Noah, and she was not about to pry into the matter, even though she suspected it had partly concerned her.

"Quite an improvement over last night," he said evenly, but he did not meet her gaze as he applied a fresh dressing and bound it with a clean bandage.

Now that she was here, Annora was at a loss about how to approach the subject uppermost in her mind. She pretended intense engrossment in observing Lucas at work until he picked up on her silence.

"Was there something you wanted?" he finally asked.

"Yes, actually." She nibbled the inside corner of her lip momentarily, then pressed on. "My trial month is about up."

He nodded as he kept working. "And I suppose you're wondering if you still have a job."

"No, not . . . exactly. I've decided to . . . seek employment elsewhere."

He stopped his ministrations and stood to his feet, eyeing her with that piercing gaze she had once considered annoying. Now it seemed different somehow. Challenging. Unnerving. And with Lucas towering over her, Annora felt more vulnerable. It was all she could do to ignore the jittering that started up in her stomach and slowly made its way down to her knees. She knew that if she dared look into his eyes for more than a second or two, he'd discover the depth of her true feelings.

"That's why I've come to speak to you," she blurted before she changed her mind. "I would like someone to drive me into town later today so I can make other arrangements." She ventured moving her gaze upward from his middle shirt button so she could make out his expression.

"This is what you want?" he asked, narrowing his eyes as if reading her thoughts.

Annora's first impulse was to say no, but honesty was the last thing she could afford right now. Even if she were positive it was natural for brothers to come to blows occasionally—and she couldn't imagine such a thing—just knowing she had been the cause of the rift in this family was unforgivable. It must never happen again. "It's what I've decided. I do believe the implied agreement was that either of us could nullify the arrangement."

"That's news to me. But if it's what you want, I'll see that you get there."

His swift acquiescence caught her off guard. What had she been hoping for—his flat refusal? An argument, at least? She gave herself a mental shake. "Thank you. I'll go and start packing."

He gave a noncommittal nod and resumed his earlier task.

But as she turned and walked away, Annora felt a marked change in the atmosphere, and she was aware of his eyes staring after her. She couldn't afford to dwell on what he must be thinking of her . . . not when so much of her concentration was being used just to keep her legs going.

Informing Melinda and Amy of her decision was even harder. The pair spied her through her open doorway in mid-afternoon, after Annora lugged her trunk atop her cot and began filling it with her belongings.

The hoop Melinda had been rolling fell to the ground, and she charged into the lean-to, her little sister a mere step behind. "Hey! What are you doin', Miss Annora?"

"I . . . um, have to go away."

"You mean, to visit somebody?" Amy wanted to know.

Annora shook her head and continued folding garments and stacking them in neat piles. "No. I mean, I'm leaving and going someplace else."

"But—but—" Even as the six-year-old's eyes swam with tears, she swiped them away in anger, her lower lip quivering. "I thought you loved us."

"I do, sweetheart. I love both of you very, very much."

"Then why are you leavin'?" she insisted.

"Who will take care of us?" Amy whimpered.

Knowing she should not have expected to escape easily from this heart-stopping pair, Annora sighed and quit packing. She gathered the girls into her arms and sat down on the foot of her bed with one youngster on either side of her. "When I first came here, it was only for a short time. You know, a trial. None of us expected it to be forever. Well, now my time is up, so I'll be moving on. Your pa will take care of you again, he and your uncle Noah. And you've both become such good helpers, I'm sure that with all four of you working together, you won't have a problem keeping everything looking clean and nice. You'll see."

Amy turned her eyes up to Annora. "But we don't want you to go away—like our mama. We want you to stay and live here with us."

"Well, we can't always have things the way we want them," Annora began.

"You mean, you don't want to stay," Melinda accused, her eyes brimming again.

"No, that is not what I mean," Annora said gently, brushing some stray dark hairs out of the child's face. "The fact is, the time has come for me to do what's right. For everyone."

Melinda hiked her chin. "It doesn't seem right to me. Or fair, either. Not when we need you."

"I'm truly sorry you feel that way, sweetheart," Annora said softly, "but I'm afraid this is how it must be."

"Then . . . then . . . just . . . go!" Melinda railed between clenched teeth as she sprang to her feet. "You don't love us, and . . . and . . . I wish you never ever came here!" And with that, she bolted from the room in tears.

Amy didn't say a word. She stared reproachfully up at Annora for a few seconds before going rigid and pulling free. Then she stomped out of the lean-to with one scathing glance backward.

Yes, I do love you, my darlings, Annora's heart called after them in silence. *But you're not the only ones I love . . . and that is the problem.* Her own eyes smarted, but she determinedly blinked back the tears. Hard as it was to deal with the way Lucas's daughters were hurting, maybe it was all for the best. They had gone somewhere by themselves to sulk. They were angry now—and perhaps feeling somewhat betrayed—but eventually they would get over it. At least she wouldn't have to tear herself away from two little girls who were sobbing their hearts out in a wrenching scene she'd never be able to erase from her memory.

She had not been packed for long before Lucas rapped at her door. "The wagon's hitched up. So whenever you're ready—"

"I'm ready now," Annora replied, amazed that her voice had not wavered. She opened the door and motioned toward her trunk and valise, then watched as her employer effortlessly hefted the ungainly travel chest to his shoulder. She donned the bonnet that matched her green traveling ensemble and followed him to the wagon, the handle of her valise held in both hands.

After Lucas situated the luggage in the wagon bed and handed her up to the seat, Annora searched everywhere for a glimpse of Melinda or Amy, but they were nowhere to be seen. She tried not to let it bother her that the girls were cheating her out of the chance to wave good-bye, to reassure them that things would turn out all right in the end.

Drawing a stabilizing breath, she relaxed her shoulders and composed herself for departure from the place that had spared her a life of unhappiness back in Philadelphia. Odd, how on the day she had arrived, she had begged Lucas not to make her leave . . . but now, she couldn't stay even if he asked her to. Fighting tears, she shoved the unwelcome thoughts forcefully from her mind. She would have ample time later for wallowing in self-pity.

The silence cloaking the drive to Cheyenne was almost unbearable. From the corner of her eye, Annora observed Lucas's stiff posture. His face was completely blank—and he had yet to say a word.

That lasted the entire route.

When they finally came within sight of the town, Annora felt a measure of relief—which quickly faded when Lucas pulled up to the railroad station and stopped.

"What are you doing?"

"Buying your fare back East." He hopped down and went for her baggage.

"But I don't want to go there," she countered, climbing down on her own. "I haven't enough funds."

"Yes, you have. I was supposed to pay your traveling expenses, if you recall. One direction or both, makes no difference to me."

"But that's absurd. I really don't—"

He paid her no mind but strode to the ticket window. "The young lady would like to travel to Philadelphia. When's the next train thereabouts?" he asked the clerk.

"Can't get that far east right now," the man answered, peering over his spectacles. "Bad rains in Ohio. Washed out part of the track bed."

"Well, how long till it's fixed?" Lucas groused.

"Couple weeks, a month—can't say for sure."

Having overheard the exchange from directly behind Lucas, Annora breathed a sigh of relief. Perhaps he'd listen to reason now. "I planned to stay at the hotel while I seek another position," she announced.

"Makes more sense for you to come back to the farm while you wait. Then if you're still set on leaving a couple weeks from now, I won't stop you."

"Lucas, please." In an effort to keep from tapping her foot in impatience, Annora filled her lungs and then let all the breath out at once. "I'm trying to tell you, it is impossible for me to go back to Philadelphia. There's no place for me there. Just book me a room at the hotel for now and let me make my own way. Please."

He frowned and searched her face.

"Please," she repeated.

"Why does it have to be now, this minute? Can you tell me that?"

"No, I cannot."

"If it's Noah you're leery of . . ."

Annora shook her head emphatically. "This is just something I have to do. I put in the trial month we agreed upon, and now that it's over, there's no reason for me to stay. I . . . want to do something different. Something someplace else."

"It doesn't make sense, Annora. I thought you were happy with . . . with us. What am I supposed to tell the girls when I get back home and you're not with me?"

"I've already spoken to Melinda and Amy, and we said our good-byes. They'll be fine, in time."

He shook his head. But when he opened his mouth as if to speak, no comment emerged. With a sidelong glare, he retrieved her trunk and carried it back to the wagon, then drove her to the hotel. Within a half-hour, he secured a room and brought her baggage upstairs.

"Well," he said flatly, "I guess this is it."

"Yes." She feigned the brightest smile she could muster and tossed her bonnet onto the bed. "Thank you for carrying my things up for me."

His hat in his hands, he turned it around and around while he stood there in the doorway, looking for all the world as if he had something to say. Only he said nothing.

"I . . . appreciate your giving me that chance I asked for, Lucas," Annora finally remarked. "It was rather an . . . adventure, getting to know you and your darling girls."

". . . who are gonna be miserable without you around," he finished, his gaze a challenge, his expression unfathomable for an uncomfortable moment or more. "Look," he said with a huff, "if you're gonna be here for awhile, would it be all right if I bring the girls to visit now and then?"

Annora wanted that more than anything, but she knew it would only prolong their sadness. Better to make a quick break and let them get on with their lives. She swallowed and shook her head. "It's best if they let go now," she said softly.

He gave a perfunctory nod. "As you wish. Oh." He reached into the inside pocket of his vest. "Here's the rest of the money I owe for your travel, or whatever . . ."

"That's not necessary, Lucas."

"Horsefeathers, Annora!" he exclaimed. "You worked for me. Worked hard. I owe you something for that, and besides, you don't know when you'll find another job. You might need this."

She could not fault his reasoning. But neither could she bear his presence much longer without falling apart. With all her resolve, she held out her hand.

Lucas pressed the roll of bills into her palm and closed her fingers around it. When he did not let go right away, her gaze was drawn to his. "Seems hardly sufficient just to say thanks for everything."

She moistened her lips, noting the pain in his eyes, wondering if it resulted from more than just the swollen discoloration around one of them. "I was just doing my job," she said lightly, hating the high pitch of her voice yet amazed she could utter anything at all with him holding her hand in both of his and staring into her very heart and soul.

His eyes slowly roved her face, finally settling on her lips. Annora's heart refused to beat for an eternal moment.

"Well, take care of yourself, y'hear?" he said softly.

"Y-you, too," she whispered, starting to tremble inside.

With a nod and a half-smile, Lucas released his grip, then left, closing the door behind him.

Annora tried not to watch him drive away. But despite her best intentions, she gravitated to the window before he was even outside. And then the sight of him leaving town was obscured by a veil of tears.

$$18$$

*A*nnora sat up in her bed at the hotel and struggled to breathe through her stuffy nose. She felt empty. Wasted. She had not wept so hard since the loss of her parents—but then, nothing else in her life had hurt so deeply . . . until now. Her eyes burned, her head ached—aggravated even more by the raucous tinkle of piano music from a few doors down the street, to say nothing of the loud voices coming from everywhere.

She could not permit her thoughts to drift to the Brent farm, to children who in all likelihood had cried themselves to sleep, or to the dark-haired farmer with the gentle blue eyes who had managed to snag her heart in the short while she had known him. Every time she gave in to those memories, a new rush of tears followed.

Having turned to God's Word for the comfort that always sustained her through dark times, Annora was dismayed that her watery eyes couldn't focus on the words. In despair, she hugged the worn book to her breast and rocked back and forth, imagining the mental picture her father had always painted for her of being held in the arms of God. Somehow that helped. But she had a strong suspicion that pain this intense would take a long, long time to get over.

Just as she expected, the next morning, the mirror above the washstand revealed the unmistakable marks the endless night had left on her puffy face. Her swollen eyes were rimmed with pink and underscored by dark circles. But like it or not, she had to go on, make plans for her future, however bleak it seemed. She poured cool water from the pitcher into the bowl, washed and changed into a fresh day gown of rust linen, then went downstairs for some coffee.

"Morning, miss," the bookish clerk, Jenson Samuels, called from the lobby desk as Annora descended the staircase. "Breakfast is being served in the dining room, if you're interested." He indicated a set of open double doors leading from the main hallway.

"Thank you." A polite smile was about all Annora could come up with as she followed his directions.

Even eyes as tired as her own could not help but appreciate the finely laid out accouterments of the spacious room—its rich Oriental carpet and an abundance of matching wooden tables in varied sizes. She surmised that at the evening's supper hour, with the ornate gasoliers casting a warm glow over the crisp white linens and best china, it must be truly lovely.

Nodding as she passed the only other occupants, an elderly couple occupying a table in the center of the room, Annora chose a small square one for herself near a window while she waited to be served.

By midmorning, Annora was feeling more like herself. After her time of Bible reading and prayer, she threw her light shawl about her shoulders and walked the short distance to the church where she'd attended service with Lucas and his daughters. The sight assailed her with memories she could not bear to dwell on, but she hiked her chin and strode purposely up the steps, hoping to find it unlocked for meditation.

Thankfully, it was. The door squeaked open on its hinges, and she stepped inside.

"May I help you, miss?" the moon-faced pastor said as he strode toward her from the sanctuary. "Oh . . . Miss Nolan, as I recall."

"Yes, thank you for remembering me, Reverend Gardner," Annora answered, appreciating the kindness in the man's smile and bearing.

"What brings you by today, lass? A problem out at the farm? Some needed counsel?"

"Well, actually, I came by to check your public board. I was hoping to apply for a new position here in town."

Obviously puzzled, he ran gnarled fingers through his thinning hair. "You're no longer employed by Lucas Brent?"

Annora smiled and shook her head. "No, that was only temporary. I'm looking for something permanent now."

"Well. Hmm. I'm afraid I cannot think of anything suitable among the present notices. You're more than welcome to look for yourself, of course." He motioned toward the cluttered board on the opposite side of the vestibule.

Her heart sinking, Annora stepped toward it, scanning the raft of bulletins pinned every which way before her eyes. All of them seemed to pertain to men. Trail guides, surveyors, ranch hands, railroad workers . . . She exhaled a disappointed breath and turned to leave.

"Wait a minute," the minister said, rubbing his chin in thought.

Annora stopped.

"Seems a member of my flock did mention something the other day—the manager of the Inter-Ocean Hotel. One of his chambermaids became ill a week or so ago, and he was decrying how short-handed they are. If you could, perchance, fill in until their regular girl recovers, maybe a position more to your liking might open up for you. Would that be of interest?"

"It surely would," Annora replied, feeling hopeful at last. "I happen to be staying there. I'll go see about it at once. Thank you ever so much!" Resisting the ridiculous urge to kiss the man of the cloth, she bobbed in a quick curtsy instead.

"And since you're residing within such close proximity to the church," he added, a twinkle in his eye, "might I expect to see your bright face among the flock next Lord's Day?"

"You just might. Thanks again, Reverend." With a new spring in her step, Annora took her leave. But before she'd gone half the distance to the hotel, she envisioned herself walking into the sanctuary on any given Sunday and seeing Lucas and the girls . . . seated, no doubt, with a gloating Rosemary Evans. And her spirit crashed to the ground.

"Well, well," came the milliner's voice from the doorway of her shop, as if Annora's thoughts had caused the woman to materialize. "Shopping again so soon?"

Annora's mind had been so occupied with her own matters, she had forgotten to walk on the opposite side of the street, where she'd have been less noticeable. "Miss Evans." She dipped her bonneted head in a respectful greeting.

The elegantly clad woman's hazel eyes swept the street in both directions, likely searching for Lucas and his daughters. "Where is everyone?" Rosemary asked.

"At home," Annora said evasively. "I'm on errands of my own."

"How . . . interesting."

"Yes. Well, I'm afraid I'm in a bit of a hurry just now. Do have a pleasant day, won't you?"

"Indeed."

Before further comments could be drawn from Annora, she hastened on. It galled her that Rosemary knew she was in Cheyenne, for in all likelihood the woman would go out of her way to ascertain the reason for her being there. But she'd have found out soon enough anyway, since Sunday was just around the corner. With a sigh, Annora ducked into the mercantile and browsed briefly through the merchandise. Then she inquired about a rear door, and with a sigh of relief, took the roundabout way to the Inter-Ocean Hotel, where she promptly applied for the job.

To her amazement, a delighted Mr. Samuels insisted she be given a thorough tour of the facility, introduced to the staff, and put to work at once.

So began a new phase of her life.

Once again, Annora appreciated her background. Keeping fresh sheets on the beds of a huge three-story hotel and tidying the scores of sleeping chambers kept her occupied from early morning until quite late in the afternoon. And on particularly busy occasions, she was also prevailed upon to help during evening mealtime as well. Weary and exhausted, she now fell asleep the instant her head touched her pillow—regardless of the town noise. But since her job was only temporary, at least she was not asked to relocate to the servants' quarters.

The unending toil kept her too busy to think, let alone differentiate one day from another . . . so the sight of Lucas Brent's wagon rumbling past the hotel several mornings later was most unexpected. Caught by surprise, she paused in her dusting. He, Noah, and the girls were decked out in their Sunday best.

They must be on their way to church. Annora pressed closer to the window, watching after them. Part of her rejoiced to see the Brent family united again, but another part of her had to battle the urge to open the floodgates of her heart . . . to the tears never far from the surface during her waking hours.

She sighed and resumed her duties with considerably less enthusiasm.

Awhile later, as she swept the front steps, her heart sank to see Lucas drive by again . . . this time with a very animated Rosemary perched between him and Noah on the wide seat. Melinda and Amy now carried new dolls, obviously store-bought. The sight of the little ones made Annora's eyes sting.

Endeavoring not to draw attention to herself with any quick movements, she continued sweeping. But Lucas's wordless glance found her. Her heart lurched within her breast as she gave him a tiny smile and went back to the chore, determined to resist the persistent moisture in her eyes that made her turn her back to the street.

That night in the dark solitude of her chamber, she finally gave in to what she hoped would be her last fit of weeping. After all, her prayers had been answered, hadn't they? Lucas and Noah had repaired their broken relationship, the girls appeared fine. Perhaps, she told herself, they would find themselves in a complete family circle once again . . . even if it was with Rosemary as their stepmother. That was the hardest of all to swallow, but Annora prayed that God would help her to accept it.

Knowing she wouldn't be able to sleep anytime soon, she went to her trunk and removed two sheets of writing stationery. Tonight she would pour out her heartaches to Lesley.

✒

Lucas closed the storybook and ruffled Amy's hair. " 'Night, pumpkin. You, too, my other pumpkin," he said, reaching to stroke Melinda's soft cheek.

" 'Night, Pa," they both said, their unhappy little smiles tearing at his insides. Hardly a day had passed that they hadn't brought Annora's name into a dozen conversations. He was just thankful they hadn't spied her earlier that morning as they passed the hotel. Bad enough that his own pulse kicked up in that crazy way at the sight of her. He could almost picture the girls jumping over the side of the wagon bed and running to hug her. Then afterward, they'd have been inconsolable, knowing that, no, she would not be coming out even to visit, and yes, they would have to do without her forever.

He'd detected particular unease in his older daughter today. She had been uncharacteristically quiet, and just as he rose from their bedside chair, Melinda turned her troubled face to his. "Pa?"

"Yes, honey-girl?"

"Is Miss Rosemary gonna be our new mama?"

He slowly filled his lungs, then exhaled in a ragged breath. "Would you like that?"

She merely shrugged.

"I like my new dolly," Amy chimed in. "Miss Rosemary buys us pretty things. She says she wants to be our friend."

"But she's . . ." Melinda's eyes suddenly brimmed and a tear rolled down the side of her face and into her hair. "She's not Annora," she wailed, her voice catching on a sob.

"Hey, pumpkin," he said in his most soothing tone, "I know you've been kind of sad since Annora went away."

"Be-because . . . I . . . m-made her g-go."

As his daughter's tears swiftly became a deluge, Lucas bent over to pat her shoulder in what seemed to him a hopelessly inadequate attempt to administer comfort. But her words disturbed him greatly. "What do you mean?"

The six-year-old sniffed and rubbed at her wet cheeks, smearing traces of dirt into uneven smudges. "When she s—said she couldn't stay, I-I told her to g-go away," she admitted in a tiny voice. "And that . . . I wished she—she'd . . . never . . . come!" Almost hysterical now, she rolled over and sobbed into her pillow, in heart-wrenching gasps that shook her tiny frame.

When the worst began to subside, Lucas picked her up and lowered himself to the mattress, hugging her hard. "Well, I'm sure you didn't mean it, pumpkin, and Annora knew in her heart that you didn't, too. The fact that she had to leave was not your fault."

"Truly?" she whimpered.

"Truly. And everything is gonna be all right. You'll see." But even as he felt her relax, he wondered how and when that would ever be true.

❧

Annora navigated the dining room, filling water glasses for the unusually large assemblage of patrons and seeing to their various needs.

"Excuse me, miss," a portly gentleman with thick side whiskers said, waving to her from where he was seated with a group of four. "Would you mind checking on our order? We've been waiting for some time."

"Yes, of course. I'll be but a moment." Nodding, she spun on her heel and started for the kitchen.

"Why, Annora Nolan!" cried a familiar feminine voice. "How absolutely lovely to see you!"

Recognizing Hope Johnston's smiling face as she rose from a table of uniformed men and their female companions, Annora gasped at the sight of her traveling mate from the train. She stepped into a huge hug. "And you!" she finally managed. "This is certainly a surprise."

"Yes, is it not?" Reclaiming her seat, the slender young military wife gestured to the tall and fair-complexioned man in blue next to her. "Phillip, you remember my mentioning the sweet friend I made during my journey. I'd like you to meet Annora Nolan. Annora, this is my husband, Lieutenant Phillip Johnston."

"Lieutenant," she said with a nod as he rose to take the hand she offered. "I'm very pleased to meet you."

"Oh, miss-s-s-s," the heavyset man across the way reminded her pointedly.

Turning back to Hope, she winced in embarrassment. "I don't mean to be rude, but I'm on duty just now."

"Of course. But is there any chance we might have a word before I must go?" the delicate-featured woman asked.

"Perhaps, if things slow down." And with that, Annora hurried away.

Half an hour later, she spotted the group from Fort Russell as they left their table and began walking toward the lobby. Checking to make certain she wasn't needed, she hurried to Hope's side and slipped an arm about her. "I'm sorry I wasn't able to visit with you. We've so much to catch up on. How's sweet Rachel? And you? How've you been?"

"Fine, fine, couldn't be better. But I thought you were contracted to work for a local farmer. Housekeeper, wasn't it?"

"Yes, and I did. But my trial period ended, and I . . . decided to move on. I'm working here temporarily now, filling in for a girl who's ill."

"Oh. Well, how providential that our paths would cross again. As it happens, a dear friend of ours at the fort, the colonel's wife, recently suffered a mild stroke and is in dire need of a live-in companion and housekeeper. Not the most glamorous of pastimes, I'll allow—but it would provide an opportunity for us to renew our friendship. If you think you might want the job, contact me through the postmaster as soon as possible."

"I will. Thanks for telling me about it." With one last hug, Annora reluctantly relinquished her hold. "Take care, Hope."

"I will. And I do hope you apply for that position."

"I'll pray about it. Truth is, it might be exactly what I need right now."

Yes, she affirmed mentally. She knew very well what her heart needed—wanted. But sitting here in Cheyenne when that possibility was utterly hopeless . . . Besides, how many more times could she bear the sight of that wagon rolling by?

No, I'll work on that letter. Tonight.

The more Annora prayed about applying for the position at Fort Russell, the greater became the sense of peace that enveloped her. Staying on indefinitely in Cheyenne, where she'd run into Lucas Brent from time to time, would be like applying iodine to a brushburn. No, it was time to move on, give the empty chasm inside her a chance to fill with new friends, new faces.

She could not imagine any man ever measuring up to the standard her heart now required, thanks to that lonely widower from Cheyenne. She would compare every single one to him for the rest of her life. But in time, perhaps a love would come along that was almost as precious as this ill-fated one.

There was no sense in letting circumstances get her down, Annora decided. Nor was there any point in waiting for the hotel manager to inform her of the exact day when the regular chambermaid would report for duty. The sooner she posted the message to Hope Johnston expressing a willingness to become live-in companion to the colonel's bedridden wife, the sooner her shattered heart would mend. During her noon break, she would mail the letter she had written last evening.

Her mind settled, Annora changed into a full-sleeved shirtwaist, indigo skirt, and long bib apron for work. She tied a red kerchief over her hair and reported to the supply room for the clean linens the morning would require.

Jenson Samuels was waiting for her when she arrived. "Oh. Miss Nolan," he said, twisting a pen nervously in his fingers, his bespectacled gaze never quite meeting hers. "I wanted you to know we've been most appreciative of the quality of your work."

"Why, thank you, Mr. Samuels. The job was a godsend to me."

"Yes." He cleared his throat. "And it was very good of you to fill in for our Sadie. But she has recovered sufficiently to return to her duties, so I've been given the unpleasant task of informing you that after today, your services will no longer be needed. I'm sorry."

"Oh, please, don't be. I've been offered another position," Annora assured him, "and I'd already made up my mind to accept it the moment my job ends here. So I'm not in the least put out by Sadie's return."

"Well," he said, considerably more at ease. "That is welcome news. However, should you ever need employment in the future, please let us be the first to know. Your dependability and fine service have earned our highest recommendation."

"Thank you, sir. I appreciate those kind words. And I just might do that someday." Smiling, she opened the supply room door and began filling her arms with clean white sheets.

The man lingered uncertainly for another second or two before handing her a list of rooms needing her attention. Then, with a cursory nod, he left for his station in the lobby.

This being her final day as chambermaid, Annora breezed through the entire morning, returning to her room slightly after noon. She freshened up and changed into a clean dress, then unpinned her chignon and brushed her long waves, fastening the sides back with ivory combs. All the while she worked, she had thought of the letter she'd composed and how it needed to be delivered to the postmaster.

She made a mental note to do that when she finished packing most of her belongings, omitting only what would be needed for another day or two. Crossing to her trunk, Annora opened the heavy lid.

Light from the window slanted across the paper lining of the chest, and for the first time, Annora noticed a peculiar unevenness in the bottom—as if a small portion had been cut to make a hidden compartment, one all but invisible against the liner's printed design. She frowned and knelt to pry at the edge with a fingernail. It popped open, and she raised the flap.

"Mama's jewelry!" she gasped, too amazed to do anything but gape at the pieces she'd asked Lesley to sell for her. Plucking the familiar items from the velvet lining the compartment, Annora saw a folded note and recognized the young woman's distinctive stationery. Her eyes misted as she opened it.

Dearest Nora,

One day you will find this tiny hiding place, and when you do, I hope it will brighten your day. Knowing how very much your mother's treasures meant to you, neither Michael nor I could bear to sell or pawn them. Both of us had been putting away a little money toward the day when we might wed. The decision to purchase your fare as our parting gift was mutual as well as joyous. We will always consider you as dear to us as a sister. May the Lord keep His loving hand upon you always and grant you every happiness.

With deepest love,
Lesley

Annora stared through her tears at her best friend's precise penmanship. She might have guessed those two would concoct such a loving tribute to the relationship they had shared in Philadelphia. If she lived to be a hundred, she doubted she would ever again find friends so close and dear.

Pressing her late mother's possessions to her heart for a few breathless seconds, Annora replaced them inside the secret compartment, then dried her cheeks and went to gather clothes from the armoire.

A knock on the door interrupted the task before the trunk was half full. When she answered the summons, her heart skipped a beat. "Lucas!"

In a jacket and work clothes, with his hair slicked back and his hat in his hands, he flashed a sheepish, one-sided smile. "May I come in?"

"Of—of course," she whispered. She stood aside while he entered, leaving the door ajar behind him. Annora schooled herself not to stare. She could not afford to let his presence affect her, not after the limited ground she had gained over her despondency. "Is something the matter?" she managed past a huge lump in her throat. "The girls—they're all right?"

A nod.

"Chesapeake, then. Is he doing well?"

Another nod. "He's starting to show some interest in those pretty little mares that have been admiring him from afar up until now," he said lightly. Then his expression turned sober. "Actually, I came to make sure that *you're* well. You looked kind of . . . tired the other day."

"I probably was," she confessed, extremely relieved to hear that nothing was wrong with either Melinda or Amy. "I'd put in a few rather long days here, filling in for an absent chambermaid."

"Ah."

"It's . . . kind of you to be concerned, though," Annora said. She had almost used the word *sweet* but caught herself just in time. He'd think she was a dolt. *And he's merely your former employer, remember*, she cautioned herself. *Don't make more of this than it is.*

His gaze, which had casually roamed over Annora from head to toe before coming to rest on her face, now meandered about the room. It halted on the partially packed trunk. His dark brows flared. "Packing?"

"Yes. I've taken another job. Well, that is, I've been offered one and agreed tentatively. I'm just about to post my formal acceptance."

"In town?"

She shook her head. The temptation to elaborate on its being a mere three miles away at Fort Russell was almost too strong to resist. Everything within her wanted to let him know she'd still be near enough to visit, to keep in touch—but she clamped her lips together.

"I see." Moving deeper into the room, Lucas surveyed the neatly folded clothes occupying the bed and the trunk, sized up the simple furnishings and the view from the window, where he stood gazing outside without a word.

Annora had the impression there was more to his coming here than he'd related, and watching him idly strolling around her chamber somehow reinforced the notion. But he'd either tell her or he wouldn't, it was entirely up to him. Meanwhile, she repressed her growing jitters.

"Well," he finally said, expelling a whoosh of air. "You obviously have things to do. I shouldn't keep you. Wouldn't want you to . . . miss your train."

She knew he was fishing for information, but she wasn't about to give him any. Best to make the break quick. Clean.

"I'm glad to see you're all right," Lucas said again. "Real glad."

Annora gave him a polite nod. Maintaining her composure was using up every ounce of her strength. If he didn't leave soon, her nerves were going to fray completely. *Please go, Lucas. Go, before I say something really dumb.*

He focused his attention on her again, and his shoulders flattened in resignation. Three strides brought him back to where she remained rooted to the floor. "I guess this is goodbye, then."

"I guess," she murmured, wise enough not to trust her voice.

"For good."

She nodded.

"In that case, I . . . wish you well." He continued to stare, his enigmatic expression gradually turning to one of acceptance. "I'll never forget you, Annora."

"Nor I you." Raising her lashes, she allowed herself one more searching look at those dusky blue eyes of his. . . . It would have to do for the rest of her life. Only with the greatest reluctance did she finally break eye contact. "Good-bye, Lucas," she whispered, offering her hand.

His fingers closed around it, but instead of giving a mere handshake, he raised it to his lips and brushed a feather-light kiss to her skin. Then, hesitating but an instant, he left, shutting the door after himself.

The back of Annora's hand burned with his kiss, and she pressed it to her lips as her heart contracted with exquisite pain. She tried not to listen to him stride down the hall. Then the stairs.

Placing a palm over her pounding heart in a futile attempt to restore its more normal pace, she closed her eyes. *At least that was our final good-bye*, she thought consolingly. *I could never endure another.*

A dull ache filled her as she made her way to the window. The sight of Lucas's departure would likely be the final glimpse of him she would have in her lifetime. . . . And she was helpless against the need to fill her eyes with him one last time.

Where are you going? Lucas's conscience railed before he'd made it halfway downstairs. *You already lost one love. Let this one slip through your fingers, and you're a blithering idiot!* He halted so suddenly, a fellow descending a step behind crashed into him. "Sorry," Lucas mumbled and moved aside to allow the man to pass.

But she has another job. Plans. He mulled over what Annora had said, trying to recollect her exact words. *Agreed tentatively*, wasn't that it? *About to* post her formal acceptance. Which means . . . she hasn't exactly committed. In the darkness of his heart, that spark of hope was almost blinding in its brilliance. A slow smile emerged.

Could be the lamest thing I've ever set out to do. "But I'm still gonna try," he said under his breath. He retraced his steps to her room. Removing his Stetson, he raked his fingers through his hair. Swallowed. Drew a strengthening breath. Rapped.

The look on her face was absolutely priceless when the door opened. "Lucas!" A pause. "Did you . . . forget something?"

"As a matter of fact, I did. May I come in?"

Obviously confused, she backed away. "What is it?"

"You, uh, still owe me two days," he blurted, saying the first thing that came to his mind.

"What?" Her cheeks pinkened . . . a shade he quite liked.

"Our agreement, remember? For a month. Well, according to my calculations, you left two days early." Smug over the absurdly flimsy straw he'd grasped, his internal grin widened into a broad smile. "I want you to come finish out your time."

"Don't be ridiculous," Annora said in that plucky way he had grown to love. She crossed her arms.

Lucas conceded that Miss Annora Nolan was not one who could be coerced. Only complete sincerity would cut through the reserve she wrapped around herself like a feather quilt. He dispensed with the humor and took her hand in both of his, gripping all the tighter at her subtle attempt to tug free. "Look, Annora," he said soberly. "Truth is, I . . . don't want you to go. I'm asking you not to take that other job."

"B-but . . . but I . . ." Myriad emotions played across her fragile features.

Lucas hadn't had an inkling that someone so vocal as Annora

could ever be rendered speechless, yet apparently that was precisely the case. Having that first ever glimpse into the depth of her vulnerability, he knew how easily he could take advantage of her, if that was what he wanted.

It wasn't.

He did want her to come back . . . but only by her own choice. And the only way to accomplish that entailed being completely honest, baring his soul. Time would permit nothing less. He shored up his insides and filled his lungs. "What would you think of staying on at the hotel for awhile?"

"I don't understand," Annora said softly. "Why would I do that?"

"Because, it would give me a chance to court you."

She paled, and her slender brows rose high. "Y-you want to court me?"

He nodded. "I've been a rotten employer, I know—or at least, I was in the beginning. I figured a whole raft of prospects would apply for the job, giving me a chance to pick and choose the one most suitable. I never believed someone like you could possibly do—*be*—all that I needed. But you proved me wrong. You were *and are* far beyond what I ever could've expected."

As Annora's emerald eyes softened, he pressed on. "The girls absolutely adore you. And I . . ." He feasted his gaze on her delicate beauty, the inner strength of character that gave wisdom beyond her years, and his whole being ached with tenderness. "I always surmised I would marry eventually, out of duty, so the girls would have a whole family again. What I didn't expect was to ever love again in my lifetime . . . that is, until you came along. I'm in love with you, Annora Nolan."

Those beautiful eyes misted over. "I . . . Th-that's really—" She blinked away the moisture. "Do you mean that?"

"Do I mean it?" he asked huskily. With a soft moan, he smiled and drew her into his arms, not even trying to suppress the surging of his pulse throbbing against his ribs . . . against hers. "How could I not love you, my sweet Annora? You brought me back to life again. You made the house a home. You made my daughters laugh. You even made me look up again and see God. I want you to come back and be part of my life. Now. Always."

Annora could not believe this was happening. Never in her wildest dreams had she imagined Lucas Brent would think of her as a woman . . . a desirable one. She only knew that he was dearer to her than her own life. He was all she ever wanted, more than she could hope for.

"I won't rush you," he said gently. "I'm willing to give you whatever time you need to decide whether or not this is something you want, too. And, to set your mind at ease, Noah realized he'd acted like a jerk, and he assures me he'll never treat you disrespectfully again."

So many, many incredible notions were playing havoc within Annora as she stood gazing into Lucas's soul. She focused on those well-formed lips that so often—and even still—had her wondering . . . Surprising even herself, she raised to tiptoe and ever so softly pressed her untried lips to his.

Annora felt him smile as he tightened his embrace and answered her tentative invitation in a kiss of utmost reverence.

She had expected to feel a bit apprehensive in his arms, even nervous. But instead she knew only peace, as if God Himself smiled down at the fulfillment of His glorious plan.

"Is that a yes?" he whispered against her hair.

A phrase he had once used popped into her mind as she smiled up at him. " 'If the prospect pleases . . . ' "

A chuckle rumbled from deep inside as he hugged her breathless.

"I happen to love you, too, Lucas," she somehow finished. "And I would be honored to become your wife."

Love, deep and abiding, glowed from Lucas's eyes as he gazed down at Annora and slowly lowered his head, covering her lips with his in a kiss filled with unspoken promises.

When it ended an eternal moment later, he smiled. "I know two little angels who are going to love hearing our news. You have just made three people very happy."

"You mean, four," Annora whispered and slid her fingers into his big, strong hand.

$\mathcal{E}$PILOGUE

Two years later

$\mathcal{T}$he breath of early autumn wafted across the porch, stirring tendrils of Annora's hair about her face. She tucked the loose wisps behind her ear and adjusted the blanket surrounding her two-month-old son, Matthew Lucas. Soon the days would turn too cool for the luxury of sitting outside for the mere pleasure of it.

"May I please hold him, Mama?" Melinda asked as she bounded up the steps, sun streaks glistening in her dark, shiny hair.

Annora smiled lovingly at her stepdaughter. The girl had sprouted like a weed during the long hot summer, and now at eight years of age, she seemed happiest when mothering her new baby brother or helping about the house.

"Sure, sweetheart." Annora stood while Melinda took possession of the padded rocking chair and positioned herself comfortably. "Remember to hold his head," she coached gently and placed the chubby infant in his sister's arms.

"I will. Oh, look," she breathed, a dreamy smile widening her cheeks, "he's starting to get some hair again!"

"Yes, I noticed."

Chuckling to herself over how Matthew's tiny face had seemed so much rounder after losing the thick black hair of birth, Annora lightly stroked the velvety copper growth, a shade lighter than her own. His eyes, however, were the same dusky blue as his father's. "I'm going to go and see what Amy's up to. I'll be back in a few minutes."

Already absorbed in admiring the baby, Melinda only nodded.

But even as Annora stepped onto the front path, the sound of an approaching buggy carried from the lane. Pausing, she raised a hand to shield her eyes, trying to make out the two occupants of the conveyance.

Suddenly her heart leapt. Could it be?

"Lesley!"

Disregarding the propriety of her station as an old married lady and mother, Annora grasped her skirts in both hands and ran to meet the carriage.

"Surprise, surprise," her best friend said gleefully as her new husband, Michael Porter, drew up on the reins, halting the splendid dapple gray horse. Lesley clambered down every bit as unceremoniously as Annora and grabbed her in a huge hug.

"I can't believe this is real!" Annora gasped, trying to catch her breath. "And just look at you!" Easing the slender young woman to arm's length, she assessed Lesley's fashionable traveling suit and satin-trimmed bonnet, both in a rich sapphire blue that deepened the shade of her eyes and complemented her abundant honey-blond curls. Had it been anyone else, Annora would have felt conscious of her own everyday attire, but her incredible joy pushed such inconsequential thoughts aside.

"Hey, am I ever gonna get a hug?" Michael's deep voice teased as he tapped Annora on the shoulder.

She turned, and meeting the sparkle in those chocolate brown eyes, she flung her arms around his tall, muscular frame. He was clad equally elegantly in a dove gray pinstripe suit and bowler. "Oh, it's so wonderful that you've come here like this! You never mentioned a word of it."

"We wanted to surprise you," Lesley replied. "Michael's parents insisted on giving us a honeymoon trip to remember . . . so we immediately chose Wyoming. That way, we could not only take in the wonders of Yellowstone but visit you, as well." She turned a delicate rose. "Of course, I realize our dropping in on you might very well be an imposition . . . in which case—"

"Oh, I'll not hear a word of that," Annora said emphatically. "Of course you're welcome to stay with us for as long as you like. Come on, both of you, and I'll give you the grand tour, introduce you to my family—all but Noah, that is. He moved on to new adventures several months ago."

"Yes, do," Lesley agreed. "I'm dying to meet Lucas and the girls—to say nothing of your first little one."

Still smiling, Annora linked arms with Lesley and began strolling toward the recently painted house with its added rooms and neatly trimmed shrubbery, while Michael climbed back into the buggy and followed behind them.

"So, your wedding went smoothly?" Annora wanted to know. "Oh, I so would have loved to have been there, but with a new baby . . ."

"Yes, it was fine—except for the weather and the cake," Lesley said. "It poured so hard that day I wondered if anyone would bother to show up, but fortunately most Philadelphians aren't in the least put off by a little rain. A nice crowd attended—drooping hats and all. The cake, I'm afraid, didn't fare quite as well."

"Whatever happened?"

Lesley smothered a giggle. "When it was being carried to the church basement, a gust of wind caught the umbrella and tore it out of my mother's hands, leaving the icing to the mercy of the elements."

"It was rather pathetic," Michael piped in. "Especially after Mom and Dad Clark's hard work to make it special."

"I would imagine," Annora said. "But I'm sure it still tasted all right."

"Yes, that it did," Lesley said, nodding. "But what surprised me most, believe it or not, was how really sweet and helpful Mirah Thornby was throughout the entire occasion."

"You're not serious," Annora protested.

"Oh, but I am. It's amazing how a year and a half of marriage and an extremely difficult confinement can bring about some rather vast changes in a person. She was so thankful to deliver her healthy little daughter, she went through a transformation, finally confessing to her parents her horrid treatment of you. Mirah and the Baxters prevailed upon me to bring along their letters of apology. I have them in my valise."

Humbled and thankful for the answers to her prayers, Annora's spirit lightened considerably.

A look of wonder settled over her friend's fine features as they reached the porch and went up the steps. "Don't tell me that pretty little charmer is Melinda?"

"She sure is," Annora said proudly. "And a better, more loving helper a new mom could never find." Crossing to her, she laid a hand on the girl's shoulder. "Sweetheart, I'd like you to meet my very best friend in the whole world. This is Lesley CI—I mean, Porter," she corrected, "and that's her husband, Michael, coming up the steps. Les, Michael, this is my daughter, Melinda. And this," she added, gently picking up the slumbering infant, "is Matthew Lucas." She placed him in Lesley's outstretched arms.

"Ohhh," Lesley crooned, caressing the tiny cheeks with her fingertips. "He is absolutely precious. You are so fortunate, Nora." She hugged him close, burying her nose in the soft bundle as she nestled him lovingly against her.

"I gather that must be the man of the house," Michael said, tipping his head in the direction of the barn.

Annora turned to see Lucas striding toward them, holding flaxenhaired Amy by the hand. Her heart nearly burst with pride at the sight of his manly bearing, the light of love in both his and their daughter's faces.

"Thought I heard someone drive up," Lucas said, removing his Stetson and raking a hand through his hair. He swept a glance over the gathering as he and Amy reached the porch.

"Lucas, I'm sure you've heard me talk often enough about Lesley and Michael, my dear friends from Philadelphia."

"Ah . . . the ones who played such an important role in bringing our beautiful Annora into our lives. Finally I have the pleasure of meeting you. It is an honor." Flashing a warm grin, Lucas took Lesley's gloved hand and then Michael's.

"We feel the same, I assure you," Lesley said, blushing becomingly.

"Annora deserves whatever happiness the Lord brings her way," Michael offered.

"Oh, now, you two," Annora cajoled. Placing her hands on Amy's shoulders, she inched the little girl forward. "And this is Amy, our little horsewoman."

"You like horses?" Lesley asked, stooping to smile at the winsome beauty.

"Uh-huh. My pa bought me a pony. His name is Star."

"Well, you'll have to show me your pony soon, all right?"

She nodded. "Sissy has one, too, named Moonbeam. And Pa has lots of horses." She gestured toward the fenced pastureland occupied by an assortment of energetic colts and serene mares.

"I glimpsed a few as we came down the lane. I can't wait to see them all."

"Well, that will have to wait," Annora declared. "I'm sure you're both tired and thirsty. Let's go have some refreshments. The Lord has blessed us with this very special day, and we've got a lot of catching up to do."

Annora smiled up at Lucas, this wonderful man who had gifted a lonely girl with his love and his family, and she slipped into the crook of his arm. He gave her a squeeze, and together they led the happy group inside.

Hold on My Heart

By JoAnn A. Grote

To Kristy, Gideon's guardian angel

1

Chippewa City, Minnesota—1894

*E*ntering the large room, Frank Sterling immediately began searching for Amy Henderson. He acknowledged greetings from friends as he moved through the crowd of Windom Academy students but didn't allow them to distract him from his goal. Floral scents from young ladies' colognes mixed with Bay Rum aftershave popular with the male students, and both blended with the spicy pine branches, which decorated the academy hall for the Christmas party. No cigar smoke clouded the air; the students wouldn't take the chance of losing their cherished place at the Academy by breaking the smoking rule.

A female classmate at the refreshment table offered him a cup of hot apple cider rich with cinnamon, and he flashed her a smile as he accepted it. "Thanks." She giggled and blushed in response and looked away in apparent embarrassment. He found her girlishness annoying. Amy never acted immature like so many of the girls their age.

Just at that moment, he found her. He lowered his cup and drank in the sight of her.

She sat on a simple oak chair in a corner of the room, straight and tall with her usual gentle dignity. A white-globed kerosene lamp on the lace-covered oak table beside her cast light on the sketch pad in her lap and brought out the glimmers of gold in her brown hair, which swept in graceful waves to the top of her head.

Walter Bay, the man she was sketching, stood with one hand beneath his coat in a poor imitation of Napoleon's famous pose. Frank felt his lips tighten in distaste. Mr. Bay must be thirty if he was a day, half again as old as Frank and Amy and the other Academy students. Bay preferred to be called Professor, but everyone at the school knew he hadn't earned the title. He had a university education and was a successful businessman. It was for those reasons he taught courses in economics. Frank had no time for the man. "Thinks the sun can't rise without his help," Frank had told his brother, Jason.

He ran a finger beneath his starched white collar. It was mighty uncomfortable compared to the work clothes he'd broken in with his daily farm chores. Seemed he couldn't grow accustomed to wearing the scratchy collars, even though he'd been wearing them for the entire fall semester.

Amy glanced up and caught Frank watching her. Did her smile deepen, her gray eyes brighten a bit in gladness at seeing him, or was it imagination? He chose to believe what his heart affirmed. Pleasure scrolled through him.

Frank felt someone nudge him and turned. "Hi, Roland."

His blond classmate was a year older than Frank and tended toward roundness, where Frank's slim frame was muscular from years of farm chores.

"Want something stronger than that apple cider?" Roland winked and nudged Frank again. "A bunch of us are getting together later at Bjorg's place."

"No, thanks."

"Are you sure? It's a cold night. Could use something to warm you before heading back to your farm."

"I'm sure. Better be careful. If you get caught, you won't be coming back after the holiday."

"We know the rules. We aren't so stupid as to get caught," Roland blustered. "If you change your mind about joining us, let me know."

Frank was glad when Roland walked away. He turned his attention back to Amy. She was engrossed in her drawing, her hand moving with sure, quick strokes. He smiled. Go drinking? Not a chance. A year ago when he'd asked Amy to court him, her father had made it clear he'd only allow Frank to keep company with his daughter if Frank went a year without drinking or gambling.

The memory of Mr. Henderson telling Frank he wasn't worthy of Amy always embarrassed Frank and made him want to reach for the bottle he'd promised not to touch. He realized now in surprise that the memory no longer left him uncomfortable. He felt proud and strong because he'd kept his promise.

Amy had assured him that she knew he'd keep his word and that to celebrate they'd attend Christmas Eve services together. At first a year had sounded like forever. He'd strengthened his resolve by recalling the Old Testament story of Jacob's fourteen-year wait for Rachel. Jacob's wait had been longer, but Jacob hadn't had to give up drinking.

At times during the last year, Frank had almost given in and reached for a bottle. Like after a hot, sticky, dirty day on the farm, when even the night didn't bring a refreshing breeze to cool the air, and a cold beer sounded like manna from heaven. Or worse, when he saw some other man escort Amy to a dance and knew he himself hadn't the right to ask for even one dance. Amy was well worth the price of giving up drinking and gambling.

Though he and Amy hadn't discussed the situation since last December, whenever their gazes met, her eyes had shined with faith in him. Or had he only imagined it?

His year of testing would be up next week. He'd kept his promise. Would Amy keep hers?

❧

Amy handed Walter the sketch. "There you are, Mr. Bay."

He didn't take the paper from her as she expected. Instead, he leaned over the drawing, leaving it in her hand. The nearness of his cheek so close to hers awakened an unpleasant desire within her to flee. Flight was impossible, even it weren't rude. He blocked her only way of escape.

"Lovely, Miss Henderson."

He wasn't looking at the paper. He was looking into her eyes. She drew her head back and set the drawing on the table, removing his excuse for closeness. "I'm glad you like it." Her voice sounded stiffer than the dead pine needles in the decorations about the room. "I hope you'll think it worthy of a donation for the Academy." She indicated the crystal bowl, which already held a smattering of coins.

He straightened, chuckling, and drew a few coins from his pocket. "Well worth the price."

The expression in his eyes left no doubt that it was the improper closeness he believed worth the price. Amy felt herself withdrawing. Her spine pressed against the back of the chair.

A small man with a beard touched Bay's arm. "Ah, Mr. Bay, just the man I need."

Amy let out a soft sigh of relief at Professor Headley's arrival.

"Mrs. Headley and I were discussing where to hold our astronomy class next semester," the professor continued. "Would you join us at our table?"

"Of course." Walter picked up the sketch as Headley drew him away. "I was just complimenting Miss Henderson on the sketch she drew of me."

Headley darted an apologetic look over his shoulder at Amy. She hoped he understood the message of gratitude in her own eyes for his intervention.

Headley settled his hand on Bay's shoulder. "We're fortunate she offered to use her talent to raise money for us. There are never enough funds for all the Academy's needs, as you well know. About that astronomy class . . ."

Their voices faded as they moved away. Amy let her gaze drift back to where she'd last seen Frank. For the first time that evening, none of the students or faculty were sitting for her. She'd hoped Frank would take advantage of her freedom and come over, but he was visiting with members of the football team.

Her disappointment melted into delight. It was a wonderful opportunity to sketch Frank without appearing to single him out. She had sketches of him at home, but they'd all been done from memory. Her hand raced over the page, capturing the three young men in earnest conversation. She was finishing the drawing when Frank broke away from the others. A minute later he was walking toward her with a cup of cider in each hand. Her heart quickened its beat, as it always did when he was near.

"I thought you might be thirsty, Miss Amy."

"How thoughtful." She accepted with a smile the cup he offered.

For a moment she considered turning her sketch-book so he wouldn't see what she'd drawn, then decided it would appear more innocent if she didn't hide it.

"Nice party. A good send-off for the students who will be traveling a distance home for the holidays."

"Yes." The look in his eyes held a compliment which propriety didn't allow him to express since they weren't courting. Amy felt herself flush with pleasure. She was glad she'd worn her new silk trimmed with velvet, which brought out the green in her gray-green eyes.

"The girls did a wonderful job decorating the hall considering how little they had to spend, don't you think?" Amy asked to fill the emotion-packed silence that had fallen between them. "They spent hours and hours making the paper roses. I understand someone donated a barrel of evergreen boughs."

"Walter Bay donated them."

"Oh."

He grinned. "Maybe we should start a pine-planting tradition so one day the town won't need to import pine trees and boughs for Christmas. When the original settlers started this prairie town twenty or so years ago, there were trees only along the river, and now elms shade every house and street. No telling how twenty years of pine planting would change the land."

"It sounds like a wonderful idea." The part that sounded most wonderful to her was the "we" in his plan. If only it weren't simply a manner of speech.

Please let him ask me to the Christmas Eve service, Amy prayed silently. She'd waited all evening, hoping for these few precious minutes with him, hoping he would take the opportunity to ask her to the service. She tried to maintain an illusion of calm and proper womanly decorum, but inside she felt she would burst from anticipation.

A trill of piano keys quieted the crowd and brought everyone's attention to the corner opposite Amy and Frank. Young Mrs. Headley invited everyone to gather around the piano for a group sing. A violinist joined the pianist in playing "O Little Town of Bethlehem." The crowd raised their voices in song as they drifted toward the musicians.

Frank held out his hand to Amy. "Shall we join them?"

She placed her hand in his willingly and rose. His hand was calloused but his touch firm and gentle. She was disappointed when he let go of her hand after giving her fingers a quick, soft squeeze. *What did you expect?* she chided herself as they crossed the room. She knew the answer. She'd not expected, but hoped, he would offer her his arm. Couples in the early stages of courting, scattered through the crowd, stood together with the woman's hand snuggled in the crook of the gentleman's arm. It was perfectly acceptable behavior for unengaged couples.

She should have known Frank wouldn't draw her hand through his arm. Likely he considered it a liberty not allowed since he had promised her father he wouldn't court her for a year.

Frank's bass resonated beside her as he joined in the singing, sending delight rippling through her. How silly to waste this special time wishing for more when they stood together celebrating Christ's birth. She caught the melody in her soprano voice. She glanced up at him and saw his eyes smiling into hers.

As the song ended, Amy heard Walter whisper, "You have a beautiful singing voice, Miss Amy."

She jumped slightly. The hair on the back of her neck rose in a chill of surprise. She hadn't realized he stood beside her. Her murmured "thank you" wasn't heartfelt.

After each song Walter made some trifling comment to her. Normally Amy wouldn't have found this annoying, but tonight he felt like an intruder. His constant attentions prevented Frank from taking the opportunity to speak to her even casually, let alone to extend the Christmas Eve invitation she'd been waiting for all year.

Was it her imagination, or was Frank withdrawing from her as the hymn sing progressed? Did Frank think she welcomed Walter's attentions? What could she do about it without appearing rude?

After a half-dozen songs, the students took a break in their singing to present their gifts to Professor and Mrs. Headley. The young couple's devotion to the school endeared them to their pupils. Light from the kerosene lamp atop the piano reflected off tears in Mrs. Headley's eyes when she pulled from the round, blue-papered box a small hat with two pheasant feathers perkily peeking up from the back. Amy blinked back her own tears. She'd selected the gift, but it was from all the students. She'd seen Mrs. Headley's gaze linger on the adorable hat in Miss Hermanson's millinery window when they were shopping together. Mrs. Headley never spoke of the small luxuries she neglected to purchase for herself, but it was common knowledge in the village that the luxuries were willingly passed over in exchange for spending much of her husband's salary on school necessities.

Professor Headley's gift of sturdy bib overalls from the students brought laughter from all. The young man had accepted the headship of the fledgling private school, understanding his duties to include distributing the budget. He soon discovered the budget didn't provide money in these hard times following the Panic of '93 for someone to dig the well, or build the footbridge over the deep, tree-filled gully between the school and town, or any of the other numerous acts of physical labor necessary. He dove into the acts himself without complaint, but they were a hardship on his clothes, which were not suited to such labor. His mended, worn trousers and shirts were quiet testimony to the students that he hadn't money to spare on new outfits. The overalls would protect what good clothing he had left.

"That was an appropriate send-off," Frank said with a chuckle after the last lines of the last tune, "God Rest Ye, Merry Gentlemen."

"Yes." Amy smiled up at him. If he were going to ask her to the Christmas Eve service, surely he would do so now. Could he understand the encouragement she tried to send with her expression? Already chattering students were retrieving their coats. In only a moment the opportunity might be gone.

"May I see you home, Miss Amy?"

Walter's offer shattered her hopes. Frank's eyes darkened, and his face looked as though he'd pulled a drapery across it, hiding his emotions. Amy wanted to stamp her feet in tantrum like a three year old. Decorum allowed no such display.

"Thank you for offering, Mr. Bay, but that won't be necessary. Some of us who live in town are walking home together." She was relieved the arrangement gave her an excuse to decline.

Sylvia, the blond, petite girl who had served the cider, stopped beside them. "Here's your coat, Amy. The others are ready to leave." As always, her words tumbled after each other in a breathless rush.

Frank held Amy's coat for her. She wondered what it would feel like if his arms wrapped around her. Would they be as warm and comforting in life's storms as her coat against winter's harsh winds?

Sylvia flashed her smile at Frank and then Walter. Her blue eyes shone. "Would you gentlemen like to join us? We have quite a nice-sized group." She waved a gloved hand toward the door where a half-dozen men and women were gathered. "The more the merrier."

Walter accepted immediately. Frank hesitated a moment before saying, "Sure. It sounds like fun."

The anticipation of more time near Frank thrilled Amy. She'd have preferred Walter not join them, but after all, it was a large group. Surely he wouldn't expect her attention to be addressed to him.

Most likely Frank's horse was at the Academy. He'd need to return from the residential section to retrieve the horse. Certainly that indicated he wanted to spend more time with her, didn't it? Or perhaps, her more cautionary side whispered, he only wanted to spend more time with the rest of their jolly friends before returning home to the quiet of the farmhouse.

The evening was lovely, with barely a breeze. Snowflakes drifted lazily in the pale yellow light cast on the snow-covered ground by the lanterns on either side of the front door. Frank and Walter were on each side of Amy as they descended the stairs. At the bottom of the stairs, Frank fell in beside her. The shoveled path was not wide enough for more than two people.

Amy caught the glance of annoyance Walter darted at Frank before dropping back to walk beside Sylvia.

Amy turned up the large collar of her gray wool coat. The maroon velvet trim felt soft and warm against her ears, and she was grateful for it. Her hat was a fashionable affair not designed to keep one warm. Her plush maroon muffler secured the collar in place.

A couple of the boys carried lanterns. The shadows of the troupe lengthened and shortened against the snow as the lanterns swung. There were no other buildings on the prairie on the village's edge, no streetlights or stray beams from parlors to help guide their way beneath the cloud-covered sky, but they were all familiar with the path across the former field.

The light had been lit at the narrow walking bridge over the gully between the Windom land and the town. Amy could see snow dapple the brims of the men's hats and the shoulders of everyone's coats. Snow dusted the bridge planks, sparkling in the flickering light as though set with diamonds. "Careful, the bridge is slippery," one of the first to cross called back.

Amy reached for the wooden handrail when she stepped onto the bridge. She felt the slight pressure of Frank's hand at her lower back and was grateful for it. By the time they reached the middle of the bridge, she walked with confidence. Amy glanced over her shoulder at Frank. "It's not too slippery. Oooh!"

Her feet flew out from under her. She fell backward, her descent stopped suddenly when Frank's strong arms closed around her. Her head collided with his chest, and she felt her hat fall free of its hat pin. Frank's heart beat fast and strong against her back, even through their heavy winter coats.

"I have you, Amy." His breath was warm against her cheek. She barely had time to register the fact before he was helping her regain her footing. "Steady now," he whispered against her hair. He guided her gently away from the side of the bridge, moving himself between her and the railing. One arm still around her waist, he looked down into the gulch. "Looks like you've lost your hat."

Everyone was watching her, all asking at once whether she was all right or warning too late to be careful. Sylvia was giggling as usual. "You've lost your topknot, too, Amy."

Her gloved hands brushed at her hair, though she knew it was useless. The carefully pinned bun had slid from the top of her head to her neck, just behind one ear. It would probably have fallen farther if not for her jacket's high collar.

"Are you sure you weren't harmed, Miss Amy?" Concern filled Frank's question. "Did you wrench your ankle?"

"No, I'm fine. All that are hurt are my pride and my hat." She sighed slightly. "I only purchased that hat yesterday, and I did fancy it."

The near-fall had happened so quickly that Amy hadn't had time to be frightened. Now she realized she could have tumbled through the snowy night into the gulch along with her hat. She shoved suddenly shaking hands into her maroon muff. "Thank you, Frank." Her voice shook as badly as her hands. Taking a deep breath, she stepped carefully forward.

Frank's hand slipped from her back. She regretted it, missing the sense of safety, but a moment later he offered his arm. She took it, welcoming the safety back.

She was pleasantly surprised that he didn't remove his arm when they reached the path on the opposite side of the gulch. Did he allow her hand to remain snug within the bend of his elbow in case of another unexpectedly slippery path or because he enjoyed the closeness? She hoped the latter.

Yet if he still cared, why hadn't he asked her to the Christmas Eve service? In the midst of the group's bright conversation, her mind wandered over the last year.

Amy hadn't seen Frank with any other girls, not once. Chippewa City was so small that one always heard if anyone was courting, and sometimes even when they weren't, the rumor mill carried the question of maybe so. She was sure her school friends would pass the tidbit of her and Frank walking home hand-in-arm about town by this time tomorrow.

Even if Frank had managed to spend time with another young woman without the town discovering it, his sister-in-law, Pearl, would have seen it, Amy knew. Pearl was her best friend and married to Frank's older brother, Jason. They all lived on the Sterling family farm together, along with Frank and Jason's younger siblings. Quoting Alexandre Dumas, Pearl liked to say, "One for all and all for one," referring to the way the family members looked out for each other since Frank and Jason's parents died a little over a year ago.

The path meandered along the edge of the bluff overlooking the Minnesota River Valley where the oldest section of town lay. Mostly business buildings now lined the street below; most of the residences were built on the bluff. Windom Academy was off by itself on the edge of town. As they neared the houses, the smell of smoke from coal and wood fires drifted on the crisp air.

Frank stopped, looking out over the valley. "I love this view."

"I do, too," Amy agreed, "especially like this, when the lights shine through the evening snowfall."

Not many business lights were on at this time of night, but the street lamps were lit, and yellow squares shown from the saloon windows.

"Look." Frank pointed into the darkness. "People must be skating by the mill. See the bonfire beside the warming house?"

"I wish we'd thought to bring our blades." Sylvia's voice dripped disappointment.

"Let's arrange a skating party over the holidays," Amy suggested.

The others quickly agreed and decided the next night would be the perfect time.

The idea brought back to Amy memories of skating with Frank the previous winter at the Shakespearean Rink. She'd been surprised when he'd stopped beside her at the edge of the rink and asked her to skate. Many of the girls her age were hoping he'd show interest in them. He seldom did, not before and not after he asked to keep company with Amy.

She understood without Frank stating it that he was not a man who courted girls lightly. She'd wanted to honor his promise to prove his decision to give up drinking and gambling by not allowing other men to escort her during the past year.

"Foolish notion," her father had raved. "And what if young Sterling doesn't have the backbone to keep up the fight? You'll not waste your time waiting for him while other, more responsible men want to escort you."

"It isn't honorable to take the chance I might give my heart to another when I've promised him—"

"You've only promised to attend a church service with him, not to marry the man." Her father had stopped his tirade and looked over the top of his reading glasses to fix a better-tell-the-truth glare upon her. "At least you've told me of no other promise."

She'd felt her face heat. "I've made no other promise, but you made one. You promised him that if he didn't drink or gamble for a year, he could court me."

"Hmmmph. I didn't mean to imply formal courtship, only that I wouldn't object to him keeping company with you." Her father looked back at his paper. "Never told him you wouldn't be promised to someone else at the end of the year."

"I should think your promise implied I'd be free, and I intend to be free."

In the end, she'd reluctantly agreed to other escorts. She didn't tell her father she'd made a promise to herself not to allow any man to escort her more than once. "I won't tease them with the possibility of winning my affections," she'd vowed.

Joy filled her now, strolling with Frank in the midst of the warmth and laughter of friends. Still, she wished for private time together. She wanted to tell him how proud she was of him, that she knew his battle wasn't easy, that she'd prayed every day of the last year that God would give him strength. Would she have the courage to say these things if they were alone? Probably not, she admitted to herself. It would be too bold. He might think she was reminding him of their agreement to go to the service together.

The group dwindled as, one by one, they reached students' homes and said good night. There were only two girls and three young men left when they reached Amy's house. Laughing, they walked her up onto the broad porch and right to her door. "Wouldn't want you to slip again," Walter said, falling in beside her and Frank at the bottom of the steps and placing a hand under her elbow.

She stood inside the hall beside the open, etched-glass door and watched them leave, their voices and laughter fading. Did Frank glance back once over his shoulder at her, or did her wishful thinking make it appear so?

Amy closed the door slowly and rested her forehead against the glass. The heady joy of the evening began melting into doubt. Was it possible Frank had forgotten the promise to attend Christmas Eve services together?

$\mathcal{F}$ rank dismounted from his horse and tied the reins to the ring beside the horse stoop at the street in front of the Hendersons' home. He reached for the hat resting on the saddle horn, then turned and started up the walk toward the house.

"Hey, Frank, wait up."

Frank groaned. He forced a smile. "Hi." He'd forgotten Roland lived next door to Amy. He held the hat at his side, low, and slightly behind him, hoping his jacket would help conceal the dainty item.

Roland punched Frank's shoulder and winked. "I can guess what you're doing in this part of the woods. Heard you walked Miss Amy home last night."

"About a dozen of us, men and women, walked her home." Frank attempted to keep his tone emotionless.

"Hear tell it was your arm she was leanin' on."

"It was slippery out."

"Yes, it certainly was, especially in areas of the heart."

Frank gripped the hat brim tighter. *If he doesn't stop that irritating wink, I'll . . .* Frank couldn't think of anything his conscience would allow. He forced a lightness to his voice. "Think you're taking those romantic poets in English literature too seriously, Roland. You're seeing romance in everything."

Roland grinned. "Like in that fancy bonnet you're tryin' to hide?"

Frank's neck and face heated as though he stood too close to a woodstove. "Just returning the lady's hat. She lost it last night."

Roland's grin widened. "That must have been easy to do on an innocent walk on a windless night in the middle of a crowd. I guess she forgot her hat pins at home."

"Excuse me." Frank brushed past Roland without looking at him. His indignation only earned him more laughter. When he reached the porch, he glanced over his shoulder. Roland's bouncy stride carried him away down the walk.

Anger dissipated when Amy opened the door. She looked a vision to him in her rose-colored dress with its high lace collar. Pleasant surprise shown in her eyes. "Hello, Frank. Won't you come in?"

He stepped inside the foyer and held out the tiny hat. "I came to return this."

She gasped and reached for it. "I can't believe you found it. I was certain it landed in some treetop, and come spring it would house a family of robins."

"Missed the treetops. I found it perched pretty as you please on a bush."

"I do hope you didn't spend hours and hours searching for it, though I am delighted to see it." Amy turned the hat about, examining it from every angle.

It had taken him the better part of the afternoon, and the bush was taller than his five feet seven inches, but he wasn't about to say so, or mention the snag the bush caused in his good trousers. "The hat doesn't look too much the worse for spending a night in the woods. That ribbon might need replacing, but the cloth flowers and the feathers are all right, I think. 'Course, me being a man, I don't rightly know for sure."

She fingered the maroon ribbon, her eyes sparkling in a smile. "Me being a woman," she mimicked, "I expect you're right."

He grinned, happy as a horse freed to pasture just to be looking at her and teasing with her.

"Oh, dear." Amy set the hat down on a marble-topped table beneath a gold-edged mirror. "Seeing my hat excited me so much that I forgot my manners. Won't you come in and visit?"

"I'd like to see your father, if he's in."

She hesitated only a moment, darting Frank a curious glance. "He's in the library. May I take your coat? Then I'll tell him you're here."

"I don't want to disturb him," Frank said, unbuttoning his jacket.

"I'm sure he'll be glad to speak with you." She hung his jacket and wide-brimmed hat on the mahogany hall tree's marble-tipped hooks before heading for the library.

Frank began pacing as soon as she left the hall. He stopped in front of the mirror and slicked back his hair. He wouldn't be more nervous if he were intending to ask permission to be Amy's only suitor. He'd like to ask that, but he knew the time wasn't right. He loved Amy and was reasonably sure she wasn't interested in anyone else. It was her father Frank believed wouldn't agree to a formal courtship yet.

Frank knew it was unusual for a young man to ask permission to court a girl in the everyday context of keeping company without the special privileges of a formal courtship. But Frank and Amy's situation was unusual. Frank had agreed to Mr. Henderson's demand to prove himself for a year. It was only fitting he ask the man's permission to keep company with Amy.

Frank shut his eyes and took a deep breath. "Please, Lord, let him say yes. And I could sure use some strength while meeting with him."

Amy returned and led him to the library. He ignored the curiosity in her eyes. He'd satisfy her questions when he knew the answers.

The room's somber elegance tested his already-strained courage. Bookcases on all but the outer wall reached to the ceiling, filled with books bound in blue, red, and brown leather with gold lettering. Mr. Henderson cast an imposing figure in the high-backed leather chair behind the mahogany desk, a shaft of late-afternoon sunlight from the tall window touching the white hair ringing his balding head. He wasn't wearing a suit jacket, but that was the only acquiescence he'd made to casual dress, Frank noted.

Mr. Henderson removed his reading glasses, rose, and extended his hand to Frank over the desktop. "Won't you be seated, Sterling? What can I do for you?"

Both men sat down, Frank in the leather wing chair facing the desk. His heart beat hard where his Adam's apple usually resided. "Sir, I'd like your permission to keep company with your daughter."

Henderson eyed him over pyramided fingertips. "I believe I set out my conditions to your intention last year."

"Yes, Sir."

"You were to stay sober and out of trouble for a year."

"Yes, Sir. I mean, I have, Sir."

"I hadn't forgotten the year was almost up. I spoke with Sheriff Amundson, asked him what he knows about your habits. He keeps a close eye on the saloons and billiard halls since so many fights break out at those establishments." The older man's eyes didn't blink or shift.

Frank tried to keep his gaze as steady as that he faced. He swallowed hard. Why be nervous? He hadn't anything to hide. "I haven't entered a saloon or billiard hall since before I gave my word to you and Amy, not even the temperance billiard hall."

"So Amundson said." Distrust filled the older man's voice.

Frank's heart sank. What could he say to prove his case if Mr. Henderson didn't believe the sheriff?

"A man can drink outside of a saloon," Henderson observed.

"I give you my word I haven't had a sip of liquor."

Henderson leaned his elbows on the desk. "You have my permission to ask Amy if she wishes to court you. I'll be honest with you. I prefer she court a man who never had a reason to reform. If I hear you've slipped back into your old ways, you will stop courting my daughter and never speak to her again."

"Yes, Sir. I won't slip." Frank stood and rubbed the palm of his hand quickly against his trouser leg before extending his hand. "Thank you, Sir."

Amy's father's lips tightened, but he shook hands. "Mind you, I'm not granting you the right to ask Amy to enter into a formal courtship. You may ask Amy to court you, but not exclusively."

"I understand, Sir."

The thick rug cushioned Frank's steps like the cloud he felt he walked on when he left the room. *Thank You, Lord. Thank You for giving me the backbone to ask him, and thank You that he said yes.*

He found Amy in the dining room arranging red carnations in a crystal bowl on the lace-covered dining-room table. "Business completed?" she asked with a small smile.

"Yes. At least, my business with your father. May I speak with you for a minute?"

"Of course." She stopped playing with the flowers and gave him her full attention.

He'd waited so long for this moment, and now he didn't know how to start. He shored up his courage with the reminder that less than twenty-four hours earlier she'd walked home from the Academy on his arm, apparently content to be close to him. "My business with your father involves you. You might recall the promise I made to him last year."

"Yes." A sweet flush brightened her cheeks.

"I kept that promise, Miss Amy, honest I did."

"I know that."

Her quiet assurance stopped his train of thought. "You do?"

"Of course. I knew you would keep it. You aren't a man who breaks his word."

Gratitude and wonder at her faith in him surged through him. Her lashes hid her eyes for a moment, then swept up in a shy manner. "Even so, I prayed for you."

"You did?"

She nodded. "Every night."

All those times he'd struggled to keep away from drink and gambling dens, thinking he was all alone in the fight, Amy's faith and the Lord had been alongside him. It humbled him. "You made a promise, too."

Her smile lit her eyes. "I thought you'd forgotten."

"Not likely." He grinned. "I've been living on that promise. That is . . . you don't need to keep it, you know." It was easier to say after seeing her smile.

"I don't go back on my word, either."

"I know." He paused, realizing his words echoed her faith in him. "I'm releasing you from your promise."

Her smile disappeared. "I see."

He could barely hear the words. *She thinks I don't want to go to the Christmas Eve service with her.* "I'm not saying this right." He ran a hand through his hair. "I only meant I don't want you to feel obligated to . . . to allow me to escort you . . . anywhere." He watched her serious gaze searching his. "I've waited a year to ask this, and now I've messed it up something fierce."

"What is your question?"

He took a deep breath and straightened his shoulders. "Miss Amy, would you do me the honor of attending the Christmas Eve service with me?"

"Yes."

He swiped his hands as if declaring a baseball runner safe. "Only if you want to, not because you feel obligated."

One side of her mouth tipped in a smile. "That's a bold question, Mr. Sterling, but I assure you I am not saying yes from a sense of obligation."

He grinned. "Good. I mean, I'm glad." He shifted his weight from one foot to the other and back again. "Guess I should be leaving."

"I'll see you to the door."

Coat, hat, and gloves back on, Frank stepped onto the porch. "Would you like to go skating? A bunch from the Academy are going to be at the Shakespearean Rink tonight."

"Thank you, but I can't. Father's invited a guest for dinner, and I'm expected to act as hostess."

Frank nodded, only slightly disappointed. The promise of Christmas Eve made it impossible to feel letdown. "I'll see you on Christmas Eve, then." He touched his hand to his hat brim and left.

Mounted on his horse, he glanced back at the house. He didn't see her watching from the door or window, but he waved just in case.

❧

Amy leaned back against the rose-embossed wallpaper beside the front door and sighed with pure joy. With eyes closed, she relived the last few minutes. "He didn't forget the promise after all," she whispered.

"Who are you talking to?" Her father's voice boomed out, startling her.

"Just me, myself, and I." She stood on tiptoe and kissed his cheek.

"I suppose that Sterling boy is the reason you're so bubbly."

"You know he is."

"It's unseemly to be so obvious about it. You're only courting, not engaged."

She laughed at his grumpy tone and slipped a hand under his arm. "You're just a poor loser. You didn't think he'd change."

"A leopard doesn't change its spots."

"Frank Sterling is a man, not a leopard. Men can change, especially when they let God help them."

"I'd rather you courted someone who didn't have any spots that needed changing, someone like Walter Bay."

Amy wrinkled her nose. "Oh, Father, please."

"Bay has a good business head on his shoulders. He's never been in trouble with the law, which is certainly more than you can say for Sterling. Walter Bay is good husband material."

"Now who is talking engagements? And to a man I haven't even courted."

"He's interested. I see it in his eyes when he's watching you. If he asks to court you, I want you to say yes."

"I don't care to court him."

"Bay hasn't the dark good looks that make Sterling so attractive to the girls in this town—"

"Frank doesn't act the Don Juan."

"Girls aren't the only ones who talk. Parents do, too. I know girls like his looks. Bay probably seems plain and staid to you beside Sterling, but he's settled and steady, and that's a good thing for a woman."

A slight shudder ran through her. "There's something about him I can't place my finger on, but it makes me distrust him. Besides, what about Frank? You've already given your blessing to our courting."

"Permission, not blessing." He laid his hands on her shoulders. "Choosing a husband is serious business. A girl's heart isn't always the best judge of what's good for her." He sighed deeply. "I wish your mother were here to advise you about men."

And everything else, she thought. The five years since her mother's death had been hard on both her and her father. She crossed her arms and gave her father a teasing glance. "Mother would be supporting me and giving advice to you about the men in my life."

Her quip brought a chuckle, but he didn't change his tune. "You haven't let any of the many men interested in you buzz around for long. I think you're only interested in Sterling because I placed a 'no trespassing' sign in front of him for the last year."

"Father!"

"I told him he could ask you to court him, but not ask you to court him exclusively."

"I won't be one of those girls who teases men, trying to make them jealous and keep them guessing as to my affections. It's disrespectful. You know you wouldn't like it if I acted that way."

"All I'm asking is that you don't settle for less of a man than you deserve."

"I won't, Father."

He chucked her under the chin she'd raised in defiance. "Give Walter a chance. Be nice to him at dinner tonight."

$\mathcal{A}$ my was polite to Walter during the meal, but her mind drifted to Frank and the service they'd attend together in a few days. Conversation flowed easily between Walter and her father. Their common views on business and finance were apparent as they discussed the silver question, the labor element warring against capitalists, and the unemployment and poor economic conditions following the Panic of '93.

The two men had met in the library for almost an hour before dinner. She hoped that meant they'd resolved any personal business and Walter wouldn't be staying long into the evening. She sighed behind her napkin when her father instructed the maid to serve after-dinner coffee in the parlor.

Amy's years of training in deportment and duty came to her assistance as always. She smiled pleasantly while pouring coffee for the men from the silver teapot and asking Walter's preference in cream and sugar.

Walter's gaze bore into hers as she handed him the china cup. She resented his rudeness and turned her attention to serving her father.

"You have a beautiful home, Mr. Henderson."

"Thank you, but that compliment belongs to my wife. It was her gift for making a building into a home that gave beauty to this house. She and I lived in a number of homes over the years, but no others were as special as this one."

"Not many homes in this part of the country compare to it, Sir."

"It's not the grandeur that gives it worth." Mr. Henderson's voice held a hint of reproof. "It's precious because my wife loved it and because it's the last place where we were together. Amy is the only thing I treasure more than this home."

Amy felt a painful lump form in her throat. Her father had loved her mother deeply. Did life sometimes seem unbearable to him without her?

After a moment Walter cleared his throat. Amy wondered whether her father's revealing personal comments had made their guest uncomfortable.

"Are you planning to join our friends at the ice rink tonight, Miss Amy?" Walter asked. "A number of the local Windom students are gathering there this evening," he explained to Mr. Henderson.

"Amy hasn't mentioned it. I hope you two don't think you need to entertain me." He waved a hand in a dismissing motion. "Go, enjoy yourselves. If I were young and spry, I'd head down there myself."

"That's kind of you, Sir. If Miss Amy would—"

"I enjoy spending my evenings with you, Father." Amy hoped her consternation didn't show in her quick reply.

"Spoken like a dutiful daughter, but I'm sure you'd prefer spending time with your friends. Run upstairs and change clothes."

Fury set Amy's hands to trembling so that she barely kept her cup and saucer from rattling. "I wouldn't want to impose myself upon Mr. Bay, Father."

"It's no imposition, I assure you." Walter's eyes sparkled in what to Amy seemed wicked glee.

Twenty minutes later she came down dressed in her emerald green skating outfit.

"Didn't you have a new skating outfit made?" her father asked.

"I'm keeping it for the new year." She hoped to wear the new outfit with Frank. Her pleasure in it would be removed if she wore it with Walter.

She hugged her father good-bye at the door. "You practically demanded I go with Walter tonight. How could you?" she whispered in his ear. "This is a low, mean trick."

He patted her back, and his voice held laughter. "Yes, yes, I hope you have a wonderful time." He beamed while waving them out the door.

The walk to the rink through the crisp early evening air did nothing to cool Amy's temper. Even the sounds of blades against ice and voices raised in fun didn't calm the fire in her chest. She answered questions posed by Walter politely but introduced no topics of conversation herself. A sliver of guilt stabbed at her. Was her attitude unfair toward Walter? After all, her father was the one who'd pushed them together. It only appeared that the two men had conspired together against her. Or did it?

The rink brought back memories of skating with Frank the previous year. They'd only skated together a few minutes, but those minutes comprised one of her favorite times. She'd loved the way his arm held her gently yet firmly snug against his side. She'd loved his gentle but shy gaze when he'd looked into her eyes. They'd skated in lovely unison, and for those few minutes no one else had existed in her world.

And to think she'd turned down Frank's invitation to skate tonight only to be forced to come with Walter.

In the middle of the rink, a bunch of boys were playing crack the whip, their screams filled half with fear and half with fun. Older boys flirted by, dashing in and out between girls who skated sedately along the rink's edge. Couples skated arm-in-arm, the women's skirts swaying.

Amy's gaze searched the rink for friends. Figures moved in and out of the shadows and light cast by the rinkside lanterns. "There's Roland." She pointed him out to Walter, laughing. Seeing other friends lifted her spirits. "He's up to his usual pranks, skating circles around Sylvia and her sister."

"Maybe he'll keep them so busy they won't see us. Sylvia could talk the ear off a stalk of corn."

"I like her friendly manner. She never speaks unkindly of people." *Unlike present company.*

A couple whirled up to the rink's edge with a flashy turn. "Hello, Amy."

"Pearl, Jason, hello," she greeted Frank's brother and sister-in-law. Their cheeks were cherry red and their eyes bright with fun. "How nice you could make it in from the farm."

Jason pulled his wife close with one arm. "Couldn't miss a perfect skating night like this."

Walter took Amy's elbow. "Let's get our skating boots on and join them out on the ice."

Amy saw the surprise and question in Pearl's eyes at Walter's proprietary touch. Slipping her skating boots from where they'd hung on her shoulder effectively removed his hand for the moment.

Friends of all ages called and waved to them as they made their way toward the bonfire in front of the warming house. The wood smoke seemed to warm Amy's lungs before she and Walter reached the group standing about the crackling fire. She sat down on a log that was already brushed free of snow and began to unbutton a boot.

"Let me help you with that." Walter knelt in the snow in front of her.

Annoyance flickered across her chest when his hands brushed her fingers away from her boot. "Please, Walter, I—"

"Amy."

Her head shot up at the strangled sound of her name. Behind Walter stood Frank, disbelief and betrayal in his eyes.

◈

Frank didn't wait for a response. The surprise in Amy's eyes showed she hadn't expected to see him. Frank turned on his heel and headed toward the street and his horse. Pain cinched his chest like a tight saddle belt. He brushed past people, not caring whether he knew them.

He climbed into the saddle and turned his horse toward home. The sound of piano music and laughter from Plummer's Saloon down the street caught his attention. He hesitated, remembering the way amber-colored beer slid down the throat so easily, the way problems slid away after a few drinks, and the pleasant camaraderie of others who cooled burning hearts with liquor. A way to ease the pain was so close, only a short way down the main street.

He pressed his lips together tight and nudged his horse with his knees. "Let's get home, Boy."

His pain didn't ease as he rode out of town, down the straight, empty, rutted road toward the farm. The cold air didn't ease the burning in his stomach caused by the memory of Walter Bay's hand on Amy's boot. How could she allow such intimate contact only hours after agreeing to permit him, Frank, to court her?

He'd thought she wanted that as much as he did. The way her eyes lit up when he asked her to the Christmas Eve service, her assurance that she'd been praying for him, her insistence that she was agreeing to see him because she wanted to, not because she felt obligated, all led him to believe she cared.

"I'm a fool. A certified, one hundred percent fool."

He hadn't asked her to court him exclusively, or at all, he realized. He'd only asked her to attend the Christmas Eve service with him. He'd assumed she wouldn't be any more interested in courting others than he was. Evidently he'd assumed wrong.

But the worst, what cut straight into his heart, was the lie. "She didn't say she was going skating with someone else. She said she was hostessing a dinner for her father."

His horse tossed its head as though trying to look back at him and snorted. Frank patted its neck. "I'm not talking to you, Boy."

Frank had never been interested in any girl but Amy. Even when they were children, he'd liked her quiet ways. She'd always befriended the shy students at school.

She'd won his heart when they were ten. The class had spent a fun morning capturing butterflies. The next morning the class arrived at school to find all the butterflies gone. When the angry teacher demanded who had released them, Amy quietly admitted her act. He liked that she wanted the butterflies to be free, that she'd had the courage to set them free and the courage to admit she was the guilty party.

He'd watched her grow into a serene, strong, beautiful young woman. The more he learned about her, the more he admired her. That made the thought she'd lied to him all the more painful.

This afternoon his world had looked brighter than a snow-covered field in sunshine. Now even the light looked dark.

❧

Amy's heart tossed and upended like a tumbleweed rolling across the prairie. The pain in Frank's eyes insisted on interfering with her vision and played havoc with her usual smooth skating strokes. She tripped herself and Walter repeatedly. After causing a tangled heap of fellow skaters for the fifth time, she held up her mittened hands in resignation. "I'm sorry. It's my first time on skates this year."

Walter helped her to her feet and slid an arm around her waist. "My arm's available to lean on."

Amy shifted away. "I need to practice staying upright under my own power." She hoped her excuse softened the sting of her repeated moves away from him. She preferred more forthright behavior, but her father's desire that she spend time with Walter kept a guard on her tongue. The only familiarity she allowed Walter was to hold her hand over a rough patch of ice.

She excused herself twice to skate with Pearl. Walter skated uninvited beside them. His presence prevented Amy from sharing with Pearl her frustration over Walter's escort. If only she could manage a few minutes alone with her friend, she knew Pearl would relate the truth of the situation to Frank.

Amy watched in dismay as Pearl and Jason left before Amy found the private moment she'd hoped for. She had no desire to stay after Pearl left.

"It's a perfect skating night, but I'm cold, Walter."

"Some time by the fire will warm you up. There's popcorn to warm your insides, too."

"I'd rather go home."

"It's early yet."

"Maybe it's all the falls I've taken tonight that have tired me." It was worrying over Frank's reaction to seeing her with Walter that had tired her, but her mother's social training was hard to overcome. "Please don't feel you need to escort me home. I'll understand if you prefer to stay here with your friends."

His eyes glittered in the light of the lantern at rinkside. "There's no one here whose company I prefer to yours. Let me help you with your skates."

The wooden stairs leading up the ridge from Main Street to the residential streets on the prairie above were slippery with frost. Walter insisted on keeping one hand on her back "for safety" even though she kept one hand on the wooden banister. Amy reflected with an aching heart how coldly she responded to his touch and assistance compared to her reaction to Frank's care for her the previous night.

They were both breathing a bit harder when they reached the top of the steps across the street from the new, three-story brick school. They turned left and started toward her home.

"I was impressed with your sketching ability last night," Walter complimented. "Professor Headley tells me you'll be teaching an art course at the Academy next quarter."

At last a subject she could discuss with pleasure. "Yes. I'm flattered he asked me to teach. In spite of the wonderful reception my work received at the Minnesota Exhibition in St. Paul last year, I know I have much to learn."

"You're being modest."

"Not at all. I'd love to study the masters."

"What's preventing you?"

"I'd need to travel to Europe."

He stopped, a stunned look on his face. "You speak as if you were planning to become an artist."

She lifted her chin to look him squarely in the eye. "I am an artist."

"I know, but it's only a hobby, isn't it? Certainly no woman with a true feminine soul would travel about the world unchaperoned simply to study art. Besides, from what I understand, some pictures are hardly suitable for a woman to view."

Amy began walking, her stride lengthening. How dare he comment on her character and artistic ambitions? He hadn't even waited to hear what she wanted to do with her painting before condemning her interest in it. Blood pounded in her ears, warning her to calm down before speaking.

"Careful." Walter caught her elbow. "You've fallen enough on the ice tonight. You don't want to fall here, too."

She thought she needed more care with her tongue than her feet.

Perhaps the way to avoid more attacks on herself was to direct attention toward him. "What are your ambitions, Mr. Bay?"

Usually she considered the social requirement of calling young men she'd known since knee-pants days by their surname silly, though she normally complied with it. But on this occasion, the rule provided a convenient way to gently inform Walter that she wasn't interested in moving beyond friendship. Hopefully he would take the hint.

"My business is doing well in Chippewa City for the moment. I plan to eventually expand my real-estate and loan business across a broader area, perhaps relocate to a larger city."

"I'm sure you'd do well in a larger town." Everyone knew everyone else in Chippewa City. Walter might be able to draw the wool over the eyes of the older businessmen such as her father, but those closer to his own age weren't fooled by his false charm. In a city where people didn't know him so well, she thought, he might do better; although she had to admit he was doing quite well already. "Father has mentioned your fine business mind more than once."

"Ah, I'm glad to hear someone is praising my virtues to you."

This wasn't the direction she wanted the conversation to go.

They turned into the walk to her house. "I'd like to escort you to the Christmas Eve service, Miss Amy."

Surprise left her speechless. For a year she'd thought of attending the service with Frank. It never occurred to her that someone else might ask to accompany her.

At the bottom of the front steps, Walter stopped her with his hand on her arm. "Did you hear me?"

"Yes." At least he'd waited until now to ask. The painted parlor lamp in the window shed comforting light over the porch and onto her and Walter. "Your invitation surprises me. I—"

"I'm sure you've noticed my interest in you lately." Amusement tinged his voice.

Amy nodded. "Yes." She took a deep breath. "Thank you for honoring me with your invitation, Mr. Bay, but I've already agreed to join Mr. Sterling at the Christmas Eve service."

"Ah." He clasped his hands behind his back and lowered his gaze to the walk. "I'm sure you are too much the lady to rescind your acceptance of Sterling's invitation?" He glanced up beneath raised eyebrows.

She almost laughed at his conceit, for his inflection indicated he hoped she would change her mind. "Yes, I am, Mr. Bay." Amy stilled her smile. She wanted to honor her father, but she simply could not continue seeing this man. She adjusted her already straight shoulders, giving herself courage. "I must tell you that I never allow anyone to escort me more than once. I realize your invitation is a great compliment, and it is with respect for that honor that I ask you not to ask me again."

His expression didn't change. His gaze seemed to study hers, though Amy couldn't be certain in the lamplight. "Not ask you again to attend the Christmas Eve service, or not ask to escort you again to anything?"

Her fingers gripped the laces of her skates tighter, but she kept her gaze and voice steady. "Anything."

Walter burst into laughter.

Amy stared at him. No men had responded to her refusals with mirth before.

He stepped toe-to-toe with her. She wanted to step back, but she was at the edge of the walk and didn't care to step into the snow.

Walter took her chin between his thumb and index finger and jerked her chin up.

Shock rippled through her.

He brought his face close to hers. His eyes appeared black with anger. She tried to pull her head back, but he tightened his hold on her chin. "Your innocence is endearing, but make no mistake, I will escort you again, and you will welcome my escort."

He released her so suddenly she almost stumbled.

Walter stepped back. "In fact, my dear Miss Henderson, not only will we court, but we will marry."

Amy's mouth dropped open.

Walter bowed deeply. Then, with a laugh, he left.

4

*F*ury still roiled in place of Amy's usual calm the next morning. She donned an apron and joined Lina, the maid who had been with the family for ten years, cleaning the downstairs in an attempt to work off her anger. Amy's thoughts continued to center on Walter's uncouth behavior rather than on housely duties.

"Watch out!" Lina caught a china figurine before it hit the pale blue etched parlor rug. "Miss Amy, you yield that feather duster like a weapon."

"I've something prickly on my mind." She brushed back a lock of hair that had fallen from its upsweep. "Thank you for catching the figurine. Mother loved that lady. I would never have forgiven myself if I'd broken it."

"You are a pure danger in here." Lina gently took the duster from Amy's hand. "Why don't you put on a pretty outfit and get out of the house? Surely there must be something you still need to buy for Christmas."

"Perhaps that's a good idea." Amy untied her apron strings while she headed to her room to change into her tailored tweed gown. Knocking the figurine from its place on the mahogany wall shelf had jolted the fury out of her and left her with a bone-melting weariness.

Walking down to the shops in the crisp morning sunshine rejuvenated her body and spirits. School was out, and children were everywhere: playing fox and geese, building snowmen, launching snowballs from behind white fort walls, flailing their arms as they made snow angels, and filling the air with their whoops above flying sleds and shovels.

Amy's hatbox swung from her arm by its gold satin string. The pretty little hat in need of a new ribbon rested inside. By the time she reached Miss Hermanson's Millinery, she'd regained her usual serenity.

Miss Hermanson's hands fluttered about the hat. "Mm, mm, mmm. Poor thing. It's been through a bout, hasn't it? Well, never mind. I'll replace the ribbon, and it will be good as new. Of course, it will take a bit of doing, as the ribbon winds in and out over the standing feathers and flowers. The matching bow in front will need to be replaced, too."

"I know you're awfully busy with the holidays upon us, but could you possibly have it ready by Christmas Eve?" Amy gave her most apologetic smile.

The millinery artist hesitated only a moment. "For you, of course."

"Thank you. I can't tell you how much it means to me." Amy's gloved hand gave Miss Hermanson's fingers a quick squeeze. The tinkling bells above the door reflected Amy's lighter heart as she left the store.

She stopped in front of the window at Sherdahl Jewelers, her attention caught by a large snow globe. In it a couple skated, joined forever above the walnut music-box base. The image brought back the sweet joy of skating with Frank. That pleasure was immediately shadowed by the memory of his eyes when he saw her the previous night with Walter, and her heart crimped.

Amy turned abruptly, blinking back tears. *I don't remember when I've been such an emotional puddle.*

She hurried into the general store next door and turned to a display counter away from other customers and clerks, hoping to hide her telltale face. The move only brought her to a collection of mustache cups, which reminded her of Frank. She laughed at a caricature of a man with a narrow mustache with elaborately curled ends, which decorated one mug. If she and Frank had been courting for awhile, she would purchase it for him, just for fun.

No telling if he'd court her after last night. What if he didn't come to take her to the Christmas Eve service? The thought brought her up short. A moment later she shook her head. Frank Sterling was too much the gentleman to go back on his word that way. She turned from the display with a sigh.

That's quite enough of your self-pity. Think about someone else. Young people could always be found at Arnold's Ice Cream Parlor. It was just the place to get her mind off Frank.

Half a dozen Academy students were gathered about one of the tables in the parlor. Their warm welcome cheered her and convinced her she'd chosen the right place. The group was all a-chatter with holiday plans: house parties, dances, sledding, and sleighing.

Amy's enjoyment dimmed when Walter joined the group. The others' greetings to him weren't as friendly as they'd been for her, but they invited him to join in their parties. He smiled and laughed with everyone, but Amy had a hard time avoiding his gaze, which seemed pinned on her most of the time. She told herself she only thought it was so because of their altercation the night before; yet whenever she glanced in his direction, his gaze met hers with that laughing warning she'd seen in it in the dim lamplight.

When the group left, Amy purposely walked between Sylvia and her sister. Walter circumvented her attempt to avoid him by catching her elbow from behind and asking in a loud, overly friendly voice, "May I speak with you a moment, Miss Henderson? I'd like to ask your opinion on a gift for my mother."

Reluctance crawled through her, but she allowed herself to be drawn to his side in order to avoid drawing undue attention from the group. "I can't give an opinion on a gift. I don't know your mother, Mr. Bay, remember?"

"But you have excellent taste. I'm trying to choose between two perfumes. Will you stop at Heiberg and Torgerson's with me and see which scent you prefer?"

"One's preference in scent is so personal. I'm not sure—"

"Please."

She nodded curtly, wishing she hadn't been raised "to be a lady," as her mother would state it.

They said their good-byes to the others and turned toward Heiberg and Torgerson's. As soon as they were out of her friends' hearing, Amy stopped. She gently pulled her arm away from Walter and clutched her black reticule at her waist with both hands. "Mr. Bay,

I had no wish to embarrass either of us before our friends, but I have no intention of assisting you in something as personal as selecting a gift for your mother. I thought I made my feelings clear last night—"

"You made them most clear. I thought I made my intentions clear, too."

Heat flooded her cheeks in spite of the cold. "I'm sure your words were spoken in jest."

"Think again. I've something you should see." He undid the top buttons of his coat, pulled an envelope from an inner pocket, and held it out toward her.

Dread coiled within her. She took a step back, coming up against the general-store window. She didn't know why she reacted so strongly to his gesture, but she knew with absolute certainty she didn't want to touch that envelope. "What is it?"

"The mortgage papers on your home."

Her gaze shot from the envelope to his face. "That's ridiculous. Why should you have them?"

"A lot of banks have gone under in these hard times. I've bought up a number of loans, including your father's."

Her hold on her reticule tightened. "Why are you telling me this?"

"Your father, like so many men, is behind in his payments."

"You're lying. Father is extremely wise in financial matters. He'd never allow his payments to lapse, nor would he dishonor a debt."

"You're right about his intentions. He assures me he intends to pay every penny he owes."

She adjusted her shoulders. This conversation was getting tiresome. "Then I repeat, why are you telling me this?"

Walter moved casually to her side and leaned against the building. "I intend to call his loan."

It took a moment for her mind to grasp the words. "You're going to require him to pay it off completely?"

He nodded, his eyes watching her face.

"But surely the contract requires the payments to be spread over a number of years." She'd learned a few things from growing up with a father who loved business.

"The contract states the loan can be called if he gets behind in payments. He's behind, way behind."

Her heart skipped a beat. She held out her hand. "I'd like to see the papers, please." She removed the papers from the envelope and scanned the agreement. There were the awful words in black and white with her father's signature at the bottom. Walter wasn't lying. He could demand payment. Slowly she refolded the papers, returned them to the envelope, and handed them back.

"He can't pay it, you know." Walter's tone was almost gentle.

Amy couldn't understand why she didn't feel anything. She'd been furious last night and this morning at Walter's presumption that she'd marry him, yet now his challenge to her father left her numb. "Why are you doing this?"

"Do you know the best thing about money?"

She waited, watching him.

"Power. You can make people do almost anything if you have money and they don't."

Disgust made her nauseous. "What is it you want?"

"You, Amy. I want you for my wife."

5

*A*my's stomach turned over. She couldn't pull her gaze from Walter's laughing one. "You can't be serious."

"I assure you I am most serious. I will call your father's loan if you don't agree to marry me. It will bankrupt him."

She stared at him, unable to speak. *This is a nightmare. In a few minutes I'll awaken, and Father and I will have a hearty laugh over it.*

Walter touched a gloved finger to the brim of his brown derby. "I'll let you think on it until tomorrow. Why don't I take you to dinner? You can give me your answer then."

She watched him walk away, helplessness swirling through her like snow in a blizzard. Slowly anger rose up. He was lying, of course, trying to manipulate her. How could he think she would believe him? Her father was a wealthy man. Did Walter truly believe she would so easily fall into his trap?

Perhaps he only wanted her to agree to his terms so he could laugh at her. Maybe it was all a trick to repay her for telling him she didn't wish to court him.

But the mortgage papers were real.

She started toward home. Her thoughts raced faster than the heels of her boots clicking against the boardwalk. Just because the papers were real didn't mean it was true that her father was behind in payments or that he wasn't able to pay off the loan if it was called. He had lots of investments. Surely, if necessary, he could liquidate them.

What was happening to her life? She'd always considered herself a peace-filled person. The last two days she'd hardly known a peaceful moment, and all the disturbance was due to Walter Bay.

Her heart turned to the One she'd always trusted. *Dear Lord, please help Father and me, and keep us in the peace of Christ.*

Immediately Romans 8:35 flashed into her mind. "Who shall separate us from the love of Christ?"

"No one, Lord," she whispered into the winter wind that tugged at her scarf, "not even Walter Bay."

❧

Amy reminded herself of that verse more than once as the day and evening progressed. Peace was illusive, slipping in and out of her heart. "How shall I approach Father about his finances, Lord?" she asked. She was sure the Lord answered her, but she couldn't hear the answer; her mind whirled with questions and fears that made her deaf to the Lord's voice.

At dinner with her father that night, she watched the candlelight play off the crystal while she continued to study the problem. When she'd asked her father last summer if she might buy the new crystal pattern, he'd immediately said yes, as he did to all her requests. She couldn't recall a single instance in which he'd asked her to economize.

Mrs. Jorgenson stepped into the room, and Amy's gaze swerved to her. The cook surveyed the table to see whether any items needed replenishing.

"We're fine for now, Mrs. J." Father beamed at her. "This roast is done to perfection."

Mrs. Jorgenson's smile filled her broad Scandinavian face as she retreated into the kitchen.

Would Father keep Mrs. Jorgenson's and Lina's services if he were bankrupt? Amy wondered.

"Amy."

"Yes, Father?"

His eyes beneath heavy white eyebrows twinkled with amusement. "I've asked twice how you spent your day."

"I'm sorry. I guess I was woolgathering." She told him of her trip to the millinery and meeting her friends at the ice-cream parlor and the many plans for holiday parties, but left out Mr. Bay and his revelations.

"Are you attending any parties tonight?" he asked.

"No. Most of the evening parties are planned for between Christmas and New Year's. There's a tobogganing party tomorrow afternoon, but Lina and I will be baking for Christmas."

"Don't forget you begin teaching at the Academy when classes resume. You need to take time during the school break for fun."

"Preparing for Christmas is fun."

He chuckled. "You sound like your mother. Remember how she baked for days and days before Christmas and gave most of it away?"

"Yes." She smiled at their shared remembrance. "Mother loved decorating the house for Christmas, too. She always sang while she put up the greens and arranged flowers."

Her father's gaze moved slowly around the dining room. "She only had one Christmas here. We spent years planning the house before we built it."

Amy's heart caught at the tears that glistened in his eyes. It would break his heart to lose this house that he'd been so proud to give her mother. She looked down at her plate and pushed idly with her fork at a piece of roast beef. "Father, I've been wondering. . . ." Her voice trailed off. It seemed so rude to ask him about his money.

"What have you been wondering?"

"There are so many people with money problems because of the Panic. Are you . . . are things . . ."

He snorted. "Does it look like we're living at the poor farm? Don't you worry your head about money. I've always taken care of you, haven't I?"

"Yes, but—"

"And I always will." He winked. "At least until some young man takes over that responsibility."

Her smile felt feeble. His answer didn't reassure her at all.

～❧

The next afternoon Amy saw her opportunity when her father left the house "to pick up one last thing for Christmas," as he said.

"Thank You, Lord," she said aloud, entering the library. The words were barely past her lips when she groaned. Was it wrong to thank God for a chance to go through her father's papers without his knowledge or permission?

Standing with her back to the window, she faced the desk. Where to begin? She started in the most obvious place, the drawer in the middle. Why should he be secretive? He wouldn't think he had anything to hide from anyone in his own home. She sat down in her father's leather chair and looked into the drawer.

"Go away," she murmured under her breath at the guilt that tugged at her conscience.

It didn't take long to go through all the drawers. Nothing she found yielded answers to her questions. She leaned back in the chair, gripping the arms. The next place to look was the safe, of course. Her father had told her the combination months ago. "In case anything should happen to me and you need to get into it," he'd said.

She knew Walter Bay's ultimatum wasn't what he'd meant. She crossed the room and removed a set of Shakespeare's works from a bookshelf to reveal the safe. "Forgive me," she murmured, reaching for the combination dial.

It was all there: ledgers, bankbooks, stock certificates, notes for loans. She carried the stack to the desk. Trepidation tightened her chest as she opened the ledger.

It didn't take long to discover Walter was correct. Her father had lost money on his investments when the market collapsed over a year ago. She saw that he'd lent money to others during those hard times, though he'd never spoken of it. Pride in him warmed her chest. It was like him to honor others' privacy. The ledger showed most of those people hadn't made payments in months. Knowing her father, she doubted he'd pressed for payments. He'd trust the people to pay when they were able again.

The original mortgage on the house had almost been paid off when the Panic hit. He'd taken out another mortgage to cover the income he'd lost. Like so many others during these hard times, he'd purchased food and other necessities on credit. Aside from the horses, Amy found no indication of assets other than the house and its contents that could provide the money to pay off Walter.

Her teaching wouldn't pay much, not enough to cover one monthly payment. Her paintings were beginning to sell, but she hadn't sold enough to make a dent in her father's debt. She dropped her head into her hands and groaned.

What money I did make on my paintings went back into painting supplies. Why didn't Father tell me we were having money problems? Does Father know of Walter's offer to forestall foreclosure if I marry him? Is that why Father pressed Walter's virtues as a husband yesterday? She shook her head vigorously. *No, Father would never concede to such a demand. Father would have thrown Walter out of the house if he'd suggested such a thing.*

The picture brought immense pleasure. It lasted only a moment. It was within her power to save her father's reputation and the home he treasured. How could she consider saving herself at his expense?

"Lord, I beg You, show me a way to save us both."

If only there were someone she could go to with her dilemma. If only she could share it with Frank. There was no one she would trust more. But he was the last person she could tell about Walter's awful demand.

❧

When Walter arrived at the front door that evening, Amy slipped into her black wool jacket and stepped onto the porch. The smile he gave her turned her stomach.

"Good evening." He offered her his arm. "I thought we'd go to the hotel for dinner, if that suits you."

"I am not going to dinner with you."

His face hardened. "We agreed to discuss the, uh, matter over dinner."

"You decided we would do so." Amy clutched her arms over her unbuttoned coat against the winter chill. "I will not go to dinner with a blackmailer."

"Blackmailer? I prefer to call myself an astute businessman."

Amy glared at him. She saw no point in arguing with him over trifles.

He spread his arms. "Have you asked your father if what I said is true?"

"I didn't tell him of your . . . offer."

A smile formed slowly. "I didn't think you would."

"It appears you are correct concerning Father's finances." Her stomach tightened with the admission. It seemed a betrayal to her father to admit the truth to this loathsome man.

The smile grew. "Then you have an answer to my proposal?"

"Proposal? I believe you mean bribery."

"Your answer?"

Amy tapped one toe against the floor planks. "What assurance do I have that if I agree to . . . to m . . . marry you that you will keep your agreement and not call my father's loan?"

He removed his brown derby and held it over his heart in an exaggerated gesture. "You have my word."

"Mr. Bay, your word would not purchase you a cup of coffee."

His chuckle would have infuriated her if she were not already angrier than ever before. Most men she knew would take offense to the implication their word meant nothing. Walter's amusement showed her he believed she had no choice but to marry him.

"What proof do you demand, Miss Amy?"

"Your signature on the mortgage papers, saying the loan is paid in full."

His voice hardened. "That's not the deal I'm offering. If you marry me, I won't call the loan immediately. I'll allow your father to pay when he is able. That's the deal."

"I'm not so foolish as to trust you to keep that promise. In return for me, I want your signature agreeing that Father's mortgage is completely paid, including interest on past due payments. That's this year's price for a purchased bride."

"You aren't in a position to bargain."

"No?" Amy raised her eyebrows and gave him her sweetest smile. "How many men in this town will continue to do business with you once they hear you tried to buy a wife by threatening to drive her father into bankruptcy?"

Walter studied her gaze, bouncing his derby against one thigh.

She met his gaze without blinking, continuing to smile. It wouldn't do for him to know she was quaking inside. Would he guess she'd never expose her father's situation to the town in such a sordid manner, that her challenge was pure effrontery?

"You wouldn't do that, Amy. I heard your father say the only thing he loves more than this house is you. You're too much the loving, devoted daughter to allow him to lose his house and his reputation to boot."

The sliver of hope she'd held to dissolved. He was right, of course.

"Your revelations might hurt my business," Walter conceded, "but at a steep cost to your father. I admit, though, your idea has some merit. You're an only child, and your father is a widow. Upon his death, all he has will belong to us. Requiring him to pay off the loan is only taking money from myself. I won't receive it as soon this way, but I'll receive it just the same."

Horror left her speechless.

"I'll sign over the mortgage right after the ceremony," Walter conceded.

Amy shook her head slowly. "Before the ceremony."

"Oh no." He shook a finger at her. "How do I know you'll go through with the ceremony if I give the executed note to you first?"

"How do I know you will keep your promise if the note isn't signed before the ceremony?"

"It seems we're at an impasse." He grinned. "Or we would be at an impasse if you had anything with which to bargain."

What a couple we'll make, neither of us trusting the other. She shoved away the despair the thought brought to her. "Sign the note in my presence before the ceremony. We'll give it to the pastor. After the ceremony, the pastor can return it to us, and you can present it to Father."

Amy held her breath, waiting for Walter's answer. He was maddeningly slow in giving it.

"Agreed. Not much chance you'll back out in front of the preacher, not right before the ceremony."

The small triumph didn't bring her joy. "You can tell Father you wouldn't think of holding him to his debt since you're family." Amy couldn't keep the sarcasm from her voice.

"A wedding gift. I like the idea. Not many grooms make their fathers-in-law such generous gifts." His smile held self-satisfaction. "A few well-placed references, and word will spread around town. It should be great for business."

Hopelessness swirled through Amy's chest. Walter managed to turn every attempt she made to insure her father's home and reputation into another victory for himself.

Walter leaned toward her. "One more thing. I want our engagement announced at the Christmas Eve service."

6

"No!" The word burst from Amy. She struggled for composure. She simply couldn't give up the evening with Frank. "It wouldn't be proper to announce it then."

"I won't allow this to drag out."

"I've already committed to attending the Christmas Eve service with Frank Sterling."

Walter snorted. "Uncommit yourself."

"If I'm willing to break my word to him, why would you trust my promise to marry you?"

"I doubt Sterling offers the same incentive I do."

"He doesn't need to use chicanery. He's a gentleman."

"He isn't the man you've promised to marry. I'd rather be your groom than a gentleman."

"I won't agree to formalizing the engagement until after Christmas Eve."

"Immediately after."

She hesitated. She didn't want to become engaged any sooner than necessary but couldn't think of any way to extend her freedom. "All right."

"Christmas Day." Walter stepped closer. "How about a kiss for your future groom?"

"Not until you are my groom in fact."

"You are one challenging woman, Amy Henderson." Walter grinned and donned his brown derby. "I admire the fight in you. I'd no idea you had the stomach for bargaining. You might actually be good at it one day with me around for an example. Just one word of warning." His gaze hardened. "Don't ever try bargaining against me again."

He turned around at the top of the porch steps. "You and I are going to make a great team, after I train you in a bit."

A dubious compliment at best, Amy thought.

At least she wouldn't be spending Christmas Eve with him. It seemed incongruous to think of attending the service in his company. He was faithful in attending church, but if he loved God, his actions certainly didn't reveal it. She suspected his church involvement was all show, considered necessary for his image as an upstanding citizen.

She groaned as a new realization struck. On top of everything else, had she agreed to marry a man who didn't share her faith? She knew the Bible admonished against Christians marrying non-Christians. It wasn't one of the commandments, but that didn't mean she could take the admonition casually.

If she and Walter didn't share a faith in the Lord, how could it be God's will that they marry? Yet how else could her father keep the house?

"I asked You to show me a way to save myself and Father from Walter's intentions, Lord. If You've shown me that way, I haven't recognized it yet. Open my eyes to Your way and my ears to Your voice, Lord," she whispered, shivering as she watched Walter disappear into the dusk.

❧

Frank stepped out of the sleigh he'd rented at the livery and tied the dapple gray to the hitching-post ring in front of Amy's home. Light from the lantern at the front of the sleigh made moving shadows across the snow as the horse shifted.

Frank nodded a bit self-consciously at a young family walking past dressed in Sunday best. "Merry Christmas." *On their way to church,* he thought. Where he and Amy would be headed in a few minutes. This last week's confusion had dimmed the anticipation of the evening he'd looked forward to for so long. *Why did Amy lie to me about going skating with Walter Bay?* The question had haunted him.

What if when he showed up at her house to take her to church she had changed her mind?

She wouldn't do that. She was not that kind of girl.

He hadn't thought she was the kind of girl to lie, either.

Frank's feet had brought him to the front door while his thoughts wandered. He stretched his neck. Even beneath his outer jacket and suit jacket, the stiffness of his boiled white shirt and starched collar made him keep his back a bit straighter than normal.

Amy opened the door herself. She was wearing a purple dress. It had those sleeves with puffy tops that women liked. The puffy tops were decorated with purple velvet bows. The soft velvet was no match for how soft and lovely Amy's face looked to him. "You're beautiful."

Embarrassment at the bold way he'd blurted out his admiration melted away at her soft "Thank you" and the joyous look in her eyes.

Amy took a cape from the walnut shrank.

"Let me help you with that." Frank took the cape from her, and she turned her back to him. The cape was luxuriously thick and warm, the outer layer a deep shade of black velvet that seemed appropriate to protect someone as precious as Amy. A gentle floral scent wafted over him as he settled the cape on her shoulders. He wanted to enfold her in his arms but instead squeezed her shoulders lightly.

She tied the cape's satin ribbons at her throat, then picked up her hat from the marble-topped hall table and pinned it in place.

"You replaced the ribbons."

She turned to him with a smile. "You noticed."

"Would your father like to join us? I was thinking on the ride in that it's selfish of me to take you from him on Christmas Eve since you're his only family."

"How kind of you to ask. He's arranged to walk over with our neighbors, Roland's family, but would you mind if we sat with Father at the service? I've never attended a Christmas service without him."

"No, of course I don't mind."

The way her face shone was his reward. "He's upstairs. I'll just run and tell him we'll meet him at church."

Minutes later he helped her into the sleigh and climbed up beside her. As he lifted the reins, Amy laid one of her gloved hands over his and removed it in a quick gesture. "Please, may we talk for a minute before we leave?"

He turned his head to look at her, uncertainty making him hesitant, and nodded.

She clasped her hands in her lap. Her face was sober, and in the light of the lantern, he could see the seriousness in her eyes. "It's about the other night and the skating rink."

Somehow he'd known she'd wanted to speak about Walter. A burning started in his stomach. He waited for her to continue.

"When I told you I couldn't go skating with you because I was helping my father entertain a guest for dinner, I was telling the truth." Her words were coming in a rush. "After dinner Father asked me to go skating with Walter. I didn't want to, but I didn't know how to get out of it. I—I—It's important to me that you know I wasn't lying."

The weight that had sat on Frank's heart for days evaporated. "Thank you." The words sounded strangled. He cleared his throat and slapped the reins lightly. "Get up there, Gray."

The walks were full of people, swinging lanterns lighting their way. Sleighs passed in the streets. Smiles and greetings were on everyone's lips. Frank couldn't remember a time in his life when he'd been happier.

At the church he guided Gray into a long line of cutters. He took a wool blanket from the sleigh and covered Gray with it before helping Amy down.

When Amy took his arm and they walked into church together, Frank felt God had given him an incredible gift. They walked past the back pews where the high-school boys always sat and took a place in the wooden pew behind Jason and Pearl and the rest of Frank's family. When Amy's father sat down beside Amy, he and Frank shook hands solemnly.

Seated with Amy's shoulder against his, exchanging shy glances during the Christmas sermon and hymns, Frank realized the last year seemed a small time to pay for the joy of her presence. What would it be like to have her beside him like this for the rest of their lives? Could life possibly hold more for a man than that?

Thank You, Lord. Frank's heart ached with gratitude.

Sylvia and Roland stopped them on the way out of church. Curiosity shone bright in Sylvia's eyes as she looked from one to the other, but she didn't tease or ask questions about the two of them attending the service together. "A group of us are going caroling. You'll join us, won't you?"

Frank looked at Amy and raised his eyebrows. "Sounds like fun. Can you go?"

She turned to her father. "Do you mind?"

"Go along and have a nice time." Mr. Henderson waved his hands in a dismissing motion. "I'm stopping at the Reverend Conrad's open house for a bit."

"That's where the caroling will end up," Roland said.

Frank and Amy greeted and chatted with a number of friends before the caroling group headed out. "After all," Sylvia said, "someone has to get home from church before we start out so we'll have someone to sing for."

Snow was falling softly when they left the church. Amy smiled up at Frank. "It's perfect, isn't it? There's nothing more beautiful than an evening snowfall when there's no wind."

His hand covered hers where it rested on his arm, and he smiled down into her eyes. "Yes, it's perfect." Snowflakes caught on her lashes, and he wished he had the right to kiss those snowflakes away.

Frank checked on Gray before they left with the others. "It's not too cold. He should be all right."

For the next hour Frank and Amy laughed and sang praises with their friends and turned down numerous offers from those they caroled to enter their homes for cookies and cider. Frank wished the evening would never end.

The carolers chose a circular route and ended back at Rev. Conrad's home beside the darkened church.

Sylvia hurried in front of the others and held up mittened hands. "We simply must carol them before we go in."

Roland laughed. "Carol them? Those are the people we were singing with an hour ago."

Sylvia wrinkled her nose at him, bounced her hands as though conducting, and began singing. "Joy to the world—" The others joined in, including Roland, though he rolled his eyes at her.

Frank shared a laughing glance with Amy.

A movement, no more than a shadow on the snowy walk down the way, caught his attention. He recognized that weaving motion, the manner in which a man walked after he'd had too much to drink. Frank tried to dismiss the dread winding through him. Maybe the man would pass by without trying to join the group or sit down under a tree and watch the festivities in quiet.

The man staggered his way to the back of the group. Frank recognized him then. It was Tom, a balding bachelor in his forties, known more about town for his drinking than anything else. He stopped only a few feet from Frank and joined in the singing. The loud, off-tune, slurred words caused heads to swivel Tom's way. Seeing the new arrival, people shook their heads or rolled their eyes, some snickered, but no one quit singing.

Frank's heart went out to the man. He knew that Tom had no idea he was an object of ridicule. Tom was a quiet, retiring man when he was sober. A few drinks made it easier for him to be sociable, or what he considered sociable in his drunken state.

The parsonage door opened, and tall, slender, bearded Rev. Conrad and his pretty, round wife, Millicent, came out on the stoop. Guests crowded behind them. Light poured from the doorway in a golden path.

Frank liked the way the Reverend drew his wife close within his arm against the chill. Would he and Amy be like that one day, years of married life behind them and content in their life together? He hoped so.

Applause thanked the group when they were done, and Mrs. Conrad invited the carolers to join the guests. This time the group accepted.

Someone bumped against Frank and burped. A yeasty smell rose about them. "Excuse me."

Frank didn't need to look to know it was Tom, headed into the house with the others. Naturally he'd want to join in the festivities, and the drinks he'd had gave him the courage. Frank knew the Reverend and Mrs. Conrad and their guests wouldn't appreciate Tom in his inebriated state.

Frank saw the look of distaste in Amy's eyes as she watched Tom. With a sinking feeling, Frank realized he could have caused that look only a little over a year ago.

"Miss Amy," he said in a low voice, "I'm going to take Tom home. Will you wait here for me?"

She glanced from him to Tom and back again. "Yes."

Frank slipped an arm around Tom's shoulder. "Hi, Pal. Suppose we head back to your house and talk awhile?"

Tom shook his head. "I'm goin' in here. People to see."

"But there's important things I want to talk about with you."

"Important t'ings?" Tom's jaw hung so loose it almost waggled.

"Yes." Frank remembered from days standing at the bar beside Tom that Tom liked to talk about life and death and good and evil and all the subjects one might hear discussed in church, where Tom would never go to talk about them. "I have some thoughts on God and want to know what you think about them."

"Oh. A'right. Le's talk 'bout them inside." Tom took a step toward the door and would have fallen if Frank hadn't caught him. "Oops."

"Let's go to your place instead. It'll be hard to hear each other in there with all those people."

Tom frowned as though he wasn't certain whether or not to go along with Frank's proposal. He wasn't wearing a jacket. Frank removed his own and slipped it over Tom's shoulders, hoping it would be clean when he got it back.

Frank realized Amy was still beside them, though most everyone else had entered the house. "Go inside, Amy. Ask Roland if he'll help me out here."

Frank sighed deeply, watching her head toward the house. This wasn't the way he'd planned to spend this evening.

7

*F*rank tried winding his muffler about his neck to ward off a bit of the cold that assailed him, keeping hold of Tom with one hand so the man didn't sink to the ground.

When Roland arrived, they managed between them to get Tom into Frank's sleigh, all the time Tom arguing he wanted to go to the preacher's house. Frank slid the buffalo lap robe over his shoulders and took up the reins.

Tom had stopped arguing by the time they reached his little log hut on the edge of town. He was almost asleep. Frank and Roland mostly carried him through the snow on the unshoveled path to the only door. The task was made more difficult because Roland also carried one of the sleigh lanterns.

Roland lifted the lantern high when they entered. "Whoa."

Frank stared in disbelief. There was barely room to walk in the one-room cabin. The floor, bed, only chair, and table were piled high with old papers, dirty used bean cans, rags, and bottles, most of them empty. The stove, which obviously served as both heating and cooking source, was cold. Roland set the lantern on top of it.

After Frank brushed a pile of stuff off the bed, he and Roland lowered Tom to the bed. It took a couple minutes to work Frank's coat off the man. Then they tugged the filthy blanket out from beneath Tom and laid it over him.

Roland propped his hands on his hips and looked around. "Merry Christmas, huh? No wonder he was headed to the preacher's house for some Christmas cheer."

"Or for food. I don't see any here."

Frank went outside to dig some wood from a snow-covered

woodpile. Back inside, he cleared rubbish away from the stove before starting a fire. "This place is a fire trap."

Unable to do anything else for Tom, Frank and Roland headed back to the party. Frank wondered how long they'd been away. Would Amy be impatient over his absence? Frank grimaced. It was probably Mr. Henderson who was impatient, thinking Frank wasn't treating his daughter well.

As soon as they entered the house, Frank began searching for Amy. She wasn't easy to find. People of all ages and sizes filled the parsonage. Women stood about the dining-room table, discussing whose *krumkake* was crispest, whose sugar cookies thinnest, and whose fruitcake had the most fruit. The men gathered in the parlor, seated on the horsehair sofa, or one of the parlor chairs that had been drawn into a circle, discussed the silver situation and whether the coming year would bring relief from the economic depression; as well as the latest gossip that the saloon keeper had lost control of his horses the night before, causing man and beast to tumble down the riverbank. Boys chased each other about, darting in and out of the adults with barely more than a "Yes, Mother" over their shoulders when reprimanded. Girls stood or sat self-consciously straight and ate daintily from china plates filled with cookies.

Frank was wondering whether Amy had gone home when he heard her voice at his side. "Would you like some cider?"

"Thanks." He accepted the warm apple cider, spiced with cloves and cinnamon sticks. "I'm sorry I was gone so long."

"It was kind of you to help him home."

"It seemed like the thing to do at the time, but I should probably have asked someone else to take him. I didn't mean to run out on you."

"I know that."

Her understanding calmed his worry.

Frank usually preferred to sit on the sidelines and observe others socializing, but with Amy at his side, the gathering was a completely different experience for him. He loved the way Amy's glance darted to his to share something someone said or a child's antics. He loved the way people spoke to them as though they were one. He loved the way

Amy's hand remained snug within his arm as they moved about, visiting with various friends.

He stopped beside an old gentleman seated in a plush chair in the parlor. The man's hands were folded over the top of a cane, which he held between his legs. Frank laid a hand on the man's shoulder. Leaning down so his lips were close to the man's ears, he said, "It's Frank Sterling, Mr. Sutter. Merry Christmas."

The man lifted a face with clouded eyes and smiled an almost toothless greeting. "Hullo there, young man."

Amy touched one of her hands lightly to one of his. "Merry Christmas, Mr. Sutter. It's Amy Henderson. You remember me, don't you?"

Frank was glad to see she greeted the old man so sweetly.

" 'Course I remember you," Mr. Sutter sputtered. "You two sweet on each other now?" He cackled at his own audacity.

Frank's embarrassment was lost in his laugh when he heard Amy's surprised giggle. "I'm working on her, Mr. Sutter, that I am," he admitted and grinned at the shy dropping of Amy's lashes.

They listened for a few minutes as Mr. Sutter, one of the town's first settlers, spoke of early Christmases in Chippewa City.

"You must miss those days," Amy said when he paused.

"What I miss most is my wife, and a close second is her Christmas bread. She made the best *julekage* on the prairie." Sutter smacked his lips.

Frank and Amy erupted into laughter once more. *I'm glad we're at the beginning of our romance and not looking back on its ending*, Frank thought.

Mr. Henderson was still at the parsonage, as were Jason and Pearl. Frank and Amy spoke with them all. Frank's arm felt empty when Amy and Pearl went off to the kitchen to locate some *julekage* for Mr. Sutter.

"We're over here," Jason reminded him dryly, digging his elbow into Frank's ribs.

Frank pulled his gaze back from the kitchen doorway with an embarrassed start.

Roland chuckled. "Looks like you've got it bad, old man."

Frank only smiled. "Having it bad" felt awfully good.

Roland frowned at his cup of cider. He opened his jacket, and Frank saw the top of a bottle. "Either of you want to add a pinch of something stronger to this?" Roland raised his eyebrows.

"No." Jason's voice was low but cracked with anger. "And this isn't the place for such shenanigans."

Roland held up a hand as if to fend Jason off. "I'm not looking to cause trouble. Just thought a bit of the cup that cheers seemed in line with celebrating." He shot a glance at Frank.

"Did you get that at Tom's place?"

"Figured he'll never miss it."

"That's stealing."

Roland leaned closer to Frank. "You used to be a lot more fun," he said before he turned away.

Frank and Jason watched him cross the room and slap an academy friend on the back. "Think he'll find anyone to share his bounty with here?" Jason asked.

"Probably. Isn't too hard. Usually people find you." Frank remembered all too well how easy it was to identify those who might carry a flask they were willing to share.

A moment later Amy and Pearl rejoined Jason and Frank, and thoughts of liquor were drowned in pleasant companionship.

When another couple claimed Jason and Pearl's attention, Amy said, "I should probably leave soon. Father left a few minutes ago. I hate for him to be alone on Christmas."

Immediately Frank went in search of Amy's cape and his jacket. He hated to think of this evening ending, but he still had the ride home with Amy to look forward to.

He stopped to speak with Rev. Conrad, in a few private words explaining the condition of Tom's cabin and his lack of provisions. He was relieved when the pastor promised to stop and check on Tom and bring him some food later.

When Frank returned to the parlor with their outer garments, his gaze searched for Amy. He stopped abruptly when he saw Walter Bay speaking to her. From the tight way she held her shoulders and chin, she wasn't too happy with him.

Frank made his way through the thinning crowd. "Here's your cape, Amy." He nodded at Walter. "Hope you're having a nice Christmas."

Walter slid a thumb beneath the watch chain strung across his vest. "Not so good so far, but it will get better. Wish I could say the same for yours." With a grin, he turned and walked away.

Frank held Amy's cape for her. "What was that cryptic statement supposed to mean?"

"He just likes to spread unhappiness," she said quietly.

"Nothing could make me unhappy tonight," he whispered.

Frank thought he saw the glint of tears in her eyes. From joy? Was she as happy as he to be together? If the tears were real, they only lasted a moment.

Outside, a soft hiss sounded when Frank lit the lanterns on each side of the cutter. Vapors from the sulfur and kerosene blended with the fresh smell of falling snow before he slid the glass down to protect the flame. He helped Amy onto the leather seat and tucked the buffalo robe about her. "I'm afraid the brick is cold by now, but maybe this will keep you warm."

Her sweet smile thanked him.

He brushed snow from Gray's blanket before climbing up beside Amy. "Do you want to head straight home, or do we have time to take Gray for a trot along the river?"

"A ride along the river would be lovely, if we don't take too long."

Clouds hid the moon and stars, but the sleigh's lanterns provided more than enough light combined with the yellow patches of lamplight falling from windows in every home they passed. Frank took the hill road that wound down from the residential area on the prairie to river level, talking softly to Gray while guiding him down the steep incline. He'd take no chance on a runaway sleigh with Amy in it.

Globe-topped streetlights cast their beams on the couple as the cutter slid down Main Street. Frank urged Gray into a trot. The street was popular with sleighers in the evenings, when most businesses were closed and there were no pedestrians or horses to endanger. Frank and Amy waved and exchanged calls of "Merry Christmas" as they passed other sleighs.

Frank pointed out a dark, quiet saloon to Amy. It was closed for the night out of respect for Christ's birth. "I know a couple men besides Tom who are likely spending tonight in their rooms alone with a hoarded bottle."

"Wouldn't they have attended church? Almost everyone goes on Christmas Eve, even if they avoid it the rest of the year."

"These men wouldn't feel at ease in a church. The camaraderie of the saloons is the closest thing they know to a home." His heart hurt for them, especially Tom, and he sent up a silent prayer that the Lord would be with them tonight, even if they hadn't made the move to join others in worshiping Him.

"You used to drink, and you weren't like that."

He didn't hear condemnation in Amy's comment, only confusion. "I might have ended up just like them."

"But you didn't." She slipped one of her hands over one of his. "I knew you wouldn't."

"It's not so easy, Amy. People think a man can just say he's not going to drink anymore, that he can see it's hurting him and the people who care for him, and just stop. It's not that easy."

"I wish I understood better; truly I do."

It was a difficult thing for him to talk about. Just to think of sharing with her how rough it was to stop drinking scared him, made him feel . . . vulnerable. What if she thought less of him because he wasn't an iron-willed man? But if they were going to have any chance together, they had to be honest with each other.

"Your prayers helped me, and your faith in me, but it was still hard. A lot harder than I thought it would be when I told God I was quitting. If I'd been drinking as long as some of these men, I don't know if I would have made it. During the time I was frequenting the saloons, I got to know the men people call the town drunks." Memories drifted before his eyes, and sadness welled up within him like a wave.

He realized Amy was waiting for him to continue. He had to clear his throat before he could say, "Some of them have awful, painful things to forget or live with, Amy. They aren't terrible, lazy people the way town folks say. They're just people who hurt something fierce inside."

"How can we help them, Frank?"

"I guess the place to start is to remember they aren't the alcohol. Beneath the people we think we see are souls God made in His image. Souls He loves—loves as much as He loves anyone else. If we can remember that when we pray for them, maybe we can learn how to help them."

"I'll try to remember, and I'll pray."

If they hadn't been on Main Street, he would have hugged her then and there.

He'd been on his way to a lonely life with liquor for his best friend when he'd made the decision a year ago to turn his life over to God. But for that choice, Amy wouldn't be beside him now, her shoulder bumping companionably against his, her perfume bringing springtime into the winter air. Without the promise of Amy's companionship, would he have had the strength to change his life? He doubted it. *Thank You, Lord*, he repeated for the dozenth time that night.

The sleigh slid onto the mill bridge, and they looked down on Shakespearean Rink. Laughter drifted up to them from the few brave souls gliding over the ice. "I want to skate with you again, Amy."

She smiled up at him. "That would be lovely."

He slid one arm a bit stiffly around her shoulders as they moved off the bridge. It could be dangerous to drive with only one hand about the reins, but Frank felt Gray was trustworthy and gentle. More dangerous was the chance Amy would tell him to remove his arm. She didn't, instead relaxing against him, sending his heart into a pounding rhythm.

The road was a popular spot for sleigh races, but tonight there weren't many other sleighs since the moon wasn't lighting the road. Bare-branched cottonwoods stood sentinel along the river. The sleigh bells chimed saucily above the *sh-sh-sh* of the sleigh runners.

"We'd better turn back. I thought there'd be more people out tonight. I don't want to damage your reputation."

Frank needed both hands to turn Gray and the sleigh back toward town. Then he urged Gray to a stop. He slid his arm back around Amy's shoulders and risked pulling her close in a gentle hug.

Wonder wrapped around his heart at the trusting way she relaxed into his embrace.

He breathed in the sweet scent that lingered about her soft hair, then touched his lips to her neck, at that place just below the dainty, purple stones that dangled from her ear. He drew his head back slightly and, barely breathing, kissed her lips. "Amy, you are so precious," he whispered, then met her warm lips again. She surrendered a kiss so sweet his chest ached.

And finally he kissed the snowflakes off her lashes.

"We'd better get home," he repeated.

Amy's head rested against his shoulder as he drove. To Frank it seemed love enclosed them in a circle so strong it was tangible.

At the mill bridge where the streetlights again brightened the way, Amy lifted her head from his shoulder with a sigh. Frank turned to smile at her, and the feathers on her hat tickled his nose, causing them both to laugh. Such a little thing to cause him so much joy, but it did.

He applied both hands to the reins again, not wishing to embarrass Amy by a public display of their affection as they drove through town. After pulling up in front of her home, he took a decorated box from behind the seat and held it out to her.

Her eyes widened. Her gaze moved from the box to his eyes. "A gift?" She didn't take it from him.

"It's probably a breach of manners to give you a Christmas gift when we're only beginning to court, but I thought of you as soon as I saw this and wanted you to have it. If you say I must take it back, I will, but I hope you'll keep it."

Amy took it from him then. "I haven't anything for you," she said, opening the box.

"You gave me tonight."

The look in her eyes was gift enough to last him a hundred Christmases.

"Oh, Frank!" Amy pulled the gift from layers of tissue. A man and woman skated together in a glass globe on a walnut stand. "I saw this in the jewelry-store window and fell in love with it at first sight." Her eyes shined with joy. "I shall treasure it."

Her gladness warmed him.

They walked up to the house slowly. Frank hoped Amy was savoring their last minutes together as he was.

"I suppose your father is waiting for you," Frank said, looking at the lace-framed parlor window that looked out on the front porch.

"Yes. He always waits up for me, even when I'm at a house party with girlfriends. He says he worries about me more than most parents since we lost Mother."

At the door Frank lifted one of Amy's gloved hands to his lips, wishing fervently etiquette and the possibility of gossiping neighbors allowed him greater liberties. "Good night, Amy."

He started to release her hand, but she held on. "Frank . . ."

"Yes?"

"I'm so proud and glad for you that you've kept your promise to God to give up drinking. You won't change your mind, will you? No matter what?"

The urgency underscoring her words amused him. "No, Amy, I won't change my mind, no matter what." He kissed the back of her hand again and gave it a gentle squeeze. "Blessed Christmas, Amy."

"Blessed Christmas, Frank."

The snow stopped before he and Gray reached the edge of town. The livery owner had asked Frank to wait until Christmas Day to return the horse and sleigh. Gray's hooves thudded softly on the snow-padded roadway. Only a dusting had fallen, not enough to dangerously obscure the edge of the road, for which Frank was grateful. His thoughts weren't on driving but on Amy.

When the door to her house had opened, the light from the lamp on the hall table had spilled out. He'd thought for a moment he'd seen tears glittering in her eyes again. He'd always pictured Amy as a strong woman, not the type who cried easily. If he had seen tears in her eyes, he hoped they were tears of joy because the two of them were finally together.

"Blessed Christmas, Amy," he whispered again into the prairie night.

❧

Amy slipped the nightgown over her head. The rose-sprigged flannel fell to her toes in soft, comforting warmth. She sat down on the bench in front of her vanity and began brushing the hair that fell in rippling waves to her waist.

Her gaze wasn't on her mirror image but on the snow globe that sat on a lace doily on the vanity. She turned the key on the walnut base, and the couple twirled to a waltz. Amy's eyes misted over until the man and woman were only a haze.

"I should have told him." Reliving Frank's kisses, his endearments, she knew she should feel guilty, but she didn't. *It might be wrong to want this night to remember, Lord, but I do. This one night is all Frank and I will ever have together.*

She knew it was wrong to allow him to hold her, to kiss her, to believe they would continue courting. Before Frank had arrived, she'd promised herself she'd tell him right after the church service about her agreement with Walter. But then they'd gone caroling and to the open house. The opportunity presented itself in the sleigh when they left the parson's, but by then the temptation was too great.

"Frank has such a beautiful heart, Lord." Watching him with Tom and later with Mr. Sutter, she couldn't help comparing Frank's compassionate nature with cynical Walter. Her heart cried out for the love of a gentle yet strong man like Frank.

"This night has to last us forever, Lord," she reminded herself and God, trying to assuage her guilt.

Amy moved the snow globe to the bedside table, where she could watch the couple turn in the moonlight that was breaking through the clouds. She climbed into bed, pulled the pink satin comforter over her shoulders, and fell asleep in the memory of Frank's embrace.

The first thing she saw the next morning was the skaters. She smiled and snuggled further into the covers, closing her eyes and reliving Frank's kisses.

She ignored the knock at her bedroom door until it was followed by her father's boisterous, "Merry Christmas, Amy."

She leaped out of bed. How could she have forgotten the Christmas-morning rituals? "I'll be downstairs in a few minutes, Father."

Christmas breakfast and the exchange of gifts were a bittersweet time as always since her mother died. The day passed quickly and pleasantly with neighbors dropping in to visit and she and her father visiting others. Amy loved the way everyone opened their homes on Christmas Eve and Christmas Day. It made the whole town feel like family. At one point she found herself daydreaming what it might be like for her and Frank to welcome visitors some future Christmas. She closed the door firmly on that dream, remembering with whom she had promised to spend her future.

It was late afternoon when she turned from greeting the editor of the local paper and his wife to see Walter enter the parlor. Amy stumbled in her words so badly that the editor's wife looked to see what had caught the younger woman's attention.

Amy tried to recover the situation. She smiled at the couple. "I see we have more company. Will you excuse me? I must see whether the refreshments are adequate."

She picked up a crystal plate still half-filled with sugar cookies and headed toward the kitchen, hoping for a few more minutes of respite before speaking with Walter.

"May I help you with that?" Walter took the plate from her hands.

Too late. Amy bit back a groan.

"You do look lovely in that blue gown, my dear."

Amy's face heated. She glanced about quickly to see who might be near. "Don't call me by endearments." She kept her voice low.

Walter laughed, and her indignation increased. She swept through the swinging door into the kitchen. Walter followed. She tried to ignore him while refilling the plate. At least this room was empty of people. Mrs. Jorgenson had the day off to spend with her family.

Walter caught Amy's wrist in a tight grip. "You haven't forgotten our agreement, have you? I expect you to act in public as if you like me, and more than a little bit."

She looked pointedly at her wrist until he dropped it. Tossing her head, she challenged, "Why do you want me for your wife? Why not a woman who loves you and wants you as dearly as you want her?"

He chuckled. "What's the challenge in that?" He placed his hands on the counter on each side of her, trapping her. "Let's announce our engagement now, here." He gestured toward the parlor with his head. "Or rather, in there."

She pushed at one of his hands. "I need to get some cookies from the jars on the table."

He released her and leaned back against the counter. "I'm waiting for your agreement."

Agreement, not answer. She busied herself with the cookies, her back to him. Her mind darted about for a way to postpone the dreaded time. "Don't you want a special party to announce it? An engagement party? That way you can invite everyone with whom you want to share the news. This way it will only be announced to whoever happens to have dropped in for a few minutes."

"I like the gathered crowd. The editor of the paper is here. He'll be sure to include the announcement in this week's news."

"I should think a man of your importance in the community would want the announcement to be made in the proper manner."

She heard his step. Then his hands at her waist made her gasp. All too close to her ear, she heard him say, "Surely a happy bridegroom-to-be can be forgiven for announcing the joyful news a bit, shall we say, out of step with conventional demand?"

"Unhand me."

Laughing, he released her. "You are a spirited lass. I'm delighted. I thought you were one of those women who corseted her mind and emotions as well as her body."

His coarse words revolted her. "If you find me so lacking in agreeable attributes, why demand I marry you?"

He spread his hands wide. "You're the daughter of the most admired man in this part of the prairie."

"Admired but poor."

"People don't know that, and they needn't if you keep your part of the bargain."

"I'm not likely to back out, considering the cost." She turned about with the replenished plate of cookies. "Unless you have something more to say, I'm going back to the parlor."

He followed on her heels. *Like a stray dog one can't discourage*, she thought in annoyance.

When they entered the room, her father beamed and reached for a cookie. "I was wondering where those went."

Amy smiled at him with warm affection as she set the plate down. "You would have found your way to them in the kitchen before long, I suspect."

Polite and friendly laughter from gathered guests greeted her remark.

Walter rubbed his palms together briskly. "Mr. Henderson, I have wonderful news." He reached for Amy's elbow and drew her beside him, grinning down at her.

Lord, I'm not ready for this. Please, please find a way to stop it. Her gaze remained fixed on Walter's, everything within her pleading for release from her promise.

The crowd watched them. No one moved. It seemed to Amy no one even breathed.

Mr. Henderson broke the stillness. "What is this wonderful news, Mr. Bay?"

There was no release. Walter's fingers pinched her arm as if to remind her not to deny his words. "Your daughter just agreed to marry me."

"Amy!" Frank's voice filtered through the crowd's murmurs and surprised congratulations.

Amy turned toward the sound. Frank stood in the parlor doorway, his face ashen, his eyes black with pain and shock. *No!* her heart screamed. She took a step toward him but was stopped by Walter's hold.

"The little woman is surprised." She heard the challenge underscoring Walter's words. "She didn't think I'd have the courage to announce it right away like this, did you, Dear?"

"No. No, I didn't."

Frank stepped back. A moment later the front door slammed. It reverberated through her as Walter's announcement had reverberated through her life, crashing her world apart.

8

*T*he grandfather clock in the hall struck seven as Amy dropped into the satin-covered parlor chair and rested her feet on the tiny footstool. Walter had stayed until after the last guest left. Finally he left also. She felt as limp as a linen gown in a rainstorm.

She glanced down at her left hand resting on the arm of the chair. A square emerald blinked back at her from her ring finger. It felt heavy and awkward. *I hadn't thought I'd ever hate a piece of jewelry.*

Her father sat down on the couch with a sigh. He studied the crystal plate of cookies on the tea table in front of him as though it were a chessboard. He finally selected a date-filled delicacy and sat back. "I'm glad the guests left us a few cookies to enjoy."

Amy managed a tiny smile. "If they hadn't, I'm sure Mrs. Jorgenson would have made more for us."

"Yes. What would we do without her?"

His comment required no answer. She felt him watching her as he ate, but she kept her gaze carefully away from him. She was sure later she would cry, but for the moment it was all too new, too much to absorb that Walter had walked into her house and destroyed her happiness, her hopes, her life.

She felt like she had when her mother died. She hated that anything would compare to that grief, but it was so. Every part of her insides burned. When she remembered Frank's eyes, the betrayal in them, her betrayal of him—how was she going to live with that memory for the rest of her life?

Her father brushed crumbs from his hands. "Are you going to tell me what it's all about?"

"What do you mean?" She continued to avoid his eyes.

"You know what I mean. You and Walter."

Amy forced a smile. The happy bride-to-be. It was important she remember to play the role properly if she didn't want him to guess the reason for the marriage. She held up her left hand. "I thought we made it quite clear. We're to be married."

"A week ago I couldn't convince you he was worth considering as a husband."

"A lot can happen in a week." Could it ever. "We'd had a disagreement."

"When? About what?"

"At the Windom Academy Christmas party. It was a petty argument. It's not important." They'd disagreed in spirit if not in words.

"Seems a bit unusual that you spent last night with young Sterling and today you announce your engagement to Bay."

Amy smoothed a fold in her skirt's lace insert. "I was keeping my promise to Mr. Sterling."

"Is that all last night was, keeping a promise?"

She nodded.

"You seemed to be enjoying yourself, keeping that promise."

"Of course I did. We were among friends."

"And you had given young Sterling your word."

"Yes."

"It's not like you to make an important decision like this so quickly, Amy, and without discussing it with me."

She looked at him then, raising her eyebrows, trying to put surprise into her expression. "Didn't Walter ask you for my hand, Father?"

"No."

"It's surprising he didn't ask you for my hand, or for permission to ask for my hand, don't you think? He does like people to believe he conducts himself properly."

Mr. Henderson leaned forward, rested his forearms on his knees, and stared hard at her. "You're not overflowing with joy over your betrothal."

"Wait until I buy my trousseau." This time her grin was real.

They both knew how she loved new clothes. Then she remembered they were living on borrowed money. There weren't funds for a trousseau.

Her father's answering grin didn't hint at his financial truth. "Now you sound like yourself."

Amy went to him and kissed him on the forehead. "I guess the excitement of Christmas and the engagement has worn me out. I'll be my usual chipper self tomorrow, you'll see."

But as she walked up the broad stairway to her bedroom, the knowledge they were both living lies weighed down her spirit. Her father lived the lie that he was wealthy instead of bankrupt. She lived the lie that she was happy to be engaged to Walter. A week ago she wouldn't have thought it possible they would ever lie to each other.

Frank believed she'd lied to him, too, through her actions last night. And hadn't she? She'd thought only of herself when she took his kiss and embrace for her memories. If only she'd had the courage to tell him the awful truth.

If she'd told him the truth, she would have saved herself, too, for she'd felt his arms about her every moment today. "I always will; I know it."

She yanked off the emerald ring, dropped it carelessly into the top vanity drawer, and slammed the drawer shut, glad to hide from sight the reminder that she'd bound herself to Walter.

❧

Frank pitched the forkful of old hay out the calf-barn door into the wagon bed. Frustration and anger put more strength than necessary behind the pitch. The barn didn't need to be cleaned, but he had to do something, or he wouldn't be able to bear just being alive, and he didn't want to be with people.

"What's gotten into you?" Jason had demanded at breakfast.

Frank hadn't answered. He couldn't make the words form, the words that said Amy was engaged to Walter Bay. He'd pushed back his chair and headed for the barn, the place where he always went when he was hurting—out to the animals he loved and the familiar scents of straw and warm animals.

A cat rubbed against his leg. "Meow."

Frank bent to pet its golden back. "Watch yourself, Gideon. I wouldn't want you tossed out." Gideon never did have sense enough to stay away from dangerous things like pitchforks.

"Would have thought you'd learned your lesson when you lost your eye." Frank recalled finding the six-week-old kitten in the hay in the cow barn, one of its eyes lacerated and infected. He'd ached for the kitten that he knew couldn't survive. There wasn't extra money for the veterinarian to help farm cats. Cats were easily and cheaply replaced.

For some reason, this little guy hadn't seemed ready to give in to what everyone thought was inevitable. So Frank had asked Pearl's father, Dr. Matt, if he'd try to help the cat. The kind man had agreed. The eye couldn't be saved, so it had been removed to keep the infection from spreading. The kitten had taken the adjustment to one eye in stride. Its courage seemed larger than its size and earned it the name Gideon, after the tough little leader in the Old Testament.

Frank's brothers had teased him for going to so much trouble for a barn cat, but Frank didn't let that bother him. Gideon seemed to realize Frank had saved his life. He followed Frank around like a dog and snuggled against Frank whenever the opportunity presented itself, purring in pleasure.

"You trust I'm always going to see you in time to keep from hurting you, don't you, Pal?" He pushed the cat gently away. "I wouldn't hurt you on purpose, but it could happen, all the same."

Amy hurt me on purpose.

"Think about something else," he commanded himself. "Think about Tom. There's someone who's worse off than you." Or maybe not. Was there a woman in Tom's past who'd betrayed him? If so, he'd never confided it to Frank in the nights they'd drunk together. Not that he remembered, anyway.

He should probably check on Tom again, make sure he hadn't gone through all the food he'd brought him on Christmas Day. Rev. Conrad had stopped by Tom's sometime between the open house on Christmas Eve and the time Frank had arrived. He'd left some bread and Christmas baked goods and a Bible. Frank could see there'd been an attempt to pick up the place a bit. He knew that wouldn't last.

When he'd left Tom's place, he'd swung past Amy's, hoping to talk her into another sleigh ride before he returned the cutter to the livery stable. He'd known as soon as he stopped that the sleigh ride was out. Amy wouldn't be so impolite as to leave her guests. But he'd thought he might say hello.

He hadn't said hello, but she'd found a mighty powerful way to say good-bye.

Back to Amy again. Couldn't even trust his own thoughts.

He threw all his muscles behind his work. Toss a pile of old straw. *She lied to me.* Another forkload. Toss it. *She betrayed me.* Another forkload. *She promised to marry Walter Bay only hours after kissing me.*

"Why didn't she tell me she was in love with him?" he asked himself for the umpteenth time. There could be only one answer. She wasn't the woman he'd believed.

He'd thought she was as beautiful in spirit as in face: sweet, honest, strong, the true-through-and-through kind of woman.

She'd taken him for a ride. Trotted him about in front of the whole town Christmas Eve and the next day announced her engagement to Walter.

"I gave her the chance to back out, told her she didn't need to keep her promise to go to church with me Christmas Eve. So why did she? And why, above all, did she act as though she cared, even letting me kiss her?"

Because she does care for me. The words whispered through his mind.

"Fool." He stuffed the pitchfork in the straw. Sinking to the floor, he buried his head in his hands. No matter that truth showed itself in her indelicate, unfeeling actions, his heart believed in her. He felt bruised inside; every inch of him felt bruised. The pain hadn't let up for one waking moment since he'd heard Walter utter the words that changed his life: "Your daughter just agreed to marry me."

A few drinks would erase the pain—for awhile. He could easily hide a bottle out here in the barn. No one would be the wiser. He could tell Jason he was going out for a last check on the cattle at night, dig out his bottle, and on to bed. No more tossing and turning. No dreams. No images of Amy and Walter flooding his mind. For a few hours he'd be free of it all. It would be so easy.

It would destroy him, destroy his self-respect.

He wrapped his arms around his middle and bent into the pain. "Help me, Lord."

9

*T*hree days later Frank turned from pulping turnips and carrots to add to the cows' feed when Jason entered the barn. "Get the town errands done?"

"Yes." Jason frowned at the floor.

Frank straightened, a carrot in one hand, and stared at him. "Something wrong? Didn't the implement shop have the parts we need to repair the harrow plow?"

"No, but they'll have them in a few weeks."

"Shouldn't be a problem. Winter won't be over for a bit yet." He grinned.

Jason stuffed his hands in his trouser pockets. "I heard about . . . about Amy and Walter."

Frank felt like he'd been kicked in the gut. He couldn't get his breath. He turned his back to his brother. Why was he so stunned? He'd known it was only a matter of time before the family found out. He tried to speak, but a sob rose up in his throat instead.

"I'm sorry, Frank. If you want to talk about it, well, I'm around."

Frank nodded, struggling to keep the sobs within. Jason's hand patted his shoulder, and then Jason's footsteps could be heard through the straw. A rush of cold air swept over Frank as the door squeaked open and shut.

The sobs rolled out. Frank leaned against a post, helpless against the sorrow pouring from him. *Not again. I can't endure this. I just can't keep enduring this.*

No one in the family said anything to Frank about Amy after Jason's comment. Frank was sure Jason had told them not to. The lack of words didn't stem the pity in his family's eyes. Frank hated that his torn soul hung bare before them.

He arose before the rest of the family each morning and escaped to the barns or the work shed. There was always plenty to keep him busy. He needn't bother with clean clothes or shaving. The cows, hogs, cats, and dogs kept him company without feeling sorry for him. They let him talk all he wanted about Amy without offering unwanted advice. When he cried, the cats and dogs snuggled close and offered love. At night Frank waited until the farmhouse windows darkened before heading home to bed.

He could see the worry in Jason's face when they met while going about chores. Did Jason think he was drinking again? If so, he didn't say so. Frank hoped it was only the state of his heart that concerned his brother.

At dusk on New Year's Eve, Jason and Frank occupied their normal station on the wooden T-stools, milking cows. Kerosene lamps hung safely above them. As usual since the news about Amy, there was none of the singing or whistling they occasionally indulged in to shorten the chore. Black-and-white and tabby cats sat in the straw, watching and waiting. Milk hissed into the pails. In the cold evening air the cow's udders provided welcome warmth to Frank's hands.

"I'm done." Jason stood beside him, T-stool in one hand and milk pail in the other. "I'll start the separating while you finish milking Sudsy here."

"All right. I'm only half done milking her."

A couple minutes later Frank heard the milk being poured into the metal separator, though the cow stood between him and Jason.

"You haven't forgotten it's New Year's Eve, have you, Frank?"

"Nope."

"Are you going to the watch party and prayer service with us? The kids spent all afternoon shelling corn to pop."

Frank rested his head against Sudsy's huge, warm side. "Don't think I'll go. I'm pretty tired." He'd been tired unto exhaustion since Walter Bay announced his "wonderful news."

"Aw, Sudsy, no." He shook his head in disgust. "This pail of milk won't be going through the separator, Jason. Sudsy stepped in it."

Jason chuckled. "Oh, well. The cows need to be milked, whether the milk goes to us or the cats."

"I'll finish separating the milk and cream and clean the separator. You go on. The family will be waiting for you to clean up so they can leave."

"Are you sure?"

"I'm sure."

There was a pause. "I can stick around tonight if you want."

"I'll be fine. The Lord isn't stuck in the church. I'm not ready to face everyone yet."

He could almost hear Jason protesting in the stillness. Finally Jason spoke. "You'll have to get back to living sometime."

"I know." Frank didn't know anything of the kind, but it didn't seem worth arguing about. Nothing seemed worth that much effort anymore.

He waited until the family left before going into the house. It was nice to have it to himself for a change, at least at first. He supposed he should take advantage of the privacy—heat some water and take a bath—but that took so much work. He changed out of chore clothes, giving himself a lick-and-a-promise sponge bath, then settled in the rocking chair beside the kitchen stove. No sense building a fire in the parlor stove for one person. Besides, the picture Amy painted last year of Pearl and Jason hung above the sofa. He didn't need yet another reminder of her.

He opened up *The Old Farmer's Almanac* for 1895. A new year. A year he'd looked forward to like no other. What a way to start it. Instead of beginning a romance, he was more alone than he'd ever been in his life.

Jason was right, even though he'd stated it wrong. It was time to return to normal life.

Frank banked the fire in the stove and put out the lamps. Then he saddled up his horse and headed for town.

He hadn't a lantern, but moonlight on the snow lit the way. Others traveled the road, mostly headed to town for church or New Year's parties. A couple of young men from the Academy raced their cutters, sleigh bells sending a merry tune not at all in keeping with Frank's mood. He greeted people with a nod or a touch to his hat.

Sleighs, wagonsleds, and horses lined the side of the street near the church. Lanterns beside the door lit the front steps for parishioners. Sleighs were pulling up near the steps, dropping off ladies.

Frank reined in his horse at the end of the line. He hadn't dressed for church, wasn't even certain when he started out that he was headed for church, but it was the safest place for him in his present state of mind. Maybe no one would notice or recognize him if he slipped into one of the back pews.

He dismounted, tied his horse to the post, and started up the walk. The sight of Amy and Walter climbing the church steps brought him up short.

Frank spun around and stalked back to his horse, ignoring the greetings of others on the path. Once in the saddle, he barely paid attention to where he headed. Tears blurred his vision. He needed to get away, and any direction would do. The fewer people around, the better.

The downtown streets stood empty because only the skating rink, billiard halls, and saloons were open. He tied his horse in front of Plummer's Saloon. The promises he'd made to himself and Amy shouted in his head for attention. He tried to shut them out. He only wanted one night without the pain, without the ache that had filled him for the last week, without the memories. Was that such a terrible thing?

Once inside, he didn't hesitate. He strode right to the bar. Tables and chairs were outlawed in saloons in Chippewa City since the gambling-den raid above this very saloon last year, but the town fathers and the Temperance League were mistaken if they thought that kept men standing while they drank. Men seated on the floor rested their backs against the walls or bar.

A bartender in a white shirt with colorful garters greeted him with a pleasant smile. "What's your pleasure, Sir?"

"Rye."

Frank pulled off his gloves and tossed them on the counter. The place was the same as he remembered. The familiarity settled upon him like a comfortable old coat: the yeasty odor, the sounds of glasses clinking, of laughter a bit too high and too bright, of beer *glug-glugging* into glasses.

Another patron leaned on the bartender's shoulder and bent his ear, delaying Frank's drink. Frank, impatient, looked about while he waited.

Old Tom slumped in a corner. An open glass lay on the floor beside his hand. His mouth hung open. His eyes were closed. Frank figured he was asleep or, more accurately, passed out. Frank envied him. *That's where I'm headed, beyond caring about this world.*

He looked again for the bartender and caught sight of his own image in the mirror on the wall behind the bar. He barely recognized himself. Circles underscored his eyes. His normally neatly-trimmed mustache was overgrown into the scraggly beard covering his cheeks and chin.

And to think he'd almost attended church this way. His appearance would have shocked Amy. He snorted. An adverse sense of pleasure stole through him at the thought. If she saw him looking like this, maybe she'd realize how much she'd hurt him.

The bartender set a glass in front of him. "Sorry it took me so long."

Frank picked up the glass and held it near his face, smelling the amber liquid. When Amy heard he'd started drinking again, she'd know he started because he cared for her so much. Then she'd feel guilty for the way she'd treated him.

Your promise wasn't to Amy.

The words sounded in his mind as clearly as if spoken. He set the glass down with a *thunk*. Of course his promise had been to Amy, to her and her father. He'd promised he wouldn't drink or gamble for a year.

No. That wasn't quite right. He'd decided to follow Christ. As part of that decision, he'd given up drinking and gambling, but he couldn't have followed up on changing those habits if it weren't for the promise that Christ loved him and stood by him through everything.

The year was a guarantee, a show of good faith to Amy's father that Frank was serious about his commitment to the Lord. Maybe it was that year that cost him the chance to win Amy by allowing Walter Bay to win her heart, but the Lord hadn't broken any of His promises to Frank.

It still hurt, losing faith in Amy's goodness, losing the chance to win her. Walking through fire couldn't hurt any more than losing her.

He looked down at the drink still in his hand. A few of these and that pain would be gone for awhile. This glass would start it, take the edge off, give his brain that fuzzy-edged feeling.

He glanced at Tom. *I want to be as free of pain as he is at this moment, but if I let myself do this tonight, the pain will be back in the morning. I'll have to do this again and again and again until there's no stopping between drinks.*

His hand tightened on the glass. Sweat trickled out from under his hat. Without drinking, his only choice was to live with the pain. Why didn't God take the pain away so he didn't have to fight this battle?

He'll help you live through the pain, so you don't need to give up everything else good in your life to escape the pain.

He did have good things in his life: his family, the animals he loved, the academy.

Frank pulled some coins from his trouser pocket and tossed them on the counter. He took out a couple silver dollars and added them to the coins. "Make sure someone gets Old Tom home safe and sound when you close up, all right?"

"Sure thing," the bartender agreed.

"One more thing." Frank shoved the glass of untouched rye toward the barkeep. "Throw this away."

He walked out feeling taller than he had in days.

10

*A*my stood back, hands on her hips, and studied the oil paintings on the wall of the Academy hall. They looked as though they hung evenly, all but the one of Pearl standing on the farmstead porch, watching for Jason. That one insisted on listing slightly to the left. She stepped to the wall to adjust the painting for the third time.

Footsteps falling quickly along the steps leading down to the hall accompanied a cheerful whistle. Amy glanced over her shoulder to see who was coming.

"Frank." Her heart stopped, then started again, faster than before.

He stopped both feet and whistle in the middle of a musical phrase, staring at her. "Amy. I—I didn't know you were here. I had some business with Professor Headley and—" He waved a hand in a careless motion. "I guess you wouldn't care about that."

His words wounded her more deeply than any words since a boy in seventh grade had told her she was spindlier than his goat. The memory twisted amusement into the present pain. She didn't know how to respond to Frank's comment. Say "Of course I care; I care about everything that concerns you"? Such familiarity was beyond the bounds of propriety now that she was engaged to Walter.

Frank's gaze wandered from one picture to another. "Are these yours?"

"Yes." She slipped her hands into the pockets of the white apron protecting her dress. She didn't want him to see how she trembled at his nearness. Her fingers closed over the emerald ring she'd dropped into her pocket only minutes earlier. "Professor Headley kindly asked me to do a showing. He thought it would be nice for the students to see my work since I'll be teaching here this winter."

He walked along the wall, examining the paintings one by one. "I've only seen the paintings you did in school and some of your sketches. These are good. You've progressed a great deal in the last couple years." He shrugged. "Not that I'm an artist, but if it's obvious to me, it should be obvious to anyone."

His compliment was like balm to her aching heart.

Frank stopped in front of the picture of Pearl and straightened it. "This is your best, I think. I can feel the scorching summer wind that's blowing her hair and dress, and I almost smell the grain that's being harvested in the field she's looking out at."

"Thank you. Too bad you're not a buyer for the Metropolitan Museum."

"If you keep at it, maybe your work will hang there one day. After all, you won a state award last year, didn't you?"

She nodded, pleased he remembered.

"Are you going to keep it up after you're married?"

There it was, the marriage topic. "Of course. That is, I haven't thought . . . we haven't discussed it, but I can't imagine my life without painting."

"He won't mind if you teach?"

"He hasn't said so." She hadn't realized until this minute that such things might no longer be hers to decide. Marriage to Walter had meant only that she wouldn't be able to see Frank. The awareness that the marriage had further consequences staggered her.

"Maybe he'll take you to Paris to see the masterpieces there."

"You remembered." The words were out before she could catch them back.

Frank's eyes darkened, and it was as if he dropped a protective shield between them. "I remember your dream to study in Paris. I remember everything."

His gaze held hers captive. Her throat ached from repressed words, words that must never be spoken. *I remember everything, too, Frank. I always shall.*

His lips lifted in a small smile. "I remember when you came back from the Chicago World's Fair last year, all excited over Mary Cassatt's mural. You glowed when you spoke of her work."

"I'd love to meet her someday. There're so many questions I'd like to ask her. One can examine a master's paintings to see how the master obtained the results, but to actually have the opportunity to ask—"

"There you are, all excited again."

She dropped her gaze. Mary Cassatt's mural had depicted modern woman's liberation in education and professions, a contrast to a mural called "Primitive Woman," where the women were slaves to the men. Amy had never thought she'd marry a man who made her feel like a slave, but now . . .

"Why didn't you tell me, Amy?"

Her gaze jerked to his. The pain she saw cut through her. She knew, of course, what he meant: Why hadn't she told him she was going to marry Walter? "I intended to. I planned to tell you after the church service, but we went caroling, and there was Tom, then the open house at the parsonage, and then . . . then . . ."

"And then." He stepped closer, and it felt as though he gripped her shoulders and forced her to look into his eyes, though he didn't touch her at all. "Then you let me hold you." His voice was low but filled with indignation and betrayal. "You let me kiss you and believe we had chance at a future together."

Amy covered her face with her hands, unable to look on his pain any longer. "I'm sorry."

"Did you know then? Did you know even then that you were going to marry Walter?"

She nodded.

"Do you remember you promised to allow me to court you, Amy? Do you remember when I offered to release you from that promise and you refused the release? Tell me, since your word has so little importance, do you plan to keep your wedding vows?"

His steps clipped angrily across the floor as he left. A sob ripped from her breast, and tears flowed into her palms.

Frank stood in the barn doorway as light faded from the evening sky. He stuffed gloved hands into his jacket pockets and stared at the farmhouse. He didn't see the house surrounded by snow and insulating hay bales as it sat now. He saw Pearl gazing out to the harvest fields, waiting for Jason, as she stood immortalized in Amy's painting.

He remembered when Amy had started that painting, remembered coming in from the fields to find her sketching Pearl. Pearl had laughed, pleased and embarrassed all at once to be the subject of one of Amy's pictures.

He'd understood why Amy had selected Pearl and the theme, though Amy never explained it to him or anyone else in the family. The love between Pearl and Jason was living, vital. Jason wasn't in the picture at all, but a person knew from Pearl's expression that she was waiting for the man she loved and that the man she loved would come home to her.

All a man could wish for was represented in that picture.

During the last year he'd been glad for Jason that he'd found such a love with Pearl. He'd daydreamed that he and Amy would have a love that deep one day, after she'd traveled to Paris and he'd taken the agriculture course at the university.

Now seeing Jason and Pearl together only increased his pain. They were a constant reminder of the future he'd lost with Amy. Maybe one day there'd be another woman for him.

Maybe, but he doubted it.

He shouldn't have let his temper get away from him at Windom Academy today. He'd replayed the questions he'd thrown at Amy one hundred times in his mind. He'd thought he'd feel better if he asked them.

He didn't. He didn't feel one whit better. Misery just kept growing in him like yeast in rising bread.

~&~

Amy caught her bottom lip between her teeth and focused all her attention on trying to make the creamy sweep of paint bring her subject's cheek to life. She stepped back, palette in one hand, raised brush in the other, and studied the canvas with tilted head. Had she caught it, the way the light played over the cheekbone? "I think maybe I have at that, finally."

A clearing of a throat made her turn toward the door. "Yes, Lina?" She tried to keep the impatience from her voice. Sunlight was all too brief these winter days, but Lina didn't interrupt her in the studio often.

"Mrs. Sterling is here, Miss Amy. I know you aren't home to most visitors, but I thought you might be to her."

"You're right, Lina. Please show her up."

"Here? To the studio?"

"Yes." Amy laughed at Lina's surprise but understood it. She'd never accepted company in the studio before. But she had nothing to hide from Pearl.

She was still working on the portrait when Pearl entered. Glancing over at her guest, Amy said, "I'm so glad you came. Please, sit down. I hope you won't mind if I take advantage of a few more minutes of sunlight while we talk."

Pearl's practical black skirt swayed as she crossed the room. "Must I sit? I've never been in your studio before. What wonderful windows."

"I love this room. It's perfect for capturing the light. I hope Walter will build a similar room for me when we have our own home." She glanced up from her work. "Do the smells bother you? I confess, the oils and cleaning fluids are as welcoming to me as perfume."

"They don't bother me. May I see what you're painting?"

Amy stood back so Pearl could see the entire canvas.

"Why, it's Frank."

"Then I've captured him. I mean, I've captured his image."

Surprise sat squarely in Pearl's blue eyes. "Yes, but why? I should think you'd choose to paint your betrothed, not a rejected suitor."

Amy's face heated. She'd been so involved in the painting that she'd forgotten for a few minutes that her subject was inappropriate. She hurried across the room and began cleaning her brushes.

Pearl remained beside the canvas. "Surely you aren't planning to hang this in the home you'll share with Walter. Did Frank commission it?"

"No."

"Amy, what is going on? We're best friends. I thought you were looking forward to courting Frank. You've always liked and admired him. You've told me so numerous times. Suddenly you're betrothed to Walter. I don't understand."

Amy poured water from a sprigged china pitcher into a matching bowl and rinsed her hands. "You're one to talk." She tried to keep her voice jolly. "You married Jason on the spur of the moment and right after another woman broke her engagement to him."

"That was different."

"Was it?" Amy laughed, truly amused. It felt good to laugh again. She couldn't remember laughing since Christmas Day.

"Amy Henderson, I've been in love with Jason since I was knee-high to a grasshopper, and you know it. You aren't in love with Walter. At least . . . you aren't, are you?"

"Why else do you think I'd marry him?" Amy busied herself with unfastening the cover-up she wore to protect her dress while painting. Pearl knew her too well. She'd easily read the truth in Amy's face.

Pearl spread her arms to her sides and dropped them. "I can't imagine."

"Walter is a good businessman. He'll be able to support a family well, even in these hard times."

"Do you love him?"

Amy hung her smock on a marble-topped hook beside the door. "People marry for reasons other than love all the time."

"I knew it! I knew you didn't love him."

"I didn't say that."

"You didn't say you do, either. And I've another question. Is Walter a Christian?"

The question had come to Amy's mind repeatedly. Each time she'd tried to ignore it as she now tried to ignore Pearl's challenging look and query. How could she admit she'd agreed to marry a man she didn't believe shared her faith?

Pearl clutched her stomach with one hand and with the other grabbed onto the easel beside her. "Oh, my."

Amy rushed to her, slipping an arm around her waist. "What is it? What's the matter? You're white as a sheet."

"I think perhaps your oils are too strong for me after all."

Amy hurried her out into the hall and shut the door behind them. "Sit in this window seat, and try to catch your breath." She lowered her friend to the flowered chintz cushions. "Don't move. I'll get a cold compress for you."

Pearl clutched Amy's wrist. "You'll do nothing of the kind. I'm fine."

"You're not fine."

"Yes, I am." She smiled, her blue eyes shining. "Jason and I are going to have a baby. We only found out a few days ago."

"A baby! I'm so glad for you." They shared an embrace. "But are you sure you're all right?"

"Yes, the paints made me nauseous is all. I'm feeling better already now that we're out of the studio."

Amy eyed her, dubious. "The color seems to be coming back to your cheeks."

Pearl patted the cushion beside her. "Sit."

Amy sat. "Yes, Ma'am."

"Don't think for a minute you're off the hook, as Jason would say. I want to know why you are marrying Walter."

Amy hesitated, watching her hands as she played with the folds in her gray wool skirt. It would be such a relief to share everything with someone. Pearl was her best friend. If there was anyone she could trust, it was Pearl. Besides, Pearl was like a sister to Frank. She'd understand how special he was, what grief Amy felt at losing him.

"You're right. I don't love Walter."

"I knew it." Pearl took Amy's hands. "Why are you marrying him?"

It tumbled out, the whole sordid story: her father's financial state, Walter's blackmail, her betrayal of Frank's trust. "That's the worst of it, that I've hurt Frank so. He has such a beautiful, compassionate heart, and I've treated him cruelly."

Pearl drew herself up, straightening her shoulders. "You can't do this, you know. You cannot marry Walter."

"Do you think I haven't racked my brain trying to find another solution? There isn't any other way out."

"There has to be. You can borrow the money."

"From whom? Using what for collateral?"

"I don't know much about business, but Jason and Frank should be able to figure something out."

"No!" Amy shot to her feet. "I told you everything in confidence because you are my dearest friend in all the world. You mustn't tell Frank and Jason. Promise me you won't."

Pearl stood, meeting Amy's gaze. "You should have exacted that promise before you told me. I won't be party to deceiving Frank, allowing him to believe you love Walter. Nor will I sit idly by and allow you to sacrifice yourself for your father."

Amy's hands closed into fists as she attempted to stop her trembling. "Pearl, please, you're my friend."

"That's why I won't make the promise you ask of me. Would you allow me to make such sacrifices? I'm going to tell Frank tonight, and you may as well get used to the idea."

Amy watched helplessly as Pearl swept down the stairs.

11

my looked over the edge of the walking bridge into the gully below, remembering the night her hat had sailed down among trees and bushes. Everything had still seemed possible and wonderful that night. The sweetness of walking home on Frank's strong arm wrapped around her in memory.

"Amy, wait."

She turned in surprise at Frank's call and watched him jog down the path from Windom. She hadn't seen him since Pearl had left her place the afternoon before. He must know the truth by now, all the terrible truths. She shuddered, dreading facing him, and dug her chin into the collar of her coat. Her glance darted over the institute grounds. There were no other students out, but that unusual condition wouldn't last long.

When he reached her, his gloved hands went immediately to her arms. "Pearl told me."

Amy cast her gaze to the ground. "I was afraid she would."

"Afraid?" Frank bent over until she had to look into his face. "Don't you know I wouldn't let Walter Bay harm you and your father this way?"

She gasped slightly. It was the gentleness in his tone and touch as much as his words that brought tears to her eyes. "There's nothing you can do. There's nothing anyone can do. But it means the world to me that you want to help us, that you care."

"Care? I'll say I care. We'll find a way out of this together. I promise we will." His eyes were lit with a tender fire.

Her lips wobbled when she tried to smile. "It's sweet of you to say that, but the only way you can help is to understand why I am marrying Walter."

"Pearl said you don't love him. You don't, do you?"

"No, but it makes no difference."

"It makes all the difference. It's the only thing that makes any difference at all."

Students were beginning to come down the path. "Frank, you must leave."

"I'll walk you home. We can try to figure something out along the way."

Amy stepped back, pulling her arms gently from his hold. "Others are coming. I'm engaged to Walter. We can't be seen this way, and you mustn't walk me home."

"We're going to thrash this out, Amy." He didn't try to touch her again, but his tone left no doubt he meant what he said. "If you won't let me talk with you out here, I'll come to your home."

"No! Father might overhear, or Walter might show up."

"Then I'll send Pearl in to pick you up. You can come out to the farm with her. She'll be a perfect chaperon."

The other students were getting closer. Amy took another step back, shaking her head. "I don't think that's a very good idea."

"When do you want her to come? Tonight or tomorrow night?"

"Tonight, since you insist upon it." If she waited any longer, she'd chicken out for sure. "Good-bye." She turned about just as the other students reached the bridge.

❧

Amy arrived at the farm with Pearl and Jason, their spring wagon set on runners for winter. Frank came out of the house to greet them as soon as they drove into the farmyard. He helped Amy down from the wagon, his hands lingering on her waist a moment or two longer than necessary as he pressed his cheek against hers. For the first time since Walter had threatened her, Amy felt safe. She didn't believe Frank could do anything to help her, but she felt his love holding her up.

Once in the kitchen, Pearl took Amy's coat and hat. "You and

Frank can talk in the parlor. We'll keep Frank's brothers and sisters out so you can have some privacy."

Amy looked from Pearl to Jason. "Don't forget, you've promised to take me home when I say I must leave."

Frank took hold of her elbow and directed her toward the parlor. "We aren't the ones kidnapping you, remember? Of course you're free to leave when you wish."

He pulled a high-backed spring rocker close to the parlor stove so Amy could warm up after the drive. Flames danced behind the stove's isinglass. The rose-colored globe on the hanging lamp spread soft, flattering light.

Frank drew an overstuffed green chair near the rocker and sat down. He leaned forward and took Amy's hands in both his own. "Thank you for coming."

"I only came because you threatened to come to my house if I didn't."

"I hope that's not true. I don't want to hurt you—I want to help."

"I understand that, but you can't help. It will only make things worse if you insist on trying."

"How could they possibly be worse?"

"Father could lose our home. His financial straits would become the talk of the town. It would destroy his pride." Amy heard her voice rise as she spoke.

"You're not alone in this anymore." Frank slid one of his hands slowly down her arm. The steady touch helped her catch the despair that had started spiraling out of control. "You didn't take Walter's word for it about your father's debt?"

"No." She told him about the mortgage papers Walter showed her and the ledgers and account books she'd found in her father's desk. "I feel so guilty, Frank. I should have realized Father might have financial problems."

One of her tears warmed the back of her hand. Frank passed his thumb tenderly beneath her eyes, catching more tears before they dropped. His kindness only increased her tendency toward weepiness.

"I've heard Father speak of the country's hard times at our very dinner table. Like everyone else, I know the Wall Street stocks almost collapsed in '93, that hundreds of banks and thousands of businesses have failed, even strong businesses like the railroads. Father always had a head for business and more than enough money for our needs. It never occurred to me he might lose everything, like so many others."

Frank's hands rubbed hers gently. "Shh. It's not your fault."

"But I've been so selfish. I bought new furniture for the dining room last spring, and he didn't mention economizing. I had a number of new winter outfits made. He said nothing, though he had not one thing made for himself. When I asked him why not, he said what he had was fine. I didn't question it, although it's not at all like him."

"He obviously wanted to protect you from the situation. I'm sure he believes he'll rebuild his financial base, that there's no reason for you to worry."

"He won't have a chance to rebuild if Walter calls his loan."

Frank lifted her hands, touched his lips to them, and cradled them against his cheek. "I love you, Amy. Marry me. We can live here on the farm, and your father will always have a home with us."

The sweetness of his love, the magnitude of his offer over-whelmed her. It wrapped around her like a chrysalis. For a moment she couldn't speak. This tender, protective love could be hers forever, but she had to turn it away. "I shall always treasure that you offered me this, me and Father. But I can't accept."

"Don't say that. Do you truly believe the money matters so much to your father that he'd want you to sell yourself into marriage?"

Amy cupped her hand about his cheek. "You can give Father a roof, but you can't save his pride. If Walter calls the loan and takes our house, everyone will know Father lost all his money. I don't know that his pride could bear that."

"Can his pride bear knowing you sold yourself for him?"

"He'll never find out."

"He will if I tell him."

Amy shot to her feet. "You wouldn't."

Frank stood, towering over her. "I'd do anything to keep you from marrying Walter. If you loved him, it would be different. Of course I wouldn't interfere then." His eyes widened. "You don't love him, do you? You said you didn't."

"I don't. How could you think I do after . . ." After the way they'd touched each other. "If you break my confidence by speaking with Father, I'll never forgive you. Even if your revelation meant I didn't marry Walter. If you tell Father, I'll never marry you, either." Amy started toward the kitchen.

He grabbed her arm. "Amy, please."

The anguish in his voice echoed the anguish in her soul. She steeled herself against it. "Thank you for your desire to help Father and me, but you will allow me to handle my own life." She stopped with her hand on the doorknob. She'd dreaded telling him this, but he must know it. "The wedding is planned for Saturday. Good-bye."

12

emember Amy. Frank bolstered his courage as he headed down Main Street toward Walter Bay's office the next morning. *Jacob worked fourteen years for Rachel. Amy's worth at least that much to me.*

He adjusted himself to his horse's movements without an awareness of doing so, his mind on the task he'd given himself. He kept his gaze straight ahead when he passed Plummer's Saloon. Wished he'd never taken that first drink. Then he wouldn't be tempted to stop for one drink, only one, to give a nudge to his courage now.

You say You are all I need, Lord, and I sure need You now.

What he had in mind would save Amy's father's pride, if it worked, but it might destroy Frank's.

He tied his horse to the street-side railing, entered a wooden building, and headed up the steps to Walter's second-floor office. The pitch he planned to make went around in his head, as it had since he'd left home.

The odor of the cigars Walter liked filled the front room. The *clack-clack-clack* of a typewriter set a busy, modern note to the office. A young woman in a black skirt and white shirtwaist with a black bow at the collar looked up at him, and the clacking ceased. "May I help you?"

Frank pulled off his hat. "Yes, Miss. I'd like to talk with Mr. Bay."

"Who shall I tell him is calling?"

"Frank Sterling. I don't have an appointment."

The trim woman entered a door with Walter's name lettered on the frosted glass. Frank heard a murmur of voices through the closed

394

door and transom. A moment later she held the door open for him. "Mr. Bay will see you now."

Walter didn't bother to stand or offer his hand when Frank entered. Instead the businessman leaned back and his oak chair creaked. "What can I do for you?" He stuck a cigar in his mouth and lit a match.

Frank didn't beat around the bush. "I understand you own the note on Mr. Henderson's house."

The match stopped halfway to the cigar. Walter shook it out. "That's right." He lit another match. This one made it to the end of the cigar. "How'd you hear about that?"

"I want to pay it off."

Walter leaned forward, elbows on his desk. "Excuse me?"

"You heard me. I want to pay off Henderson's loan."

A short laugh burst from Walter's mouth. "Do you have any idea how far behind Henderson is on that loan?"

"Yes."

"What are you planning to use to pay it off?"

Frank's grip on his hat tightened. "I can't pay it off all at once."

"Just the back payments?"

"I can't pay them off all at once, either." Frank kept his expression carefully solemn. He knew how ridiculous his offer sounded, but he only had a couple options.

Walter laughed again, relaxing against the chair back. "Maybe you should tell me what you have in mind that involves taking over the loan without making the payments."

Frank felt a flush rise up his neck and over his face. "I'll sign over my share of the proceeds from the sale of our crops."

"For this coming year?"

"For as many years as it takes."

Walter crossed his arms and looked Frank up and down.

Frank stood still, keeping his gaze steady.

"Why are you offering to do this?"

Frank didn't answer.

"You couldn't be this crazy about little Amy, could you?"

"Yes or no, Bay?"

"No, I think."

Frank's jaw tightened. He waited.

"Definitely no."

"I'll work for you. You can add my wages to my portion of the crops."

"Mm, mm, mm." Walter shook his head. "You want that little lady something fierce."

"What's your answer?"

"I'm not looking to hire anyone." He rolled his cigar between his thumb and forefinger. "There is one thing I'd consider."

A warning tingled along Frank's nerves. Nothing Bay came up with was likely to be honorable. "What's that?"

"I like a challenge as much as the next man. I hear tell you do, too. So how about a friendly little card game? All or nothing. You win, I sign over the note to you. I win, you sign over your share of the farm and I keep the note on the Henderson place."

Frank's heart picked up its beat. The forgotten but familiar excitement of the gambling dare raced through his blood. His conscience reminded him of the promise he'd made to God to give up gambling, but it looked like this was the only way to get rid of Henderson's debt and save Amy. Was his promise more important than that? "I'll have to think about it."

"Don't think too long. The offer's on the table until midnight. If you want to give it a toss, you'll find me above Plummer's Saloon."

❧

Frank couldn't keep his mind on classes at the Academy. All day he argued with himself and his conscience over Walter's challenge. Was the bet an answer to prayer?

I asked You to show me a way to help Amy and her father out of this mess, Lord. I've tried everything that came to mind. This is the only way left. Does that mean I should take the challenge?

He'd heard too many sermons against gambling to trust it could be God's answer to his dilemma. Yet . . .

He'd offered Amy marriage, offered to take her father into their home, and she'd said no. It was important to her that her father's honor not be smirched.

He'd offered his income from the crops to Walter, offered to work for Walter, and those offers were also refused.

What else could he do? He'd spent sleepless nights wracking his brain for possibilities. He'd struck out on every idea. Wasn't it possible God's answer to his prayers was Walter's bet? If Frank won, and of course he'd win if this was God's plan, the debt would be wiped away and with it Walter's hold over Amy.

If I win, Amy won't need to marry Walter, but she won't marry me, either.

Amy and her father were as much against gambling as they were opposed to drinking. Frank hadn't forgotten his right to court Amy had been conditional on the promise he neither drank nor gambled for a year.

Mr. Henderson's cause for exacting that promise, Frank remembered all too vividly, was that Frank had been caught in a raid on what the newspaper called "the gambling den" above Plummer's Saloon, the very place Bay had set for the card game.

Frank's only consolation at the time had been that Ed Ray, another of Amy's suitors, had been caught in the same raid and consequently dropped from Amy's courters.

If I win the card game, I lose all chance at marrying Amy. If I don't take up Bay's challenge, I've lost Amy anyway.

❧

Frank's boots clunked against the narrow wooden stairs leading from the back of Plummer's Saloon up to the second floor. Laughter and loud conversation drifted up the stairwell. Smoke and the relaxing odor of drinks made from hops filled the air. The saloon was doing a brisk business, but that was normal for ten at night.

He stopped in the open doorway at the top of the stairs. He hadn't been in this room since the raid more than a year ago. He'd ended up in jail overnight and paid a fine, but the largest cost had been losing the opportunity to court Amy. Now he was back, hoping to win her freedom.

Still time to change my mind.

He pulled off his gloves, stuffed them into his coat pockets, and stepped over the threshold. The arguments hadn't stopped circling through his brain since he'd left Bay's office more than twelve hours earlier. He didn't like the choice he was making, but it was the only choice that gave him a chance to save Amy.

More tables filled the room than he remembered, probably brought from downstairs when the local law was enacted against tables in barrooms. A number of card games were going on, some with house dealers and some not. People lined a narrow table along one wall, calling encouragement to dice that danced with the people's dreams. In one corner a ball rattled as a wheel spun.

A rush of energy flooded him. He recognized it. That rush was the reason he'd enjoyed gambling.

Frank's gaze scanned the room for Walter and found him in the middle of a poker game. Frank made his way through the tables, returning greetings and turning down invitations to join in games. He stopped beside Walter's table as Walter pulled in a pile of winnings.

The irony of the situation wasn't lost on him. Mr. Henderson had tried to do right by Amy, demanding Frank not court her if he drank or gambled. She'd quit seeing Ed Ray after he had been caught gambling. Now, because of her father's debt, Amy might end up married to a man who made Frank and Ed look like amateurs in the world of drinking and gambling.

"Ah, you made it." Walter spoke around his cigar. "I was beginning to think you'd chickened out." He looked around at the others at the table. "You'll have to find a new game, boys. Next one is private between me and Sterling here."

"Hey, you need ta give us a chance ta win our money back," one of the players protested.

"Sure thing," Walter accommodated. "After the private game's over."

Frank took a seat across from Walter as one of the other players stood up. Most of the others hung around. Frank wished they'd move on but knew too well they wouldn't. A private game, no joiners allowed, might be high stakes. Could prove entertaining.

"Buy you a drink?" Walter asked.

"Sarsaparilla."

"Oo-oo-oo. Tough man."

The group about them guffawed. Frank smiled but didn't change his order. Not that it wasn't tempting. A drink would take the tension out of his shoulders. But even if he hadn't vowed to stop drinking, he didn't want alcohol crowding his thinking tonight.

Vowed not to gamble, too.

He pushed the thought away.

Walter called out to a young, mustached bartender who went downstairs to get the drinks.

"What's your pleasure?" Walter's eyes mocked Frank while he shuffled the cards.

"Your choice." His heart raced, but he tried to keep a calm demeanor. Nothing worse than a card player who couldn't keep a poker face. Easier to keep it if he started with it.

Walter announced his choice.

Frank gave one curt nod in agreement.

"What're the stakes?" the man who'd given Frank his chair asked loudly. "Gotta know the stakes before the hand's dealt."

Amy's happiness.

Walter pulled folded papers from his inside jacket pocket and tossed them on the table. Frank picked them up, unfolding them to scan them. The man behind his chair leaned close for a look. Frank pressed the papers to his chest. "This is private, George."

George stuffed his hands in his trouser pockets and took a step backward. "Private stakes in a public card game. Never heard of such."

The note appeared legitimate to Frank. He refolded the papers and laid them on the table, then pulled a note from his own coat and tossed it across to Walter.

Bay had no compunction with allowing others to see Frank's stakes. "Your share of the farm?" a man standing beside Walter burst out.

Heat flooded Frank's face, then receded so quickly he almost felt faint. If he went through with this game, the town was sure to find out about Henderson's financial troubles. George was right; high-stakes games didn't stay secret. Why hadn't he realized it before? Win or lose, he'd place Amy's father in the exact position she was trying so desperately to avoid.

But what else could he do? In less than a week Amy would be Walter's wife, and then nothing could change her fate. *There's no other way I can help her.*

13

Is God limited to my help? The thought shouted in Frank's mind.

Walter's grin mocked him as he set the paper with Frank's signature down beside the Henderson note. "Nothing left to do but get started." He accordioned the deck between his hands.

"I want a new deck."

"Sure thing." Walter nodded at George. "Get us a new deck, would you?"

George hurried off. Walter and Frank stared at each other, Walter blowing smoke and grinning.

Frank tried to pray, but the question of whether he was limiting God kept getting in the way. Could he possibly trust God to help Amy, trust Him enough to walk away from this card game that appeared his only opportunity to save her?

His answer arrived at the same time George returned with the new deck of cards. Limited trust was no trust at all.

Frank pushed his chair back. "I've changed my mind."

Walter, new deck in his hands, stared openmouthed. "What?"

Frank reached for the note promising his share of the farm and stuck it in his pocket. Henderson's note remained on the table, looking innocent. Just pieces of paper, but the promises in them had the power to change lives.

Walter's laughter, loud and triumphant, stung Frank like whiplashes as he strode to the door.

❧

Amy's thoughts strayed again and again from the temperance-meeting speaker. The applause at the end of the speech startled her back to the church and the meeting. She joined belatedly in the clapping.

"Penny for your thoughts," Pearl whispered with a smile from the seat beside her.

"You wouldn't want them at any price." Self-pity wasn't worth the sharing.

The applause stopped as another speaker was introduced to the Women's Christian Temperance League. Amy listened to figures about alcohol that she could barely comprehend. More than a billion dollars was spent on alcohol every year in the United States, even during these hard times.

"How could that be?" the speaker asked. "How can people waste money on alcohol when there isn't enough to keep a roof over their family's heads?"

When the speech was over, Amy confided to Pearl, "I used to ask that same question in that same self-righteous tone."

"Which question?"

"'How can people waste money on alcohol when they can't afford to keep a roof over their family's heads?'"

Pearl frowned. "You don't ask that any longer? I do."

"I think Frank answered it for me, at least partly. He explained the people who drink heavily often do so to try to ease their pains and fears."

"The pains and fears are still there when they get done drinking."

"Yes." Amy didn't have the courage to say that for the first time in her life she could understand a person's desire to forget the painful places in life, even if for only a few hours. Not that she planned to re-sort to drinking herself, but in understanding that desire to escape, those who drank to excess had become more real to her. She realized in some ways she was just like them. If she hadn't been raised to be-lieve Christ was sufficient in times of trouble and joy alike, would she have sought a way to forget her fears and responsibilities, even if it hurt the people she loved?

The WCTL president took the stage. "Before we adjourn in prayer, there are some questions I hope you will give serious consideration in the week ahead. Do you know any boys or young men who are beginning to drink? If so, have you pleaded and pleaded and pleaded with God for them? Have you felt as much real concern over them as you have over your winter coat or hat or a piece of furniture?"

She led them in a closing prayer, but her remarks left an impression on Amy's heart. Before Frank had laid his heart before her a year ago, she'd prayed for people to give up drinking but not with her heart and soul. Only because she cared so deeply for Frank had she learned to give depth to her prayers.

Was he tempted to go back to drinking because of the awful manner in which she'd treated him? If so, she was sure he'd fight the temptation, but she hated the pain she'd inflicted upon him. *Please, Lord, be with him. Lend him Your strength. Uphold him with Your everlasting wings.*

The meeting adjourned, and the women gathered about the refreshment table. Amy stayed in her seat, not eager to mingle. Beside her, Pearl rummaged through her reticule.

"Pearl, won't you change your mind and stand up for me at the wedding?"

"I should say not." There wasn't a second's hesitation in her answer. Pearl's hands stopped, and she grinned. "Unless you change your mind and your groom."

Amy didn't find her answer amusing. "I'd like you beside me. It would make it easier."

"Why should I make it easier for you to do something I think you shouldn't do at all?"

Mrs. Headley from the Academy and another woman stopped beside them. Amy thanked them for their excited congratulations on her upcoming wedding. She tried to appear happy and gracious. With dismay she realized they were only the first. It was the earliest opportunity for most of the women there to express their wishes, and Amy found herself surrounded.

When she was finally able to politely withdraw, she grasped Pearl's arm lightly. "Quick, let's get out of here before other wellwishers descend on me."

They collected their coats from the cloakroom. In the narthex,

Pearl laid her hand on Amy's arm. "Has Walter told you that Frank spoke with him yesterday?"

"No." Dread made Amy's heart feel weighted. "What did Frank say?"

"Perhaps it's not my place to tell you, but I think you should know."

Amazement and gratitude flooded Amy when she heard Frank had offered the income from his crops and even offered to go to work for Walter. It humbled her to be loved that much. When Pearl told of Walter's offer to put Mr. Henderson's note up as stakes in a card game, Amy paled. She wasn't certain what was worse, the insult to her father or the fear that Frank had agreed to the game. "Did . . . did Frank?"

"Of course not," Pearl shot back.

Relief washed through her. "Good."

"Though he said he considered it. He only wants you and your father free of that man." Pearl pulled something from her purse and handed it to Amy. "Frank asked me to give this to you."

A wave of gratitude swept through her. She didn't know what was in the small brown book, but the fact that Frank wanted her to have it told her that he continued to forgive her for the pain she'd brought to him. She rubbed a hand lightly over the cover, admiring the gold cross and the words. *The Shadow of the Rock.*

"He sent a note with it," Pearl said. "I put it inside the front cover. I need to be getting home. I hope I see you again before the wedding."

Pearl climbed up into the spring wagon and started down the street. Amy watched her friend and the wagon disappear, thinking about the incredible sacrifices Frank had offered to make for her. If it weren't for this painful place in their lives, if it weren't for Walter keeping them apart, she might never have known the depth of Frank's love.

Amy opened the book and removed a folded piece of paper:

> *Dear Amy,*
> > *Page 187.*
> > > *Always,*
> > > *Frank*

She touched the word "always" with the tip of her index finger.

She flipped through the pages. The book was a collection of Christian readings, poetry, and the words to songs. She turned to page 187, curious. The reading on that page was titled "Hold On, Hold In, Hold Out." She read the first verse:

Hold on, my heart, in thy believing!
*   The steadfast only wins the crown.*
He who, when stormy waves are heaving,
*   Parts with his anchor, shall go down;*
But he who Jesus holds through all,
*   Shall stand, though heaven and earth shall fall.*

"Oh, Frank," she whispered. Her eyes misted. The Lord must have known she needed this encouragement. How sweet that it came through Frank, that he understood she needed it. Whatever came, she would hold to Jesus and trust Him to hold her up.

❧

Amy walked slowly along Windom Academy, fingers clasped lightly behind her back, looking at the pictures in her showing. Her students had viewed them earlier that day. It had given her a strange sensation to have her paintings viewed not only for enjoyment but also for instruction.

She shook her head. "My work isn't worthy, Lord," she spoke into the empty room. "I've so much to learn."

Would Walter allow her the opportunity? Perhaps by this time next year they would have a child, and her desires and commitments would be elsewhere.

"Your work is worthy."

Amy spun around at Frank's voice, her hand flying to her lace-enclosed neck. "I thought I was alone."

He leaned against an oak table set against the wall opposite the paintings. "Don't ever belittle your work. You might have more to learn—I expect that's true about everyone in every line of work—but you know more than most people in these parts. You offer the students here a lot."

"Thank you. I should remember to value the Lord's gift instead of judging it." She pressed her lips together hard and shook her head. "You were right about Walter's attitude. He told me he will allow me to continue teaching through the winter because the academy is counting on me, but after that he expects me to devote myself to . . . to being Mrs. Bay."

"I'm sorry."

She nodded. What else could either of them say about Walter's decision? "Thank you for the message, 'Hold on, my heart!' How did you know it was just what I needed?"

"I knew because it was just what I needed."

There were so many things she wanted to say and couldn't that her chest ached from the weight of them. "I wish things were different."

"You can change them."

Amy turned her back to him. "I can't. You know I can't. How can you attack me that way?"

His hands cupped her shoulders. "I didn't intend it as an attack." He turned her gently to face him. "I've been thinking lately a lot about the Bible story of Jacob and Rachel. Do you remember it?"

"Of course. Jacob loved Rachel and worked for her father for seven years for the right to marry her. Then her father deceived him. Jacob married Rachel's sister. He worked seven more years before Rachel's father allowed them to marry."

"Rachel's father manipulated Jacob and Rachel's lives and Rachel's sister's life, too. I wonder how they felt about his interference? I wonder if they resented it as much as I resent Walter running our lives."

"I resent it, too." Her words came out in a cracked whisper.

"I know."

He touched his lips to her temple. His arms slid around her shoulders, drawing her against his chest in a tender embrace.

Amy rested her head against him. She shouldn't allow his touch, but her heart belonged to him. He made her feel cherished. If God by some miracle gave her a way out of the marriage to Walter, she hoped to marry Frank. Whatever happened, of one thing she was certain: She loved Frank Sterling.

"During the last year when I was struggling to stay away from drinking, I held onto your trust in me to help get through."

Shame washed over her. "And in the end I wasn't able to keep my promise that we'd court."

"I'm not accusing you. I'm trying to apologize, to tell you I was wrong. I made my promise to stop drinking when I told Christ I wanted to follow Him and His ways. I was wrong to tie that promise to you." His hands framed her face, and she trembled as he looked deep into her eyes. "I could only stop drinking for myself, with Christ's help, not for you. That's what I've learned since you became engaged to Walter."

Her smile was shaky. " 'He who Jesus holds.' "

"Yes." Frank took her hands in his. "I thought you were perfect, Amy, but you're not. Only Christ is perfect. Remember how Rachel's father manipulated Rachel's life?"

She nodded.

"With the very highest intentions, you're manipulating your father's life."

Amy tore her hands from his. Anger and hurt made it seem her heart pounded in her ears.

"I'm sorry, Amy, but it's true." Frank reached to recapture her hands.

She stepped back, placing her hands behind her. "Don't touch me."

"Listen, please. I know you're trying to save your father from embarrassment, to save him from losing his house. But you aren't trusting him to be man enough to face his own responsibilities. How do you think your father will feel when he learns about your sacrifice after you're married and he can't change what you've done?"

"He won't find out."

"Do you honestly trust Walter not to tell him?"

She saw the pity in his eyes and hated it. He was right, of course. Walter wasn't trustworthy. But what could she do other than hope this one time would be different?

"How will your father feel when he discovers you haven't let him decide how to handle his own debt or decide what sacrifices he's willing to make for himself? Your loving intention is to give your father a gift by marrying Walter, but you're taking away your father's right to run his own life, the way Rachel's father took that right away from his daughters and Jacob, and the way Walter is trying to take it away from us."

"No! You're willfully misinterpreting everything." Tears streamed down her face, but she was past caring. "You don't care about my father. You only care about yourself. You'll say anything—all these awful things—to stop me from marrying Walter."

"Amy, you couldn't save me from drinking, and you can't save your father from his problems. It may seem you can for awhile, but in the end, each person, with God's help, has to rescue himself, even your father."

"Go away." She buried her face in her hands. "Please, go away."

She could barely hear his footsteps leaving over the sound of her sobs.

$$\textbf{(14)}$$

rank rushed through the front door of Windom Academy and down the stone steps, blind to the snow-covered prairie before him. He'd known he was risking her anger in trying to make her see things from her father's perspective, but that didn't stop it from hurting. Would she forgive him one day, or would she allow this to fester into hatred? If she married Walter, it might be easier for her if she didn't love another man. Still, already the estrangement between their hearts left his soul scorched.

The winter wind whipped hard little snowflakes into his face. He pulled up his jacket collar and wrapped his muffler around his neck against nature's fury as he headed toward the shed where the horses were kept.

A drink would take the edge off the wind's chill—and the chill of Amy's anger.

He pushed the thought away. Would he always face that temptation? If only he could be done with it once and for all. He had no intention of drinking again, but the thought did creep in every time he faced something hard.

The smells of straw and horses were welcoming in the dark shed. He lit a kerosene lantern that hung beside the door. His boots crunched in the straw as he crossed the shed to saddle his horse.

The shed door creaked open, letting in a shaft of sunlight and gust of wind and snow, then creaked shut. "Frank Sterling, you in here?"

"Over here, Professor Headley, by the lamp." Frank settled a saddle blanket over his horse's back. "Come spring, we need to build a decent stable," he said, only half joking.

The professor sighed. "We could barely afford this shed, even with the students doing the labor. Money is tight."

Frank grunted as he lifted his saddle from the straw. "That it is. Tight everywhere." *So tight it's strangling the life from Amy and her father.*

Professor Headley leaned against the post on which the lamp hung, his hands stuffed in his coat pockets. The light cast shadows over the slender man's angular face beneath his derby.

"Frank, there are some questions I need to ask that I'd rather not. I meant to ask you to come to my office to talk, but I didn't catch you before you left the building."

Surprise mixed with trepidation sent a warning through Frank's chest. Had the professor overheard him and Amy? Was he going to accuse Frank of besmirching Amy's honor? What else could the professor possibly question that would be a delicate topic? Frank had to swallow twice before he could speak. "Ask away, Professor."

"You know the Academy allows no leniency if a student is caught drinking or gambling."

Frank's hands froze on the saddle belt he'd just cinched. "Yes, Sir."

"Someone reported to me this afternoon that you'd been seen coming out of Plummer's Saloon a few nights ago." Professor Headley's voice sounded almost apologetic.

"You're asking whether it's true."

"Yes."

"It's true I was in the saloon."

"I see."

The disappointment in the kind man's voice cut into Frank's chest. "I didn't drink any liquor, and I didn't gamble, though I admit I came close on both counts. I'm not proud of that."

"I'm glad to hear you only came close. Unfortunately, the school rules say you will be suspended from classes until this matter is resolved."

The pain in Frank's chest grew. "How do I go about clearing myself of the charges?"

"You'll need to find someone to confirm your statement that you didn't drink or gamble while inside the saloon. Then it will be up to the directors to decide whether they believe you and your witness."

Witness. Sounded like a court of law. Might as well be for the sentence they could impose on him. "I'm sure I can find someone to stand up for me."

"Be aware that the word of anyone who was in the saloon with you might be considered suspect by the directors."

He hadn't thought of that, but it made sense. "Thank you for the warning. Is there anything else, Sir?"

"The man who brought the accusations to me is one of the directors."

"Am I allowed to know who it was?"

"Walter Bay."

Hope plummeted. *I should have known.* It was like Walter to do this. He'd have a good laugh over it, knowing Frank would never tell that he'd been at the saloon to meet Walter, never reveal Amy's secret by telling of Walter's challenge.

"Is there anything else, Sir?"

"No. Except . . . I'm sorry, Frank."

Frank nodded. "Good day, Sir." Numbness set in as he led his horse from the shed into the sharp sunlight. How much more could go wrong in his life?

❧

Amy slumped against the wall across from her paintings. Her handkerchief was sodden, she had a headache, and her stomach muscles hurt from crying, but still the tears came. Frank's arms had provided a refuge, albeit a bittersweet one. Then his words turned everything into bitterness. How could he have been so cruel? Didn't he understand how difficult it was for her to marry Walter? It was so important to her that Frank understood.

"Amy?"

At Mrs. Headley's voice, shame and consternation increased the weariness in the wake of Amy's sobbing.

The professor's wife slipped her arms around Amy's shaking shoulders. "My dear, what is it? Nothing's happened to Walter, has it?"

Amy could only shake her head. Words wouldn't come through her sob-filled throat.

"There, there. Cry it out, whatever it is." Mrs. Headley patted Amy on the back gently.

"I don't know wh-what's g-gotten into me," Amy said in a sob-stutter when she could finally speak. "I n-never c-cry." Of course, she knew exactly what had caused the crying spell, but she couldn't possibly admit she was crying because she loved one man and was marrying another.

Mrs. Headley handed her a clean handkerchief. "Wedding jitters. Every bride is entitled to at least one good cry."

Amy looked curiously at the headmistress. Mrs. Headley wasn't much older than she. "I can't imagine you crying before your wedding. You and the professor are so dedicated to each other."

"I admit I've never been happier. But marriage changes a woman's life forever. It's a sensible woman who questions whether she is doing the right thing when she marries."

"It's a joy to see the way you and your husband work together for the academy."

"We love the academy. It's exciting to see it grow, but some aspects are difficult."

Amy dabbed at a lingering tear. "I know the funds have been difficult to raise."

"That isn't the worst of it." Mrs. Headley sighed. "One of our students was seen frequenting a saloon. It's always sad when we have to ask one of our young men to leave the school, but we must guard the morals of the other students."

Amy nodded.

"I'm especially disappointed this time," Mrs. Headley continued. "My husband and I try not to play favorites, but just between you and me, we did especially like Mr. Sterling."

"Frank?" Shock jolted the last of the sobs from her lungs.

"Yes. Such a polite, intelligent young man."

Amy grasped Mrs. Headley's arms. "When was he accused of being at the saloon? Was it Plummer's Saloon?"

Mrs. Headley gasped. Her eyes widened.

Amy dropped her hold, mortified at her behavior. "I'm sorry. I didn't mean to grab you that way. It's just that it's so important. When was Frank accused of being at the saloon?"

"I'm not certain. It was within the last few days."

"Oh, no." Had Frank known of the accusations when he and she argued, Amy wondered? It would be so like him to spare her the knowledge. If he were dismissed from the Academy, it would be for attempting to help her. She should be devoted to Walter, yet everything she learned about Frank, everything he did, increased her admiration and love for him.

"Amy, what can you possibly know about this?" Mrs. Headley's words held not only curiosity but a hint of disapproval.

Amy's thoughts raced. If she told what she knew, she'd expose to Professor Headley the very things she'd tried so hard to keep private. If she saved her own reputation and her father's, Frank might be expelled. Attending the academy was so important to him.

She took a deep breath. "I think I'd better speak with your husband."

The professor wasn't in his office or in the rooms in Windom Academy that he and his wife shared. Mrs. Headley and Amy finally learned the professor had gone to get some supplies at the general store. Mrs. Headley invited Amy to join her and the students who roomed at the Academy for dinner, but Amy declined. She was glad when Mrs. Headley went to oversee dinner, leaving Amy to relax in the room that served as the Headleys' parlor.

A simple kerosene lamp on a small parlor table was lit against the early winter evening darkness. Amy paced the small, sparsely furnished room, praying. "Hold on, my heart," she encouraged her soul.

Professor and Mrs. Headley entered the parlor following dinner. Almost immediately Mrs. Headley left the room on the pretense of hanging up his outer coat and derby. Amy was grateful for the woman's courtesy in offering them privacy. The professor invited her to sit in an oak rocker, and he sat across from her in a stiff-backed chair. "My wife tells me you believe you have knowledge concerning Mr. Sterling's frequenting of Plummer's Saloon. I find this difficult to believe, but I'm willing to listen."

"You will keep this in confidence, Sir?"

"As much as I am able. The situation will be brought before the directors, of course. If what you say truly relates to Mr. Sterling's guilt or innocence, it may be necessary to share it with the directors."

Amy caught her bottom lip between her teeth. She'd convinced herself of the need to expose her situation to Professor Headley, but to the directors? Secrets didn't remain secrets once one began sharing them. Little by little they leaked out into the community. *But if I don't tell, Frank will be suspended.*

She took a deep breath, lifted her chin, and looked the professor squarely in the eyes. "I believe you will understand the need for discretion when you hear my story. Mr. Sterling was at the saloon because of me."

A log broke and crashed in the fireplace. The flames cast strange shadows across the professor's face.

"Miss Henderson, are you aware of what you're saying?"

She flushed but kept her gaze steady. "Perfectly." She explained succinctly about her father's inability to pay his mortgage and Walter's offer to Frank to put the note up for stakes in a card game. She left out that her engagement to Walter was a result of blackmail.

The professor rested his elbows on the arms of the chair and pyramided his fingers. "Do you know whether Mr. Sterling participated in this card game?"

"No, he did not."

"How do you know this?"

"His sister-in-law told me."

"If Sterling was intent on saving your father's honor, why did he change his mind?"

"I can't answer for him, Sir."

A knock at the door made her jump. The professor answered the door and ushered in three guests: Frank, Jason, and a young man who looked vaguely familiar but whom she couldn't place.

Shock at the sight of her filled Frank's eyes.

A tremble rippled along her nerves. Earlier Frank had accused her of interfering in her father's life. Would Frank hate her now for interfering in his own life?

15

Frank stopped short. "Amy. I mean . . . Miss Henderson, I didn't expect to see you here." He whipped his hat off.

Jason and the other young man followed suit.

Frank eyed Amy nervously. He'd never imagined he would see her here the night before her wedding.

"What can I do for you young men?" Professor Headley asked.

"We're here about that incident we discussed earlier." Frank hoped the professor realized the need for discretion. "I didn't know you had company. We can come back another time."

"You may have arrived right on schedule." The professor nodded at Amy. "Miss Henderson believes she has knowledge that may help your case."

Frank felt the blood drain from his face. "I don't think that's possible, Sir."

"It seems unlikely to me, too," Headley agreed, "yet she wishes to speak on your behalf. Perhaps you have something to say which will make her contribution unnecessary?"

"I hope so." He glanced at Amy. Her cheeks were rosier than he'd ever seen them indoors. Anguish filled the eyes that looked back at him. He turned to the professor. "You've met my brother, Jason. I asked him to accompany me when I went to find a witness to my actions at the saloon. I didn't want to be accused a second time of drinking while I was there." He nodded toward the other man. "This is Mr. Peters, a bartender at Plummer's. Mr. Peters, this is Professor Headley."

The men shook hands.

"I assume Mr. Peters is here to shed light on your activities?" Headley asked.

"Yes."

Headley turned to Peters. "And what do you have to say, Sir?"

"Frank here, he came into the saloon, all right, but all he ordered was a sarsaparilla."

"Are you certain?" Headley questioned. "Isn't it hard to remember what one person ordered?"

Peters grinned. "Not when it's sarsaparilla. Not many men come to a saloon for a tame drink like that."

"Were you the only bartender that night?"

Peters hesitated. "I was the only bartender in the room Frank here was in."

"I understand Mr. Sterling was invited to join a card game at the saloon."

Peters's gaze shifted to Frank, then the floor, then back to the professor. "Card games and gambling ain't allowed in Chippewa City."

Frank recognized the apprehension in Peters's eyes and understood it. Frank wasn't allowed to drink or gamble if he wanted to remain enrolled at the Academy, but there was no law against selling liquor in the saloon. There was, however, a law against gambling. Peters didn't mind verifying the sarsaparilla, but he wouldn't threaten his job by admitting to the gambling. Where had Headley heard about the game? Surely not from Amy.

Peters stepped toward the door, worrying his hat brim. "Uh, I need to be getting back to work."

Headley held the door for him. "Thank you for coming."

"Yes, thanks," Frank added.

Jason offered to take Peters back to the saloon and then return for Frank. "I expect you and the professor need to have a few more words."

Headley closed the door behind Jason and Peters, then leaned back against it, arms crossed over his chest. "It appears there's a lot more here than meets the eye, Mr. Sterling. Miss Henderson tells me Mr. Bay asked you to join him in a card game with a note for stakes, a note on her father's house. She says you backed out of the game. That seems strange, since evidently you went to the saloon for the sole purpose of participating in that game."

How much had Amy told him? Frank didn't want to reveal more of Amy's situation than she had already done. "I wanted to get that note out of Mr. Bay's hands, Sir. I don't trust the man and don't like to see Mr. Henderson in debt to him. But I made a promise to give up gambling over a year ago. In the end, I couldn't go through with the game. Just didn't seem good could come from breaking my vow that way."

Headley rubbed a hand over his beard. "If we bring this situation before the directors, it's certain there will be questions that no one involved with the gambling at Plummer's will be willing to answer honestly. I know there's something you two aren't telling me, but I'm going to accept your word, because I can't imagine why Miss Henderson would lie for you about this, Mr. Sterling."

Relief poured through Frank, both for himself and for Amy. "Thank you, Sir."

"Thank you," Amy echoed.

Headley pursed his lips. "Mr. Bay isn't a student at the Academy, but he is a director. I don't like the idea of allowing a director to get by with behavior that results in expulsion for a student. Yet I can't expect you to speak against your betrothed, Miss Henderson."

"No, I couldn't do that." Her voice was soft.

"And you, Mr. Sterling?"

"I think not."

"No, I didn't think so." Professor Headley shook his head slowly. "I don't know for certain what's happening here, but I have my suspicions. Yes sir, I definitely have my suspicions, and they aren't pleasant. I suggest you two spend some time searching your hearts—alone— and a lot of time on your knees."

Frank accompanied Amy to the front door of the Academy, where they waited for Mrs. Headley to join them. When Jason returned, they would take Amy home, with Mrs. Headley chaperoning. It would take a bit of time going back and forth, but with Amy marrying Walter in twenty-four hours, her reputation needed to be protected more than ever.

"I'll never forgive myself for putting you in this position," Frank told her, "and never stop thanking God that you cared enough to speak up for me to Professor Headley."

Amy leaned against the door, watching out the window. "I didn't tell him Walter is blackmailing me into marrying him. I hadn't that much courage."

"I'm glad you didn't." The words came out more fervently than he'd intended. He cleared his throat. "I wish . . . I wish you loved Walter."

She swung around, and surprise sat large in her eyes.

"I mean it. Since you're determined to marry him, I wish you were crazy in love with him. I want you to be happy every moment of your life."

Her face gentled into a smile so sweet he thought he could hang the stars on it. "I want the same for you, Frank."

He ached to hold her and never let her go. At least it brought some comfort to know she understood he loved her, and she loved him.

Mrs. Headley's footsteps clipped along the hallway on her way to join Frank and Amy.

Frank allowed his gaze to tell Amy one last time that he loved her, but all he said was, "Hold on, Amy. Hold on."

16

my sat in front of her walnut vanity, watching the mother-of-pearl-backed handle move back and forth in smooth strokes as she buffed her nails. The grandfather clock in the first-floor hallway sounded dimly in her room. Five strikes. Two hours until the wedding. In a little over two hours in the parlor downstairs she'd become Mrs. Walter Bay.

The trunk beside the tall walnut shrank was filled with her clothes. Only the suit she planned to wear after the wedding remained in the shrank. A few things still covered her vanity: the brush, comb, and buttonhook that matched her nail buffer; the jewelry she planned to wear with her gown; the little brown book from Frank with its brave gold cross on the front; the miniature skaters in their glass dome.

She wished she and Frank had a dome to protect themselves from the pain of the years to come.

A quiet knock at her door brought her from her reverie. "Come in."

Pearl stuck her head inside the door. "Am I still welcome?"

"Of course." Amy set the buffer carelessly beside the matching vanity accessories and stood, meeting Pearl with a hug in the middle of the room. "What are you doing here?" A terrible thought filled her with dread. "Is Frank all right?"

"He's fine physically. Wallowing in misery, of course." Pearl took a deep breath. "I know I told you I wouldn't stand up for you at your wedding, but I've changed my mind, if you'll have me."

Amy threw her arms around her friend again, joy and relief flooding her. "I'd love to have you."

"If you asked someone else, I'll gladly take my place as a simple guest."

"No, I've asked no one else. You and Jason are the only friends I asked to the wedding. Father asked a couple friends, as did Walter. Walter hasn't any family here. Lina and Mrs. Jorgenson are helping with the guests. I thought if I must have someone stand up for me, I would ask one of them at the last minute. I didn't want anyone but you. I'm so glad you changed your mind."

Pearl sat on the edge of the brocade-covered bedstead and sighed. "I'm embarrassed to say it took Frank to bring me to my senses. He reminded me we need to honor others' decisions, even when we don't agree with those decisions. He said, 'God gives us free will. We should honor each other as much as God honors us and not try to force our will on others.'" She raised her chin in a defiant manner. "I may not believe marrying Walter will make you happy or that it's a good answer to your problems, but you have the right to marry whomever you choose, and I'll love you even when you're Walter's wife." She wrinkled her nose. "I may need to continue thinking of you as my friend Amy instead of Mrs. Walter Bay to keep my good intentions, though."

A laugh bubbled up from Amy's chest, and she dropped down on the bed beside Pearl. "Thank you. I thought I'd lost everyone important in my life except Father." Amy hadn't the slightest doubt that Pearl's presence was a gift from both their heavenly Father and Frank, and as such, Pearl was doubly, triply welcome.

Pearl laid her hand on the small bulge at her middle. "Is it in poor taste to stand up for you in my condition?"

"It's always perfect etiquette to act in love for another, isn't it? It must be wonderful to be expecting a child with the man you love." Frank would make a doting father and a doting husband to the mother-to-be. Sadness at what might have been dampened the spirits Pearl's arrival had lifted. Amy refocused her thoughts with determination. She'd chosen to marry Walter, whatever the reason. No use remaining a weeping Wilma about it. "Besides, you aren't large enough yet for anyone to more than suspect you're expecting a baby."

Pearl ran a hand along her turquoise silk skirt. "I wore my best gown for your wedding. It's last year's Christmas gown, altered for my condition, of course. I've let out a number of outfits already. Soon I'll need to give in and make something more appropriate from scratch, though it seems such an extravagance in these hard times."

There it is again, Amy thought, *the awareness of the need to economize. Am I the only person who went along blissfully unaware of the Panic's effect on daily life? I've thought only of myself. No wonder Father and I are in this unsavory situation.*

Joy shone forth from beneath Pearl's comments regarding the necessary work and economy in accommodating her growing size. Amy envied her. Raising children with Frank would have been wondrous fun. He'd make a marvelous father. She shuddered to think what kind of father her possible children had to look forward to in Walter.

Pearl straightened her back. "Here I am going on about myself when we need to get you ready for your wedding. Your gown is exquisite!" She moved quickly across the room to the shrank, where an ivory satin gown hung.

Amy followed slowly. "I tried to convince Father that one of my other new winter gowns would do as well, but he insisted I have the latest thing. I couldn't think of a way to argue him out of it without revealing my knowledge of his financial affairs." She fingered the puffed shoulders above narrow lace sleeves. "I'd hoped the dressmaker would solve the situation for me by insisting she couldn't make the gown so quickly. I'm afraid she worked night and day to complete it."

"And completed it beautifully." Pearl pulled the gown out from the shrank to view the back. "Oh, my. We'd best begin dressing you now. It will take hours to fasten all the satin-covered buttons on the back and sleeves."

Everything inside Amy withdrew, revolting against donning the gown that represented the demise of Amy Henderson and the birth of Mrs. Walter Bay. She removed her wrapper and laid it over the end of the bed, wishing desperately that time would stop moving.

It seemed hours later that Pearl fastened the last button.

"Finally." Amy heaved a sigh. "My feet are giving out."

"Don't sit down. You'll wrinkle your gown."

"Wish I'd thought of that before putting it on. I still haven't done my hair."

Pearl glanced about. "I can stand on the vanity bench while I work on it." They laughed at the sight they made while she piled Amy's thick, soft brown hair in a bouffant topknot. She tucked orange blossoms around the knot. "Beautiful. Do you have a veil?"

"No."

"Jewelry?"

Amy put on a pair of simple drop pearl earrings. Then she took from the vanity drawer a gold bow pin with a delicate oval, etched gold locket attached, and pinned it to the left breast of her gown. *Above my heart*, she thought.

She met Pearl's glance in the mirror. A frown crinkled her friend's brow. "Um, I don't think that's the usual jewelry to wear with your bridal gown."

Amy ran her fingertips lightly over the cool gold. Not even with Pearl would she share the full truth about the locket. The front opened to reveal a timepiece. The back held a secret opening. Inside was a picture of her mother on one side. The other held a miniature painting she'd made of Frank. She told Pearl a partial truth. "The locket belonged to my mother."

The frown cleared. "Then of course you must wear it. I wish I'd had something of my mother's to wear at my wedding." Pearl laid a gentle hand on Amy's shoulder.

Amy covered Pearl's hand with her own, a pang of empathy touching her heart. "Weddings seem meant to be shared with mothers, don't they?"

Their gazes met again in the mirror. Pearl dashed away a tear from her lashes and smiled. "What's next?" Her tone obviously meant to break the emotional moment.

Amy hesitated. "Do you remember the painting you saw me making of Frank?"

Pearl nodded.

"I can't keep it. There's no telling what Walter might do if he saw it. I can hardly leave it here in the house. Father would wonder if he came across it. Will you take it home, please?"

"You know I will." Pearl rearranged a curl in front of Amy's ear. "If you don't mind my saying so, I think that's wise. Anyone who saw it would know immediately that you care deeply for him."

Amy's heart tripped. She hadn't realized she'd exposed her love for Frank to the world in that picture. As an artist it was a compliment. As a woman marrying another man, well. . . . "It's in the shrank, wrapped in a soft cloth. I'd like Frank to have it. I suppose it's inappropriate to give it to him, but then," she shrugged and gave a sharp little laugh that rose from her shattered heart, "it seems everything about my life is inappropriate."

"They say time heals all things," Pearl said softly.

"They?"

"People who've lived a lot longer than you and me."

People who hadn't loved Frank Sterling and married Walter Bay. What did they know? She took a deep breath. " 'He who Jesus holds through all, shall stand, though heaven and earth shall fall.' "

"Yes, thank God. Um . . . I think you've forgotten something, Amy."

Amy raised her eyebrows in question.

"Your ring."

Amy removed the emerald ring from the drawer and slid it on her finger. It felt like the weight of the world.

There was a loud knock at the bedroom door.

"Come in, Lina," Amy called.

The door opened. "It's not Lina. It's the proud papa coming to see his daughter one last time before giving her away."

Tears distorted Amy's image of her father's round smiling face above his formal black cutaway coat and white shirt and vest. The words "giving her away" struck her as especially and awfully true. She didn't want to be given away. She didn't want to go away at all.

"Amy's a lovely bride," Pearl assured him. "I'll give you two a few minutes alone. I'll be down the hall on the window seat if you need me." She closed the door behind her.

"Let me look at you." Mr. Henderson's voice was softly gruff, and Amy knew he was having difficulty keeping a check on his emotions.

She turned around slowly. When she stopped, she saw his eyes had reddened.

"Mrs. Sterling is right; you are a lovely bride. The loveliest ever, except for your dear mother." He reached for Amy's hands. "I do wish your mother could be here today. I don't know that I've ever told you, but she'd be busting her corset stays in pride over the woman you've become."

"Father!" She giggled at his unusual language. She suspected he used it to add levity to the situation.

"I hope Walter will brings as much happiness to your life as your mother did to mine." He glanced about the room with its embossed floral wallpaper and pale blue window hangings. "Remember how many hours you and your mother spent planning this room? Nothing would do but that you had the exact shade of blue you wished in the hangings and that your bed be the finest your mother could find."

"I do remember." Amy smiled at the heart-warming remembrance.

"Some of my fondest memories lie in planning and furnishing this house with your mother." He lifted his big round shoulders in a self-conscious shrug. "More to the truth, she and I planned it, and she did the furnishing." His gaze swept the room, and he sighed. "It's a mighty big house for a man to ramble around in alone. Maybe I should think of selling it."

Amy's heart faltered. "S-sell it? Mother's house?"

"She did love it, but she has a better one now."

"But . . . but the memories. Could you bear to leave them behind?"

He shook his head, smiling down at her. "Oh, Sweetheart, don't you know we never the leave the memories behind? They live in our hearts."

Confusion turned her mind to balls of cotton. She'd thought it would all but kill her father to lose this house, but now he spoke of selling it. Frank's accusation from the day before leaped into her thoughts: "You're taking away your father's right to run his own life."

Pearl had just commented on honoring others' rights to make

their own decisions. Honoring. The word used in the command, "Honor your mother and father." Was not trying to save them from their problems without allowing them a chance to decide whether they wanted the help a form of honoring them? Frank and Pearl were honoring Amy's decision. *Would I want my father making sacrifices for me without giving me the chance to make my own sacrifices, my own decisions?* The answer flashed sure and swift in her soul. *No, I wouldn't want Father to lie to me, even to save me from something awful.*

"Why the frown?" Her father lifted her chin. "A bride should wear a smile, and a radiant one at that."

Amy took a deep breath. "I think we need to talk."

"Now? It's almost time for the wedding to begin. There'll be plenty of time to talk afterward." He chuckled, his stomach stretching the coat buttoned across it. "It's not as though Walter's carrying you across the continent to live. His house is only a few blocks from here."

Amy laced her fingers together in front of her. "I'm sorry to keep the guests waiting, but what I have to say needs to be said now or not at all."

"Sounds ominous." His voice was light, but she could see the concern in his eyes. Worry for her, no doubt.

"I'm afraid I've acted high-handedly and pridefully."

His brow furrowed in confusion. "About what?"

"You."

"Me?"

Amy nodded, catching her bottom lip between her teeth. She searched for a way to begin. "I've tried to solve a problem for you without letting you decide whether you want me to solve it."

His round cheeks shook with his chuckle. Relief danced with the amusement in his eyes. "I thank you for wishing to help me, but I can't imagine any problem of mine which you could solve, especially behind my back."

"I thought the same thing a couple of weeks ago."

"What happened then to make you so wise?" A remnant of his chuckle reverberated in his chest.

She dropped her gaze to the floor, unable to meet his eyes. Sorrow over the pain she knew her revelation would cause her father made her throat feel swollen and sore. It took an effort to speak, and the words came out a whisper. "I found out you're behind on the mortgage on this house and have lost most of your money."

A moving shadow brought her gaze up. Her father had grabbed the bedpost with one hand. His face was ashen.

Amy gasped and reached for him. "Father!"

17

Mr. Henderson waved his free hand and shook his head. "I'm all right."

His words didn't reassure Amy. He looked ill. Why, oh why, hadn't she left well enough alone?

He sat down heavily on the bed. "How did you find out? When?"

"A week before Christmas. Walter told me."

"Walter?" Disbelief filled his still-whitened face. "I suppose he thought you had a right to know since you're going to be his wife." He shook his head slowly. "I wanted to spare you the worry of it all. Everyone is living on credit these days. My business contacts have been understanding in extending me time. I hoped I could get by until you married. I don't mind so much for myself losing my money, but for you. . . ."

A small cry escaped her. She dropped to her knees, heedless of her dress, and grasped his hands. "I don't care about the money for myself. My concern is for you. I didn't want you to be embarrassed in front of your friends and business associates."

"Most of my business associates already know I've lost money in my investments and can't pay my bills. It's a little embarrassing, yes, mainly because I've believed an honorable man pays his debts. But everyone is having money trouble since the Panic. I hope if I hang on long enough, I'll eventually be able to pay those who have trusted me by extending me credit."

"What if the people you owe demand the money? Can't they force you to . . . to sell the house, for instance, to raise money?"

"Yes, and if they demand their money, then it's only right I sell the house or anything else I can to raise it. Of course, in the present economic situation there aren't many who can afford this place, even at the reduced price the times demand." He frowned. "Just how did you plan to solve my money problems? Did you sell a painting for a stupendous price and forget to tell me about it?"

"I wish." She laughed in spite of her heavy heart. She was glad to see color returning to his face. "My plan won't solve all your money problems. Only one."

"I'm still mystified. Which one?"

"The mortgage."

His thick white brows met in confusion. "Walter hasn't demanded payment on the note."

"Not from you."

"Who else would he demand it from?"

Amy saw the truth begin to dawn in his eyes.

"He asked you to pay it? His own betrothed?" Shock and scorn saturated his words.

"After a fashion. He, um, said he would demand immediate payment in full if I didn't marry him, and—"

"What?" He shot to his feet. His lips trembled in anger. "He dared demand that of you?"

She rose hastily, almost tripping on her gown. "Yes, but—"

"Is that the only reason you're marrying him?"

"Y-yes."

"Why that . . . that . . ." He started toward the door.

"Wait." Amy put her hands against his chest. "Please, try to calm down."

"Calm down? Just wait 'til I get my hands on that young rapscallion." He stepped sideways, and her hands slid from his chest.

She grabbed his arm. "Father, wait."

He stopped, impatience in every line of his face.

"Please don't do anything rash, Father. You've always told me to think things through completely before making a decision. This house means so much to you." She held up a hand as he started to speak. "I know you told me you're thinking of selling it, but I think you weren't completely honest with me. You aren't thinking of selling because I'm leaving the house, are you? You're thinking of selling because you can't pay the mortgage. My leaving only makes it easier."

He started to protest.

She interrupted him. "Your honest answer, Father."

His gaze searched hers a moment. Then his shoulders dropped slightly. "You're right. But that doesn't mean—"

"I love you, Father. Walter promised our marriage will pay the mortgage in full, including all back payments. I know this is not the way you would choose to pay this debt, but if you need me to do this, I will do it willingly."

His eyes suddenly teared, and Amy found herself wrapped in his embrace. "You are the most precious thing in my life. I want your happiness more than I want my own. We have wonderful memories in this house, but I can leave the house and take the memories. The thought of you as the wife of a man who would blackmail you into marriage . . . it makes me see purple."

Amy pressed back her own tears.

Her father awkwardly patted her shoulders. "Come on, now. Our guests are waiting. I'm looking forward to telling that worm of a man that there isn't going to be a wedding."

They headed for the door hand in hand.

Pearl met them in the hall. "Amy, Walter is waiting for you in the library. He said there's something you two need to discuss before the ceremony and that you'd understand."

The note. How could she have forgotten he'd agreed to sign the note as paid in full before the ceremony began? "Yes, I understand."

"You are running a bit late," Pearl reminded apologetically.

Mr. Henderson grinned. "Later than you think."

Amy threw her arms around Pearl. "We're not getting married."

Pearl gasped and returned the hug. "That's wonderful!"

"Would you tell Walter I'll be right down?"

"I'll be delighted to tell him. Wish I could be there to see the look on his face when you give him the news." Pearl gave Amy's hand a conspiratorial squeeze before she hurried downstairs.

Amy explained quickly to her father why she and Walter had planned to meet.

Her father shook his head, a glint of a smile in his pale blue eyes. "Pretty smart of you to get him to agree to signing the papers over before the ceremony. If you weren't a woman, you'd make a great businessman."

"What do you want me to tell Walter?"

"I thought we already decided the wedding is off."

"I mean about the papers."

His sigh lifted his chest and strained at his white vest buttons. "I admit it's tempting to allow him to sign off that the note is paid in full before telling him the wedding is off, but it wouldn't be truthful."

Amy gave a small sigh of relief. "No, it wouldn't."

"There's no reason for you to face him now. You can stay in your room until I've spoken with him and dismissed the guests."

Amy took her father's arm and urged him toward the stairway. "I'm going with you." The scent of flowers from the parlor below enwrapped them.

"No need for you to be there. This is between us men."

"I'm the one who almost married him. I'm the one who is breaking a promise."

"A promise obtained through deceit," he reminded her in a vigorous whisper, obviously aware of the guests in the parlor.

"A promise just the same." She spoke for his ears alone. "It's only honorable that I face him with the withdrawal of that promise. And you are the one who taught me about honor, after all."

"All right," he agreed with a grudging tone. "But if things get ugly, I expect you to leave."

"Oh, I think it very likely things will get ugly." She avoided agreeing to his request. Happiness bubbled up in her until she felt giddy with it. "Things have been ugly since Walter demanded I marry him."

Amy glimpsed the wedding parlor through the doorway as they passed it on the way to the library. A lace-covered table set along one wall glimmered with crystal and silver wedding gifts. Sobering guilt quieted her runaway emotions. Friends and relatives had sent the gifts as a way to rejoice with Amy and Walter in what they believed was the couple's joy in finding each other. She'd return all of the gifts, of course.

There would be questions about the dissolving of the engagement at such a late hour: questions asked point-blank by the bold, left unspoken by the discreet. Amy would share the truth with no one but Pearl and Frank, but the questions spoken and unspoken would be hard to face.

In the library the desk lamp banished the early evening darkness with a mellow glow cast through the umber globe and lent a deceptively peaceful atmosphere to the room. The fireplace, which warmed the room when her father used it as his office, held only logs ready to light, and the air was chill.

Walter leaned against the desk, watching the door. He looked more commanding than usual, Amy thought, in his black cutaway wedding suit and black patent shoes. His hair was parted fashionably in the middle and the light brown waves so oiled that they glimmered in the lamplight. The proper black cane rested beside him. His cloth wedding gloves fit his hands like soft skin. He held the papers. Amy could hear the quiet slap as he idly bounced them against one palm.

Walter's eyes widened in surprise at the sight of Mr. Henderson with Amy. She saw the question in his eyes, but he said nothing as she and her father came around the desk. Her father sat down in his desk chair. Amy stood beside him, one hand resting on the tall leather chair back.

Together they'd face the enemy, she thought, restraining a giggle.

Walter obviously didn't see anything amusing in the situation. "The wedding should have started fifteen minutes ago. Our guests are getting impatient. Let's get this business over." He opened the papers and laid them on the desk, then began to open the gold-covered ink bottle. "I thought Amy planned to give you the executed agreement after the ceremony, Sir, but I guess this will do just as well. I asked Mrs. Sterling to lead Rev. Conrad in. I suggest we ask him to keep the agreement for safekeeping until the vows are said, as we originally planned, Amy."

Mr. Henderson picked up the papers. "That won't be necessary."

Walter's gaze darted to Amy's. Suspicion darkened his eyes. "What's going on?"

She pressed her lips together tightly. She'd leave this in her father's hands. She sent up a silent prayer asking her heavenly Father to give her earthly father wisdom and restraint.

A quiet knock sounded at the door and Rev. Conrad entered. He stopped just inside the room and stared at the group about the desk, looking unaccustomedly uncertain.

Is the tension in the air so strong he can sense it? Amy glanced at her father. Would he ask Rev. Conrad to leave? Surely he didn't need to safeguard the document now.

Mr. Henderson nodded at the pastor, then turned his attention back to Walter, handing him the folded paper. "You won't need to sign this. My daughter isn't for sale. Not at any price."

Walter's jaw dropped. He accepted the note without seeming to realize it was in his hand. "What—?"

Amy dared a glance at her father out of the corner of her eye. His gentlemanly voice had been steady and calm, but his eyes glittered with anger. Her hand tightened on the chair back.

Mr. Henderson smiled thinly at the pastor. "Reverend, would you explain to our guests that the bride and groom have changed their minds?"

The slender, bearded pastor was the most reserved man Amy knew. His usually passive face registered shock, but he said nothing. She suspected the pastor knew of other marriages that had been called off at the last minute but expected he hadn't heard the intended groom accused of purchasing his intended bride before.

"Wait." Walter held up a palm toward the pastor, but his glaring eyes were upon Mr. Henderson.

Amy caught her breath.

"There's still time to change your mind, Amy," Walter said, still looking at her father. "I assure you I am going to collect on this note, one way or another." He held the note out.

Mr. Henderson ignored it. "I suggest you collect in the normal business way, Mr. Bay. Now I have a choice for you to make. You may leave the house now, before the guests are dismissed, or you may wait for their condolences."

Walter, his face mottled with anger, stuffed the papers beneath his cutaway jacket. He grabbed his silk top hat from the corner of the desk. With a jerky movement, he picked up his black cane.

The shift in his expression was so swift Amy barely caught it before he struck out with the cane, swiping it across the desktop.

Leather desk blotter, stationery, paperweight, books, inkwell, and pen flew.

Her own screams mingled with those of her father and Rev. Conrad.

Her father leaped back.

Amy lunged toward the lamp, catching it as it teetered after a book clipped the edge of the lamp's base.

"I'll be back." Walter stalked toward the door, settling his top hat on his head as though nothing were abnormal.

"Wait," Amy called. She set the lamp back on the desk, noticing blue ink blotched one lace sleeve.

Walter turned around and waited, hands on his black walking stick in such a normal gentlemanly stance that a sense of the bizarre flashed through her.

She lifted her gown slightly while picking her steps through the mess he'd caused on the floor. When she reached him, his lips stretched in a thin smile. "Change your mind?"

"I only wanted to return this." She pulled the hated emerald from her finger and held it out.

His hands tightened on the top of the walking stick. The thought flashed through her mind that he might again use it as a weapon, this time against her. The knowledge left her trembling, but she resisted the urge to step backward.

Rev. Conrad moved quickly but quietly beside them. He took the ring from her and held it toward Walter. "I think this is best, Mr. Bay, don't you?"

Only respect was evident in his voice, and Amy wondered how he managed it.

Walter hesitated a moment longer, then snatched the ring, stuffed it into a pocket, turned, and left.

"I'll never wear emeralds again," Amy said fiercely. She turned to the pastor. "Thank you." She knew he'd stood beside her, hoping to protect her if Walter lashed out at her with the walking stick.

The crashing of the front door as it was slammed shut reverberated in the house. Amy wondered whether her guests were stretching their necks to see who had been so improper.

"It appears you chose wisely in ending the engagement," Rev. Conrad said quietly. "I'm sure I don't need to tell either of you that I won't repeat what I've witnessed here."

This time Amy's father joined her in thanking the pastor.

"Would you still like me to dismiss the guests?" the pastor asked.

Mr. Henderson grinned. "I'd like that pleasure for myself."

Amy laughed. "I know it's not possible, but it would be nice if the guests could stay. Mrs. Jorgenson and Lina are prepared to serve refreshments. I've more to celebrate now than I did before the wedding was cancelled. Of course, we'd never live down the notoriety."

Her father joined in the laugh, and even the serious pastor smiled.

"We do have a lot of food," Mr. Henderson agreed. "Perhaps it wouldn't be too indiscreet to ask the Reverend here and his wife to stay and join us in enjoying some of it." He raised thick white eyebrows in question.

Rev. Conrad smiled. "Mrs. Conrad and I gladly accept your invitation."

"Perhaps we can ask Pearl and Jason," Amy added. She knew Pearl and Jason would join in her spirit of celebration, even if in silence: celebration of freedom from Walter and, more important, celebration of the chance for her and Frank to discover whether their love was as real as they believed.

❧

Amy must be married by now. Frank didn't have a pocket watch in the barn with him, and the evening seemed especially long with the knowledge of Amy's wedding taking place, but surely the vows must have been spoken by now. The thought burned Frank's heart.

He set the T-stool into the straw beside Sudsy. Sitting down, Frank leaned against her warm side with a sigh. "Hi, Sudsy, girl. Did you have a long day, too?" Patient Sudsy was as usual the last cow to be milked. Gideon and two of his female friends took up spots nearby, close enough to be available for a sampling of milk, yet far enough away not to be kicked by Sudsy's hooves.

The milking took longer than usual since Frank was doing it alone. Jason and Pearl were at the wedding. Frank's younger brother and sisters had been invited to Pearl's parents for dinner and to spend the evening. Frank was glad for the solitude. He hadn't the energy or desire to be around anyone. The barn with its familiar smells and the animals he loved was the most comforting place for him.

Gideon jumped onto his knee, stood on his hind legs, and burrowed his head beneath Frank's chin. "Need a hug, Gideon?" The cat always liked to snuggle. "Or do you think I'm the one who needs a hug?" Frank stopped milking to pet the cat. "Maybe both of us need a bit of loving." He hated to admit to himself how much that cat's show of affection meant to him.

Sudsy turned her head to see why Frank had stopped milking and protested noisily. Frank chuckled. Gideon's balancing act was hard to milk around. Frank set him on the ground with reluctance. "Sudsy's going to be mighty upset if I don't finish milking her soon."

He went back to business, gratitude warming his chest. What would he do without these animals? "Wonder how Amy's going to manage without her painting." He imagined that would be as awful for her as life for him without his animal friends.

"Maybe it wouldn't be so bad losing Amy to Walter if he loved her." Gideon responded with a meow and a rub against his legs.

What kind of a bleak, miserable life was ahead for his fine, sweet Amy?

He snorted. "She's not mine."

Gideon leaped to his shoulder and settled there, purring loudly in his ear. Frank gave him an absentminded pat and went back to the milking.

Was he ever going to stop hurting?

A drink would make things better. The familiar thought flowed into his mind as it always did when everything looked bleak and hard and hopeless. He turned from it in the way that was becoming habitual. He knew it would come back and he'd need to push it out of his mind again. He was beginning to think it was going to be like the milking; you did it over and over again, day after day, for the rest of your life.

He'd been so excited when Amy had promised that she'd allow him to court her if he stayed sober for a year. What good was his commitment to the Lord anyway, when people like Walter Bay could ruin his life and Amy's? He'd committed his life to the Lord, given up drinking and gambling, and trusted God to show him and Amy a way out of this situation with Walter. As far as he could see, God wasn't honoring their commitment to Him at all.

That's not true. It's only frustration talking.

He hadn't asked any promises of God when he'd decided to follow Him. God hadn't promised him Amy would love him. God wasn't forcing Amy to marry Walter; that was Amy's choice. A misguided choice from Frank's viewpoint. It was a coward's way out to blame God because life wasn't turning out all peaches and cream.

Jacob hadn't hid from life when he found he'd been deceived by his father-in-law into marrying the wrong woman after seven years. He'd just buckled down and worked another seven years.

"Won't do me any good to wait another seven years for Amy. She's Walter's wife by now and lost to me forever."

Maybe one day God would bring another woman into his life he could love, though he doubted it.

He hoped Amy wouldn't regret every day of her life that she'd married Walter. Frank had told Amy that he'd learned to trust that God had a bigger plan than he could see when life was hard. Maybe living with Amy would change Walter, make a better man of him. Was that God's plan in what seemed a horrid mess?

"Help her, Lord. Somehow please make this marriage turn into something good for her," he whispered.

The barn door creaked. Frank's heart plummeted. The others must be home. He hadn't expected them so soon. Or maybe it was later than he thought. "I'm over here," he called out. "Just finished the milking."

"Down you go," he said, lifting Gideon from his shoulder. "Time to do the separating." He'd tell Jason he'd be glad to finish up himself, gain a little more time alone. He patted Sudsy and pulled the pail of warm milk from beneath her. Boots crunched in the straw, carrying Jason closer.

Frank stood, pail in one hand and T-stool in the other, and turned to greet him. Shock barreled through him. He stared in disbelief at Walter in his silk top hat, fancy full-length overcoat, and shiny dress shoes. His walking stick made a hollow staccato sound as he bounced it against the barn floor. He seemed an apparition, he was so out of place in a barn. Had he come to gloat? "Walter! What are you doing here?"

"As if you don't know."

"Know what?" Frank looked over Walter's shoulder into the darkness of the barn. "Did you come alone?"

"Did you think I'd bring Amy?" Walter's lips twisted in a sneer. "Think I'd be so obliging as to bring her to you?"

"Bring her to me?" Frank felt awash in confusion. Excitement began to stir. He didn't know what was going on, but one thing was certain. Walter wasn't with Amy. "Shouldn't you be celebrating with Amy and your wedding guests about now?"

Walter shoved one of Frank's shoulders. "Stop testing me!"

Milk sloshed over Frank's legs and into his boots as he stumbled backward. "Hey!" Gideon and his companions darted away, out of reach of human feet.

"I know you're behind this," Walter raged. "If you didn't want Amy for yourself, her father would never have found out about my agreement with Amy. She loved him too much. She'd never have let him know she was marrying me to save his precious house." He shoved Frank again.

Frank stumbled into Sudsy. Trying to avoid her hooves and not hurt her with the stool, he sidestepped, barely regaining his balance.

Walter pushed at him once more, but this time his hand glanced off Frank's shoulder.

Frank dropped the stool and pail into the straw that hindered him and lifted his arms to defend himself. He didn't want to fight; he wanted to find out what had happened between Walter and Amy. Apparently the wedding hadn't taken place, but he didn't dare hope that was the truth. "I didn't say anything to Mr. Henderson."

Walter gave a short bark of a laugh. "You think Amy would?"

"No, of course not." Frank tried to work himself away from Sudsy and the other cows. If Walter insisted on a fight, Frank didn't want to land beneath any hooves or somehow harm the cows.

He'd told the truth. He didn't think Amy would tell her father the reason she was marrying Walter. He'd sure tried to convince her to often enough. "What did her father say?"

"What do you think he said? He called off the wedding."

Joy washed through Frank. "He did?"

Walter growled and slashed out with his stick.

Frank leaped back. The stick missed its mark. His heart was racing now.

Walter swung again.

Frank grabbed the stick and flung it away into the darkness. He heard the soft plop when it landed in the straw.

He didn't like the way the cows were getting restless. They were grumbling their protests, shifting about. They'd moved away from the lantern that hung on the post where he'd been milking. The light's rays were dim in this part of the barn. No telling what they might fall over or step in. "If you want to fight, let's go outside."

Walter tripped over a T-stool and swore. Picking up the stool, he tossed it at Frank.

He dodged. It struck his arm. He grunted and winced from the blow but kept moving toward the barn door, walking backward so he could keep an eye on Walter. He bumped into a post. Darted a glance over his shoulder and adjusted his path. Looked back at Walter.

Walter's body blocked Frank's view of the lantern, but Frank saw its light glint off something in Walter's hands. The pitchfork!

He glued his gaze to the tool-turned-weapon. Fear tunneled up his backbone and prickled his hair. He reached toward heaven with a wordless prayer, feeling his way backward with his work boots.

"Walter, you don't want to do this. You can marry most any woman you want." The straw crackled beneath his boots.

"You think this is just about Amy?"

Frank's gaze flicked to Walter's face and back to the fork. "It's about the money? You still hold the note on Amy's father's house. You're one of the most successful men in town and half the age of most of the businessmen."

"It's not Amy, and it's not the money."

"What then?" Frank's arms swung wide in frustration.

Walter lunged.

Frank dove to the side.

The tines of the pitchfork caught Frank's open jacket and drove into the wood of a stall.

Walter chuckled. "You're about as harmless as a pinned butterfly." He leaned into the fork's handle. "It isn't about Amy or money, Sterling. It's about power. It's all about power."

The quiet way he spoke caused fear to burn like a whitehot coal in Frank's stomach.

Walter pulled on the pitchfork. He couldn't get it unstuck. He tugged, lost his balance, and fell back into the straw, striking his head on the other side of the stall.

Sweat dampened Frank's hands as he jerked one arm out of its sleeve and worked on releasing the other, watching Walter all the time.

Walter rubbed his head, swearing. His arm bumped something leaning against the stall, and he turned his head to see what it was. He stood and picked up the shovel from beside him.

Desperation sickened Frank. He wrenched his arm free at last. The suddenness unbalanced him. He heard the shovel *whoosh* as Walter swung it. Then something slammed against the side of his head. The last thing he heard was the straw crackling against his head.

He wasn't sure how much later something small and damp and scratchy against his eyelid awakened him. He turned his head. Pain crashed through his skull, and he gasped.

The rhythmic scratchiness started again against his eyelid. He tried to reach to brush it away. It took all his strength. The heaviness of his arm, the slowness with which it moved, seemed like part of a bad dream. His hand touched something warm and furry. "Gideon," he whispered—or tried to.

The straw-covered floor beneath him vibrated. He tried to think what could cause such a thing. It was the cows, he realized. The cows were bellowing. It sounded like they were trying to get away from something. Curiosity grew in him. He started to open his eyes, but that made his already aching head feel like someone was taking a hatchet to it.

"Meow. Meo–o–o–ow." Gideon bumped his head against Frank's chin.

The cat was sure being insistent.

The odors of straw and dirt and animals mingled with something that shouldn't be there. Something scary. Something that hurt his nose and throat and eyes.

Smoke!

18

*A*my closed the door behind the last of their departing guests. She slipped her hand beneath her father's arm, and he patted her hand as they walked slowly toward the parlor.

The room had already resumed much of its everyday air. While Amy'd been upstairs changing from her ink-splattered wedding gown into a simple white shirtwaist and black skirt, the parlor had also undergone a transformation. Her father, Rev. and Mrs. Conrad, Jason, Lina, and Mrs. Jorgenson had removed the gifts and the large satin bows that had decorated the room, as well as many of the flowers. Most of the food had been removed from the dining room to the kitchen, including the cake over which Mrs. Jorgenson had labored so many hours. Gratitude for her father's and friends' thoughtfulness warmed Amy.

A couple large bouquets remained and perfumed the air, but Amy didn't mind.

Mr. Henderson sat down on the sofa. He'd removed his black cutaway coat and white vest and collar. He looked comfortably homey in his white shirt with the top button open.

Amy settled beside him, facing him. "I'm glad the Conrads and Sterlings stayed for coffee, Father. Visiting with them washed away some of the . . . awfulness of the evening. I'm not certain awfulness is a word, but I can't think of another that adequately describes the horror I feel whenever I realize how close I came to marrying Walter." A shiver ran through her at the thought.

Her father grunted in agreement. "It's enough to give a man apoplexy."

Amy's laugh rang out. It felt so good to laugh freely and easily again.

"It's the truth," Mr. Henderson insisted. "To think I urged you to see Walter, to give him a chance to court you. I should have trusted your instincts about men."

"A compliment like that could go to a girl's head."

"Tease me if you must. I deserve it."

Amy's soft chuckle died. "All my instincts weren't wise. It's true I've never trusted Walter, though I didn't have a specific reason not to at first. My instincts on how to handle his threats against you weren't sound.

"I lost count of how many times I asked God to show me what to do. I kept wondering whether Walter was a Christian. I knew it couldn't be God's will to marry Walter if we didn't share a love for Christ. I'm ashamed to admit I refused to face the issue. I knew if I did, I'd have to tell Walter I wouldn't marry him, and I'd have to tell you everything, and you'd lose the house. I see now that telling you everything was what God wanted me to do. My doubts about Walter's faith were the answer to my prayer for guidance."

"Your actions came from love. I hate that Walter used your love for me against you, terrorized you that way, and blackmailed you into agreeing to marry him. I hate that he played my friend while planning behind my back to steal you away." His round cheeks grew ruddy. "Most of all, I hate that you believed I loved this house and money and my pride more than I loved you."

"But I don't." Amy leaned toward him and rested one of her hands on his arm. "You don't understand. I didn't tell you about Walter's blackmail because I knew you loved me too much to allow me to marry him to save you."

He patted her hand, his eyes damp with tears. "I'm glad you told me before it was too late."

She still didn't like to think of him losing respect in the eyes of the townspeople and other businessmen, but Frank was right: Her father's life was his own to lead. "Frank convinced me to tell you."

"Sterling?" His white brows rose in surprise. "Wanted you for himself, I suppose."

"I hope so." Her lips quirked in a mischievous smile. "Seriously, he said I should show you the respect of allowing you to make your own decisions about your life."

"I'll make sure to thank him." He sighed. "Another man I misjudged, it seems."

"Frank is a good man, Father. He's kind and compassionate and strong and wise and—"

His laugh bounded out. "Sounds like you're more than a little fond of him."

She felt herself blushing. Her fingers played with the locket she'd moved from the wedding gown to her blouse. "I am."

"Expect he'll be coming around now that Walter's out of the way."

"I expect." Joy danced in her heart at the prospect. "Where do you suppose that will be?"

Her father frowned. "Where will what be?"

Amy sobered. "Us. What will we do now? Walter will take the house, won't he?" It was more a statement than a question.

"Yes, I'm sure he will. Another man might have given me warning, allowed me time to sell the house and try to regain enough money to pay off the loan, but not Walter."

"Frank offered a solution. He asked me to marry him. We'd live at the Sterling farm, and you would be welcome to live there with us."

Her father swallowed hard before replying. "I appreciate his offer, but I'm not about to allow you to marry another man just to put a roof over our heads."

She twisted the locket and smiled. "I wouldn't marry Frank just to put a roof over our heads."

"You and young Sterling need to court properly for awhile before you marry. From the way you speak of him, he sounds like as fine a man as I could want for you. But you need to discover if what you feel for each other is truly love or only admiration blown out of proportion by the separation I forced on you this last year. Besides, Frank's still attending school. Didn't you tell me he wants to attend the university in St. Paul, too?"

"Yes, to take the agricultural course there."

"Don't you still want to visit Paris?"

"Paris will wait for me." That dream seemed unattainable, considering her father's financial state. She didn't imagine Frank would have enough money for them to travel to Paris. Even if he did, she doubted the farmer was interested in dawdling around the city while she visited the Louvre and tried to obtain audiences with the famous painters in France.

"All the same, I think it's time I found some paying work instead of waiting around for my investments to regain their health. Things might look bleak, but I'll find a place for us. It won't be fancy like this, but I promise you a roof over our heads."

Amy rested her head on his shoulder. "I've no doubt you'll keep that promise."

Funny how peace fills me now, she thought, *when it looks like we're going to be penniless.* "We have each other and God. We're going to be fine."

❧

Heading back to the farm from Chippewa City, the runners on the Sterlings' wagon sang over the prairie snow. *Sh-sh-sh-sh.* The wagon rode smooth, rocking and sliding over the snow-covered road. It was a treat compared to the rough rides over the rutted summer road.

Frank and Jason's younger siblings snuggled beneath lap robes on top of the hay in the wagon bed. Pearl's mother had warmed bricks for the ride home. An invigorating chill against their cheeks encouraged the Sterlings to keep the robes pulled up to their chins.

They sang into the night, silly ditties that reflected the fun of a night free from the farm for the youngsters. Sleigh bells jangled on the two horses in accompaniment to the voices. For Jason and Pearl the songs were a release from the tension of a day that had started with dread of Amy's wedding but ended in joy.

"I love the prairie sky on winter nights." Pearl snuggled close to Jason on the wagon seat. They shared the thick buffalo robe. Their feet rested on two warmed bricks. The children's singing allowed her conversation with Jason to feel private. The moon reflecting off the snow brightened the night until lanterns weren't needed. Distant lights could be seen from farmhouse windows scattered across the prairie. The air was crisp, occasionally warmed by wood smoke or coal smoke from a nearby farm. "Do you remember what Byron calls the stars? 'The poetry of heaven.'"

Jason chuckled. "No, can't say I remember, not being a reader of poetry."

"I like you anyway."

"I should hope so, since you're stuck with me."

Pearl rubbed her head against Jason's shoulder. "I'm glad Amy isn't stuck with Walter."

"Amen," he agreed fervently. "I've been mighty worried about Frank since Amy became engaged to Bay. Frank was hurting something fierce. I wonder whether Amy and Frank will begin courting now that Bay's out of the way. I know Frank's crazy about her, but do you think she likes him? I mean, as much as he likes her?"

"Oh, yes." Pearl smiled, remembering Amy's painting of Frank. Pearl wasn't delivering the painting to Frank after all. There was no need since the wedding didn't take place. "I'm so glad for both of them. I remember how awful it was when I didn't know whether you loved me."

He winked at her. "And how wonderful it was when we discovered we loved each other."

"It's still wonderful."

Jason took one hand from the reins and reached across her lap, making sure the buffalo robe was tucked firmly about her. "Are you and our little one warm enough?"

She nodded. His concern for them warmed her more than the robe.

He slid his arm around her shoulder, squeezed her gently close, and whispered in her ear, "Just think. Before next Christmas we'll know that little tyke face-to-face. Can't wait to hold that baby."

Pearl laughed, patting her stomach lightly. "You haven't much choice, Sir."

He drew his arm back. Pearl wished he'd left it but knew he didn't feel safe driving one-handed. One never knew when the horses would take a fright from a strange shadow or unexpected noise or a wild creature darting out of a ditch. It seemed to her the horses were acting a bit skittish now, though she couldn't see a reason. They were tossing their heads slightly and nickering in a nervous manner.

She glanced at Jason. Worry lined his face.

"What is it, Jason?"

"I don't know. Do you have a good hold? I don't want you slipping off the seat if they balk."

She gripped the edge of the seat, but her mittened grip didn't feel as secure as she'd like. She reminded herself that Jason was strong and a good driver. What was causing the horses' fright? Was there a wolf or other predator hiding out here somewhere? There wasn't much place for anything to hide. The snow revealed every shadow. The only trees were those around farmsteads.

The wagon lost its smooth journey as the horses' pace grew jerkier. The kids stopped their singing; first fourteen-year-old Andy, then thirteen-year-old Maggie, and finally six-year-old Grace. Andy's head popped up over the seat back. "What's going on?"

"Not sure." Jason clipped his words. "Get back down, and see the girls stay down, too."

Andy obeyed immediately.

They'd almost reached the drive leading to their farm. Pearl could see the row of poplars that lined the long drive from the road to the yard. Blue shadows cast by the trees stretched across the snow.

"Almost home." Relief underscored Jason's observation.

Something tugged at Pearl's brain. Something wasn't right, but she couldn't place her finger on it. Something about the air, but what? There wasn't anything unusual in it: the cold, the hay from the wagon bed, the strong scent of the buffalo robe, smoke from their farmstead—but Frank was home so the stoves should be lit.

"Jason, the smoke. It smells stronger than usual to me."

Jason's glance met hers for a moment. She saw the concern in his eyes, but he said nothing.

He pulled on the reins. "Who–o–a. Slow down, boys. Time to turn." The horses followed the leading of the reins and turned onto the drive.

They'd only traveled a third of the way when Pearl saw it. It was only a flash at first, but she knew. Fear rippled down her spine. "The barn, Jason. The barn's on fire."

He took it in with one glance. "Move!" He slapped the reins, leaned forward, urging the horses on. "Hold on!"

Pearl held on. She grabbed the top of the footboard with both hands, trusting her grasp there better than on the seat. She heard Grace begin to cry. Pearl's gaze stayed on the barn. Only a narrow streak of flame flared out. The barn wasn't engulfed. If it were, they'd have seen it. Fire couldn't hide on a moonlit, snow-covered prairie.

The crackling of the fire and cries of frightened animals filled the air as they neared the yard. The two farm dogs barked wildly, racing alongside the wagon. Jason slowed the horses to a stop and threw the reins to Pearl. "Tie them. Maggie, Grace, get some buckets from the kitchen. Come with me, Andy." He leaped down from the wagon and started at a run. "Frank must be in the barn."

Frank and the animals, Pearl realized as she and the others followed Jason's directives. Her mind raced. What had happened? How had it started? Why hadn't Frank released any of the farm animals? Was he in the barn? In the house? Had he gone into town? Had he been so downhearted over Amy's marriage that he'd finally given in and started drinking?

She ran onto the porch, almost slipping on the wooden steps. She grabbed an iron bar and swung it in a circle again and again, ringing the triangle used to call the men from the fields. Its noise battered her ears. Was the clanging loud enough to catch their neighbors' attention?

Maggie and Grace stumbled past her toward the well, the buckets making it difficult for them to run.

Pearl tore toward the barn. She had to help the men get the animals out. Where was Frank? *Dear God, help us!*

$$\left(\begin{array}{c}19\end{array}\right)$$

*S*moke!

The realization seeped into Frank's brain. The smoke meant fire. The cows' and horses' terrorized screams tore at his heart. He struggled to rise, pushing against the floor with his arms. They bent like prairie grass before a storm. *Help me, God, please.*

He kept trying. If he didn't get out, he'd never see Amy again. He rolled against the stall wall and managed with great effort to little by little sit up against it. *I have to get to Sudsy. Have to get the animals out. It's only You and me, God.* The smoke burned his eyes and nose. His head pounded worse with every movement. His eyes blurred.

But his arms and legs were getting stronger. The shovel Walter had wielded against him was lying beside him. Using it to lever himself, Frank pushed and pulled himself to a standing position.

He half dragged the shovel with him, half leaned on it for support as he moved toward Sudsy. The fire seemed nearer her than the other animals. He couldn't be sure. His vision doubled and tripled images. The fire licking along the outer wall supplied light so he could tell where to go. The flames would feed rapidly on the straw. Every moment counted, and a tortoise could move faster than he could.

He was almost there. "It's all right, Sudsy." He laid a hand on her flank.

She lurched.

Frank lost his balance and started falling.

"Frank!"

Was that Jason? Frank wondered as he landed on the floor. The jolt caused an eruption of stars in his head. With an effort, he tried to roll away from Sudsy's hooves.

Then Jason was kneeling beside him, tugging beneath his arms, dragging him into a sitting position. "Frank, are you all right? Can you stand?"

"Need a little help." Why did his words slur together that way? "Sudsy . . . the cows . . ."

"Andy will get Sudsy. Let's get you outside."

Frank felt one of his arms pulled over Jason's shoulder, and then Jason lifted him to his feet. He tried to walk, but Jason moved too fast.

A blast of cold air hit them.

"Pearl, hold the door," Jason demanded.

She gasped. "Is Frank all right?"

"I'm not sure," Jason said as they moved past her into the outdoors. "Get out of here."

"I'll help Andy with the animals."

"No!"

She disappeared into the barn. Didn't surprise Frank. Pearl was that kind of person.

Frank drank in the cold air. "I'm all right." He pulled his arm from his brother's shoulder. He tried to steady himself, but he swayed despite his best effort. "Get the animals out."

"Frank—"

He could see the indecision and anguish on Jason's face. "Get them out!"

Jason grimaced and turned back to the barn.

Andy was leading Sudsy and another cow through the door.

"Thank God." Frank sank into the snow. He hadn't the strength to go back into the barn. Would the others be able to get the animals out in time?

A shadow caught his attention. Their neighbors, Thor and his wife, Ellie, were rushing into the yard. Gratitude rushed over Frank in a wave. If Thor had seen the fire, maybe other neighbors had as well.

"Meo-o-o-ow." Gideon stood on his hind legs and looked into Frank's face.

Frank ran a hand along the thin, fur-covered back. "I'll be all right, Gideon, thanks to you. Here I thought you were a cat, and all along God knew you were an angel."

Ellie knelt beside him. "What are you doing out here with no coat? And what happened to your head? It's bleeding."

"It is?" He lifted a hand to the place that pounded. Sticky. "Guess the fire caught my attention."

Frank allowed her to help him toward the house. More neighbors were entering the yard as they crossed it, some on snowshoes, some on horseback, some in a wagon on runners. Animals freed from the barn were rushing about the yard. People called to each other and the animals. The fire snapped and popped and made its own wind. A haze of smoke dulled the star-sprinkled sky. Cinders drifted down like misshapen, dirty snowflakes.

Frank turned his back on the melee. Guilt tugged at him, but he knew he'd be more hindrance than help.

Ellie helped him to the green plush sofa in the parlor, then found a cold wet cloth for his head before returning to the yard.

Frank lay on the sofa, the cloth pressed to his head, and stared out the window for a long while, watching the flames leap and listening to the frantic sounds. He prayed for his family and friends and for the animals.

And he prayed for Amy. Thank God she'd escaped marriage to Walter. What happened to change everything? What had her father found out, and how?

Finally he could fight the pain and exhaustion no longer, and he slipped into sleep.

He was awakened an hour later by Pearl's father, Dr. Matt Strong. The doctor cleaned Frank's head wound, bandaged it, gave him some headache powders, and told him to stay awake for awhile. "Your blurred vision worries me. Could have a concussion."

"I'm not seeing double anymore."

"Just the same, stay awake."

"Guess I'll have some of that coffee I smell. One of the ladies must be brewing it for the people fighting the fire."

"You have a lot of good neighbors out there."

"We sure do." Frank touched his bandaged head gingerly. "How did you hear I needed you?"

"Jason sent one of the neighbors for me."

"Glad he did." Flames still brightened the world outside the window. "How are things going out there?"

"As you can see, the barn's still burning. Afraid that will be a total loss. Jason thinks all the animals were saved, though."

Frank rested his head against the tidy-covered sofa back. "Thank the Lord." He felt suddenly relaxed. He hadn't realized his muscles had tightened like a spring against what he might hear.

Dr. Matt patted Frank's knee. "I'll get you that coffee."

It was a long night. The Chippewa City volunteer fire department joined the farmers in fighting the fire, but by morning the barn was a smoldering mass of burned timbers in a puddle of melted snow. Silos and the grain that had filled them lay in ashes also. Smoke was thick in the yard and even in the house, though the house had escaped the flames.

Neighbor women filled the kitchen, serving a breakfast of sausage, potatoes, toast, pie, and coffee in shifts to the men. The Sterlings' friends, who had spent the night fighting for them, continued to work, gathering up the animals and taking them home to their own barns until the Sterlings could make other arrangements.

Frank joked, "It will be interesting going visiting to do the milking. Should we wear our dress suits and take our calling cards?"

The crowd of soot-covered, weary neighbors at the breakfast table chuckled politely. "Don't you boys worry none about milking today," one of the farmers ordered. "We'll all take care of the cows boarding in our barns."

The assistance wasn't a joke. It was beyond the power of humans to repay such kindness. The Sterlings thanked each of their friends with quiet, simple words of gratitude straight from their hearts. It was accepted with self-conscious shrugs or nods and averted looks and mumbles that the Sterlings would do the same for them if the need arose and "there but for the grace of God. . . ."

Dawn brought exhaustion, curious townspeople, and the Hendersons.

Frank's gaze hungrily sought Amy's. He had a dozen questions to ask, and questions filled her eyes, too. There was no privacy in which to ask them with the house full of people.

"Are you all right?" she asked, looking at the bandage on Frank's head when they had a moment beside each other.

"I'm tired, dizzy, and my head pounds like a blacksmith beating on an anvil, but Dr. Matt promises I'll recover." Even the pain lightened now that she was with him.

The neighbors and firefighters from town drifted out. A few ladies remained to help clean up in the kitchen. The Sterlings, the Hendersons, and Dr. Matt retired to the parlor and closed the door. The family hadn't had a chance to discuss the night's events, and though their bodies ached for their beds, their hearts needed answers. Only six-year-old Grace gave in and slept.

Frank took hold of Amy's hand and drew her down beside him on the sofa. A rosy glow colored her cheeks, but she allowed him to keep her hand in his. The simple trust he felt from her put a glow around his heart. Last night in the barn he'd thought he might never see her again. The need to touch her now was irresistible. He saw from their glances that the others in the room noticed his and Amy's connection, though no one commented on it.

Jason led out with the question most on everyone's mind. "What happened last night, Frank? How did the fire start?"

Frank shrugged. "I don't know. I have some suspicions, but I don't know for sure."

Jason grimaced. "I had some suspicions, too, when I found you in the barn last night unable to stand and slurring your words."

Frank felt the startled glances of the others on him. Amy's fingers tightened about his. Was she telling him she trusted him, even now?

"I owe you an apology," Jason said. "It was your head wound that was the problem. At first I thought you'd been drinking and hurt yourself when you fell. Then I found this." He held up Frank's chore jacket. "I couldn't think of any reason you'd take it off on a winter night and attach it to a stall with a pitchfork."

A collective gasp filled the room.

Frank patted Amy's hand, hoping to reassure her.

"Why don't you tell us what happened, Frank?" Jason suggested. "As much as you can recall, from the beginning."

So he did. He started with Walter's arrival while he was milking Sudsy, through the attack, to Gideon's gentle yet insistent awakening.

The cat's loyalty earned laughter, which relieved some of the tension Frank's story had built within the family.

"I'll never belittle your pet names again," Jason promised. Addressing Amy, he added, "The way cats multiply around the farm, no one bothers to name them except Frank. He has a name for every one of them. For that matter, he has a name for every cow and hog."

Amy's radiant smile told the room she approved of Frank's attachment to the animals he cared for.

Her father returned to a more serious topic. "So you don't know whether Walter Bay set the fire?"

Frank shook his head. "No. As I said, I have my suspicions, but I can't prove them. I have questions, too. If Bay did set the fire with the purpose of killing me, why not start it closer to me? Or why not just hit me again with the shovel? I wasn't in any shape to fight back."

He felt Amy's shudder and wished he'd been less graphic.

A horrible thought drained the blood from his face. "Has anyone seen Walter? He couldn't . . . Is it possible . . . ?" He couldn't make himself put it into words. What if Walter had been caught in the fire and no one had looked for him because no one but Frank knew he was there?

He knew from the way the room went completely still that everyone understood what he hadn't said.

Andy gave them all release. "Bay wasn't caught in the fire. One of the first neighbors to show up last night saw him."

A collective sigh of relief went up.

"Are you sure?" Frank asked.

Andy nodded. "The neighbor mentioned it at breakfast. Thought it strange Bay was heading for town when he knew everyone else was headed here to help. Then thought maybe Bay was going to raise the alarm with the fire department."

"I don't think so." Amy's soft voice trembled. "If his intentions were honorable, why didn't he pull Frank out of the barn first and try to save the animals?"

No one had an answer. Horrified glances were exchanged among the group.

A chill settled in Frank's bones. To think sweet Amy almost married that cold-hearted man. He drew her hand beneath his arm and pressed it close.

Jason stood. "Since you're not in any shape to go anywhere yet, Frank, I think I'd best ride into Chippewa City and tell Sheriff Amundson our suspicions. Bay may have already left town or be getting ready to leave. If he's still in town, he must know Frank isn't dead and will tell about the attack."

"But I have no proof he set the fire." Frank didn't like the idea of accusing Walter without proof, as much as he disliked the man.

"I think we still need to report his actions," Jason argued.

Dr. Matt and Mr. Henderson agreed.

Pearl stood, stifling a yawn. "I think the rest of us should get some sleep."

"I'd like another cup of coffee before I leave," her father said. "I've some stops to make before I head home, and a cup to keep my eyes open would be appreciated."

Mr. Henderson, Amy, and Frank stayed behind when the others left the room. Dr. Matt brought in his cup of coffee and joined them, settling himself in the high-backed oak rocker.

Mr. Henderson sat on the edge of the green overstuffed chair, rubbing his palms together, and cleared his throat. "I owe you an apology, Frank. I offer it now, complete and without reservation."

Surprise lifted Frank's brows. "You owe me an apology? Why?"

Dr. Matt started to rise. "Sounds like I've barged in on a private discussion."

Mr. Henderson waved him back to his seat. "You may as well stay. Not many secrets in a town this size. Besides, you're related to Frank through Pearl, and families have a hard time keeping secrets." He turned back to Frank. "I told Amy awhile back that I didn't want you two courting. I didn't think leopards changed their spots."

Embarrassment surged over Frank. He couldn't look at Amy's father or Dr. Matt, so he looked at his and Amy's joined hands instead.

"I was wrong." Henderson's voice was firm. "Amy told me so, and she was right."

"Thank you, Sir." Frank supposed he should feel pride. Instead he felt humbled. "I think, though, that you were wise demanding that I prove my change of heart by abstaining from liquor and gambling for a year. I took my decision to change seriously, but I didn't realize when I made it how tough it would be. Then, too, lads are beginning to pay attention to Maggie, though she's only thirteen. I realized I wouldn't want any men who court her to drink."

"I'm glad you understand." Henderson smiled. "I also wish to thank you. Amy told me of your offer to allow me to live with you if you two marry."

Dr. Matt sat up quickly, choking on his coffee.

Amy and Frank exchanged laughing glances.

Mr. Henderson held up an index finger. "On this, Dr. Matt, I would appreciate your discretion." Turning his attention back to Frank, he continued. "Although I'm grateful for your offer, I must decline. You've proven yourself an honorable man, and obviously Amy is willing to accept your attentions. But marriage is a lifetime contract, and I believe a little more courting time is in order for you two before any hard and fast decisions are made regarding matrimony."

"Yes, Sir," Frank agreed. "If it's not too bold to ask, what do you plan to do? About Walter, I mean, and his demands. He does still plan to foreclose on your home, doesn't he?"

Dr. Matt sputtered over his coffee again. "Foreclosure, attempted murder, marriage possibilities. This is rather a lot of serious conversation for this early in the day, don't you think?"

They joined in a hearty laugh.

"To answer your question, Frank," Mr. Henderson responded, "I fully expect Walter to foreclose. I don't know yet what Amy and I will do, but we'll work something out."

"Will you need a place to live?" Dr. Matt asked.

"Yes, we shall, and I am going to look for a job."

"If you need something until you get back on your feet, I could use someone to manage my drugstore. The apartment over the store will be vacant the end of the month, too."

Mr. Henderson beamed. He walked over to Dr. Matt and held out his hand. "I'd be honored to work with you. And we'd be glad to move into your apartment, wouldn't we, Amy?"

"Yes, definitely."

Frank was pleased she didn't hesitate at all in her response and thrilled at the way the Lord was supplying a way for them.

"We should leave soon, Amy," Mr. Henderson said, "and let Frank get some rest. If Dr. Matt is willing, I'll just have a cup of coffee with him in the kitchen before we go. Talk a little business."

Frank rubbed a hand over his chin, hiding his grin. He was pretty sure the business talk could wait. Mr. Henderson was giving him and Amy some precious minutes alone to say good-bye . . . and hello.

Dr. Matt stood up. "Yes, indeed, another cup of coffee is just the thing. About that foreclosure; maybe I could loan you enough to get you up-to-date on the payments. Would you like to consider it?"

The two men walked out of the parlor, pulling the door shut behind them.

"I feel foolish," Amy said. "I acted so much the martyr, thinking only I could save Father from certain destruction. Since I took your advice and told Father about Walter's blackmail, everything seems to be working out fine for Father."

"You weren't acting foolishly. You acted out of love." Frank shifted to face her. He cradled her face between his hands, touching her as tenderly as he was able. It was a gift to be allowed to touch this precious woman. "I just want to look at you," he whispered, happiness welling up within him. "I was afraid I might never see you again."

A sweet smile gentled her face. "I want to look at you, too. Listening to what happened to you last night—" She shuddered. "You might have died, and that would have been my fault, too."

He laughed softly. "You take way too much responsibility for the things that happen to other people."

"If I hadn't gone along with Walter's perverted plan to begin with, he wouldn't have had any cause to attack you."

"No? I don't think we can understand the way his mind works.

Let's forget him for awhile. Let Jason and Sheriff Amundson worry about him."

Her smile returned. "That sounds like a good idea."

"May I kiss you, sweet Amy?"

Her lashes swept low and lifted in a shy, entrancing move that hid, then revealed eyes reflecting his own longing and happiness. "Yes," she whispered and closed her eyes.

He touched his lips softly to hers for the length of a heartbeat. Then again, his hands still framing her face. His lips moved to one eyebrow, and then the other, barely brushing them, then back to her mouth. His arms slid around her, drawing her to him as the kiss lengthened. One of her arms slid about his waist in a slightly hesitant manner, and she rested against him.

When the kiss ended, he brushed his lips back and forth over hers lightly and whispered, "I love you, Amy. I love you with all my heart and soul."

"I love you, too. I thought I'd never have the right to say those words to you."

He buried his face in her neck and held her close, rejoicing in her love. "I wish we could marry now, tonight."

She laughed softly at his fervent tone.

He drew back slightly with a sigh. "I suppose your father's right that we shouldn't marry so soon." He traced her cheekbone with an index finger. "It will be fun courting, don't you think? We can go sleighing. I can walk you home from classes, carrying your books. This spring we can join the other couples out on the Academy steps in the evenings."

There were other things to discuss, like how they'd manage to send Amy to Paris and how many children they hoped to have one day, but there was plenty of time for that. Now that Walter was out of their lives, there would be time for everything.

"Don't forget ice skating," Amy said, continuing his list of courting activities.

"Hmm. We could do that tonight."

She shook her head, laughing at him again. "Not likely, with that cut on your head." She sobered. "It must hurt horribly. Are you still dizzy?"

"Yes, but I'm not sure if it's from the wound or from your closeness."

"Silly boy," she whispered, surprising and delighting him with a quick kiss.

"I won't be a boy by the time I'm through with school and we can marry."

"I'll wait as long as you ask me to wait. What else is there for me to do? You hold my heart."

The promise in her eyes settled every question he'd ever had about her love. A deep peace filled him. "And you hold my heart, Amy. Forever."

He sealed their promises with a kiss.

Meet Me

with a Promise

By JoAnn A. Grote

For Charlie

rank Sterling knocked on the oak door at the top of the narrow indoor stairway and waited. He'd traveled 130 miles, from St. Paul to Chippewa City on the edge of the prairie, to see Amy. He shifted his wide-brimmed brown hat from his right hand to his left and shifted his weight impatiently from one foot to the other.

From the street below he'd seen the mellow glow of lamplight filter through the lace curtains in the window of the second-story apartment Amy Henderson and her father shared above Dr. Matt Strong's pharmacy. One of them must be home.

Were those footsteps? He stopped fidgeting and straightened. The brass doorknob turned, and the door opened. His heart quickened at the sight of Amy in a simple white shirt-waist and dark blue skirt, her pale brown hair in the popular upsweep, as usual. "Hello, Amy."

The green-gold eyes he loved widened. Joy filled her face and reflected in his heart. "Frank."

She threw her arms about his neck, and he caught her to himself. The familiar lavender fragrance filled his senses.

The uncharacteristic spontaneity of her greeting warmed him. He realized suddenly what was meant by the saying "Home is where the heart is." This was his home, no matter where he lived. Home was with Amy, in her arms, in each other's hearts.

"The war's come, Amy." His voice broke slightly on the words. He hugged his fiancée close, trying to surround her with enough love to protect them both from what the future might hold.

"I know." Her hug tightened a moment before she released her hold. She stood in the circle of his arms and played with the collar of his brown corduroy jacket. "Word arrived in town over the wire at the railroad station yesterday. Men galloped through the streets, shouting the news like Paul Revere calling out the minutemen. I'm afraid the editor of the *Chippewa City Commercial* is a bit miffed he wasn't the one to break the story to the town."

Frank managed a lame laugh at her joke. He knew from her high, bright tone that she was trying to be cheerful and brave for him. He'd play along.

She gave his collar a final pat and stepped back, breaking the circle of his arms. "My, what am I thinking, keeping you out here on the landing? Come in."

He followed her into the living area, reaching quickly to grasp one of her hands. She darted a surprised smile at him over her shoulder. He squeezed her hand and returned the smile.

His gaze swept the small room. Fine furniture from the large home the Hendersons once owned crowded the room: mahogany tables, pale blue satin parlor chairs and matching brocade sofa, and the grandfather clock that once stood in their hallway. There was no hallway for the clock here. A fine gateleg table was tucked in one corner, covered with lace and bordered by two chairs with needlepoint cushions. The corner was the Hendersons' current dining area. There was no dining room in the tiny apartment. In the opposite corner stood Mr. Henderson's imposing mahogany desk.

Pale blue velvet draperies hung beside exquisite lace undercurtains, further remnants from the home on the hill, the home that had been the envy of the town. Porcelain figurines rested on tables and graced shelves. Books from her father's once pretentious library filled the walls and were piled here and there on the thick Persian carpet. The lamp on the piecrust table before one of the two windows in the room sent light through the pink roses on the painted globe.

The panic of 1893 had wiped out Mr. Henderson's investments and taken the house, but he and Amy never complained about their cramped new home. Frank admired their attitude. It had made him love Amy more than he had before her father's financial disaster.

The silence of the apartment registered on him. "Isn't your father home?"

"He's meeting with Dr. Strong about some missionary board business before tonight's prayer meeting."

Frank took a step toward the door. "I shouldn't stay." He didn't want to hurt her reputation. All it would take in this small town was one person discovering they were here alone and Amy would be top gossip news for days.

A rosy blush tinted Amy's cheeks. "I was so excited to see you that I forgot Father isn't here to act as chaperon. Would you like to go to the prayer meeting? It's a special one because of the war. It begins in about twenty minutes."

"I can't think of a more appropriate place to be right now than at a prayer meeting with our friends." He glanced at the parlor stove's grate to see if a fire needed to be banked before they left. No light shown through. The late April evenings were still cool, but the Hendersons had chosen not to heat the apartment. He opened the door and stood just outside on the landing to wait for her.

Amy slipped on a blue jacket that matched her skirt. The jacket nipped in at the waist. It's wide lapels and popular leg-o'-mutton sleeves increased the impression of a willowy frame. After adding a matching hat and gloves, she put out the lamp, and she and Frank left.

Frank liked the familiar feel of Amy's fingers tucked into the crook of his arm, her shoulder brushing gently against his as they walked, the soft sound of her skirt swishing as her shoes kept up a light *tap-tap* beside his heavier tread on the boardwalk. The realization their time together was limited caused an ache in his throat and chest.

He tipped his hat to the lamplighter who was busy lighting the lamps along Main Street against the darkening twilight. Most shops had closed for the day, and there weren't many people walking or riding along the street.

Flags waved from every storefront. Red, white, and blue bunting draped from balconies and the tops of buildings. It hadn't taken the nation long to break out in a nationalistic fervor.

"Flags are everywhere in St. Paul, too," Frank told Amy. "On the trip out here, flags and bunting flew from every station and from farmhouses, too. Even saw a milk farmer with a flag perched on his wagon. Stores have about run out of flags."

"Here, too."

They started up the steps leading to the top of the ridge. Most businesses were built along Main Street near the river at the bottom of the ridge. The homes and churches perched on the prairie above.

"I didn't expect to see you, Frank. It's Wednesday. Didn't you have classes?" She stopped suddenly and stared up at him with questioning eyes. "Surely the university didn't close because of the war?"

He gave a short laugh. "Hardly. I came home to see you." He pressed her arm closer to his side. "You know I joined the National Guard a few weeks ago."

"Yes, after the *Maine* was fired upon."

"I joined because I believe we as a nation should be prepared to fight for others who are struggling for their freedom. Maybe I was naive, but I believed if Spain knew we were serious about helping the Cubans gain their freedom, Spain would withdraw from Cuba. We now know Spain is ready to fight us to stay there."

"Yes, unfortunately for everyone."

"I don't want to kill anyone, Amy. I don't even like killing the hogs and chickens we raise on the farm. And I'm not sure if Spain meant the *Maine* to hit the mines in Havana Harbor. Like everyone else, I hate that we lost the 266 men who were aboard on a peace mission, but my conscience won't let me stand by and do nothing when we can help the Cuban people. The stories we hear about the way they've been treated by the Spanish—" He couldn't think of words to tell how the horror affected him.

Amy squeezed his arm. "I know. It's impossible to imagine people treat others the way the news stories say the Cubans are treated. Herded into guarded camps surrounded by barbed wire and hunted down like animals. I read that almost two hundred thousand Cubans have been killed."

Frank nodded. "Yes, almost a quarter of their people."

They walked along the boardwalk that edged the top of the ridge. Across the road, houses looked out over the river valley. Children darted among the houses, hiding behind bushes and trees. "Ally, ally, ally in free!" they heard a girl call.

Amy smiled up at him. "Remember playing that when you were a child?"

"Yes, but I played with my brothers and sisters on the farm, not with my neighbors, like you must have done being an only child."

"It was fun just the same. How was your trip out today?"

"Fine. Long. The train seemed crowded for a weekday. Everyone was talking about the war, of course."

Two boys darted across the street. Frank and Amy stopped as the boys ran past and down the slope. One carried a wooden rifle. The other a wooden sword. "Remember the *Maine!*" the second boy cried.

Amy shivered and drew closer to Frank. He laid his hand over her fingers where they rested on his arm. "It's only play," he said quietly.

She nodded and smiled brightly. "I just had a chill. I should have expected it would turn colder now that the sun's down. Spring afternoons feel so warm after the long, cold winter."

Her bravado didn't fool him, but he didn't challenge it. He was glad for her courage. It was easier to face than the fear she must feel at the thought of the war. It was easier to face than his own fears.

The simple event silenced the announcement he'd traveled almost all the way across Minnesota to make to her. The words filled him and pushed to be told, but the dread of seeing her eyes darken in sadness and fear kept the words inside. He suspected she knew what he'd come to say, but as long as the words were unspoken, they could pretend there was escape from the truth.

More people and carriages filled the walks and streets as they passed the tall brick high school and neared the church. He was pleased to see his brother Jason's horses and wagon hitched outside. He'd be able to ride back to the farm with Jason for the night. Besides, Jason and the rest of the family had to be told, too.

People greeted Frank and Amy with surprised, happy faces as the couple neared the church. There wasn't time for long hellos since the church bells were announcing the prayer meeting was about to begin. Frank knew that wouldn't be the case following the service. Neighbors and family would want to know what he was doing home in the middle of the week. It wasn't his nature to lie to them.

It wouldn't be right not to tell Amy before she overheard him telling others. He drew her aside just outside the tall, heavy wooden doors. "I have to tell you. I should have told you earlier, I know, but . . ."

The soft lines of her sweet young face drooped. Her eyes lost a bit of their light, as if to ward off a blow, but her gaze met his unflinching.

He took a deep breath before continuing in a whisper. "The first troops for the war are to be called from the National Guard. I expect the call to come any day now. That's why I came home, to say good-bye."

❧

Amy sat between her father and Frank on the hard wooden pew. She followed the words of the prayers issued by Reverend Conrad and others, her heart pleading their essence as never before. Prayers for a quick war, for few casualties, for victory and freedom for the Cuban people rumbled out in Reverend Conrad's deep, comforting voice.

Let Spain change its mind, even at this late hour, Lord, Amy's own heart pleaded. *Let war be averted and the Cuban people win their freedom without further bloodshed. If this can't be, please bring Frank home safe to me.*

The prayer rang over and over inside her head. Frank had to come home. He had to. All her plans were wrapped up in him. How would she be able to go on if he didn't return?

Tears heated her eyes. She batted them back. She wouldn't let herself cry. She wouldn't burden Frank with her own fears. He needed to know she supported him in his decision.

Frank's family filled the pew in front of them: his older brother, Jason; Jason's wife, Pearl; their three-year-old son, Chalmers, and three-month-old daughter, Viola; seventeen-year-old Andy; sixteen-year-old Maggie; and ten-year-old Grace. With their brown hair and wide faces, none of them looked anything like Frank. Amy loved his almost black hair and matching thin mustache, the somber dark eyes that were as black as his hair when he was angry, the square jaw, and quiet, reserved manner.

Frank's parents were no longer with them; they'd been killed in an accident five years earlier. Grace and Chalmers kept turning to peek over the top of the pew at Frank with big grins. Normally their antics amused Amy. Tonight their actions were bittersweet.

Frank squeezed her hand. Her eyes misted over once more. She didn't look at him but kept her gaze on her lap. Frank had been right. This was the best place to be, surrounded by their friends and family, seeking God's comfort and help. It was absolutely the perfect place to be.

After the service, Frank's family surrounded him with hugs and the question Amy knew they'd ask. Friends broke through the family circle to ask the same question. "What are you doing home in the middle of the week? Did the university kick you out?" followed by friendly laughter.

Amy kept a smile on her face through all the answers, through the repeat of the same answer so many times she lost count. She hated the answer.

"You must be so proud of him," people said to her over and over. She nodded and said, "Yes, I am."

It was true. She was proud of him. Proud of his beautiful heart that cried out against one group of people trying to over-power another. Proud that he was the kind of man who was more than talk, the kind of man who stood up for what he said he believed.

And completely terrified he might not come home alive.

The town's young men formed a tight circle around Frank, soon forcing most of his family aside.

"Wish I'd thought to join up with the guard," Roland, a redheaded young man who'd attended the local academy with Frank, blustered. "Maybe I'll volunteer for the navy instead, though."

"Me, too," Frank's brother Andy agreed. "We might need the army to get the Spanish soldiers off the island, but I'd sure like to have a shot at their ships. After all, they blew up the *Maine*. That's what started all this."

Pearl, who was standing behind Amy, gasped. Beside her, Jason groaned.

Amy studied Andy uneasily. He wasn't that much younger than she and Frank, but Andy seemed barely out of boyhood.

The smile on Frank's face died. "Are you serious, Andy?"

"'Course I'm serious."

Jason shook his head. "We need you on the farm, Andy."

Andy pushed back a hunk of his straight brown hair and jutted out his chin. "The country needs me, too. I'm almost eighteen. I won't need your permission to sign up."

The group about them fell silent. Jason and Andy glared at each other. Feet shifted as the group watched the brothers.

Frank slipped an arm around Andy's shoulders. "Let's talk about your plans at home tonight."

Andy grinned at him. "Sure."

The conversation started up again slowly with Roland asking Frank how he'd come to join the guard.

Amy watched Andy, disquiet filling her spirit. Andy and Frank had squabbled for years, as so many brothers did. Suddenly Andy was acting like Frank was a hero because he was likely to be in a war soon. Would Frank try to talk Andy out of following him into the service, or would he encourage Andy to join up? It would be difficult enough for their family to have one of the brothers in danger. Amy hoped Andy could be persuaded to stay home. She grudgingly acknowledged to herself that the farm couldn't possibly sound as exciting to a boy Andy's age as fighting in a war.

Her gaze traveled around the ring of young men and boys. Their eyes were lit with unsuppressed excitement. Their voices were loud with it. All of them were eager to be part of avenging the Cuban people and shoving the Spanish out of the Western Hemisphere. They reminded her of the two boys who'd run across her and Frank's path earlier, playing at war.

Reverend Conrad broke through the circle of young men. His bearded, lean face and deep-set eyes were sober as he rested one of his hands on Frank's shoulder. "I hear you're likely to be called up soon."

"Yes, Sir." Pride and excitement shone in Frank's eyes.

"I wish we'd known sooner. We could have prayed for you tonight during the meeting. You can be sure we'll be praying for you from here on."

"Thank you, Sir. That means a lot to me."

Amy smiled her own thanks to the preacher. The promised prayers gave comfort, reminding her that whatever happened, she and Frank were wrapped in the love of the Lord and their friends.

"So you're going to be a soldier." A round man, so short he barely reached Frank's shoulder, slapped Frank on the back.

It apparently took Frank, who was engrossed in conversation with Jason, by surprise. He stumbled forward a step, coughing. Turning, he recognized his friendly attacker and grinned. "Hi, Shorty. Yes, I'm with the guard."

Shorty hitched at his trousers. "Nothing like fighting for your country, no siree." His lips twisted into a proud, tight smile.

A tall, lean, wrinkled man beside Shorty snorted. "A lot you know about it. You didn't fight for your country. You fought against it, you low-down Confederate."

Shorty's ruddy complexion grew redder. "Did so fight for my country, Slim Anders. We'd withdrawn from the Union, as was our right. We were dragged back into it kicking and screaming."

Slim rested both hands on the top of his cane and leaned over Shorty. "And you're still screaming about it. Think you'd have enough sense to thank us Yanks for letting you stay part of the greatest country on the face of the earth."

Shorty's eyes narrowed. *"Letting us stay?"* He reached up and pointed one of his index fingers at the bottom of Slim's nose. "We had a pretty good country of our own. That's why the Union didn't want us to go. We're the part that makes this the greatest country on the face of the earth."

The group around them chuckled. Amy smiled. They'd all heard the same arguments and more every time the two men were within speaking distance of each other. They'd been arguing since they arrived in Chippewa City almost thirty years ago.

Frank raised his hands, palms out. "Truce. This is a house of peace, remember?"

"Hmmmph." Shorty crossed his arms over his chest. "At least in this war the North and South will be fighting together against the same enemy."

Slim nodded curtly. "You finally got something right." He patted Frank's shoulder. "You do us proud in this war, young Sterling, you hear?"

Frank grinned. "Yes, Sir. I'll do my best."

Amy noticed Reverend Conrad had begun putting out the lamps. She touched Frank's arm and nodded in the direction of the preacher. "I think it's time to leave."

They and the group around them filed down the aisle toward the door. They walked slowly, letting Slim set the pace. He was so tall and sure of himself that Amy tended to forget he had a wooden leg. As far as she could tell, it only slowed down his walking. The man was spry of mind and as energetic as a man half his age. In spite of the way he and Shorty bickered, both men were loved by the community. She couldn't imagine the town without them.

Once outside, Jason turned to Frank. "Pearl and I are heading over to Pearl's parents with the young'ns to visit. You can meet up with us there later and ride back to the farm, if you'd like."

"Thanks, I'll do that."

Jason jerked his thumb toward the line of wagons and horses hitched along the street. "There's an extra lantern in the wagon box if you need one."

"Good. Amy and I didn't think to bring one along, and her father already left with Dr. Strong."

Townspeople who lived along the way kept Frank and Amy company as they walked, exchanging pleasantries. A group of older boys followed behind, singing "Rally 'Round the Flag, Boys." The words sent icy shivers down Amy's spine.

She was glad when the last of the boys and their families turned to their homes, leaving her and Frank alone. The lantern of blackened tin swung from one of Frank's hands, making shadows on the boardwalk.

Amy and Frank started down the wooden stairs that ran from the top of the ridge to Main Street. Once they reached the street, there would be no privacy. The stairway to the apartment was private, but her father would arrive home soon. She desperately wanted a little more time alone with Frank. "Do you think we could stop here for a few minutes and talk?"

"Here?"

She heard the surprise and hesitance in his voice. The ridge was covered with brush, making the steps a secluded area. She knew it had a reputation as an area for spooning couples in the warmer months. Her cheeks heated, and she was glad Frank couldn't see them color in the dark. "I only want to talk with you alone." She sat down on the cold wood.

Frank sat down beside her and set the lantern a couple steps below them. "We shouldn't bump it there." He slipped an arm around her and pulled her close. "Ah, Amy, I'm going to miss you awfully."

She rested her cheek on his shoulder. "I'll miss you, too." It felt so comfortably familiar, being with him like this. She loved the way it felt to be in his arms. "What will happen with your education, Frank? Will the university allow you to graduate without completing this year's studies?"

"I'll go back when the war's over. Everyone says it won't last long."

No one had thought the War Between the States would last long, either, if she remembered her history lessons correctly.

"My graduation will just have to be postponed." He cleared his throat. The sound was loud in the night, so close to her ear. "I'm afraid the wedding we planned for June will have to be postponed, too. I'm so sorry, Amy."

She nodded against his shoulder, his corduroy jacket soft beneath her cheek. Her throat was thick with unshed tears. She couldn't speak, but it didn't matter since there were no words that could change things. War was one of the unfightable things in life. Leaders decided to wage war, and the lives and plans of their countrymen went up in smoke.

Amy felt Frank's lips warm against her temple. She didn't dare lift her lips for his kiss, afraid she wouldn't be able to hold back the tears.

"I know it seems unfair," he whispered. "We've waited so long to be together. There're so many things we fought to have the right to be man and wife. I'll never forget how close I came to losing you to Walter Bay."

Amy shuddered. "Don't remind me." Walter had tried to coerce her into marrying him to save her father's house, on which Walter held the mortgage. Amy had thought she was being noble, agreeing to marry the man to save her father's home. Thanks to Frank, she'd finally realized her father wouldn't want her to sacrifice herself that way. Walter now resided in prison. "I had a narrow escape."

"*We* had a narrow escape, my love. We've had a lot of escapes. If it weren't for your father refusing to allow me to see you unless I quit drinking, no telling what my life would be like now." He pulled his head back, and she glanced up at him. "I expect you wouldn't have stuck by me if I'd kept up the drinking and gambling."

She smiled. The lantern didn't cast enough light to see his features, which were further shadowed by his hat brim. "I suppose you're right, but it's so hard for me to believe you ever did those things. I never saw you drunk."

"For which I'm eternally grateful."

This time she had no qualms in meeting his kiss. It was warm and gentle and sweet and filled with his love, as she remembered. How long after tonight until they shared a kiss again?

A sliver of an idea slipped into her mind. She blinked in surprise. Blinked again. The idea put out a root into her heart. It wasn't all that far-fetched, was it?

She fingered one of the bone buttons on Frank's jacket. "Frank, about the wedding . . ."

"Yes?"

"We wouldn't have to postpone it. We could cancel it instead."

She felt him stiffen. It seemed even his breathing stopped for a moment. "Cancel it?"

"Well, not exactly cancel it. What's the opposite of postpone?"

He pulled back slightly. "What are you talking about?"

"The wedding."

"I know, but—"

"Do we have to get married when you get back from the war?"

"I thought you wanted to get married." His voice was defensive, threaded with confusion. "I thought you loved me. That's why we planned the wedding, isn't it? Isn't that what we've wanted for years?"

She laughed softly, joyous in the knowledge of his love for her. "Yes, that's what we want. So why wait? Why not get married right away, before you leave?"

$$2$$

*M*arry now? Tonight?" Frank jerked back and grabbed Amy's shoulders, a jolt of energy rushing through him.

"Yes, or as soon as possible." He felt her breath soft against his face with her quiet laugh. "Why not?"

"Why not? There are a million reasons why not."

She slid her arms around his waist. Her lips touched his cheek in a quick, warm kiss. "No, there's not. We love each other, and we want to be married. There are not a million reasons we shouldn't be married right away. There's not one reason we shouldn't."

"There's at least one very good reason, and you know it. You just don't want to admit it." He grasped her shoulders again and pushed her gently from him. Her suggestion was all too tempting when she was so close. He stood up to further break the intangible bond.

She rose quickly, all but destroying his attempt at defense. The lavender scent she wore melded once again with the spring earth smells. "What is that reason?"

"Are you sure that's what you want, for me to put it into words?"

Even in the darkness he could see the outline of her face, see her chin lift. "Yes. Say it."

"I could die, Amy. I might not come back." The anger in his voice shocked him. "I could die," he repeated, forcing a softness he didn't feel to the words.

"Why should that keep us from marrying?" she challenged. "I'd be as alone then whether we married or not."

He was sure she knew he would like to be married as much as she wanted it. "You haven't thought this through."

"To what conclusion?"

"If we married, we might have a child."

"Yes."

The love and happiness in the word almost crushed his resolve. "That can't happen, Amy."

"Why not? You love children."

"It's irresponsible to father a child when a man knows he might not be there to raise it."

"No man knows he'll be there to raise his children. It doesn't take war to kill a man. Your sister Grace was only five when your parents died. Besides, not all soldiers die when they go to war—not even most of them."

Frank groaned and wrapped his arms around her. "You are too convincing for our own good."

She leaned against his chest, her shoulders shaking in soft laughter. "Does that mean you agree to my proposal?"

"I'd love to, but I can't." He sighed. "You know I'm right about this, Amy."

She wasn't laughing any longer. "You'll come back, Frank. You must." She paused, and he suspected it was to swallow the desperation he heard in her words. "But on the slight chance you don't, if we marry, you might have a child keeping part of you alive."

He understood now what she wanted—a way to keep him and their dreams and their love alive if he didn't make it back. "It wouldn't be fair to the child," he whispered. "We mustn't pretend that it would be."

He pulled her closer and rocked slightly, wishing he could comfort them both. He wanted to tell her it would be all right, he'd be back, but he had a bad feeling about this war. Not about his decision to fight in it—the Cuban people's freedom from Spanish tyranny was worth risking his life.

"When I return, we'll have so many babies, we'll need two houses to hold our family."

"Enough babies to fill our arms and hearts will be fine." Tears mingled with her words.

Frank wasn't sure how long they stood that way, holding each other, speaking only with their hearts. Finally he picked up the lantern, and he and Amy walked to her home. His chest felt as though it would explode with his love for her and with the fear they wouldn't have the life together they'd dreamed of for so long and the fear that their babies would only live in their dreams.

❧

Frank leaned back against the side of the wooden wagon box with his younger siblings. Old quilts and fragrant, scratchy straw lessened the jolts slightly as the family headed down the rutted country road under the stars toward home.

Jason's son, Chalmers, slept in Frank's lap, oblivious to the bouncing. Frank studied the round face resting trustingly against his chest. Chalmers's expression beneath pale brown curls was calm in the moonlight. Remembering his discussion with Amy only an hour earlier, Frank's chest expanded in gratitude for this cherished time. Would he ever cradle his and Amy's son in his arms?

He glanced across the wagon bed at Andy. The boy's head rolled easily back and forth with the wagon's movements. His eyes were closed, and his arms crossed over his chest. Frank was pretty sure his brother wasn't sleeping but rather choosing to ignore the rest of the family's friendly chatter to show his anger at Jason. Frank felt sorry for him, walling himself off that way, but maybe his sullen ways were better than subjecting everyone else to his rage.

When they arrived at the farm, Andy took the still-sleeping Chalmers from Frank and started toward the house. Pearl followed with baby Viola. Maggie ran ahead to open the back door off the porch and light a lamp.

Frank reached to help his youngest sister, Grace, out of the wagon bed. The ten year old hugged him tightly about the neck, refusing to be lowered to the ground. Her giggle tickled his ear, and he laughed with her.

"Better get down, Pumpkin," he warned, "or you'll have to help me rub down the horses."

"I don't mind." Her hold didn't slacken a whit.

"On second thought, you're too short to help with the horses. You barely reach their bellies."

"I'm not either that short."

"I'll have to set you down to work on the horses. What if you fall asleep in the barn?"

Her giggle rose. "You'd carry me into the house."

"I might forget you."

"No, you wouldn't."

She was right, of course. "Jason, I'll be out to help unhitch after I take Grace inside."

Grace's game continued in the kitchen, where Maggie had lit the kerosene lamp on the red-and-white oilcloth-covered table. It took the promise that the youngster could help him milk the cows in the morning to convince her to release her hold.

"Can I shoot milk to the cats right from the cows?" she pleaded.

He ruffled her hair. "We'll see how good your aim is."

Frank smiled as he hurried across the farmyard in the moonlight to the large red barn, his shoes kicking up dust. He would have been impatient with his youngest sister for such a performance in the past. Knowing he might be called to battle changed his attitude toward even such previously insignificant exchanges.

Smells of animals and of fields freshly plowed for spring seeding and of leaves budding out drifted on the night air. The windmill creaked as it turned in the prairie breeze. A wolf howled somewhere out in the night. Stars blinked, and the moon hung in a sky that seemed to go on forever. Frank drank the night in with all his senses and wondered what night was like in Cuba.

Jason was finishing unhitching, while the horses stamped impatiently outside the barn door. The horses needed no urging to enter the barn, where rest and water and food waited. They went right to adjoining stalls. The saddle horses in nearby stalls whinnied a greeting.

Andy brought buckets of water for rubbing down the horses. Together the three brothers made sure the horses had fresh water, hay, and corn.

Frank performed the chores, all the time aware of enjoying the feel of the barn at night: the creak of the building; the strong, warm smell of the horses; the cats watching patiently, then darting into the straw in the hope of catching any little creature foolish enough to stir; the larger animals moving about and crunching straw beneath their hooves.

When the duties toward the horses were completed for the evening, Frank patted each of the horses' necks. "Be sure you're good to these guys while I'm gone," he admonished his brothers.

"I'll take good care of them," Andy promised. The brothers started for the door. Andy reached for the lantern and shot Frank a grin. "At least until I enlist."

He can't wait to leave the farm and ordinary, everyday life, and I can't wait to get back to the farm and ordinary, everyday life. Maybe there'll be a miracle, and the Cubans will be allowed their freedom, the Spaniards will go home, and Andy and I and Amy can stay home and live plain, dull, ordinary lives.

Please, God.

❧

Frank rode one of the saddle horses to town the next morning after helping Jason and Andy milk the cows. He smiled, remembering Grace's play with the cows and cats. Her attempts at milking were short-lived.

He'd taken a few minutes to say good-bye to his favorite cows, especially Sudsy, and Gideon, the one-eyed golden tabby cat who'd been a good friend since a kitten. He was going to miss those animals. He already missed them while attending the university, but that was different.

Even the fields he passed triggered unfamiliar emotions within him. For the first spring of his life he wouldn't be here when the fields turned green with new crops. He wouldn't see the crops grow tall and lush, see them waving in the summer breezes, hear the wind clatter through them, or watch the sunlight and shadows play over them. Would he be back in time for harvest? Those people most optimistic about the United States' power might consider it possible, but he doubted it, even if the war was short.

On reaching town, he made only one stop before heading to Amy's. He tried to keep his desire to be alone with Amy at bay during a meal of scalloped oysters with Amy and her father. As soon as Frank felt he could politely do so, he suggested that he and Amy go for a walk.

The couple didn't speak of where to walk but, as if in unspoken agreement, headed behind Main Street toward the river that wound through the valley beneath sheltering cottonwoods.

Some of the cottonwoods stood in water, for winter's melting snows made the river high. It rushed over its banks in a muddy, dangerous wash along its usual path and beyond. The flooding wasn't high enough to threaten the businesses on Main Street this year, but farmers' fields on the other side of the river lay beneath swirling water.

Frank selected a spot beneath a cottonwood not far from the edge of the water. He removed something from his jacket pocket and spread his corduroy jacket on the ground. "Sit here, Amy."

"That isn't necessary. I don't want to get your jacket dirty."

"Better my jacket than your skirt. Besides, the air is warm, but the ground still holds a bit of winter's chill. I wouldn't want you to get cold."

"I should have thought to bring a quilt."

Nothing talk, Frank thought. Nothing but unimportant details to hide the fact that inside they both felt like the careening waters before them, out of control and running over life's familiar edges.

Seated beside her, he reached for one of her hands and wished she weren't wearing the blue cotton gloves that matched the blue background in her dress. He couldn't recall ever seeing her outside without her hat and gloves. He was accustomed to Pearl and his sisters often going without both outside at the farm.

Frank touched the brim of her hat with his index finger. "I don't think I've seen your hair uncovered in the sunshine since before we entered high school."

Her cheeks flushed and her lashes lowered. "It wouldn't be

proper." She shifted slightly until her shoulder rested partly against his shoulder and partly against his chest. He sighed in contentment at her closeness.

He held out the maroon velvet box he'd removed from his jacket pocket. "This is for you."

Her eyes widened in surprise. She opened the box and gasped at the sight of the tiny ruby heart set on a silver ring. "Oh, Frank, it's beautiful."

He tenderly removed her glove, then slipped the ring on her finger. Her hand trembled slightly. He touched his lips to the ring and then lifted his gaze to hers. "I wanted you to have something, something you could keep with you all the time to remind you that I love you. I'll always love you. I'll go on loving you even if time stops."

Tears brightened her eyes. Then she was in his arms, her arms around his neck. "I love you, Frank." Her tears tumbled over and flavored their kisses.

The thought that they should perhaps not be so intimate within sight of the backs of some Main Street buildings gave him only momentary pause. He held her close, feeling her heart beat strong and quick against his chest.

After a few minutes, she pulled back slightly in his arms. Her hat, pinned so primly in place with a pearl-studded pin before they left the apartment, hung askew over her left ear. She laughed self-consciously and removed the hat, setting it on the grass beside them. Her hair tumbled in loose waves from its topknot.

"I have something for you, too." She fumbled in her lace reticule and pulled out the folded brown paper he'd seen her slip into her apron pocket earlier. She handed it to him, her eyes shining above flushed cheeks.

He removed the red twine tied about the small package. It was fun to receive something unexpected from her. It didn't matter what the package held. "Feels solid," he remarked.

She only smiled, her eyes bright with expectation and the joy of giving. He leaned forward and kissed her lightly on the lips.

She pushed at his chest gently with her fingertips. "Open it."

He grinned at her eagerness and obeyed. A silver pocket watch embossed with a simple vine design lay in his hand. It wasn't expensive, but it must have cost her dearly. She and her father hadn't money to spend on extravagances.

"I want you to have something with you always to remind you of my love." Her voice was just above a whisper, almost drowned out by the splashing of the water rushing past. "My love, too, will live past time."

The words grew in meaning, connected as they were to the little time remaining before he left. He clutched the watch in his hand, unable to speak for the lump in his throat.

Amy unclasped his fingers from the watch. "Open it."

He pulled his gaze from her face and opened the watch-case. Opposite the watch face was a picture of Amy.

He slid his hand behind her neck and pulled her toward him. Their lips met in a sweet, lingering kiss. "The gift is perfect. You couldn't have given me anything I'd treasure more. I'll keep it with me always."

Her eyes told him that he and his heart had said just the right thing.

Amy cleared her throat and pointed to the still-open watch-case. "That is telling me it's time we started back. I have an art class at the academy this afternoon. It's the only class I teach today."

Regret that their time alone was ending washed through him, but he snapped the watch shut and stood.

Amy pushed at her loosened locks of hair, rearranging hairpins until the topknot again felt secure, then pinning on her little blue hat. She pulled her glove on over the ruby ring, and they reluctantly stood up, Frank putting on his jacket.

The couple walked slowly, her hand in the crook of his arm, shoulders brushing, treasuring these last few minutes together and the simple touches that seemed so intimate.

Mr. Henderson was just coming down the stairs of the second-floor apartment when Frank and Amy reached the first-floor pharmacy. They had barely exchanged greetings when they were interrupted. Feet sounded in a running, thumping pace on the boardwalk behind them. "Sterling! Frank Sterling, wait up!"

The three turned toward the voice. Frank's friend Roland was running toward them from the direction of the train station, his open jacket flapping and his red hair windswept. His right hand held a yellow paper, which he waved over his head as he ran.

Roland stopped beside them. "Glad I caught you." He gasped for breath between sentences. "I was headed for the livery. Planned to ride out to your farm to let you know." He waved the rectangular piece of paper in Frank's direction.

Frank took it. He read it silently and felt the blood drain from his face. The stiffening went out of his knees. He lowered himself to the wooden bench in front of the pharmacy.

"What is it?" Amy grabbed the paper from him, fear drawing her eyebrows together in a frown. Her father peered over her shoulder.

Roland didn't wait for them to read the news. "The state guard's been called up. They're ordered to assemble in St. Paul tomorrow at Camp Ramsey with a day's cooked rations."

It's too soon, Frank thought. *Too soon.*

He'd known it was coming, but in spite of all his talk of it the last couple days, he felt numb all the way through. *It's too soon.*

⟨ **3** ⟩

t's too soon, Amy thought. *I'm not ready for him to leave yet, Lord.*

She rested one of her hands on her chest. She could feel her heart beating as steady as always. How could that be, when she felt numb from head to toe?

Amy felt a hand on her shoulder and turned to see her father's sorrow-filled gaze upon her. "Maybe you could put together some food for him to eat on the train back."

She nodded.

Frank stood up. He removed his hat with one hand and pushed the fingers of his other hand through his hair. "That would be nice, thank you. Roland, would you mind riding out to the farm and letting my family know?"

"Sure. Already told the others at the station that I was heading out there. They won't be expecting me back for awhile."

"You can take my horse. I left it at the livery when I rode in this morning. Is it too late to catch a train back to St. Paul?"

"Leaves in an hour."

"Not much time." Frank settled his hat back on his head.

Roland was breathing easier now. He pulled his shoulders back and lifted his chin in a manner that made Amy think he was feeling important as the bearer of this awful news. He held out his hand. "In case I don't see you before you leave, good luck, old man. Give those Spaniards what for."

As Roland left, Amy turned toward the door to the apartment with a heavy heart. Frank and her father followed.

She was grateful her father went to his desk when they entered the apartment, again leaving her and Frank alone in the kitchen.

Frank leaned against the cupboard while Amy sliced and buttered bread and put it in a tin lunch bucket for him. Her chest ached from unspoken words, but she didn't know what the words were, only the feeling of them.

"Can you spare any of that great pie you made this morning?" There was a forced lilt to Frank's voice.

Amy kept her back to him and managed to put a touch of lightness in her own voice. "I think I could spare a piece or two." Her jaw quivered. She clamped her lips shut. *I won't break down. I won't make this harder for him.*

She sliced the pie. As she put the pieces in the tin pail, she heard her father clear his throat loudly just before entering the kitchen. "You two youngsters ready to head to the train station yet?"

Frank straightened and picked up the tin pail by its handle. "Yes, Sir. Amy has packed me a fine lunch. I'm afraid I've taken the last of your pie, though."

Mr. Henderson patted his sizable stomach. "Oh, I think I'll make it through until the next pie is baked. It's near time for Amy's class."

Amy gasped and pressed her palms to her cheeks. "I forgot all about it." Her stomach clenched at the thought of going to the academy instead of seeing Frank off at the station.

"Forget about it you should." Her father's voice boomed out. "You've a young man to take care of here. I'll go to the academy and tell them the class is cancelled for today."

"Thank you, Father." Amy gave him a hug. The clenching in her stomach loosened somewhat.

Amy clung to Frank's arm on the way to the train station. She kept her chin high, her gaze straight ahead, and a smile on her lips. She nodded to the townspeople they met on the way but didn't attempt to speak to anyone. She needed to keep her determination intact or she'd break down in tears before Frank left. That wasn't the way she wanted him remembering her when he was in Cuba.

Frank and Amy kept watch on the road, looking for his family. The Sterling wagon clattered into the train yard, the horses at a trot, only five minutes before the train was scheduled to leave. Jason and Andy were still in their field clothes.

Andy was the first out of the wagon. He ran up to Frank and shook his hand fiercely. "Sure wish I was going with you."

"Sure glad you're not," Frank shot back with a grin.

"I'll get there yet, you'll see."

Maggie and Grace embraced Frank, tears large in their eyes. Grace bawled outright when Pearl took her from Frank's arms.

"I was afraid we wouldn't make it in time," Jason said. "You never saw a team hitched up so fast." He pumped Frank's hand in a handshake and thumped him on the arm. "We'll miss you. Watch yourself."

"I will."

They stared at each other, continuing to pump each other's hands during the awkward silence.

They were only a year apart in age, Amy remembered. What must it be like to say good-bye to someone who's been part of your life for more than twenty years?

A whistle blew. A conductor called, "All aboard!"

Frank darted a look at the train and turned back to Jason. "Don't forget to pray for me."

"Every day."

Frank reached for Amy's hand and led her a few feet away. "I don't care what any of Chippewa City's old biddies say. I'm going to kiss you good-bye right here in front of anyone who wants to watch, Amy Henderson. If anyone has the nerve to say anything to you, you tell them they're only complaining because they're jealous."

His unexpected joking dashed her tears away from the surface.

He was as good as his word. He hauled her into his arms and kissed her long and hard, as if to make the memory of it last forever.

The whistle broke into their world. "Last call!" the conductor warned.

Frank loosened his hold and pressed his cheek hard against hers. She wanted to beg him to promise he'd come back to her, but she wouldn't allow herself to ask him to make a promise he had no way to know if he could keep. Her chest ached with the effort it took to keep the words to herself.

"You know I hate to leave you, don't you, Amy?"

She nodded, biting her bottom lip, and rested the palm of her hand against his chest. "Your beautiful heart is the reason I love you. I know you have to help those people."

He placed his palms on each side of her face and smiled into her eyes. "If I get back, Amy, meet me with a promise."

If. "What . . . what promise?"

"That you'll still marry me."

Her grin burst across her face, and joy and love flooded her. "I will. I will marry you when you get back."

With a lurch, the train started chugging along the track, the whistle blowing so loud that Frank yelled his last words. "Remember, I'll love you even if time stops!"

Then he ran for the train, grabbing the long handle beside the steps and jumping on board, the tin lunch pail swinging from one hand. He stood on the step and waved.

Amy watched and waved until the train was out of sight, all the time praying, "Bring him home to me, Lord. Bring him home."

❧

Five days later, headlines screamed, "Victory at the Battle of Manila." The people of Chippewa City were wild with rejoicing all day long and into the night.

Amy scoured the newspaper for knowledge of this war that had invaded her tiny prairie town, threatening the life of the man she loved.

The news came by way of Spain, whose government received the information by wire from Manila. Although President McKinley hadn't received word directly from the American officer in charge, he was convinced the report was accurate. "Why would Spain lie about losing the battle?" he asked.

A United States naval officer was quoted as saying the war would not be won with just the defeat of the Spanish soldiers on the ground at Cuba. He believed the Spanish fleet must be destroyed and, along with it, Spain's ability to access the island.

The United States under Commodore Dewey had attacked the Spanish fleet near Manila Bay on May 1, only days after Frank reported to the campgrounds at St. Paul. According to the article, all the Spanish ships in the Philippines were destroyed and many Spaniards killed. The United States lost no ships and only one man, who died of heat stroke.

Notes from Frank arrived almost daily. Amy treasured every one, although they were short and contained primarily mundane information about life at Camp Ramsey: new blue uniforms, living in converted stables on the state fairgrounds, training hours on end. His signature was always accompanied by a simple drawing of a watch face, which recalled to her his words, "I'll love you even if time stops."

Frank wrote that he was now part of the Thirteenth Regiment of Minnesota Infantry Volunteers. The long, proud name was soon shortened to the Thirteenth by Minnesotans and the press.

On May 17, Amy received a note in which the scrawled handwriting showed Frank's obvious haste.

May 16, 1898

My dearest Amy,
I've only a moment snatched from packing to write this.
We're mustering out today. The Thirteenth is heading for San Francisco. Please tell my family. I'll write when I can.
All my love always,
Frank

The two other Minnesota regiments, the Twelfth and Fourteenth, had been mustered out to Camp Thomas in Georgia for further training. The Thirteenth was headed to Manila.

"I thought only navy men would be sent to Manila," Amy said to her father.

"Evidently the war secretary wants the infantry there, too."

The idea made Amy uneasy. "Do you think Frank will be safer in the Philippines than in Cuba?"

"Is any place safe in a war?"

The helpless look on her father's face only increased Amy's own helpless feelings. She fled to the riverbank where she and Frank had spent so many beautiful moments of their last afternoon together. There she poured out her fear and pain to the Lord.

After an hour or so, she allowed some peace to replace the distress she'd nurtured in her heart. She wiped away the last of her tears and heaved a shaggy sigh. "Lord, it seems since Frank left, not only words but every thought and feeling I have is a prayer."

At the end of May, President McKinley called for more men. Minnesota was ordered to raise almost another thousand to join the regiments already in the field. The governor put out a call for volunteers, as there wasn't another guard regiment available.

Chippewa City and the surrounding county created a volunteer company. Young men left their families and farms and small-town jobs eager to prove their bravery and embark on the adventure of war with the men with whom they'd grown up.

Frank's sister Maggie started a group of girls who met every evening to make up linen bags for the soldiers. In the bags they placed a Bible, needles, thread, and a thimble. Amy thought it was a wonderful idea and joined the group whenever she could. She wrote Frank about the group, and he wrote Maggie, praising her efforts.

To Amy the country seemed turned upside down. Every train that came through town carried volunteers to St. Paul. Amy joined other young women from the Women's Christian Temperance League at the station, handing out cookies and coffee to the new soldiers who hung out the windows waving and grinning at their admirers on the platform. Along the tracks, children and young women and men waved scarves, handkerchiefs, and flags to cheer the soldiers on their way.

The town band sent the local volunteers off with renditions of the ever popular "Rally 'Round the Flag, Boys," as well as "The Star Spangled Banner," "Stars and Stripes Forever," and the romantic song too close to Amy's heart, "The Girl I Left Behind."

Maggie's group passed their linen bags to the volunteers, who accepted them with cheerful smiles.

Other scenes at the station were foreign to the sense of decorum with which Amy had been raised and seemed counter to the town's moral fiber. Young women met the trains with bouquets of early spring flowers and small budding branches and bestowed them along with kisses on soldiers, young men they'd never met or barely knew. There was a sense of the carnival about it all that lacerated Amy's heart.

She knew she wasn't alone in her pain. She saw it in the hooded eyes of mothers and fathers who sent their sons off to war. She witnessed a few couples who, like her and Frank, were deeply in love and hated to part. She relived the terrible sense of her heart tearing in two every time she saw such a parting.

Roland, the telegraph clerk who'd raced down the street with the notice of Frank's call to duty, joined the volunteers. Amy couldn't imagine jolly Roland in a battle scene. Petite, blond Sylvia saw him off at the train station. Tears filled the eyes of the usually bubbly girl. The couple often attended social events that Amy and Frank attended. The couple's friendship had grown slowly over the years into courtship.

Amy saw Andy at the station saying good-bye to friends and knew he wished he were joining the volunteers.

Slim and Shorty, the veterans of the War Between the States, met most of the trains, too. They cheered the new soldiers on. They recounted to anyone who would listen tales of the battles in which they'd fought. Amy was amazed how the two men, who had been enemies for years, now grew unified in their hatred of Spain. It saddened her that it took hatred and a common threat for the men to become friends.

The newspapers announced the first battle between the American infantry and the Spanish in Cuba had taken place on June 24. Amy's first thought was gratitude that Frank hadn't been part of it. Her second thought was shame and a prayer for those who lost loved ones in the battle—for the loved ones on both sides of the war.

It seemed eons before Amy received another letter from Frank, this one sent from Honolulu. He had started the letter the day he left San Francisco and continued it every day the ship traveled between California and Hawaii. Amy rejoiced over the length of the letter and the bits of his new life that he shared with her.

June 27, 1898

My dearest Amy,

    We left San Francisco today under General Arthur MacArthur. We sailed out of the harbor to a chorus of ships' steam whistles and guns. Flags and handkerchiefs flew from the shore and harbor.

    We passed through the Golden Gate and on out to sea. That lady greeted us with winds and waves that made the prairie winds seem tame by comparison. Breaking a bronco is easy next to riding the Pacific's waves. I joined most of the others in a bit of seasickness, though it's nothing compared to my homesickness for you.

He spoke of the long days on ship, the simple fare, and the heat.

    You never saw a thousand men so glad to put their feet on land as we were when we arrived in Hawaii. Took awhile to get our land feet. When we did, we swarmed through Honolulu's streets. The islanders presented us with wreaths made of flowers, which we wore like necklaces. The flowers reminded me of you and the floral fragrance you like to wear. I pressed a blossom in the pocket-size Bible I carry.

    I'll send you a letter whenever I can, but I don't know when the next opportunity will arise. Know I am thinking of you every day and love you always.

The familiar watch face adorned the letter at the end of each day's writing. Amy rested the palm of her hand over Frank's signature and imagined she touched the hand that wrote it.

She wondered if he knew that while he was in Honolulu, Congress had voted to annex Hawaii.

It seemed strange to think of Frank seeing parts of the world she might never see, experiencing sights and sounds and smells she might never experience. What did it feel like to sail the oceans, she wondered. What did the waves sound like against the hull of a ship? What did the flower wreaths that he said reminded him of her smell like?

Had he heard of the Battle of San Juan Hill in Cuba? Did he know that on July 16 the fighting in Cuba came to end with the signing of what were called "The Articles of Capitulation"?

The voyage took about a month. That would put him in the Philippines the end of July or perhaps the first week of August if the seas were rough or the stopover in Hawaii lasted longer than expected.

Amy felt as though she walked in a cloud of joy from the moment she heard of the peace in Cuba. Surely the troops in the Philippines would be sent home soon. "Perhaps Frank's ship will dock only to turn right around and come back," she said to her father.

"Time will tell."

The cloud darkened when an epidemic of typhoid fever broke out among the Minnesota volunteers in St. Paul in late July.

"I'm so glad Andy didn't join the volunteers," Pearl told Amy after a prayer meeting. "How awful to think of young men's lives threatened in camps on our own soil."

"Yes." Amy hugged her Bible to her chest. "Father says it's the same in every war."

"At least here we know the men will receive the best of care, with clean beds and enough medicine. Apparently the soldiers nearer the battlefields haven't that luxury."

"Doesn't it make you wish you could join Clara Barton and her Red Cross volunteers? It brought tears to my eyes when I read of their work with our men in Cuba."

"It takes a special kind of bravery to do what they do. I admire them, but I know my place is here, taking care of my family."

"Yes, I'm sure you're right." *But I don't have a family to raise. There's only Father, and he doesn't need me the way Pearl's children need her.*

A chill ran through Amy when she read of another battle in the Philippines the night of July 31 and August 1. She scanned the article, frantic, until she'd assured herself the Thirteenth Regiment wasn't involved. On another page she saw a short article, only a paragraph long, saying the Thirteenth arrived in the islands August 1.

The hope and joy that had filled her upon the cessation of fighting in Cuba dissolved. She wished she were with the Red Cross, that she had the knowledge to help the wounded, that she was in the Philippines and could help Frank if he were wounded.

"But I don't have the knowledge, and I can't help anyone," she lamented to the Lord while seated along the banks of the river.

The flooding waters of spring had receded. The river no longer swirled angrily or hurled along whatever it caught in its path. The dark waters flowed peacefully, sun-dappled beneath the cottonwoods that shaded her. If only the country's angry flood had receded, too, she thought. She'd like to feel as peaceful inside as the river before her appeared.

"If there were only something I could do." She straightened. "Maybe . . . maybe I can help after all."

Two days later she entered Camp Ramsey. At the post hospital, she spoke with the officer in charge. "I have no training as a nurse, but I can sit with men who are ill. I can bathe their foreheads, help feed them, change their bedding, and pray with them. I don't care how mundane it is. I will do anything, just let me help."

The officer's eyes and cheeks were sunken with fatigue. His gaze searched hers. "You don't know what you are asking. We are fighting a serious disease, an often fatal disease."

"I do know. That's why I'm here."

"Have you no one at home to care for?"

Amy removed her left glove and held out her hand. The tiny ruby flashed from her finger. "The man I love is with the Thirteenth in the Philippines. I only hope he has all the help he needs should he be injured or fall ill."

"He will most likely return. Most soldiers do." His smile barely touched his tired eyes. "You want to be alive when he comes home."

"I want him to come home alive. Every man in this camp has a mother or sister or loved one who wants him to come home alive, too. I want to help them."

They stared at each other across the desk. Amy forced herself to keep her gaze steady and her hands from trembling. She sent up a prayer that he would accept her offer.

He stood and gave a curt little bow from the waist. "Thank you, Miss Henderson. I will be honored to have you with us. I hope that man in the Philippines knows what a fine woman he has waiting here for him."

The following days were the longest and most exhausting of Amy's life, but also the most rewarding. She helped with laundry, fanned and bathed feverish patients, prayed with them when they were frightened, held glasses of water for them when they were too weak to hold the glasses themselves, fed them, wrote letters to loved ones, read letters the patients received, washed dishes, cleaned lamp chimneys and trimmed wicks, and did anything else asked of her.

In every patient's face, she saw Frank's face. To every prayer for a patient before her she added a silent petition for Frank's safety. She experienced in a new way a sense of connection with all people through the Lord's love and learned in every painful place there is a blessing.

Amy's conviction that she'd made the right choice in volunteering solidified when young men from her county began appearing in the hospital beds. She spent time with each one, promising to take messages to loved ones if needed.

Hurrying about her duties, she spotted a familiar red-haired young man in one of the beds. "Oh, no, not Roland." It took her a couple minutes to compose herself before she could approach his bed with a smile.

She held one of his hands between both of hers. "Hello, Roland. It's Amy."

Feverish eyes opened. "Amy. Heard you were nursing."

"Helping out. I'm not a nurse."

His eyes closed. "Not supposed to be like this."

She leaned over to hear him better. "What isn't?"

He didn't answer immediately. She waited, sensing him gathering his strength to continue talking. "War. S'posed to fight, not get sick like this."

She smoothed back his hair, which was wet with sweat. "Rest, Roland. Spare your strength."

"Want to talk while I can."

"You have to believe you'll get better."

"Don't think that's going to happen."

"Would you like us to pray together?"

A minute passed before he responded. "Think God will listen to me? I've been living pretty rough."

Amy knew what he meant. Frank had expressed concern over Roland's drinking. The academy had suspended Roland for it. Frank had remained friendly with him, hoping to help his friend. "God knows none of us are perfect."

She sat at the edge of the bed, holding his hand. Her prayer was simple. At the end he joined her in an "amen."

His fingers gripped hers when she stood. "Can you stay a little longer?"

Duties called. She hesitated. "Of course." She sat down again and spoke of happy memories, times she and Frank had spent with Roland and Sylvia.

"If I don't make it, will you tell Sylvia I love her?"

The lump that suddenly filled Amy's throat made it difficult to answer. "Yes, but she knows it, Roland."

"Should have asked her to marry me. Tell her I wish I had."

"I'll tell her."

Another patient lay in Roland's bed when she came to the ward the next morning. Roland hadn't made it. Working the long day was difficult with the knowledge of his passing swelling her heart. Back at her own simple cot that evening, Amy wrote to Sylvia. The government would inform Roland's family of his death, and Roland's family would inform Sylvia. But the government wouldn't tell Sylvia of Roland's love for her.

Several of the patients, as they regained health, showed interest in Amy as a woman. When they did, she showed them her ring and spoke of Frank. To a man, they told her they hoped he would return to her.

One of the things the patients liked best was the little sketches she made of them and the camp on the letters she sent to their families. She took care the sketches didn't show the ravages of the disease. It filled a special place inside her to know that finally her talent, which had seemed so inadequate in this war, was being used to help others even in such a slight way.

Recalling the work of Frederic Remington and Howard Chandler

Christy, who recorded the war in Cuba in sketches for *Harper's Weekly* and *Leslie's Weekly*, she made sketches of camp and hospital life and sold them to the *St. Paul Pioneer Press*.

She wrote Frank of her decision to volunteer at the hospital and described the humble tasks that made up her days. She had no idea when or if he would receive her letters, but she continued to send them.

Two weeks after Amy's arrival, Camp Ramsey reverberated with joy. Shouting and cheers and singing and gun salutes by the healthy volunteers marked the news that Spain and the United States had signed a peace protocol. That night Amy smiled as she said her evening prayers. She slept better than she had since Frank left for the war.

Two days later, she picked up a newspaper after a long day at the hospital and read that the day after the peace protocol was signed, the Thirteenth had fought its first battle at Manila.

$$4$$

rank grinned as he walked away from mail call. The mail had been a long time catching up with the regiment, but the letters from his brothers and sisters in addition to those from Amy made it worth the wait.

He dropped down beneath a palm tree, welcoming the shade, and placed the letters in the sand beside him. Pushing his broad-brimmed, high-crowned campaign hat back from his forehead, he picked up the envelopes and arranged them in the order post-marked. He was determined to read them in date order, though he was sorely tempted to read all of Amy's letters first.

He rubbed the palm of his hand over the beard he'd grown since leaving San Francisco and opened a letter from Andy. His younger brother had finally turned eighteen in August, but he hadn't joined up yet. He was waiting for the typhoid epidemics in the camps to pass before enlisting.

Maybe he won't enlist at all, Frank thought, *now that Spain has signed articles of capitulation in both Cuba and Manila.*

Frank opened the first letter Amy wrote in August, ignoring the man who sat down beside him until the man spoke.

"From that silly grin on your face, I expect that's a letter from your favorite girl, Sterling."

"You've got that right." Frank lowered the letter, only mildly annoyed at the interruption. Dan Terrell had become a good friend since they arrived on the Philippines. The two had fought side-by-side during the Battle of Manila, making their way through the city by ducking behind and climbing over garden walls and scurrying for cover beside native huts and wattled fences.

Frank pulled out his pocket watch, opened it, and handed it to Terrell.

Dan looked at Amy's picture and whistled appreciatively. "She's a pretty lady. How'd a guy with a face like yours get so lucky?"

Frank retrieved his watch with a grin and snapped the watch cover shut. "Charm. Need lessons?"

Dan chuckled, brushing from his forehead the brown hair that curled in the island's moist heat.

"How about you?" Frank asked. "You have a special lady waiting for you back home?"

Dan looked out at the thatch-roofed huts before them. "No. My lady died."

Frank was stunned into silence for a minute. "I'm sorry. I didn't know."

Dan nodded, still staring straight ahead.

Frank swallowed, trying to moisten his suddenly dry throat. "What happened?"

"Horse-and-buggy accident last winter. The buggy tipped over, and Belinda—that's my wife—her neck was broken."

His wife? "Were you married long?"

"Two and a half years."

Frank tried to imagine how awful it would be to lose Amy that way. Even the possibility of her death was too painful to consider. "Do you have any children?"

"We were expecting our first child when Belinda had the accident."

Frank's stomach tightened at the drawn look on Dan's face and the hollow sound of his voice. Frank couldn't think what to say to his new friend. A letter stuck out of Dan's shirt pocket. Frank indicated the letter with a wave of his hand. "Looks like you received news from somebody today."

Dan looked down at the envelope as if surprised at its existence and grunted. "From a friend." He drew it from his pocket, fingering the envelope as though undecided whether or not to open it. "Belinda and I rented his farm."

"Where was that?"

"Southeastern Minnesota, near Northfield."

"I'm from the opposite side of the state. Aren't you going to read the letter?"

"Sure." Dan tore the envelope open and unfolded the letter.

Had he wanted to wait to open it, to draw out the experience? Frank wondered. *Hadn't Dan received any other mail?* Frank cleared his throat. "Do you have any family back home?"

Dan didn't look up from the envelope. "My folks died from diphtheria back in '88. Had a sister and brother once, but they died when they were kids."

"My parents are dead, too." Frank glanced at his pile of letters and thanked God for his brothers and sisters.

Turning back to Amy's letter, he began reading it slowly, savoring every line as he had done with each letter before.

> *I've envied the Red Cross nurses who helped the wounded in Cuba. Are there Red Cross nurses in Manila? I wish I were there, close to you. I wish I were a nurse and could help if you were injured.*

Frank was fervently glad she wasn't a nurse. The last thing he wanted was for her to be in a battle area.

> *You've perhaps heard that typhoid fever is ravaging the Minnesota volunteers at Camp Ramsey. I've volunteered to help in the camp hospital.*

"What?" Frank shot to his feet.

Dan looked up at him. "Is there a problem?"

Frank had to try twice before he could make his voice work. "It's Amy. She's . . . she's volunteering at Camp Ramsey, helping with a typhoid epidemic."

"Is she a nurse?"

Frank shook his head vigorously. "No."

He was aware that Dan rose and stood beside him, waiting for him to finish the letter. Frank scanned the page, his heart racing as fast as it had the first time he faced enemy fire.

"She must be one terrific lady to do that," Dan offered.

Part of Frank wanted to burst with pride that she would offer herself so selflessly. The rest of him felt nigh on to bursting with fear. How could she do this to them? What if she caught the fever and died? What if he made it home from Manila and she was no longer there to share his life? How could the life he went back to possibly be worth anything without her?

He dropped to his knees, the letter shaking in his trembling hand. He grabbed the pile of unopened envelopes. He tossed aside all but those with Amy's handwriting.

Dan squatted beside Frank. "What is it?"

"I have to see if she caught the fever."

It was now mid-September. The last letter from Amy was dated August 13. The irony of the date was not lost on him; the day he first experienced battle.

Amy had been alive that day. He tore the envelope open and scanned the letter. Only mundane news, wonderful everyday news of her chores at the camp, of plans to move the camp to Fort Snelling in an attempt to break the epidemic's hold, of her assurance she still hadn't contracted the disease and was as strong as ever. He skimmed past the lines over which he would normally linger, those telling of her love and how much she missed him.

He pawed through the unopened letters from his family. There were no envelopes postmarked after Amy's last letter. That made sense, since it took about a month for the mail to make it to the Philippines from the States. It didn't give him much comfort. Amy could be lying in a Fort Snelling hospital bed right now, her body raging with fever. Or worse.

He felt Dan's hand on his shoulder. "She was all right when the last mail was sent," Frank told him.

He drew up his knees and rested his arms on them, then buried his face in his arms. He was too afraid to even cry. *Keep her safe, Lord.* His silent prayer screamed inside his head. *Keep her safe.*

Amy must have felt like this, Frank realized. This was what the fear felt like for all the women waiting at home for the men they loved to return from the war: numbing, terrifying.

He picked up her last letter again. Hot fear twisted inside him like a living thing. He understood for the first time that when she wrote the letter, she hadn't known whether he was alive or not. And he knew he had to do the same thing for her that she did for him with every letter. He'd write her back, tell her how proud he was of her, tell her the everyday things of his life here in Manila, avoid the horrible aspects of war, tell her he loved her, and pretend he wasn't wondering every minute whether she was alive or dead.

✦

Amy breathed deeply of the pine-scented air in the large hall, which was decorated for the Christmas party at Windom Academy. "It's good to be back, Mrs. Headley."

The slender, thirty-year-old brunette beside her stepped back from the picture she'd just hung on the wall. "I do wish you'd call me Mary. You're an instructor here, not a student. I consider you a friend and hope you consider me one also."

"Yes, I do." Mary and her husband, the director of the academy, had become trusted confidants since Amy began teaching art there four years earlier. "I can't tell you how much I appreciate your husband offering me back my teaching position now that my volunteer work at the fort is over."

Mrs. Headley patted Amy's sleeve. "We're glad you came through your experience without becoming ill from the fever. It seems a miracle."

"To me, too, although I'm not the only person working with the patients who didn't contract the disease."

Mrs. Headley studied the painting hanging in a wide tortoiseshell frame on the wall. Amy fought the desire to leave and not look back, a desire familiar to her whenever someone examined her work for the first time.

"It's lovely," the verdict came. "A perfect companion piece to the photograph beside it."

"Thank you." Amy's gaze slid to the photograph, which also hung in a tortoiseshell frame. In it, a woman stood in a parlor, her eyes cast down, her stance and facial expression showing sorrow; a young man in army uniform stood in the open doorway, his arms outstretched toward the woman, his own face expressing his yearning to stay.

Amy hated the photograph. It spelled out her life all too well. Half the homes she entered had a copy on a wall. When Amy saw a copy hanging on the wall at the academy, her frustration boiled over. She'd immediately gone to her studio at the school and started the painting that became her response: a young woman with arms spread in welcome, joy shining from her face, and a returning soldier walking through the door with matching joy radiating from him.

Mrs. Headley held the door leading to the classroom hallway. "Have you heard when Frank will return?"

"No. When the guard was called last spring, the men were told they would serve for two years or the duration of the war. He may not be home for another year and a half."

"A pity. I know you and he would like to start your life together."

Amy gave her friend a quick hug. "Thank you for understanding and for your prayers. You needn't tell me you are praying for Frank and for me and for us as a couple. I know you are. It makes everything easier to bear, knowing you and others are carrying us in your hearts and prayers."

Amy pulled on her mittens as she left the building, walking down the steps and across the snow-drifted walk toward the ravine-spanning bridge that led toward town and home. When would Frank be back, she wondered. When would this awful war be over and Frank return?

❧

In spite of the peace protocol, the war in Manila continued after Christmas and into spring. The war was no longer against Spain but instead against the Filipinos who wanted to re-establish their own government. The days and weeks and months dragged by for Amy. The Thirteenth was finally relieved in March of its duty guarding the city of Manila against its own people.

"Does this mean Frank will be sent home soon?" Amy asked her father eagerly, looking up from Frank's letter.

His reply was the same as always. "Time will tell. Only God knows."

Frank's next letter didn't bring welcome news of his impending return.

> *My regiment was assigned to guard the railroad, which runs*
> *north of Manila, against the Filipino insurgents. Looks like I'll*
> *soon travel even farther from the city. Today I was reassigned to*
> *an expedition into the interior of Luzon, another island.*
> *Unfortunately this means I won't be sending or receiving mail for*
> *awhile. Know that I'm thinking of you every hour.*

The letter sent chills along Amy's arms. Her heart trembled at Frank's news, and she sent up yet more prayers. He didn't need to spell out for her that this was not a Lewis-and-Clark type of expedition. The soldiers would be trying to flush out insurgents.

On a bright, clear day in May when the people on the Minnesota prairie were rejoicing in the warmth of spring, Amy opened her apartment door to Frank's sister-in-law, Pearl.

"What a lovely surprise. Do come in. I'll put on the coffee pot."

Pearl stepped into the parlor. "No, no coffee."

Amy stared at her, puzzled. Pearl's face was pale, her eyes filled with pain.

Amy's heart swelled until it seemed her ribs must burst from the fear and dread. "It's Frank, isn't it?"

Pearl nodded. She licked her lips. "He's wounded."

"How . . . how bad is it?"

"We don't know. We've only received notice he's been wounded in action." Pearl spread her arms in frustration. "We don't know what kind of wound, or how serious it is, or if he's being treated in the Philippines or sent back to the States. We don't know anything. Jason is trying to find the answers."

Amy pressed the palms of her hands to her face.

Pearl slid her arms around Amy's waist and hugged her close. "I'm sorry, Amy. I'm so sorry."

Amy moved her trembling arms stiffly about Pearl's shoulders. "I . . . I want to be with him. I have to find him. He needs me."

Amy felt the warm moisture of Pearl's tears against her cheeks and realized in amazement that there were no tears in her own eyes. All she felt was the full yet hollow place fear had carved in her chest and stomach. "I need to do something to help him. There must be something I can do, somewhere I can go to help him. Where can I go?"

"Jason will find out. Until then, your love can be with Frank, Amy. Your love and prayers can be with him."

If he's still alive. The words flooded into Amy's mind. She shut her heart hard against them.

❧

Amy fought her fears for almost a week while Jason battled for information detailing Frank's condition. Each day Amy listened for the train that brought the mail and hurried to the post office as soon as she thought the mail might be sorted.

"You almost beat the train today," the postmaster greeted her on Friday. "There are three letters here for you from that soldier." He drew them from a mail slot and handed them to her.

"Thank you." It seemed to Amy her heartbeat drowned out her words.

"I heard about young Sterling getting wounded. I hope it's not too serious. He's a good lad."

Amy smiled her thanks. Turning, she hurried toward the door. On the outside steps she almost ran into Pearl.

Pearl glanced at the envelopes in Amy's hand. "Are any of those from Frank?"

"All of them. I haven't opened them yet." Amy didn't want to admit she was afraid she'd break into tears when she read the letters.

"I've come into town each day to check on the mail. Jason and I are too anxious to hear from Frank to wait the extra hours for any letters to be delivered at the farm. I'll be right back out."

Amy waited beside Pearl's wagon. The wagon bed and horses gave her a sense of privacy. Amy barely noticed the creaking wheels and harnesses of passing wagons or the dust that rose from horses' hooves and settled on her spring-green hat and gown.

She glanced at the envelopes in her hands, wondering which, if any, contained news of Frank's condition. "Oh, no," she whispered. Her heart sank to her stomach. The handwriting on one of the envelopes wasn't Frank's, but it was addressed to her and had his name in the return address.

Her fingers felt frozen. She stared at the envelope, wanting to know what news it contained yet terrified to know.

Pearl hurried up to her. "Only one letter from Frank for Jason." She held it up.

Amy looked at it. "Frank wrote it. It's his handwriting."

"Of course it is." Pearl frowned in puzzlement.

"This one's not." Amy realized her friend didn't understand the significance. *But she's never written a letter for a soldier who couldn't write his own.* Amy tore the envelope open slowly. The rip of tearing paper seemed ominous. As if by not opening it anything awful would be kept contained. If only it were that easy.

> *May 12, 1899*
> *Philippines*

Dearest Amy,

It seems the war has really caught up to me. I'm glad to tell you I'm no longer on the expedition on Luzon. Unfortunately, that's because I'm in the Red Cross hospital. I met up with an insurgent and lost.

Don't be afraid for me, Amy. I'm wounded, yes, but I'll pull through. The doctors did their best work on me and the nurses are following it up with great care. So promise me you won't worry. I won't be able to get the rest the nurses insist upon if I think you're worrying.

Amy's voice caught in a sob. She pressed the fingers of one hand to her lips. The sudden mist in her eyes made the words look wavy.

Pearl touched Amy's arm but waited silently for her to regain control. Amy's voice wavered when she continued reading.

> *You might not hear from me for awhile. They're shipping me back to a fort hospital in the States.*
> *You may have noticed the handwriting is easier on the eyes than my handwriting. One of the nurses, Miss Patchett, is writing it for me. She insists that rest includes not writing letters. I've insisted she put in this explanation. I've spoken to her about you so often she says she'd know you if she met you on the street.*
>
> *Love,*
> *Frank*

Amy searched in vain for the usual clock face. Frank must not have told Nurse Patchett to include it. The omission added to Amy's sadness.

Pearl grabbed an edge of the letter and scanned it. "He doesn't say where he was wounded."

"No."

"He sounds cheerful."

Amy folded the letter slowly. "He probably doesn't want to scare us." She'd met many patients like that at the fort. They wanted messages sent to their loved ones but didn't want to frighten them. The letters of those who died from the fever often sounded the same in tone as those of the soldiers who lived. The knowledge ignited a burning pain inside her. "He must be weak since a nurse is writing the letter for him."

"Maybe he wrote one of these other letters."

He hadn't.

The letter seemed to cheer Pearl and Jason and their family, though Amy wondered whether they simply tried to keep hope alive for her. Surely they knew, as she did, that if Frank's wound wasn't serious, he wouldn't have been sent to the States for treatment. Instead he'd have been treated at the Red Cross hospital in the Philippines and returned to duty as soon as he was considered able-bodied.

The news of Frank's wounded condition spread throughout the small town and countryside. People stopped Amy everywhere she went to ask about him and express their concern. Reverend Conrad and the congregation prayed regularly for Frank. Amy hoped Frank could feel all the love poured out for him.

She was relieved to finally receive a letter announcing he was back in the States. She tried to ignore the pang of fear she felt that the letter was written by another Red Cross nurse.

> *You needn't play Florence Nightingale and come see me,*
> *Amy. No man likes to be visited by his lady love when he must*
> *play the invalid. I assure you the doctors and nurses here are*
> *giving me the best possible care.*

Sighing, she ran her fingers over the signature, wishing it were truly his. The watch face was again missing. She wished Frank had asked the nurse to draw it. Immediately she scolded herself. "Don't act so petty, Amy Henderson. It's enough that he's alive and that you've heard from him again. There are many women not this blessed."

But the longing remained.

5

When spring quarter at the academy ended, Amy felt at a loss. She couldn't remember a time when her painting hadn't pleasantly filled her days. Now she paced the school's studio, staring out the windows at the prairie sky and picturing Frank in a hospital bed. The oil paints dried on her palette before she remembered to apply them to canvas.

Letters from Frank no longer arrived in bunches. He'd written often before he was wounded, even though the letters weren't mailed as soon as they were written. Now the letters dribbled in, at first weekly, then farther apart. The loving phrases that had brought color to her cheeks and joy to her heart were no longer included.

Amy told herself if Frank were writing the letters himself, they'd come more often and be more personal. She worried that he wasn't writing his own letters yet. She longed to visit him, but he continued to insist neither she nor his family travel to the hospital. Amy had to admit to herself that the cost of such a trip would be prohibitive, but she'd find a way to cover the cost if he wanted her with him.

Church, Bible class, Women's Christian Temperance meetings, and caring for the home she shared with her father weren't enough to keep her mind from worrying.

"Visit us at the farm," Pearl suggested when Amy complained to her after a Sunday church service.

"You don't need me underfoot." Amy slid the strings of her ivory lace reticule over her wrist. Fingering the frayed cuff on her yellow linen sleeve, she sighed. "I need some new dresses, but I hate to spend the money on a seamstress."

"You don't need a new dress, just a new cuff." Pearl examined the material. "That's not badly frayed. A bit of lace on each cuff should cover the wear nicely."

Amy lifted her brows in surprise. "Honestly?"

Pearl laughed. "Of course. Haven't you ever freshened up an outfit that way?"

"No. You know I don't sew except to stitch on buttons and mend hems, as you taught me." Amy tried to keep the impatience from her voice. Growing up, she hadn't thought about the new gowns the dressmaker made for her each season. She hadn't wondered what other women did when their clothes wore out. It made her ashamed to realize how little she'd understood the way most people lived. Since her father had lost his money in the depression, she'd gained respect for the discipline and ability to live on little means.

"I'll gladly teach you more. We can start with freshening this gown. Perhaps you have some lace at home you'd like to use on it. Otherwise you can purchase some. Bring it out to the farm along with the dress."

"I can't let you neglect your work for mine."

"I've no intention of neglecting my work. I'll show you what to do. It will be fun. We can visit while we work."

"I'm all thumbs when handling a needle. You probably can't understand that, since you're one of those amazing women who can look at articles about cute needlework items on the women's pages in the newspapers and know how to follow the instructions."

Pearl's laugh pealed out. "Quit pouting. Sewing takes practice, like everything else in life. Come out to the farm. Evening would be best. Harvest is starting, and my days will be filled from sunup to sunset."

"You don't help the men in the fields, do you?" The thought of petite, feminine Pearl doing the work of field hands shocked Amy.

Pearl's eyes danced with laughter. "We hire men to help with harvest. Our neighbor, Thor, helps, too. In return, Jason and Andy help with his fields. Feeding everyone keeps me and Jason's sisters busy."

"May I help?"

Pearl looked taken aback at the offer. "Why . . . certainly, if you'd like, but please don't feel you need to offer."

"I need to learn to be a farm wife for Frank."

Pearl nodded. "The days are long and hot. Wear something old and cool and bring a work apron."

"May I bring some food?"

"Just bring your willing spirit."

Amy started for the farm early the next morning but not early enough to beat the farmers to the fields. The men and their machines and horses and the crops were silhouetted against the pinkish-orange horizon. Dust rose behind her buggy from the dirt road and met the grain dust from an amber field under harvest.

"The men like to get into the fields while it's cool," Pearl told Amy when she arrived at the farm. "It will warm up soon enough as the sun moves higher."

Pearl unharnessed Amy's horse. Amy watched carefully and asked questions and did as Pearl directed her. Amy had never harnessed or unharnessed a horse before. She was determined to remember how to do it.

"I'll get Maggie to rub the horse down for you." Pearl turned toward the house.

Amy took her apron from the buggy seat and fell into step beside Pearl. "Don't you need Maggie's help in the kitchen?"

"The horse needs to be rubbed down before it's turned out to pasture for the day."

Amy sighed deeply. "I don't know anything about life on a farm. I don't even know how to rub down a horse. Why Frank wants to marry me is beyond my understanding."

"Because you are fine and beautiful, through and through." Pearl grinned and linked arms with Amy. "Rubbing down a horse is one of the easiest things to learn, but we'll let Maggie take care of it for you today."

The cheerful yellow-and-white-walled kitchen was already warm and filled with the smells of coffee, eggs, ham, and apple pie. Bread rose beneath clean muslin cut from a flour sack. Maggie rolled piecrust on the work table in the middle of the room. Grace stood at the iron sink, working away at the stack of breakfast dishes. The girls greeted Amy with smiles that made her feel hugged and welcomed.

Viola sat in the middle of the linoleum floor, banging two kettle tops together. Pearl nodded at her. "She's noisy, but at least I know where she is."

Seeing the attention focused on his little sister, Chalmers hurried over to kneel beside her. He tried unsuccessfully to convince her to exchange the noisy lids for an old wooden spoon.

Amy grinned. She loved the casual, busy hominess that was so different from the small, quiet apartment she and her father shared.

At Pearl's request, Maggie headed outside to take care of Amy's horse.

"Where would you like me to start?" Amy asked.

Grace turned, her hands deep in the dishwater. "Can she dry the dishes for me, Pearl?"

Pearl hesitated. Amy suspected Pearl had another chore in mind, but she agreed to Grace's request. The ten year old kept up a lively conversation about a new litter of kittens and the field hands. Amy gave the child her full attention and found herself sincerely interested in something other than her worry for Frank for the first time in weeks.

Amy liked working in Frank's home. It made her feel closer to him. She and the Sterling girls planned a party for Frank's homecoming while they worked. Whatever his wounds, the doctors wouldn't release him until he was healed. He might need time to regain his strength, but a nice picnic where family and neighbors could welcome him home shouldn't be too tiring. In fact, they were sure it would prove healing.

At noon Jason, Andy, and the hired hands, hot and hungry, came into the farmyard. Jason and Andy led teams of horses to the barn.

The men washed up at basins set along a wooden bench on the porch. Long board "tables" had been set up for the men beneath some cottonwoods so they could enjoy their meal in the shade. The women moved about in a flurry, carrying food and pitchers and coffee pots to the table. While the men ate, the women hovered about the tables, filling each plate or cup as soon as it was emptied.

The quick wash-up had removed the worst of the dirt from the men's faces and hands, but it hadn't removed the aroma of hard work. It seemed to Amy the smells of grain, earth, sweat, and the kerosene used to keep flies and mosquitoes at bay drowned the smells of the food. From the men's comments, the food smelled as enticing to them as ever, maybe more than usual. Amy was amazed at the amount of food the group consumed.

She smiled, watching Chalmers and Jason together. The boy insisted on sitting in Jason's lap the entire meal. Chalmers told his father all about his day, augmenting his limited words with animated gestures and facial expressions. Jason's gaze was soft as it lingered on his son. Amy believed she could see the love in his touch when his large, tanned, calloused hands tousled Chalmers's soft, pale brown curls.

The sight caught at her heart and awakened a craving. Frank loved children. She longed for the day when she would see their son seated on Frank's lap.

When the men had finished the last of their coffee and pie, the horses were retrieved, and men and horses headed down the dusty road back to the field.

The women relaxed then, enjoying their own meal. The respite was over before Amy felt ready, but she cheerfully helped carry dishes inside and began to wash them.

Soon the entire routine from the morning started over in preparation for supper. The kitchen was hotter than in the morning. If the open screened windows and door helped, Amy couldn't tell it. Her scalp and clothes were damp from perspiration, as were Pearl's and Maggie's.

After the evening meal, the men went back to the field and the women once more cleaned up the dishes. Finally Amy and Pearl walked out onto the porch.

The windmill stood tall against the darkening twilight sky. The breeze turned the windmill blades slowly, sending out a continual creaking noise. Evening insects joined it in a chorus. Dozens of tiny birds dove and darted over a nearby field.

"What are those birds?" Amy asked.

"Swallows. They always appear this time of night in August."

The peace of the setting sun sank into Amy's bones and spirit. She leaned against a white wooden post and sighed. "The cool breeze feels good. I can't remember ever being this tired. Is your life always like this?"

"No." Pearl rested her hands on the railing beside Amy. "This is one of the busiest times of the year."

"That's good. I was beginning to fear I hadn't the stamina to be the kind of wife Frank needs."

"He needs the kind of wife who loves him, who thinks she is the most blessed woman on the face of the earth to be married to him. That's the kind of wife every man needs."

Amy thought Pearl looked very content after the long day. "That's obviously the kind of wife you are." She smiled. "I'm glad you're happy with Jason."

"I am." Pearl returned her smile. "I won't pretend this is the only busy time of year. We put in long days all spring, summer, and fall. Jason and the boys take care of the fields and livestock. The girls and I take care of the home, but I like the feeling that we're building this life together. I guess a lot of people think it's a hard life, but it's a deeply joy-filled life also."

Amy removed her apron and laid it over the railing. She repinned tendrils that had loosened from her topknot, then brushed ineffectually at wrinkles in her blue-and-white-striped work dress. *The day has taken its toll on my appearance*, she thought.

"I brought my yellow linen and the lace, as you suggested," she told Pearl, "but I haven't the energy to work on them now."

"One thing about mending, it can always wait." Pearl untied her apron and lifted it over her head. "This is the part of day I like best. When the chores are done, Jason and I like to step outside and just be still together, watching our little world."

Amy let her gaze rove over the farmyard and nearby fields. She imagined Frank standing with his arm around her shoulders, enjoying the quiet with her. How long before they stood together here? Each day that passed brought them closer to their life as man and wife. *Farmer and wife*, she corrected herself with a smile.

Maggie and Grace came across the farmyard together, home from walking the cows and horses in from the pasture. Jason and Andy walked into the yard from the drive and met the girls at the bottom of the porch steps.

Jason mounted the steps, nodded at Amy, and headed for the washbasins. "Chalmers and Viola asleep already?" he asked Pearl.

"Yes, I guess the excitement of all the people around wore them out."

Jason grunted. "Hardly see those two these days."

Grace stretched her arms high over her head and yawned. "I'm going to bed, too." She hugged Pearl, then Jason. Wrinkling her nose, she shook her head. "Ugh. You stink."

"I'll go in with you, Grace." Maggie opened the screen door. "I'm pretty well all in myself."

Andy followed Jason to the basins. "I'll hook up your horse and drive you into town as soon as I wash up here, Amy."

"Thank you, but I can drive myself back."

"No women leave our farm alone at night." Jason's tone left no room for argument. He kissed Pearl's cheek. "I'll be back when I'm done with the milking." At the bottom of the steps, he turned to look back. "Thanks for your help today, Amy. Mighty nice of you."

Andy bounded down the steps after Jason. "Should only take a few minutes to get your buggy ready, Amy."

Amy could barely see the brothers in the darkness as they walked toward the barn together. "I feel so guilty. They've had such a long day. Now Andy is looking out for me and Jason has to milk the cows alone. Some help I am."

Pearl rubbed her hand lightly on Amy's sleeve. "I'm glad you were here today. And Andy would rather drive you into town than milk cows, you may be certain."

Golden lamplight fell through the window and screen door, out over the porch, casting shadows. *Maggie must have lit a lamp*, Amy thought. Within minutes, moths softly thunked and fluttered against the screens. Smells of livestock and fields and trees washed away the clinging odors of the day-long cooking.

The sound of horses' hooves softly thudding on the drive caught Amy's attention. She turned her gaze toward where she knew the drive entered the yard. Two lit lanterns bounced in the dark, and she knew from their height that they hung on either side of a buggy. "Are you expecting someone, Pearl?"

"No. I can't imagine who it could be at this hour."

The buggy stopped in front of the house but too far away for the light from the kitchen to illuminate it.

"Hello," Pearl called.

There was no response.

The buggy lanterns revealed the shadow of one person, but the buggy top hid his or her features.

The person half-stood to get out of the buggy, and Amy could see it was a man. An excitement started, a stirring inside her. The man moved somewhat awkwardly as he climbed down, but there was something familiar about him, something—

"Frank!"

6

*A*my darted down the steps and over the path to the buggy, her heart racing, joy flooding her senses. She flung her arms around Frank's neck. "Frank! Oh, Frank, you're home. You're truly home." She pressed her lips to his cheek.

"Amy." The word was a hoarse whisper on the warm breath at her ear. His arm tightened about her waist, and he held her close against his chest. She felt him stagger slightly and step back under her fervent greeting. Guilt stabbed her. He'd been in a hospital for months. Naturally he'd be weak.

She loosened her hold, and he lowered her until her shoes touched the ground. Her hands rested on his shoulders. Even through the khaki shirt he wore she felt a difference. He'd lost muscle during his recuperation. Her heart trembled at the knowledge. *But he's home. With rest, he'll regain his strength.*

"What are you doing here, Amy?" Tension and confusion mingled in Frank's quiet question.

"Welcome home, Frank." Pearl's greeting awakened Amy from the world that included only her and Frank. She stepped back from Frank's arm to allow Pearl to greet him properly.

He couldn't have stopped at her home before coming here, Amy realized. If he had, her father would have told Frank she was here. As much as Frank loved his family, the Frank she knew would have come first to her. Why hadn't he let anyone know he was coming home?

An aching, tugging fear started in her stomach. She recognized it immediately as an extension of the fear that she'd tried to ignore for weeks—the fear that Frank was pulling his heart away from her.

Frank leaned down and touched his cheek to Pearl's. "How's my favorite sister-in-law?"

"It's so good to have you back."

"It's good to be back."

Watching them, unease tightened Amy's chest. Something was wrong. She wasn't certain what it was, but he didn't move like himself. Perhaps she was imagining it, reacting too strongly to his unexpected return. She frowned, watching him and Pearl. It was hard to see him clearly in the light from the buggy lanterns.

Running footsteps were quieted only slightly by the dirt as Jason and Andy came toward them, calling Frank's name. Before they reached the buggy, the back door slammed and Maggie and Grace joined in the race. A dog ran alongside them, barking as though he'd caught their excitement.

"Whoa." Frank gave a shaky laugh and stepped back against the buggy wheel. "I'm glad to see everyone, but I can't take you all on at once."

Laughter greeted his comment. Amy knew the laughter wasn't due to the humor as much as to their overwhelming happiness that he'd returned.

The family tossed questions at Frank.

"Did you get in on the last train?"

"Why didn't you tell us you were coming? We'd have met you at the station."

Andy pounded on Frank's shoulder in greeting. "You got here just in time to help with the milking. Sudsy's waiting for you."

Jason reached to shake Frank's hand. Grace dove in between the two men and threw her arms around Frank's waist. "I missed you."

Amy knew then, in an instant. The wound was to his right arm. She knew by the way Grace's arm pulled his khaki sleeve, the part below the elbow, tight against his body.

Grace gave a small cry and pulled back. "Where's your arm?"

Everyone stilled. In the darkness Amy could sense the horror and fear on the faces turned toward Frank.

That's why he came home this way, in the night, without telling anyone. That's why he didn't stop to see me before coming here. That's why I've felt him pulling away from me. He was afraid we'd react just like this, as if he were . . . damaged.

She slid her hand beneath his left arm and squeezed his arm gently. She pressed her cheek against his shoulder and looked into his eyes, trying to put all the love she could into her gaze. "I'm so glad you're back. I've missed you horribly."

The muscle beneath her fingers tensed. "I've missed you too." He looked at the others. "I've missed all of you."

A chill ran through her. He'd intentionally generalized the sentiment.

Her and Frank's actions stirred the others back to life. She heard a small gasp of a sob and saw Grace wipe tears from her face. Pearl slid her arms around the girl's shoulders and drew her back against her skirt.

"Well, you don't need to stand out here all night," Jason blustered with a cheerfulness that appeared false. "Come inside. Andy and I can take care of the horse and buggy. Rent it from the livery?"

"Yes." Frank didn't move.

Jason turned to Pearl. "Any of that coffee left? Must be some pie, too." He looked back at Frank. "Harvesting today. You know what that means. Lots of vittles."

Frank nodded.

"There's pie," Pearl assured. "The coffee is cold, but we can heat some up. The coals are still warm from the pies we baked this evening."

"Don't bother. Some milk would taste good."

"Say, we forgot the cows." Andy started toward the barn.

Amy thought Andy seemed inordinately glad to escape. He must have forgotten that he was about to drive her back to town, she thought. Or maybe he knew she wouldn't want to leave now or expected Frank to drive her back.

Frank tugged his arm gently from Amy's hands. He reached into the buggy and pulled out a leather satchel.

Jason grabbed the satchel handle. "I'll get that."

"I've got it." Frank's voice was tight but even.

Frank led the way toward the house, carrying the satchel. A sense of strangeness and loss swept through Amy. It was unlike him to walk on and leave her behind. *I'm acting petty. This must be horribly difficult for him, and I'm thinking only of my bruised feelings.* She took a deep breath and followed the others.

Maggie hurried ahead of Frank when they neared the door and reached to open it for him.

In the kitchen, Frank set the satchel down and took a deep breath. "Mmm. Home cooking." He pulled a chair out from the oak kitchen table and sat down. Grace sat beside him and Jason across from him.

Amy wanted to sit beside him, but he made no move to indicate he wanted her there. He didn't even look at her.

She gathered plates from the open cupboard, while Pearl sliced the pie and Maggie brought cold milk from the oak icebox.

"How are the crops?" Frank broke the tense atmosphere with a question for Jason. "Too dark to see much on the drive out."

Amy was sure Jason had kept Frank informed on crop conditions with the letters he wrote every few days, but now Jason answered as though he'd never mentioned them, his voice too cheerful.

"Wheat's great. No rain when it was in pollen. Not one hailstorm hit. Heads so thick you wouldn't believe and some as long as my forefinger. Running thirty-five bushels to the acre."

A hungry, jealous look passed over Frank's face. "What about the turnips? Get them sowed last month?"

Jason nodded. "Yep. Last week of the month, same time Dad always insisted we plant them."

Amy watched Frank while she worked. He'd always had high cheekbones and a slender face. Now the beard he'd grown couldn't hide that his cheeks were sunken. Gray circles made his eyes look deeper set than normal. His brown khaki military shirt hung on him. Her throat ached with the love she wanted to express to him, the assurances she wanted to give him that she loved him whatever his wounds.

Only the forks striking ironstone plates and moths plunking against the screens sounded while the family ate. Frank, who had been right-handed, used his left hand with more skill than Amy expected. *Of course, he's likely been feeding himself for quite awhile at the hospital*, she thought.

Amy remembered the meals earlier that day, the teasing and friendly banter. How different from this simple shared dessert.

It should be a joyous time, a time of rejoicing. Was it his attitude or hers and his family's that made it more a funeral than a celebration? She searched her mind and heart for a way to make his return what it should be, to make him understand they were all thrilled he was alive and home among them. Nothing seemed adequate.

"The neighbors all ask about you, Frank," Pearl said a bit too brightly. "They'll be glad to hear you're home."

Frank pushed the last bit of crust on his plate about with his fork. "Did you finish the harvesting today?"

"No," Jason answered. "I think tomorrow will be the last day. We'll move on to Thor's when we're done here."

Frank's chair scraped across the linoleum as he pushed it back. "I'm pretty bushed. If you don't mind, I'm going to turn in."

In an unintelligible jumble, Pearl, Jason, and Maggie assured him all at once that of course they didn't mind.

Frank picked up his satchel and walked across the large kitchen, toward the door to the steps that led upstairs.

Amy watched him, her heart racing. He couldn't leave without speaking to her, if only a few words. She couldn't bear it. She willed him to turn around with each step.

When he reached the door to the stairway, he set down his satchel, then reached for the brass door handle.

Pearl was up in a flash. "You'll need a lamp. I'll light one for you."

Amy pushed her chair back and hurried across the room. She knew the family was watching, that they would hear every word, but she was beyond caring. She wanted to fling her arms around Frank and hold him until he could feel her love passing between them.

Instead she reached for his hand. He shrank back a bit from her touch but not completely. Was he afraid to show rudeness to her in front of his family? she wondered. She folded her hands around his hand and spoke quietly. "I'm glad you're home. I hate the things you've endured, but I'm so glad you're alive and back with us. I love you."

Time seemed to stretch forever while she waited for him to respond. His gaze searched hers somewhat warily. She thought he grew more tired before her eyes. "I'm all in, Amy. Can we talk another time?"

"Of course."

He tugged his hand lightly, and she released it.

Jason came across the kitchen with a newly lit kerosene lamp, and he and Frank headed upstairs.

The ache in Amy's chest grew to enormous proportions. *He didn't say he loves me, not once.*

❧

Frank set his satchel on the floor beside the bed. A colorful, light-weight quilt protected the double bed, though the weather was too warm to sleep under it. Frank sat down on the bed with a grunt, while Jason set the lamp on an oak stand near the head of the bed. Along the wall opposite the bed stood the simple oak washstand, a linen towel hanging on the side next to Andy's razor strap, and a white galvanized bowl and pitcher on top beside Andy's razor.

Frank brushed the palm of his hand across his bearded chin. He didn't care for the beard, but he didn't trust himself to shave with his left hand.

Lace curtains waved gently at the open windows. The wonderful smells of a summer night on a Minnesota farm—smells of earth and animals that he'd missed for more than a year—drifted into the room. An owl hooted in the night. The windmill creaked background music.

"Room looks the same as it did the night I left."

Jason turned. "Not much changes around here." His Adam's apple jerked as he swallowed. "About the threshing tomorrow—"

Frank tried not to sigh. It exhausted him just to think about facing simple questions like this. He rested his right ankle on his left knee and tugged at his boot. "I don't think I'd be much help. I wear out pretty fast these days. Amazing how getting wounded takes the stuffing out of you."

"Sure. 'Course you'd be tired. Anyone would be."

Frank grimaced at Jason's stumbling.

"Uh, do you need help with . . . anything . . . before I head to bed?" Jason asked.

"No. I can get my clothes off. Takes a bit of jerking and twisting, but I can do it. Good night."

"Yeah." Jason walked slowly to the door and turned around. "What Amy said downstairs, that goes for me, too. I wish this . . . this . . ."

"I lost my arm. You can say it."

Frank and Jason stared at each other. They didn't break their gaze as Jason continued slowly, "I'm sorry, sorrier than I've ever been about anything in my life, that you lost your arm. If it had to happen to one of us, I wish it were me."

"Don't pity me." Frank's anger flashed full-blown and brought him to his feet.

Jason flinched and raised an arm in a swift motion as if to protect himself.

Does he think I'm going to attack him? Frank wondered, then reminded his brother, "I knew the risks when I enlisted."

"Yes, I guess you did." Jason lowered his arm. His shoulders drooped.

He looks as weary as I feel, Frank thought, so he tried to keep the anger from his voice as he said, "You'd better get some sleep. You've had a long day, and tomorrow won't be any shorter with all the harvesting."

Jason nodded and reached for the door handle. "I'm glad you made it back alive. I laid awake many nights fearing I'd never see you again, praying you'd come back." He raised his arms slightly and let them drop back to his sides. "Good night."

As Jason turned to leave, Frank thought he saw the lamplight reflect from tears in Jason's eyes. The moment was so brief that Frank wondered whether he'd imagined the tears.

Pity. The one thing above all he wanted to avoid, that he knew people would feel, that he didn't want them to feel for him.

He rubbed his eyes with his thumb and forefinger as he heard the door close gently behind Jason. *It's not true*, Frank thought. *It's not true that I knew the risks when I enlisted. I knew there was a risk I'd die and wouldn't be able to spend a lifetime with Amy. I thought if I made it back,*

I'd pick up my life where I laid it down when I left. I never thought I'd come back like this.

The anger at Jason dissolved, leaving Frank even more tired. He sat down on the edge of the bed. *I've bungled it badly. I should have written them about my arm. Shouldn't have sprung it on them this way.*

But each time he'd thought of putting it down with ink on paper, he'd panicked. Once the words were written, his loss would become too real. He'd be forced to face his fears about the way people would react, the fear that they'd stop seeing him as Frank and start seeing him as Frank-the-man-with-one-arm.

And there was Amy. He hadn't wanted her to have a chance for pretense, to pretty-up her reaction. He'd wanted to know her true and honest feelings. Maybe that had been unfair, but he wasn't sorry for his choice.

Leaning back against the pillows, he pulled his watch from his pocket. He pressed his thumb against the trip mechanism, and the cover popped open. His gaze lingered on Amy's image as he held the case near the warm lamp. With a sigh, he set the open watch down on the bedside table.

When he'd awakened in the hospital after the surgery on his arm, the first thing he'd asked for was his watch. He'd fumbled to open it. It had stopped.

He let himself relive the moment Amy recognized him, the joy in her voice, the way it felt to be in her arms again, the soft, eager kisses against his cheek. If he didn't experience anything else good for the rest of his life, he'd have that moment—the memory of her gladness at seeing him again.

It would need to be enough.

❧

Amy stared out her bedroom window at the dark, shrub-covered hillside behind the building. She released the lace curtains she'd been fingering and hugged herself, sorrow overflowing in tears but never lessening.

The room was dark. Clouds covered the moon. Amy's heart felt as devoid of light as the world about her.

She hadn't known it was possible to hurt this much. For over a year she'd longed and prayed for Frank's return. Now he was home. Or was he?

It was as though he'd built a wall between them. She saw the wall reflected in his eyes, felt it in the way he drew back from her touch. Had he stopped loving her? She'd always heard that absence made the heart grow fonder, but Frank's absence appeared to have separated them not only in body but in heart.

Tears fogged her view through the window. She drew a shaky breath and moved to the bed, fingering the button at the collar of her white shirtwaist.

I should wash up and change into a nightgown, she thought, *but I'm so weary.*

She lay down on the old pink satin comforter. The faint scent of lavender rising from the lace-edged pillowcases didn't hide the cooking odors still in her hair and clothing. She twisted a tendril that had come loose from the topknot earlier that day.

"Oh, my." Realization stilled her finger. Dismay swirled through her stomach. She hadn't thought until now what a mess she'd been when she greeted Frank. As much as she wished she'd looked her best for him, she knew his distance wasn't caused by her mussed hair and rumpled, sweaty blouse and skirt.

"I don't think I can bear it if he no longer loves me, Lord," she whispered into the darkness. She tried to picture the future without Frank and couldn't see a future. "Let him still love me, please." She wanted to repeat the prayer and repeat it again, then again, as if repeating the request would increase the likelihood God would answer as she wished.

If we'd married before Frank left, he would have come home to me instead of the farm. I could have held him and surrounded him with love, maybe enough love to absorb his pain or at least to lessen it.

What but love—hers, his family's, and his friends'—could help ease the pain and fear of learning to live without his arm? He was obviously pushing away her love and his family's. Was he pushing away God's love, too?

Please heal his heart, Lord.

In the face of Frank's pain, the other prayer her heart persisted to cry out—that God would keep Frank's love for her alive—seemed selfish.

She yearned for sleep to come and anesthetize her fears, but it didn't. She turned her mind away from her fears and chose instead to remember the moments beside the buggy when she and Frank held each other close, and there was nothing in her heart but joy, thanksgiving, and great love.

7

rank laid back in the tall prairie grass beside the pond and breathed deeply, luxuriating in the scent of wild grass, prairie flowers, and earth. He stared into the cloudless morning sky and felt his heart almost burst in gratitude that he was back in the place he loved best, back in a place of peace.

He shifted his broad-brimmed felt hat over his forehead and closed his eyes, sighing in contentment. Here no one would order him to shoot someone. Here he needn't dodge bullets or swords. Here he needn't quiet his breathing to hear whether the enemy was near. Here he could relax amid the medley composed of the chirping of crickets and grasshoppers that crawled benignly over him, booming prairie chickens that hid beneath the waving grass, croaking toads on fallen logs, and warbling red-winged blackbirds that bounced on pussy willows at the pond's edge.

He felt rich amid the ordinariness of the prairie.

Abruptly his hat lifted, and rays from the early morning sun fell full on his face. His eyelids flew open.

His brown hat dangled inelegantly above him from the mouth of his favorite cow. He grabbed for the hat, his laughter ringing out. "Sudsy, you remember our game."

Frank stood up, settled his hat back on his head, and rubbed Sudsy behind one ear. With a sigh, he started back to the farmstead, the tall grass bending beneath his boots.

He was entering the barn when he heard horse hooves, the creak of a harness, and the rattle of wheels. He turned to see who was driving into the yard. Amy.

For a moment, he felt frozen to the spot. Impulsively, he stepped into the barn. Maybe she hadn't seen him.

He took a deep breath, closed his eyes, and clenched his fist. This was ridiculous. As much as he wanted to hide in the dark depths of the barn from the rest of the world, he couldn't do that forever. "Might just as well get used to facing people right off."

No one he'd rather see less at this moment than Amy. "Probably why she's here," he muttered, opening the heavy door. "Some sense of humor You've got, Lord."

Amy was already climbing down from the buggy, her back to him. She steadied herself with one hand, while the other hand held the skirt of her blue-and-white-checked cotton dress out of the way.

He stepped up behind her. "Let me help you." He reached to grasp the elbow of the arm with which she clutched her skirt.

He missed as Amy gasped and turned her head quickly to look over her shoulder. "My, you startled me."

He reached for her elbow again to steady her, and this time he succeeded. Memories of the many times he'd helped her from buggies and wagons, often catching her to himself with both arms for a stolen kiss, filled his chest with painful longing. The gentle floral scent she wore increased his awareness of her. Her straw hat, decorated simply with a ribbon that matched the pale blue in her dress, hid her face while she watched her step.

As soon as Amy stood steadily on the ground beside him, he released her elbow.

"Thank you, Frank." She looked up at him, her green eyes searching his face. Was she wondering why he hadn't sought her out last night?

Uncomfortable under her scrutiny, he shifted his weight and peered into the buggy. "Anything in here you need?"

"Only the aprons that are lying on the seat."

He stepped up, balancing carefully, and reached for the aprons. A wooden easel caught his attention. When he handed her the aprons, he indicated the easel with a jerk of his head. "Why did you bring your painting things?"

"They're still in the buggy from yesterday." Amy's gaze darted away, and she shook her head, laughing softly. "Yesterday was my first day helping during threshing. I've been wanting to paint a field scene and thought I might have time yesterday in between rushes of work. I'm sure you know how mistaken I was in the belief there'd be empty time to fill."

He chuckled, genuinely amused at her sweet innocence and ignorance of farm ways. Almost immediately followed a sense of surprise that she'd so soon and easily slipped under the barricade he'd set up against her.

Quickly, he reached for the driving rein. "I'll take care of your horse. You can go on up to the house." The words came out in a harder tone than he'd intended. *Perhaps that's best*, he thought.

"Pearl showed me how to unharness yesterday. I can help you."

"I don't need your help." Anger sprang up with the quickness of lightning. It was bad enough he wasn't carrying his share of the threshing. "I don't need help from a woman to unharness a horse and rub it down. I've been doing this since I was knee-high to a grasshopper."

Amy looked as if he'd struck her.

He pressed his lips together hard to keep back the apology that leaped from his heart and turned to his work. She'd accept more easily what he had to say later if he allowed this wound to fester.

After caring for Amy's horse, Frank sat in a pile of fresh straw inside the barn. Rubbing down a horse had never wearied him this much before. He could hardly keep his eyes open.

The sound of the draft horses from the field being led into the barn awakened him. He stood up almost before he was fully awake, not willing to be caught sleeping by his brothers or by any of the others who'd spent the morning working hard in the fields.

He stepped around the end of a stall and saw Andy and Jason with the horses. "Need a little help there?"

His brothers glanced at each other, then at him. He understood that wary look. "I can rub down a horse and give it feed and water."

"Little help would be nice," Jason said evenly.

Frank found his will was stronger than his body. His nap hadn't restored the strength lost from his work with Amy's horse and the walk to and from the pasture with the cows. He was acutely aware that he performed far less than one-third of the work. By the time the brothers were ready for dinner, Frank's shirt and hair were soaked with sweat.

His heart beat wildly as he followed his brothers out to the planks-on-sawhorses tables where the workers had already finished their main meal and started on the pies. He grinned. *Haven't been this nervous since I first asked Amy to allow me to court her.*

He'd just as soon avoid meeting Thor and the hired workers—many of whom had worked the Sterling farm for years—but he figured he might as well get it over with. Have to happen sometime. Besides, if he was going to stay jittery about letting people see him with only one arm, he'd need to become a hermit.

The idea has its merits, he thought, watching heads swivel to face him.

Greetings poured forth from the gathered friends before Frank reached the washbasins on the back porch. He grinned, feeling self-conscious. "If you don't give me a chance to wash up, you better sit upwind of me, folks."

They laughed and allowed him time for a lick-and-a-promise wash job.

When he returned to the table with his brothers, the welcome-homes started all over. He nodded and smiled and shook hands awkwardly with his left hand as he walked toward an empty seat. He seated himself and began to fill his plate from the serving platters and bowls the women had replenished. "Sorry I'm not joining you fellas in the field today. Hate to seem a slacker. I'm mostly back to snuff but still wear out pretty quick."

Shifting bodies and ducked heads revealed the group's unease at his oblique reference to his injury.

"You weren't a slacker serving yer country," the bulky man beside him said fiercely.

"You betcha." Swedish Thor from the neighboring farm bobbed his head in agreement.

"This time next year we won't be able to keep up wit' you," a bald Norwegian across from him asserted.

Frank's heart warmed to their desire to make him feel normal and comfortable, though part of him held to resentment that, like his family, they appeared trying too hard to act cheerful and ignore his arm.

Pearl set a golden-crusted pie on the table. "Guess a war hero has a right to rest a bit." Her chin stuck out in belligerence, and her eyes flashed, challenging the men to contradict her.

"I'm hardly a hero." Frank dropped his gaze to his plate and stuffed a forkful of mashed potatoes into his mouth. Why did women say such fool things? He thought his sister-in-law was wiser than most about the things that hurt a man's pride.

"You are to us." Thor's soft Scandinavian accent didn't hide the sincerity behind his words.

"Lemonade, Frank?"

His heart skipped in surprise at finding Amy beside him with a creamy porcelain pitcher in one hand and a glass in the other. There was a small smile on her lips and question in her eyes. He sensed the question was more about what he felt toward her and how he would react to her than about lemonade.

"Lemonade would hit the spot, thanks."

He allowed himself to study her while she poured. The heart-shaped ruby in the ring he'd given her flashed in the sunlight. His heart crimped at the memory of the many dreams that ring represented. A white apron with ruffles and a couple small kitchen splotches now covered the blue-and-white-checked gown. He found it unexpectedly endearing to see her at his home looking so housewifely.

The domestic term frightened him. He couldn't allow himself to imagine her part of his everyday life in such a homey and wifely manner. He yanked his gaze from her.

Thor grinned. "When are you two hitching up?"

Even Frank's ears heated at the question. Hired hands watched with curious and laughing eyes.

Frank jabbed his fork at a piece of meat. "We haven't had time to discuss it. I only got back last night, you know."

"Better get her to the altar fast." Thor's advice was given with a laugh in his voice. "There are a couple young men in town itching for a chance to court her. They've held back out of respect while you were away serving your country, but if you don't marry her soon, you'll have a fight on your hands for her." Thor's eyes danced beneath his shaggy gray-blond brows.

Frank forced a grin and wondered what Amy, who still stood beside him, was thinking.

Amy's soft voice interrupted the laughter. "You might tell your friends that Frank Sterling is the only man for me."

Laughter erupted again as Amy moved to the next man to offer lemonade.

Guilt twisted Frank's heart, though he continued to grin to keep up the charade. To avoid facing Amy or the others, he gave his attention to pouring gravy over a second helping of potatoes. *When I was in the Philippines, I thought life was going to be easier if I ever returned home. Instead, I'm just dodging bullets of another kind.*

❧

Frank spent the afternoon alternately wandering familiar pastures and the edges of fields and taking catnaps, sometimes in the barn and sometimes in a fragrant, shady spot outdoors. He avoided the farmyard where the children played and the house filled with womenfolk. It distressed him that he fatigued so easily from such little physical effort. By suppertime, his shoulder and arm ached.

He joined the others for supper, finding it easier to face the group the second time. After the meal, the men went back to the fields to steal a couple more hours of work from the day. The women went back to the kitchen to clean up the dishes. Maggie and Grace went to the pasture to bring the cows back.

Frank sat beneath the maple tree. A small breeze had come up, rustling the leaves above him and chasing away the mosquitoes. He scratched the golden tabby cat in his lap. "Good old Gideon. I was gone so long I was sure you'd forget me. Old faithful, that's you." The one-eyed cat stretched its neck and kneaded Frank's thigh. "At least I know you don't care that I came back slightly the worse for wear."

He leaned his head back against the tree trunk and sighed. He'd told Amy they'd talk this evening. He dreaded that talk. "I'm going to need some help, Lord. It's going to take all the courage I can muster; a whole lot more courage than it took to go to war."

"What will take more courage than going to war?"

He started at Amy's question, and Gideon jumped from his lap. "I didn't hear you come up."

"You said you wanted to talk with me after supper."

"Yes." He stood up.

"So, what will take so much courage?" Amy repeated, smiling up at him.

He recognized the guard she put on her smile and knew it was caused by his abrupt attitude toward her thus far. With a sinking sensation in his chest, he realized that after this talk, he might never again receive the smile of complete welcome he was accustomed to from her.

8

*A*my clasped her hands together behind her. She was glad she'd bolstered her own courage by washing her face, straightening her hair, and dabbing a bit of Pearl's violet water to her wrists and neck.

She tried to hide her nervousness from Frank with a smile. He looked altogether too guilty for her comfort. "Apparently you intend to keep that object of courage a secret."

Frank hooked his thumb in his trouser pocket and rested his shoulder against the tree trunk. "It was nice of you to come out and help Pearl the last couple days."

"I'm glad to do it. Besides, I've so much to learn."

He frowned. "About what?"

"All the things a good farmer's wife needs to know." Amy spoke lightly, hoping to disguise the fear that caused her throat to feel as if her heart were lodged in it.

He took a deep breath.

Her fear multiplied.

"Amy, I don't think we should marry."

Her stomach tightened. "Why?"

"I'm not the man I was when I asked you to marry me."

Hope surged through her. He hadn't said the words she'd most feared. He hadn't said he no longer loved her. "You mean because of your arm? Surely you don't think something like that could change my love for you." Impulsively, she stepped closer to him and rested the palm of her hand on the front of his shirt. She could feel his heart beat. "It's your heart I love. Losing an arm can't change your heart."

"Don't be too sure."

His sharp tone jerked her gaze to his eyes. Their usual brown color looked black with emotion.

"War does change people, whether they're wounded or not."

"But—"

"I don't know what my life is going to be like from here on out. I don't even know whether I'll be able to support myself, let alone a wife and family."

"Other men do, men like Slim. Well, Slim doesn't have a wife and family, but he has a job."

"He's a store clerk."

She couldn't suppress a smile. "Aren't store clerks as respectable as farmers?"

"The job's not as physically demanding."

"I know it will take time to learn to do things with one hand." She raised her gaze to his and gentled her voice. "I'll wait as long as you feel you need, but I would rather marry soon. People who love each other need to be beside each other at times like this."

"You don't understand." His voice was as quiet as hers had been.

The fear that hope had routed only a minute earlier gripped her again. Since she threw herself into his arms when he arrived the night before, he hadn't hugged her. He hadn't kissed her once. Even now he hadn't touched her.

"I'm not asking to postpone the wedding, Amy. I'm saying I'm not going to marry you."

"But I told you, it doesn't make any difference to me that you lost your arm." Her fingers clutched his shirt.

"It makes a difference to me."

"You know that I mean it doesn't make any difference in how I feel about you."

"And I mean that it makes a difference in whether I want to marry you."

The conversation was spiraling out of control. Amy took a deep breath, but it barely lessened the panic in her breast. "If you'd lost your arm in a farming accident or even in the war after we married, you wouldn't expect me to reject my vows or stop loving you, would you?"

"There's no sense imagining situations. We have to live with life as it is."

Amy could barely hear herself think for the roar fear made in her ears. She pressed her fingers against her temples and stared over Frank's shoulder, trying to bring clarity to her thoughts.

"Amy, I'm sorry, but it's for the best."

She wanted to slip her arms around his neck and hug him close until he admitted he still cared for her, that it was only his silly fears that made him change his mind about the wedding. How could she hug him when he was trying to push her out of his life?

She lowered her hands. Her gaze searched his. "You haven't said you no longer love me."

He continued to meet her gaze evenly.

Her heart regained its equilibrium. "You *do* still love me."

"It wouldn't be loving to marry you now. You'd be marrying a stranger. I told you, I'm not the same man who left here over a year ago. I don't want you to marry me, then discover you don't love who I am now. What if you found you didn't love me and stayed with me out of pity or duty? You deserve a better life than that."

She didn't believe he wasn't the same person, but he kept insisting it was so. She studied his face, looking for answers she couldn't find. "Do you think it is noble to give up our dream of a life together?"

His gaze didn't falter, but he didn't answer.

"You do think it's noble." The knowledge sent anger pouring through her veins. "I don't think it's noble. I think it's horrid that you are turning away the greatest thing, the only thing, I have to give."

How could she convince him their love was strong enough to survive his wound? Her mind was too filled with pain and anger to think clearly. The realization she was shaking increased her frustration. "If this is what you choose, there's nothing left to say."

"It's what I choose."

The soft, even tone chilled her as much as his words. "Good-bye then."

She started toward the house to collect her things. After half a dozen steps, she turned around. Frank was standing where she'd left him, watching her as she'd known he would be. "I guess you've changed after all. The Frank Sterling I know would never have walked away from us. He was convinced through and through that God meant us to be together, that we were God's gifts to each other. The Frank Sterling I know believed in us. He would have slain dragons to keep us together."

He simply stared at her with those dark eyes and the look other girls had called brooding when they were in school. She'd always felt she could read his heart in his eyes. Now he wanted to keep her out of his heart and its secrets.

Amy whirled and headed for the house again. Andy opened the screen door when she reached it. She gave him a large smile. "Would you have time to hitch up my buggy?"

"Sure, glad to do it. I can ride into town with you, too."

"Thank you, but I don't think that's necessary."

Andy smiled. "I forgot. I suppose Frank will be driving you home."

"No, but it's not dark yet. The sky is clear, and the twilight should be bright enough for me to drive safely." Amy was glad it wasn't dark yet. It would be mortifying if she started crying in front of Andy on the way home.

She kept her smile in place as she hurried through the warm kitchen, still redolent with baking and cooking odors, past Pearl, who was putting away dishes and pans. Her face felt tight with her smile, and her eyes wide and hot with tears that wanted to escape.

In Pearl and Jason's bedroom, she retrieved her hat. She turned to the mirror but barely noticed her reflection as she positioned the hat on her head. "Ouch."

"Did you hurt yourself?" Pearl's anxious question broke into Amy's jumbled thoughts.

"Stuck myself with the hat pin." Amy placed the pin properly on her second attempt, though it took an effort to control her shaking fingers. She smoothed her hands over her hips, hoping to keep the shaking from Pearl's notice. "There, I think I'm ready to go now."

Pearl gave Amy's shoulders a gentle squeeze. "What's wrong? Did you and Frank argue?"

Amy didn't want to answer. To put Frank's decision into words might give it life. But Pearl was her best friend, and likely Frank would tell her and the family of his decision soon anyway. Had he told them already? "He doesn't want to marry me."

The shock on Pearl's face assured Amy that her friend hadn't known of Frank's decision. "He can't mean that, Amy. He's loved you for years. You're the only girl he's cared for in his entire life."

"Nevertheless, he insists he won't marry me."

Pearl's arms enclosed Amy in a hug. "He's just upset about . . . about his arm and all. He'll change his mind when he's feeling better. I'm sure he will."

Amy held tightly to her friend. "I hope so." The words sounded thick with the tears Amy struggled to suppress. "Will you walk out to the buggy with me? I don't think I can speak to Frank now should he still be there."

"Of course."

Amy picked up her ecru lace reticule from the bed and slid its strings over her wrist. In the kitchen she retrieved her dirtied aprons from the wooden peg beside the door. She wished good night to Grace. Then she stepped quickly through the doorway onto the porch. She wanted to escape into a solitary place and examine her conversation with Frank piece by piece. Perhaps she'd missed something. Perhaps she could find a way back for them.

Relief and regret mixed within her when she saw Frank still standing under the maple. She turned her gaze from him and walked quickly beside Pearl to the buggy.

"He's all ready for you." Andy patted the horse's neck. "If you want to wait for a few minutes, I can drive into town behind you. We forgot all about returning the buggy and horse Frank rented from the livery last night."

"That's a kind offer, but I think I'll start out right away." Amy was glad no one was insisting on driving back in the buggy with her. "It's nice to know that you'll be coming along behind me soon in case I have trouble, though."

Pearl gave her another hug. "I'll be praying."

Amy hugged her tighter, surprised to find she didn't want to let go of this friend who cared about her pain. She recognized the gift in holding someone now that she was deprived of hugging Frank.

She drew a shaky breath and released her friend. "Do you need my help tomorrow?"

"No. The men are done here for the time being. Tomorrow they start on Thor's farm."

"I'm sure Frank will find that a relief." So did she.

She refused to allow herself to look toward Frank when she directed the horse toward the drive. As she left the farmyard behind, it felt as though she was leaving the only whole and unhurt part of herself behind as well. The woman she took with her was only shards of the woman who had waited all these long months for Frank to return from war.

❧

Frank leaned against the tree and watched Amy ride off down the drive in the twilight. It felt as though someone's fist was wrapped around his heart. "I'm not sorry," he whispered. "I'd do it again in a minute. She'll be happier this way in the end."

She deserved a whole man, a man who could support her well. One day she'd see that for herself. He'd rather it wasn't as his wife. He couldn't bear the thought of someday looking into her eyes and seeing, instead of love, distaste or pity or resignation.

He could still see the pain and disbelief in her eyes when he'd told her he wouldn't marry her. Her pain had sliced into his heart. It had taken all his strength not to take back the words, not to catch her close and say nothing on earth could ever make him leave her.

It hurts her now, but she'll get over that. He brought his hand to his chest. *I'll get over it, too, one day. Hearts don't really break.*

Yes, they do, a thought slipped through.

But it couldn't be true, because he could feel his heart beat. It was as strong now as the day he was born, though his heart felt crushed.

We'll get over this. When we're sixty and gray-haired, we'll run into each other at the general store or church and smile when we remember how once we thought we couldn't live without each other.

"But for now, please help her, Lord. Help us both."

❧

The men moved along to Thor's farm with the jointly owned thresh-ing rig the next day, but there was still work to do in the Sterlings' fields. When Jason and Andy headed off to the neighboring farm, Frank headed to the Sterlings' oat field and began tipping shock butts to the sun to dry out the dampness from the ground.

Like most fieldwork, the chore had always been time consuming and tiring, but his muscles had mostly been up to the work from the time he was a boy. Today he started out with every muscle in his body screaming, already worn from yesterday's toll.

He forced himself to work through the pain. He was glad for a chance to experiment with different ways of handling the shocks be-fore working in front of his brothers' and others' eyes. After a bit of trying, he found he could use the top of his short arm to help balance the shock and do the work of turning with his hand. The first time it worked, joy jolted through him. He'd done it!

The joy remained through the next hour, but it became a calmer joy. His muscles continued to protest as he pushed them to obey his urgent need to become a useful member of the family again. He kept checking the height of the sun, wondering whether it had always moved so slowly in its path across the sky.

He stopped earlier than usual for the cheese, bread, and apple lunch he'd brought out to the field in a tin pail. His body insisted on the nourishment. He took some powders for the pain in his arm, washing them down with a drink of water.

The sun was barely halfway to its noon height, and already his shirt was soaked with sweat. He was tempted to remove it, but he hadn't kerosene with him to keep away the bugs. Not caring to be-come their lunch, he kept his shirt on.

Satisfaction filled him with sweet calm when he looked on the shocks he'd tipped. He went back to work with his energy slightly restored but his muscles still protesting. Now that he had the hang of tipping the shocks, his mind wandered more often from his work. Its destination was always Amy.

Fatigue and pain drove him home from the field earlier than in the past. He barely had energy to wash up before climbing the stairs to his room and throwing himself across the quilt-covered bed. His last thought before falling asleep was that, if God especially blessed him, his dreams would be free of the girl he loved and the pain of separation from her.

❧

Frank left the noise of wagons, buggies, and horses behind and entered Dr. Strong's pharmacy with Pearl. He'd only been home a week, but that short time working in the fields had been rough on his weakened muscles. Hope for relief brought him to the doctor. He left Pearl at a display of kerosene lamps near the front of the store and proceeded toward the back of the shop and the door to Dr. Strong's adjoining office.

It's almost as much a general store as a pharmacy, he thought with amusement as he passed a glass display counter with dainty porcelain gift boxes. Shelves filled with jars of every shape and size—clear, opaque, or clay—lined the walls behind the cabinets. Flowing black script on the jars identified herbs, salves, and other remedies.

A small wooden sign on the office door announced a patient within. A short oak bench beside the door invited him, as the next patient, to wait in relative comfort. Frank chose to browse the store instead.

He stopped short at the sight of Amy. She stood in front of a shelf of shaving mugs, her back to him. He wobbled between speaking to her or going back to the bench and hoping she wouldn't see him. He longed to talk with her, if only to hear her voice again, but how would she react? He hadn't seen her since their confrontation at the farm last week.

Talking with her won the battle. He removed his broad-brimmed brown hat. His boots sounded loud to him as he crossed the wooden floor, but she didn't turn around. He stopped behind her and cleared his throat.

"I'd like this mug, please." She turned around with a large porcelain shaving mug in her hands and a friendly smile on her face. The smile froze when she saw him. "You."

"Morning, Amy."

"I thought you were the clerk. I'm buying a gift for Father. It's his birthday. His shaving mug is chipped and—"

"I'm sure he'll like this one." He hadn't often seen her this flustered. She looked tired. The rich green of her dress accented the green in her eyes but didn't disguise the circles beneath those eyes. Wasn't she sleeping well?

"Mrs. Johansen, who used to be our cook, is baking a cake. With all my practice my cakes still can't compare to hers. Of course, she has won the blue ribbon at the county fair for her cakes for the last five years running."

"Amy—"

"She's joining us for dinner. That will be nice. We don't invite company as often as we once did."

"Amy—"

She paused in her uncharacteristic chatter. A slight frown creased her brow. "What are you doing in town in the middle of the morning?"

"I came to see Dr. Matt."

Her gaze dropped to his arm.

"Yes, because of my arm." He took a deep breath. "Truth is, they gave me morphine in the hospital."

Her gaze flew to his, and her eyes widened. "Morphine?"

He nodded, trying to appear nonchalant about it. "I've heard tales of what happens to men who keep taking morphine. I refused it as soon as I could bear the pain without it, though some of the doctors recommended I continue it. I'm out of the strong pain powders I finally talked them into giving me instead. I'm hoping Dr. Matt can give me something."

"I hope so, too."

"Amy, how fortunate I ran into you." Pearl walked up to them briskly, her yellow-and-white dress a spot of cheer in the dark shop.

"Do you still want to learn how to refresh the collar and cuffs on your dresses?"

"Yes, but I realize you haven't time to teach me now."

"Things are still busy at the farm. They will be for months. I have enough time to help you, though."

"That would be wonderful. I probably need to buy some material and lace."

"We could look together while Frank is busy here. I have some items to pick up at the general store anyway." She lifted her brows in friendly question. "You don't mind meeting us there when you're done with Father, do you, Frank?"

"Of course not."

A creak notified Frank the doctor's office door was opening. A glance over his shoulder verified it. Gray-haired Dr. Matt stood in the doorway and smiled at an equally gray-haired woman while patting her hand in a reassuring manner.

"I'd better grab him before someone else does."

Pearl grinned and shook her head. "I want to say hello to Father first. I promise to only take a moment." She hurried toward the doctor.

"Rather nice to have a doctor in the family, isn't it?" Amy smiled at Frank. "He gives everyone the best of his services, of course, but I imagine even good-hearted doctors have a special place in their hearts for family."

"Hard to imagine what Pearl's life would have been like if Dr. Matt and his wife hadn't taken her and her brother into their home when their father left." Frank shook his head. "I never understood how any man could leave a two-year-old daughter and a five-year-old son, just walk away and never come back."

"It seems especially cruel that he left right after their mother died. You'd never suspect that Pearl's life started that way. She has such a positive outlook on life."

A glimmer of hope slid into Frank's heart. If Pearl could heal from such wounds, surely it was possible for God to heal him, too. Frank pulled his thoughts back to the present. "Wish your father a happy birthday for me," he said to Amy.

He wished he were celebrating it with them. Then again, he

thought as he crossed to the office, her father would probably rather strike him down than share a meal with him. Not many fathers merrily welcomed men who walked out on their daughters.

Slim was seated on the oak bench when Frank left Dr. Matt's office a few minutes later. The old veteran stood up with a stiff, jerky movement, but if his joints hurt, his face didn't reveal it. A smile shone from a myriad of wrinkles. "Young Sterling, as I live and breathe. If you ain't a sight for sore eyes, I don't know what is." He reached out with his right hand to shake Frank's, realized his error, and held out his left instead.

Frank put his hat on his head to free his hand to shake with Slim. "Good to see you."

Dr. Matt leaned against the doorpost. "You here to see me, Slim?"

"Sure am, Doc. Like to take a minute to talk with our hero here first, if you don't mind."

Doc nodded. "You know where to find me." He entered his office and left the two veterans alone.

A quick glance about the store assured Frank that Pearl and Amy had left. He had time to talk. "Appreciate the sentiment, Slim, but I'm hardly a hero."

Slim's smile disappeared. "I know what war is like. Every soldier is a hero. Either that or a fool or both."

Frank chuckled. "Both, I think."

"Probably so. Saw you talking to that pretty young lady of yours earlier. Yes, sir, you're a lucky man coming home to her."

"She's a fine woman, that's certain, but she's no longer mine."

"Throw you over when you came home with that arm?" He didn't wait for an answer. "Well, good riddance to her, I say. Women are all alike beneath those soft, sweet faces. My girl did the same to me when I came home from the war with this." He slapped his palm against the thigh above the wooden leg. "Said she wanted a whole man. Said she knew I'd understand."

Frank's stomach turned over. "I'm sorry." It was the first he'd heard of this woman. How had Slim endured her betrayal? If Amy had acted that way . . . "You never married?"

"Met a couple ladies I considered courting. In the end, I just couldn't trust them." He leaned closer and said in a loud whisper. "I don't tell that to just anyone, you know."

"I'll keep your confidence."

"Sorry about Miss Henderson. I thought she was the type to stick by a man no matter what."

It seemed cruel to correct Slim's misconception that Frank was a fellow victim of a betraying woman, but to allow it to stand was unfair to Amy. The way gossip flew around this town, if he didn't straighten out the facts, everyone would be prattling off the wrong story by lamp-lighting time.

Frank cleared his throat. "You're right about Amy. She isn't the type of woman to walk away from a man because he loses an arm. I don't want people thinking she is. I'm the one who walked away."

"You have a woman like that and you walk away?" Slim crossed his arms over his chest and shook his head.

"Excuse me." A plump woman in her forties stopped beside them. "Are you two waiting to see the doctor?"

"Doc's waiting on me," Slim informed her. "Best get in there." He nodded at Frank. "Glad you got back, even if you aren't all in one piece. And I'm not talking about your arm." He pointed at his head and chuckled as he stepped toward the office door.

Frank didn't join in the chuckle. Thoughts of the woman who betrayed Slim clung to him as he went about his day. Thank the Lord, Amy hadn't been repulsed by him. Adjusting to a future without her was difficult enough under the present circumstances. He could only imagine the depth of the pain if that bleak future was the result of Amy's revulsion.

Maybe Slim was right. Maybe he was a fool to walk away from Amy. But his love for her meant he wanted life's best for her.

His boots clunked against the boardwalk as he walked toward the general store. *Please give her a beautiful life, Lord. And if it's not too late after all these years, please heal Slim's heart.*

His own heart clenched. *Will I end up bitter like Slim because I walked away from Amy's love?*

9

"ello, Amy." Pearl looked across the kitchen from where she stirred a large pot with a wooden spoon. Little Viola perched on one of her mother's hips and stared diligently into the pot. "I saw Maggie helping you with your buggie and horse, or I would have gone out to help you."

Maggie patted Amy's arm. "She's getting good at unhitching."

Amy set her basket on the kitchen table. "I think you're flattering me. I do believe I'm getting better at it, but I'm still not comfortable doing it myself. I'm afraid I'll undo something in the wrong order and mess myself up."

She crossed the room and held out her arms. "Hello, Viola. May I hold you today?"

Viola shifted her wide-eyed gaze from the bubbling pot to Amy, considered the offer in silence, then with a sudden move leaned toward Amy. The women laughed as Amy drew the girl into her arms. "You are the sweetest thing." Amy dropped a kiss onto Viola's forehead.

"She's been a rascal today," Pearl confided. "Every time I turned my back for even the briefest moment, she'd find something dangerous."

"The beetle wasn't dangerous," Maggie protested with a grin. "Just untasty."

Amy wrinkled her nose. "Ish."

Pearl nodded. "Exactly."

"This looks much better than beetles." Amy glanced at the golden mixture bubbling on the stove. "Mmm. Applesauce."

"Mmm." Viola pressed her lips together and moved them back and forth. "Mmm."

The women laughed, delighted by the girl's simple imitation.

Pearl lifted her eyebrows and smiled at the girl. "Where is Amy?"

Viola frowned slightly, then pushed a pudgy finger into Amy's cheek.

"That's right," Pearl praised. "Can you say Amy?"

Viola's finger went into her mouth. "Mmm."

Maggie brushed her hand across Viola's curls. "Don't feel bad. She can't say Maggie yet, either, and I work on it every day with her."

"Uh. Uh." The little girl wiggled in Amy's arms.

Amy laughed. "She gets her ideas across pretty well without words. I think she wants to get down, but I don't dare put her down here so close to the hot stove."

Maggie reached for Viola. "I'll take her outside."

Amy's heart felt the emptiness when Viola settled into Maggie's arms. She'd so often dreamed of raising children with Frank. Now that dream appeared dead, along with so many others.

"I do worry about this winter," Pearl confided as the screen door banged closed behind Maggie. "Now that Viola's learned to walk, she usually runs instead. Even with all of us watching, she's almost too quick for us sometimes. Can't let our guard down for a minute. This winter the stove will be heated almost all the time and the parlor stove, too. I told Jason we should fence them off. I was only partly in jest."

"I'm sure you will all watch over her and keep her safe."

Pearl sighed. "We try."

"Where are Grace and Chalmers?"

"I sent them outside to play. Chalmers has been into trouble all day today, just like his little sister. He was determined to help Andy carry out the pail of stove ashes this morning. Of course, he tripped on the porch steps."

"Did he hurt himself?"

"No, but he was gray from head to toe."

Amy smiled. "You're very fortunate, you know, to have this wonderful family."

A sweet smile grew slowly across Pearl's face. "Yes, I do know."

"I wasn't sure whether I should come out today."

"Why? I expected you. You aren't in the least in the way."

"I don't think Frank would agree. Is . . . is he home?"

"He's outside somewhere. Probably in the barn. I never saw a man or child who loves animals the way Frank does." Pearl pulled the iron pot to a covered burner. "This can cool now. Let's move the table and a couple chairs over by the window. We'll be able to see our stitches better there, and it will be cooler."

Amy settled her chair beside the window, welcoming the breeze, which caused the curtains to wave gently into the room. She glanced up at a sampler on the nearby wall. "I've always loved that sampler. 'Charity hopeth all things.'"

"Frank and Jason's mother made it." Pearl leaned against the back of her chair and looked at the sampler. "I treasure it. It was a great strength to me during the months right after Jason and I married."

"It must have been difficult. You not only married Jason but his family."

"That wasn't the difficult part. At least, it didn't seem difficult. I don't think I've ever told anyone the truth about Jason's proposal."

Amy touched Pearl's arm gently. "You needn't confide anything in me unless you want to."

"I want to." Pearl took a deep breath. "As you know, I loved Jason since we were children. I was ecstatic when he asked me to marry him. But almost as soon as I said yes, he indicated he wanted a wife to help him with his younger brothers and sisters. His parents had died only a few weeks earlier. Then I realized he hadn't said he loved me. He didn't mention love at all before he asked me to marry him or for a long time after the wedding."

Amy stared at Pearl, shocked. "But he is so in love with you. It's in the way he looks at you and moves around you so naturally and, well, just everything about the way he is around you."

A blush brightened Pearl's cheeks. "Now, perhaps, but not back then. I asked the Lord to let Jason love me. And I kept hoping. I read every verse on hope in the Bible I could find. I needed to know more about hope because it was so hard for me to hope for Jason's love." She laid her hand over Amy's. "I'll be hoping for you and Frank, too."

Tears welled up in Amy's eyes. "Thank you." She took a deep

breath and lifted the linen towel from its protective position on top of the basket. "We'd best start our work."

Amy pulled the yellow linen gown from the basket. "I probably shouldn't waste the time on this one. Summer is almost over."

"There'll be more hot days yet. This is the gown we bought the lace for, isn't it?"

Pearl explained how Amy could replace the frayed linen cuffs with ruffled lace. Amy gave her full attention. Seated on the oak kitchen chair, she began removing the cuff with care so she didn't tear the sleeve.

Pearl brought a man's brown cotton shirt out, sat down beside Amy, and began removing the shirt collar. "This needs turning," she explained in response to Amy's questioning look. "There's a sheet that needs redoing, too, but I haven't time for that today."

"A sheet?"

"Yes. The middle is quite worn."

"How can you hide that?"

"I can't hide it, but I can make it last longer. I'll tear it down the middle and restitch it back together with the edges in the middle."

"You are a marvel, Pearl Sterling."

"Hardly that."

Amy lifted the detached yellow linen cuffs. "There. Now what?"

Pearl showed her how to place the lace, overlapping it at even intervals to form a dainty ruffle, anchoring the lace with pins. The stitch required was simple but tiny.

Amy worked at the table, her concentration wholly given to pinning the lace. When she completed pinning it to one sleeve, she placed her porcelain thimble on her finger and began making careful stitches.

She shook her head, keeping her attention on her work. "I am so ignorant. I never knew people redid their clothes and sheets. I barely know how to sew. Maybe Frank is right not to marry me. Maybe he needs a wife who knows all the things I don't."

"That's only your fear talking. Frank needs a wife who loves him as much as you love him."

Amy managed a shaky smile. "That's what you always say. I'm glad you do."

" 'Charity hopeth all things.' "

"Maybe it would be wiser for me not to hope, but I don't know how. Most of the time I'm certain Frank will come to his senses and realize we are meant to be together. I keep reminding myself that I have to be strong for him. I always knew there's much for me to learn to be the farm wife he needs. But now it's even more important when chores are so much more difficult and time consuming for him. I'll need to take care of the house and garden and chickens. Will you teach me to milk a cow?" She looked up from her stitching.

Pearl laughed. "I'm afraid not. Frank tried to teach me once. Jason was furious. He said he didn't want his wife to smell like cows." She leaned forward, her eyes sparkling, and dropped her voice slightly. "I thought it a rather good reason not to do the milking."

Amy joined her in a chuckle, but she didn't change her mind. Things were different for her and Frank—or they would be when Frank remembered God meant them to spend their lives together. If he remembered.

"Jason is awfully worried about Frank. We all are, but Jason especially. They were so close growing up, though for a time after their parents died, there was a rift between them."

Amy nodded. "Frank told me. He thought Jason was trying to take over their father's place in the family. Frank wanted to go to school to learn more about agriculture, and Jason told him they couldn't afford it."

"Since Jason is the oldest, he naturally felt the responsibility of running the farm and caring for the family fell to him."

"All Frank could see was his world falling apart." Amy understood Pearl's need to defend Jason's behavior, but Amy felt the same need to defend Frank. She was glad their friendship could withstand the truth and that it was always kindly spoken to each other. "Frank always loved farming. It's all he's ever wanted to do. He said Jason never wanted to be a farmer. He wants to be an architect. That's what you told me, too."

"Yes."

"Frank felt Jason was stealing his future."

Pearl's hands stopped in the middle of a stitch. Surprise stood large in her eyes. "I didn't know that. Jason never intended to take the farm away from Frank. He only wanted to keep the farm going to support the family."

"Frank knows that now. He was only eighteen at the time and grieving over the loss of his parents, the same as Jason. Frank said it took a long time for him to understand that Jason felt as though his calling had also been stolen when their parents died. Giving up the profession for which he'd trained must have been a painful sacrifice for Jason."

"It was." Pearl lowered the brown material to her lap. "Those were awful days for everyone." She caught her bottom lip between her teeth.

Amy saw the gleam in her friend's eyes. "I know that look. You've a secret and can't decide whether to share it."

"You always keep my confidences, but this involves other people."

"Then follow your conscience." Amy went back to her stitching.

For a minute, only sounds coming through the window were audible: the breeze rustling the leaves of the lilac bushes near the porch, a cow making an announcement to another cow out in the pasture, bees buzzing busily among the flowers beside the steps.

Amy's thoughts quickly turned from her friend's secret to Frank. He seemed always central in her thoughts. What exactly was he doing now? Did she hover in his thoughts as he hovered in hers?

"Oh, I want to tell you. Jason won't mind." Pearl leaned forward, the cotton shirt a pile in her lap, her eyes sparkling. "Jason is working at his architectural design again."

"Why, that's wonderful. Is he designing something special? Has he sold his designs?"

"Yes and yes. He's designed homes and outbuildings for a few people over the years since we married but not enough to make much money from it. He didn't try to sell his designs himself. First Thor asked him to design their new farmhouse after the fire burned down their old home. The next year another farmer asked him to design a home. People liked his work and recommended him to others. He's designed maybe half a dozen buildings now."

"That's wonderful. Why is this a secret? I'd think he'd want people to know."

"He hasn't the time to put into it to make a living at it. Now he's been asked to submit a design for the new bank and for the bank president's house as well. He's barely slept lately, between that and harvest. He starts after the field work is done and works by lamplight late into the night." Pearl's face softened, and Amy knew her friend was picturing her husband at work. "When he begins designing in the evening, he's exhausted. But it doesn't take long for him to become so involved in his work that he forgets his fatigue." She grinned. "Until morning, that is."

"If he's awarded the contracts for these buildings, maybe it will be the step he needs."

Pearl picked her work back up and shook her head. "I don't think so. Jason wouldn't leave the farm now. He feels Frank needs him here."

"Has he told Frank that?"

"No, he'd never do that. He doesn't want Frank to feel he's a burden."

Sadness gave a heaviness to Amy's chest. "Frank will sense it," she said quietly.

"I hope not."

Amy didn't insist, but she knew in her heart Frank would know his brother was sacrificing for him. She wanted to believe it would make Frank feel loved. She knew instead that he'd feel pitied and hate it.

She changed the subject. "How is Frank's health? He looks tired."

"He is awfully tired, I'm afraid."

Amy didn't like the frown that furrowed Pearl's forehead. "He insists on working every day," Pearl continued. "'I'll carry my own weight,' he says, but he can't do much yet. It takes very little to wear him out. Father warned him to rest more, but Frank won't hear of it. And of course, the pain is difficult for him sometimes."

Remembering that Frank had refused morphine, Amy shuddered. He was in so many kinds of pain, and she was shut out from helping him relieve any of them. Was there anything in life more horrible than knowing you couldn't help someone you love?

They soon set aside their mending to prepare lunch. Pearl encouraged Amy to continue her stitching, but it made Amy uncomfortable when she could be helping Pearl. Soon a roast was braised and placed in the oven. A trip to the garden was a refreshing change from spending the morning indoors. They washed the potatoes and carrots beneath the outside pump, the cold water chilling their hands.

Maggie volunteered to pick fresh corn for lunch. She brought back a basketful. Amy joined Pearl and Maggie on the back porch steps, husking the corn. Amy liked the sweet smell of the large yellow kernels. She liked the silky feel of the tassels. She liked the friendly conversation. She liked working in the sunshine, so different than working alone inside her tiny apartment kitchen.

She did not like the occasional worm she found.

Viola had no such compunctions. The women spent almost as much time keeping Viola from searching for the creatures in the discarded husks as they did husking.

All the time she worked, Amy thought how she'd love to be living this life every day, performing simple homely duties like preparing a meal for Frank, working with his family, feeling one with them. For years she'd believed this would be her future. *I can't believe Frank has chosen that this won't happen for us, Lord. I can't believe he won't come back to us again. I won't believe it.* Time and again she blinked back tears, trying to hide from her friends the pain that never ceased.

Maybe if I'm around Frank, he will change his mind, she thought. *Surely seeing me will make it harder for him to forget the love we shared.*

Yet part of her wondered whether keeping hope was wise. Would the pain increase if she allowed herself to hope and Frank didn't change his mind? *He must change his mind*, her thoughts insisted. The verse on the sampler rang through her head. *Charity hopeth all things.* How could hope not be wise when the Bible spoke of it so highly?

At noon while Amy joined Pearl and Maggie in the kitchen with last-minute preparations, her heart picked up its beat. The mixture of joy and trepidation left her feeling uncharacteristically giddy, though she hoped she appeared calm, happy, and nonchalant.

She heard the three brothers at the basin on the back porch before she saw them. Jason was the first to enter the kitchen. The smells of earth and sweat and kerosene entered with him and mingled with the kitchen odors. Amy had found the smells of the working men unpleasant at first. Now the smells only spoke the happy fact that the men were home from the fields.

"Papa." Delight filled little Chalmers's voice when he spotted Jason entering the kitchen. The boy raced across the room, arms outstretched.

Viola, who'd been happily banging a pot lid against the floor, turned at the word "Papa" and squealed with joy. The pot lid was forgotten as she stood and headed for her father in a run.

Jason swooped Chalmers into his arms. "Hello, Son. Have you been a good boy for Mother?"

"Yes. Have you been good?"

Laughter filled the air.

"I've been working," Jason replied, setting Chalmers down and lifting Viola, who had wrapped her arms around his denim-covered leg.

"I do believe you avoided our son's question," Pearl teased, wiping her hands on her apron. "What could you possibly have been doing out in the fields but behaving yourself?"

Jason dropped a kiss on her cheek. "I'll never tell."

Amy loved watching the little family. Was there anything more wonderful than spending life surrounded by those you loved?

She knew the moment Frank entered the room. She glanced up from the bread plate she was filling to smile at him.

His brown eyes were stormy.

He didn't greet her. The slight dampened the giddy feeling, but Amy continued to smile. She didn't want anyone to see how strongly his anger shook her. Why was he so unfriendly? He hadn't acted that way at the store last week.

At least I'm not seated next to him or directly across from him, she thought as she took her seat following grace. Frank sat on the other side of the table but at the other end.

Filling plates from the overflowing platters and bowls kept everyone's attention for a few minutes. Jason and Andy quickly assured Pearl that the meal "hit the spot."

Amy glanced at Frank while accepting a bowl of cucumbers and onions in vinegar from Pearl, who sat beside her. Frank's tan showed the time he'd spent in the fields since arriving home, though his face didn't show the typical farmer's hat line yet.

He squinted in a frown and rolled the shoulder of his wounded arm.

The movement tightened her throat.

Was he in pain? Was the medicine Dr. Matt gave him sufficiently strong to fight the discomfort? Likely Frank was also battling the normal aches that anyone would feel upon entering back into life after months in a hospital. A little sigh escaped her at the thought of how much he faced.

Frank looked up and their gazes met. She chanced a small smile.

He didn't return it. He turned his attention to his meal.

Amy took a bite of potatoes, but she'd lost her appetite.

A couple bites later she realized the usually talkative family was quiet. It only made her more uneasy believing she and Frank were causing discomfort for the others. Even Viola and Chalmers weren't chattering.

"Frank's had some news about his division," Jason finally announced.

Everyone looked at Frank.

He laid down his fork. "The Thirteenth is coming home. They embarked August thirteenth."

Andy shifted in his chair. "Does that mean they're through fighting?"

Frank nodded. "It will probably be awhile before they're mustered out. They'll land in San Francisco. I suppose they'll travel to Fort Snelling in St. Paul after that."

"Maybe you'll see some of the men when they get back," Jason suggested.

"Not likely. None of them are from around here." Frank still hadn't cracked a smile.

"What about that man you've received letters from?" Pearl asked. "I think you said his name is Dan."

"Dan Terrell. He's from the other side of the state. Not much chance we'll see each other."

Amy remembered Frank mentioning Dan's name often in his letters. "Mr. Terrell is from the Northfield area, isn't he?"

"Yes." The quick glance Frank gave her wasn't friendly. She felt as though it was a warning to keep silent. Did he not even want such a simple reminder that he'd once shared his life with her?

Silence fell on the group again. Amy was aware the family darted looks from her to Frank and back. She hated their discomfort and her own. Why did Frank insist on acting as though the two of them were feuding?

Frank cleared his throat. "There are farms in the Philippines; at least there were farms there before we arrived. Our camp was in a peanut field."

No one said anything, but they gave Frank their full attention.

"Not a day went by but I thought about that poor farmer. Land he'd toiled over, his livelihood, his support for his family—and we slept and ate on it." He looked up, and his gaze moved from one to another around the table. "What if that were our farm? What if an army camped in our fields? What if armies shot at each other around our buildings and animals?"

The quiet, almost emotionless tone added to the chill his words sent through Amy.

Frank's gaze shifted to Chalmers, who chewed on a piece of buttered bread. "What if armies were in our fields shooting at each other around Chalmers and Viola?"

Everyone was still. They'd all stopped eating. The horror Frank presented made Amy feel sick to her stomach. She suspected the others' reactions were similar.

"The farmer will be able to clean up his field now." Frank lifted his fork. "Quite a chore, I imagine."

Jason cleared his throat. "Yes, I should think so."

No one spoke after that. Amy's thoughts whirled around Frank's war experience. How many awful things were trapped inside his mind? Her heart ached for him.

Amy didn't finish her meal, nor did Maggie, though the others managed to do so. The pie Pearl had baked that morning wasn't touched. No one had the stomach for dessert.

After the men left, the girls began clearing the table. "Why don't we sit on the porch and rest for a few minutes while the girls wash up the dishes, Amy?" Pearl led the way, carrying Viola propped on her hip.

Amy's composure had outwardly held together during the meal, but now that she was alone with Pearl, it broke. She pulled a lace-trimmed hanky from her apron pocket and caught the tears that spilled onto her cheeks. "I never thought Frank would ignore me like that, especially in front of other people."

"I didn't either." Unease threaded through Pearl's quiet reply.

"I suppose he thinks by coming out here I'm trying to push my way back into his life. He's using his silence to yell at me that my attempt is not going to work." Amy hugged herself, as though by doing so she could force her pain to leave.

Pearl shifted Viola from one hip to the other. "You're my friend. You're a friend to all of us. You're always welcome here."

"Thank you."

"Oh!" Viola reached out a pudgy hand, her fingers opening and closing. Amy followed the child's wide-eyed gaze. Viola's fascination was caught by a Monarch butterfly, which flew over the pansies beside the porch with grace. The child squirmed in her mother's arms, anxious to get down and run after the butterfly.

Pearl laughed. "Oh, no you don't, Viola. You'll never catch the butterfly, no matter how hard you try, but you'll trample my flowers in the attempt."

The picture brought a small smile to Amy, but it also tugged at her heart. "Do you know how blessed you are?" The tears clogging her throat caused the words to waver.

Pearl's gaze met hers. She nodded. "Yes, I do. Which makes seeing Frank trying to push away his love for you and seeing how painful that is for both of you all the harder to watch. I'm so sorry, Amy. I wish there was something I could do."

Amy gave a strangled little laugh. "So do I. I'd better leave. I shouldn't have come in the first place."

"Frank will come to his senses eventually."

Amy remembered Pearl's statement half an hour later as she turned the horse and buggy from the farm drive onto the narrow road. She had to believe Frank would come to his senses. She had to keep hoping. *If I don't, how can I bear to face the future, Lord?*

Frank's treatment of her at lunch rolled back into her mind. How could he treat her that way? Her face grew hot at the memory. Anger surged in a wave from the embarrassment. Her back straightened. The muscles in her face tightened. "How dare he?" She flicked the reins to hurry the horse to a pace more in keeping with her anger. "There's no reason for him to act so . . . so . . . childishly. He could act civil toward me."

She nursed the anger along, feeding it excuses and painful memories the way she fed kindling to a fire. The anger relieved the pain somewhat.

"How dare he try to make me feel I'm wrong to visit Pearl?"

Guilt wiggled into her thoughts. She'd known, hoped, she might see Frank when she visited Pearl for help with her mending. Of course, he knew that, too. How could he not?

The anger unraveled a bit back into pain. She immediately threw in another piece of mental kindling. The reason for her visit didn't justify his refusal to act like a gentleman. There was no need for him to purposely build thick walls between them. Did he think she was going to storm those walls, to force a confrontation, to force him to admit he loved her?

Truth weakened her defenses. She would storm those walls if she knew how. She would attack his defenses if she believed doing so would force him to admit his love.

Clarity struck so swiftly that she pulled the horse up short. It neighed in protest.

Frank knew what he was doing in building the walls. He wanted to feed his own anger. What better way to protect himself?

Wasn't she welcoming anger to protect herself from the pain of losing his love?

"You wouldn't choose anger to avoid pain, dear Jesus. I won't choose it, either. But this is a new path for me, Lord. Show me how to love him the way You love him, without anger and without insisting he return my love."

The desire to tell Frank what she thought of his behavior still whispered in her thoughts. She struggled to put those temptations away. "What would You say to him in my place, Lord?"

The thought came swift and sure. *My wish for him is the same as for all My children. I wish him love and peace and healing.*

Amy took a deep breath and closed her eyes. "Dear Lord, please bring love and peace and healing into Frank's life. Amen."

She opened her eyes, flicked the reins, and urged the horse to start. Queen Anne's lace, purple thistle, and daisies danced in the wild grass along the roadside. She hadn't noticed them earlier; she'd seen only her anger and pain.

Enduring her own pain wasn't nearly as searing as feeling his.

10

*S*ummer slid into colorful, pungent autumn. The green of leaves, grass, and fields muted into golden and brown relieved by splashes of burgundy. Corn harvest filled farmers' days. Huskings and harvest dances livened the evenings. V's of geese patterned the sky at dawn and dusk. The full orange harvest moon commanded the night.

Amy stayed away from the farm. She threw her energy into preparing for the fall classes at Windom Academy. When she wasn't working on class preparation, she spent all the hours she dared spare painting. Attempts to capture the glories of autumn demanded concentration. She welcomed the respite, however brief, from thoughts of Frank.

For the first time in her life, she dreaded attending church. It meant seeing Frank. Sometimes he honored her with a solemn nod of recognition. More often he ignored her, talking with other people and avoiding so much as a glance in her direction. She was certain he was as aware of her presence as she was of his. The pain twisted her insides and made concentration on the worship impossible. She left every service with a prayer asking God's forgiveness for her inattention.

"I'd spend the morning with my thoughts more on the Lord if Frank weren't there," Amy grumbled to Pearl.

Fall term at the academy didn't bring the relief for which she hoped. A friendly camaraderie existed between most students and the small faculty. The returning students' questions and her reply became a refrain: "Yes, Frank did return from the war. Thank you for asking after him. He's wounded but alive. We've cancelled our plans to marry." The inevitable expression of sympathy followed. "Thank you."

Then the smile and attempt to redirect the conversation. "What about you? How was your summer?"

A number of male students from the academy had joined the service after war was declared. None of them made it to the battlefields. Amy knew she was more deeply grateful for that fact than were the young men who'd so eagerly offered themselves. Now some of the women came up with an idea that rapidly gained favor: a celebration honoring all the young men in the area who had joined the service because of the war.

"The pictures of the soldier leaving for and returning from war will be perfect for the celebration," Mrs. Headley told Amy. "We'll hang them in a conspicuous place at the reception."

"Oh, no, please." Amy sought frantically for an excuse, any excuse but the true one. "The print of the soldier leaving is so well known. People will think it presumptuous if my painting of the returning soldier is shown beside it."

The headmaster's wife patted Amy's hand. "My dear, the townspeople will think it most appropriate, I assure you. The people are as proud of your talent as if it were their own."

Amy smiled weakly. She considered Mrs. Headley a friend, but even to her she didn't want to admit her fear.

Everyone in town knew she'd expected to welcome Frank home to her arms like the woman in her painting welcomed home the soldier. Everyone knew Frank broke their engagement. People might not speak to her face of the similarity of the painting to her expectations, but she was certain they'd be thinking of it.

For Amy, the celebration was only another expectation of pain at seeing the man she loved. She helped prepare for it with a heavy heart.

❧

I feel like a stranger here, Frank thought, looking at the crowd in the academy hall.

Men in military uniforms filled the rectangular room. He'd lived among military men for over a year. *Why don't they seem familiar?*

Dan Terrell, who Frank had unexpectedly met in St. Paul just a week before, leaned close. "The man who spoke at the presentation earlier said none of these men fought in the war, right?"

"Right. It seems the entire group got no farther than one of the stateside camps."

"Battled typhoid fever but not the Spanish or Filipinos."

"That's the way I understand it." Frank smiled. "So that's it."

Dan raised his eyebrows in question. "What is?"

"That's why I feel like a stranger among these men, even though they were in the military and I've known most of them all my life."

"I think after a man's fought in a war, he's a stranger for the rest of his life to everyone who hasn't fought in one." The words were spoken matter-of-factly.

Frank looked at his friend. Dan met his gaze steadily.

This was one of the reasons he treasured Dan's friendship, Frank realized. They spoke the truth to each other, the truth they often wouldn't admit to others. They spoke it straight out, without waxing maudlin about it.

Dan indicated a table across the room. "Those refreshments look mighty tempting. What say we check them out? My stomach is growling."

"That's Amy at the right end of the table, the one serving punch."

"So that's why we're standing over here starving. You're avoiding her."

Frank and Amy's friend, Sylvia, and Mrs. Headley stopped to welcome them, relieving Frank of the necessity of replying to his friend's all-too-accurate observation.

Frank had always thought of Sylvia as rather the silly sort, though good-hearted. Now she wore a sober air. He knew instinctively that she was thinking of Roland, wishing he were here, remembering he would never be with her again in this lifetime.

Frank took hold of one of her hands. "I'm sorry for your loss. Roland confided in me how much he cared for you. I couldn't believe it when Amy wrote me that Roland died from the typhoid. I'll miss him. We had a lot of good times together."

Her eyes misted over. "Thank you."

"Do you remember that night years ago when a group of us walked home from a Christmas party together?"

She nodded. "The party was held in this very room."

He'd forgotten that. "Amy slipped on the walking bridge that spans the ravine."

"And her hat went tumbling into the gorge below." She laughed.

"That's right. The next day I searched for it. It took me hours, but I finally located it up in a tall bush. I took it over to Amy's house to return it. In front of her house, who do I run into but Roland. He spots the hat and starts teasing me about it. That was before Amy and I started courting. I was one embarrassed fellow, I can tell you."

She gave his hand a squeeze and smiled. "Thank you for sharing such a fun memory."

Sylvia and Mrs. Headley moved on.

"Brave enough to face Amy yet?" Dan asked. "Or will I be obliged to bring you punch and a piece of one of those incredible looking cakes?"

Frank shot him a dirty look and headed across the room. Well-wishers stopped them every few steps. "You've met nearly the entire town," Frank told Dan as they reached the refreshment table.

"Not this lady." Dan smiled at Amy. "Aren't you going to introduce us?"

Amy blushed.

Beneath the calm, polite exterior Frank struggled to maintain, he seethed. He'd ignored Amy for two months. Dan knew he'd broken up with her. Why was he insisting on putting them in this position? "Dan, this is Miss Amy Henderson. Miss Henderson, this is Mr. Dan Terrell. We—"

"Mr. Terrell, I'm delighted to meet you." Amy beamed at Dan. "Frank wrote me about you."

"I hope he said as many nice things about me as he told me about you."

Frank caught the pleased look Amy darted at him. He felt his face heat. "Dan—"

"Miss Henderson, we are about to faint from hunger and thirst. May we sample some of that spicy smelling punch you're dishing out?"

She laughed, filled a crystal cup with the golden liquid, and handed it to him. "Would you like a cup, too, Frank?"

He nodded.

Dan pointed to two pictures on the wall above the table. "Those are certainly appropriate. I've seen copies of the one with the soldier leaving before, but the one of the soldier returning looks like an original oil painting."

"It is," Amy admitted.

Frank studied the picture of the returning soldier. The man and woman in the painting looked as though they could walk right off the canvas they were so alive. Their love for each other and joy in their reunion shone from their faces, from every line of their bodies. Frank knew in an instant that Amy had painted the picture from her heart, knew that he was the man in the picture and the woman was Amy, though the faces in the painting weren't theirs.

"You painted this." He continued staring at the picture as he spoke to her.

"Yes."

He couldn't take his eyes off the picture. His heart drank in the love she'd expressed for him in it. She'd laid her own heart open for the world to see how much she loved him and how deeply she longed for him to return from the war to her. He knew he shouldn't allow himself to welcome this. If he let down the barriers he'd put up against her, it would be difficult rebuilding them. But he was so tired of all the battling with life he'd done the last couple months, of all the battles he envisioned before him in the years to come, that he yearned for a respite, even if only for a moment.

"When did you paint this?" he asked when he could speak again.

"Soon after you were sent to the Philippines."

"You didn't tell me."

"No. Paintings are hard to express in words."

"Frank told me you painted, Miss Henderson, but I had no idea the extent of your talent."

"Thank you, Mr. Terrell."

"Did you paint the picture hanging in the Sterlings' parlor—the one of Pearl's parents?" Dan asked.

"Yes, I did. It was Jason's gift to Pearl for their first Christmas. I painted it from an old photograph of the couple on their wedding day. Pearl lost her parents when she was only two, so the picture meant a great deal to her."

Dan's brown eyes seemed to light up. "I wonder if you'd be so kind as to paint a portrait of my wife and I on our wedding day from a photograph, like you did Pearl's parents."

"I'll be glad to paint it for you. Is it a gift for your wife?"

Dan set his cup on the table. "I'm a widower, Miss Henderson."

She touched the back of his hand in a quick, spontaneous gesture. "I'm so sorry. I'll begin the painting as soon as possible. I teach art here at the academy, so you can send the photograph to me here. How will I deliver the painting to you? You live near Northfield, I understand."

"Not anymore. I'm a resident of this county now."

Frank decided it was time to explain. "Dan and I ran into each other in St. Paul last week."

"At the parade?"

"Yes." President McKinley had traveled to St. Paul to personally review the Thirteenth in its final march before mustering out. Frank had been surprised at the pride he'd felt marching before the country's most important man. It had been both joyful and painful to see the men he'd fought beside. Strange that only among them did he feel completely comfortable without his arm.

The only time he'd felt uncomfortable that day was when he'd been presented a medal for bravery. What was brave about doing what you had to in a life or death situation, he'd wondered.

He'd thought about Amy so many times during the parade day. Had she attended? If so, she hadn't attended with his family. He'd purposely refrained from asking Pearl. He didn't want to admit he still cared.

He hoped Amy had seen the parade.

He shifted his thoughts with an effort. "Dan's agreed to stay at the farm through the winter."

Dan grinned. "That's a nice way of saying I'm the latest hired help."

"He's a good farmer. We need someone like him around the farm."

"You've never seen me working as a farmhand," Dan reminded him in a wry tone.

"I've seen you under fire. I know the kind of man you are." At Dan's embarrassment, Frank changed the subject. "I'm ready to head back to the farm if you are, Dan. Much more of this celebrate-the-returning-hero stuff, and our heads will be too large to fit through the barn door come morning."

It was with reluctance that Frank said good night to Amy. He was fiercely glad for the excuse Dan had given him to ignore the walls he'd so carefully and firmly built up since arriving home. Still, he had every intention of putting those walls back in place immediately.

After all, the soldier Amy painted had returned with both arms intact.

A few weeks later, Amy stood in the academy art studio, surveying the canvas on an easel with a critical eye. She'd completed the painting days ago and hadn't looked at it since. She'd wanted to distance herself from it in order to view it with a semblance of objectivity.

Did her figures look as much like Dan Terrell and his wife in their wedding picture as possible? Did they look as lifelike as her abilities allowed? Would a little more shadow beneath his bride's chin help, or had she caught the lighting correctly?

Finally she gave a satisfied nod. "Yes, it is as good as I thought."

The afternoon was crisp and clear. She had no more classes scheduled. Even though it was only two days before Thanksgiving, no snow or ice had turned the roads into threatening passages. She would deliver it to Mr. Terrell that afternoon.

Amy pushed back her eagerness at the possibility of seeing Frank and concentrated on packing the painting with care. The painting was dry enough to deliver with only limited danger of damage.

The fields were either black after their turning by the plow or stubbly. Amy knew that to some people the November landscape seemed barren compared to the lush August fields she'd passed the last time she'd visited the farm. The artist in her saw beauty in patterns and shadows in the late fall fields.

As she entered the farmyard, her gaze searched for Frank. He wasn't in sight.

He'd acted curt toward her at the reception honoring the veterans last month, but at least he'd spoken to her. Since then when they'd run into each other at church each Sunday, he'd said hello and smiled. He'd taken part in conversations she'd had with Pearl and Jason. Twice he'd shared a laughing glance with her when a comment by Jason elicited a common memory. Surely God must be healing Frank's wounds.

The process seemed agonizingly slow to her, but at least her hope that Frank would return to them appeared possible and not a silly flight of fancy.

Amy was tying the horse to the hitching rail when Andy came out the back door. "Need some help unhitching your buggy, Miss Amy?"

"No, thank you. I don't expect to be here long enough to unhitch. I've come to deliver a painting to Mr. Terrell. Is he home?"

"He and Frank are in the barn, sharpening tools. I'll fetch him for you."

Pearl held the door for Amy as she carried the painting into the house. The kitchen was warm and inviting after the chill outside air. Sunshine brightened the large room. The pleasant aroma of coffee from the huge enameled pot on the stove welcomed them.

The large oak table stood near the stove. Maggie, grasping the wooden handle of the sad iron, bent over the work shirt on the ironing board, which rested on the table and a nearby kitchen chair. At the other end of the table, Jason studied architectural drawings. Grace sat on the floor, pointing out pictures in a catalog to Viola and Chalmers. Amy suspected it was Grace's responsibility to keep the little ones away from the hot stove and irons.

Amy laid the painting on the table. A moment later, Dan entered the house. Disappointment slipped past Amy's defenses when she saw Frank wasn't with him.

Excitement filled Dan's slender face. "Andy said you brought my painting, Miss Henderson. I didn't expect it for another month at least."

Dan drew off his gloves and began cautiously removing the protective cloth. The family gathered around to watch.

At a cold rush of air, Amy looked over her shoulder toward the kitchen door to see Frank enter the room. His gaze met hers, and the friendly welcome she saw warmed her heart.

Amy turned her attention back to Dan. Frank stepped up beside her, and the awareness of his presence tingled along her nerves.

When the painting was completely uncovered, Dan and his young bride looked out at the assembled group from the canvas. Compliments for the work poured out.

"It's wonderful, Amy."

"Beautiful."

Dan said nothing.

Was he disappointed? Amy dared a glance at his face. Tears welled in his eyes.

She looked back at the painting. The bride and groom stood beside each other. The bride's large brown eyes beneath thick brows looked confidently toward the future she expected to share with Dan. "Your wife was beautiful."

"Yes." The word was a husky whisper. "Yes, she was beautiful; beautiful through and through." He cleared his throat and tried to continue. He cleared his throat again. "The photograph can't compare to this, Miss Henderson. You've put color and life and warmth into it. It's almost . . . almost like seeing her standing before me again." A tear slid down his cheek. He didn't bother to brush it away.

The intensity of his love and longing for his wife twisted Amy's heart. She suspected the others in the room felt it also, for all fell silent. Frank squeezed her shoulder, and she knew that he, too, felt the sense of reverence for this couple whose life together had been too brief.

"I'll take it to my room now." Dan picked the painting up and turned to Amy. "I'll pay you our agreed-upon price, of course, but no amount of money can pay for what you've given me. Thank you."

No one else in the room moved until Dan entered the stairwell and closed the door behind him. Then throats cleared and people went back to what they'd been about before Dan entered. They walked quickly, moved items noisily, and spoke brightly as if they felt a desperate need to break the spell of Dan's lost love.

"It's your best work yet, Amy." Frank's voice was low and a bit rough with emotion.

Before she could thank him, he started toward the parlor. The small bit of kindness and warmth he'd shown her left her feeling hugged. Was this a sign he was reconsidering his decision about them?

"You'll stay for coffee, won't you?" Pearl asked. "Maggie made apple and cranberry pies this morning. The coffee will warm you for the ride back."

"That's a tempting argument." Not nearly as tempting as spending more time near Frank.

"I'll get your foot warmer." Andy headed for the door. "Might as well heat it up while you're eating."

"Should I unhitch the horse?"

"It'll be all right," Andy assured. "You don't expect to be here more than an hour, do you?"

She assured him she didn't. She hung her coat and muffler on the wooden pegs beside the door, then reached to remove the pins from her hat. "Can I help with anything?"

"Oh, no. Make yourself to home." Pearl entered the pantry. A moment later she returned with a pie. "Maggie, set the ironing board aside so there's room at the table for everyone. I'd invite you into the parlor, Amy, but the stove isn't lit in there. Our teeth would chatter so they'd threaten to break the cups."

In spite of Pearl's insistence that Amy needn't help, she gathered cups from the open shelves and brought them to the table. Then Amy, with an easy familiarity in her friend's kitchen, located the sugar and cream and began pouring coffee. Pearl sliced pie, and Maggie set out a plate of cheese. Andy brought in the metal foot warmer and set it on the stove, then at Pearl's request went to ask Dan to join them for coffee. In the midst of it all, Jason continued to work over his sketches.

Frank entered the room with a copy of *Farm, Stock, and Home* and sat across from Jason. As usual, Frank's presence made all Amy's senses stand up at attention.

Andy returned looking solemn. "Dan says he'll be down in a few minutes, that we should start without him."

The family all took seats at the table. Chalmers climbed up on Frank's lap. The boy pointed to a picture in the magazine. "What's that?"

"It's Uncle Sam, lassoing the Philippines."

Chalmers frowned, obviously not understanding the cartoon. "I don't know Uncle Sam."

The family chuckled.

"I guess you don't at that," Frank replied with a twinkle in his eyes.

The spark caught at Amy's heartstrings. This was the most relaxed and happy she'd seen him since he returned home. Chalmers's blond curls brushed against Frank's brown flannel shirt. The boy appeared completely trusting of Frank and not at all put off by Frank's wounded arm.

Pearl touched Jason's shoulder. "Won't you put away your work for a few minutes and visit with us?"

He grinned sheepishly and stacked the papers in a pile on the end of the table. "Sorry. When I'm working on plans, I tend to get so involved, I forget the world around me."

"I do the same when I paint," Amy told him.

Chalmers slipped down from Frank's lap and took the magazine with him. "I want to show Dad."

Frank agreed, but Amy thought he looked slightly disappointed as the boy left.

Frank didn't invite Amy to sit beside him, and she hadn't the courage to do so uninvited. Instead she sat at the other end of the table where she could easily see him.

She lifted Viola onto her lap. "Will you sit with me?" The little girl stuck a fingertip in her mouth and studied Amy for a moment, then grinned and rubbed her forehead against Amy's shoulder. Amy rested her head against Viola's for a moment, amazed as always at the softness of Viola's curls.

Amy looked up and caught Frank's gaze on them. She blinked at the hunger in it. In the next moment the hunger was gone as completely as though she'd imagined it. *Had I?* Amy wondered. *Do I only want to believe he longs for us to have a family of our own as much as I do?*

When Frank cut into his piece of pie, Amy noticed how red and chapped his fingers looked.

"How did Dan's wife die, Frank?" Pearl asked.

Frank told them what Dan had shared with him while they were in the Philippines. "He still misses her a great deal, as you saw."

Heavy footsteps on the stairs prevented more questions. Dan joined them at the table with an apology for his tardiness. His red-rimmed eyes made Amy wish there were something she could say or do to comfort him.

"Dan and I started a list of tools we'll need to replace," Frank told Jason. He named a few. He could as well have spoken in another language for all the names meant to Amy.

Pearl smiled across the table at her. "Would you and your father join us for Thanksgiving? We'd love to have you."

"Thank you, but Mrs. Jacobson is already planning our little repast. It would disappoint her terribly if Father and I changed our minds." Would Frank regret her absence? Had he requested that Pearl invite them?

Out of the corner of her eye, she saw Frank move his wounded arm as though to reach for something. He bumped the plate into his coffee cup. Milky brown liquid poured across the table onto Jason's papers.

Frank and Jason leaped to their feet in the same moment. Frank grabbed the cup and righted it.

Jason whipped the papers from the table. He shook coffee from them, splattering it across the linoleum. "Why don't you watch what you're doing?"

"It was an accident." Frank's face was redder than Amy'd ever seen it. "Besides, the table's no place for your work, not when people are eating."

"That's no excuse for clumsiness." Jason took the towel Pearl handed him and dabbed at the papers.

"I suppose you could do better with one arm?"

The heat in Frank's cold tone sent fear through Amy. She fought the desire to reach out to him with a restraining touch. It would likely only increase his anger.

Viola's fingers closed around Amy's collar. Fear filled the child's eyes as she stared at the men. A moment later she burst into sobs. Amy hugged her close, whispering shushing sounds against her hair and rocking.

Chalmers followed Viola's example with a wale.

"Stop arguing this minute." Pearl wiped up the spilled coffee from the table. "You're upsetting the children."

"This is a farm." Frank ignored Pearl's demand and continued his tirade in a louder voice. "You're wasting time designing buildings for other people when there's plenty of work inside our own buildings and outside that needs doing. Andy and Dan and I bust our britches keeping things going while you sit inside and play with those papers."

"*Those papers*, as you call them, bring in money the same as the crops."

Frank slammed his fist on the table and leaned across it, glaring at Jason. "I'd like to see you draw those sketches if you lost your drawing hand."

Maggie gasped.

Everyone stared at Frank.

You've gone too far. Stop before you say anything worse, Amy pleaded silently.

"Frank, calm down." Andy scowled at him. "It was an accident, like you said. No call to get in a huff."

"And you." Frank swung toward his younger brother. "You begged to join the service before I left. Bet you're glad now that Jason didn't allow it. Haven't heard you say you wish you'd fought in the war, not since I came back like this." He raised his wounded arm.

A flush spread up Andy's neck and covered his face.

"Frank." Dan's calm voice urged Frank with one word to stop and think.

Jason dropped the papers onto the table. "You came home after the war insisting you could pull your own weight around here. When

I said to take it easy, you accused me of pitying you. You know, little brother, there isn't anyone who comes close to pitying you as much as you pity yourself."

"And you don't feel sorry for yourself?" Frank gave a sharp laugh. "You've always resented sacrificing your dreams of becoming an architect for the farm. You didn't think I could run this place even when I had both hands. You had to play the family martyr when Mother and Father died."

A grayish tinge seeped beneath Jason's tan. "You want to run this place? You go ahead."

"Jason." Pearl clutched his arm.

He jerked his arm away. "Pearl and I and the kids will move into town. I've enough requests to bid on buildings now to give architecture a try. You go ahead and run this place by yourself. Run it into the ground for all I care."

"You'd like that, wouldn't you? It would prove you're the only Sterling son capable of running Dad's farm. Fine. If you want to leave, you go right ahead." Frank stormed to the door and grabbed his jacket from the wall pegs. Without waiting to put the jacket on, he left, slamming the door behind him so hard the house shook.

Except for the children's sobs, it was as though everyone had turned to stone. Frank's anger stunned Amy. She'd never seen his face twisted by fury before. *By pain.* The thought flashed through her mind. She knew instantly it was true—the anger was caused by incredible pain.

As Amy turned to hand Viola to Maggie, Pearl remonstrated with Jason, and Dan headed toward the door.

Amy touched Dan's sleeve. "I'll go." She reached for her coat and put it over her shoulders, not taking time to slip her arms into the sleeves.

Dan hesitated.

He thinks I'm the last person Frank wants to see now, she realized. "I won't stay if he chases me away."

"He's hurting."

His understanding of Frank and care for him warmed her heart. She was glad Frank had such a friend on the farm. "I know." She hurried out the door.

(11)

*A*my leaned against the wooden support and watched Frank currying a horse. Did the horse need it, she wondered, or did Frank simply need a way to release his angry energy without hurting himself and others?

She'd known he'd come to the animals he loved. She'd always appreciated the way he cared for animals. Their companionship comforted him, but today she wished he'd come to her for comfort instead.

"I thought I'd find you here," she said quietly.

Frank whirled. "What are you doing here?"

"Are you all right?" She crossed her arms over her chest, hugging herself beneath her jacket, wishing she could hug him instead.

"All right?" He made a sound that was half laugh and half sob. "Of course I'm all right. After all, the doctors said I was healed. They sent me home. I must be all right."

Shock stung her to silence. She struggled to keep her feelings from showing.

He raised his wounded arm. The sleeve hung flat and loose below the elbow. "Do you see a forearm and hand here? No? They're there in my dreams at night. They're there in my mind when I think about something I'm going to do. Know what's scariest? I feel them sometimes. Then I do things like I did today. I reach for something, and the truth throws itself in my face—and in everyone else's, too."

That's what happened in the kitchen, she realized. Frank felt friendly and calm and ordinary. Then he reached for the glass, and the accident embarrassed him and reminded him of his wound, and the pain of it burst out in anger.

Amy's throat ached with a sob that fought for release. *Don't let me cry, Lord. He needs me to be strong for him now.*

"Do you remember before the war, Amy, when I told you I had to fight? I still believe it's important to fight for other people's freedom. That's why I enlisted."

"I remember."

"That's not how I lost my arm, fighting for other people to be free."

"I don't understand."

"Did you read in the newspapers about the Filipino people? Like the Cubans, they fought the Spanish for their freedom."

She nodded. "The insurgents. They thought when we destroyed the Spanish fleet and forced Spain from the Philippines, they could reclaim control of their islands. Our government said no, that the Philippines are ours as the spoils of war."

"Right. So instead of fighting to free the Cubans, I fought to keep the Filipinos from gaining their freedom." The wild tone that had frightened Amy was gone.

She spoke cautiously. "Most Americans think the Philippine citizens did gain their freedom by becoming part of our free nation."

"During the Revolutionary War, the British felt the American colonists should be content to be part of Britain," Frank replied.

She couldn't argue with that.

"A lot of the men I fought beside hated the Filipinos. I don't think they hated them when we landed, but they grew to. They used nasty terms for them. They thought of the insurgents as lesser people, the way some white people still think of black people."

"How horrid."

"Yes, it is. At first I thought the men who felt that way were horrid, too. Then I realized many of them were only protecting themselves. Fighting the Filipinos went against everything they'd been raised to believe. The only way they could justify it was to find a way in their own minds to make the Filipinos wrong."

His understanding of his fellow soldiers amazed her and reminded her of all the reasons she loved him. She wished she dared tell him so.

He brushed his hand over his hair. "I can't even be angry at the Filipino responsible for my arm. He fought for his freedom. I was the one in the wrong, trying to keep that from him."

"Do you think God allowed you to lose your arm to punish you?"

"No. I don't know why God allowed it, but I don't think He was punishing me." Weariness weighted his words.

"God knows your heart, Frank." She walked slowly toward him. "He knows you joined the service to help people, not to take their freedom away. It's your heart God looks at."

A little of the strain in his face eased. "Thanks for reminding me."

Everything within her yearned to comfort him and help him heal. She rested her palm on his arm.

He jerked back. "Don't."

"I'm sorry." Rejection seared through her like a physical pain. "I only wanted . . . I hate to see you hurting like this."

He stepped away from her. His eyes looked emotionless. "I shouldn't have told you all that."

"Why not?"

"I didn't mean it as . . . as an invitation to renew our . . ."

"Our engagement?"

He nodded. "Go home, Amy."

"But—"

He raised his arm and let it drop against his side. "I don't know how to be only friends with you, and there's nowhere else for us to go anymore."

"There could be, if you weren't so stubborn. Life is never perfect for anyone, Frank. Can't you see that only makes it more important not to waste the gifts God gives us—those gifts that make the hard places easier and entire days bright and beautiful? Surely God wouldn't want us to waste our love for each other."

"I don't want to marry you."

Amy caught her breath. The words, so stark and cold, hit her like arrows. "I don't believe you." She blinked back sudden tears.

The muscles in his face tightened, but he said nothing.

"You think you aren't whole because you have only one arm.

Don't you know neither of us will ever be whole until we're together, living as one as God intended?"

She spun about, not waiting for him to answer. Straw crunched beneath her shoes as she rushed through the barn and out into the bright, chill daylight. Tears tumbled after each other down her cheeks as she hurried to the farmhouse. In the kitchen, she grabbed her things, aware of the Sterlings watching her in stunned silence. She hurt too much to care what they must think.

On the way back to town, her mind replayed the conversation with Frank. Then she remembered another conversation with Frank when he had said, "I'm not the man I was before I went to war. The war changed me."

She'd told him it couldn't change him. But maybe it had. Today he'd revealed a tiny piece of what he experienced in the war. What he chose to not reveal must be horrendous. How did a man live with the memories of war?

"Please, Lord, heal his heart and bring him peace."

It was her constant prayer. How could he possibly return to her if he didn't heal?

What if God heals him, but Frank doesn't return to me?

Amy caught her breath at the thought. It didn't seem possible Frank wouldn't want to spend his life with her if his heart healed. They'd loved each other for so many years. Surely he couldn't ever love another woman.

What if he could? She forced herself to face the possibility. Would she want his heart healed if it meant he spent his life with someone else? "Yes, Lord," she whispered. "Please heal him, even if You use the love of another woman to do so."

"But . . . what about love hoping all things, Lord?" Her question brought a rueful smile. Already she was trying to convince God to only heal Frank in a way that brought him back to a life with her.

God didn't force people into His will. He didn't force them to love Him. She couldn't expect God to force Frank to come back to her, either. Part of loving someone was allowing them to make their own choices.

"If he doesn't come back, what will I do?" For a moment, all she could picture was an empty future. She took a deep breath and brushed at a stray tear. A lot of women lived without the men they loved. There were a number of widows in Chippewa City. Some retreated into lives made up of nothing but self-pity. Most built useful lives. They gave their love to their family and neighbors. They might miss the one they loved, but they found life still had beautiful and bountiful places.

I can do that, too. I have more than most women. I've my painting and teaching, in addition to Father and my friends. Gratitude eased the constriction in her chest from the separation from Frank. Amy lifted her chin and threw a promise out on the breeze. "I'm not going to waste this life, God. I'm not going to let my heart shrivel up because Frank won't marry me. I'm going to make a fine life with the gifts You've given me."

Maybe Frank would never return to her, but God wouldn't leave.

At least Frank is alive, she thought. She tugged on the reins, and the horse stopped. She removed her left glove and watched sunlight play over the ruby heart in her ring. Slowly she pulled the ring from her finger. "I love you, Frank. I'll always love you. If you can't heal with me in your life, I'll accept that. But please let the Lord help you heal, whatever it takes." Amy opened her reticule and dropped the ring inside.

❧

Frank set the kerosene lamp he'd carried down from his bedroom on the kitchen table, then walked over to the window. Staring out at the mist-shrouded moon, he sighed and leaned his forehead against the cold glass. He felt weary to his bones.

His mind drifted back to Amy and their conversation in the barn. His heart savored the love she'd showed him. What kept her loving him? He'd been cold toward her for months, and she never retaliated in kind. She only kept loving him.

It frightened him the way his anger had exploded today. He could still see his family's shocked faces and hear the children crying. He loved those children. More than anyone else, they'd accepted him as whole when he returned with his wounded arm. Chalmers had been open in his curiosity and questions about the arm, but he never acted like the injury made Frank a freak. He hated that he'd frightened the children.

"Forgive me, Lord. Help me never to let my anger get out of control like that again."

Years ago when he drank heavily, before he decided to live as he believed Christ would want, he'd fought with Jason. It seemed he'd been angry all the time back then. His anger today reminded him of those times. That he hadn't physically harmed anyone was only slight consolation.

The explosion reinforced his conviction that Amy was better off without him.

At a sound behind him, he turned. It was Dan. "You couldn't sleep, either?"

Dan stretched his arms over his head. "No."

"The nightmares again?"

"Yep. You, too?"

"No. Not tonight."

Nightmares from the war disturbed their sleep more nights than either liked to admit. They'd wondered aloud to each other whether the dark dreams would ever leave them for good. It seemed a man should at least have sleep to escape life's horrors. Neither of the men told the others in the house about the dreams. They didn't speak of the war much to others at all—not the true war. They shared funny or interesting sidelights. The things of nightmares remained only between them.

Dan leaned against the wall next to the window and crossed his arms over his chest. "You had an interesting day."

Frank shrugged.

"Wasn't like you to argue so fiercely with your brother. I'd have thought you'd seen enough fighting in the Philippines to last you a lifetime. Guess I was wrong. You came back home to fight with your family and the girl you love."

"I thought you'd understand." Frank didn't look at his friend.

"Their lives are so different from ours." He pointed to his temple. "In here."

"So you push your family out of your life. Are you trying to prove you don't need them?"

"I'm not trying to prove anything."

"Is it such an awful thing to need people? Everyone needs others, even people with both arms."

"I didn't say—"

"God put us in a world filled with people. Do you think He did that so we'd be alone? I think He did it because He means for us to lean on each other and work together. You and your brothers are running a farm here, raising crops to feed people. That's a noble calling. Isn't it worth working together?"

"I don't have any choice but to lean on others, thanks to this arm."

"What about Amy?"

Frank swung around and settled his hand on his hip. "You're sticking your nose way too far into my business."

"You and I have been through more together than most people. We've always spoken the truth to each other. I'm not planning to stop now. If you don't like it, you can send me packing along with everyone else in your life."

Frank sighed and wiped his hand over his face. "No."

"So, what about Amy?"

"What about her?"

"You've admitted to me you still love her. I know you think you're doing her a favor stepping out of her life, but she obviously doesn't see it that way."

"She's better off without me."

Dan shook his head. "Amy isn't the kind of woman to quit loving you because you lost part of your arm. You do her a disservice if you think she is." He pushed himself away from the wall. "I'd give anything in my power to have my wife back for just one day or even five minutes. I wouldn't love her one iota less if she came back missing an arm." He started toward the stairway door. "Good night."

"It's not the arm."

Dan turned around. "What?"

Frank took a deep breath. "I said, it's not the arm. I didn't know that until tonight. All this time, I thought it was the arm. I thought I was doing the honorable thing, not burdening Amy with a crippled husband." He told Dan what he'd shared with Amy in the barn. "Tonight I started thinking about the nightmares and all the other things you and I don't talk about. That's when I realized my arm is like . . . like a symbol, always reminding me of how much I've changed inside. I'm not the same person I was when I left for the war."

"None of us are."

"Do you think it's fair to Amy to marry her like this, while I have nightmares when I'm asleep and nightmares when I'm awake?"

"She loves you. She'd be good for you."

"I wouldn't be good for her. I appreciate your advice on most things, but Amy is off-limits from now on."

They stared at each other. Finally Dan spoke. "All right."

Frank breathed deeply in relief. He didn't want to argue with his friend. "Did I ever tell you about the dream I had in the hospital?"

"The nightmares?"

"No, just the opposite. In this dream you and I were walking down a path together. Christ walked with us, larger than life, His arms spread out as though to guard and bless us. We were surrounded by the most intense sense of peace."

Dan was smiling by the time Frank finished describing the dream. "I'll take that dream over a nightmare any time."

"I didn't know what to make of the dream at first, the part about you and me together. You were still in the Philippines. I was in a hospital in the States. Didn't know if we'd ever see each other again. Now here you are, standing by me closer than any of my old friends. Maybe that's what Christ meant to show me, that both of you would . . . you know. Sometimes I think you're the only one who understands what I've been through."

"That goes both ways. Besides, with Christ walking alongside, a man can handle a heap of hard places."

"You've said something there." Frank straightened. "Guess I've put myself in a harder place than necessary, all but kicking my brother off the farm."

Dan grinned. "You might say."

"I've been home three months. I think it's time I stop wallowing around in self-pity. Are you planning to stick it out with me here on the farm?"

"Just try to get rid of me."

"Then let's start rebuilding our lives. From this point on, when one of us starts slipping into discouragement, the other shores him up."

"Sounds good to me."

"You may do more than your share of shoring up."

Dan shrugged. "I doubt it. Life has a way of evening things like that out. For now, I suggest we try to get some sleep. Dawn won't wait on us."

As they climbed the stairs together, Frank reflected on the part of the dream he hadn't shared with Dan. Frank had been walking between Dan and Amy. Christ's arms had encompassed them all.

Am I walking away from a blessing God intends for me by walking away from Amy, Frank wondered, *just like she accused me of doing today?*

*A*my turned from the pharmacy counter with a packet of headache powders for her father in her hand. A familiar image stood silhouetted against the sunlit window at the front of the store. She hurried toward him. "Hello, Jason."

"Hello, Amy." He smiled and pushed back his broad-brimmed gray felt hat. "What are you doing out in this weather with nothing but that shawl for protection? Don't you know it's winter?"

"I only ran down for some headache powders."

"I forgot you live upstairs."

"Pearl told me you and the family are moving into town this week."

He nodded. "Yes. We moved in yesterday. Renting a house at the top of the hill. It's a bit small for all of us, but we can make do for awhile."

She struggled to maintain composure. "I know Frank's accusations angered you, but I didn't think you meant it when you said you'd leave the farm. Jason, how could you leave him alone out there?"

"He's not alone. Dan Terrell is staying with him."

"Only two men for the entire farm. You know it's too much for Frank."

The smile with which he'd greeted her was gone. "Frank and Dan will get along fine. Frank and I apologized to each other the day after our argument. When I threw out the idea of moving to town, it was just anger talking. But the more I thought about it, the more I thought it was a good idea."

"But—"

He lifted a hand to silence her. "The only way Frank is going to learn to rely on himself is if he's forced into it. Without all of us around, he won't be embarrassed when he can't handle something the first time. Since it's winter, he can take most things at his own pace."

"You honestly believe he can do it, that he can be a farmer on his own?"

"With some hired help, I think he has a good chance. He's a natural-born farmer, Amy. He knows when it's time to plant just by the feel and smell of the soil. Sometimes I think he knows what the animals are thinking. If he doesn't have me and Andy to lean on, he'll see for himself that he can handle it. You'll see."

She hoped he was right. Frustration made her feel restless. Frank seemed bent on making life more difficult than necessary, pushing away everyone who loved him.

"You're the only one left who can help him, God," she whispered, climbing the steps to the apartment.

❧

Amy stood before an easel in the academy studio where she taught, admiring the painting of a student from her last class. The young man had caught the elusive quality of shadow moving across a field of grain. Only another painter would know the difficulty in capturing that.

The student was easily the most talented she'd worked with. He'd never worked with oils before her class. It thrilled her to know she'd helped bring out his God-given talent.

"Miss Henderson?"

"Yes?" Amy turned toward the door, expecting a male student behind the respectful inquiry. Instead Dan Terrell stood in the doorway, broad-brimmed felt hat in hand. "Mr. Terrell, this is a surprise. Do come in." She darted a glance about at the room and laughed. "There's nowhere clean to offer you to sit down, I'm afraid."

"I've never been in a place where people paint pictures before." His gaze moved about the room slowly. "It's fascinating. Must be nice to work in a room with huge windows like this. Is the smell of paint always this strong?"

"No. We're working with oil paints right now. Sometimes we work with watercolors or just sketching. Does the smell bother you? It does some people. I can open a window if you'd like, or we can go out in the hall to talk."

"No, it doesn't bother me." He grinned. "As to opening a window, I had enough fresh Minnesota December air riding into town."

She returned his grin. "And what brought you here, Mr. Terrell?"

"I came to pay you for the painting. Meant to pay you when you brought it out to the farm, but . . ." He hesitated, worrying the brim of his hat.

Embarrassment tightened Amy's chest at the remembrance of that afternoon. She forced herself to meet his gaze. "But I rushed off."

"Yes. Anyway, here's the money." He dug it out of his pocket and handed it to her. "Doesn't seem nearly enough for what that painting means to me."

"I'm glad you like it, Mr. Terrell." Without counting it, she dropped the money into a pocket on the front of the white painting smock she wore to protect her shirtwaist and navy blue skirt. "I'm sorry about your wife. How long ago . . . when did the accident happen?"

"Two years ago. Still have a hard time believing it."

"I understand that."

His gaze searched hers. "I think you do." He took a deep breath and began worrying his hat brim again. "About that afternoon at the farm . . . I know it's none of my business, but there's something I'd like to say."

Trepidation sent a warning along her nerves. "I'm not sure—"

"Please, Miss. Let me start. Then if you don't want to hear what I'm saying, ask me to stop and I will."

"All right." She slid her hands into the pockets of her smock.

"Frank's a good man, Miss Henderson."

Amy smiled. "We agree on that."

"What I mean to say is, it's not like him to get so riled as he did with Jason. Sometimes he just doesn't know what to do with all the pain that's built up inside him."

She nodded. "I know. I haven't always understood that. I think Frank learned a long time ago, when he stopped drinking, that pain makes people do things that seem unkind or unwise. He told me that years ago. I tried to understand it then, but I don't think I did completely until he came back from the war."

Dan's shoulders lowered a bit at her response, as though some tension went out of them. "He's got a whale of a lot of healing to do, Miss, and I don't just mean his arm. War leaves a lot of nasty pictures in a man's mind and a lot of questions." He heaved a sigh. "War throws strange bedfellows together. Frank and I fought alongside rich men, poor men, fine men, and not so fine men. One of the men in our regiment belongs to one of the richest families in St. Paul. Bryant's his name. Couldn't find a better fellow if you searched the entire earth. Did Frank tell you how he lost his arm?"

Amy frowned, trying to follow his quick change of subjects. "No. He never offered to, and I never had the courage to ask him to relive the experience."

"There was a soldier in the Thirteenth who didn't like Frank. Didn't like me much, either, but he especially didn't like Frank. Name was Elias Goodworth." Dan shook his head. "Misnomer if I ever heard one."

"Why didn't he like Frank?"

Dan shrugged. "Not sure exactly. It started when he discovered Frank and I don't drink. He'd make comments about how if we couldn't handle a stiff drink we weren't manly enough to be decent soldiers. We never bothered retaliating. At first some of the other men snickered at Goodworth's comments. Eventually, most of the men learned that Frank and I weren't shirkers when it came to fighting, and they quit joining in Goodworth's sarcasm."

"I should think so."

"During one battle, Goodworth was close to Frank and me. Frank was only a yard or so away from him. An insurgent—that's one of the Filipinos we were fighting—seemed to come out of nowhere. He lunged toward Goodworth, his sword drawn. Goodworth didn't even see him. Frank dove for Goodworth. Shoved him out of the way. The Filipino's sword came down full force on Frank's arm."

Amy gasped. She crossed her arms over her chest in a sudden movement, as if to protect herself from the pain that lashed her.

"Far as I know, Goodworth's never even thanked Frank. But Frank's never once spoken ill of Goodworth."

"Frank told me he couldn't be angry with the Filipino, that the man was only fighting for his freedom. Frank never mentioned Mr. Goodworth."

"I expect there's a lot he hasn't mentioned to you. I know he loves you. He's afraid if he marries you, he'll bring all the pain he's dealing with right into the marriage with him. He doesn't think that's fair to you." Dan's smile was reflected in his eyes. "I think you're a strong enough lady to handle that. I expect he thinks so, too, but he loves you too much to want you to have to face his problems."

"Isn't that what love is for?"

Dan stared at the floor. "That's exactly what Belinda would have said." His voice was soft. He swallowed hard before continuing. "I'm afraid Frank has a long way to go before he will let himself admit how much he loves and needs you. I'm not sure he ever will."

She nodded slowly. Pain filled her chest until it felt her rib cage must burst from it. "Thank you for telling me about . . . about how Frank . . ."

"Sure. Frank might not appreciate the way I'm sticking my nose in here, but I thought you had a right to know."

"I'm glad you're his friend. He needs someone now, and he won't let me or his family close."

"He trusts me because I was there. I saw what he saw. I have the same memories. I came back with both arms intact, but a lot of things I still need to figure out, just like Frank." He told her briefly about the nightmares.

Footsteps and cheerful voices in the hall caught Amy's attention. "I'm afraid my next class starts in a few minutes."

Dan straightened his shoulders. "I'll be going then."

"Thank you for coming. It means a great deal to me to know these things about Frank. I'll know better how to pray for him now."

Dan lowered his voice as students began entering the room. "I'm not sure he will let himself come back to you."

Amy heard the regret in his voice. It echoed in her heart. "I know, but at least I understand him better."

She tucked the revelations away in her heart to reflect on later and turned to bring order to the class.

∾

Frank slung the T-stool into the straw, sat down on it, and began milking the brown-and-white cow. "Sorry the job goes so slow with only one hand, Sudsy."

"Me-eow."

Frank glanced over his shoulder but continued to milk. The one-eyed golden tabby cat balanced on top of the stall wall. "Careful, Gideon. You know you have a habit of forgetting you can't see on the side you're missing that eye. You've fallen off that wall more times than I've seen Christmas."

Frank turned his attention back to the cow, relaxing to the rhythmic hissing of the milk into the pail.

Gideon jumped down from the wall to Frank's shoulder.

Frank laughed. "I'm not going to squirt any milk your way while you're up there." He brushed his cheek against the cat's. "You haven't let living with one eye get you down, have you, Fella? You're the best mouser on the farm. Think I'll learn to handle living with one arm as well as you've learned to live with one eye? At least Dan's standing by me this winter."

Although he'd lived on a farm all his life, everything seemed new to Frank now. Chores he could practically do in his sleep before the war needed his full attention to perform with one hand. On some days, things as simple as tying a knot could make him so frustrated he wanted to give up farming for good.

Dan stood by him through all the struggles. "Nothing lost," he'd say when Frank couldn't get something right the first time. "Try again."

Dan pulled his own weight, but he never jumped in to do things for Frank without first giving Frank a chance to try them himself.

Initially, Frank had been terrified. For all he'd harangued Jason, accusing him of taking responsibility for the farm away from him, Frank discovered he was scared to death at trying to run it himself.

As the months passed, Frank grew more competent at performing the chores. And as his abilities grew, his frustration at the world dissipated. Work didn't knock the stuffing out of him the way it had when he'd just gotten out of the hospital. Instead it was building back the muscles he'd lost.

The first time he lifted a sack of feed that would have taken him two hands to lift before the war, the realization sent a jolt of elation through him. He laughed out loud and looked in wonder at the sleeve stretched tight over his bulging muscles. *I can't wait to show Amy*, he thought. Instead he kept the news to himself and was rewarded by Dan's comment two weeks later on his growing strength.

It helped that Frank had only the relatively easy chores of winter to do as he began rebuilding his strength. Caring for the livestock, cleaning the barn and stables, repairing and cleaning tools and equipment, and going through seed catalogs with Dan filled most of his waking hours. Learning to ride a horse and handle a team while driving a wagon was a challenge that at first frightened, then excited him as he became more accomplished.

Often as Frank worked, Dan's words about the importance of farming came back to him. Frank found it healing to his soul to think of his work as something that blessed others.

The frequency of those times when nightmares woke him with racing pulse, drenched in sweat, decreased. As he began to trust in his physical abilities and began to see beauty in the world again, he discovered himself clinging to new hope: the hope that Amy was right about him, the hope that beneath all the things he'd seen and experienced in the war was a man who at the center was kind and good and strong in Christ.

But as far as Frank could tell, his heart hadn't healed at all. Amy was still the first person he thought of when he awakened and the last thought on his mind at night.

He and Dan celebrated Christmas in town at the house Jason and Pearl were renting. Seeing Amy at the Christmas Eve service was especially painful. Later that night he shared with Dan the story of a Christmas Eve years earlier.

"When I first asked Amy to court me, I'd just decided to live for Christ. I'd been drinking and gambling pretty heavy for awhile before that. I was making a new start. Amy's father didn't trust my change of heart. He said Amy couldn't see me until I proved I was a changed man by not drinking or gambling for a year. I was crushed. Then Amy said she believed in me, and we'd celebrate my success by attending the Christmas Eve service together when the year was over."

"And did you?"

"Yes." Images of that night drifted through his mind. The pleasure of her faith in him and of that evening together filled him with the joy of the love they'd shared, and he smiled. "Her faith in me helped me through a lot of tempting times that year. I used to compare that year to Jacob's years of work to earn the right to marry Rachel. Remember that Old Testament story?"

"I do. Sounds like you and Amy have been through a lot together."

"Yes."

"Maybe too much to throw it all away?"

Frank grinned. "Maybe I talk too much. Did you hear Professor Headley tonight?"

"That's a pretty abrupt change of subject."

Frank ignored the jibe. "The professor asked if I'd give some classes on agriculture and livestock. He said there are so many young men in the area going into farming—men who can't afford to learn the latest methods at the university like I did—that this might be a good way to share my knowledge."

"I think that's a great idea."

"So do I. At least until spring, when there's so much to do around the farm."

It would also give him a reason to be near Amy. Frank wasn't ready to change his mind about their future, but it would be nice to see her more often. Just to be around her would be a blessing.

Even in his daily Scripture readings he was reminded of her. Sometimes it seemed he couldn't open the Bible without his gaze lighting on a reference to married love. He hadn't realized before that there were so many such verses.

He became aware of them first when he opened to Proverbs 31 and read how blessed a man is who has a virtuous wife, "for her price is far above rubies." The comparison to rubies, the stone in the ring he'd given Amy, only made the words cut quicker to his heart.

Seeing two cows huddled together against the chill winter winds one afternoon reminded him of the verses in the fourth chapter of Ecclesiastes he'd read the night before: "Two are better than one; because they have a good reward for their labour. For if they fall, the one will lift up his fellow: but woe to him that is alone when he falleth; for he hath not another to help him up. Again, if two lie together, then they have heat: but how can one be warm alone? And if one prevail against him, two shall withstand him; and a threefold cord is not quickly broken."

It brought back the memory of Amy's theory that their love for each other was a gift from God to make the hard places in their lives easier.

Were the Bible verses he kept coming across a coincidence? Was God trying to push him back to Amy?

The verse that struck him most forcefully was Proverbs 18:22: "Whoso findeth a wife findeth a good thing, and obtaineth favour of the Lord." Frank's immediate thought was that finding Amy had indeed been a very good thing. His second was that obtaining favor of the Lord sounded like a good thing, too.

His third was that he didn't believe that finding him had necessarily been a good thing for Amy. Marrying might be good for him, but it would definitely not be good for her.

❧

Frank hummed a popular tune as he hurried through Windom Academy in early March, headed for the hall where Amy's picture of the returning soldier hung. Ever since he started teaching at the academy, he'd avoided the painting, though his heart had longed to see it again.

It was a tangible reminder of the love Amy had once held for him. His mind warned him that seeing it would only open him to more pain.

His heart won out.

He stepped into the large hall and stopped short. His heart slammed against his rib cage. Amy stood before the picture. While he watched, she reached up and removed it from the wall.

Running into her hadn't been part of his plan. They saw each other often at the academy. That was inevitable. But usually there were students or other faculty members around. It was nice being near her, seeing her laugh or her eyes warm in sympathy with another or sparkle in excitement with a shared idea. Still, he never sought her out alone.

Now he took a step back, hoping to slip away undetected. Instead he bumped into the door.

Amy looked over her shoulder. "Hello, Frank."

He gave up the retreat and walked toward her. The sadness in her eyes grabbed at his heart. Did she see the same thing in his eyes, the regret that they weren't together? He pulled his gaze away and indicated the picture she was holding with a nod of his head. "Taking it down?"

"I'm taking it home." She laid it face down on two pieces of cotton-wrapped wood. "The war is over."

"Yes." He supposed for most people it was over. He wondered if it would ever be entirely over for him. "People are ready to move on." Like he and Dan were trying to do.

"Some people, anyway." Amy pulled the cotton ties from the wood protectors behind the back of the picture and secured them.

Was she indicating that she wasn't ready to move on? More likely she thought he was not moving on.

He watched while she wrapped a large piece of white cotton around the painting and tied it in place with twine. Pain sliced through him when he saw she no longer wore the ruby-heart ring he'd given her before leaving for war. Immediately he reprimanded himself. What kind of fool was he to think she'd wear the symbol of his love for her the rest of her life? Isn't this what he wanted, for her to leave them behind the way the war must be left behind?

"I hope you're enjoying teaching," Amy said. "The students are enthusiastic about your classes."

The knowledge sent a thrill through him. "Glad to hear it. I hoped they'd find the classes useful, but you never know."

The smile he knew so well lit her face. "Yes. It's like that for all of us."

It was nice, knowing they shared this experience. "The students speak highly of your classes, too. And of you."

"Thank you for telling me. Teaching is a great blessing to me." Amy picked up her gray, thigh-length wool coat with maroon trim from a nearby table and started to put it on.

"Let me help you with that." Frank grabbed one shoulder of the coat. Surprise jolted through him. He'd forgotten for a moment he had only one hand. He couldn't hold the coat properly. For all his improvement in handling farm chores and animals, helping a woman into a coat made him feel awkward and inadequate.

Amy didn't appear to notice. She managed to slip her arms inside the sleeves with grace.

The light floral fragrance she wore wafted to him. He'd forgotten that such close proximity held that pleasure.

She turned around. "Do you mind if we talk for a minute?"

"I thought that's what we were doing."

"I mean about us."

"Amy—"

"I won't beg you to come back to us, I promise."

Is that how she thought of them, not as two separate people in love with each other but as one unit called *us*? Funny how right that felt to him, even though he'd torn that unit apart. "All right. What did you want to say?"

She took a deep, shaky breath. "I want to thank you for all the beautiful things you brought into my life. You taught me so much about love—not only love between a man and a woman but love for others."

"I taught you?" He smiled. "You are the most loving, gentle, strong woman I know. I'm sure you taught me more than I taught you."

"No. Years ago, after you'd given up drinking, you told me that men who drank heavily weren't evil; they were only trying to heal some deep pain in their lives. I tried to understand, truly I did. A few months ago you told me a little bit of what you face because of the war, and I began to understand more about the wounded places inside people."

"I don't want—"

Amy touched the palm of her hand to the front of his jacket. "I know you don't want to talk about those wounds. I'm not asking you to. I'm only trying to say that because of you, I think I understand God's love better. I think I'm a more loving person. I want you to know that I treasure that gift from you."

Her revelation overwhelmed him. "I don't know what to say."

"You needn't say anything."

He watched in silence while she pulled on her gloves, pinned on a small maroon hat, and wrapped a plush maroon muffler around her neck.

She picked up the picture.

He reached for it. "I'll carry it for you."

She hesitated.

Anger flashed through him. Resignation followed. He'd told Dan once that the missing arm was only a symbol of the changes inside him. It was a symbol, but not *only* a symbol. He chose not to act from his anger. He purposefully softened his voice. "It's all right, Amy. I won't drop your painting. My arm is a lot stronger now."

She allowed him to take it. "Thank you. I didn't think you'd harm it."

He mentally kicked himself. He should have known her concern wasn't for the painting.

They walked together in silence through the building to the front door. Outside, a horse and buggy were tied at a hitching post near the bottom of the stone steps. "Professor Headley is letting me borrow his horse and buggy to take the painting home," Amy explained. "I hitched up the horse before going to get the painting. I'm becoming quite accomplished at hitching and unhitching. I'm quite proud of myself." She beamed.

"You should be." He beamed back at her, finding pleasure in her excitement at mastering the task he'd learned to perform almost before he could remember.

Wind swept across the snow-covered prairie and pulled Amy's maroon plush muffler into a banner. It yanked Frank's hat from his head. It danced and rolled along the ground. "Hey!" Carrying the painting, he couldn't retrieve the hat.

Amy ran after it, making three futile grabs before capturing it. They laughed together as she placed it back on his head and tightened the cord, which he seldom used, beneath his chin.

The closeness of her laughing eyes and the lips that had shared kisses with him so many times was painfully sweet. He wanted to pull her close and hold her forever. If his hand wasn't clutching the picture between them, he might give in to the temptation to do just that, he realized.

Amy's laughter died. Her hands rested on his shoulders. "Why do you think . . ."

"Why do I think what?"

"Why do you think our love was put through so many tests? We went through so much and waited such a long time to be together. Then the war came and destroyed everything."

"I don't know, Amy." He wished he could make the sadness in her eyes go away. He didn't know how to do that without asking her to marry him again, and he was certain that wasn't the right thing to do. He didn't even have two arms to hold her anymore.

He broke the invisible cords binding them together and put the picture in the buggy. He steadied her as she climbed up into the buggy. "Be careful, Amy. The roads are still pretty rough with ice and snow."

"I'll be careful."

He watched the buggy start down the road across the plateau toward town, the wind whipping the horse's mane in a picturesque dance. "Take care of her, Lord. Make her happy."

His fanciful thoughts wondered whether the wind carried his prayer heavenward.

Amy forced herself to keep her attention on the road, though everything within her urged her to look back at Frank. Was he watching her drive away? When they were courting, he always watched until she was out of sight. She'd done the same when he'd left her.

She both loved and hated that Frank worked at the academy. He only taught two courses, and his classes didn't meet every day, so at least he wasn't around constantly. It was painful seeing him so often when he chose for them not to be together. It was nice to look across the tables at lunch and see his eyes light up while he talked with faculty or students. Was it her imagination, or was he truly growing in confidence, learning he wasn't only his body, that he had so much to offer others?

Whenever she found herself begging God to bring Frank back to her, she made herself stop. "God has a plan for my life, with or without Frank," she'd told Pearl. "It's still hard to believe we'll never be together again, but sometime I'll get used to it."

"Have you seen anyone else?" Pearl had asked.

"No."

"I can't believe none of Chippewa City's young men have come around."

"A few have asked to escort me on occasion," Amy admitted. "I'm not ready to replace Frank yet. My heart still feels bruised. For now I'm spending my time with Father or my work and once in awhile helping out your father."

Dr. Matt had asked her to do simple nursing for patients on occasion since her experience at Camp Ramsey and Fort Snelling. At first she'd felt her training wasn't adequate, but he assured her he would not ask anything of her that was beyond her ability. Mostly she helped care for older patients, allowing their families some time to rest. It was rewarding work. And it helped fill her time and keep her from feeling sorry for herself.

"Maybe getting to know some other men would be a good idea," Pearl suggested in a gentle manner. "You wouldn't need to fall in love with someone else right away."

Amy laughed. "As though one plans such a thing." Her smile died. "I think I need to heal from Frank's leaving a bit more first."

Maybe Pearl was right, Amy reflected as she pulled the horse to a stop in front of the pharmacy and her home. Maybe the only way she would ever rout Frank from her heart was by making the commitment to allow another man to fill his place. But she wasn't ready for that yet. She expected it would be a long time before she was ready for another love.

$$\left(13\right)$$

rank opened the top drawer of the mahogany desk in the parlor and looked down at the yellowing newspaper pages. Pearl had tried to get him to look at them before she and Jason left the farm, but Frank had refused. The pages contained articles about Camp Ramsey and Fort Snelling during the time Amy spent there. Pictures Amy had sketched of life in the camps and hospitals were included in some of the articles.

He hadn't dared open his heart to the pain of looking at the clippings before today. The short time he'd spent with Amy in the snow in front of Windom Academy had renewed his longing to know more about what she'd experienced. Maybe the fact that her painting of the returning soldier was no longer available for him to see whenever he chose had sparked the interest.

He lit the hanging lamp with its globe of painted roses and sat in the plush green chair beneath it, clippings in hand. He read every word, examined every sketch of army life and patient life in the camps, imagined Amy in the midst of it all with the sick and dying soldiers. And let the tears fall.

❧

By the end of March, spring began to show its face on the Minnesota prairie. Snow showers spattered occasionally across the land, but for the most part they were short-lived and often mixed with rain. Prairie roosters boomed announcements of spring's promise from ridges at sunrise and sunset, and prairie hens responded with excited squawks.

As much as Frank enjoyed teaching at the academy, he was glad to return to the fields. Walking behind the team working the harrow tested his mettle. There were no handles to grasp, only the reins. He and Dan had worked hard with the horses during the winter months, teaching them to respond to verbal commands in addition to the urging of reins. It paid off now in spades. Frank's heels dug into the soft, turned soil as he trudged back and forth across the fields. The work left his arm and calves stiff, but his spirit soared. Wonderful, to face a challenge like this and conquer it.

More than once he fell in the conquering. While walking behind the drag, his heels would slip in the moist earth or the horses would jerk him off balance, and he'd land on the ground. At first the falls frustrated him. Then he remembered that he'd had many similar falls in the fields before the war. Everything couldn't be blamed on his arm.

On beautiful spring days, he felt sorry for the people working in cities. He loved watching spring unfold into summer. The prairie sky, which so many thought of as empty, was filled with ducks and geese making their way north, followed by the crane. The birds' cries added to the joy of the day.

Frank swallowed his pride and asked Andy to help on the farm. He was pleased that Andy quickly agreed. When Jason offered to help out, too, Frank could have leaped with joy. Instead he merely nodded and said, "I'd appreciate that."

"I can't work every day," Jason qualified. "I've my other work to do, but it doesn't take up all my time yet."

"Farm still belongs to all of us," Frank reminded him. "Up to you whether you choose to work it or not, though I'd be glad for your help."

"I hope one day to be able to support my family working as an architect. Maybe when that day comes, you'll want to buy my part of the farm."

"We'll talk about it when and if the time comes."

It felt strange at first to have his brothers turn to him as the leader at the farm. They knew what needed to be done, but Frank was the one who determined who did what and when on a daily basis.

Wheat was sown first, early, when the chill was barely out of the ground. Corn was sown next. The earth changed daily, the fields and meadows growing greener and more lush until in June the land pulsated with life everywhere: crops, prairie grass, fragrant wild flowers, birds, grasshoppers, chirping crickets, flies, mosquitoes, and prairie dogs.

As Frank worked, verses from Ecclesiastes repeated in his mind day after day. "To every thing there is a season, and a time to every purpose under heaven: a time to be born, and a time to die; a time to plant, and a time to pluck up that which is planted."

One evening, over biscuits and salt pork, Frank told Dan, "I feel like one of those hard kernels of seed corn. They look as dead as I felt when I returned from the war. Now they're green plants growing taller every day, filled with life, able to bend before the wind. I'm beginning to feel alive again, too."

All his life, working the land, he'd watched spring and summer follow fall and winter. He knew from the watching that God always brought a form of life out of every kind of death. Frank began to feel the stirrings of excitement within his chest. What would his new life look like?

Some things would never change. Some wounds would take years to heal, and their scars would always remain. Challenges would continually need to be faced. But there was beauty in the world, and strength was returning to his body and soul.

"For awhile I thought life would never be good again," he admitted to Dan. "Now I know it will be."

Even without Amy, he admitted to himself.

Frank was delighted one day by the sight of a red fox racing out of the cornfield and across the road, its tail flying straight out behind it. The beauty of the creature delighted him.

He remembered his father telling him as a boy that an injured fox hid away by itself until it healed.

That's what I've been doing, he realized with sudden clarity. He'd withdrawn from the world as much as possible to heal the wounds left from the war. A hope he hadn't allowed himself before stirred within him. Maybe one day he'd be healed enough to allow Amy back into his life. If she still wanted him by then.

❧

Amy awoke smiling. Morning sunshine softly reached through lace curtains to brighten her bedchamber. Mourning doves cooed from the ledge outside her window. She stretched luxuriously, still wrapped in the sense of peace and joy she'd felt in her dream.

Closing her eyes, she recaptured the images from her sleep world. She and Frank walked along a path. Between them walked Christ, holding their hands. Everything was bright.

Did the dream mean Christ was bringing her and Frank together again? That was the hope her heart leaped to first.

Maybe the dream meant that although they weren't together—for Christ was between them—Christ walked with them both. Surely that was true regardless of whether she and Frank spent the rest of their lives together. This morning, feeling the peace and joy in Christ's presence in the dream, Amy knew it was enough that He walked with each of them, wherever life led.

❧

One day in mid-June, Frank was surprised to receive a letter from a man he'd fought beside. "It's from Timothy Bryant," he told Dan, tearing open the envelope.

He scanned the letter quickly. A thrill darted through him. "He's coming out this way. Plans to be here for the Fourth of July."

"What's a city man like him want out here on the prairie?"

"Says he's planning to run for a congressional seat this year. Wants to get in some stomping this summer. Wants to start here with the Fourth celebration. Then take in the fairs in late summer."

"Not a bit surprised he's interested in politics."

"Wants to stay with us when he comes out. It will be good to see him again."

Timothy Bryant arrived the Saturday before the Fourth. The three former soldiers sat up late into the night reminiscing. It surprised Frank to realize all the memories weren't filled with horror. There had been times of camaraderie and humor, too.

And the war had brought good friends into his life. Bryant, born to an affluent Minneapolis family, wouldn't be in Frank's home, acting as comfortable as one of his farmer neighbors, if it weren't for the war.

Dan showed Timothy the picture Amy had painted.

"This is very well done," Timothy praised. "Who is the artist?"

"Amy Henderson. You remember the girl Frank was always talking about, don't you?" Dan asked, grinning at Frank.

Frank frowned at him.

Timothy turned to Frank. "I'm surprised to find such talent out here on the prairie. Where did she study?"

"She took some classes at the University of Minnesota in St. Paul."

Timothy studied the picture closer. "I know a thing or two about painting. My parents have quite a collection of work by the finer artists. I'd like to see more of your Amy's work."

"She isn't my Amy." Frank darted a look of disgust at Dan. "But I think she'll agree to let you see more of her paintings. I'll ask her tomorrow."

The 1900 Fourth of July celebration planned by the county was the most elaborate Frank could remember. The county fathers were bent on celebrating the United States' expansion of its manifest destiny with the addition of Hawaii and the Philippines. Frank wasn't so sure that expansion was the country's destiny. He was surprised when Reverend Conrad asked him to speak at church the Sunday before the Fourth. He tried to decline.

"I've nothing worth saying. I know some of the townspeople consider me a war hero, but I'm not."

"Speak to them about what you told me, about the healing. It's not only wounded soldiers who need to heal from the war, you know. The whole country needs to heal, whether we admit it or not."

That's how Frank found himself preaching one-half of the sermon on Sunday morning. Reverend Conrad had been part of Chippewa City since the town began. Frank felt Reverend Conrad's introduction was a sermon in itself.

"Chippewa City is a babe as towns go. It's only thirty-odd years old. It grew from scratch here on the prairie at the meeting of the Minnesota and Chippewa Rivers after the Sioux were forced to leave this land. We struggled with growing pains, the same as our nation has struggled. Many of you older people lost husbands, wives, and children to things like diphtheria epidemics or the blizzard of '88. We almost lost the battle against the grasshoppers in the seventies. A lot of farmers and townspeople moved farther west at that time. Then there was the panic of '93. Yes, we've been through a lot in this town's short life. Two years ago we were drawn into another battle. Fights for freedom in two little island countries drew men from our own county. Here's one of them to speak on battles and healing. Our own brother, Frank Sterling."

Frank felt awkward walking up the aisle to the podium before the altar. He was glad he'd badgered Dan into joining him.

He laid his Bible on the podium and opened it, then looked out over the congregation. He and Dan hadn't told anyone except Bryant that they'd be part of today's service. He saw curiosity in Jason's eyes. Bryant sat beside Andy. Amy and her father sat behind Jason's family, as usual. Frank avoided Amy's gaze. Slim and Shorty sat up front, Slim clutching his cane, both watching Frank in eager expectation.

Frank cleared his throat. "Most of you know my friend, Dan Terrell. We fought together in the Philippines."

Cheers and applause surprised him. He'd grown accustomed to people praising him for fighting but hadn't expected it during the service. When the congregation quieted, he continued.

"Dan's agreed to help me out here. We're not planning to tell you about our war experiences in the Philippines. This Fourth of July, along with celebrating the birth of our country, a lot of people are celebrating the victory in the Spanish-American War. Dan and I would like to suggest we celebrate the peace God has restored. As the reverend indicated, every one of you has had your own wars. You may want to celebrate peace and the end of wars and battles in your own lives.

"Dan and I aren't planning to speak our own words much. We'll be reading from Ecclesiastes three, verses one through eight. Seems to us, this about says it all."

He cleared his throat and began. "'To every thing there is a season, and a time to every purpose under the heaven.'"

Dan read, "'A time to be born.'"

Frank purposely roughened his voice in anger. "'And a time to die.'"

"'A time to plant.'"

"'And a time to pluck up that which is planted; A time to kill.'" Frank saw Amy flinch at the words and his tone.

"'And a time to heal,'" Dan read in a gentle voice.

"'A time to break down.'"

"'And a time to build up.'"

"'A time to weep.'" Frank kept his manner angry.

"'And a time to laugh.'"

"'A time to mourn.'"

"'And a time to dance.'"

"'A time to cast away stones.'"

"'And a time to gather stones together. A time to embrace.'"

"'And a time to refrain from embracing.'"

"'A time to get.'" Dan's voice seemed to beg Frank to look at the good.

"'And a time to lose.'" Frank challenged. Then, with a sense of grudging reconsidering, "'A time to keep.'"

"'And a time to cast away. A time to rend.'"

"'And a time to sew.'" Frank's voice was softer now.

"'A time to keep silence.'"

"'And a time to speak.'" Frank's voice grew louder, more assured, calmer. "'A time to love.'"

"'And a time to hate; A time of war.'"

"'And a time of peace.'"

The congregation was still as Frank and Dan took their seats. Frank wondered whether the words would mean as much to anyone in the congregation as they meant to him.

After the service, many people stopped to tell him and Dan how much they appreciated their sermon. Amy's thanks meant the most to him. He could see she'd struggled with tears and knew the words had touched her.

He introduced Timothy Bryant to her and saw the sweet modesty reflected in her eyes when Bryant praised her work. Frank was pleased

when Amy agreed to allow Bryant to see more of her work before they
returned to the farm.

❧

Amy was glad the day was sunny, the light bright through the large
windows in the studio at Windom Academy. The light presented her
paintings at their best.

She was surprised at the interest Frank's friend showed but kept
her curiosity in check. She stood back and allowed Mr. Bryant to
study the paintings at his leisure. He took time to give his full attention to each, one by one: Chalmers sitting on Frank's lap; Pearl on the
back porch of the farmhouse staring out at the fields where Jason
worked; Slim and Shorty at the depot waving flags at a departing
train; Slim in a church pew with a ray of light through a window ac-
centing the wrinkles in his face and the sad longing in his eyes; Viola
in a smocked gown squatting in the grass to examine the first violets
she'd seen in her young life.

Finally he turned from the paintings. "You have the gift, Miss
Henderson."

"Thank you."

"Many artists can paint a portrait that looks like a real person.
Only a handful paint portraits of people's hearts and souls. You are
one of the few."

Amy blinked back sudden tears. How did he know she'd started
seeing that way? How did he know when she painted, she tried to
capture the wonder and the pain and the love and the wounds?

She hadn't even known to paint what she saw of a person's heart
until she began to understand Frank's wounds. She hadn't known until then that it was possible to see another's heart, let alone paint it.

Mr. Bryant smiled at her. "I know the owners of a fine art gallery
in St. Paul. I'm sure they'd love to do a showing of your paintings.
May I bring one to them as an example of your work?"

Amy darted a glance of joyful surprise at Frank. He nodded, grinning. "Tim's parents are collectors. You can trust his judgment."

"I—I—I don't know what to say, Mr. Bryant," she stammered.

"A simple yes will suffice."

"Yes." She laughed. "Yes."

"I'd like to buy one of your paintings myself." He pointed at the canvas of Viola and the flowers. "This one. My wife would love it."

Amy hesitated, loathe to let the painting go.

Mr. Bryant appeared to misunderstand her hesitation. "I'll wait, however, until the showing. That way you will be sure I pay a fair price for it. My friends won't allow your work to be sold for less than its value."

"You seem very sure your friends will like my work as well as you do."

"I am."

Amy allowed herself to share another joy-filled glance with Frank. How wonderful that he had been the one to bring this opportunity into her life. *Thank You, Lord, for allowing him to be here to share this moment with me.*

❧

Behind the curtain that provided privacy for Dr. Matt's patients, Frank struggled only slightly as he slipped his shirt on.

Dr. Matt patted Frank's shoulder. "Your arm's healed well. Must have had a good surgeon in Manila."

"Mm."

"You're fortunate gangrene didn't set in. Battlefield hospitals are filled with patients losing the battle with gangrene. If you'd succumbed to gangrene, you'd likely have lost the rest of your arm, if not your life."

"I know." Frank's response was subdued. Usually he resented the implication that his wound could have been worse, feeling the attitude belittled his loss. Hearing it from Dr. Matt was different. Frank knew the physician had seen worse cases. For that matter, so had Frank. "Saw a few of those cases in the hospital."

"Nothing like a hospital to make a man grateful for what he'd consider a trial otherwise."

"That's saying something." Frank's mind filled with images of patients he'd seen at the hospital. "When I was in the hospital I felt just like you said, grateful. I admit I was worried about getting on with life with only one arm and worried about how people would react. But mostly, I was glad to be alive and glad I wasn't in worse shape."

Dr. Matt lifted graying eyebrows. "Something change?"

"Yes. Me. I let myself get bogged down in self-pity. Let myself?" Frank snorted. "I drove straight into the bog, like I planned it."

"Don't be too hard on yourself. It's a major adjustment for anyone, what you've gone through."

"Well, I'm still alive. I guess that's a pretty good sign God has a plan for the rest of my life. No sense kicking about that."

"Have you been kicking?"

"Like a bronco. Lately, though, I'm beginning to feel like I've got my feet under me again."

Dr. Matt nodded brusquely. "You'll make it. Some men don't when life gets tough, but you will. I've seen you make it through other hard places. Let's head out to the apothecary, and I'll get you those pain powders."

When he left the apothecary, Frank climbed the stairs to the Hendersons' apartment. He'd received a letter from Bryant the day before. Enclosed with it was a letter for Amy. Bryant had asked him to deliver it.

It took more courage than Frank liked to admit to climb those stairs. He'd barely spoken to Amy's father since returning to Chippewa City. Whenever they saw each other at church, Mr. Henderson was cordial, but he never smiled. Frank couldn't blame him. He stood before the door to the apartment, took a deep breath to steady his courage, and knocked. He slid his hat from his head before the door opened.

"Frank. This is a surprise."

Not a happy one, Frank surmised from the older man's scowl. "Hello, Sir. I've brought some mail for Amy."

"She isn't home." Mr. Henderson stepped back. "Won't you come in?"

Frank entered reluctantly. He set his hat on the table beside the door so he could pull the letter from his pocket. "Here you are, Sir."

Mr. Henderson held the envelope at arm's length and peered at it. Then he appeared to remember the wire-rimmed glasses he held in his other hand. He put them on and looked at the packet again. "Oh, yes. From your friend Mr. Bryant."

"I'll just be going, Sir." Frank reached for his hat.

"No, please, stay for a few minutes."

Frank hesitated.

"It was a nice thing you did for her, showing that man her paintings." The words were said in a grudging tone.

"She's a talented artist."

"Yes. Amy tells me I'm not to be angry with you for breaking your engagement."

Frank stared at him, surprised to silence.

"She says you have every right to change your mind about marrying her, and she wouldn't want you if you don't want her." Mr. Henderson shook his head. "Have to tell you, Son, I'm not so forgiving of your treatment of my daughter as she is."

"I don't know that I deserve forgiveness, Sir. I do know Amy deserves a better man than me."

"You're not expecting an argument on that point, I hope."

"No, Sir." Frank made himself stand still and face Mr. Henderson's accusing gaze.

Finally the older man nodded, as though he'd made a decision. "There's something I'd like you to see. Come over to my desk."

Frank followed him across the room to the corner where the elegant mahogany desk from the Hendersons' more prosperous days stood near the window. Clipped newspaper articles and books covered the top of the desk.

On one corner stood the music box Frank had given Amy for Christmas years ago. On top of the walnut base a man and woman skated within a crystal snow globe. His heart caught at the sight. He'd bought the music box for Amy because ice-skating held special memories for them. Would life ever again seem as innocent and beautiful as it had the first time they'd skated together at the millpond?

Mr. Henderson nodded toward the piles on the desk. "This is Amy's project. Go ahead and look."

Frank stepped backward, shocked at the idea of invading Amy's privacy. "I don't think so, Sir."

"Nothing personal here." Mr. Henderson held up a newspaper clipping. "No secrets; just news about the war."

"The war?" Almost against his will, Frank read the headline of the article Amy's father held toward him.

"Amy reads everything she can find about the war, on all fronts. She pours over soldiers' personal experiences and pictures published in the papers."

"Sounds gruesome."

"Yes, I thought so. Hardly a proper topic for feminine pursuit."

Frank agreed with the sentiment. He couldn't imagine sweethearted, refined Amy thrilling to war stories. "I thought she hated war."

"She does. But she loves you." Mr. Henderson shook his head. "I don't know why, but she does."

Frank's neck and face grew warm from shame.

Mr. Henderson shuffled some of the papers and lifted a book he found beneath them.

Frank recognized it: Teddy Roosevelt's tales of the Rough Riders in Cuba. He'd heard others speak of it. Experiencing war firsthand had left him with no desire to read of others' battles.

"My daughter fills her mind with all of this for only one reason."

Frank met Mr. Henderson's gaze. "And that is?"

"To understand you better. She doesn't want to remain oblivious to the things you've seen."

"I wouldn't want her to see what I've seen!"

The tense lines in Amy's father's face softened, and so did his voice. "Of course you wouldn't. No gentleman would want any woman to know the horrors of war."

"Especially not Amy."

"I've told her it's not necessary. She insists it is."

Frank stared down at the cluttered desk. Consternation drained away into wonder that Amy loved him enough to do this for him. Even though he'd pushed her away, tried to keep her from his life, she'd struggled to understand him, his pain, his world. She'd struggled to give love to him when he wasn't aware of her efforts. Her choice reminded him of Christ's choice to become part of humanity and experience man's struggles.

Love enwrapped him in such a tangible manner, it felt almost like being held in Amy's embrace.

Mr. Henderson held out the letter from Timothy Bryant. "Maybe you should deliver this to Amy yourself. She's at Windom Academy, painting."

❧

"Funny thing about watches."

Amy whirled around at the sound of Frank's voice. Blue paint dripped from the tip of the brush she held in her right hand. Frank sat on a stool near the door of the studio. "How long have you been here? I didn't hear you come in."

He grinned and nodded toward the canvas behind her. "You were a bit engrossed in that painting. As I was saying," he held the watch she'd given him before he left for the war, "it's a funny thing about watches."

A little thrill ran through her that he still carried the watch.

He started winding the watch. She could hear the soft action of metal against metal. "Watches stop keeping time if we don't remember to wind them," he continued.

She wanted to giggle at his philosophical tone. "I've noticed that."

He looked up from the watch, smiling. "It took me awhile to learn how to wind this with one hand."

Her heart skipped a beat at the simple fact. Even the watch she'd given him to remind him of her love had become something that reminded him of his wound. But . . . his eyes didn't hold the look of pain today. She wasn't sure what was happening, but if he was willing to spend a few happy minutes with her, she wasn't about to protest.

"Sorry. I got sidetracked. What was I saying?"

He didn't look like he'd forgotten. He looked like he was teasing her.

"You were saying what a funny thing it is that watches need to be wound."

"Mm. Yes. I mean, watches are supposed to keep time. But time can't be kept, can it?" His voice softened. His gaze met hers, unwavering. "It can't be kept, and it can't be stopped."

"No," she whispered, suddenly feeling breathless.

"I told you once that I'd love you even if time stopped."

"I remember."

"Time doesn't stop. Neither has my love."

Amy caught her breath, hardly able to believe what she was hearing. "Frank—"

" 'To every thing there is a season,' Amy, 'and a time to every purpose under heaven.' Since you gave me this watch, I've been through times of war, times of mourning, times of casting away, times of healing. Lots of times. For awhile I forgot time doesn't stop, and after war comes peace, and after mourning comes dancing. I tried to forget there's a time for embracing and a time for loving. I was afraid those times were behind me and would never come again."

Amy trembled. She longed to go to him, but he'd distanced himself from her for so long that she hadn't the courage to without his express invitation.

He stood and slipped the watch into his trouser pocket. He crossed the room slowly, his gaze never leaving hers. When he reached her, he removed the palette from her left hand and set it down on a nearby table. Then he took the brush from her and laid that down.

He faced her from about a foot away. "Ecclesiastes tells us there's a time to keep silence and a time to speak. I've kept silent a long time. Tim Bryant says you see into hearts, so I guess it won't do me any good to keep pretending I'm strong and tough where I'm not. I'd like to believe I'm ready for a time of love again."

Confusion dampened her joy. Why, if he loved her, did he keep this distance between them?

Her confusion must have shown, for he held up his hand as though in warning. "I haven't treated you well for the last year. I don't know if my time of being ready to love again coincides with your time of being ready to love again. Maybe you need a time of healing, a time of healing from the wounds I've inflicted on you. If so, I understand."

Now she saw the pain in his brown eyes clearly and the hope behind the pain. Her own hope leaped to life in response. "You haven't done anything unforgivable. Besides, isn't it love that heals wounds?"

The tension in his face melted away into a smile. "When I left for the war, I asked you to meet me with a promise . . . the promise that you'd still marry me."

"I remember."

"I'm a bit late claiming that promise. Or perhaps claiming is too strong a word."

Joy burst from her heart. "My promise still holds."

Finally he took the step that bridged the distance between them. Amy closed her eyes and sighed in deep contentment as he pulled her close in his embrace.

For many minutes they stood like that, glorying in the gift of being together. It felt so familiar: the way his head rested against hers, the way his shoulders felt beneath her hands, the sound of his heartbeat beneath her cheek. It was the place that felt most right to her of all places on earth.

"I hate that I haven't two arms to hold you, Amy." His whisper was rough with anguish. "I can't help it. No matter how much I try not to mind, I do."

"I know, my love." Tears misted her eyes. She blinked them back. She ached to make his pain go away, but she'd learned over the last year that it wasn't in her power to do that. "But what's most important is that your heart holds me."

"Even if time stops." His lips touched her temple, kissed the edge of her eyebrow with the lightness of a feather, moved at long last to meet her lips. His kiss was warm and sweet and lingering.

He pulled away only far enough to whisper against her lips, "I love you, Amy. I'll always love you."

For so long she'd wondered whether she'd ever hear those words again. They were sweeter to her than any other words could possibly be.

For a long while they were lost in each other's embraces and kisses, speaking their love for each other, rejoicing that they'd found each other once more, shyly revealing how much they'd missed each other during the last two years.

More than an hour passed before Frank asked, "Will you marry me after harvest is over?"

Amy smiled mischievously. "Do we need to wait that long?"

He caught her close again with a laugh. "If you come out to the farm as my wife before then, you won't have time to finish the paintings for your show."

"What show?"

He released her then and pulled an envelope from his pocket. "This came today from Tim Bryant."

She opened it eagerly and scanned its contents. "You're right, Frank. His friends want to do a showing of my work in November." She could hardly believe so much happiness was coming to her at one time. A thought stopped her. She looked up at Frank. "Will you mind if my work is shown? I probably won't have much time to paint after we're married."

"Between being a farmer's wife and raising our children, you mean?" His eyes twinkled.

She felt herself blush at his reference to children. She leaned against him, smiling. "Yes."

"We'll find a way for you to paint. Like Tim said, you have a gift for it. Besides, I want paintings of all of our children."

Amy laughed, lifting her eyebrows in teasing query. "All of them? How many are you planning?"

"As many as the good Lord grants."

Amy relaxed into his kiss, thanking God that at last they had returned to the time to love.

CROSSINGS®
THE BOOK CLUB FOR TODAY'S CHRISTIAN FAMILY

A Letter to Our Readers

Dear Reader:

In order that we might better contribute to your reading enjoyment, we would appreciate your taking a few minutes to respond to the following questions. When completed, please return to the following:

Andrea Doering, Editor-in-Chief
Crossings Book Club
401 Franklin Avenue, Garden City, NY 11530

You can post your review online! Go to www.crossings.com and rate this book.

Title _____ Author _____

1 Did you enjoy reading this book?

❏ Very much. I would like to see more books by this author!

❏ I really liked_____

❏ Moderately. I would have enjoyed it more if_____

2 What influenced your decision to purchase this book? Check all that apply.

❏ Cover
❏ Title
❏ Publicity
❏ Catalog description
❏ Friends
❏ Enjoyed other books by this author
❏ Other _____

3 Please check your age range:

❏ Under 18   ❏ 18-24
❏ 25-34   ❏ 35-45
❏ 46-55   ❏ Over 55

4 How many hours per week do you read? _____

5 How would you rate this book, on a scale from 1 (poor) to 5 (superior)?
_____

Name_____

Occupation_____

Address_____

City_____ State_____ Zip_____